The Roommates

by

Vikki L. Jeanne Cleveland

Published By

Kitty Literature Publications

Salem, IL 62881-1831

vikki@cfc93.com

Printed/Distributed By

Lulu Enterprises, Inc.

3131 RDU Center Drive, Suite 210

Morrisville, NC 27560

www.lulu.com

As always, dedicated to the precious memory of my beloved mother,
L. Jeanne Cleveland,
and to
Elouise Greenwood,
who helped to fill the void in so many ways.

Part I: The Roommates/June, 1984

CHAPTER ONE

Has it happened to me? Have I been jilted?

Although Siara Nealy strained to see as far down the foliage-canopied road as possible, there was no distant billowing of dust to signal Prescott's arrival.

Did his wife refuse to give him a divorce? Did he decide that marrying me was too much trouble?

She pushed a sudden, disturbing thought of Connor firmly aside. Prescott had said not to worry about anything.

He said I should trust him...

He was supposed to be speeding down the road to meet her.

Trust him...

He was supposed to be leaping from his car now and taking her into his arms passionately and impatiently.

Trust him...

Hours later, as the sun sank mockingly into the tree-lined horizon, she finally realized that she couldn't trust him at all.

"Trust me," Jordyn Nealy said as she rolled out of bed and pulled on her jeans.

"Trust you? You're the one who was so all-fired eager to go to a motel after dinner. Now you want to leave after...after just one time, which is not like you at all, and you insisted on driving your own car to meet me here. So if you're not off to meet another one of your boyfriends, what else am I to think?"

"Would you be offended if I told you I really don't give a damn what you think, Farm Boy?"

"Damn you, Jordyn..."

She smiled. Things were so much safer between them if she could make him angry now and then. Still, she felt vaguely uneasy whenever the smile faded from his face.

"Look, Farm Boy," she said to mollify him. "I have to leave because Sari needs me."

"Sure."

"Really. I can feel it. Siara needs me. It's the twinstinct. Remember? I told you about it."

Luke Johnson lay back and dropped his arm across his eyes. Shrugging, Jordyn sat on the edge of the bed to pull on her sandals. A moment later she felt his finger tracing the smooth contours of her back, left exposed by a halter-top.

"You know I love you," he said.

"It would be so much better for both of us if you didn't."

"Would marrying me really be so terrible?"

"I'm a city girl. I wasn't made to be stuck away on your farm and used for breeding like your cows. Besides, I don't look good in gingham and bread dough."

"You know my mom well enough. She's hardly confined to the farm, and I've yet to see her in either gingham or bread dough."

"I thought we got this straight already. No strings."

Luke stretched and casually folded his arms behind his head. "The way I see it, you must feel something for me. We've been seeing each other for a long time."

"You're hung like a prize bull. I like that in a man...any man. It doesn't have to be you."

His amber-flecked eyes burned with anger. "Damn you, Jordyn."

"Call me tomorrow." She squeezed his crotch playfully. "I'll make up for tonight."

"Maybe I have other plans."

"Suit yourself," she called as she left the motel room. "I'm going home now. Really."

Jayme McCray looked up from her word processor. "It's getting late. Won't Wallis be worrying about where you are?"

"Naw." Harlan Oakes peered into the tiny refrigerator in the corner of Jayme's office. He wanted beer, but there was only diet soda and yogurt. "She knows I'm here. She don't worry none when she knows I'm with you."

Jayme winced, even though she had been hearing him butcher every grammar rule in the book for many, many years.

"I don't know whether I should be flattered or not..." She tapped out another paragraph to her article. "Most women don't like their husbands hanging out with other women."

"She knows me and you has been like brothers since we was kids."

Gritting her teeth, Jayme typed furiously without responding.

"Is somethin' wrong, Jae?" he asked.

"If the Cardinal fans can forgive you your transgressions, I can, too. I've been forgiving you a lot longer than they have anyway." *And for lots more than "booting one."*

Harlan made himself comfortable on Jayme's desk. "I need a favor, Jae."

"Favor? Ah, I knew there had to be some ulterior motive behind your sudden sociability."

"Huh?"

"Never mind, Harlan. What do you need?"

Propping her chin on her hand, she stared at her unfinished story. Because today's game had started at noon, she hoped to be home by dark for once. Harlan, of course, wouldn't care too much about what she wanted.

"What I want is a woman to have my baby," he told her.

Jayme rubbed her tired eyes. "I must have dozed off. For one silly moment I thought you said you want a woman to have your baby."

"I did. Wallis ain't able, y'know."

Or willing, Jayme thought meanly.

"And she wants a young'un in the worst way. So we got this idea, see...from one of them lady mags Wallis reads. With all this talk about suffragette mothers..."

"I think you mean surrogate mothers."

"Yeah, them. We just thought it'd be a good idea. Only I ain't gonna jerk off in no test tube some strange broad's gonna shove up herself."

"So you...and Wallis...thought you'd ask me to shove it up myself." *I know where I'd like to shove it.*

"No. Ain't nothin' like that. Gimme some credit for some sensitivity, for Chrissake."

"Sensitivity? I'm impressed. You've been reading the 'Word Power' section in *Reader's Digest.*"

"I'm tryin' to be serious here. There ain't gonna be no test tubes. We'll do it normal."

"You mean...you mean..." Jayme locked her fingers together. "You mean you and me TOGETHER like this?"

"Yeah."

"And Wallis agrees to this?" *She's up to something sneaky again.*

"Well, yeah. It was her idea, if you wanna know the truth. You're the one female in the world she ain't jealous of. She knows we been like..."

"Like brothers. You've used that compliment on me before."

The irritated look that had settled on Jayme's face suddenly softened as her eyes narrowed in sly speculation. *Don't be so hasty, Jae old girl. Think this one through carefully.*

"I'll need some time to think about it, Harlan. It's quite a big favor you're asking."

"I'd do it for you!"

You're so stupid, Harlan. So adorably stupid.

"Go home, Sport. Tell Wallis I'm considering your request."

Darica Cervantes hurried to unlock the door to the house she shared with the Nealy twins and Jayme McCray. Relieved, she saw that she was the first one home this evening even though it was nearly eight o'clock. Since she had promised to make spaghetti for Jayme and Siara tonight, she worried all the way home that she was too late. Evening mass had lasted longer than usual, and then, after faithfully lighting three candles, she had paused to confer with Father Jonathan about plans for St. Mary's Fall Festival.

Setting out everything she needed, she tossed together a salad and readied the garlic bread for toasting. These preparations finished, she relaxed. Everything could be finished in half an hour...if the girls still wanted to eat this late. Darica checked her watch. Since Jordyn had a dinner date tonight, maybe Jayme and Siara had decided to eat out, too. Maybe they had waited for Darica to come home, and when she was late...

Oh dear, oh dear, oh dear...

She climbed the stairs to her room and gently tucked her rosary away in her jewelry box.

I try so hard to do things right, and nothing happens as I plan.

Settling comfortably in her rocking chair, she sighed and opened her Bible, absently fingering the unique bookmark she herself had made so many years ago. Fleetingly she thought of Alvito, just as she did every night when she opened her Bible. Then, just as quickly, she snapped her mind closed to his memory as she buried herself in the comfort of the Scriptures.

Not long afterward she heard the slamming of a car door. Pulling her curtain aside, she saw Jordyn getting out of her red TransAm.

But Jordyn was supposed to have a date.

Did I make another mistake? I must make more spaghetti and garlic toast so that Jyn won't think I forgot her.

Darica tucked the bookmark into her Bible, which she lovingly placed on the table by her rocker. Allowing herself to think again of Alvito, she whispered the familiar words, seeking the absolution she could never be certain she would receive.

"Forgive me, Heavenly Father, for I have grievously sinned..."

CHAPTER TWO

"Have you heard anything from Sari?" Jordyn asked as Darica walked into the kitchen. "Her car's not back yet. Shouldn't she be here by now? It's after eight."

"Twinstinct again?" Darica asked. Both she and Jayme had learned to trust that uncanny, silent communication that could take place between the sisters even when they were separated by miles. "Twinstinct" the girls' father had called it.

Jordyn was pacing now. She was the active twin, always moving or fidgeting. Strange how two people who looked so much alike could be so different in everything else. So different, in fact, few people had trouble telling them apart.

"Do you know where she's supposed to be?" Darica asked as she turned on the stove. She, too, felt the need for activity. Though younger than the other girls, she felt somewhat maternal about them, especially about Siara, the quiet twin, for whom Darica felt the most affinity. Jayme and Jordyn called them "Sari and Dari, the Mouse Sisters." Darica liked having a nickname, and she liked having a nickname sister, too. Three nickname sisters if she could count "Jae" and "Jyn."

"It's her day off," Jordyn was saying. "She's likely to be anywhere, probably with that doctor friend of hers. My twinstinct hasn't been picking up good vibes about that bastard."

"You mustn't judge someone whom you've never met."

"You don't like her seeing him any more than I do."

"He's married."

"An insignificant detail," Jordyn said. "He's playing her for a sucker, and the feeling I have is that she's just been suckered real good."

"The doctor may not be like that. We don't know the man."

"But I know MARRIED men where Sari's so damn gullible about men period. Easy prey for some old lech."

Though Darica harbored much the same opinion, she kept her remarks to herself. Jordyn was already worried enough, and now she was opening and closing cabinet doors for no reason other than she needed to keep moving.

The sound of an approaching car stilled her, and she leaped to the kitchen door.

"Damn!" Jordyn resumed her pacing. "It's Jae."

"Hi, guys!" Jayme sang out, sweeping into the kitchen. "You didn't wait supper for me, did you? You're such a sweetheart, Dari. Didn't you have a date with your farmer, Jyn? Hey, listen. The most incredible thing has happened. Just wait until you hear...and neither of you is listening to a word I'm saying, are you? What's wrong? Is something wrong?"

"Siara's very late," Darica told her. "We're a little worried."

"A lot worried," Jordyn corrected.

"Oh." Jayme picked a lettuce leaf out of the salad bowl and sat down at the table.

"I'm sorry, Jae," Jordyn said, still fidgeting around the kitchen. "I didn't mean to shoot you down. What's your news?"

"It's about Harlan and me."

"Is he finally leaving Wallis?" Darica asked. "Or is Wallis leaving him?"

"Oh, no, nothing like that. But he and Wallis have done me the honor of asking me to be the surrogate mother of their child."

Jordyn stopped her pacing as Darica fumbled her spaghetti spoon onto the floor.

"You can't seriously be happy about THAT!" Jordyn said, staring at Jayme.

"But I'm delighted."

"Hasn't that man treated you badly enough?" Darica ventured gently as she picked up the spoon. "Now he wants to use you in a disgusting way...like a...like a laboratory rat."

"Ah, but you're missing the point." Jayme chewed serenely on a lettuce leaf. "The only rat is my beloved Harlan. Everything else will be perfectly normal. The baby will be conceived in the usual way...by Harlan and me."

Darica lost her grip on the spaghetti spoon again. "Jayme! You mean you would...with Harlan...when he's so MARRIED? And to someone like Wallis?"

"So you've decided to be Hunky Harlan's brood mare." Jordyn resumed her pacing, though less briskly and more thoughtfully now. "It's about time you decided to give it up, but I hardly think this is the way or place to start. Harlan's a hunk, but he's...he's..."

"A doofus," Jayme admitted.

"And Dari's right about how he's treated you. He's been using you since you both were kids though he's too stupid to realize it. You, however, should know better. Are you going to let him get by with this...this...THIS?"

"I now have this golden opportunity to have the love of my life...for a while anyway...which I've decided is better than never at all. And it will be for longer than Wallis thinks. Even she wouldn't expect ME to be sneaky enough to accept their kind offer and then take steps to prevent the planting and subsequent harvest, so to speak."

Jordyn grinned knowingly and said to a puzzled Darica, "Birth control pills, Mouse."

"Oh, Jayme…"

"Don't be so scandalized, Dari," Jayme laughed. "These days even good Catholic girls use birth control pills."

"How in the world do you think I've survived intact all this time?" Jordyn asked. "Of course, no one's ever accused me of being a good Catholic girl."

Darica's face reddened. "Could we talk about something else, please?"

Jordyn laughed at Darica's apparent discomfort. "It wouldn't hurt you to find yourself a hunk, Dari. Virginity's un-American in a woman your age. It's downright blasphemous in Jae's case."

The red tinge on Darica's olive-toned skin deepened though neither Jordyn nor Jayme noticed, for at that moment another car pulled into the driveway.

"It's Sari," Darica told them, glad for the diversion.

Jordyn threw open the kitchen door just as Siara stepped slowly onto the back porch.

"He didn't show up, Jyn," she said, dully at first, but then her words spilled out with a renewed flood of tears. "I waited for hours, and he didn't show up. We were going away, just for a while, until he could get a divorce. I was going to call you from Nevada. We were going to Reno to be married as soon as his divorce was final. I knew you would worry if I told you ahead of time. I worried that even if I didn't tell you, you would know it and try to talk me out of it. I thought I knew what was best for me this time. Only he didn't show up. He never intended to show up, did he, Jyn?"

"Sit down, Baby," Jordyn urged soothingly. "Sit down and talk it all out to us. You'll feel better for it. And Jae has some news that will make you smile. Hey, Jae, bring out the wine, will you? We'll toast your success… such as you seem to think it is…and drown Sari's sorrows."

And end up giggling, Darica added to herself. *We always giggle after wine.*

She turned off the stove. No one would be eating for a while.

CHAPTER THREE

"Are you really going to do it, Jae?" Siara asked, her words slightly slurred, although perfectly understood by the three other girls, whose hearing was slightly slurred.

"You betcha." Jayme's hiccupping sent them all into fits of giggling.

Darica smiled. She had known they would end up giggling. Wine and girl talk could cheer up anyone, especially girl talk with friends as close as they all were.

Like family, Darica thought, sniffling as her eyes filled with tears. *They're my family now. And Sari's hurt...my fellow Mouse Sister...her dreams destroyed...by a man...as mine were. Something should be done about men like that.*

"Looky here," Jayme said. "Dari Mouse is on a cryin' jag."

"One glass of wine too much," Siara explained.

"One BOTTLE of wine too much." Jordyn frowned into the second empty bottle. "Perhaps we're drunk. Y'all think we're drunk?"

"Oh, Jyn..." Siara gulped suddenly. "I think I'm becoming ill..."

"Take a few deep breaths, Baby. You'll be okay."

"Maybe we should eat something." Darica stumbled to the stove. "I bet Sari hasn't eaten all day. I made spaghetti."

The spaghetti, however, had long since coagulated into one big glue ball, the lettuce in the salad had wilted, and the garlic bread had dried to an unappetizing crust.

"We could make croutons out of the bread and dump them into the spaghetti sauce," Darica suggested apologetically.

Jayme wrinkled her nose. "What a revolting thought."

Jordyn slapped her hand against the table. "We'll send out for pizza. Large deep dish with extra everything okay with everyone?"

Receiving only queasy moans in response to her question, Jordyn phoned in the order while Jayme rummaged for another bottle of wine.

"Maybe coffee would be better?" Jayme asked when her search turned up nothing interesting.

"And soberize myself?" Siara leaned back in her chair. "I prefer being drunk. I feel better that way...though you better heat up the spaghetti sauce, Dari, because I won't last until pizza gets here. Suddenly I am very hungry."

Her sister hugged her unsteadily. "A definite sign of recovery, Sari Mouse. Any thought about what you wanna do to that asshole doctor?"

"I'm not a big revenge advocate. Can't we let things be? Chalk it up to experience and all that?"

"And let another man come out on top? Men always think they have to be on top. I'm sick of 'em gettin' the jollies while the women get the tears...'specially now that it's my baby sister on the receivin' end. Sick, sick, sick, y'hear!" Jordyn flopped into the chair next to Siara and heaved a dramatic sigh of exasperation.

"Though Jyn is obviously farther gone than any of the rest of us, I gotta agree with her." Jayme dumped a pound of coffee into their coffee maker. "This guy needs to be taught a lesson."

"I agree," Darica said as she set out mugs. "Something should be done about men like that. They'll only keep on hurting people unless something is done."

Jordyn raised her eyebrows in surprise. "What's this? Our gentle Dari Mouse has a vindictive streak in her?"

Darica twisted her fingers together nervously. "It's just that I can't bear seeing Sari hurt so much while that man is probably laughing about it and not caring one bit about what he's done. Oh dear...I'm sorry, Sari. I didn't mean...didn't mean...to be so blunt..."

"Don't apologize, Dari. He IS probably laughing about it, and he doesn't care about what he's done to me. I've no one to blame but myself. All of you...and Connor, too... tried to warn me in one way or another, and I wouldn't listen."

Tears traced down her cheeks.

"Now, none of that, Baby." Jordyn wiped her sister's face with a dishtowel. "None of that. Dr. P.D. Chadburn isn't worth a pot of rat piss, much less the tears of my sweet baby sister."

Jayme smiled wickedly. "Are you sure his name is Prescott, Sari? Maybe his real and true name is something like Prick Demon? Or Penis Disability..."

"Listen to Doris Day here," Jordyn laughed. "A little wine fills her head with perverted thoughts. I like that in a friend."

"Doris Day...Doris Day..." Jayme tapped her fingers against the coffee pot. "Doris Day...*Lover Come Back*...that gives me a gloriously inspired idea..."

Jordyn grabbed the pot of water away from Jayme and passed it to Darica. "Finish the coffee fast. Jae's drunker than we thought."

"I'm serpectly pober, and I have a werpectly ponderful idea." Jayme laughed at their doubtful expressions. "I happen to be in perfect patrol of myself. And I have a gloriously inspired idea, from watching a bajillion old movies late at night in lonely hotel rooms during those endless road trips. It might be a great way to get even, if you were serious about getting even, that is."

"Will we have to be drunk to do it?" Jordyn asked.

"No. Just bold and brazen." Jayme smiled at Jordyn. "I'll be bold, and you can be brazen."

"What's the plan?" Jordyn asked, suspicious of the gleam in Jayme's eyes.

"*Lover Come Back*," Jayme explained. "Doris Day gets mad at Rock Hudson. To get even, she lures him out to a secluded place in the country, talks him out of the car and out of his clothes, and then she takes off in the car and leaves him there stark ravin' naked. Couldn't we arrange something like that for ol' Penis Disability? It would certainly seem appropriate to the occasion if you ask me."

Darica shook her head. "We could never do anything that theatrical."

"YOU couldn't," Jordyn said, "but I sure as hell could."

Jayme's grin brightened. "Exactly what I was thinking."

"It would never work," Siara told them. "Prescott would be too suspicious. Jordyn looks very much like me, you know. That's why we're twins."

"Now is not the time to start being a smart-ass, Baby. That's exactly why this could work so very well, you see. I...being the insatiable slut this town thinks I am...don't frown at me like that, Sari...you know it's true...I'll go to visit Dr. C because I'm so terribly curious about what manner of man could possibly worm his way into my shy baby sister's pants. I figure he must be real hot stuff, see, and it's only natural that a sex fiend like me would want to check it out."

"He would never believe it," Siara said. "He knows how close we are, and he knows that you would never flirt with my...someone I was interested in...once."

"But, Baby, that's over and done with now. He's history for you, and you're mending your broken heart just fine, so why shouldn't I have my turn?"

"If I didn't know you were doing this for me, I'd be jealous."

"Good! If I can convince you, he should be easy."

"The clincher is he'll be jumping at the chance to slime up the sheets with sisters, twin sisters especially," Jayme said. "So he won't be thinking things out too clearly. Horny men never do."

"Let's hope that Dr. Chadburn doesn't watch old Doris Day movies," Darica said quietly.

"So what if he does? He'd never suspect that HE was being set up. Men's egos don't work that way..." Jayme tapped a finger against her lip.

"What else you dreaming up here, pal?" Jordyn asked.

"Oh...nothing real vital to the plan...but it would kill two birds with one stone, so to speak. I need a doctor to put me on the pill, so if I were to call Dr.

Prick Demon and request his last appointment of the day, you'd have a better idea of when to stop by and arrange your rendezvous."

"He does usually remain in his office for an hour or so after his receptionist leaves and before he goes to the hospital for his rounds," Siara told them sadly. "Sometimes he would call for me to join him then...t-to help him unwind after a long day he said."

"I'll help him unwind all right," Jordyn growled. "And then I'll wind him right back up and make a bow with his weenie."

"That wasn't in the movie," Jayme pointed out.

"So I'll ad lib. I've always been good at improv. Do you have access to a camera with an infrared lens, Jae?"

"I can probably scrounge one up from one of the photogs at the paper. Just what are you planning to ad lib anyway?"

"We'll want pictures, won't we? Sari, that place in the country where you met him...are there trees and bushes enough for you to hide yourselves and your car?"

"Sure...but surely we shouldn't WATCH..."

"Surely you should. Otherwise why do it? And be sure he knows you've been watching when you vacate the premises after me."

Darica cleared her throat apologetically. "Is there something I can do besides being there to watch? I know you'll think I'm silly, b-but I don't think I should see...could see him without his clothes on."

"There's no need to explain, Dari Mouse," Jordyn assured her. "We know you close your eyes even during Fruit of the Loom commercials."

"But I want to do something to help."

"Why don't you make us *chile rellanos con queso* for afterward?" Jayme suggested. "I'll eat lettuce for a week if I can look forward to your *chile rellanos*."

"With lots of wine." Siara's voice trembled. "I'll need it."

CHAPTER FOUR

"Yes?" The young, blond receptionist smiled around a wad of gum.

Jayme tried to put just enough nervousness into her voice. "I'm the doctor's three-thirty appointment."

"Mrs. Hudson, right?"

"Miss Hudson. I won't be a Mrs. for a few weeks yet. That's why I'm here...to get started on the...well...you know."

Jayme tried her best to blush as she fidgeted with her mother's engagement ring, lovingly presented to her by her father on her thirteenth birthday.

"Have a seat, please. The doctor will be with you soon. We're a little behind today."

"Miss Doris Hudson" sat down in a chair close enough to the receptionist's window for conversation. Gratefully she noticed that the waiting room was otherwise empty.

So far, so good, she thought, taking a deep breath. What had seemed like a great and fool-proof scheme a week ago when their reason was soaked in Riunite now seemed rather foolish in the sobering light of day.

Jayme, however, did need to see a doctor about that necessary prescription.

And Jordyn was adamant about avenging the hurt to her sister.

So here Jayme sat as "Miss Doris Hudson" because Dr. Chadburn would recognize her real name from Siara's talking about her roommates to him.

Jayme cleared her throat and hoped her look of wide-eyed innocence was believable. "I'm nervous. Isn't that silly?"

"Nervous?" The girl was obviously surprised.

To her I look like a senior citizen who should have been around the block a few dozen times, Jayme thought.

"There's no need to be nervous," the blonde was saying. "Dr. Chadburn is an excellent doctor."

"It's just that I've never had this kind of checkup before. It won't hurt, will it?"

"Of course not."

"I wonder what his wife must think about his...having to do checkups like this."

"Dr. Chadburn isn't married, but even if he were, these examinations are merely routine procedures in a doctor's workday."

Jayme hoped her startled look flew by the receptionist's notice. "No wife you say? I thought all established doctors were married..."

"Not this one," the girl replied happily. "He just has other...priorities."

And I bet you're one of them, girlie, Jayme thought. *Wait until the girls hear this. Poor Sari. Jyn will want to castrate this creep, and I may help her do it.*

"Miss Hudson?"

A moment passed before Jayme remembered that she was Miss Hudson.

"Oh...yes?"

"If you will follow me, we'll get you ready for the doctor now."

Jayme followed the girl, whose hips swayed so much that Jayme was thankful for the wide hallway.

"In here, Miss Hudson. If you'll undress, then put on this gown, I'll be back in a moment to check your weight, temp, and BP."

Undress? You mean EVERYTHING?"

"Yes, ma'am. How else can the doctor examine you?"

The girl left as Jayme pondered the disgusting things she always seemed to be doing because of Harlan.

Certain that her face was still red from the examination, Jayme left the doctor's office to meet the twins at the drugstore soda fountain four blocks away. As doctors went, Jayme considered, ol' P.D. seemed competent enough, although she herself had always been too healthy and too busy to bother much with doctors.

At least, she now had the prescription she wanted although she would wait until she was closer to St. Louis to get it filled. Too many people knew her here in Applewood for her to get a prescription for "Miss Doris Hudson." Fortunately the doctor and his wiggly receptionist were relative newcomers.

He had been unable to conceal his surprise about the intactness of her nether regions. Probably he encountered few thirty-three-year-old virgins either at or away from his work.

Would Harlan be...be what?...thankful...impressed...pleased that Jayme saved herself for him? Maybe the knowledge would jolt him into realizing that they belonged together...Harlan and Jayme...Jayme and Harlan...Jayme Oakes...Mrs. Harlan Oakes...

"Hello, Jae. You look deep into something, and I can probably guess what...or who it is."

Mrs. Harlan Oakes.

Jayme sucked her breath in sharply. "Hello, Wallis. What brings you to Applewood? Rather a dull place for someone with your interests, isn't it?"

"My HUSBAND insists upon visiting his parents whenever he has an off day during a home stand. I thought I'd see what artifacts I could find in your quaint little shops here."

You're the artifact, and Harlan's folks can't stand the sight of you. "Spending some of Harlan's new million-dollar contract?"

"Why shouldn't I? I negotiated it for him. Besides, he denies me nothing. The boy is positively devoted to me."

When Jayme flinched, Wallis's emerald green eyes gleamed with catty satisfaction.

"Have you decided about that little matter Harlan discussed with you?" Wallis continued casually.

"As a matter of fact, I've been giving it a lot of thought."

"I thought you would."

Wallis smiled smugly, and though Jayme had resolved to remain cool whenever Harlan's wife provoked her, she now felt the need to attack.

"Why are you so willing to let another woman go to bed with your husband? Thinking maybe you can get him for adultery and get a big divorce settlement?"

"Don't get your hopes up, Jae, dear. Divorcing Harlan is the farthest thing from my mind. He's worth more to me as my husband. Being the wife of a celebrity is very satisfying, and very profitable. As for adultery, well... this hardly counts because the whole thing is my idea. You may thank me profusely if you like."

Jayme flushed darkly. "Why me? Why choose me when women advertise to do this...this service these days?"

"I thought Harlan explained that part to you. The poor dear has this absolute dread of having to jack himself off in a hospital room to get the job done, and the only way he'll do it is the old-fashioned way...you know, Jae dear...fucking. That limits the field considerably."

"To me."

"To you."

"What makes you so damn sure about me?"

"When have you ever denied Harlan anything? Why should you start now, especially about something you've been itching to do for years? Just don't lose sight of the fact that Harlan is and will be MINE. In fact, the boy is even more devoted to me because of my unselfish acceptance of the whole idea."

"You're a bitch."

"Why, thank you, Jae. I consider that my most useful talent."

"Call me 'Jayme,' please. Only my friends call me 'Jae,' and I hardly think you qualify."

"Is that any way for a maid of honor to talk to the bride?"

"I did that for Harlan, not for you."

"And you'll do this favor for him, too."

"Suppose I say I won't?"

"You might say that to me, but you'd never say that to Harlan."

"What's wrong with you that you can't do this yourself? You're not THAT much older than Harlan and I."

"Meow, Jae dear. If you feel you must know, I...miscarried at an early age...and, yes, Harlan knows about it. My frail constitution prevents my conceiving again...though God knows Harlan and I have tried often enough. Perhaps you'll enjoy yourself. Harlan fucks like a mink, and he's rather well endowed. Maybe you can pick up a technique or two to help you trap a man later. It's a shame to see you wasting yourself waiting for Harlan to marry you. He never will, you know. I've guaranteed his commitment to me by agreeing to this whole silly idea."

"Maybe I'll raise Harlan's child myself. Did you ever think of that?"

"And give up a career that lets you travel with the team and see Harlan every day seven months out of the year? I don't think so, Jae dear. Just as I don't think that even in this you'll say no to Harlan. Of course, we'll make sure that everything is strictly legal...just in case. But, no, I have no worries whatsoever. Nothing that I can't take care of anyway. I'd really like to stay and chat further, Jae dear, but I must finish my shopping. I'm meeting an old friend later to wrap up some very old and annoying business. Being Harlan's wife is not without its headaches and responsibilities no matter what you may think."

Bitch, Jayme thought as she turned from Wallis and entered the drugstore. *Bitch and double bitch.*

"We saw," Jordyn said as Jayme joined the twins in a booth. "Quite a conversation you two seemed to be having."

"Oh, how I hate that woman. But she'll not have things her way this time." Jayme flashed them the prescription paper.

"How did your appointment turn out?" Siara asked softly.

"Now I know why I've been avoiding that kind of checkup all these years. It's all very...undignified."

"That's not what she meant...Doris," Jordyn told her. "Am I ready to go on?"

Jayme studied the older twin. Jordyn's blond hair fell in soft curls over bare, tanned shoulders. The fabric of her strapless sundress was white and silky and hugged her body seductively at every curve...all in sharp contrast to Siara's denim skirt, ruffled gingham blouse, and ribboned ponytail.

"You look ready enough," Jayme said. "What a hussy you are."

"Thanks, pal." Jordyn's deep blue eyes shined with excitement for the challenge ahead.

"I don't know about this," Siara said then. "Maybe we shouldn't proceed..."

"We'll stop now if you really want to, Baby...but I'm hoping you won't. That asshole needs a lesson taught to him, and it's not often we females get a chance to teach lessons to assholes."

"Besides, he's a bigger asshole than we imagined," Jayme added, drinking from Jordyn's glass of diet soda. "According to his receptionist, the doctor is not married."

"What!"

Two pairs of identical blue eyes filled with identical amazement before tears glazed one pair and anger flared in the other.

"B-But from the first he always s-said..."

"Did you ever see a wife or hear a wife?" Jayme asked gently.

"N-No..."

"Well, then, I'd say you were snookered from day one," Jordyn said.

"Oh, Jyn..." Siara buried her face in her hands. "I was such a fool."

"Just inexperienced, Baby. After a while you learn not to believe ninety-eight percent of what a man says, and you can never be too certain about the other two percent. Now quit your boo-hooing. I've got work to do. Dr. Chadburn is probably in need of diversion to help him unwind from a very tiring day."

"We'll head on home and eagerly await your report," Jayme said as Jordyn stood up to leave.

"I am woman, hear me roar!" Jordyn proclaimed as she breezed out the door.

"Would you mind driving back alone?" Siara asked once her sister was gone. "I'd like to walk for a while."

"But it's nearly six miles back to the house."

"I'll walk to the college. It's not that far, and I can take a taxi from there. I really need to be alone for a while."

"Okay, but don't wander around too long. Jyn will want you there when she gets home, and she'll have my head for leaving you unchaperoned right now."

"I'll be fine."

"It's against my better judgment, but I can understand your wanting to be alone for a while."

"Thanks, Jae. I need some alone time to organize my thoughts and feelings, especially now that I know that Prescott was deceiving me the entire time we were together. Don't worry about me. I'm stronger than Jyn thinks I am, and this experience has made me even stronger, maybe even strong enough to handle a man like Prescott Chadburn."

For some reason Jayme was disturbed rather than comforted by the determined look on Siara's face.

CHAPTER FIVE

"Dr. Chadburn? Dr. Prescott Chadburn? I hope I haven't caught you at an inconvenient time."

His back was turned to the doorway as he gathered papers into his briefcase.

"Actually I do have a personal appointment in a few minutes. My receptionist is gone for the day, but if you—"

He turned around then, recognition causing him to bite off the words. Because the girl looked so much like Siara, yet so different, too, he knew this visitor must be the beloved twin sister. A guarded look settled on his face though he tried to be casual as he snapped his briefcase shut.

"If you're here about Siara, I really must tell you that—"

With the grace of an experienced dancer, Jordyn glided across the floor until she stood directly before him. Interest had sparked in his eyes with each willowy movement she made. Jordyn wasn't surprised. He had, in fact, noticed the bait as soon as she showed it to him. A few more nibbles and the sucker would bite. He was no different from any other man whose brains and emotions were tucked away in his Jockey shorts...older than what appealed to her though she could see the attraction for Siara, who would be easily taken in by a distinguished, gray-at-the-temples type, like their father. Macho hunks scared Siara to death.

"Siara was right about one thing." Though she felt stupid doing it, Jordyn kept her voice whispery soft. She knew men slobbered over voices that were more bedroom than brain. "You are very attractive. I was curious to see what kind of man could lure my little sister out of her shell."

Dr. Chadburn cleared his throat as he tried to maintain control of his body, which had become too aware of Jordyn's closeness...her perfume...her husky, sexy voice...her bare shoulders...her fingertips skimming along the hairs of his arm without touching the skin.

"Is that why you're here, Miss Nealy...just curiosity?"

"Call me Jordyn. I like to be on a first-name basis with the men I intend to fuck."

She trailed her hand lightly around him as she moved to pull herself up onto his desk. Allowing her dress to slide up and reveal most of her thighs, she placed her arms far enough behind her to thrust her breasts temptingly upward. The office air conditioner cooled the room enough that her nipples were rigid points against the soft fabric of her sundress, as she had intended. He would, of course, think she was overcome with desire for him.

"What about your sister?" he asked, his throat obviously dry.

"What about her? It was a new experience for me, you know, her having a man I hadn't...known first. I didn't like it at all. Of course, I would never move in on Siara's territory, but you're fair game now. You did dump her, didn't you?"

"Actually *dump* is somewhat harsh. I needed to end it, you see. Siara is a sweet girl, but she became much too serious...and too possessive. I recognized that tendency in her early and tried to stifle it by telling her that I was married, but then she started talking marriage anyway. I knew it would be best for her if—"

Jordyn laid a finger across his lips.

"You don't need to explain anything to me. I know that Siara is a hopeless romantic. Right now she thinks her heart is broken forever, but she'll bounce back okay. I should thank you for letting her down so easily. Will you allow me to show you my gratitude?"

"What do you have in mind?"

"You surprise me. What do you think I have in mind?"

After she placed his hand on her thigh, she fought the urge to slap him away when he began caressing her leg.

"You're not much like your sister, are you?" he asked.

"I like to have a good time. Unfortunately Siara's conscience has always interfered with her having a good time. However, I have no such bothersome conscience. Can YOU show me a good time?"

"I think I have the necessary qualifications." When he was certain that Jordyn had not come to rant at him for wronging her sister, his confidence swelled along with his manhood. "But I do have this important appointment in a few minutes..."

"I'm free tonight." Jordyn wriggled off the desk and drifted away from him. "If you're interested."

"I'm interested," he said. "There's this quiet little restaurant I know...a little run-down and off the beaten path, but—"

"I'm not interested in eating with you, Doctor. I think you can feed me just fine with what you have...on hand."

When surprise sparked in his eyes, she continued, "Do I shock you? Didn't Siara tell you that I'm the town nympho? No...she wouldn't...she thinks I'm wonderful. But then so do all the men I've enjoyed...and I do enjoy my men. The thing is, I do have this one man who thinks he's my boyfriend...my big hulking boyfriend who can become quite mean when he gets jealous. He doesn't understand this NEED I have, you see, and I must be very discreet about how I get this need satisfied. He has tons of money, and I'd hate to lose a chance at it. Do you understand what I'm trying to tell you, Doctor?"

He pressed her hand against his crotch. "Maybe this will take care of your need."

Jordyn struggled to keep from laughing in his face. "Mmmm...I'm sure it will. Do you have this effect on all your women?"

He smiled. "I've had no complaints. Perhaps I can share one of my favorite places with you. I have some land in the country, very secluded. A bottle of wine, a blanket under the stars, an incredibly beautiful woman...I find that quite titillating. Perhaps you'll enjoy such a setting?"

"It sounds wonderfully delicious. I love feeling the night air on my naked skin. We'll have to take my car though...so that my boyfriend won't see it parked somewhere and get suspicious. He checks up on me a lot. Is nine an okay time for you?"

"Nine is fine," he said as she turned to go. "A kiss to last us till then?"

She kept her back to him. "If I kiss you now, you'll surely miss your appointment. A girl like me has very little will power with men like you. Let's wait until nine. You bring the wine. I'll bring the blanket. By then I'll be all hot and juicy for you."

She left the office quickly, making a sick face as soon as she was in the corridor. *God, what a typical male egotist pervert,* she thought. She would enjoy seeing the doctor get exactly what he had coming to him. *Which is not coming at all,* she thought with a satisfied smile.

Her TransAm was parked in front of the drugstore, and she walked the few blocks briskly, laughter burbling within her as she thought of the encounter with Siara's doctor. Child's play. Handling men was child's play. She couldn't understand why women always seemed to have so much trouble...

A familiar blue and white Bronco was parked beside her car. Luke's Bronco. Whenever she saw Luke, she was both pleased and impatient with him. No other man could love her the way he did. At six-feet-six, he had huge shoulders from years of farm work, and the black tee shirts he wore stretched to show every bronze muscle. In the summer his light-brown hair was sun-streaked with red and gold, and his smile flashed brilliantly white against his rugged, tanned face. Sometimes his amber-brown eyes would melt in warmth when he looked at her. More often, however, they snapped in fiery anger at her, for she could not, would not commit herself to this farm boy, even if he was the very best she'd ever had in bed. Being a farmer's wife was not her idea of a fun way to spend the rest of her life.

"Waiting for me, Farm Boy?" she asked him now.

He smiled down at her from the truck. Suddenly Jordyn felt very warm.

"Actually I'm waiting for Lissa. She's in the drugstore buying her weekly fix of teen magazines. But when I saw your car, I thought this might be a good place to wait."

"Finding a thirteen-year-old sister hard to handle?"

"All women are hard to handle, especially when they get older. So, where you been?"

"If you think it's any of your business, I've been to see a doctor."

"Been sick?"

"Does a girl have to be sick to see a doctor?"

Luke looked hopeful. "Are you pregnant?"

"Good Lord no! Are you crazy? I'm too smart to let that happen."

"Oh." He tapped his fingers against the steering wheel.

"You sound disappointed."

"If you were, we'd have to get married, wouldn't we?"

"Think again, Farm Boy. What makes you think you're the only man who's had his dipper in my ice cream lately?" *Jesus Christ, he has been the only one for a long time now. Maybe I am sick!*

Luke rubbed his hand across his eyes. "Why do you do this to me, Jordyn?"

"Do you want me to lie instead?"

"No...but you could be a damn sight more tactful about it, especially since I've made no secret of my feelings for you."

"Sorry."

Jordyn was saved from further comment when Malissa Johnson bounced out of the drugstore with her arms filled with teen magazines.

"I really hit the jackpot, Luke. The new *Teen Beat* has a centerfold of John Stamos."

"Life has meaning again."

"Father Jonathan has asked us to perform at the Fall Festival," Jordyn told Malissa, "so don't spend so much time staring at John Stamos that you forget to practice."

"I'll be a star, and then John Stamos can look at MY centerfold in *Teen Beat*."

As Jordyn and Luke laughed together, he reached out to brush a bit of hair away from her face, his eyes that warm, melting amber-brown.

"Maybe we can catch a movie later tonight?" he said softly.

Cursing silently, Jordyn prepared herself for the firestorm. "I can't tonight. I already have plans."

"I see," he said, jerking his hand back. "Well, have yourself a damn good time."

His tires squealed as he pulled away from the curb. The effect was spoiled, however, when he almost immediately had to stop for a red light.

"Bye, Jyn!" Malissa yelled, laughing as she leaned out the window to wave.

Jordyn waved back, smiling as Luke reached angrily across the seat to pull his sister back inside the truck.

CHAPTER SIX

"Where is everybody? I expected an eager audience, and all I get is you." Jordyn tossed her keys onto the kitchen counter and sat down at the table with Jayme, who was surrounded by notes for a feature she was writing about a Cardinal rookie.

"I have no idea where Dari is," Jayme said. "Afternoon mass probably. Your sister was supposed to walk to the university and then catch a cab home. She wanted to be alone for a while."

"Well, damn. What a letdown."

"Thanks a lot, pal."

"Why aren't you working in the study?"

"I'm more comfortable here. I always feel like I'm intruding when I'm in your dad's study."

"Nonsense. No one but Connor ever uses it. I'm sure both Daddy and Mama would have been delighted to see it used by a famous reporter like you."

"You seem especially gushy. I take it things went well."

"Very well. The fucker was putty in my hands."

"Aren't all men?"

"True. Very true." Jordyn helped herself to Jayme's Diet Rite.

Laying down her pen, Jayme stretched her arms over her head. "I did some checking with my stepmom. P.D. has been spending some quality public time with some widowed chick with mega bucks over in Willow Grove, someone very active in charities and church work."

"So that's why he went to such extremes to mislead Sari. P.D.'s charities-and-church lady wouldn't like sweet young things hanging all over her boyfriend."

"Next time we'll check with Gwynnie BEFORE Sari starts up with a new guy."

"IF she ever does. This episode hurt her self-confidence pretty damn bad. She was never involved with anyone before ol' Doc C reared his ugly prick. She's always been too sweet and shy for what most guys look for in a date. She's the kind they settle down with after they've sown their wild oats with gals like me. I've tried to tell Sari that, but she never has believed me. She thinks she's unappealing."

"Did you point out that you do quite well with the exact same equipment?"

"It's no wonder I've worn myself out keeping the men in this town happy. I've had to pick up the slack for my roommates. Siara's too shy and insecure. You're too hung up on Harlan. And Darica's too afraid of sinning."

"We appreciate your efforts in our behalf."

Jordyn stood up and paced around the table. "I think I'll start supper."

"Dari's making *chile rellanos*, remember?"

"I know. But she's gone, and you're too busy to be any fun. Even when there's no game, you're busy."

"It goes with the territory." Jayme drummed her fingers on the table. "Sometimes I wonder why I bother. There are more important things in this world than a bases-loaded walk in the bottom of the ninth."

"Harlan is why you try. No mystery there."

"Except to Harlan."

"You're making progress though. At least now you'll get to fuck him."

"Leave it to you to put romance in its proper perspective."

Jordyn grinned as she randomly tossed some items out of the refrigerator. "I'm a firm believer in the therapeutic value of sex."

"No wonder you're so healthy."

"Healthy, and..." Jordyn turned to face her roommate. "Would you believe I'm nervous?"

"Nervous? You? About what?"

"Tonight's extravaganza with the doc. This kind of stuff may work for Doris Day, but I'm not so sure about it working for me."

"I can't believe you're nervous about something that is so simple compared to stuff that you...and we have done and gotten away with in the past. Remember Hudson Turner? And your nasty uncle?"

"I have a spooky feeling this time though."

"Stage fright, that's all. We're rounding third and heading for home. What could possibly go wrong now?"

A car roared into the driveway then, throwing gravel as it skidded to a stop.

Jordyn peeked out the window. "It's Darica. She looks excited about something."

"Jyn! Sari! Jae!" Darica shouted, racing into the kitchen. "You won't believe it! He died and the office burned! God's judgment! It's God's judgment!"

"Calm down, Dari." Jordyn grabbed Darica's arm to keep her from rushing blindly around the kitchen. "Who's dead? What office? You smell like smoke. What happened?"

Darica gulped for breath. "The doctor was dead...Dr. Chadburn was dead. And then the office...on fire...it burned so fast. I was going to talk to him...to appeal to his Christian decency...for Sari...only...only...and the firemen are there now...and the POLICE. He was murdered. I KNOW he was murdered...I need to wash my hands...I MUST wash my hands..."

Jordyn's eyes locked on Jayme's as both girls noted Siara's absence. For the next half hour, Jayme talked quietly to Darica in an effort to calm her while Jordyn paced, peeked out the window, and paced some more. Finally she saw Siara walking around the cluster of trees that bordered the end of the driveway.

Jordyn ran out to meet her sister. "Where have been, Baby?"

"Just walking for a while," Siara murmured dreamily. "Just walking...and talking...and getting my heart back on track..."

Jordyn wrinkled her nose then, somewhat fearfully as she detected the smoky smell on her sister's clothing.

Part II: Jordyn and Siara Nealy/1957-1984

CHAPTER ONE

When the doctor first told Amelie Nealy that she and her husband, Devon, could probably expect twins, she felt a twinge of dismay. They really couldn't afford even one child although they had happily resigned themselves to making Devon's salary as a teacher cover the added expenses somehow. With Devon working for his doctorate in the evenings and during summer vacations, he certainly couldn't take a part-time job. Nor did Amelie want him to, for his career dream was a professorship, hopefully in Applewood at Mosby Scheffers…not a large college, to be sure, but well-respected in the academic world of Illinois.

Equally out of the question was Amelie's taking a job. For someone so educated and enlightened, Devon was frustratingly narrow-minded about working wives, especially pregnant ones. Amelie smiled wryly. Doubly so for one pregnant with twins.

"Hello, my darling," she called to him as she entered their three-room apartment.

He was sitting at the kitchen table with textbooks piled around him as he worked on his lesson plans. With his lesson planning and paper grading out of the way before dinner, he could concentrate on his own studies later.

"How's it going, my love?" she asked, hugging him from behind as she kissed the top of his head. His hair was thick and dark and beginning to gray at the temples.

"The planning's almost finished, but the grading will take forever." Removing his rimless glasses, he rubbed his eyes. "One of these days I'll learn not to assign themes for Friday."

"Your beautiful brown eyes are always so red and tired by the end of the week. Can't you save some of this for later in the weekend?"

"I'd like to spend some time with my lovely wife this weekend." He drew Amelie onto his lap, wincing slightly as her full weight pressed against his legs. "Another few pounds and I'll have to hoist you with a crane, Mel."

"You say such pretty things to me, darling. Kiss me, and I'll think about forgiving you."

His kiss was gentle, and she sighed as she cuddled against him.

"Now tell me what Dr. Davies had to say." As he nibbled at her ear, he wondered if he should break the romantic moment by telling his wife that she was cutting off the circulation in his legs.

"Can't we wait until later for boring doctor talk? We need some quiet family time right now...just the four of us."

"Four? You, Baby Nealy, me, and if you've brought home a stray cat, Amelie, you'll both sleep in the hallway."

"We'll all have to sleep together, Devon my darling. Baby Nealy is a plural."

"Plural?"

"As in more than one...which two is...more than one."

He forgot the numbness in his legs. "You don't mean... you CAN'T mean..."

"Twins, Devon my love. Baby Nealys. Or is it Babies Nealy? Whatever way is correct, isn't it wonderful?"

"How could you do this to me, Mel?"

"I absolutely refuse to take full responsibility, so quit trying to pass the buck."

"Whatever will we do? We'll have to move for sure now...and soon."

"There's the house on Meadow Lane."

"Even if we could afford it, sweetheart, it will take a lot of time and money to fix it up...and we have neither."

"Correction, darling...neither of us has the money, but I have lots of time. Oh, Devon, I am so dying to get my hands on that house, and it can't be on the market too much longer before someone else grabs it. We don't need to do anything major for a while...just enough to make it livable until you finish school and get on at the university."

"IF I get on at the university."

"You will. I'm sure you will. Even Dr. Cuthbertson says so, and he's head of the English department."

"There's still the immediate money problem, sweetheart."

Amelie took a deep breath and plunged ahead. "Now don't bull up on me without our talking this through, my love. Your sister is sure Blair can get us a loan at his bank."

"So you're already plotting and planning with Bonnie..."

"Don't be angry. She knows how much we're going to need a bigger place, and this house is a terrific bargain. Even you said so."

"Where do we get the extra cash for repairs?"

"Bonnie is sure Blair can arrange it for us somehow...and so that our monthly payments won't be much more than our rent is now, or would be if we rented a bigger apartment. Our folks are standing by ready to co-sign if necessary. If we don't do this now, darling, we will have to rent a bigger place, and that will be just so much money going towards someone else's equity. Besides, in another year you'll be a professor at the university, and money won't be so tight for us."

"You have it all planned, don't you, Pollyanna?" Smiling, he stroked her soft, blond curls. "What will we do for furniture? What we have will barely fill a single room in that house."

"We can make do until we can afford more furniture, and Bonnie and your mother and my parents are sure to have a few things they'll let us use. Please, Devon. Please say yes."

"I hate the thought of accepting a favor from Blair. I love Bonnie dearly, but she has lousy taste in men."

"Blair is quite good-looking in a rugged sort of way, and he works very hard to stay in shape."

"Should I be jealous?"

"Of Blair? Not in a million years. I like my men gentle, tall, and slender...amazingly like you, in fact."

"You told your mother that I remind you of Ichabod Crane."

"My mother has a big mouth. Now back to Blair."

"He's a son of a bitch, and Bonnie was crazy for marrying him, no matter how rich he is...or will be...supposedly."

"Love makes us all crazy. After all, I never considered Ichabod Crane particularly sexy until I met you. And quit straying off the subject. I'm not letting you weasel out this time. If you don't want to ask Blair for a favor, think of it as a favor from Bonnie. She'll be doing all the persuading."

Devon patted her belly. "I don't have any choice, do you? I'm outnumbered three to one."

"Oh, Devon!" Amelie hugged him fiercely. "I love you, I love you, I love you! Let's go to bed, and I'll show you just how much."

"Before dinner? How decadent you've become, sweetheart. Are you wanting a try at triplets?"

"Are you going to resist me?" She grinned mischievously as she unzipped his trousers.

"Have I ever been able to resist you?" Picking her up to carry her the few steps into the bedroom, he grunted, "Think Blair can loan us enough extra for that crane?"

CHAPTER TWO

The house at Three Meadow Lane was a throwback to the days when rooms were added as needed with little regard for overall architectural appearance. Devon was indeed thankful for the clusters of trees that hid the awkward structure from passers-by. Though the house had originally been a two-story salt box, fifty feet square, single-story additions had been built onto either side, the room on the left beginning flush with the front of the house, and the addition on the right beginning about five feet back, but ending flush with the back of the house. Perhaps Devon's aesthetic instincts would not have been offended if the three sections presented even a hint of uniformity. Though attached, each section maintained its own uniqueness, differing in every detail from the style and color of the shingles to the color of the paint. What was left of the paint anyway. The entire exterior needed new paint badly. In that, at least, there was uniformity. Layers of old paint had curled and warped so much that Devon could break off large chunks of it.

He surveyed his new kingdom doubtfully. Tangles of bushes, overgrown weeds, a driveway that was little more than a dirt path...and that was just the outside.

Inside was a nightmare of peeling and faded wallpaper, cracked plaster, sagging floors, tarnished light fixtures with questionable wiring, and antique plumbing that trickled rusty water. For some reason he could not understand, Amelie was absolutely enchanted with the whole monstrosity...to the point of hysteria, Devon thought. He should never have married an interior design major.

As Devon began to attack the grass, he sighed the sigh of a martyred husband who caters to the crazy whims of his pregnant wife.

* * *

"But you must have a study, Devon. I insist. There's plenty of room with four bedrooms upstairs and those huge additions."

"Why haven't I won a single argument since we bought this house?"

"Because you're smart enough to realize I'm always right, darling."

So part of the "house money" had gone to buy Devon a huge second-hand desk, which Amelie stripped, stained, and lacquered for him herself. Bonnie donated a few bookcases that had been stored in the Eldred basement and bought Blair a new padded swivel chair for his den so that she would have a good excuse for giving Devon the "old" one. Together Amelie and Bonnie painted the walls of the room pale gold and waxed and buffed the neglected hardwood floor until it shined. Borrowing her mother's Singer, Amelie made curtains from a handsome gold, brown, and cream linen-look fabric. Even with Devon's awards and degrees framed and grouped on the wall behind his desk, the end result had a distinctly unfinished look because of the sparse furnishings.

Nevertheless, Amelie was pleased that Devon would no longer have to work at the kitchen table. Devon, too, was delighted with the room and touched by the thoughtfulness of his wife and sister.

From that moment, he resolved to rein in his doubts and to trust his wife's taste, resourcefulness, and common sense in renovating their new home.

They were visited one Saturday morning by several Scheffers engineering students, who swarmed throughout the house, checking, repairing, and replacing electrical wiring. "Extra credit field trip," their instructor, Henry Gillette, said, though Amelie seemed prepared enough, Devon noticed, with sandwiches, cookies, and cherry Kool-Aid. When Devon looked to his wife for an explanation, she merely smiled as her blue eyes twinkled impishly.

That same afternoon, undergraduates from Scheffers English department…many of whom Devon had privately tutored through the horrors of the required composition courses…showed up to help with the scrubbing and painting. One student, the son of a plumber, set to work in the bathrooms and kitchen, and soon steady streams of clear water replaced the rusty trickles. Devon knew there had been plotting afoot when stately Dr. Cuthbertson showed up in painter's bibs, asking to be put to work.

"Kinda reminds you of a Judy Garland-Mickey Rooney movie, doesn't it, darling?" Amelie said happily as she wiped the cherry Kool-Aid mustache off her husband. "By the way, did you know that Dr. Cuthbertson's niece is married to Henry Gillette?"

Soon, with the help of family and friends, Amelia's magic had transformed the house on Meadow Lane. Each room had been painted or papered, the plumbing and electrical wiring fixed, and floors braced, waxed, and buffed. An assortment of used or borrowed furniture kept the rooms from standing empty. "Early hand-me-down spaciousness," Amelie said lovingly.

Outside, continuous mowing was bringing the lawn under control, and Bonnie was pampering the rose bushes discovered amid the jungle. She had also pruned the rhododendrons around the house and planted marigolds. Blair was bullied into buying gravel for a proper driveway though he refused to become involved with scraping and painting the exterior of the house. Consequently, Devon and Bonnie with their mother and Amelia's parents did most of the outside painting, refusing to let a grossly huge Amelie on a ladder.

The tri-colored shingles would have to wait until later, but the fresh white paint certainly did a lot to make the place look worthy of human habitation…and that, Devon thought, was a definite improvement.

Knowing that Amelie longed for blue shutters, Devon took money for them out of Gaylord, their huge glass piggy bank where they were hoarding money for a down payment on a new car. Amelia's mother took Amelie for a ride in the country, carefully staying away long enough for Devon and his father-in-law to install the shutters. The surprise bought a flood of tears from Amelie and, Devon swore, sent her into labor, with the twins arriving six hours later.

Ironically, the twins were born on different days and in different months: Jordyn Eve made her squalling entrance at 11:55 p.m. on July 31, and Siara Dawn entered the world more quietly at 12:03 a.m. on August 1, thereby establishing early that though they were identical in appearance, each would steadfastly maintain her own identity.

* * *

With the twins settled into a daily routine and the bare essentials of the house taken care of, Amelie began a room-by-room decorating campaign, deterred only when money ran low, as it often did, even after Devon was, as predicted, accepted as an assistant professor at Scheffers. To overcome this minor financial annoyance, Amelie began "advising" a few of Bonnie's friends about their decorating concerns, for which she received "monetary gifts of appreciation" and numerous recommendations to other women who needed her guidance.

Though Devon was fully aware of his wife's growing popularity, he did not, at first, realize that Amelie had sneaked a potentially profitable business into their home. When he did realize what was happening, he pursed his lips tightly and pouted in his study while Amelie and Bonnie calmly drank their iced tea in the kitchen, certain enough of Devon's sense of fair play to know he would resign himself to the situation sooner or later in spite of his views on working mothers.

An hour later he came into the kitchen, "for a glass of cherry Kool-Aid," he said. Then, sitting at the table with Amelie and Bonnie, he sulked in silence, waiting for one of them to say something in surrender. The women, however, recognized his strategy and held their ground quietly until he, at last, relented.

"I suppose I can live with it," he said, "since it's not an office job or factory work that will keep you away from home all week. And you are very good at it, sweetheart. I shouldn't deprive others of your talent."

"Thank you for understanding, my darling." Amelie smiled as she wiped the cherry mustache off her husband's lip.

* * *

"Now blow out the candles, darlings, while Daddy snaps your pictures."

Amelie puffed her cheeks out to show her daughters what was expected of them, but they only looked at each other and giggled before plunging their hands into the chocolate frosting.

At three years old, Jordyn and Siara continued to show everyone that their twinness extended only as far as their identical blue eyes, white-blond hair, and dimples. Where Siara was content to study the chocolate stickiness on her fingers with all the seriousness of a scientist looking through a microscope, Jordyn was streaking the frosting on herself and her sister, giggling as she looked sideways at her parents to see if she was going to get into trouble. Because today was her birthday, however, Amelie and Devon merely smiled indulgently as Aunt Bonnie and Uncle Blair, Grandy Grace, and Pappy Dan and Mammy Min laughed as though Jordyn had done something wonderfully clever. Reveling in their obvious adulation, Jordyn tried even harder to entertain, digging out a hunk of cake and hurling it into the face of her twin, who promptly began to wail in distress. Though she seldom cried herself, Jordyn was crushed at having brought such anguish to her sister, whom she now hugged and patted with a chocolate-covered hand. After a few sniffles, Siara managed a brave smile.

"Jordyn," Amelie explained, "takes her responsibilities as the older sister quite seriously."

"And Siara," Devon added, "is a little quicker to pick up on things. But Jordyn is definitely the bolder of the two at exploring and checking out something new. When we took them to Nanette's last week to get them started in dance and gymnastics, Jordyn jumped right in, but Siara wanted no part of it. In fact, Nanette recommended that we wait a while to start Siara because she seemed so afraid."

Amelie grinned. "But we saw Jordyn showing Siara what they had done that day in class, and Siara was following along perfectly, until she noticed that Devon and I were watching her. I hope she's not that shy when she starts school."

"Jordyn will watch out for her, sweetheart."

"They look so much like you at that age, Amelie," Min said proudly, gazing at the twins with grandmotherly devotion.

"Except for Jordyn's stubborn set of the mouth." Grace Nealy nodded knowingly. "She inherited that from Devon for sure."

"We think Siara will be the intellectual," Amelie said as she stood and raised her paper cup toward Devon, "like her daddy, who's just been given a full professorship at Scheffers."

"And Jordyn, will be just like Mommy," Devon laughed as he waved away the family's congratulations, "using her devious woman's wiles to twist some poor intellectual around her little finger."

"No doubt about it..." Blair belched on the last of the beer he had brought to the party. "They'll be real heart-breakers someday. The bucks will be standing in line for a chance to get into their pants."

"Blair!" Bonnie's embarrassed admonition was harsh. "Try not to be so smutty-mouthed around family."

"If a guy can't be smutty around his family, then who the hell can he be smutty with?" Blair belched again as he lit one of his fat, black cigars and puffed smoke into Bonnie's face.

"From what I've heard, you don't have too much trouble finding an audience for your smut."

There was an awkward silence as Amelie sneaked a worried look at Devon, whose lips were pressed together so tightly the surrounding skin was white.

The grandparents hovered around the twins, three adults stuffing cake down two children and trying very hard to look too busy to have noticed anything disagreeable.

Amelie cleared her throat. "More cherry Kool-Aid, darling? Devon is an absolute addict when it comes to cherry Kool-Aid. Did you see the roses, Bonnie? They're in full bloom now and absolutely gorgeous. You've done wonders with them, Bonnie. And to think Devon was ready to mow them down when we moved in..."

"You're babbling, sweetheart," Devon whispered.

"So give me some help here, darling."

"Say...Blair...Dan...why don't we take the girls into the living room and let the ladies clean up in here?" Devon suggested, still angry with his brother-in-law but ready to help his wife restore the congenial atmosphere. "The Cardinals are on television this afternoon I think."

"Great!" Dan bellowed in relief. "I've been dying to see the game."

"Sure, why not?" Blair stabbed out his cigar in a plate of melting ice cream.

"Your father's never been that interested in baseball before," Min whispered to Amelie.

"Hush, Mama. Just help me clean up the girls and let the men watch the game."

While the ladies busied themselves with clearing away the cake and ice cream no adult had bothered to eat, the men settled in the living room with the twins. Pappy Dan studied a picture book with the ever-solemn Siara as Blair...in a rare display of avuncular affection...bounced a giggling Jordyn on his lap. For some reason Devon could not clearly identify, he was disturbed by his brother-in-law's attention to his older daughter.

He would have been even more concerned had he seen that Jordyn was being gently bounced on Blair's swollen manhood.

CHAPTER THREE

"I think he acts that way just to upset Bonnie," Amelie said later that night. The twins had long since been put to bed, and Amelie and Devon nestled together in their bed as they enjoyed their alone time and the peace and quiet after the day's confusion.

"I keep telling you that Blair is that way naturally... a peasant playing at being a prince," Devon said. "I think Bonnie is noticing it, too...finally."

"It's not so much that as her suspecting that he has a few girlfriends on the side. The girls at the bank play up to him, and he eats it right up. Bonnie says he spends a whole lot of time working late these days. She seems more angry than hurt."

"It's a blow to her ego, not to her heart."

"How can you say such a thing about your own sister?"

"Who could possibly love Blair? He's crude, rude, boring, and boorish. Bonnie is a wonderful sister, but she has always been too attracted to money and position. I watched her discard one boyfriend after another if she thought she was trading up. But she made a mistake with Blair. For all his sneaky ways, he has gone as far at the bank as he's going to go. There's no room at the top for a pig. Blair will never reach the pinnacle of success Bonnie envisioned, and I'm sure she's been quite a shrew about it, too. I could almost feel sorry for Blair if I didn't find him so contemptible. I do feel sorry for Bonnie. She's stuck and will never divorce him because she'd have to admit that she made a huge mistake."

Amelie sighed. "I feel a little guilty. Everything is so perfect in my life...two beautiful daughters and a wonderful, loving, and successful husband...our home is becoming just like the home I've always dreamed about..."

"You're no slouch yourself, my love. Thanks to your own talents, we can park a new Buick in the driveway and still put money in the girls' college funds."

"Does my working still bother you any? Sometimes I worry that you're just being a good sport because you love me."

"If your working made you any less a wife or mother, I'd be complaining at the top of my lungs. However, you, my darling wife, manage to handle everything in your usual superb fashion. I have never felt neglected, and I can be very selfish about sharing you."

"I love you, Devon."

"Of course you do. Another wonderful thing about you is that you...unlike Bonnie...have great taste in husbands. Now why don't you show me how much you love me in that wonderful way you have..."

Sometime later, as they drifted into peaceful, sated sleep, a pensive three-year-old crept back to her own bed after gently closing the door to her parents' room. Jordyn had discovered that by opening the door a crack, she was able to hear and almost see some interesting activity in her parents' bed.

* * *

"Go ahead to your meeting," Blair told Devon. "I'll stay with the kids until Bonnie and Mel get back."

Devon hesitated, telling himself that he was foolish for being so apprehensive about leaving his six-year-old daughters with their uncle. He had no real choice in the matter anyway. Amelie, who had been shopping with Bonnie in St. Louis, had called to tell him they would be delayed by a flat tire, and Devon's departmental meeting was one he couldn't miss since he was being considered for assistant department chairman. For a moment he thought about calling one of the grandparents, but then decided that such a move would be rude and unexplainable to Blair, who had come by to pick up Bonnie.

"I've got to wait for Bonnie anyway, old boy," Blair continued, "and how much trouble can the girls be asleep?"

"Well...if you insist. Mel should be back in an hour or so, and I'll not be much longer than that. The girls should sleep at least that long. The cold medicine the doctor gave them makes them sleep quite soundly."

"Quit your worrying and go, will you? I'll watch a little television until someone gets home."

"If you're sure you don't mind. Thanks, Blair."

After Devon was gone, Blair settled in one of the comfortable over-stuffed chairs in the living room. A football game flickered at him from the television set, but he wasn't that interested in the action. Instead he puffed on one his big, black cigars and thought about his sister-in-law. Classy, sassy Amelie. *Wonder what it'd be like to put it to her,* Blair considered, knowing that Amelie would never be a willing partner.

Bonnie was getting fat and sloppy, though he had stopped going to her for his satisfaction even before she began to pick up weight. The girls at the bank were more inclined to refuse him these days unless he promised them some expensive gift or job perk. Blair didn't think he was so repulsive that the gifts and perks were necessary. He had some influence in the bank...though not as much as he liked people to believe he had...and he had managed to maintain his athletic physique from his college football days. So what was the problem? Occasionally he was even forced to jack himself off here lately. And for the first time ever he had actually paid cash for a piece of ass from some St. Louis call girl who wasn't worth the price she demanded even if she was only fourteen as she claimed to be.

"Where's Daddy?"

Blair squinted through the cigar smoke at the sleepy-eyed youngster standing in the doorway.

"Which one are you?" he asked, for he could never tell the twins apart as easily as everyone else seemed to.

"Sari. I'm Sari, and I want my daddy. I don't feel good. My tummy hurts."

"Your daddy's at a meeting." Blair rubbed his crotch thoughtfully and studied the girl for a moment before he continued speaking. "Come to your Uncle Blair, honey. I'll try to make you feel better."

Siara eyed her uncle suspiciously. Unlike Jordyn, who always laughed and giggled with him, Siara had never much enjoyed being around him. She much preferred Aunt Bonnie, who didn't stink like beer and cigars.

"Come to your Uncle Blair, honey. Maybe I can make your tummy feel better."

Needing the comfort of an adult, even if it was Uncle Blair, Siara padded across the room and climbed onto his lap. When the smoke from his cigar made her choke, he quickly put it out.

"See, honey. Uncle Blair wants to make you feel better."

Blair raised up her nightgown and rubbed his hand over her stomach. "Is this where it hurts? Is Uncle Blair making Siara feel better?"

The drone of his voice relaxed her, and she nodded sleepily as she leaned against him. When her eyes closed, he slid his hand into her panties.

"I not hurt down there," Siara murmured, pushing weakly at his hand.

"Does it make you feel good when I rub you there, honey? It makes me feel good. Can you make me feel good like I'm making you feel good?"

"I'm sleepy. I want to go to bed now." Siara struggled feebly as she tried to sit up.

"Okay, honey. I'll take you up to bed, but first I want to give you a present."

"What is it?"

"A...a sucker. You like suckers, don't you?" When Siara nodded, he continued. "I have a big sucker for you, honey. You can lick my big sucker."

"Where is it?"

"In my pocket. Right here in my pocket, honey. I'll show you..."

He unzipped his trousers and pulled out his cock. He'd been hard ever since he began thinking of Amelie. Siara certainly resembled her beautiful mother...only younger, of course...and more innocent...and untouched...

Blair's balls ached with excitement.

"That's not a sucker," Siara said doubtfully.

"It's a...a peppermint stick. See how red and delicious it looks. Put your mouth on it. Suck it...suck it hard..."

"Don't want to. My tummy hurts."

"Put your mouth on it, honey, and you'll feel better. Suck it hard, and you'll feel better..."

"Please...no...I don't want to..."

"Suck on it...now!" He forced her head toward his crotch.

The ferocity in his voice frightened her as much as the throbbing purple and red monster poking at her face.

"I don't want to," she cried. "Please don't make me. I don't want to!"

Her pleas were muffled as Blair forced his engorged penis into her mouth. Siara gagged once, twice, then vomited chicken soup and orange juice all over his lap.

"You goddamn, fucking brat!" Blair yelled, hurling Siara to the floor as he jumped up.

Siara did not wait for him to comment further. Running upstairs, she locked herself in the bathroom. She squeezed half a tube of toothpaste directly into her mouth and brushed her teeth until her gums ached. Then, after shedding her soiled nightgown and panties, she filled the bathtub with steaming hot water and scrubbed her body until her skin was red.

Cautiously she peeked around the bathroom door, then ran to her bed, pulling the covers over her head as she shook uncontrollably.

She was still shaking when her mother returned. Adult voices drifted up the stairs, then silence, then footsteps on the stairs, and her mother's gentle, soothing voice.

"Are you all right, darling?" Amelie pulled the covers away from Siara's head and placed a cool hand on the girl's fevered forehead.

Siara's teeth chattered. "I-I-I'm-m c-cold, Mom-m-my."

"Well, no wonder, darling. You don't have a nighty on." Amelie selected a flannel gown from a bureau drawer and quickly dressed her daughter. Then, wrapping a blanket snugly around the child, she rocked Siara gently until the shivering stopped.

"I...I...b-barfied on Uncle Blair, Mommy."

"So he told me. But don't fret about it, darling. It was an accident. Uncle Blair isn't mad."

"He...he tried to make me eat his peppermint stick, Mommy. I didn't want to. It was nasty."

"Peppermint stick? Blair brought you candy? And it made you barfy on him?"

Siara nodded, relieved that her mother understood.

"You must forgive your Uncle Blair, darling. He's not used to little girls, especially sick little girls. He was just trying to be nice to you."

"But, M-Momm-my..." Siara began to shiver again.

"What is it, darling?"

"I...I...Uncle Blair...n-never m-m-mind. Just m-make m-m-me warm again, Momm-my...please..."

CHAPTER FOUR

"Did you throw out my mascara?" Jordyn asked, rummaging through her sister's dresser drawer, where she hid all the make-up their mother had forbidden her to wear. No one ever suspected Siara of disobedience.

Siara looked up from her book. "Why would I throw out anything that makes you look like such a cute little raccoon? I like raccoons."

"Very funny."

"Maybe Mama found it this morning when she put away the underwear."

"I wish she'd mind her own business."

"Mothers do have a silly notion that their children are their business."

"Whose side are you on anyway?" Jordyn asked indignantly.

"Mama's this time. I don't like your slopping make-up all over your face. You look too much like Mia."

"First of all, I do not slop on make-up. I expertly apply it. And what's so bad about looking like Mia? Next to you and me, she's the best-looking girl in Applewood."

"But she's a...she's a...a..."

Jordyn laughed. "*Slut* is the word you're too polite to say. I know what people think about Mia."

"Do you want them thinking the same thing about you?"

"I don't give a Fig Newton what people think. I just like to have fun, and fun is very hard to find in Podunk Applewood, Illinois. Mia, however, always seems to locate what fun there is."

"Her kind of fun is different though. She's a senior in high school. You're only fourteen."

"I've been told that I look like I'm seventeen. With a little make-up, I'm betting I can pass for eighteen. I hope I can pull it off anyway. Those frat guys might not be so eager about a lowly high school freshman."

"What frat guys?"

"Didn't I tell you? Mia's current lay is taking us to a Kappa Chi Nu party tonight."

"You're going to a college fraternity party?"

"You bet."

"Do Mama and Daddy know?"

"Of course not. And you're not to tell them. Why do you think I talked them into playing cards at Blair and Bonnie's?"

"Oh, Jordyn..."

"Don't start in on me, Baby. I get enough lectures from Mama. Besides, she's a fine one to be talking about MY behavior. She and the ol' man go at it so much it's a wonder we don't have a houseful of brothers and sisters. She must take a mighty powerful birth control pill is all I can say."

"Jordyn!"

"It's true. I've seen them a lot of times going at it so hard I thought the bed would fall."

"You wouldn't have seen anything if you hadn't been sneaking around. How could you do such a thing?"

"I was curious. Who's a girl to learn these things from if it's not her parents?"

"Please don't do it anymore, Jyn. Promise me you won't, or I'll tell them what you've been doing."

Jordyn grinned. "You don't worry me. You'd die of embarrassment before you got a word out. But I will stop peeking in on them. They're sorta boring actually...same old stuff all the time. Mia has some really great books they should look at."

"I refuse to discuss this anymore."

"At least be excited for me. Tonight is my big chance at Hudson Turner. He's got to be the dreamiest, the sexiest, the handsomest..."

"The oldest. He's at least twenty if he's on the varsity football team at Daddy's college."

"So what if he is twenty? I kinda go for older guys. Those our age are such babies, and most of them have pimples...gag! If you're so worried about my virtue, come with us. We'd be a real sensation, you and me. Hud would surely notice."

"I don't enjoy parties. You know that. I'm staying right here with *Ivanhoe*."

"On a Saturday night? Really, Sari...sometimes I worry about YOU. You read entirely too much. At least let us drop you at Aunt Bonnie's. Blair is always good for a laugh or two, and you can keep mentioning to Mama and Daddy that I'm at the movies for a double feature. That'll keep me covered until eleven."

"I'd r-rather not."

Jordyn combed her fingers through her long, blond hair. "What is it with you and Blair anyway? You cringe every time you're around him. He's not such a bad old boy, except for smelling like beer and cigars, and getting a little handsy sometimes, but I don't mind that so much. He's kinda handsome for an old fart, and he tells great dirty jokes."

"I'd rather not talk about Uncle Blair, please."

Jordyn stared at her sister. In almost every other instance, the twins shared between themselves a telepathic communication their father called "twinstinct." For some reason, however, Siara had purposely closed her mind to Jordyn where Blair was concerned.

"Well," Jordyn said to break the silence that made her feel awkward, "I guess I'll have to raid Mama's hoard of face paint. I can't go to the party looking like a ghost."

"You'll get into trouble. She'll notice."

"ANY trouble I get into will be worth it if I can get my hands and body on Hudson Turner."

Siara only shook her head, her smile ruefully indulgent as she continued reading.

After borrowing a few items from their mother's vanity, Jordyn swept into her own bedroom, its untidy confusion a sharp contrast to Siara's meticulous organization.

With a surge of motherly inspiration, Amelie had made the twins' bedrooms identical in every way but color. Where Siara's room was mainly pristine white with pastel pink accents, Jordyn's was pink with white accents. Though such planning was probably clever, Jordyn felt uncomfortable in the midst of so many frills and ruffles. She had asked her mother about redecorating the room in red velvet and black lace…asking once, only once, for Amelie had been so horrified that Jordyn was afraid to ask again.

She's just not used to the fact that her babies are growing up, Jordyn thought, scrutinizing her cosmetic effects in the mirror. *Well, one of her babies anyway.*

Jordyn was pleased with herself for keeping a secret of her own from Siara: tonight was the night she intended to relinquish her bothersome virginity. To Hudson Turner.

CHAPTER FIVE

"You'll get more if you pump it first."

Jordyn's heartbeat quickened as she struggled to maintain her outward calm. Hudson Turner pumped the beer keg, then filled her plastic cup.

"I'm disappointed," she said with more boldness than she felt. "That you meant the keg, I mean."

"We certainly can't have one of our most beautiful guests disappointed, can we, Jordyn?"

"You know my name?"

"Steve and Mia pointed you out to me...not that I hadn't noticed you before, especially in this crowd of barbarians we seem to have attracted tonight."

"Do you use that line on all the girls, or were you saving it especially for me?"

"I've saved everything for you, baby doll. I have often dreamed of the day that a blond goddess would walk into my life."

"Blond goddess, huh?"

Jordyn licked her lips and turned to the crowded room. Though she knew she was supposed to be captivated by Hudson Turner's smooth compliments, she was, in truth, resisting the urge to laugh out loud.

"So, what's with the beer drinking?" she said after a while. "Aren't you in training or something?"

"Beer has all the vitamins and minerals necessary to build strong bodies."

"I can see that."

"I'm pleased that you noticed. Maybe you'd like to see more. Beer also enhances a man's virility. Why don't we find a nice, quiet place to talk about it?"

"Your virility, you mean?"

"I bet you have ways of enhancing a man's virility, too," he whispered, trailing a finger beneath her chin.

Jordyn swallowed. This was it, her moment of truth. A twinge of nervousness was soon replaced by warmth that swelled within her. It was not an unfamiliar feeling to Jordyn, who had first felt the tugs of yearning while sneaking peeks of her parents in bed. Later Mia was able to provide the necessary details with descriptive stories of her dates with college men. And Jordyn had spent a lot of time with Mia's collection of "sex texts" and their graphic instructions, illustrations, and photographs.

"You want to or not?" Hudson Turner asked.

"Just like that? We've known each other less than ten minutes."

"I know what I like, baby doll, and I know what you like, too. Steve said you're hot for me, so why waste time with meaningless preliminaries? We're both after the same thing, aren't we?"

The warmth within her had become an aching urgency, more intense than anything she had ever experienced before, in fact. Mia had told her how to bring herself some small satisfaction when these cravings took control of her body, but Jordyn had always felt slightly embarrassed by having to do such things to herself.

No more of that, she thought now, as she looked Hudson Turner squarely in the eye.

"Yes, we are after the same thing," she said. "So why are we standing here wasting time? Let's go have a look at that virility of yours."

Jordyn supposed that at some later date she would look back on this moment with fond amusement. In the meantime, however, her mind was teeming with fragments of information culled from Mia's recommended reading material. Oddly enough, her current mental condition reminded her of how she felt before taking Mr. Beckle's history final the year before. If she had failed that test, her entrance into high school would have been delayed. Therefore, Siara had questioned and drilled her so thoroughly and saturated her brain with so many confusing facts and details, Jordyn had trouble concentrating on the test and passed with the lowest possible grade.

Now, when she was concentrating on technique, the urge began to ebb; and when she focused her attention on the pleasure rippling through her, she could remember nothing about method.

So much for romance, she thought, *but, then, I'm not here for romance.*

"Oh, baby doll," he was panting into her ear. "You are a beauty, a real beauty."

"How can you tell in the dark?"

"Oh, I can tell, baby doll. I can tell."

His hands stroked and rubbed, caressed and fondled every bare inch of her. Jordyn's skin was ablaze with sensation as his mouth enclosed one of her rigid nipples. Arching her back and thrusting herself toward him, she groped for his manhood.

"There, baby doll. Touch me there," his hoarse whisper implored.

The size and turgidity of him startled her, and she was momentarily panicked at the idea of having such a hard shaft rammed into her. Just then, however, his fingers discovered the center of her passion. With a pleading moan, Jordyn spread her legs and pulled him to her, gasping as he entered her, pressing against him as she tried to draw him deeper into her desire.

Thrusting himself at her once, then twice, Hudson Turner suddenly rolled off her and sat on the edge of the bed. He appeared to be gasping for air, and Jordyn worried that she had, in some way, injured him.

"What's wrong? Did I do something wrong?" she asked.

"How would you know one way or another?"

"What do you mean by that?"

"I mean, kid, why didn't you tell me you're a goddamn virgin?"

"Does it matter?"

"Does it matter! It sure as hell does! I'm not a cherry buster, and I'm not about to become one now."

"How noble of you."

He ignored her sarcasm. "Noble has nothing to do with it, kid. Most girls get all kinds of silly notions about their first times, and I don't need that kind of hassle."

Jordyn really wasn't surprised by his attitude, but she needed relief only a man, this man could give.

"Maybe I'm not like most girls," she ventured hopefully.

"No. I'll give you that. You're not like most girls."

"So..." Jordyn would stop short of begging, but she did want him to realize that they had started something she surely wished he would finish.

"So, come around again when you've had some experience. We'll talk about it then."

As he fished around on the floor for his clothes, she asked, "And for now?"

"For now I'm going to see if Brynda Barlow is still hanging around."

"Brynda Barlow?"

"She's a Greek groupie. I got blue balls because of you. I'll probably get sloppy seconds, thirds, or eighths by now, but it can't be helped this late in the evening. I can't waste any more time tracking down another available babe."

"I'm sorry I inconvenienced you," Jordyn snapped.

"Don't be like that, kid. If you want to play games with me, you have to follow my rules." As he zipped his pants, he turned to her. "By the way, do I want to know how old you are?"

"No," she said vengefully, "you don't. Unless your thing is fucking fourteen-year-olds."

"That's what I was afraid of."

He left the room then, quickly.

Jordyn covered her face with a pillow, trying to suffocate her anger, humiliation, and frustration.

"Someday I'll get you for leaving me like this, Hudson Turner," she vowed as she slid her hands between her legs.

CHAPTER SIX

Jordyn padded over to the mirror. Her critical inspection affirmed that she looked PERFECT for tonight. She wore no make-up but a touch of mascara to make her eyes look big and vulnerable...*like Bambi's,* she thought with a giggle. Her hair was sweetly clean and curled and tied up with pink ribbons on either side of her face. Beneath her short, ruffled nightgown, she wore only sheer bikini panties, which she had purchased especially for this occasion.

If all went according to plan, tonight Jordyn would start accumulating that experience on which Hudson Turner had placed so much emphasis. Jordyn wasn't going to waste her time with amateurs. She was going right to an expert...she hoped.

That events could happen so conveniently and so quickly only proved to Jordyn that tonight was indeed THE night. With Amelie and Devon at the convention in Minnesota, the twins had to stay somewhere for the weekend. Amelie would never allow her fourteen-year-old daughters to stay alone, unprotected and unchaperoned. When Blair and Bonnie had, of course, offered to take the girls for the weekend, Siara produced a convenient invitation from one of her school friends. Being away from Siara, even for the weekend, was harder than Jordyn thought it would be. They had never been apart for that long in all their lives. Still, Jordyn realized that her twin's absence was necessary if her plan was to work. If Siara suspected anything, she would have locked Jordyn in leg irons before allowing this plan to be actuated.

The plan was simple: Jordyn was going to seduce her Uncle Blair.

Both her aunt and her uncle were being marvelously cooperative. Aunt Bonnie had gone to bed early with one of her sick headaches. Even now Jordyn could hear her gentle snores from across the hall, where she slept alone. Because Blair and Bonnie had had separate rooms for years, Jordyn was spared the necessity of feeling guilty because of her aunt, who obviously cared very little about her husband's sexual activities.

For his part, Uncle Blair liked to stay up late, drinking beer, smoking cigars, and watching television. Jordyn was certain that her uncle would not be indifferent to what she was offering tonight. There had been too many sloppy, lingering kisses from him and too many hugs that lasted too long and gave him an excuse for brushing against her breasts. He was certainly never that affectionate with Siara, whom he ignored as studiously as Siara avoided him.

Jordyn brushed guilt-provoking thoughts of her sister out of her head. Nothing was going to interfere with her plan tonight.

At his desk in his den, Blair Eldred sat surrounded by empty beer cans and an ashtray full of cigar butts. Friday nights were for enclosing himself within a comfortable beer-hazy cocoon. He no longer found satisfaction in weekly trips to St. Louis. In truth, he had never found that much satisfaction to begin with. Having to pay for the use of a female body had been somewhat demoralizing to him. Recently he'd had a few encounters with girls from the university. Some of them, he had discovered, worked their ways through school by spreading their lovely legs. In this pursuit, however, he was tempting fate. He was too close to home for the comfort of anonymity, and The Bank would look unkindly on any such transgressions.

"Uncle Blair?"

Blair squinted through the fog of cigar smoke. *Jesus Christ,* he thought in something close to panic. *Why did she have to come down here NOW and looking like THAT?*

"What is it, kid?" he asked with a sense of déjà vu. He hadn't forgotten his encounter with Siara eight years before, although God knew he had tried. Blair knew that Siara remembered, too, though she had chosen to remain mercifully silent. He was thankful enough that he stayed away from her, easy enough to do since Siara carefully avoided him.

But Jordyn...ah, here was a different story...a different story indeed. For a moment Blair dared to be almost hopeful.

"Are you real busy, Uncle Blair?"

"I guess I can spare you a few minutes." Blair shook a few of the beer cans until he found the one that still had beer in it. "Wanna beer?"

"No...well, not a whole one. Maybe I could have a sip of yours?"

Eleven years of dance instruction had instilled in Jordyn a natural lissomness, which she used to her advantage now. Blair was fully aware of every graceful step she took toward him and every fluid sway of her hips. Jordyn was conscious of his awareness. The knowledge made her feel strangely triumphant, and powerful as well, sensations she savored, especially after the humiliation she had suffered because of Hudson Turner.

She laid her hand lightly against his chest as she took the beer can from him. Then, sipping daintily, she sat on his desk, facing him as she spread her legs just enough to give him a peek of her sheer panties. When she leaned over to return the beer to Blair, the top of her nightgown opened enough to reveal budding breasts, pink with the promise of future lusciousness. Blair gulped loudly, then passed his tongue slowly over his dry lips.

"Uncle Blair, do you think I'm desirable?"

Blair sputtered in his beer. "What kind of question is that to ask your uncle?"

"Who else could I ask? Daddy? He'd surely have a heart attack. And you and I have always been...close. Haven't we?"

"I suppose we have."

"You opinion is important to me. You see, there's this boy that I really, really like...an older boy...and he won't take any serious notice of me. That's when I got to wondering...if I'm desirable or not. Do you think I am?"

Blair swallowed, hard. "Well...I guess that given the right circumstances, I might think you're desirable."

"What would those right circumstances be?"

"Something other than uncle-niece circumstances."

"But we aren't related by blood."

"There are those who would say that our lack of blood ties doesn't change anything."

"What do YOU say? Be honest. I'll be honest with you. I've always thought you're attractive."

"You're just a child, Jordyn."

"Then you haven't been looking, Blair."

"I've been looking."

"I read somewhere that in one culture it's the responsibility of a revered uncle to...to introduce his niece to the wonders of life."

Blair tried unsuccessfully to light his cigar. "What is it you're suggesting?"

She moved from the desktop to her uncle's lap, her knees on either side of him as she pressed fully against him. When she felt his hardness pushing against her, a sense of victory pulsed through her, elevating her own passion.

"Wh-Wh-What are you doing?" Blair dropped his cigar and the match, and the beer can balanced on the arm of his chair fell to the carpeted floor with a foamy foomp.

Jordyn buried her face in her uncle's shoulder and sobbed, as best she could anyway. She was not without a certain dramatic talent, but she did have trouble mustering real tears.

"Hey, kid, don't do that..."

His voice was hoarse as he patted her back in an awkward attempt to comfort. When Jordyn's arms slipped around his neck and she pressed herself even more tightly against him, Blair was stripped of the last vestiges of will power. In a single, urgent motion, he slid Jordyn's panties off her and laid her back on his desk. Empty beer cans rattled to the floor as he fumbled at his zipper. He was oblivious to everything but the maddening necessity of ramming his engorged member into this silken pool that could offer him relief. Unmindful of the barrier that guarded her virginity, he shoved himself into her hard, once, twice, then once again. The third thrust brought his climax, a sudden spasm that racked his entire body with waves of mind-numbing delirium.

Beneath him Jordyn lay quietly, biting her lip to keep from crying out in pain. She felt as if she had been ripped apart by a telephone pole. Reason told her that Blair had done something wrong, for she felt no release from the grip of her own passions. Even when Blair pulled out of her and away, she felt unpleasantly full and torn. She wasn't even sure she could walk without looking like some old, bow-legged cowboy who had been in the saddle for a month.

She said nothing to him because she could think of nothing to say. Instead she picked her panties up off the floor, her one thought to get away from this fiasco. With a certain satisfaction, she noticed that she had bled on his desk blotter.

A cold shower followed by a hot soak in the tub had relaxed her so that sleep came easily. She hadn't been sleeping long, however, when the click of the bedroom door opening awakened her.

"Jordyn?" Blair whispered as he sat on the edge of the bed. "Are you asleep, honey?"

For a moment Jordyn considered faking sleep, but such deception was pointless. She had to face him sometime.

"I'm awake."

"I came in to apologize," he said.

"No need. I got what I asked for."

"No, Jordyn, you didn't."

"What do you mean?"

"Without going into details, I'll just tell you that I was physically incapable of ...of teaching you...making you enjoy it, too, I guess is what I really mean. I'm more in control now...if you still want to learn...if you still want me to be the one to teach you..."

With rising excitement, Jordyn considered her uncle's offer. She wasn't naive enough to believe he had come to her for purely charitable reasons. He was horny was what he was, and in the mask of darkness, Jordyn smiled slyly. She would give him what he wanted, and she would control him.

If it worked with Uncle Blair, wouldn't it work with other men, too? Especially younger, less experienced men...

Like Hudson Turner.

"It's very lonely in this big bed alone, Uncle Blair," she said, reaching for him in the dark.

His bathrobe was open, and she ran her hand along his thigh until she touched his rigid manhood. He wasn't as big as Hudson Turner, but a girl couldn't always start at the top.

He gasped as she touched him. Then, sliding beneath the covers with her, he pressed his hands between her legs, stroking her until she began to wriggle and moan with ignited passion.

"We'll take it slow and easy this time, darling Jordyn," he whispered. "You'll be wanting a steady diet of your Uncle Blair after tonight..."

CHAPTER SEVEN

"Mama can't yell so loud since it's my own money I'm spending on my own make-up," Jordyn said as she applied a third coat of mascara, more in defiance than from preference.

"At the rate you use that stuff, a part-time job won't pay you enough to keep you supplied," her sister observed.

Siara's only make-up was some pink-tinged lip gloss and a light dusting of face powder to take the shine away. On this particular Friday, both twins were preparing to go out, an event that totally surprised Jordyn, who had accepted that her sister preferred books to boys.

"I don't use that much," Jordyn said. "Besides, the bank pays me very well. If you weren't so stubborn about accepting a favor from Blair, he'd get you on there, too. He did offer, you know."

The offer had come on the twins' sixteenth birthdays two months before. Amelie and Devon gave the girls a new blue Mustang, paid for, in part, with money bequeathed by grandparents who had all died, sadly, within the past eighteen months. From Aunt Bonnie and Uncle Blair each girl received a gold watch, identical, of course, except for the special inscription on the back of Jordyn's: the "Love, B" Blair secretly arranged to have engraved after Bonnie selected the watches.

Blair then offered the girls part-time jobs at the bank. Though Siara politely but quickly refused, Jordyn eagerly jumped on the opportunity to earn her own spending money. Even with the money Blair was always giving her, Jordyn never seemed to have enough for all her clothes and make-up. She realized that the bank job was another of Blair's schemes for some time alone with his favorite niece, but so long as the money was good, she didn't worry overmuch about what she had to do to get it.

"I'd rather work in the college library," Siara said now, tying the belt to her pink dress. "Daddy has some influence with some dean who's in charge of hiring. Have you seen my pink hair ribbon?"

"The last thing in the world I'd be keeping track of is a pink hair ribbon."

Jordyn looked critically into the mirror at her tight, low-cut, black knit shirt and snug jeans tucked into knee-high boots. With a thoughtful frown, she tugged the neckline farther down to expose the cleavage she was so proud of. Not all high school juniors were so fortunate. Siara was, of course, another exception, but Siara also took great pains to conceal her endowment. Around her neck, Jordyn carefully knotted a black silk scarf, "borrowed" from her mother's lingerie chest.

"Working with a bunch of books would be right up your alley," Jordyn admitted once she was finally satisfied with the scarf. "But working for Blair is a whole lot easier. He's a pussycat to work for, and he's usually the only boss type that hangs around by the time I get out of school."

"Mama said that Uncle Blair is upset that you won't go to Florida with him and Aunt Bonnie over Christmas break."

"Blair will have to learn he doesn't always get what he wants, especially from me."

"What do you mean by that?"

"Nothing you'd understand, Baby. So, tell me about this big romance between you and Stanley Klosterman."

"It's not a romance. It's just a date."

"A date for you is a major event. I can count on one hand the number of guys you've accepted though I know you've had more offers than that."

"Most boys are so...so aggressive they scare me. Besides, I haven't had that many offers. Most boys are disappointed I'm not like you. They think I'm dull and boring...especially if they compare me to you."

"You're too sweet to put out for them like I do only they're not honest enough to admit it."

"Jordyn!"

"It's true, Baby. I like sex. Why should I be a hypocrite about it? I've more or less given up on high school boys though. They don't do it for me anymore."

"Is that why you sneaked out to see Mr. Dillard the other night?"

Jordyn raised her eyebrows in surprise. "I thought you were asleep."

"I was sitting at the window and looking at the moon, and I recognized his junky old car. You're lucky it didn't awaken Mama and Daddy."

"High school chemistry teachers can't afford fancy cars. Would you believe me if I told you he was helping me with a chemistry problem?"

"You don't even take chemistry. Mr. Dillard is your study hall teacher."

"But chemical reactions have always fascinated me...especially where male hormones are involved. So where are you and ol' Stan going?"

"The Little Theater is performing *Camelot* tonight at the university auditorium. Where are you going?"

"To a Kappa Chi Nu party. I'm hoping Hudson Turner will show up."

"Didn't he graduate last year?"

"He's back as a grad student."

"I thought you swore off him and Kappa Chi Nu parties a long time ago."

"I'm not finished with Hudson Turner...yet," Jordyn smiled mischievously at her sister. "But I will be after tonight..."

CHAPTER EIGHT

Stanley Klosterman fidgeted in his seat. Being with Siara always seemed to bring him to this uncomfortable condition, and he wondered how he could rearrange himself without her noticing. She was such a little Puritan. Such a beautiful, little Puritan.

So far, he tallied, they had had three dates. Four if he could count the trip to the university library to research for the Elizabeth Barrett Browning project they worked on together last spring. Miss Barstow gave them an $A+$, and Siara dazzled him with one of her shy, sweet smiles that gave him an immediate hard-on right there in English class. Stanley kept his notebook in his lap for the rest of the class period.

Yet in all this time and with all this bridled desire, he had not tried even once to kiss her. There was something about Siara that discouraged the attempt, an aura of ethereal untouchability. She was like the statue of the Virgin in St. Mary's. One could pay homage to her, but one couldn't touch her. Stanley always felt incredibly guilty for all the sexual fantasies he had about Siara, but he continued to have them. Some of his nighttime dreams were so vivid, in fact, that he spotted his sheets with those tell-tale stains that drew disgusted frowns from his mother and knowing smirks from his dad.

After three dates...no, four...maybe he could hold her hand, at least. Surely his gentlemanly restraint had earned him that meager reward.

When Stanley looked at Siara now, her lovely, blindingly blue eyes were focused on the stage where King Arthur was vocalizing his advice on how to handle a woman. Stanley listened carefully to the song, but the king didn't seem to know any more than he did. And the king had Merlin to advise him.

Stanley decided on the bold approach, mainly because he was afraid he lacked the emotional endurance for anything subtler. Sneaking a sideways peek, he saw Siara's hands gracefully folded in her lap. With one quick, desperate movement, he lunged to clasp her slender hand within his own. Perhaps this strategy might have worked had he not overlooked one minor detail: the half-full cup of Coke he had balanced on the arm between their seats.

Flinching as Stanley knocked the cup loudly into her lap, Siara gasped, dismayed as a brown stain spread across her dress. He dabbed at her skirt helplessly with his handkerchief and mumbled his apologies, but Siara merely stared at him as the people around them shushed his flustered attempts to atone for his blunder.

"Why did you do that, Stanley?" Siara asked, her eyes so painfully accusatory he would have willingly placed himself before a firing squad as penance for his foul deed.

Flushing with embarrassment at the impatient commands for silence hissed by several members of the audience, Siara grabbed the handkerchief from him and fled to the ladies' room where she could assess the damage to her dress.

Stanley slumped in his seat, miserable in his defeat and certain that Siara would never speak to him again.

"Are you sure you won't be mad at me forever for ruining your dress and making a scene and causing you to miss part of the show?" Stanley asked meekly as he escorted Siara to her front door.

"I told you I'm not mad. Now would you please stop fretting about it so much? You just spilled Coke on me, for goodness sake. It wasn't like it was a vat of boiling oil or anything. Now THAT would have made me mad."

She smiled at him to ease his concern. In truth, she had been rather upset with him for his unexplained clumsiness, but his continuous self-reproach afterward had caused her irritation to ebb.

"But your dress...I ruined it. I'll pay to replace it or have it cleaned...whatever needs to be done."

"Don't worry about it. Mama will fix it. She's very clever."

"I hope you're right. You're so beautiful in that dress...but then I think you're beautiful in everything you wear."

"Why, Stanley, what a lovely compliment. Thank you. And thank you for taking me to see *Camelot* tonight. I enjoyed it. Really I did...in spite of the little accident we had." She smiled at him again and turned to open the door. "Well...I guess I'll see you Monday at school..."

"Siara, wait..."

She turned to face him again. "Yes, Stanley?"

Stanley shuffled his feet and pulled at the collar of his shirt. In the glow of the porch light, his bulbous nose was a red bloom of flustered self-consciousness. He was a unique person in that only his nose reddened when he blushed, but this particular gift of nature had brought him little contentment over the years as he was forced to endure countless references to a popular reindeer with the same distinction.

Siara, however, understood his shyness. In fact, she found his bumbling attempts to woo her rather endearing. He might not have been the best-looking boy in class, but he was the most gentle and polite. Siara knew he wanted to kiss her good night. She had never allowed a boy to kiss her before. Though she couldn't say that she wanted Stanley to kiss her now, she was curious about what kissing felt like.

"Is there something you want to ask me?" she prompted as she stepped toward him.

Her soft voice gave him some hope. "I thought that maybe...since we...you and I...have been...seeing each other for a little while now...maybe you'd do me the honor of...of...letting me kiss you good night?"

"You want to kiss me?"

"Yes..." He croaked and cleared his throat. "Yes, I do."

"That's a lovely compliment, too."

"Then...you'll let me?"

"I'd be honored," she murmured as she tipped her face up to his.

After that concession, she was uncertain of how to proceed, so she waited for Stanley to make the next move.

He swallowed, closed his eyes, and lowered his face toward hers, hoping all the while that he had aimed correctly. Etiquette did not allow for opening one's eyes to re-aim in the middle of a kiss.

Siara's eyes, however, were open. Open so that her curiosity about the mechanics of kissing would be satisfied.

She should have closed her eyes, however, for her curiosity was soon replaced by an uneasiness that mushroomed into a body-devouring fear.

In the dim illumination of the porch light, Stanley's fleshy, rubescent nose wasn't a nose anymore as Siara was suddenly six years old again, and the red thing hovering before her face was the ugly, pulsating monster Uncle Blair had forced into her mouth.

Siara screamed, not once but continuously, and ran, panic-stricken, into the house, leaving Stanley to agonize over what horrendous misdeed he was guilty of now.

CHAPTER NINE

He'd been eyeing her from across the room for most of the evening. Someone he thought he should remember but couldn't. Someone he'd certainly like to make a few memories with now. But he couldn't appear too anxious. That was uncool. Unmacho. Besides, he was a graduate student now. She was probably an underclassman. Though with that body...those tits...

Jordyn smiled slyly and sipped her Coke. Plain Coke. No whiskey tonight. She needed to be in full control of her mental and physical faculties.

Without actually looking at Hudson Turner a single time, she had been fully aware of his scrutiny, even as she flirted audaciously with the college men who always congregated around her. She had already singled out one of these men for later. She would need his services when she was finished with Hudson Turner. After all, she was only human, and Hud the Stud would certainly be in no condition to take care of her.

Winking at the Greek god sitting next to her, she glanced briefly but obviously at his crotch. His face brightened considerably at her signaled suggestion.

"Later, Adonis," she whispered to him. "I have to...pay off a debt first. I promise you I'm worth waiting for."

"I don't doubt that at all." He ran his hand up her thigh. "My room is on the second floor, last room on the right. My roommate went home this weekend for his sister's wedding, so we won't have to worry about any interruptions."

"You'll be so into what I'm doing to you, you won't notice an interruption even if there is one. Give me an hour, and I'll meet you in your room. If you'll have your clothes off already, we can save bunches of time. I'm so hot for you, I can barely stand up."

"You don't need to stand up, beautiful. Just lie down and spread your legs."

"You'll find that I'm a lot more mobile than that," Jordyn laughed.

"I'm looking forward to it."

"So am I, Adonis. So am I." She stood up and leaned down to kiss him lightly. "Now scoot on up to bed, and I'll be there soon to tuck you into me."

Knowing that she was getting appreciative looks from many of the men in the room, including Hudson Turner, Jordyn moved slowly to the bar, exaggerating the natural sway of her hips just enough to emphasize her sensuality without appearing ridiculously pretentious. She added some whiskey to her Coke this time, then turned to scout Hudson's current location. He was making his own way to the bar, casual and unhurried as he directed his attention at everything and everybody but Jordyn, who was not fooled by his pretense. She knew he was coming to the bar to contrive an accidental meeting.

Because she had a deadline of sorts to meet, she decided to make things easier for him.

"Hello, Hudson Turner. You're still in training for the Budweiser Olympics I see."

He tried to look surprised. "Well, hello to you, pretty woman. Do I know you? I surely wouldn't forget someone as lovely as you are."

Jordyn smiled up at him as she stirred her drink with her finger. "We met...briefly...two years ago. You told me to come back when I'd had some experience. So here I am, handsome. Experienced and still craving your bod like crazy."

A gamut of emotions registered on his face in rapid sequence: surprise at her bluntness, pensive confusion as he tried to remember, stunned wariness when he did remember, and finally smiling anticipation as he surveyed her womanly form. Her blue eyes glittered with definite knowledge of how to please a man. Hudson could barely keep his tongue from dragging on the floor.

"What exactly do you have in mind, baby doll?"

"If you have to ask me a question like that, maybe YOU aren't experienced enough for ME."

"I was trying to make polite conversation."

"Politeness is a waste of time. Take me to the nearest bedroom."

"You don't fool around, do you?"

"Oh, but I do." Jordyn grinned as she recalled their previous discussion. "Why waste time with meaningless preliminaries? We're both after the same thing, aren't we?"

"That's a fair conclusion," he said, taking her hand. "Let's go, baby doll. I'm quite interested in seeing what you've learned in the past two years."

Hudson Turner closed the bedroom door. When he reached to turn on the light,

Jordyn set her drink and purse on the dresser and laid her hand on his.

"Please, Hud, no lights."

"But I want to see you, baby doll, and what I'm doing to you and you to me."

"So do I, but let's save that for later. First I want to get to know every inch of you by touch. I know you think I'm silly, but I've been dreaming of this moment for so long. You want to make my dreams come true, don't you?"

"I'll see what I can do, baby doll."

"Once isn't going to be enough for me tonight. I've been waiting too long. Does an old man like you have enough stamina to keep me satisfied?"

"I'm sure I'm still UP for the challenge."

Jordyn laughed at his attempted witticism. In the darkness he couldn't see her narrowed eyes or the unpleasant grin on her lips.

"Oh, Hud, you are so clever. Will you mind terribly if I make a few requests along the way? After all, this is my dream...my fantasy coming true."

"I'll make every fantasy you've ever had come true," he whispered into her ear.

"I...I need to go into the bathroom for a sec. There's something I need to...insert first. We don't want any accidents, do we?"

"God no!"

"Will you be naked and ready and waiting on the bed for me when I return?"

"Will YOU be ready for ME?"

"I've been ready for you for two years."

She pulled him to her and blistered his lips with the fire of her kisses. When she finally turned him loose, he was panting heavily, and Jordyn was sure that drool was leaking from the corners of his mouth.

"Hurry, girl!" he breathed as he immediately began to strip off his clothes.

"Your every wish is my command." She unzipped his pants and slid her hands inside. "I'm going to make sure you never forget tonight, Hudson Turner."

Slowly she withdrew her hands and then skimmed her fingers over his bulging crotch.

"I'll be back in a few minutes," she said, gathering up her purse and her drink. "Just a few tiny minutes."

In the bathroom across the hall, she leaned against the wall and fought back an attack of giggles.

I'll guarantee you won't forget tonight, Hudson Turner, she thought. *And you won't forget me either.*

She took a small tube and an envelope out of her purse. Making sure the cap was on tightly, she tucked the tube into her cleavage for safekeeping and then emptied the contents of the envelope into her Coke-and-whiskey. With the handle of a toothbrush she found lying on the sink, she stirred the drink until she was sure her special ingredient was dissolved.

Cascara sagrada.

Thank you, Mr. Dillard, for making tonight possible. You fuck like a tired, old man, but you do know your chemistry.

And he had access to so many interesting things. Like cascara sagrada, an extremely potent laxative. And the special quick-dry epoxy resin used primarily in the construction of airplanes.

Jordyn smiled at her image in the mirror as she raised her drink in tribute to her own ingenuity.

"Are you ready for me?" she called softly as she entered the bedroom.

"Why don't you see for yourself, baby doll?" he called from the darkness.

Jordyn resisted an urge to hoot out her scorn for his overly confident male ego. When her eyes were accustomed to the dark, she saw his shadow stretched out on the bed, and she walked toward him slowly. He sat up and pulled her down beside him, guiding her hand to his shaft. His immensity excited her, and she momentarily considered abandoning her original plan.

"Think you can handle that, baby doll?" he asked, drawing her closer to him.

His arrogance brought her to her senses. "Careful...you'll make me spill my drink."

"Your drink? Are you still carrying that thing around?"

"I didn't know what to do with it, and I've had my limit for the night if I want to keep alert for the next few hours. Will you finish it for me?"

"I don't want the damn thing. Set it on the nightstand or some place and take your clothes off."

"We can't just leave it sitting around. With all the activity, it might spill and make a stain. I don't want to get you into any trouble."

"Why didn't you pour it out in the bathroom?"

"I forgot," she said contritely. "Besides, my mind was filled with you. Please, finish it for me, Hud, so we can get down to business. You don't want me worrying more about spilling my drink than fulfilling your needs, do you?"

"Oh, all right. Give me the damn drink." He grabbed the plastic cup away from her and emptied it in a few loud gulps. "Sometimes I think you women do these stupid things just to see how high you can make us jump for a little pussy."

"You've hurt my feelings now," she pouted. "I would never resort to anything so sneaky"

"So I apologize, and you can start with your fantasy already."

"I think I've changed my fantasy." She stifled his protest by laying her fingers over his lips. "While I was in the bathroom, I had this delicious image of lowering myself right onto you."

"We can do it that way. Oh, baby doll, yes, we can do it that way with no problem at all."

"But you're so big, Hud. I'm a little...concerned."

"I won't hurt you, baby doll. You're gonna get a pussy full of pure pleasure."

"Still, would you mind lubing yourself up a little while I get undressed? I found some stuff in the bathroom. I'd feel better if you used it."

"Woman, you better be worth all this extra effort. Give it to me..."

"Oh, I'll give this and lots more to you, darlin'."

Grinning triumphantly, Jordyn handed him the tube of epoxy resin. Because she could see only shadows in motion, she listened carefully as he unscrewed the cap and contents of the tube over his erect penis.

"Please use a lot of it, darlin'," she purred, pantomiming the motions of undressing. "I need for you to be all slick and wet when I impale myself on your magnificent cock."

A wet, squooshing sound told her that he was spreading the substance liberally, and, for the time being anyway, probably enjoying the sensations he was giving himself as he anticipated the sensations she would soon be giving him.

"What the hell is this stuff anyway," he asked suddenly. "It doesn't smell like anything I have ever used."

Jordyn's laughter bubbled in her throat until she could hold it back no longer.

"Hey," he called to her. "What's so funny? And why aren't you...aren't you...what in the...what is this? What is this stuff you gave me? Jesus Christ! What have you done to me? My hand is stuck to my...what was in that goddamn tube? WHAT HAVE YOU DONE TO ME?"

"I believe that you've done it to yourself," Jordyn said cheerfully.

Hudson tried to be calm. "Okay, you've had your fun. Now do whatever you have to do to get me loose."

"But, baby doll, I don't know what to do to get you loose. Maybe you should consult a specialist, maybe a cocktologist. You do have a sticky problem on your hands."

"You're not funny!"

"But you surely are."

He began to flail on the bed as he tried to roll off and stand up. "You bitch! Do something! You've got to do something. You can't leave me like this!"

"You left me in an uncomfortable condition two years ago. We're even now."

"I never did anything like this to you. Great God in Heaven, I don't even remember your name!" He managed to get to his feet and stagger toward her. "But I'll find it out, and when I do—"

Jordyn grabbed her purse and opened the door for protection. He couldn't follow her into the hallway in his present condition.

"And when you do, you'll do nothing," she said. "I'm only sixteen, and I don't think a man your age is supposed to be tampering with a young thing like me. What do they call it? Statutory rape? Contributing to the sexual delinquency of a minor? Whatever. It wouldn't look too good on your record. I can look very innocent when I want to, and I have a great talent for telling convincing lies. Well...since you have things firmly in hand, I'll be on my way."

As she was leaving, she turned back to him. "Oh, by the way, you can expect another little surprise in about...oh, ten to fifteen minutes I'd say. Just another little reminder that I may let men fuck me, but I don't let them fuck WITH me. Remember that."

She waved at him and closed the door on his oaths and threats. She could still hear his shouting when she reached the last room on the right, just down the hall. Without knocking, she threw open the door and rushed inside, heaving a huge sigh of relief as she locked herself in.

"You're late," her blond Adonis called from his bed.

"I was unavoidably detained." Jordyn scanned his naked form as she unfastened her jeans. "Besides, good things come to those who wait."

Minutes later, as she settled herself joyfully upon his huge and hard manhood, she heard the wet, explosive bursts from down the hall, faint but distinct in the quiet of the second floor. The cascara sagrada had moved through Hud's body right on schedule. She smiled, and a sudden image sent her into fits of laughter: Hudson Turner yanking himself around the room by his own penis as his bowels unloaded themselves loudly, violently, and uncontrollably. Too bad the bathroom was all the way across the hall.

"Want to let me in on the joke?" her companion asked.

Jordyn was saved from answering as Hudson Turner's voice boomed throughout the Kappa Chi Nu house.

"Herb! Ed! Trevor! Somebody! Get up here! I need help! Hurry! SOMEONE, PLEASE HURRY!"

The man beneath Jordyn groaned and lifted her off him. "I should go see what the problem is. Hud sounds like someone is trying to kill him."

"There are others who can help him, others who aren't so...busy, right?" She traced his lips with her finger. *I'll be damned if I let Hudson Turner be responsible for leaving me horny again.*

He smiled at her for a minute and then pulled her leg across him. "I suppose you're right."

"By the way," Jordyn said guiding him into her again, "which one are you anyway? Herb or Ed or Trevor?"

CHAPTER TEN

"Where have you been?"

Jordyn cringed as she closed the front door. *Jesus Christ, I'm only half an hour past my curfew,* she thought. *That's better than I usually do.*

"Sorry, Daddy." She mentally prepared herself for the verbal barrage. "I forgot to wear my watch."

"We'll discuss that later," Devon told her grimly. "Right now we want you to go upstairs and talk to your sister."

"Sari? Is something wrong with Sari?" Jordyn looked anxiously from her father to her mother.

"We don't know," Amelie said, struggling to keep her voice calm. "She won't talk to us. Maybe she will to you."

"But what happened?"

Devon wrapped a comforting arm around his wife. "Siara was out on the front porch saying good night to her date, that Klosterman boy, and the next thing we knew, she was running up the stairs screaming, hysterically."

"That boy tried to rape her, Devon," Amelie said tearfully. "I'm sure of it."

Jordyn peered at her mother in mild astonishment. "Don't be silly, Mama. Stanley Klosterman couldn't rape himself out of a brown paper bag."

"Perhaps you can provide us with another explanation?" Devon asked, staring at his daughter's smudged mascara and tousled hair.

"I really can't tell you anything, Daddy." Jordyn tried very hard to look innocent. "But I'll go up and see what I can get out of Sari. I'll go up right now...unless, of course, you need me for anything else first?"

"No..." Devon waved toward the stairs. "Talk to Siara. We'll be waiting in our room after we lock up down here."

Jordyn raced up the stairs before her father could be inquisitive again. She found Siara in the bathroom, sitting on the floor by the toilet.

"Sari? Baby, what's wrong?" Jordyn asked, kneeling beside her sister.

"I...I have been sick."

Jordyn laid her hand on Siara's forehead. "You don't have a fever. Did you eat something that disagreed with you?"

"N-No. I...I was just sick."

After soaking a washcloth in cold water, Jordyn gently wiped her sister's face. "You weren't drinking beer or anything like that, were you?"

"Of course not. Mama and Daddy would kill me if they caught me doing such a thing."

"The trick is not to get caught. I've managed to stay among the living. Are you feeling better now?"

"I th-think so."

"Then let's get you to bed." Jordyn pulled Siara up and draped an arm around her shoulders. "You're shaking like a wino with D.T.'s. Are you cold?"

"I'm not cold. I'm...I'm...oh, Jyn. It was awful...so awful..."

Tears gushed down Siara's cheeks then as Jordyn quickly led her to the bed.

"You'll be okay, Baby," Jordyn crooned softly as she rocked Siara in her arms. "Tell me what's wrong, and I'll take care of it. Don't I always take care of you? Tell me what's wrong, and I'll make it better."

"He...he tried to...tried to...and I couldn't...I just couldn't, Jyn. Something is wrong with me that I can't...and...he stained my dress, too...my new pink dress..."

Because Siara was alternately sniffing, hiccupping, and choking on her tears, Jordyn was unable to understand all the words, but she thought she understood what Siara was trying to communicate.

"Stanley did that? Stanley...stained your dress?"

Siara nodded, her eyes glazed with tears. "I...I know he wasn't expecting more than any boy would...and I was c-curious about what it was like...but then I couldn't do it...and Stanley...he...something must be wrong with me..."

"Nothing is wrong with you, Baby. Nothing at all. You're too good and sweet for the dirt-bag boys in this town. Now you lie back here and go to sleep and forget about Stanley Klosterman."

"But shouldn't I...shouldn't I...talk it over with him...or something?"

"Leave Stanley Klosterman to me," Jordyn said, tucking the blanket around Siara and turning off the light. "I'll take care of him. You sleep."

"Thank you, Jyn," Siara murmured, closing her eyes. "I'm so lucky to have a sister like you. I love you, Jyn."

"I love you, too, Baby. Now sleep."

Jordyn sat on the edge of the bed and held her sister's hand until Siara fell asleep. Seeing Siara's dress lying on the floor by the bed, Jordyn picked it up, straining her eyes in the darkness until she could see the faint outline of a stain contrasted against the pale pink of the dress.

"Even Stanley Klosterman," she muttered through clenched teeth. Imagine that. Their mother had been right about him.

Too bad the tube of epoxy resin was still at the Kappa Chi Nu house.

But there were other ways of getting even with Mr. Stanley Klosterman.

Her thoughts on her battle strategy, she walked slowly to her parents' bedroom. To their expectant stares, she said only, "She was frightened by a snake in the grass. Don't worry. I have everything under control."

* * *

Jordyn's opportunity to set her plan into motion came late the next morning. With Siara and Devon buried in a mountain of books in the study and Amelie off shopping with Bonnie, Jordyn was alone upstairs as she sneaked into her parents' bedroom to use the phone there.

She had been rehearsing for the part all morning in the solitude of her room, and now, as Stanley Klosterman answered his telephone, he had no cause to doubt that he was talking to Siara Nealy herself. He was, in fact, so overcome with joy at the call that any differences between Siara's voice and Jordyn's impersonation went completely undetected.

"I m-must apologize for last night," Jordyn said in Siara's gentle, hesitant way.

"I was rather...concerned about what happened," Stanley gulped, "but so long as you're all right...that's all that matters to me. I never dreamed you'd be so scared."

"You overwhelmed me."

"I overwhelmed you?" Stunned, Stanley quickly sat down before his weakening knees gave way.

"After last night, I f-feel you're the one boy I can be completely honest with. May I be completely honest with you, Stanley?"

"Of c-course you can. A good relationship is built on honesty."

"Do you want to have a relationship with me?"

Stanley pulled at his collar. "You've got to know that I do...especially after last night."

"I want a relationship with you, too, even though you must have doubts after the way I acted. I guess you picked up on my innermost desires before I realized them myself."

"D-Desires?"

"I had a long talk with myself, Stanley. I know you're too nice a boy ever to try anything...well, you know, intimate in nature...unless you really had strong feelings for the girl and thought she had the same kind of feelings for you. I have to admit to some strong feelings for you, Stanley. You made me feel so good being that close to you last night, only I acted weird because…because, well, I've been raised to believe that such feelings for a boy are wicked. Do you think I'm wicked, Stanley?"

"No…never!" Stanley placed the phone book in his lap as his mother walked by him. "I've f-felt that way about you a long, long time."

"Do you…do you think it's possible that we…that you and I could be falling in love?"

Stanley's eyes bulged. Siara Nealy was actually talking to him about being in love! That she would even venture such a question made him bolder.

"Well…we do get along well, and I think you're the greatest girl I've ever met. So it's possible we're falling in love."

"That's so sweet, Stanley. You're the sweetest, kindest boy I've ever known. That's why…that's why…oh dear, this is so difficult for me to say though I feel it with every fiber of my being."

"You don't ever need to be afraid to say anything to me, Siara…darling." His nose reddened at his own audacity.

"Then I shall say it straight out. I want you to make love to me…really make love to me…and we'll just forget about last night since it wasn't what either one of us was expecting."

He thought, for a moment, that he was hyperventilating, but eventually the buzzing in his ears subsided and he heard her soft voice calling to him in distress.

"Oh, Stanley, you really think I'm wicked, don't you?"

"No…no…not at all. You just surprised me. I never dreamed that…that it was possible you felt that way."

"Does my…inexperience matter to you? I know that you're far more experienced than I, but maybe you could teach me how to please you?"

"Siara…I…I…" *Oh, God, what do I do now? Lie to make it sound good? No. Not to Siara. I can't lie to Siara.* "Actually there have been no others before you. But we can learn…together."

"Oh, Stanley, you make me tremble so. Do you think that…maybe we could…see each other tonight?"

"Of course we can. What time shall we…shall I come by for you?"

"There's one slight, little problem. Mama and Daddy are a little unsure of you after last night…though I tried to explain…without explaining EVERYTHING, of course. So maybe you shouldn't pick me up here. I'll meet you at the university library…about seven?"

"What if your parents find out? They'll really be against me if we start sneaking around, and I don't want them hating me, especially if we're going to have a…a relationship."

"They won't be mad forever. Besides, won't it be exciting…being in love in secret…like Romeo and Juliet?"

"Romeo and Juliet ended up dead."

Jordyn forced a pout into her voice. "Don't you think I'm worth the risk?"

"Of course you're worth the risk," Stanley said quickly. "Where in the library shall we meet?"

"I'll be waiting right outside the front doors for you. Don't be late…please. I'm so anxious to make up for that…misunderstanding last night."

"I'm the one who should make up for last night."

"Oh, I'm sure you will…Stanley dear."

Jordyn's plan was not without its complications, the most minor of which was thinking of a good reason why she would want to borrow any of Siara's clothing. The girls had not dressed identically since they were old enough to voice opinions about their wardrobes, and Jordyn's closet was filled with outfits that were inappropriate for the role she would play that night.

The major obstacle was Devon, who decided to restrict Jordyn's social activity for a week as punishment for her tardiness the night before. Because she knew a display of temper would only extend her sentence another week, she submitted meekly to the decree while she plotted an alternative course of action.

The solution was so obvious that she was back in her father's study within the hour as she humbly requested permission to spend the evening in the college library so that she could research for a paper she was writing for American history. When Devon looked at her suspiciously over the top of his glasses, her eyes widened in innocent sincerity as she told him that he could even drive her there himself after dinner and pick her up when the library closed at ten o'clock. Devon relented although he was not entirely convinced, even when Jordyn asked to use his faculty library card.

Smiling at him gratefully as he handed her the card, Jordyn turned to her sister, who had been watching the exchange with suspicions of her own.

"Could I borrow something to wear tonight, Baby?" Kari asked.

"You want to borrow some of my clothes?"

"I really need to get this research done, and at the risk of sounding conceited, if I go to the library looking like me, the guys will start...well, you know, talking to me, and I won't get anything done. But if I look like you—"

"No boy will be interested in giving you a second look."

"That's not what I meant at all. Everyone there knows you are a serious student, so they won't bother you. If I look like you, they won't bother me. See?"

"Sometimes even I think you are rather strange, Jordyn."

"But you manage to love me in spite of it, don't you, Baby?" Jordyn grinned at her sister and turned to leave.

Devon cleared his throat. "Just what is the topic of this historical masterpiece you're working on? Maybe I have something here that can get you started."

"I don't think so, Daddy. It concerns the changing roles of women in our history, and you really are something of a male chauvinist. I'm out to prove that women are not the weaker sex."

"You're not thinking about burning your undergarments at any equal rights demonstrations, are you?"

"Oh no, Daddy. In my mind being equal to men is a step backwards for us."

Jordyn blew him a kiss and quickly ran up the stairs to her room.

Men! They are such fools. Even Daddy...sometimes.

CHAPTER ELEVEN

With thirty minutes to wait before Stanley was scheduled to arrive, Jordyn decided to test her disguise on the people working in the library, most of whom knew Siara well because she spent so much time there, either alone or with Devon. Jordyn also wanted to check out a few books that would, she hoped, convince her father that her intentions for the evening were legitimate.

As soon as she opened the front door to the library, she assumed her sister's serious and scholarly demeanor. Tonight her blond hair was pulled back in a simple ponytail adorned only by a pale blue ribbon that matched the sweater and plaid skirt she had borrowed from Siara. The skirt was not, of course, nearly so short as the fashion of 1973 mandated, and the sweater hung loosely from her shoulders. Siara always bought her sweaters a size larger than she actually wore whereas Jordyn was inclined to buy them a size smaller...unless Amelie exercised a motherly veto.

Jordyn concentrated on walking as Siara walked, with her eyes demurely downcast and each step a shy request for permission to take another. Siara always walked as if she was afraid of trespassing onto someone's private property. Jordyn, on the other hand, never merely entered a room...she barged into it, so she had to restrain her own usual confident, exuberant stride now.

She knew her deception was working when the librarians and aides on duty greeted her with her sister's name. Smiling at them timorously, she bit her lip, lowered her eyes again, and walked on to the stacks, territory which was alien enough to her that she paused in confusion as soon as she was completely alone.

How in the world was she going to find the books she needed in this baffling assortment? Siara usually gathered whatever research materials Jordyn needed for reports. Card catalog. Siara said something about a card catalog. Jordyn had envisioned a glossy-papered catalog full of birthday and Christmas card selections until a laughing Siara tried to explain this special research innovation. However, Jordyn had not been interested enough to pay attention to the explanation.

What do I do now?

She had to have a book or two with her when her father picked her up. Siara would never have to ask for help in a library. Siara was as familiar with the library as Jordyn was with frat house bedrooms.

"Hi, Stacks."

Jordyn jumped and turned around. The spectacled man who was smiling at her was tall and scholarly. Though the dark hair that curled around his ears was beginning to gray, he didn't look much older than twenty-five.

"You aren't Siara," he said in embarrassed surprise. "I am sorry."

Now what?

Tell him that he was right and blow her cover? Or try to persuade him that she really was Siara and maybe screw up something her sister had going here?

What the hell, she decided. This wasn't the guy she was out to deceive.

"That's okay," she said finally. "We do look an awful lot alike. It was a natural mistake."

"You must be Jordyn."

"You know me?"

"Siara speaks of you often."

"She does? Who are you anyway? You're not leching after my sister, are you?"

He laughed though his face reddened at her question. "Siara said you are outspoken, and now I will have to agree with her. I am Connor Sanderson. I work in the English department here with your father, and for that reason alone, I would never…lech, as you say, after one of his daughters. I have tremendous respect for him…and for Siara. She is an exceptionally intelligent and gifted young lady."

Jordyn arched her eyebrow. "And if she were a few years older, you'd lech after her anyway."

Although he continued to smile, Jordyn noticed that a slight coolness edged into his voice. "Any man who has anything less than honorable intentions where your sister is concerned is not worthy of her time or her company."

"Then you and I have something in common, Mr. Sanderson. That's exactly how I feel."

She glanced at him sideways as she considered flirting with him a little. No…not until she knew what Siara's feelings about him were…and probably not even then. Connor Sanderson reminded her too much of her father.

"Why do I feel as if I just passed a test of some kind?" he asked her.

"A girl can never be too careful where her baby sister's concerned. Now, since you know Siara and Daddy so well, perhaps you can help me out. Unlike Sari, I'm pretty well lost in here, and I need some books for a paper I'm writing. Can you help me, Mr. Sanderson?"

"I would be honored, Miss Nealy," he said, gallantly offering her his arm, a gesture that Jordyn found amusingly old-fashioned, but strangely pleasing, too.

"So," Connor Sanderson was saying, trying his best to be casual, "tell me why Siara isn't here to help you find her way. Does she have a…a date tonight?"

Why, he does have a thing for Sari, Jordyn thought, studying him carefully.

She would have to keep an eye on Connor Sanderson. But, first, there was Stanley Klosterman to deal with.

Jordyn jumped into the car before Stanley could get out to open the door for her. He had even worn a tie for the occasion, she noticed with a stifled smirk, a tie and about half a bottle of after-shave...even though he had no reason to apply a razor to his face.

She settled into the seat and folded her hands primly in her lap. "Hurry, please, Stanley. I am so afraid we'll be seen by someone who will tell Daddy. If he were to forbid me to see you, I don't know what I would do."

Stanley pulled away from the curb so quickly that the tires squealed and Jordyn was thrown against the door.

"Sorry, Siara," he mumbled. "I g-guess I'm a little nervous."

"Do I make you nervous?"

"It's not you. It's just that there's...there's something about this that doesn't seem quite right. I'm not sure we should be sneaking around like this."

"Do you want to take me home then?" Jordyn said with quiet distress. Siara would never react with anger or irritation.

"No," he replied quickly. "I want to be with you no matter what."

"I am so glad." She smiled at him and then lowered her eyes. "Do you think that it would be permissible to sit somewhat closer to you? You know...really close...as all the couples we know do?"

"C-Couples?" Stanley's nose began to glow in the dark.

"You and I...we are a couple now...aren't we?"

"I'd like for us to be."

Jordyn slid across the seat until she was sitting right next to him. Stanley gulped as he felt her pressing against him. He nearly strangled when she casually laid her hand on his thigh.

"Where are you taking me, Stanley...darling?" she asked as she tried to hide her amusement. As soon as she placed her hand on his thigh, she detected the swelling in his trousers.

"Where would you like to go, Siara...dear?"

"I...I really have no idea. I thought that you would know about things like that."

"Well…"

Stanley slumped in his seat. The only place he knew was Belix Bottoms, the party and making-out place frequented by most of the high school students. Though he would be thrilled to be seen there with a beauty like Siara Nealy, the need for secrecy prohibited that selection. Maybe later, when he and Siara were an established couple and they didn't need to sneak around on her parents. Would she accept his class ring tonight anyway? He had cleaned and polished it just in case. But in the meantime, where would they go to…to consummate their relationship? Stanley shifted slightly in his seat to ease the tightness in his trousers.

"Well…"

"You said that already, Stanley darling."

He cleared his throat. "I guess we could get a m-m-m-m-motel room."

"Won't that be terribly expensive?"

"Nothing is too expensive if it's for you…Siara dear," Stanley said, mentally postponing the purchase of the new tape deck for his car.

"You're so sweet, Stanley. But I really don't think a motel room is necessary. We couldn't get one without arousing numerous suspicions. Maybe we can…park somewhere…where we can be all alone?"

"The thing is…I…I…I don't exactly know where a place like that is."

"We could try the old stone quarry."

He stared at her in surprise. "The stone quarry?"

"Jordyn told me about it. It is very secluded, and not too many people appreciate its possibilities…Jordyn says."

"Does Jordyn know about us…about tonight?"

"Of course she does. We tell each other everything. And I really needed some expert advice and encouragement. Do you mind?"

"Well…no. It's just…just that…sometimes Jordyn…well…scares me."

"Scares you? How?"

"She's so…so forceful."

"Most boys like her that way."

"Most boys aren't…intimate with her sister. Some strange feeling tells me that she's not too pleased about your…uh…about us." He cleared his throat in nervous embarrassment as his nose flamed brightly.

"You are quite perceptive. She was not pleased. I guess she is rather protective of me, and she does fuss over me like a mother hen sometimes. However, I am sure when tonight is over, she will be pleased with what happens between you and me."

"You're going to tell her EVERYTHING?"

"Why, tonight will be so special, Jordyn will know every detail without my saying a single word. It's like that sometimes with twins, you see. I won't have to say a single word to her."

CHAPTER TWELVE

"What is it, Devon darling? You look so strange."

After hanging up the phone, Devon sat by Amelie on the sofa as Siara looked up expectantly from the homework spread on the floor around her.

"It's one of those situations that's rather unpleasant, yet it has its humorous side, too. I am not quite certain how I should react."

"Share it with us, darling, so that we can be uncertain with you. I'm definitely intrigued."

"I am not so sure that Siara should hear."

"I am sixteen years old, Daddy," Siara said, frowning at her calculus paper. "What could Connor possibly have to say that I can't hear?"

"CONNOR, is it? I shall have to keep an eye on that young man. He probably called here to talk to you. You surely had plenty to say to each other before you finally turned the phone over to me."

"Really, Daddy…" Siara flushed darkly. "We like to talk about books. That's all. Besides, he's an old man."

"He will appreciate that observation. I surely do, especially since I am almost old enough to be his father."

Smiling, Amelie touched her lips to his. "For an old man, you've managed to stay frisky enough. Now quit your stalling and tell us what Connor had to say."

"I owe Jordyn an apology, Mel. I really thought that she was up to something, but Connor saw her at the library and even helped her find some research material. Isn't it interesting how her little disguise didn't fool him? He must know Siara better than we thought."

"Daddy!" Siara's brow wrinkled with exasperation. "Mama, he's stalling again."

"I agree." Amelie pulled his face toward hers and growled playfully, "Talk, pilgrim, or you'll be de-friskified tonight."

"That, my dear, is cruel and unusual punishment. Nevertheless, I'll humor you. Just remember that you asked for the details. Connor called to tell me what happened to one of the graduate students last night at one of those fraternity parties. A boy from the business and finance department…that Turner boy."

Siara's gasp interrupted him.

"Is something wrong?" he asked his daughter.

"N-No. I…I just remembered something…a…an assignment I had forgotten about. Go on with your story."

"Well…the boy has always been rather cocky…obnoxiously so. Mel, remember my telling you a few years ago that he expected us to give him a passing grade in a composition class because he was on the football team and because his father is supposed to be an influential politician in Indiana? The fact that he was an academic idiot with a belligerent attitude wasn't supposed to matter to us. How he managed to qualify for graduate school I shall never understand. Money and power can be quite persuasive I suppose."

"Stop your editorializing and get to the good part," Amelie said. "What happened to him?"

"He was the victim of some fraternity prank last night. Somehow or another…Connor was not too sure of the exact details…Turner's hand became glued to his…to his…male appendage."

Amelie giggled. "Connor's making that up."

"No, he was quite serious…though he was rather guffawing while he recounted the story. Mr. Turner made few friends in the English department. Anyway, to add the proverbial insult to injury, the lad experienced a horrendous case of diarrhea while he was…in that inconvenient condition. He found himself in quite a mess…literally and figuratively."

Amelie's giggles exploded into tear-producing laughter as Siara bit her lip and tried to appear engrossed in her calculus.

"Now, Mel, this is not that funny. I actually feel a touch of sympathy for the lad. His condition could be rather serious."

"In what way, darling?" Amelie said, trying to control her giggling.

"The glue was some kind of super-bond epoxy. Turner had to have his hand surgically removed from his…from his…uh…"

"Male appendage," Amelie said helpfully. "Who was the perpetrator of this dastardly deed?"

"Turner isn't talking…except to request that his transcripts be sent to a college in Indiana. As soon as he has recuperated, he is returning home. It's rather disturbing that something like that could happen on our campus."

"Don't be such a snob. College students are the same everywhere, even at Scheffers. Besides, that Turner thug deserved to be a sucker in a prank, though I'm sorry the results were so serious. Even so, I admire the mind that thought the whole thing up. I wonder how she got him to do it."

"She?"

"Had to be a girl. No guy could have persuaded him to glue up his…male appendage."

"Well…" Siara said loudly as she quickly gathered her homework. "I will head upstairs now and go to bed with *King Lear*. Good night."

She kissed her parents and ran upstairs.

"Our Siara is not quite so worldly as she thought," Devon said, nuzzling his wife's neck.

"She's a sweet little prude about so many things. Sometimes I worry about her."

"Jordyn is the one we should worry about. She is just the type who would talk a boy into gluing his…his male appendage to his hand. Say, where was she last night anyway?"

"Don't be so suspicious. She went to a dance at the Teen Center last night. Then I suppose she and some boy drove out to Belix Bottoms."

"I'm not supposed to be suspicious about THAT?"

"You and I spent some time at Belix Bottoms once upon a time, darling. I recall a time or two you even let me play with your male appendage."

"Amelie!"

"You can't deny it."

"We were going steady and on the verge of being engaged."

"Siara comes by her prudery naturally."

"Mere moments ago you were commenting on my friskiness."

"I'm partial to frisky prudes. I'll show you how much after you pick up our frisky daughter at the library."

Jordyn had no definite plan in mind for what she was going to do to Stanley. She knew only that she was going to do SOMETHING to him. The little twerp was not going scot-free after what he had done to her baby sister, no matter how much he obviously liked Siara.

Actually, Jordyn considered, Siara had probably brought it on herself, however unwittingly. Poor ol' Stanley. The heat of desire had been too much for him. When a geek could go berserk and jump on an unwilling female body, well…it just proved Jordyn's theory: men were penis-motivated in everything they did. The old brains-in-the-crotch syndrome.

Even her father was not immune, though he was less silly about it than most other men. Her mother was no fool. She used his innate male weakness to get her way on countless occasions. Just the slightest hint that there would be no fun in bed that night would make her father fall all over himself to please his wife.

Jordyn had watched this loving manipulation carefully. Over the last two years, she had perfected her own technique to the point that she was supremely confident of her dominance. Even older men had fallen victim to her wiles. Like Uncle Blair. Like Mr. Dillard.

Stanley was no challenge at all.

In the light of the dashboard, she could see the near panic on his face. He had been guiding his old Chevy slowly over the weed-plumed mounds around the quarry for several minutes now, wanting to stop, yet afraid to stop because he wasn't sure about what to do once he did stop. Some benevolent fairy godmother must have taken pity on him. As they encountered a particularly steep mound of dirt, the car lurched forward and died. At least Stanley had the presence of mind to pretend that he had intended to stop at that very spot all along.

"Well…this seems like a good spot."

"Yes…it does."

In the awkward silence that followed, a plan came to Jordyn. Leaning forward casually, she began to fidget with the knobs and buttons on the dashboard.

"What are you doing, Siara?"

"I am more nervous than I thought," she said, pushing at the cigarette lighter for a second time. "I am not even sure what to do first. What do we do first, Stanley?"

He loosened his tie. "Well…I guess we…we could…k-kiss."

Oh, Lord, she thought, slightly nauseated. *I never thought I'd really have to kiss the twerp. The things I do for Siara…*

She leaned toward him and puckered her lips. As Stanley's mouth bumped into hers, his bulbous nose squished against her face. Overcome by an urge to laugh, Jordyn parted her lips lightly and took a deep breath to restrain her giggles. Stanley considered the opening an invitation to ram his tongue into her mouth.

Choking, Jordyn bit down on his tongue.

"Siara! That hurt!"

You didn't do me a whole lot of good either. What in the world were you trying to do? Lick my tonsils?"

"That's kissing. French kissing. The kind of kissing that lovers do."

"Are you sure that's the way it's done?"

"Well, almost sure."

"Something didn't seem right."

Jordyn fiddled with the knobs on the dashboard again. She would have to hurry this little rendezvous along, not only because she was running out of time, but also because she could not stand much more of Stanley the Twerp Klosterman.

"Stanley...maybe we should act more like lovers."

"What do you mean?"

"Maybe we should...b-be more intimate with each other. Would you think I am terrible if I said that I would like to touch your...your...well...you know what I want to touch...don't you?"

"Siara..." Stanley squeaked and cleared his throat. "I...you want to...to touch my...my...me?"

"I feel strange being this direct...darling...but I must be back at the library in time for Daddy at ten. And I am so anxious to...to make up for last night. So couldn't we...get started? That is, if you still want to?"

"Oh, Siara, I do. You don't know how much I do."

"Then you will have to start. You are the one who knows how."

As Jordyn continued to twist and push the knobs on the dashboard, Stanley nervously unzipped his pants and, with trembling fingers, pulled out his hardened penis. When he slid his arm around her waist, Jordyn turned to him and reached automatically for his exposed manhood.

"Why, Stanley," she said with honest surprise. "You're enormous."

But that didn't change the fact that she owed him for what he had done to her sister.

Using her left hand to stroke his swollen member, Jordyn endured the slobbered kisses he pressed upon her as he fumbled beneath her sweater in an effort to unhook her bra. With her right hand, Jordyn removed the cigarette lighter from its plug. Stanley was too preoccupied to notice its hot glow in the darkness. Nor did he realize that Jordyn's fidgeting with the dashboard knobs was a ruse to keep the lighter hot until she needed it.

"Oh, Stanley...Stanley..." she panted into his ear to keep him distracted as she aimed the lighter at his crotch. "You make me feel so good...so good..."

By now Stanley had managed to free her breasts, and in triumph he pulled he sweater up. Looking down to gaze upon her moonlit loveliness, he saw the lighter poised just inches from his manly tool. Only then did he feel its heat.

"Great God in Heaven, Siara!" he yelped, jerking away from her. "What are you trying to do?"

The hand that had been holding him so gently now grabbed hold of him firmly.

"I'm not Siara, you cock-sucking twerp. If you had a brain in your head, you'd have realized it."

"Jordyn? B-But…but WHY?"

"You know why, you pervert," she hissed, twisting his penis sharply and smiling when he groaned in pain. "Did that hurt, Stanley? Think about how much it hurt my sister when you rammed that ugly thing into her."

"Wh-What?"

"Don't play dumb now that you're cornered." Jordyn pressed the lighter against the top of his now-shriveled penis. Stanley recoiled in blind terror, but the lighter, though warm, was no longer hot enough to do him any damage.

"Damn," Jordyn muttered, tossing the lighter aside and gripping Stanley even more tightly.

He grabbed her wrists. "Please…I don't know what you're talking about. I would never do anything to hurt Siara. All I did was try to kiss her."

"You're lying."

"I'm not. Honest, Jordyn. I swear it."

"Then how do you explain the dark stain on her dress?"

"I spilled a Coke on her."

"Coke?"

"When we went to see *Camelot*. I knocked it over, right into her lap."

"You're telling me you didn't rape her…or try to rape her?"

"R-Rape her? Did Siara tell you that?"

"Well…no…not exactly."

"I just tried to kiss her, and she started screaming and ran into the house. That's all it was, Jordyn. I swear it…on my mother's grave I swear it."

"Your mother's still alive, Stanley."

"When she has a grave, I'll swear on it. Please, Jordyn…"

Jordyn let him go. He collapsed with a relieved sigh while Jordyn frowned thoughtfully.

"I think," she said finally, "I should have a long talk with my baby sister."

When Stanley began to stuff himself back into his pants, Jordyn reached for his hand.

"Don't do that, Stanley," she told him, laughing when he flinched from her touch.

"Wh-What are you going to do to me now?"

"Fuck your socks off, sweety. I figure I owe it to you."

Sighing, she pulled her sweater over her head and unzipped her skirt.

"B-But, Jordyn…"

"Relax, Stanley. You'll enjoy it. You can even pretend I'm Siara if you want to, but after tonight it would be a good idea for you to steer clear of the Nealy sisters."

Stanley vehemently nodded his agreement as Jordyn lowered her mouth onto him

.

CHAPTER THIRTEEN

Siara was lying on her bed reading when Jordyn peeked into the bedroom. "Are you busy, Baby? We need to talk."

Siara closed her book. "Poor King Lear wasn't getting too much of my attention anyway. I have been waiting for you to come home."

After shutting the bedroom door carefully behind her, Jordyn stretched out on her stomach beside Siara.

"We look more alike now than we have in years," Jordyn said, tugging on her twin's ponytail and then untying the ribbon around her own ponytail.

"You wanted to look like me tonight, remember?"

"I thought I had done a pretty good job of it, too, until I ran into a friend of yours at the library...Stacks."

Siara's face reddened. "C-Connor said he had seen you there."

"He didn't waste any time in getting home to call you."

"He called Daddy, not me."

"I bet. I'm very curious about this nickname he's given you. With all those baggy sweaters you wear, I'm surprised he knew so much about what you look like underneath. Have you been holding out on me?"

Siara's blush deepened. "He calls me that because that's where we always seem to bump into each other...in the stacks. We're library acquaintances, that's all."

"And I'm the Virgin Mary."

"What did you do to Hudson Turner last night?"

Jordyn rolled onto her back and lifted a leg into the air. "What makes you think I did anything to him?" she asked casually, poking her thigh in her daily check for signs of fat.

"Connor told Daddy that Hudson Turner was a victim of a fraternity prank last night, and he had to have surgery to separate his hand from his...from his..."

"Penis?" Jordyn asked with a raised eyebrow.

"Yes," Siara said faintly. "That's what he had to have his hand separated from."

"No kidding? Surgery?"

"That's what Connor said. He also said that Hudson Turner is transferring to a college back in his home state."

"I can see where he wouldn't want to show his face…or anything else…on campus after last night."

"Did you have anything to do with the prank?"

"Are you sure you want to know?"

Siara considered the question. "Probably not. I look guilty enough for things that I already know for sure that you do."

"God has gifted me with a low guilt threshold," Jordyn grinned. "Though He seems to have given my portion of it to you. Sorry 'bout that, Baby."

"Did you know that Hudson Turner's father is a prominent politician in Indiana?"

"Really? Good news for me. Hud will be even less likely to admit he was dabbling with an underage girl. His daddy won't want that kind of scandal."

"Jordyn, please be careful. Sometimes you are so…so…"

"Forceful?"

"Well…yes…something like that."

"Funny you should say that. A friend of yours said the very same thing about me tonight…to me, in fact, though at the time he thought I was you."

"Whom are you talking about?"

"Stanley Klosterman."

"Oh." Siara opened her book and flipped over a few pages. "Was he at the library?"

"Long enough to pick me up."

"What?" Siara stared in surprise at her sister.

"Without going into details you don't want to know, I'll just say I wanted to get a few things straight about what happened to you last night. Somewhere along the way I got the impression that he tried to rape you."

"Rape me? Stanley? Oh, Jordyn…"

"Don't look so distressed, Baby. Stanley straightened me out in a hurry…when I nearly ripped his dingus off."

"Oh, Jordyn…you didn't!"

"No, I didn't, but I was ready to. The thing that's really worrying me is that a simple kiss upset you as much as if he'd really tried to rape you. Forgive me for saying this, but that's not normal, unless you're a nun or something."

"I was just frightened. That's all."

"Of a kiss? Why?"

"I don't know. I just was."

"You're holding out on me."

"Please don't badger me about it. It's no real problem."

"It will be if the same thing happens the next time a guy tries to kiss you."

"The solution is simple. I won't let any guy kiss me."

Jordyn moaned loudly. "That's no solution. In fact, it's a fate worse than death."

"To you maybe. Not to me."

"Are you going to get mad if I nag you about this?"

"Are you going to get mad if I won't talk about this?"

"Siara…"

"Jordyn…"

Jordyn sighed in surrender and took her sister's hand. "I worry about you, you know."

"Then we are even. I worry about you, too."

After a moment of silence, Jordyn asked, "Surgery, huh?"

"Surgery."

"Wow. I wonder what his dingus looks like now."

* * *

Jordyn leaned back in her uncle's chair and propped her feet up on his desk. Blair was checking to be sure that all the other bank employees had gone and that all the doors were securely locked before he returned to his office. It was a common ritual. Jordyn had actually come to regard it as part of her job description: filing financial reports and credit applications, answering the phone, typing letters, and screwing Uncle Blair.

There were tougher ways for a seventeen-year-old to earn money.

Though Blair failed to excite her anymore, she never complained, and she rarely refused him…unless she had something, or someone, better to do. Blair doted on her, and Jordyn did not want to alienate his generous devotion. Besides, she was rather fond of the old guy.

Tonight, however, she had other ho-hum things to think about.

She had to get home to study for a damn algebra final. If she wanted to graduate on Friday, she had to pass the final or she wouldn't get the math credit she needed. Making cheat notes for an algebra test wasn't easy, and since her algebra teacher was a woman, studying, with Siara's guidance, was Jordyn's only recourse.

Unless...

She played with an idea until her uncle returned.

Jordyn knew that something different was on Blair's mind as soon as he opened the office door because he did not immediately shrug off his jacket and unzip his pants. Instead he patted his coat pocket, smiled, and reached for Jordyn's hand.

"We need to talk, darling Jordyn," he said, pulling her gently toward him.

Jordyn sighed. She hated Blair's attempts to be romantic. Screwing one's uncle was one thing; being romantic with him was quite another.

Still, she didn't want to hurt his ego. Maybe being romantic was the way he coped with some hidden guilt he experienced over their relationship.

However, since her psychology grade was only slightly better than her algebra grade, she probably shouldn't be speculating.

"Uncle Blair," she said, carefully emphasizing the *Uncle* as she always did when he became effusive, "I hope you won't be too disappointed with me. I have to get right home to study for a final. If I don't pass it, I won't graduate with Siara."

Blair kissed the palm of her hand. "I'll be disappointed, yes, but never with you. Can you spare an old man a few minutes before you leave?"

Jordyn recognized her cue. They had played this scene often. Part of the job description.

"You're not an old man. *Mature* or *experienced* would be more appropriate for you."

"You make me feel so good in so many ways. I want to show you how I feel by giving you your graduation present a little early."

Interest sparked in Jordyn's blue eyes. "Present?"

Reaching into his pocket, Blair fumbled out a small box that he presented to Jordyn.

"Oh, Blair, you do spoil me."

She kissed him quickly and opened the box. She was stunned to silence when she saw the diamond ring inside.

"Well," he said. "Do you like it?"

"It's a beautiful ring. I love diamonds, especially big diamonds like this one. But it looks like an engagement ring."

"It is an engagement ring. I'm asking you to marry me."

Jordyn's mouth fell open. Blair's bombshell had destroyed her ability to speak again.

"You...you...can't be serious," she finally managed to say.

"I can see you're surprised. I knew you would be. At first I myself didn't think it could be possible, but the more I thought about it, the more possible it seemed."

"What about Aunt Bonnie?"

"I'll divorce her, of course."

"You make it sound so easy."

"It won't be easy. I know that. There will be a thousand and one complications, but I love you so much I don't care. We'll be the talk of the town, Jordyn. Not too many girls your age become wives of bank vice-presidents."

"I don't disagree with that at all."

Jordyn groped behind her for the desk and sat on it heavily.

Damn. The old fart is serious.

Serious enough to think that she would actually accept his proposal. What would she do now? Venting her true feelings was out of the question. She couldn't be that cruel to someone who was temporarily insane. Besides, such rejection would be tantamount to killing the goose that was laying her golden eggs. Jordyn needed those golden eggs. She had plans for her future.

When in doubt, stall. As long as possible.

"I won't be eighteen until the end of July, and Dad will never give his consent."

"By the time we get all the complications out of the way, like Bonnie, you'll be old enough, so we won't need Devon's consent."

"A lot of people will be upset. Shouldn't we kinda let everyone get used to the idea gradually? Dad moved heaven and earth to get me into Scheffers, and I really want to give college a try. A banker's wife shouldn't be an airhead."

"You can still go to school after we're married."

How could I possibly concentrate on my books with a handsome man like you at home? And I really don't want to be upsetting Dad and Mama with this right now, especially if it's just a matter of using a little self-control for a few years."

His face sagged pitifully. "What you are saying is that you don't want to marry me."

"What I am saying is I don't want to marry you now." *Or ever.* "I'm trying very hard to make a mature decision, Blair. Resisting you isn't easy."

She pressed her body against his. Sliding his arms around her waist, Blair lifted her for a kiss.

"I don't suppose I have any other choice," he said reluctantly. "Will you wear the ring?"

"On a chain around my neck for now."

"I'm still telling Bonnie I want a divorce. The sooner, the better."

"Whatever you think is best," she told him with only a little guilt. Aunt Bonnie would be better off without him.

"Would it do any good to ask you to stay away from those college men?"

She replied to his question carefully. "No college man can ever change the way I feel about you."

Briefly touching her lips to his, she left quickly before he could ask any more difficult questions.

* * *

Siara sat on the folding chair, clenching and unclenching her hands in a nervous rhythm that increased in tempo as the ceremony progressed. Where Jordyn always had little trouble impersonating Siara...and even relished the challenge the deception provided...Siara was nearly paralyzed with terror when circumstances required that she impersonate her vivacious sister. Not that Siara impersonated Jordyn that often. Never, in fact, until this week when she had to be Jordyn twice.

Once to take the algebra final in Jordyn's place...a simple exercise for Siara, who was exempted from all her own finals because of her perfect grade point average.

And now to sit alphabetized among two hundred graduating seniors of Applewood Community High School while Jordyn sat at the front of the class, ready to give the speech that Siara, as valedictorian, had written, but was too timid to present before an audience.

Though Jordyn placed little importance on her academic progress and studied accordingly, she had never asked Siara to take a test for her before. Nor would Siara have considered such duplicity had the situation not been so unusual. She certainly didn't want one little test to hold up her sister's diploma. When Jordyn offered to give the valedictory address in exchange for Siara's taking the math exam, Siara was relieved to be offered such an equitable solution to both their problems.

Still, Siara glanced periodically into the crowd of assembled parents, relatives, family friends, and well-wishers as she waited fearfully for someone to reveal the fraud with loud, indignant oratory. Jordyn was so good at being Siara, but Siara made a very inadequate Jordyn.

If their parents ever realized what was going on, both twins would be in serious trouble. This apprehension in itself was enough to unsettle the modicum of composure she had managed to retain. But Uncle Blair's steady and intense stare nearly sent her screaming from the auditorium. Only her innate sense of decorum kept her seated throughout the proceedings.

As Superintendent Rayburn introduced Applewood's latest valedictorian, Devon squeezed Amelie's hand tightly. The speech his daughter had written was excellent, of course, but he had fretted right along with her over its presentation. Siara was such a shy dove that speaking before an audience was traumatic for her. He hoped that the theatrical coaching Jordyn had given her would be as helpful as the coaching Siara gave Jordyn for that algebra final.

So far, so good, Devon thought with a relieved sigh as he returned Amelie's proud smile. Actually, Siara was doing quite well. Both their little girls were growing up.

Connor Sanderson leaned forward in his chair and shook his head in amused understanding. Stacks wasn't behind the podium. Jordyn was up there pinch-hitting for her beautiful, brilliant sister. A quick look at Devon and Amelie told him that they were unaware of the switch. He certainly wouldn't spoil the evening for them or for the twins. After all, Siara had written the speech herself. A literary melody he thought when Devon first showed it to him. Did who presented the speech really matter so much? Wasn't Laurence Olivier a better Hamlet than Shakespeare could have been? His eyes softened as he captured the real Siara within his gaze. Surely Aphrodite had not been so lovely, and certainly not so nervous. If only she were a few years older.

Blair and Bonnie studiously avoided all body contact though they sat next to each other. That afternoon, Blair had asked his wife for a divorce. Surprisingly, there had been no scene. No tears, no angry words, no pleading for a second chance. Bonnie hadn't even ordered him out of the house. In fact, she had calmly asked him to attend the graduation ceremony that evening with the family as planned for the twins' sake.

Could the old girl be up to something? Not that it mattered to him. Soon he would be free to show his darling Jordyn the proper attention in public. Attention befitting a lover rather than an uncle. He knew he would be able to persuade her to change her mind about waiting. She was crazy about him. Hadn't she singled him out for her first sexual experience? Wasn't she always eager and waiting for him in his office at the end of their workday?

What a sensation their engagement and marriage would make! Stuffy old Devon would choke on his Chaucer, and Amelie…well, she would probably try to be understanding. What a mother-in-law Amelie Nealy would make. What a coup for Blair Eldred, having the sexiest wife and the sexiest mother-in-law in Applewood. Members of the board of directors would certainly notice.

He smiled as he focused his eyes on his beloved. She seemed uncharacteristically nervous tonight, but, of course, he had given her a lot to think about this week. Maybe he could sneak a few kisses later. He couldn't wait to tell her about the long weekend he had planned for them in St. Croix.

Later, in the lobby, Jordyn waded through an ocean of caps and gowns as she tried to find Siara. She knew that Siara would need a few reassuring words even now that the graduation was safely over. This week had not been an easy one for her baby sister. In truth, Jordyn herself had been somewhat concerned about Siara's taking the algebra final, for Mrs. Ruebler was a formidable old bat. Fortunately, however, Mrs. Ruebler had averaged grades throughout most of the test, and except for frequent checks for cheating, she paid little attention to Siara, who had further protected their scheme by deliberately missing several of the exam problems, enough to prevent suspicion while insuring a passing grade.

Yet Siara had been just as nervous tonight with Jordyn on the front lines.

Jordyn stopped to scan the crowd. Their parents were standing with Aunt Bonnie and Dr. Sanderson over by one of the exits. Then she saw Siara standing patiently, waiting for a gap in the milling throng so that she could inch her way toward them. *Siara will never shove her way through*, Jordyn thought as she pushed toward her sister.

Blair, Jordyn noticed, was standing on the fringe of the crowd behind Siara. An instant later, he reached for Siara's hand and pulled her back into the dimly lit corridor that led to the coaches' offices. The hallway door closed immediately behind them.

Quickening her pace, Jordyn shouldered and elbowed her way through to the corridor.

Siara lay unconscious on the floor while Blair knelt beside her.

CHAPTER FOURTEEN

Jordyn pushed Blair aside and gathered Siara into her arms.

"What did you do to her?" she asked her uncle angrily.

"Jordyn? But I thought…I thought…oh, God…"

He stared first at one twin and then at the other. Finally he whispered hoarsely, "I thought she was you."

"I asked you what you did to her."

"I kissed her and she fainted. I swear, Jordyn, I thought she was you."

Jordyn well remembered the incident with Stanley Klosterman. Still, she looked at Blair doubtfully. "Are you sure that's all you did?"

"Well…maybe my hands did brush against her…her chest once or twice. I swear, Jordyn, I thought she was you."

"Didn't you suspect anything when she didn't respond to your pawing?"

He smiled sheepishly. "I thought you were being playful."

Jordyn's irate admonition was interrupted when Siara stirred.

"Jordyn?" Siara mumbled, her eyes tightly closed as she shook her head. "Jordyn, don't let him do it. Please don't let him do it again…"

"Who, Baby? Don't let him do what again?"

"The peppermint stick. Uncle Blair's peppermint stick. Don't let him stick it into my mouth again. Please, Jyn, don't let him…"

As Jordyn held her sobbing sister against her, she realized what must have happened. Murderous fury flaring in her eyes, she looked around for Blair.

He was already gone.

"Is she all right?" Connor and Devon asked in unison when Amelie and Jordyn came downstairs.

"Oh, sure," Amelie replied, slipping an arm around Devon's waist. "The tension of the week got to her is all. There's no cause for alarm. She's resting comfortably now."

"Giving that damn speech did it," Devon said with a frown. "We should never have allowed her to do it. She doesn't have the proper temperament for public speaking, and the strain was too much for her."

Jordyn lowered her eyes as Connor stared at her.

Damn, she thought. *He knows what we've done.*

Obviously he hadn't narked on them. He'd never do anything to get Siara into trouble.

"I'll sleep with Siara tonight," Jordyn said finally, "just to make sure she's okay."

Devon's brows arched in surprise. "Are you forgetting that all-night graduation party you wheedled, pouted, and ranted to get permission to attend?"

"I'd rather stay with Sari. She needs me."

"You're right, of course. Thank you, Jordyn." Devon rubbed his hand over his face to brush away the sudden rush of involuntary tears.

Amelie, however, was not fooled.

"Still think we need to worry about Jordyn?" she whispered into his ear.

Devon shook his head and leaned down to kiss Jordyn's forehead.

"You're a good girl, Jordyn."

Jesus Christ, Daddy's getting sloppy. What is there about graduations that causes everyone to freak out?

"Just don't tell anyone," Jordyn said. "You'll ruin my reputation. I'll go up to Sari now if it's okay with you. I'm sorry your little family get-together fizzled, Mama."

"No problem, dear. The cake and ice cream will keep for a day or two, and there's always a steady supply of cherry Kool-Aid around here. I am a little worried about Blair though. Bonnie's the one who usually gets the sick headaches. Maybe I should call to see how he is."

"You do that, Mama."

Jordyn quickly turned toward the stairs, but Connor touched her arm to stop her and handed her a package wrapped in white tissue paper.

"Would you give this to Siara?" he said awkwardly. "It's a book of poetry I thought she might enjoy."

"Sure, Dr. Sanderson."

Jordyn's knowing wink brought the color into Connor's face. Laughing, Jordyn ran upstairs to her sister.

"Jordyn?" Amelie whispered, laying a gentle hand on her daughter's brow. "Are you awake, darling?"

"Yes, Mama. I'm awake."

"How is Siara? Has she been sleeping?"

"Sleeping fine. Don't worry."

"I just talked to Bonnie. Blair is feeling much better."

"Yippee."

"You handled everything very well tonight, dear. We are so proud of you. You did a tremendous job with Siara's speech, too."

"You knew!"

"Of course, I knew. Mothers always know...even a few things they'd rather not know, but we won't go into that. I suggest that we not make any confessions to your father though."

"Thank you, Mama," Jordyn said, surprised by the curious swelling in her throat.

"I'm going to bed now. I just wanted to check on Siara and tell you about Blair. Bonnie says you're to report to Mr. Someski next week at the bank, by the way. She and Blair are leaving for St. Croix on Monday. A second honeymoon she says. I didn't know your uncle could be so romantic."

When Siara woke up screaming a few hours later, Jordyn grabbed her quickly and clamped a hand over her sister's mouth.

"Shush, Baby. You'll wake up Mama and Dad, and they'll be asking all kinds of questions that we don't want to answer."

Trembling, Siara nodded her head and choked back the screams as Jordyn held her tightly, rocking her in a gentle, soothing rhythm.

"It's all right, Baby," Jordyn said. "I understand now. I could kick myself for not understanding a whole lot sooner."

"I...I thought he'd leave me alone forever after that time. Why didn't he?"

"He thought you were me."

"You? But he was so...so intimate."

"Since this seems to be the night for revelations, I might as well tell you that we've been fu—having sex for over three years."

"Oh, Jordyn...please tell me that you are making that up."

"I'd be lying if I did, but if it makes you feel any better, his party with me is over."

"What if he gets nasty about it?"

"He can't get too nasty. I'm sure he doesn't want his tendencies made public. The worst he can do is fire me, which I don't think he has the guts to do. Besides, I'm quitting before he gets back from St. Croix."

"Why is he going to St. Croix?"

"To get away from you and me. I'm not too surprised. It shows what a low-life coward he is. Sari...how long ago did he...well...you know?"

"A long time ago. We were in first or second grade."

"Oh, Lord, that's even worse than I suspected. Do you want to talk about it? It might help. You know I won't tell anyone."

"Just your knowing helps. I should have told you a long time ago, but I...I was so ashamed."

Siara covered her face with her hands and began to cry again.

"No, Baby, none of that. YOU certainly have nothing to be ashamed about. It's not your fault Aunt Bonnie married a horny old pervert."

Siara's sobs turned into hiccupping giggles. "Oh, Jyn, we are a pair, aren't we? Imagine what Daddy and Mama would say if they knew all our secrets."

"Mama knows a lot more about what's going on than she lets Dad think she does. It's a pleasure to watch her operate."

"Have you told them you want to quit your job? They might not think it's such a good idea with both of us starting college in the fall. I know they've saved up for our college and all, but still..."

"But still they shouldn't have to foot the whole bill, especially since I didn't get a scholarship like you did."

"I didn't mean it that way."

"I know you didn't, but that's the truth of the matter anyway. The thing is that Nanette has asked me to work for her...teaching dance at the studio. She doesn't get around so well since she broke her hip last year, and it seems like a good job for a theater and dance major. You'll be working in your stacks, Stacks, and I'll be working in my leotards."

"You will probably like working for the studio better than for the bank, and I will like your working for Nanette better than for Uncle Blair."

"Baby...you realize, don't you, that your...experience with Blair is why you're so...shy around men?"

"Do we have to talk about it?"

"You need to work it out of your system. Poor Stanley Klosterman would probably agree with me."

"'Poor' Stanley Klosterman has girls hanging all over him these days."

"I asked a few of my friends to play up to him, and once they discovered his endowment, he did okay on his own."

"Stanley has an endowment?"

"His dingus, silly. It's bigger than a space-age missile."

"Jordyn!"

"I just wanted you to know what you missed."

"Jordyn!"

"I'm only teasing you. But I am serious when I say you need to talk about what happened, if not to me, then to someone else. Like a counselor."

"I could never tell anyone but you."

"So talk to me then."

"Please, not now. Maybe later. Isn't it enough that you know what happened? It's enough for me. Really."

"I disagree with you, but we'll play it your way...for a while."

"Thank you."

"But we will talk about it. There's a man out there somewhere who will thank me for pulling you out of this phobia of yours, and he could be as close as Scheffers."

"I don't understand what you mean."

"Connor Sanderson, silly."

"Don't you be silly. He's a friend of Daddy's."

"He'd like to be friendlier to you."

"He's just a friendly person. That's his way. He's friendly with everyone."

"He didn't give me a graduation present."

"He didn't give me one either."

"Think again." Jordyn leaned over the edge of the bed and groped around for the tissue-wrapped package. "He told me to give this to you. It's a book of poems he thought you might like."

"Teasdale," Siara said, taking the package. "It must be Sara Teasdale."

"Who's she?" Jordyn turned on the bedside light as Siara unwrapped the package.

"She was a poet. Oh! I was right! It's her *Collected Poems*. Connor said that I write like her...lyrically gentle he says."

"Sounds to me like Dr. Sanderson knows you pretty well."

"Don't read more into it than there is. Our relationship is strictly academic. He is much too old for me."

"Dad says he's only twenty-eight."

"And I am only seventeen, and I don't need a boyfriend of any age, so please hush. I'll probably have Connor as an instructor sometime in the next few years, and I'll feel uncomfortable around him if you continue teasing me about everything he says or does. He would die of embarrassment if he knew we were having this conversation."

"So do you want to talk about something else since we're both wide awake now?" Jordyn asked as she turned off the light.

"Yes, please."

"How about Stanley Klosterman's dingus?"

"Jordyn!"

Both twins exploded into a fit of giggles then, and they continued giggling until Devon's stern voice ordered them to be quiet and go to sleep.

CHAPTER FIFTEEN

"You're sure you'll be all right alone?" Amelie asked, hugging her daughters again. "Blair and Bonnie will be happy to have you stay with them while we're gone."

"Mama, we're twenty-one years old," Jordyn said. "We don't need babysitters."

"We have been staying by ourselves for years now," Siara ventured gently. "We'll be fine. You and Daddy go on to the convention and have a good time."

Devon put on his best look of authority. "Now, Jordyn, don't you go wandering around St. Louis by yourself when you're finished with your commercial. Wait for Connor and Siara to pick you up at the studio door. Then you can wander around all you want...so long as Connor is with you."

"I really wish you hadn't imposed on him like that," Jordyn said, her lower lip jutting forward.

"It's no imposition," Siara told her sister. "While you are shooting, we can visit the Bellefontaine and Calvary cemeteries."

"Good Lord, why?"

"Sara Teasdale is buried at Bellefontaine and her benefactor, William Marion Reedy is at Calvary. Kate Chopin, too, though I don't count her among my favorites."

"I'm sure she will be crushed."

"She's dead, Jyn. Otherwise she wouldn't be allowed to stay in the cemetery."

"College is bringing out your smart-ass tendencies, Baby. Or is Connor bringing you out of your shell?"

"Jordyn..."

"I know, I know...he's a friend of Dad's and merely your dedicated faculty advisor. If I had a nickel for every time I've heard that over the past three and a half years, I wouldn't have to wear myself out modeling and making commercials."

"I thought you were getting ready for Hollywood."

"I hope," Devon said, "that Hollywood is getting ready for Jordyn."

Amelie wiped traces of cherry Kool-Aid off his mouth. "Perhaps we should wire ahead and warn them that she's coming, darling."

"Oh, I don't think that's necessary. They are already accustomed to natural disasters out there...you know, earthquakes...the San Andreas fault..."

"Make fun of me all you want." Jordyn fluffed her hair and struck a dramatic pose. "If I forget to mention you all during my acceptance speech for the Academy Award, remember that you deserved it."

"We'll keep that in mind, darling," Amelie told her as a horn sounded in the driveway. "That's Bonnie. She's a little early. I do hope the plane is on time. I hate waiting. Grab the bags, darling. I have the tote and your briefcase. Siara, Jordyn, you two behave yourselves and watch out for each other. And no cutting classes this morning just because we're gone and you have a commercial tomorrow, Jordyn. The name of our hotel is on the pad by the phone, and if you need anything, you know to call Bonnie or Blair, of course. Now, have I forgotten anything? Oh yes…we love you, darlings. Now give us a kiss, and we'll be on our way."

The twins kissed their parents dutifully and stood by grinning as Amelie and Devon left the house in a whirlwind of baggage and Amelie's "did-you-remembers."

"Why do I already feel lonely for them?" Siara asked as Bonnie's silver Cadillac disappeared from sight, and silence settled throughout the house.

"Because you're a sentimental weakling. You have to be tough like me."

"You miss them, too. You can't deny it. My twinstinct tells me I'm right."

"Does your twinstinct tell you to go on to class without me? I'm staying home to rehearse."

"Mama said—"

"Mama won't know if my baby sister keeps her mouth shut. This particular commercial could be my big break. The director's next job is some project in L.A., and his sister-in-law's best friend is a cousin of the wife of a big producer out there."

"Are you really that serious about Hollywood?"

"You bet. Why else would I care about some old fart's genealogy? That damn ring Blair gave me for graduation gave me funds for a fancy photographer for a fancy portfolio, so I'm set. The way I figure it, I'm a natural. I'm gorgeous. I can dance. I can act. I can probably even sing if I have to. And I'm not adverse to warming a casting couch here and there."

"But Hollywood is so far away."

"I'll be so rich, I can jet back to see you any time I want or fly you out to see me…if you can take your nose out of a book long enough. You're crazy for going to grad school, especially since you don't want to teach."

"I could never get up in front of a bunch of people I don't know. I'll be quite happy as a research librarian specializing in American literature. I may even write a few scholarly articles and books along the way."

"You're becoming an academic nun."

"You are being overly dramatic. I am quite content…except for…for…"

"For what, Baby?"

"Sometimes I get this eerie feeling that Uncle Blair is just waiting for another opportunity to do something awful to us. He always seems to be staring at us with a weird look on his face."

"Aunt Bonnie has him firmly in hand these days…much to his dissatisfaction I'm sure. So don't you ever worry about him again. Nothing can happen to us now."

"Are you going to read all night, darling?" Amelie scooted across the bed and tipped the book away from Devon.

"Do you want me to be the only English professor at the convention who hasn't read Dr. Thursby's new book?"

"You can read it later, handsome. If you have any strength left."

"What do you have in mind for me?"

"After all these years you have to ask a question like that?"

Amelie took the book from him and tossed it onto the floor.

Devon removed his glasses and drew her into his arms. "I've been overruled again, haven't I?"

"Do you mind?"

"You know I don't. Is that the new nightgown you bought for the trip?"

"You've been so busy with Dr. Thursby, I didn't think you'd ever notice."

"I noticed all right, and now that I have noticed, you won't be needing it anymore tonight."

He caressed the gown off her body as she snuggled against him.

"Ah, Mel, your lips and your body are as familiar to me as my own, yet each time I kiss you, each time I make love to you, I am filled with the same wonder and excitement as the first time we kissed or made love."

"That was a lot of years ago, my darling. It hardly seems possible that it's been so long. Do you realize that I've been in love with you nearly all my life? And each year it gets a little better."

"Loving you is as natural to me as breathing and as impossible to control as a heartbeat."

"I should let you read Dr. Thursby more often. You've become quite poetic tonight."

"Shall I compare thee to a Summer's day?"

"Devon darling? Do you have to talk so damn much…"

The smell of smoke awakened her.

"Devon? Devon, wake up. Something isn't right."

"Hmmm? What is it, Mel? What's wrong?"

"Smoke. I smell smoke."

Devon sniffed the air. "Good Lord, you're right."

Quickly he jumped out of bed and ran to the window. The scene before him filled him with panic, but he swallowed back the fear as he turned to Amelie.

"Mel…sweetheart…the hotel is on fire. For some reason the alarms didn't sound. Throw something around yourself. We have to leave…and fast."

"How bad is it?"

"Hurry, Mel!"

She wrapped her bathrobe around her while he pulled on his pants.

"Devon…our bags…"

"Just your purse," he said, hurrying to the door. Carefully he placed his hand against the panel. "Oh, Lord…"

"What's wrong?"

"The door is hot…extremely hot."

"We'll have to find another way out then."

He could keep the helplessness out of his eyes no longer. "There is no other way. We are…trapped…"

"We can't be! The firemen will get us out through the window."

"We're on the fourteenth floor, darling."

"Don't be silly. They can get us out. We just have to let them know we're here."

As she turned to run toward the window, Devon grabbed her arm.

"No, Mel. Don't look. The fire is all around us. They will never be able to get to us in time."

"What can we do? We have to do something! What can we do?"

"I don't know. God help us, I don't know."

He recognized the terror in her eyes though she tried to smile bravely.

"Hold me, Devon?" she whispered.

He pressed his face against her hair as he wrapped his arms around her.

"I love you, Amelie."

"I love you, too, my darling. Oh, Devon…the girls…our babies…"

The only response he could manage was to tighten his hold on her.

At first the rumbling was distant, like the approach of a behemoth locomotive. But within seconds the thundering roar surrounded them, and Devon and Amelie Nealy disappeared in a fiery collapse.

CHAPTER SIXTEEN

"Oh, look, Jordyn. There's Aunt Bonnie's car. I wonder what she's doing here."

From the back seat of Connor's battered Volvo, Jordyn leaned forward for a better look. "Mama probably sent her over to see if we washed our dishes and made our beds."

"I washed our dishes, but you didn't make your bed."

"I had better things on my mind. Hey, we'll have a party tonight to celebrate. Maybe we'll even let Blair join us, and we can call Mama and Dad and tell them the good news."

Connor carefully parked his battered old car at a respectful, but still convenient distance behind Bonnie's Cadillac. "You shouldn't drop out of school and buy a plane ticket just yet. The director...what's his name?...Wolfgang?...may have been feeding you a line to hook an eager, blond fish."

"His name is Wohlgenmeier, and you don't need to be such a spoil-sport, Connor," Jordyn told him with a pout. "This L.A. project is his big break, and he says it could be mine, too. I'm sure he was serious, and I didn't have to take my clothes off. That should count for something."

Color rushed to Siara's face. "Jordyn! Please don't say things like that in front of Connor!"

"I'm just trying to prove to him that someone appreciates my talent and potential."

"I have never doubted your talent or your potential," Connor said as he opened the car door for the girls. "Now, could I beg a glass of cherry Kool-Aid from you ladies before I head home to a depressing pile of compositions, most of which were written by freshmen here on football scholarships. I don't expect an enjoyable evening at all."

"Won't you stay for Jordyn's celebration...or at least for supper?" Siara asked, tugging on his sleeve. "I promise not to let Jyn do any of the cooking."

"Not tonight, Stacks," he said with a regretful smile as Jordyn frowned at both of them. "If you want to see O'Neill's *Strange Interlude* on Sunday, I must finish those papers tonight. However, I will let you make me a sandwich. It's been a long time since lunch."

"A picnic in a cemetery in twenty-degree weather," Jordyn sniffed as she opened their front door. "You're both nuts. Cemeteries are for dead people. Oh...hi, Aunt Bonnie...Uncle Blair..."

Blair and Bonnie stood up simultaneously as the twins and Connor entered the living room. When Jordyn realized that Bonnie had been crying, she instinctively reached for Siara's hand.

"Something's happened," she whispered.

Bonnie took a deep breath as a fresh flood of tears spilled from her eyes. "Something HORRIBLE…"

"Perhaps you should sit down first?" Blair suggested.

His voice was gentle, but Jordyn did not miss the anticipatory gleam in her uncle's eyes.

Connor stared dully at the paper in his hands. The writing on it might as well have been hieroglyphic for all the sense it made to him. Suddenly nothing made any sense. Not in a world where people like Amelie and Devon Nealy could meet such tragic deaths.

His current despair went beyond the fact that he had lost his two best friends. Siara had lost her parents. Her beloved mother and father. Connor felt her loss as keenly as his own.

There had been no surprises in the reactions of the twins to the tragic news brought to them by their aunt and uncle. Siara collapsed, weeping hysterically, and Jordyn comforted her. Though tears welled in her blue eyes, Jordyn did not cry, but her ashen face and trembling lips revealed the grief bottled within her.

When Blair suggested that the twins stay with him and his wife for a while, Siara crumbled so completely that their family doctor was summoned to administer a sedative. With Siara finally ensconced within the merciful insensibility of drugged sleep, Jordyn politely, but firmly refused her uncle's invitation though both Blair and Bonnie continued to badger her on the matter. Nor would Jordyn permit Bonnie's moving into the house on Meadow Lane, although Jordyn refused this offer less strenuously than she had Blair's. There was no need for the inconvenience to their aunt, she had stressed. She and Siara would take care of each other, and Bonnie was just a few minutes away if the twins needed her.

Blair would handle the arrangements for bringing Amelie and Devon back to Applewood, and then the twins would make the necessary decisions…with their uncle's guidance. Jordyn voiced no resistance to these recommendations as she ushered Blair and Bonnie to the door later in the evening. Through it all, Jordyn's face remained calm, though pale, and her expression firm, yet strangely vulnerable.

In that moment she looked more like Siara than she ever had.

When she and Connor were alone, she turned to him immediately and asked him to stay with them that night, admitting to him that she didn't really feel very strong at all. She needed to borrow from his strength, and Siara would need his comfort.

So he went home long enough to get his papers and a change of clothes while Jordyn secluded herself in her room.

When he looked up at her now as she slowly descended the stairs, he knew that she had finally surrendered to her tears. Her eyes were puffy and red-rimmed, but she would never let anyone witness the actual shedding of a tear. Not Jordyn.

"Is Siara still sleeping?" he asked as she moved listlessly around the room.

She nodded and plucked absently at the living room drapes.

"You never did get that sandwich and Kool-Aid, did you?" she said finally. "I'll get them for you now."

"Don't bother. I'm not hungry anymore."

"Nonsense. You've got to eat." She turned to him suddenly. "If I don't have something to do, I'm going to go nuts, and you'll have to zonk me like we did Sari."

He wanted to hug her, but knew with fair certainty that such a gesture would not necessarily be comforting to this young lady who needed to trust her own strength and independence right now. What he could do was help her bolster that tenuous façade.

"You may make me a sandwich if you make one for yourself," he said. "I bet you haven't eaten since breakfast."

"Not even then, but I'm not hungry…"

"If I eat, you eat. Even Wonder Woman needed occasional nourishment, you know."

"Wonder Woman also managed a happy ending for every episode. I think we're more than a sandwich away from one of those…"

"Do you want to talk?" Connor asked later when they had finished enough of their sandwiches to say that they had eaten something.

"Maybe later. Right now it's enough that you're here. Aunt Bonnie would have turned into a raving lunatic eventually, and I would've had to take care of both her and Siara. And Blair…well…let's just say that he has a way of making a bad situation even worse, especially for Sari."

"Don't feel that you have to be everyone's guardian and caretaker."

"Not everyone's. Just Sari's. And I'm pretty sure I'll have some help…won't I?"

When the phone rang then, Connor smiled in shy relief. "Saved by the bell, as the saying goes."

Jordyn responded with a faint smile of her own as she picked up the phone.

Mr. Wohlgenmeier. Of course. He had talked to some people in L.A., and when he left for California in three weeks, Jordyn could be with him. Of course, she would be handed a decision like this at a time like this. Of course, of course, of course…

Of course, there was only one decision she could make…

"I've changed my mind, Mr. Wohlgenmeier," she said firmly. "I'm sorry for any inconvenience I created for you."

She cradled the receiver slowly, reluctantly.

As if she is hanging up on a dream, Connor thought.

As she dropped into a nearby chair and covered her face with trembling hands, he went to her, kneeling before her and taking her hands gently into his own.

"You didn't have to so that, Jordyn."

"Do you really think I could go so far away and leave Siara here alone."

"She wouldn't be alone."

"Maybe not actually alone, but lonely…for me…especially now. And I would be awfully lonely for her, to tell you the truth. I can't break up a matched set, can I? I've gotten so used to being a twin, I'm not sure I'd like being solo."

"For Siara's sake I am glad about your decision. However, you must consider your own needs."

"Hey, I can take care of my needs any time, anywhere. Haven't you heard?" The flippancy drained from her quickly. "Listen, Connor. I really need to get out and walk or run or something. Would you keep your ears open in case Sari wakes up? I left her door open, so you should be able to hear her if she…needs anything. If you could just check in on her now and then…"

"Of course. But should you be out alone this late?"

"This is Jordyn Nealy you're talking to, remember? This is what I have to do for me if I'm going to be any good for Siara."

"Just be careful."

"Don't worry. I've been a big girl nearly all my life." After retrieving her jacket from the hall closet, she peeked back around the corner. "If Sari should ever ask about…about the L.A. deal, and I'm sure she will eventually, our story is that Mr. Wohlgenmeier decided that I wasn't right for the role. Can a decent guy like you manage a lie like that to the woman he…um…respects so much?"

Connor tugged at the neck of his shirt. "I think I can manage a bit of prevarication for such a noble reason."

Jordyn managed a weak smile. "While you are prevaricating, try not to blush so much, okay?"

Connor wasn't sure whether he actually heard Siara's crying or merely sensed that she needed comfort. Whatever the case, he threw his papers aside and bounded up the stairs and into her room.

She was lying with her face buried in the pillow to muffle her sobs as Connor sat on the side of the bed and pulled her into his arms. Reacting more from intuition than from experience, he whispered her name in soothing, reassuring tones. Guiltily he thought of how good she felt sheltered within his arms, this girl who had become a woman before his eyes. This girl who was the daughter of his best friend.

Forgive me, Devon, for having such thoughts about your little girl.

But would Devon have been all that surprised? Or even that adverse to this sudden hope swelling within Connor's heart?

What was the adage? When God closed one door, He opened another. Had last night's tragedy in some way opened a door that Connor had been afraid to open himself?

Let's face it, Sanderson. You've been waiting for Stacks to grow up for over five years now.

When her tears subsided, he cupped her chin within his hand and wiped her face with a corner of the sheet. Brushing back her tear-dampened hair, he ventured a chaste kiss to her brow. As he was considering the possibility of another, less chaste kiss, on her lips, she spoke to him in that shy, soft voice that had always been ethereally musical to him.

"J-Jordyn has always said you remind her of Daddy. You must adopt us for sure now, Connor, so that I won't feel quite so...so orphaned."

Connor closed his eyes and swallowed his disappointment. "I'll always be here for you, Stacks...however you want me."

Why do I feel as though I've just suffered another loss? he asked himself as she nodded her appreciation and laid her head against his shoulder.

February. A time when winter had one final fling before spring stroked it into hibernation with a patient, but persistent hand.

Jordyn turned her jacket collar up to fend off the stinging bite of an icy-breathed night. She should have grabbed a heavier coat before leaving the house, but her one thought at the time was to get out. To get out into the night where she could look up into a star gemmed sky and imagine that she had somehow wandered into the Twilight Zone. That she could turn around now and go home and her mama would be there chiding her for going outside in such a light jacket and her daddy would look at her sternly over his glasses before his face was softened by a cherry Kool-Aid smile.

But that couldn't happen now, could it? Her mama and daddy were...dead. Oh, God...DEAD.

She began to run then, her footfalls padded by a sodden cushion of decaying leaves, remains of last autumn's brilliant cascade of colors.

Autumn to winter.

Color to decay.

She ran faster. Until the trees and houses bordering the road were but a blur. Until her nose and throat burned from sucking in the night air. Until her side knotted in pain.

Still she ran.

In the distance she saw the lights of Applewood's business district. Civilization. Out of the Twilight Zone and into reality.

Painful, painful reality.

When the neon glow of the city lights fell fully across her face, she slowed her pace. She exhaled in rapid puffs, whitely visible in the rainbow luminescence. She would need to rest before heading back home.

Six miles she had come without realizing the distance, but the six miles back would be a different story. And she didn't want to bother Connor for a ride.

Where to now? The thought of socializing seemed somehow repugnant, but she did need something to drink. Burkey's was the logical choice. The good thing about bars was that even in the midst of a hundred people, she could be alone if she wanted to be. And Jordyn definitely wanted to be alone.

After digging through her pockets to see how much money she had with her, she found a small table in a secluded corner of Burkey's, as far away as possible from the bar and the Saturday night losers on the prowl for female company.

The waitress seemed only mildly surprised when Jordyn ordered plain grapefruit juice. Jordyn seldom drank anything stronger than fruit juice or wine anymore. Alcohol had lost its glamour as soon as she became old enough to drink legally. Besides, she didn't much like the way the stuff befuddled her mind and muddled her reflexes.

Though right now a little mind befuddling and reflex muddling sounded quite tempting.

Jordyn closed her eyes tightly and shredded a napkin into a forlorn pile of tiny, ragged pieces.

"No charge," the waitress said as she set the juice on the table. "I heard about your parents on the radio. I'm so sorry..."

"Thanks. Me, too..."

Jordyn tried to smile, but she knew the result was a pitiful, etiquette-mandated facsimile that would fool no one. Still, she was unexpectedly touched by the girl's gesture. Jordyn usually had little use for sentimentality, but tonight everything seemed alarmingly out of kilter.

Fortunately the waitress seemed neither to need nor to expect any further response as she continued clearing glasses off tables and taking new orders.

Pushing the tattered napkin pieces around with her glass, Jordyn wondered why she had even come here. She wasn't that thirsty anymore. Maybe she had needed the reassurance that only neon artificiality could provide. The world had not gone suddenly crazy on her...it had always been this way. Persistent consistency. How comforting that nothing had changed.

Jordyn laid her head down on the table. *I'm going nuts here,* she thought in panic. *Nuts, nuts, nuts...*

"Hey there, blondie. Looks to me like you've had one too many and need a ride home...a long ride home...like through that stone quarry that turns you on so much."

Jordyn raised her head. "Buzz off, Thad. I'm not in the mood."

"Since when? You're easier to spread than warm peanut butter."

"Find yourself someone else to slobber on. I'm not interested."

"Impossible. I'm what every woman dreams of."

"Go harass someone else and leave me alone."

"Aw, c'mon, Jyn. It's getting late, and I'm so horny I could fuck a duck."

"You're so drunk you wouldn't know the difference. Just go away and leave me alone, okay?"

"Not okay..."

He lunged across the table and sent her glass crashing to the floor. In the jovial din of a normal Saturday night at Burkey's, the breakage went unnoticed except by those sitting at the tables closest to Jordyn. Even those weekend celebrants, however, were too preoccupied with their own pursuits and conquests to give much attention to Thad's drunken attempts at primitive seduction.

Since Jordyn was denied the theatrical satisfaction of throwing her drink into his face, she cocked her arm, intending to administer a stinging slap across his sloppy leer.

Suddenly, however, to Thad's surprise as well as her own, he was jerked off the table and set roughly on his feet.

"The lady does not want your company," an amber-eyed giant growled. "Now get out of here before I decide to help you out."

One look at the six-foot-six tower of muscle convinced Thad not to argue, and he shrugged and staggered away as the titan bent down to pick up the broken glass on the floor.

"Thanks," Jordyn said. "Do you work here? I've never seen you here before."

"My cousin Sandie works here." He nodded toward the waitress who had served Jordyn. "I came in to give her a ride home, and then noticed that you might be having some trouble here. Sandie told me about your folks, ma'am. I'm real sorry. I wondered why you weren't at the dance studio today."

"You were at Nanette's?"

"Almost every Saturday. My little sister Lissa...Malissa...Johnson is in one of your classes. I usually take her there and fetch her home afterwards. I...I've noticed you a time or two, and Liss likes to talk about you. I guess I kinda encourage her to talk about you."

"In other circumstances I'd probably be flattered, Mr. Johnson."

"Luke. Call me Luke. In other circumstances, Miss Nealy, I might be forward enough to ask to take you home."

"You may call me Jordyn. And I do need a ride...that is, if your cousin won't mind."

"She's already stood me up." When he grinned at her, his eyes sparkled warmly. "One of her boyfriends happened by, and she says she'd rather catch a ride with him. Imagine that."

"Oh...so...we'd be...alone...'"

Her implication did not offend him. In fact, his face softened with understanding.

"I'll take you straight home, ma'am. In other circumstances, I might ask your permission to make a detour, but I know that you...have other things on your mind right now."

"Thank you for realizing it. Most men wouldn't."

"I have to tell you that I have ulterior motives."

"Such as?"

"I've been racking my brain for months trying to think of a clever way to make myself known to you."

"You could have introduced yourself when you picked up Malissa."

"You were always so busy with the young'uns...and, well, a farm boy like me isn't real comfortable around ballet slippers and tutus."

"I guess we're starting out even, Farm Boy. I'm not real comfortable around harness boots and fertilizer."

"Thanks for the ride home, Luke."

As she placed her hand on the door handle, her shoulders sagged for an unguarded moment before she again rallied her composure.

He leaned across the seat and gently squeezed her arm. "Hey, are you going to be all right?"

"I...I will be...eventually. Right now I have to look as though I am."

"Why do you feel that way?"

"People expect it, and my sister needs me to be that way."

"What do YOU need, Jordyn?"

"I'm not sure. There are so many thoughts spinning around in my head. The only thing I can focus on is that Siara needs for me to be strong. So maybe that's what I need...her needing me."

"Is she a lot younger than you?"

Jordyn smiled wanly. "In a lot of ways, yes. But in actual time, only eight minutes."

"Oh...twins..."

"Identical twins though we're about as different as two people can be. Still, we've always been close, closer than most sisters, and that will help us both right now."

"Were you and your sister real close to your folks?"

"Sari was, especially to Daddy. I didn't think I was...until today when it was too late for me to do anything about it." When tears welled in her eyes, she quickly turned her head and fumbled with the door handle. "The damn door won't open."

"I really should be getting me a new pickup one of these days. The only way you can open that door is from the outside."

"Well, get out and open it."

"No."

"No?" As astonishment widened her eyes, tears escaped onto her cheeks. Quickly she brushed them away and then tried unsuccessfully to roll down the window.

"Window's broken, too," he told her calmly.

"What the hell do you think you're doing here?"

"You kinda like to be in control of things, don't you?"

"What the goddamn hell is that supposed to mean?"

"Do you always swear this much?"

"Only when I'm angry."

"Am I making you angry?"

"Yes, Farm Boy, you are. Now get your goddamn ass out of this goddamn truck and open this goddamn, fuckin' door before I kick the goddamn, fuckin', son-of-a-bitchin' window out."

"I can't remember the last time I heard so many swear words spoken in one breath. I think maybe it was the locker room a few years back when I was playing football for Oklahoma State."

"You're on the verge of getting your balls crushed."

"That could make for an interesting evening. So long as it's me you're mad at and not yourself."

"You're trying to mix me up."

"Just the opposite. Admit it. You've been mad at yourself all evening over what happened to your folks. Even if you had been there, you couldn't have saved them."

"That's not the point."

"Then what is?"

"Why should I tell you?"

"No special reason…except that I'll listen because I have nothing better to do, and you aren't going anywhere right now. So tell me…what exactly is the point?"

Jordyn growled and yanked furiously on the door handle. When it came off in her hand, she stared at it for a moment as if it was some alien creature that had suddenly appeared in her hand.

"Okay, Farm Boy," she said, struggling for both words and composure, "the point is that I was up last night primping in front of a mirror and practicing my lines for a fuckin' department store jeans commercial while my mother and father were being cooked alive."

"What do you think you should have been doing instead?"

"I…I…oh, hell, I don't know. Something more…more noble I guess."

"Like discovering a cure for cancer?"

"You're being ridiculous."

"If you think about it, so are you."

After a moment's silence, she continued more calmly. "I wasn't even home today when their bodies were identified. I was in St. Louis shooting that damn commercial while my sister and her friend were wandering around a…a cemetery. God, how morbidly ironic that turned out to be. The police in Minneapolis had to call the police here, and the local boys called my aunt and uncle. All that time Mama and Daddy were…were dead, and Sari and I didn't know. We should have known."

"How could you have known? Even your aunt and uncle apparently didn't know until the police contacted them. It happened too late to make the morning papers, and unless you just happened to catch a newscast on the car radio, there was no way you could have found out."

"So I should have been listening to the news…"

"Do you usually listen to the news?"

"Well…no. We didn't even have the radio on today. We were too busy talking about things that suddenly seem profoundly insignificant."

"Quit laying a load of guilt on your shoulders, Jordyn. Nothing you did or could have done would've changed a thing."

"I could have been a better daughter. I'm no angel. My mom and dad deserved to have angels. They got one in Siara, but I certainly tipped the scale back to zero. I lied to them. I sneaked around and did things I knew they didn't approve of…"

"Most kids do that at some time or another."

"I did it more than most, and like I said, they deserved better. They didn't deserve to die like they did either. They should have grown old and gray together and died peacefully in their sleep with a flock of grandchildren and great-grandchildren left behind to mourn them. Instead they…they were trapped on one of the topmost floors, and the hotel collapsed around them. They must have been terrified. I keep having these scenes in my head…of them realizing they're about to die, of them falling and burning and being in pain…oh, God, since it had to happen, I pray they didn't have to suffer…"

She covered her face with her hands until she was sure she could speak again without crying. "The police told Uncle Blair that they found my mom and dad locked in each others' arms. They must have fallen that way. Through the fire and the fall and everything collapsing around them, they held on to each other. I'm trying to find some comfort in that."

He waited until he knew she was in control of herself again and then slid across the seat.

"Would you let me hold you just a bit?" he asked. "After what you just told me, I think I need a hug or two."

Jordyn looked up into his eyes before yielding to his suggestion. "You're not fooling me for one minute, Farm Boy."

"I didn't think I was, but you do feel better now, don't you?"

"Yes," she said, pressing her face against his jacket. "Yes, I do."

Jordyn reached across the bed for Siara's hand. "Are you sleeping, baby?"

"I can't sleep anymore. I keep thinking."

"Yeah. Me, too."

"I keep thinking it has to be a bad dream. Things like this don't happen to people like us."

"Dying happens to everyone sooner or later."

"Why couldn't it have been later for Mama and Daddy?"

"Some people would call it fate or God's will I suppose. I think it was just their dumb luck to be in the wrong place at the wrong time."

"Maybe we should have gone to mass more? We weren't too good about going after Mammy and Grandy died."

"Don't be silly. That wouldn't have changed a thing."

Siara moved closer to her sister. "Jordyn...do you think we're being punished?"

"For what?"

"We both have done things in our past that were...punishable...haven't we?"

"I haven't been a paragon of virtue, but I can't remember anything you've done that's been so awful. Unless you've been holding out on me."

"Uncle Blair. I'm being punished for Uncle Blair."

"Bullshit. Blair is the one who will roast in Hell for that. You were nothing but an innocent victim."

"Do you think there really is a Hell...and a Heaven? I have been thinking about that, too."

"If there is a Heaven, Mama and Daddy will make the cut for sure."

"But you're not certain there is a Heaven, are you?"

"How can anyone be certain? It's one of those faith things. You either buy it or you don't."

"How scary if there is to be nothing afterward. An end with no beginnings...it makes life seem so scientific and impersonal. Thornton Wilder said in *Our Town* that there is something eternal in all of us...our souls...and I do believe in souls. Souls make people good like Mama and Daddy or bad like Uncle Blair. So if I believe in the eternity of souls, I must believe in Heaven, too."

Though Jordyn was not so easily convinced, she said nothing. Siara had found some comfort in her conjectures, and Jordyn would not deny her sister that consolation. Instead, she squeezed Siara's hand, a response that was noncommittal, but reassuring.

"There is something else I have been thinking about, Jyn."

"What is it, baby?"

"The way Mama and Daddy were found...you know, holding onto each other. They loved each other so much, and I know this may sound strange to you, but I really do feel quite strongly about it. Jordyn, I think they should be buried together."

"Of course they'll be buried together."

"I mean REALLY together...in the same c-casket."

Jordyn pondered the idea for a moment. "I think you're right," she said finally. "But is it possible? Can it be done? There might be a regulation or something, and people are bound to think we're crazy."

"When have you ever let anything like that stop you?"

"Only never."

"With my brains and your bravado, we'll be okay...won't we? I've been thinking about that, too."

"We'll be fine, Baby. You can count on it."

CHAPTER SEVENTEEN

"**W**hy the hell should I believe a fuckin' thing you say, you asshole?"

Jordyn slammed her hands down on the desk and glared fiercely at her uncle.

Blair calmly lit a cigar, puffing serenely as he visually recorded every curve and swell of his niece's womanly form.

"The way I see it, you don't have much choice in the matter. Your parents named me executor of their estate…such as it is…and until all the legalities are satisfied, I'm in charge of the purse strings, darling Jyn. I can drag out everything for as long as I want to…especially in view of the fact that I am suing the hotel…in behalf of my grieving nieces, of course…for the negligence that led to the deaths of their parents."

"You have no authority. Siara and I are twenty-one. We don't need a guardian."

"As executor, it's my duty to uphold the conditions of your parents' will. Among those conditions is the stipulation that I oversee your financial affairs until you and Siara reach your twenty-fifth birthdays."

"So you're going to financially blackmail us into doing anything you want over the next three and a half years."

"That's an unkind way of phrasing the business arrangement I have in mind. In fact, we can both benefit from what I have in mind…so long as you're…cooperative?"

"Eat one, Blair. I'm not cooperating with a damn thing you have in mind. Siara's working. I'm working. We'll get by. Besides, you'll have to give us some sort of household allowance or face an investigation by the board of directors. I won't hesitate a minute to drag them into it."

"Perhaps you should reconsider. First of all, currently there isn't that much cash flow. Devon and Amelie depleted their savings to get you through school and to have your house rewired and rerooted. There will be insurance and an annuity and whatever your father paid into his pension fund, but all that will take some time and wading through a lot of red tape. Of course, the lawsuit I've filed in your behalf should eventually leave you girls comfortably situated, but the pace of justice and restitution is very slow. In the meantime, there are bills…the mortgage on the house for four more years, the Lincoln that your parents bought last month, the funeral expenses…and let's not forget Siara's plans for graduate school. You girls are working only part-time, hardly enough to cover all these expenses without my help. You can, of course, sell the Lincoln, but I'm sure you won't want to lose the house. Though I'm certain that Siara will sacrifice grad school, I'm equally certain you won't let her."

"You son-of-a-bitchin' bastard…"

"Darling Jyn, is that any way to talk to your uncle? Didn't I show my love and family devotion to you girls by helping you get your parents buried the way you wanted them buried? That was no easy accomplishment, my sweet. I had to pull some strings and grease some palms."

"Love and devotion had nothing to do with it, you fucker. Aunt Bonnie agreed with us and made you do it. Maybe I'll talk to Aunt Bonnie now and tell her what you're up to."

"Talk away. If the old girl gives me too much hassle, I'll walk out on her, and you will have accomplished nothing but the destruction of your aunt's marriage, which would be very humiliating to her though not necessarily heart-breaking. Bonnie and I may not have the most loving relationship in the world, but we did manage to reach an understanding a few years ago that has worked out rather well for both of us. Of course, I had to pay dearly for the meager marital privileges she agreed to bestow upon me. You'll remember the trips to Europe, Hawaii, the Bahamas, and Vegas…the ermine coat…the new Cadillacs every year…the new house on Walcott Road. In exchange she took a more active social role in my career, and I have to give her credit…she has been a definite asset these past few years. She's even been a steady source of sex, grudgingly so, but it was part of the understanding. Of course, it was like fucking a cold, dead fish, but it did offer a small measure of relief. Still, I've missed you, Jordyn. Which brings me to the terms of our business arrangement…"

"Forget it, Blair."

"If you turn me down, I'll have to go to Siara."

Jordyn lurched across the desk and grabbed his tie.

"You stay away from Siara!" she hissed, yanking his tie until his face reddened.

Gripping her wrist, Blair yanked her across the desk, ignoring the papers that avalanched to the floor.

"Then be more agreeable."

"Fuck you…"

Blair unbuckled his belt and unzipped his pants. "That's exactly what I have in mind…"

* * *

Siara chewed on the end of her pencil as she studied their ad. After making a final change in the wording, she handed the paper to her sister for approval.

"Wanted: two amiable and trustworthy female housemates to share expenses. All the comforts of home plus the privacy of your own bedroom. Call Jordyn or Siara Nealy at 555-1144 for an interview."

"Print it." Jordyn handed the paper back to Siara. "The sooner, the better."

* * *

With unveiled curiosity, the twins eyed the woman sitting across from them.

Auburn hair that captured the sunlight from the window. Brown eyes that could probably be kindly and warm except for the nervousness that flickered there. A woman slightly older than the twins, but obviously more ill at ease.

"Dad remarried recently," she said by way of explaining why she was looking for a place to live, "and I really think he and Gwynnie deserve some privacy in spite of their protests to the contrary. They were both so worried about my moving out...I had to promise to find a place in Applewood. With me working in St. Louis County, they were afraid that I'd find a place in the city and get raped or killed. You know how parents can b-be...oh, God, I'm sorry. I shouldn't have said that."

She flushed darkly as her brown eyes filled with apologetic embarrassment. Jordyn and Siara exchanged meaningful glances before flashing identical smiles of understanding.

"We know what you mean," Siara said, her smile becoming wistful with remembering.

"I...I had your father in a few classes," Jayme McCray ventured hesitantly. "I was more into journalistic writing than creative writing, but I learned a lot about literary style from him. That's why your ad attracted my attention. I recognized your names, and since you evidently need to rent a room, and I need to rent a room...well...for a reporter, I'm really screwing up this explanation, aren't I?"

"You write for a newspaper?" Jordyn brightened at the thought of an association with a source of free publicity. "Do you write a society column?"

"No..."

"Book reviews?" Siara guessed, intrigued by anyone who wrote anything for a living.

"Nothing quite so glamorous or cerebral. I'm a sports writer."

"Sports?" Siara asked. "You mean like figure skating, swimming, and tennis?"

"Like baseball mostly...sometimes football and hockey...occasionally soccer, golf, and tennis. Another reason why your ad attracted my attention is that a room is really all I need since my editor has...finally...seen the wisdom of sending me on the road with the Cardinals."

Jordyn was immediately interested. "You get to travel with a baseball team?"

"This year I do. I am pretty excited about it."

"I would be, too. All those gorgeous, muscular bodies! Do you go into the locker room?"

"My paper received the necessary permission from the organization. It helps that I grew up with one of the players. In fact, he and my father are probably the reasons why I was given the Cardinal assignment. Dad's editor of the local paper, and every now an then he's been known to smooth my way a little. I'm one of those shamelessly spoiled brats who are not opposed to parental intervention when necessary, and here I am rambling on about parent things like an insensitive moron. I'm sorry..."

"Nonsense," Siara assured her quickly. "We're adjusting well. You won't have to guard your every word when you move in with us."

"When? You mean…you want me?"

"Of course we do," Jordyn said. "Especially if you'll pass out my phone number to all the baseball players."

"But…but don't you two need to consult each other alone or something?"

"We already have," Siara said, laughing with her sister at their new roommate's bewildered expression.

* * *

Siara hung up the phone.

"I knew it. I just knew it. Father Jonathan has discovered our sins, and he's coming to tell us that we are responsible for keeping Mama and Daddy in purgatory."

Dropping onto the couch, she wrung her hands while her sister stared at her in total disbelief.

"For someone so smart," Jordyn said, "you can certainly come up with some stupid ideas."

"Why else would Father want to see us if it's not about our souls…and Mama's and Daddy's?"

"Get a grip on yourself, Baby. First of all…and I'm telling you this for about the bajillionth time…you have done absolutely nothing sinful. And Mama and Daddy would not be stuck in purgatory for MY evil deeds…assuming, of course, there is a purgatory and assuming that I may have done a thing or two to displease the Main Man. It's every man for himself in a situation like that."

"Just the same, we should start going to mass more regularly…at least on weekends."

"Oh, good Lord…"

"Maybe we should go to confession, too?"

"Father Jonathan doesn't have enough time or stamina to hear everything I'd have to tell him."

"You need to be more serious about this."

"And you need to be less serious, so once again we manage to balance nicely."

"If he is coming to discuss our souls, promise me you won't be flippant."

"I promise I won't be flippant."

"And you'll go to mass with me this Sunday?"

"Don't expect miracles. I'm never up in time for mass. Saturday nights take too much out of me. Maybe Jae or Connor will go with you?"

"Jae's getting ready to leave for spring training, and Connor thinks churches are nothing but social institutions…and he's Baptist anyway. Please, Jordyn?"

"I've got a date with Luke Johnson this Saturday night. What's he going to think if I tell him I have to be home early so that I can get up for Sunday mass?"

"He'll think you are a good little Catholic girl."

"That's the last thing I want him thinking!"

"What do you think of our new roommate, ladies?" Jordyn asked later when she, Siara, and Jayme were alone.

"She's awfully quiet," Jayme said, grinning. "It'll take some getting used to after all the chatter in the locker room and then your mouth in perpetual motion here."

"Thanks a bunch, pal. Get me into the locker room, and you'll really see a mouth in perpetual motion…"

"I'm sure the guys would love having you have them," Jayme told her, "but go easy on your overt expressions of carnal cravings for a while. Darica doesn't look strong enough right now to handle your special kind of candid lust."

"Father Jonathan said there was trauma in her life though he didn't say what it was." Siara chewed on her lip. "She does have sad eyes. The poor thing was dead on her feet, too. I'm not so sure she should start her new job tomorrow. It's too soon."

"She went to bed early enough," Jordyn said. "She'll be fine in the morning."

Jayme leaned forward, her brow furrowed with concern. "She looks awfully young. I hope we're not harboring a runaway."

"Father Jonathan said she will be twenty in May," Siara said. "Father wouldn't fib to us."

"But would she fib to him?" Jordyn asked.

Jayme shook her head. "She's too much like a shy, little mouse to be a fibber."

"And Father wouldn't have brought her here if there was any question about her acceptability," Siara said. "Besides, she is very devout. When I was helping her move in, I noticed that she was particularly and reverently careful with her Bible and her rosary."

"Great!" Jordyn smiled. "Darica the mouse can go to mass with my sister the mouse on Sunday!"

CHAPTER EIGHTEEN

Jordyn stared into the flickering light from the movie screen. Though the last thing she usually wanted to do on a date was sit in a movie theater for two hours, she had been quick to suggest it when Luke asked her what she wanted to do that evening. She needed some time to think, to sort through her options. Of course, she could have canceled the date, but for some reason she had been almost excited about going out with Luke Johnson. Now there was a problem in the making: her feeling that way about a man could leave her open to all kinds of nasty situations. Proceed with caution.

In the meantime, there were other more urgent problems to deal with.

Her uncle…

And Nanette's offer…

Blair, of course, wasn't too pleased with his nieces' plan to circumvent his financial authority. Though the girls still had to go to him for some of their living expenses, the rent money from Jayme and Darica limited the extent of his control. Jordyn had already dropped out of school so that she could teach extra classes at the studio…a change in plans she had not yet told Siara about. Nanette was getting too old to handle the grind and, in fact, wanted to retire and sell the studio.

To Jordyn.

An investment suited to Jordyn's talents and capabilities. An uncle who was a banker. A pending settlement from the hotel fire.

Jordyn was the logical successor.

Though Nanette didn't want to put any extra pressure on Jordyn, the fact was that Jordyn's job would not be guaranteed if the studio was sold to someone else with his "own people." And the studio was no white elephant. It was thriving…drawing students from as far away as St. Louis and Terre Haute. Nanette had the all-important contacts that could generate moneymaking opportunities for her students. Commercials mostly. A few had danced at the Muny, one was a Dallas Cowboys Cheerleader, and two others had danced on television for Dean Martin and Carol Burnett.

A good investment. A sound investment. A perfect investment for Jordyn.

The problem was money. More specifically Jordyn's lack of it.

Blair was the obvious solution. He could arrange a loan for her with very little trouble. He WOULD do it, too, if Jordyn agreed to certain non-contractual terms of compensation. However, having to ask him would be unpleasant and demeaning. Fulfilling his demands would be even more unpleasant and demeaning.

Jordyn slumped in her seat as her face contracted into a pensive frown. Maybe she could try other banks. Certainly SOMEONE would realize that the studio was a good investment and that Jordyn was a good business risk. However, the other bank and loan companies in Applewood would be suspicious about her not getting a load from her own uncle. If Blair Eldred wouldn't risk money on his niece, something was wrong somewhere...

Maybe a bank in St. Louis...a certain long shot. While working for Blair, Jordyn had realized that banks did not loan money to single women...especially young, single women...without collateral and cosigners and liens on the women's firstborn children. The unfairness of such blatant discrimination galled her, but she could do little to correct a system that was so universally accepted.

She fought a sudden surge of anger. She couldn't get sidetracked by any liberationist crusades. Her one concern now was to get the money for the studio. The desire to own it was overwhelming her more than any passion she had ever felt for a man.

Plan. She must have a plan. A plan and counter plans in case the initial plan did not work.

Okay.

Blair.

She would save him for the very last resort.

The first resort. The long shot. St. Louis. She would try banks in St. Louis. She would ask around to see if any of her friends had connections with any banks there. Getting a loan was easier with connections. Getting anything was easier with connections.

Next resort. The other bank in Applewood. And the savings and loan. She wasn't optimistic enough about these possibilities even to rate them long shots. Word would filter to Blair, who would have the satisfaction of knowing that he finally had Jordyn pinned to the mat. This knowledge would decrease Jordyn's bargaining power with him if she was forced to seek his assistance.

Still, she had to try. Maybe she could lay some sob story on the other bankers...tell them she didn't want to trouble her uncle with such a huge request after all he had done for her and her sister. A forlorn expression. A single tear. The newly orphaned girl trying to be brave and strong. It might work.

If she needed a cosigner along the way, Connor might agree. Yes, she was certain that he would help her as much as he could. He of all people knew that Jordyn was shrewd and resourceful enough to maintain, even advance the success of the studio. And Nanette would be around to assist in the transition of ownership.

She must finalize everything before Blair had a chance to interfere. If he did find out and then she had to go to him to beg his help...well, she wouldn't even think about that. She would concentrate on success rather than failure. Having to ask Blair for help would be bitter failure.

"Jordyn? Are you ready to go now, or do you want to stay to see the movie again?"

"Hmm?" Jordyn's blue eyes blinked in the suddenly blaze of house lights.

Laughing, Luke reached for her hand. "All this time I thought you were so engrossed in *Ice Castles*, and you were really a million miles away. I think I'm offended."

Jordyn presented him her most electrifying smile. "Is there any way I can make it up to you, Farm Boy?"

His amber eyes glowed as he helped her into her coat. "I'll do my best to think of something."

"Milk! I can't believe you're really drinking milk."

Staring at Luke suspiciously, Jordyn leaned back in her seat. She felt his arm, hard and strong behind her along the back of the booth Sandie had somehow commandeered for them in spite of the boisterous horde at Burkey's. As strobe lights throbbed with the penetrating rhythm of rock-'n'-roll, Jordyn's pulse throbbed with anticipation.

"I got early morning chores," he told her. "Wouldn't do for me to be hung over. Besides, I've never had much of a taste for alcohol. It reminds me of horse liniment."

"And just how much horse liniment have you drunk over the years?"

As he grinned, his eyes flashed warmly in the pulsing light. "Just enough to put hair on my chest, ma'am."

"It certainly didn't stunt your growth any," she said smoothly despite the sudden fever that tickled her body. "Did you say you played college football?"

"At Oklahoma State. Even considered going pro until I tore up my knee my junior year."

"You can't be a local boy. I would have noticed you for sure."

"I was born and raised in Oklahoma…worked a small farm there with my dad. We sold the place and moved north when Dad's brother…Sandie's step-father…died about five years ago…a year after I graduated college. Uncle Bob left Dad three-fourths interest of the spread we have now. The other fourth is Sandie's though she doesn't want it. I'm buying her out as I can afford it. Of course, she has a home there no matter what. We're the only family she has left and vice versa. She has her eyes set on a big-city career though, soon as she's through college."

"What career does she have in mind?"

"She wants to be a clinical psychologist."

"Then the big city is the place for her. Opportunities around here are rare unless you're a scholarly type content with university life."

"Is that what's been bothering you tonight? Graduation coming up before too long, and you're not a scholarly type content with university life…"

"Why should that bother me? I'm thankful I'm not a scholarly type. I have a lot more fun than Siara does. What was your major?"

"Agriculture. Mom kept trying to push me toward doctoring or lawyering, but I'm happy down on the farm. So, are you going to tell me or not?"

"Tell you what?"

"What's been eating at you all evening? There's been something on your mind besides me and that skating movie…which, I might add, I would never have sat through for any girl but you."

"Thank you for the sacrifice."

"Does the sacrifice entitle me to know what's bothering you, or should I mind my own damn business?"

Jordyn toyed with the straw in her drink. "I dropped out of school."

"Why, Jordyn? You're graduating in three months."

"I…want to work full time for Nanette."

"Want to or need to? Are you and your sister having financial problems?"

"Nothing we can't handle. The thing is that Nanette wants to sell the studio…preferably to me…and I want to buy it. It's a good investment, and as we've already determined, career opportunities are not abundant around here."

"Are you having trouble with financing?"

"Too early to tell. I haven't looked into it yet. I was just thinking about how to look into it, what options are available to me and all. If worse comes to worst, I can go to my uncle. He's a banker."

"You say that like you'd rather ask Ted Bundy for a business loan."

"Without going into details, I'll tell you that you are very close to being right."

"I wish I was in a position to offer you some help. I don't want worries in your head when you're out with me."

"I'm not worried, but I was preoccupied…with financial strategy…back at the theater. If you really want to help me, you can preoccupy me with something else now."

"That's what I had in mind…"

"I can't believe this. You brought me right home." Crossing her arms, Jordyn glared at him.

Luke turned off the truck. "I bet you expected me to stop at a motel somewhere along the way."

"The thought crossed my mind."

"This is our first date, ma'am. A man can expect a few kisses from a lady on a first date, but not a few hours in a motel room."

"I never said I was a lady."

"Then it's time someone started treating you like one so you can start being one in your own eyes."

"Your cousin's the psychologist, Farm Boy. You should stick to your plow."

"Do I still get my kisses?"

"Do you kiss as well as you plow?"

"Even better, though I haven't had as much practice. Maybe you should judge for yourself?"

"I can't believe this," Jordyn muttered, pulling him toward her. "First milk, and now only a few kisses. You better be a damn good kisser, Farm Boy…"

* * *

Crossing one leg over the other, Jordyn swung her foot in nervous agitation. She hated to be kept waiting, and Ms. Konstance Fletcher had already kept her waiting fifteen minutes. Ms. Konstance Fletcher, loan officer at the Trust and Savings Bank of St. Louis and mother of Francesca Fletcher, Nanette's former student who was the Dallas Cowboys Cheerleader. A tenuous connection, but the only one that Jordyn had managed to uncover.

The prospect of doing business woman to woman increased Jordyn's optimism. Another woman would be more understanding of Jordyn's plight and, therefore, more willing to loan her the money in spite of the financial stigma of Jordyn's being a single woman. Surely Ms. Fletcher understood ambitious drives. She was an officer in a large bank…with an office and a secretary…and her own important meetings with the board of directors.

"Ms. Fletcher has been unavoidably detained with the directors," the secretary had smiled while ushering Jordyn into the office. "You can wait for her here. She shouldn't be much longer."

Much longer. Twenty minutes was more than "much longer" on Jordyn's timetable.

"Miss Nealy?"

Jordyn whirled around in her chair.

The secretary was peeking around the doorframe and smiling apologetically. "Ms. Fletcher just called in to say she'll be tied up much longer than she expected. Do you want to wait, or shall I schedule another appointment?"

Jordyn tried to keep the impatience out of her voice. "How much longer until I can see her? I drove over from Illinois."

"I really can't say. Sometimes these meetings drag on forever. Ms. Fletcher's been so busy with administrative affairs lately that she hired an assistant. Perhaps you'd like to talk to him?"

"How long will I have to wait for him?"

"He can see you now I think. Shall I send him in?"

"Okay. Send him in."

Him. A man. Jordyn squared her shoulders and revamped her battle strategy.

"Miss Nealy?"

The voice was familiar enough to send a prickle of dread through her. She turned in her chair to face Ms. Konstance Fletcher's new assistant:

Hudson Turner.

CHAPTER NINETEEN

"Connor? Are you busy? I really need some advice." Siara entered Connor's office hesitantly, her eyes downcast and her hands tightly clasped.

"I always have time for you, Stacks." Quickly Connor stood up and pulled a chair for her over by his own. "Here…sit down. You look particularly distressed this morning. Jyn must have told you what she did."

"You already know? You never mentioned it last night at the library."

"She came by here yesterday afternoon. She asked me not to tell you because she wanted to tell you herself."

"It is my fault, isn't it? She dropped out of school to support me so that I can stay in school."

"Jyn delayed telling you because we were afraid you would react this way." Connor leaned forward and took her hands into his own. "You have really been piling a heap of guilt on yourself lately, and all of it is totally unwarranted. Jyn and I talked at length about that, too."

Siara looked up, startled. "Jordyn told you about…about EVERYTHING?"

Connor squeezed her hands for reassurance. "No details, but I am not so stupid that I cannot deduce some specifics from what she did say."

"What…exactly…did she tell you?"

Siara's voice was hushed and her face pale. Connor instantly regretted telling her about his conversation with her sister.

"Only that because of something your uncle tried when you were a little girl, you have been weaving every bit of guilt you can accumulate into an emotional hair shirt in an attempt to mortify your sinful soul."

"Jordyn said THAT?"

"Actually the words are mine, but the thoughts are hers, and I concur."

"Jordyn should never have told you anything."

"She and I are the two people in this world who care most for you now. You realize that, don't you?"

"I know," she murmured.

"Do you trust me?"

"Of course I trust you."

"You realize that if I advise you to do something, I am motivated only by your best interests?" When she nodded, he continued. "I want you to talk to a counselor."

"About my graduate studies?"

"About your parents...about how their deaths are affecting you..." He studied her face for any sign of emotional retreat. "About the situation with your uncle..."

"I couldn't...I could NEVER..."

"Please listen to me, Siara. Your parents' deaths have apparently triggered some potentially destructive guilt mechanism within you. For now the results aren't psychologically crippling, but your guilt inclination is evinced in your thinking that Amelie and Devon were killed to punish you for something that was totally beyond your control and in no way your fault. I am also guessing that this same incident is a factor contributing to your rather monastic attitude about relationships with men."

"Perhaps my attitude is rather monastic, but it is surely no aberration. You yourself seldom date."

Connor carefully avoided her eyes. "My priorities don't allow for dating. Taking up a woman's valuable time when my thoughts and inclinations are...directed elsewhere is hardly fair."

"My thoughts and inclinations are directed elsewhere, too."

"Very well. I will concede that point to you. However, I won't surrender my original assumption that you are overly vulnerable right now, and unless you resolve this childhood trauma within your own conscience, you are perpetuating a condition that can eventually bring you grievous emotional problems. Yours is a situation that has happened so often it's tragically clichéd. Jordyn and I cannot sit idly by and watch it happen to someone we love, especially when we are in a position to recognize the danger signals and neutralize the problem before it assumes serious proportions."

"You both are over-reacting to something that is truly trivial so far as my state of mind is concerned. I am handling everything rather well I think."

"Just a few moments ago you were upset because you felt responsible for Jordyn's dropping out of school."

"I am responsible."

"Your sister has never been an academic wonder, Stacks. Her GPA is abominable. The only classes she makes fairly decent grades in are her drama and dance classes, and she cuts those so often she doesn't do as well as she should. Her time could be spent so much more profitably if she were doing something she felt really dedicated to. The truth of the matter is that Jyn wanted to drop out two years ago, but Devon had his heart set on seeing both his daughters graduate from Scheffers.

"Now that this possibility of her buying the studio has developed, I will do everything I can to insure that she has her chance for success simply because that's what she wants...just as I will insist that you go to graduate school because that's what you want. Jyn's decision had nothing to do with your financial situation. In fact, the studio will probably put a bigger strain on you girls for a while. Jyn, however, is doing what is right for her, and you will be doing what is right for you, and that's the way it should be. There is absolutely nothing in this whole scenario that you should feel guilty about...unless you persist in moping about and burdening Jyn with even more worries about you. You could ease your sister's mind considerably by agreeing to talk to a counselor."

"I haven't even really talked to Jordyn about...about what happened. She only knows that it did happen. I could not possibly elaborate to ANYONE."

"I am no expert, but my profession has given me some counseling experience. Can you talk to me?"

Color drained from Siara's face. "No! Especially not to you! It would be too much like telling Daddy."

Connor turned his head so that she would not see the pain flash across his face. "There are a few other possibilities I can think of...if you will agree to talk to someone...if not for yourself, then for Jordyn."

"You know I would do anything for Jordyn. I don't want to be a source of distress for her. If she is that concerned..."

"You will agree to some kind of counseling?"

"I...I will try. I just don't know if I can. Jordyn has encouraged me to talk with her, but my throat and tongue seem to become paralyzed if I try to elaborate. If I am unable to talk to Jyn, how can I possibly talk to a stranger?"

"Actually a stranger might be easier for you to talk to. Shall I call Father Jonathan for a recommendation or call Scheffers Student Services?"

"I...I really don't feel comfortable with either of those suggestions."

"We might consider Jordyn's suggestion then. The cousin of this boy she's dating is working on a master's degree in psychology. If you talked with this cousin, you would have the benefit of someone with a certain amount of expert knowledge while possibly easing yourself into a qualified counseling situation."

"Is that what you think I should do?"

"I prefer for you to see a professional counselor now. However, you should do what you are most comfortable with."

"Or the least uncomfortable with. I will never be comfortable, and I still say this is much ado about nothing."

"All we want you to do is try, Stacks. Shall we call it preventive medicine...to ease your sister's mind and mine?"

A sigh quivered off Siara's lips. "Very well. I will talk to the cousin...or try to..."

"I can be happy with that compromise, if not totally agreeable to it. You do realize that I am always available if you need me?"

"I know. Jyn and I are fortunate to have a friend and guardian like you."

Another twist of the knife in my heart, he thought, *and she doesn't even realize it...*

"I do feel a certain amount of responsibility for your welfare," he said. "Your parents were my best friends, and, of course, I have developed quite a...a fondness for you...and Jordyn, too...of course..."

"I guess that is why she came to you with all this. I don't always listen to her when she is telling me something for my own good. She hardly ever pushes for anything that is for HER own good if she thinks I would be hurt in the process. She was counting on my listening to you as I always listened to Daddy."

Ah, Stacks…you are bleeding my heart into a withered husk…

"That's what I am here for," he said with forced cheerfulness. "However, you will not be getting off so lightly, Stacks. I expect you to cook me supper tonight, and after Darica has gone upstairs to her Bible, you and Jordyn and I will sit down together and discuss the day's events. I am hoping your sister will have some good news about her conference with that lady banker in St. Louis."

"You're making that up, Jordyn. You have to be making that up." Siara passed a cup of hot coffee to Connor and sat beside him on the sofa. "Things like that don't happen in real life."

Stretching her legs out in front of her, Jordyn yawned and, through half-closed eyes, studied the couple across from her. Poor Connor. He might think he was concealing the pained longing in his puppy-brown eyes, but Jordyn wasn't fooled. As for her sister…well, sometimes Siara could be such a ninny about things that were so damn obvious. Jordyn hoped that some day Connor's patience would be rewarded. Now that he had convinced Siara to talk to Sandie Johnson, Baby Sister just might wake up and see Connor as a man rather than a clone of their father.

"There he was as big as life, Baby," Jordyn said, stifling another yawn, "and looking like a harbinger of death as soon as he recognized me."

"Whatever did you do?"

"I certainly didn't ask to see his surgery scars. I did what any brave and resourceful woman would've done under similar circumstances. I skedaddled…as quickly as my lovely legs would carry me."

Connor cleared his throat. "Shall I ask whether this particular bit of irony is in any way connected with the unfortunate…uh…prank perpetrated on Mr. Turner several years ago?"

"You don't want to know, Connor." Siara smiled into his eyes, but Jordyn was the one to notice the emotion that flickered there before he concentrated on the coffee steaming in his cup.

"What will you do now, Jyn?" he asked finally.

"Tomorrow I'm going to Applewood Community, and if they turn me down, I go to Blair."

"No, Jordyn…" Siara whispered in dismay.

Connor set his cup aside and leaned forward. "I don't want you going to your uncle for anything."

"I may have no other choice."

"There is one other way…maybe. Let me buy the studio."

"You?" the twins chorused.

"Perhaps obtaining the necessary loan will be easier for me...a man...an older man. I can purchase the business from Nanette, and you, Jordyn, can in turn buy it from me by making monthly payments large enough to cover my monthly responsibility to the bank."

Without even a moment's consideration, Jordyn shook her head. "I truly appreciate what you're wanting to do, but there's no way I'll let you go out on a limb like that. What if the studio loses money...or I run into unforeseen financial problems...something happens that I can't work...a student gets hurt and files a lawsuit...you could be either partially or totally stuck with a legal and financial mess."

"I trust you enough to take the chance, and I have a little money put away to cover any problems."

"And you wouldn't have to ask Uncle Blair for anything," Siara said, her face filled with the knowledge of what Jordyn would have to do to get that much money from their uncle.

"I can handle Blair. Hey, didn't you tell your fellow Mouse Sister you'd take her some warm milk about now?"

Siara glanced at her watch. "Yes, I did. Warm milk helps her sleep," she explained to Connor. "Sometimes she has these horrible nightmares. Perhaps SHE should have a conversation with Luke's cousin."

"Dari will barely talk to us, Baby."

"She's improving. She's just shy and timid. I can understand how she feels."

"That's why she stays so close to you whenever she's out of her room. You're birds of a feather...or mice of a feather. I think Jae and I scare her a little."

"She will be all right once she discovers that you have a marshmallow center."

"I do not have a marshmallow center, Siara Nealy, and don't you be telling anyone that I do."

"Not even Luke?"

"Especially not Luke."

"He probably knows it already anyway. You have surely seen a lot of him these last two weeks."

"That will end as soon as I bed him down once or twice...depending on how good he is. Right now he's merely a challenge."

"That was a very unladylike thing to say in Connor's presence."

"Connor has known about the facts of life for years now, Baby. Now go tend to the milk, will you? I'm tired and would rather not be awakened by one of poor Dari's whimpering fits tonight."

Siara withheld any further chastisement of her sister when she realized that nothing she could say would influence Jordyn toward verbal discretion to lessen

Connor's red-faced discomfiture. Shaking her head, she went to the kitchen while Connor finished his coffee and Jordyn yawned loudly and rubbed her eyes.

Connor was grateful for an opportunity to aim the conversation in another direction. "You've been losing sleep over this whole situation, haven't you?"

"Night times are my best times for uncluttered thinking these days. I am so busy at the studio during the day, and I've been out with Luke in the evenings a lot. Something's got to go…and that will be Luke as soon as he—"

"So," Connor interrupted quickly, "are all details arranged with his cousin?"

"She and Sari are meeting for coffee this weekend. We'll see how that goes before we make any long-range plans."

"Speaking of long-range plans, you should reconsider my business proposal. It's a reasonable and logical solution to your situation."

"I disagree. The offer came from your heart, not your head. Let me do it my way. If I fall flat on my face, at least it's my nose that's smashed, not yours."

"I don't want you to ask your uncle for any favors. From what I can deduce, he would…exact a very high rate of interest from you."

"I'll do what I have to do to land on my feet…even if that means lying on my back for a while."

When Connor's face flushed darkly, Jordyn grinned and winked at him. "You and my sister really make a great pair, you know. When are you going to do something about THAT?"

"I d-don't know what you are talking about."

"The hell you don't. Even Jae noticed it, and she was around you and Sari only a couple of times before she took off for sunny Florida with all those gorgeous baseball bods."

Connor leaned forward again, his eyes urgently serious. "I hope you haven't been teasing Siara with this? I will admit…to you…that I hold your sister in extremely high regard. However, she isn't ready to be receptive to that kind of relationship with a man. Perhaps someday when she is ready…well…I'll still be around here somewhere…"

Bewildered, Jordyn shook her head. "First Luke, and now you…perfect gentlemen to your last breaths. Don't men ever get divinely and uncontrollably horny anymore?"

* * *

Visibly amused by his niece's dilemma, Blair settled back in his chair and gazed at Jordyn over fingertips that he pressed together rhythmically throughout her presentation. She had come to him well prepared with facts, figures, projections, and proposals. No promises. Not of the sort he was waiting for anyway. He knew, however, that those promises would come later.

He had been anticipating this moment of triumph for several days because word of her attempts to secure financing from other sources had filtered to him. The young man who called him from Trust and Savings in St. Louis had not known that Blair Eldred was the uncle of Jordyn E. Nealy. Hudson Turner had said only that he was calling banks that the young lady might try to con into a loan. She was, Mr. Turner advised, highly unstable and irresponsible though she did possess certain persuasive talents that might disguise those unfavorable qualities. Professional courtesy from a fellow banker? Blair suspected that Mr. Turner had a personal reason for the professional blackballing.

Blair suddenly realized that Jordyn had stopped talking and was now watching him expectantly. He felt almost guilty about not paying attention to her presentation because she had obviously worked so hard on it.

In time she would have enough money to cover any loan she could acquire now. Contrary to what he had told the girls, Devon had provided well for his girls although Blair was doing little to expedite the realization of any benefits. Until the twins reached their twenty-fifth birthdays, he could do as he pleased. After that, they would be grateful to him for managing their finances so well. Jordyn would want to keep her beloved uncle happy. If all went according to plan, he might even ask her to reconsider his marriage proposal.

She would certainly be the prize jewel in his career and personal crowns.

"Well?" Jordyn asked, narrowing her eyes as he licked his lips.

"Time for the only collateral you have to offer me, don't you think?"

CHAPTER TWENTY

"I don't owe you any explanations, Farm Boy, so just leave me alone and go tend to your cow shit." Gripping the phone receiver tightly, Jordyn cursed her uncle and his demands on her time and energy.

"This is the third time in the last two weeks you have broken a date with me. You do owe me an explanation." Though Luke spoke softly, Jordyn could well visualize the anger snapping in his amber eyes.

"I'm flattered you're keeping score. We certainly haven't been doing anything else worth scoring."

"Is that what all this is about? You're mad because I won't sleep with you?"

"Now there's a typical egomaniac male assumption. For the record, SLEEPING with you has never been my intention. Maybe I just don't like you."

"I don't believe that."

"You wouldn't, of course."

"If that were the reason, you would have told me by now. Girls don't continue going out with guys they don't like."

"So now I am discontinuing going out with you."

"Just for tonight…or forever?"

"Forever would be the best thing for you."

"I can't agree with that."

"Look…you need to find yourself someone to slop your chickens and can your soybeans…some sweet, young thing who'd be happy down on the farm."

"I don't want a sweet, young thing. I want you."

"You really know how to charm a girl."

"What do you expect from a mere farm boy?"

"Right now I don't have time for any involvement."

"Sex isn't an involvement?"

"Not to me. But you seem to think it goes hand in hand with all kinds of stifling commitments. Some people play tennis or collect stamps. I fuck. If I can't get it from you, I'll get it from someone else."

"So that IS what's at the bottom of all these cancellations."

"Actually no. I was sidetracked."

"Then what is?"

"I'm working my ass off at the studio, and there are certain…family responsibilities I have to take care of."

"I thought Sandie was making some progress with Siara?"

"Yes, she is, but it's not just that. I'm getting pressure from several different sources right now. I can't handle the additional pressure of a…a relationship."

"I wasn't aware that I was pressuring you. I don't want to add to your problems, but I don't want you to cut me out of the herd either."

"So long as you realize that you are part of a herd. Tying myself down with only one guy is not my style."

"Would you change your mind if I changed mine…about us…bedding down together?"

"You are such a prude. If you fucked me, I would not change my mind…though it would be a time-saver, now that I think about it. I wouldn't have to waste valuable time looking for a date who isn't quite so noble."

"You really have a way of dumping romance right into the gutter."

"Romance is for people who have time to waste. I don't have that luxury right now."

"Okay, you win. I'll pick you up in an hour, and we'll go right to a motel."

"Pay attention, Farm Boy. I told you I can't see you tonight."

"When can you fit me in?"

Jordyn did not miss the impatient sarcasm in his voice.

"Are you free tomorrow night?" she asked, stroking his ego with a sweet murmur.

"Yeah, I can get free. May I take you to dinner first, or do you want to…to couple as soon as I get you into the truck?"

"Depends on what I am most hungry for then. I'll have to let you know…"

* * *

Siara fanned the photocopies out on the bed in front of her. In the dim glow of her bedside lamp, the white paper blended with her snowy sheets so that the black typed characters on the pages appeared like lines of tiny troops assembled and ready to march relentlessly into her mind. Invaders? Or liberators of the embryo of anxiety that had taken seed on a long-ago winter day?

If even Jordyn and Connor thought she hovered on the brink of an emotional abyss, then there must be a problem. Siara had to admit that sometimes her lack of normalcy bothered her. She did not date as other girls her age did, nor did she even want to. Once she had considered that she had lesbian tendencies lying dormant within her, but after careful deliberation, she had dismissed that thought as even more ridiculous than her wish to lead a celibate life.

Siara lay back against the pillows. What was it like to feel consuming passion of the kind that provided so much fuel for books, plays, and poetry? Surely she was missing out on something special since everyone seemed so preoccupied with it. Had the experience with her uncle really imprisoned her sexual instinct, a possibility Sandie had suggested? Had this same incident burdened her with shame…unreasonable though it was…shame that had transformed her soul into a guilt-sopping sponge…Sandie's speculative metaphor?

Not that Siara had provided Sandie with any actual details. Goodness no. Sandie, however, seemed to understand anyway…to understand and expect Siara to be shy and hesitant with a stranger. Siara, in turn, was grateful enough to try her best to be cooperative and had eagerly accepted the suggestion to read various case studies concerning other incidents of child molestation. Then

Sandie and Siara could discuss the relevant case studies with the same informed objectivity as Siara used in debating literary points with Connor.

Both Jordyn and Connor applauded the idea simply because it was so well suited to Siara, who had to agree that talking about someone else's childhood trauma was easier than talking about her own, whatever similarities happened to exist.

The trick now was to make herself read the case studies. Like taking a foul-tasting medicine with no spoonful of sugar to make it go down.

Grabbing a pillow and hugging it tightly, Siara closed her eyes and reached for one of the case studies.

"Let's get this over with, Blair," Jordyn said, loosening the scarf around her neck. "I'm tired, and I want to go to bed."

Blair settled in his leather chair and pressed his fingertips together. His self-satisfied smirk made Jordyn uneasy.

"You'll be in bed soon enough…though don't count on much rest."

"What do you mean 'in bed'? What's wrong with here in your office like we usually do?"

"I'm only thinking of you. Don't you find it rather degrading and uncomfortable here?"

"An office is the place for business transactions, and any fucking done by you and me is just that…a business transaction. Don't be fooling yourself into thinking it means anything more to me."

"Contrary to what you may think, I'm actually glad you feel that way. Since this is a business arrangement and since you're the one who owes me, I have a certain amount of latitude in deciding just how you'll pay off certain conditions of your debt."

Jordyn stared at her uncle suspiciously. "I'm not doing anything weird with or for you."

"I doubt that you'll be asked for anything weird. Just the usual application of your various talents will suffice."

"I don't have time for bullshit. Just tell me what the hell it is you think I'm going to do for you tonight."

"Very well." Blair lit one of his huge, black cigars. "Tonight I am subletting you, so to speak. I want you to entertain an out-of-town colleague of mine. And when I say entertain, I mean you're to make him as happy as he wants to be made."

"You and your out-of-town colleague can go to hell for entertainment. I won't provide his fun."

"Do I need to remind you that you are heavily indebted to me…and that I can make things very difficult for you…and for Siara?"

"So you've stooped to pimping now?"

"And guess what that makes you, darling Jyn."

His lips curled complacently in response to her glare. Mentioning her sister had secured her cooperation, unwilling though it was. Siara was definitely Jordyn's area of vulnerability, and Blair would not hesitate to aim his attacks in that direction to insure Jordyn's obedience. Though he didn't actually relish the idea of turning Jordyn over to that Turner fellow for the evening, he was curious to determine the limits of his control. Now he knew: there were no limits.

"Someday, Blair," Jordyn was saying, "when you're a sick, old man, I'll ask Aunt Bonnie if I can take care of you."

"Do I dare to hope that you'll do so out of the love and devotion bestowed by a grateful niece?"

"Not even close. My reason is simple: I want the pleasure of watching you die, and I'll make your passing as hard as I can."

"I'm already hard. So you can take care of me before your date with Turner."

Jordyn's scowl dissolved into wide-mouthed astonishment...tinged with just a bit of apprehension. Blair's eyes narrowed slyly.

"Wh-Who did you say I am to meet?" She tried to mask her uneasiness by casually sliding off her shoes and pantyhose.

"Turner. Hudson Turner," Blair replied. "Don't bother with your dress. There's no time. Just take your panties off. Turner's from a St. Louis bank that's looking into some investment property around here for a client of theirs...foreclosure property we've been trying to unload for months. So you can see why I'm anxious to keep him in an agreeable state of mind. Now if you will just sit here on my desk, you can make me agreeable, too..."

The names and recorded experiences were snarled within Siara's mind...an untidy bundle bound with a tragic cord of childhood trauma:

Two-year-old Cynthie, who had been raped by her male babysitter so violently that ten years later she was still undergoing corrective surgery...

Tanita, whose rape at sixteen by an older brother and his friend eventually necessitated her prolonged stay at a mental facility...

Zandra, whose parents had introduced her to the techniques of sex when she was five so that she could perform with other adults in front of movie cameras...

Phaedra, who beginning on her thirteenth birthday, had been forced to participate in the bestial and orgiastic rites of the religious cult ruled by her father...

Et cetera, ad infinitum...

Siara's mind embraced these innocent children who had suffered so unfairly. She willed each of them a happy ending though the case studies reported none. All Siara knew was that these girls had received or were now receiving professional help as they endured the painful process of exorcising their psychological demons. Specific details of their progress were not included in

Siara's photocopies. The stories themselves were enough to place her on the threshold of understanding.

She was ashamed for having felt...well, so ashamed. Now there was a curiosity Sandie would love to cope with. Siara's experience was certainly not so severe as the indignities inflicted upon the poor girls in the case studies. Yet her own situation had certainly affected her in some way, the seriousness of which was yet to be determined.

Stacking the photocopies into a neat pile, she lay back on her bed and created the happy endings she wanted each of the girls to have. She must give them happy endings or she would never get to sleep, and she had promised to attend early mass with Darica the next morning.

Her mission of imagination was quickly accomplished, for happy endings were easy to create...and rather stereotypical with all girls eventually finding peace and contentment with gentle, loving husbands and gentle, loving children.

Not unlike the happy ending Siara envisioned for herself.

Except for the addendum that placed Blair somewhere on a distant tropical island inhabited by cannibals.

Actually, Siara admitted, she wasn't so unhappy now. She just did not feel like a normal, complete person, and she could not determine why. Maybe Sandie could help her sort through the dilemma.

Or Jordyn. Siara could talk to Jordyn now. Siara had heard her sister coming upstairs a few minutes before. Funny. Jordyn had not peeked in as she normally did when she returned from a date.

Twinstinct told Siara that something was wrong.

Worried, she jumped up and hurried into the bathroom that connected the twins' rooms. Jordyn's door was closed, but for once Siara did not bother with social amenities as she threw the door open.

Jordyn was lying on her bed in the dark.

"Go back to bed, Baby," she said.

Alarmed because Jordyn's words were muffled and indistinct, Siara flicked on the overhead light. Jordyn covered her face, but not before Siara saw her sister's bruised lips and blackened eye.

CHAPTER TWENTY-ONE

Jordyn winced as Siara pressed the ice bag gently against her eye.

"This is my own fault," Jordyn said. "I should have been more careful, especially when he wanted to tie my hands to the bed frame…"

"I don't need details," Siara said, but then she quickly added, "unless you NEED to share them."

Apparently Jordyn needed to share them.

"What the hell, I thought, so he's a little kinky. Maybe I'll go along and show him that I really meant the little speech I laid on him earlier in the evening about letting bygones be bygones and all…chalk my previous antics up to an immature high school mentality, y'know. Then maybe he would be more agreeable to Blair, too.

"But then he started hitting on my face, and there was nothing I could do but lie there and take it. I wasn't going to give him the satisfaction of seeing me scream or, God forbid, cry. Then I guess he wanted to prove to me that he could still perform like a man in spite of the surgery to his dingus. He was none too gentle about it either. If a man can make MY twat hurt, you know he's ramming it home pretty damn hard…"

"Ssssshhhh, Jyn, please, no more details." Siara touched her fingers to Jordyn's bruised lips. "You should rest."

"Okay, Baby, no more details. Just get me some aspirin…a dozen or so should help…"

"Do we need to call the police?"

"Absolutely not. Think of the hassles that would create, not to mention the negative publicity for the studio. Besides, a lot of people in this town would think I got what I deserved."

"Don't talk like that."

"My reputation doesn't exactly qualify me for the nunnery, y'know. If I weren't such a damn good instructor…and Devon and Amelie's daughter…I'd have been branded with an *H* for *whore* and run out of town."

"That's not true. You just get some strange pleasure from thinking that way. And *whore* begins with a *W*."

"Then *harlot* should begin with a *W*, too. Damn, a girl can't trust anything to be consistent in this world…"

As Siara pressed her uncle's telephone number, she maintained her tenuous control only by conjuring the image of her sister's battered face. The spasmodic trembling within her was difficult to ignore, but she braced herself for the moment that Blair answered the phone.

"Hello?"

"Uncle B-Bl-Blair," she said in a small, frightened voice, her mouth and throat suddenly dry. "This is Siara."

"Siara?" He was as astonished as she was anxious. Siara had never called him for anything before.

"I am c-calling about J-Jordyn. That man beat her up, Uncle B-Blair."

"Someone beat up Jordyn? Who? Is she all right?" Blair's hand began to tremble.

"She'll be all right, though b-bruised and sore for a while. It was that man you made her go out with…Hudson Turner. He beat her up, and you should do something about it."

"Does she want to press charges?" Momentarily forgetting his niece's physical condition, Blair frowned at the possibility of an unexpected obstacle to his deal with Trust.

"She says no police."

He exhaled loudly in relief. "Thank God for that."

Siara chewed her lip and squeezed the receiver. "You are the reason why she was with that man. You should assume some responsibility for what happened."

"How was I to know this would happen?"

"You know now, and you should do something."

"What do you want me to do, Siara…beat the guy up?"

"It seems a reasonable way to start."

His eyebrows shot up in surprise. Was this really his meek, scared-of-her-own-shadow niece?

"That man is twenty years younger than I am, Siara."

"Age differences were never much of a concern to you before."

Her audacity startled even her. Blair was stunned to silence. Seconds passed awkwardly before he could muster any words.

"All I can do is make things a little difficult for him at his bank."

Her sudden rush of courage dissipated, and she was unsure of how to end the conversation.

"Thank you," she said faintly.

Panic-stricken at what she had done and confused about what to do next, she slammed down the receiver and ran upstairs to her room.

* * *

As he watched Hudson Turner sign a stack of papers, Blair unconsciously assumed his favorite position of power and observation. Zeus on Mt. Olympus…comfortably settled on a leather throne…fingertips pressed together.

Actually the Turner boy wasn't so unlike Blair at that age. Ruggedly handsome. The muscular stockiness of a football player. Average intelligence. Not brilliant, but unscrupulous enough in a socially acceptable way to be successful. Blair could almost admire the kid.

Except for this thing with Jordyn. Blair would let her know that he planned surreptitious retaliation in her behalf. Someday the girls would appreciate their uncle. Someday Jordyn would appreciate him as a man rather than an uncle...

Hudson Turner finished his signing with a flourish and pushed the papers toward Blair.

"That should take care of everything, Mr. Eldred," he said with a businesslike smile.

Blair examined the papers carefully. "Quite right, Mr. Turner. It has been an honor to deal with Trust and Savings."

"Thank you for your hospitality."

"I hope the company I provided for you last night was satisfactory."

A flash of anxiety in Turner's eyes was instantly concealed as he busied himself with loading his briefcase.

"Quite satisfactory. Did you happen to ...uh...speak with her today?"

"No." Blair lit his cigar with slow, languid motions. "I haven't seen or spoken with the girl since yesterday afternoon. Why do you ask?"

Turner could not camouflage his relief. "No special reason. I thought I might have the pleasure of running into her here. I thought she worked for you."

"She doesn't work here. She was returning a favor."

Turner was even more relieved. "She's a very beautiful woman," he said generously, his confidence restored. "Thank you for providing me with her...um...company."

"Actually she's always been a beautiful girl. I've known her since she was in diapers." Blair eyed Turner through a veil of cigar smoke. "She's my niece."

Turner's briefcase dropped open, and papers spilled onto the carpet. Hastily he crammed them back inside.

"I'll be on my way now, Mr. Eldred," he said, backing toward the door. Papers peeked out of the closed briefcase at odd angles.

"Have a safe trip," Blair called. The door slammed behind a retreating Hudson Turner.

Blair waited until he was finished with his cigar before he instructed his secretary to get Ms. Konstance Fletcher at Trust and Savings in St. Louis on the phone for him.

As he waited, he leaned back and pressed his fingertips together. In truth, he didn't much like women bankers. They all were overly defensive because they felt that they had something to prove. A man couldn't even smile at one of them without being accused of something sneaky and underhanded. However, a woman would be more inclined to sympathize with his story about his poor, recently orphaned niece being brutalized by Ms. Fletcher's representative. Such unforgivable conduct from one of their colleagues. And Blair's niece was a fledgling businesswoman, too, who deserved greater respect from a man. Blair was certainly disappointed with banking's new crop of executive material. Wasn't there something Ms. Fletcher could do to take care of the problem since St.

Louis was her turf? He had done all he could by persuading his niece not to press charges...not for the sake of the boy, but in order to preserve the good name of banking, Trust and Savings in particular...

Turner would be virtually defenseless with Ms. Fletcher. What could he say to defend his behavior to another woman?

Now, could Blair feed all this bullshit to Ms. Konstance Fletcher without laughing in her pretty, liberated ear?

Jerking open the door to Luke's truck, Jordyn jumped inside and slammed the door quickly behind her.

"I was coming to your front door to get you," Luke told her.

"Totally unnecessary. I've lived here all my life and can find my way to the driveway unassisted."

"So it's going to be one of those nights." He started the truck. "Do you often wear sunglasses after dark?"

"It's my new image. Don't you think I look delightfully mysterious?"

"Who can tell? You're too far away. I thought we were up to the part where you sit over here by me."

"This is part of my new image, too."

"I liked your old image better. Where do you want to go to dinner?"

"I'm not hungry."

"Oh, for Chrissake..." He turned off the truck. "What's the problem now, Jordyn?"

"What makes you think there's a problem?"

"You're acting strange, even for you. Are you nervous...about tonight?"

"Don't be ridiculous. I'm hardly a jittery rookie." She did not see his wince.

"So what is the problem?" he asked.

"No problem. Now get this pile of junk started, and let's go somewhere to fuck."

He winced again. "Could you please use a more polite word?"

"Is there one?"

"*Making love* seems civilized enough."

"We're not in love."

"There is always the remote possibility that someday we could be."

"Not in this lifetime, Farm Boy, so don't be getting any stupid ideas. I don't need that kind of hassle. If you want to fuck me, crank this heap up and get going. If you want to fall in love, let me out now and go find yourself a little homespun farm girl."

"Damn you, Jordyn," he said.

But he started the truck.

Jordyn grabbed Luke's hand before he could turn on the motel room light.

"No lights," she said quickly. Then, realizing he would expect some explanation, she added, "We'll have more fun finding everything without them."

"That's the last straw." He led her to the bed and set her down. "I may not be the smartest man in the world, but I know when someone is trying to hide something from me. You haven't looked me square in the face since I picked you up, and I want to know why."

As he switched on the bedside lamp, Jordyn flinched from him, but not before he had seen her.

"Did that guy you met at Burkey's last night do this to you?" His mouth was a grim line as he pulled the sunglasses away from her face and stroked her still-swollen lips with hands that were surprisingly tender considering their size and strength.

"How did you find out?" she asked, annoyed with herself for feeling guilty about his finding out.

"My cousin works there, remember? Maybe you wanted me to find out about him?"

"I thought Sandie was off last night. She and Siara had dinner earlier."

"Merle called her in to cover for someone. I don't much appreciate being stood up for another guy, Jordyn."

"I thought we got this straight yesterday. I don't owe you any explanations or any faithfulness."

"I'm not talking explanations or faithfulness. I'm talking about courtesy and treating people right. You broke a date with me to go out with some creep."

"I have better taste than that, Farm Boy. Hudson Turner hardly qualifies as competition even for you. He's one of my uncle's slimy business associates, and Blair asked me to…keep him company while he was in town. That's the first, last, and only explanation you'll ever get from me. So take your clothes off and fuck me."

"Damn you, Jordyn," he said.

But he took off his clothes. And hers.

The size of him did not disappoint her. His patient tenderness, however, exasperated her. She needed immediate relief.

Grunting with frustration, she grasped him and guided him into her. When his immensity and the residual effects of her encounter with Hudson Turner made entry momentarily uncomfortable, she winced and shifted beneath him.

He stopped instantly, poised above her, panting as he struggled to hold his own desire in check.

"I'm sorry, Jordyn. I was trying to go slow so I wouldn't hurt you. I guess I'm…I'm…"

"Built like King Kong," she murmured in appreciation. "Don't apologize for it, and for Chrissake don't stop now…"

CHAPTER TWENTY-TWO

Hearing a car stop in the driveway, Luke peered out his living room window. His pulse quickened when he saw the long, light blond hair brushed gently by a summer breeze. Just as quickly, however, he realized his mistake, and disappointment squeezed his heart. Siara, not Jordyn. Of course, not Jordyn. She would never demean herself by setting her dainty foot on a farm.

Luke starred out across the neatly trimmed lawn toward the barns and outbuildings and the acres of pasture and crop land. Jordyn had it in her head that the Johnsons lived like sharecroppers. Because Luke wasn't a bragging man, he hadn't told her anything different; because he was proud of their spread, he wanted her to see it for herself.

In a time when farmers were losing acreage through foreclosures, he and his father were showing a profit through careful management, a little luck, and a lot of hard work and adaptability. Nothing that would make them millionaires, but enough to keep them all comfortably and to provide for Lissa's future. Enough for Luke to provide for a wife.

Jordyn.

He lost track of the times he had asked her to marry him. However, he knew the number equaled the times she had refused him. Actually *rejected* was a better word, for Jordyn's refusals were neither gentle nor tactful. Repeatedly she told him that the only reason why she continued to see him was that he was great in bed.

He tried not to think of all the other men who shared a bed with her.

Why he continued to see her brought him no contentment either: he loved her.

Luke opened the front door just as Siara raised her hand to knock.

She smiled uncertainly. "You are very prompt."

"I saw you in the driveway." He grinned with genuine affection for Jordyn's little sister. "I guess you're here to see Sandie. She's upstairs packing. Come on in."

"I brought her a going-away present. I know she's excited about living in New York, but I'm truly going to miss her."

"We all will, but this is what she has been working for. She'll be staying with a friend of Mom's for a while, so we're resting a little easier about her being away from home and in the big city."

"I would never have that much courage…to leave my hometown and go to a new city alone."

"Some people are lucky enough to realize that grass isn't always greener in other fields." Luke's mouth tightened as he again thought of Jordyn.

"That's your Jordyn frown, Luke. I've seen it too often not to recognize it."

"Usually when you're trying to explain to me why your sister has broken another date with me."

"Please be patient with her. She truly cares about you."

"She has a damn strange way of showing it."

"You're the only man she has dated so often and so long."

"She also continues to date every other man who gets within flirting distance."

"Her philosophy is safety in numbers. I can give you a whole list of reasons why she feels she can't settle down with one man right now. Chief among them is her obsession with the studio. Now that we have the insurance settlement from the hotel fire, she has all kinds of grand plans. Of course, her vision is commendable, but it's also a bit of self-delusive rationalization."

"You're talking over this farm boy's head."

"Jyn has this tough-gal image that she perpetuates, but in actuality, she is like…like…well, like her brownies…rock hard on the outside, but soft and mushy on the inside."

Luke tried his best to appear casual. "Supposing a guy wanted to get through to the soft part? How would he go about it?"

"By osmosis."

"I'm sure that make sense to someone with an advanced degree, but you're talking to a simple man with a simple degree in ag."

"When does Jyn give you the most grief…like standing you up and breaking dates and talking about other men?"

"Usually right after I've asked her to marry me or told her that I love her…you know, the usual stuff that makes a girl act like a b…witch."

"Now, Luke," Siara chided softly, "sarcasm about my sister will not endear you to me at all. Don't you see that all that love and marriage talk is a dent in her brownie?"

"Have you been spiking your cherry Kool-Aid?"

Siara smiled shyly at this teasing. "What I am trying to tell you is to be patient. Forgo the love and marriage talk for a while. Let her think she's getting her way. Then little by little, you will be absorbed right through her protective shell and into her soft heart. She won't even realize what is happening if you don't draw her attention to it. What you've been doing wrong is drawing her attention to the fact that she is letting a man get too close to her. Then she tries to drive you out, and you have slowed the osmotic process. Understand?"

"Yes, I do…which may not speak well for my sanity."

"Talk to Sandie. She is the expert."

"You seem pretty knowledgeable yourself."

"I read a lot, and with Jyn I have a special advantage our daddy called twinstinct. Trust me…someday Jyn will realize that you've become such an important part of her life that she'll be willing to change her mind about a few things."

"Thanks for the advice. I sure hope you're right."

"Of course I'm right. We blondes aren't dumb anymore, not since the ERA."

Laughing, Luke motioned her toward the stairs. "Go on up, Einsteinem. Cuz is in her room somewhere. Finding her with all the boxes, trunks, and suitcases in there is the tricky part."

"You are coming to our birthday party, aren't you?" Siara asked as she started up the stairs. "Sandie is taking a later flight so that she can be there."

"It's hard enough for me to hear about Jordyn's other men. If I had to watch her with one…"

"I'll tell you a secret. There are not so many other men anymore. She just wants you to think there are."

"Why?"

"She's protecting that brownie. Please come. This is an important birthday for us…our twenty-fifth. After midnight tomorrow…well…I'll just say that Jyn is making the final payment on a debt that has been burdening us…Jyn in particular…since our parents died."

"If it's that important to you, I'll be there."

"Good! And one more bit of advice…if Jyn offers you any brownies, decline…unless you have good dental insurance."

Blair had installed a couch in his office two years before when he realized that Jordyn would never submit to the comforts of a motel room with him. Although he gloried in his power over her, he hesitated to become too demanding, especially since that fiasco with the Turner kid.

Much to Blair's irritation, Hudson Turner had somehow retained employment at Trust and Savings though his position had been precarious for a time. Blair guessed that Ms. Konstance Fletcher lacked the authority to discipline the boy adequately. After all, she was only a woman shielded by a fancy title, a figurehead selected to placate the equality zealots.

That his circle of influence might not extend to a St. Louis bank never occurred to him. He felt invincible after resuming his regular visits with Jordyn. So invincible that he easily overlooked Jordyn's total lack of desire for him.

However, lately her visits had become less frequent. By the end of the day, Blair was simply too tired to perform. To Jordyn's credit, she did not ridicule him as he had feared. Nor did she mention his age or his graying, thinning hair despite the fact that she was not the most tactful person in the world.

Her apparent patience and understanding refueled Blair's hopes that maybe Jordyn had fallen in love with him in spite of herself. After all, she had agreed to be with him tonight, the very night before the birthday when she would gain control of her own finances.

Blair stretched out on the couch. While the champagne chilled, he would take a nap so that he would be well rested when his future bride arrived. He didn't want to disappoint her tonight when he asked her, again, to marry him.

"You shouldn't have been so extravagant, Sari!" Sandie said, winding the key on the music box. She smiled at the tune: "You've Got a Friend."

"I want you to have something to remember me by when you go to New York." Siara wedged herself carefully between two piles of clothes on the bed.

"I will never forget you, and I will definitely miss you. Whenever I get homesick, and I'm sure I will more often than I care to admit, I'll play this music box to cheer me up. Thank you."

"I'm the one to be thanking you. I'll never be the aggressive, vivacious femme fatale that you and Jyn were hoping for, but I am more confident about…well, just being me. So you can count me as your first successful patient."

"You aren't a patient. You're a friend. Besides, you were never in any real emotional or psychological danger. You merely needed an objective ear to talk into…so that you could work through some concerns on your own…the same thing Jordyn and Connor had been trying to help you do. Only from them it sounded like nagging…nagging from the heart, but still nagging. You accepted it from me. That's the way it is with family situations, fortunately for psychologists. Otherwise we'd never get any business."

"You underestimate your ability. You made me comfortable about talking to you, which was no easy task. I feel…friendlier with people now, people besides Jordyn and Connor and Jae and Darica. I think I may even have helped Dari overcome some of her shyness. She was the first person I had ever met who was shier than I. So you helped not just me, you see."

"I would really feel like I'd accomplished something professionally if I could get you to—"

"Date?" Siara shook her head. "Why are you and Jyn so concerned about my dating? Don't measure your success by the number of boyfriends I accumulate. For one thing, I'm not interested, and for another, they aren't interested. The phone doesn't ring all day with offers for me. All of them are for Jordyn."

"There's interest out there. You just choose to ignore it," Sandie said, thinking of Connor. "One of these days, you'll open your eyes to it, and when you do, I want you to promise me you'll do something about it."

"To make you happy, I'll promise. However, don't be expecting any wedding invitations within the next couple of weeks."

"There is one other loose end we haven't taken care of…your uncle. I know he's a pile of poop, but until you make your peace with him, you'll never be at peace with yourself."

"You'll come closer to getting that wedding invitation from me, Sandie. I won't feel peaceful about him until one of us is dead…"

While Blair pumped away over her, Jordyn lay still and silent as she pondered how she wanted her studio enlarged with her share of the insurance money. She could add a few classrooms, maybe even a small auditorium so that she wouldn't have to rent the high school's every time she planned a recital.

And advertising.

Students had crossed the river from Missouri for years to study under Nanette Bakerman…and then Jordyn, who had lost none of the clientele in the transition of ownership. In fact, she gained a few students.

Some well-planned newspaper and radio advertising…maybe even something on the cable stations…featuring her own students, of course. She could even begin some kind of placement service for her students to set them up with modeling gigs and commercials. Nanette might even agree to handle it. Retirement was not agreeing with her, and she spent most of her time hanging around the studio anyway. Although an arthritic leg restricted her mobility as an instructor, she would be perfect as an agent. She had the contacts…she knew the girls' talents…she was anxious for anything that would keep her busy…

Jordyn suddenly realized that Blair was slobbering all over her neck. Frowning impatiently, she closed her eyes so that she wouldn't have to look at him.

Would he never be finished? He was working so hard now his face was florid and grotesque. If she hadn't felt a strange need to make this final payment on her debt, she wouldn't even be here tonight. Tonight was a kind of thank-you for the huge hotel settlement he had negotiated for the twins. And he was being a good sport about turning over control of their money though, as Jordyn had suspected, she and Siara had never been in such dire financial straits.

So one more time for old time's sake and that was it. If she never saw him again, there would be no void in her life.

At midnight tomorrow, both she and Siara would be free of their uncle's yoke.

'Gad, Blair was really huffing and puffing tonight. Maybe she should have been more helpful. He was practically gulping air.

When he collapsed onto her, she thought, *Good…he's done.*

But he continued to gasp.

And then he clenched his chest…

And the wetness that was spreading between her legs was not…

Frantically she pushed him away from her. His eyes rolled back into his head and he sagged against her. Dead.

CHAPTER TWENTY-THREE

"Is Siara back, Dari?" Jordyn whispered into the phone.

"She's in the shower."

"What about Jae? Is she home from the game yet?"

"She got home about an hour ago. Do you want to talk to her?"

"I want to talk to you all," Jordyn said. "Put Jae on the phone downstairs. Then drag my sister out of the shower and share the upstairs phone with her."

"What's wrong, Jordyn?"

"Don't ask questions now. Just do what I said and hurry!"

The urgency in Jordyn's voice sent Darica sprinting up the stairs after Siara as Jayme fielded the telephone receiver that was hurled in her direction.

"Jyn? Is this you?" Jayme asked, bewildered.

"Yeah, it's me."

"What in the world did you say to Dari?"

"I'll give you the details when I get you all on the line, but I could be in trouble. Big trouble."

"For Pete's sake, Jyn, what have you done now?"

"I think I killed Blair."

"Omigod…"

Siara picked up the phone then. "Jordyn, what is going on? Darica's running around up here like Chicken Little."

"I've killed Blair, Baby." She permitted Siara and Darica one chorused gasp before she rushed on with her story. "Now don't ask any dumb questions, and don't be giving me any lectures…any of you. There's no time. The thing is I was giving Blair his good-bye fuck, and the bastard had a heart attack on me, and I mean right on me. He's lying on the couch now, deader than a witch's toenail. What the hell am I going to do?"

"Are you sure he is dead?" Siara asked hoarsely.

"Positive. No pulse. No heartbeat. No breath. What am I going to do? I've got to do something!"

"What do you want to do?" Jayme asked calmly.

"What kind of dumb-ass question is that? Obviously I can't be caught here like this!"

"It would enhance your uncle's reputation, maybe even begin a legend."

"Dammit, Jae, we're talking about a real live dead man here!"

Siara broke in quietly, "That real live dead man finally got what he deserved. We owe him no courtesies, do we?"

"Of course not. But what about ME? Think about what this mess could do to the studio. It won't do Aunt Bonnie a whole helluva lot of good either."

"Then get out of there as quickly and as quietly as you can," Siara told her. "You and Blair are…were alone there, right?"

"Yes, but I can't just leave him like this. There will be questions...an autopsy...evidence that will eventually point to me. I don't want any cop running ballistics on my—"

"We get the picture," Jayme interrupted. "What we've got to do is get you out of there and think of some reason for him to be there...like he is. Did he fool around with anyone else?"

"I doubt it. No other girl would touch him. I wouldn't have myself except for certain circumstances beyond my control. God, why didn't I just tell him to go fuck himself today and be done with it?"

Thoughtfully, Jayme twisted an auburn curl around her finger. "You might be on to something there, Jyn. Make him look like he was...pleasuring himself when the heart attack got him."

"You mean fix him so he looks like he was jacking off?"

"Exactly."

"Isn't that tampering with evidence?"

"For Pete's sake, YOU didn't kill the man. He died of natural causes, and by doing so, he managed to drag you right back into a mess right when you were about to rid yourself of him. We're not covering up any crime."

"Do it, Jordyn," Siara urged. "And then get out of there. The cleaning people come in at ten. Aunt Bonnie took them hot cider and cookies last Christmas, and I helped her carry everything."

"But what do I do? I've never seen a man jack off. My proximity makes such a thing unnecessary."

"What's to know?" Jayme asked. "Wrap his fingers around his whackydoodle, and then vacate the premises."

"If you want it to be convincing, you must do more than that."

"Who said that?" Jayme and Jordyn asked together.

"Darica did," Siara said, totally incredulous.

Darica closed her eyes and swallowed. "Y-You should put some of his clothes back on him, Jordyn...b-but keep his trousers pulled down around his ankles...and a towel or bunch of Kleenex to make it look like he was going to clean himself up afterward...and...and...if you can m-manage it, a dirty p-picture or something for him to be looking at..."

"Blair keeps his monthly supply of smut magazines in his desk," Jordyn began. "My God, Dari, how do you know all that?"

"I...I had a b-brother once," she mumbled, her face darkly red. "Please... none of you ever mention this again. Ever..."

"Well..." Jayme cleared her throat to bridge an awkward silence. "Jyn...uh...be sure to...to clean up everything that is obviously from you...like blond hairs and such. You'll have to work fast. There's something about the way the blood settles after an hour or so that could arouse suspicion if we're not careful. Hopefully the heart attack will be so obvious the coroner won't be too curious. And the cops will laughing themselves silly over the way the old boy apparently checked out."

"Do you really think we should do this to Blair?"

Siara's voice was stern. "It's his reputation or yours, Jordyn. He owes us."

"You're right, Baby."

"Can you do this alone?" Jayme asked. "Should I drive in to help you?"

"I can manage. Too much coming and going would attract attention. Geez…coming and going got me into this mess tonight…"

Only Jayme seemed to understand what she meant. "You've always said that men are dying to have their way with you."

As Siara and Darica were pondering this new turn in the conversation, Jordyn said, "You guys stay there, and if anyone asks, I have been there all evening, okay?"

"You got it," Jayme said without hesitation, and Siara and Darica nodded their agreement.

Jordyn hung up the phone and got to work.

Jordyn's hand shook slightly as she set down her empty glass. Her roommates had met her at the door just over an hour after she talked to them. Though curiosity filled their eyes, they asked no questions as each offered some token of support and sympathy. Jayme thrust a tumbler full of Coke-and-whiskey into Jordyn's hands; Darica brought her a plate of cookies and a pillow to cushion her feet on the coffee table; Siara clutched her sister's hand, squeezing it periodically as Jordyn told them what the cleaning people would be discovering within the next few minutes.

"I even used a magnifying glass from his desk to check for blond hairs," she said rolling her head against the back of the sofa. "Do you know what it's like looking at a man's dingus and maracas through a magnifying glass?"

As Siara studied the ceiling and Darica the carpet, Jayme swirled her amusement around in her mouth. "I think I can safely say that none of us has experienced anything even remotely similar."

"I cleaned him up just enough to keep me in the clear. I didn't want to be too picky. Some of his mess had to be there to set the stage for whoever finds him. Thank God I wasn't wearing perfume. The scent would have been impossible for me to get rid of in such a short time."

"We were beginning to worry," Jayme told her, "but we didn't dare call. We couldn't be sure what was going on there."

"I had trouble getting the fucker into his shirts. He just had to be wearing a tee shirt, of course. And he was a heavy son of a bitch. I propped him up with some sofa pillows, and that was no easy job either.

"The rest of it was a breeze though. I put his socks on him and bunched his shorts and trousers around his ankles. Then I scattered a few of his smut rags on the floor after laying a real juicy one across his legs. I placed his hand just close enough to his dingus to be convincing, and I wadded up some toilet paper on the couch beside him. I must admit I did a damn fine job.

"Then I hightailed it out of there. Thank God Blair gave me the key to the alley door a long time ago. I was able to lock the outer door behind me…and Blair's office door has a button lock, so I could lock that behind me, too, and make it look like he had locked himself in his office for his little interlude with Miss Slut-of-the-Month."

"Are you sure no one saw you?" Jayme asked.

"Positive. I was very careful. But we might have a problem if anyone saw my car parked at the studio. I usually leave it there and walk the few blocks to the bank, which could work for me or against me. I can say I wasn't at the bank, but I can't claim that I was home with you girls."

"You may not have been here with us," Jayme said, "but who's to say we weren't at the studio with you? With the party tomorrow night, you needed us to help you with some paperwork and cleaning so that you can take tomorrow afternoon off, right?"

"Jae, you are a delightfully devious young lady."

"In a man's world, we have to be. And sometimes even that isn't much of an advantage."

Jordyn recognized the flash of heartache in Jayme's wry smile. "That's because some men are too dumb to realize the obvious. Want me to mention any names?"

"The list is too long, but I'm sure Harlan's name is at the top of it. For such an talented athlete, he specializes in setting records of dubious worth."

"Is four wives in eight years a record?"

"It is in Applewood."

"Applewood will have something else to talk about as soon as the news about Blair hits the streets. What a humiliation for the guy."

Siara squeezed Jordyn's hand again. "Please don't feel guilty over what has happened."

"I don't feel guilty, Baby. I feel scared. This could get serious if anyone gets suspicious."

"You didn't do anything wrong. If Uncle Blair had survived the heart attack and you did nothing to get him medical attention, you might have been guilty of something. But he died. And he would be just as dead now if you had called someone in."

"We'll be sure you have an alibi if you need one," Jayme added.

"I don't feel particularly good about having you guys lie for me in something as serious as this."

Darica finally entered the conversation. "We don't count it as lying. It's more like protecting the innocent."

"Thanks, Dari. I'm not used to being an innocent, you know. Just to be sure, maybe you can say a prayer or two in my behalf?"

"God does work in mysterious ways." Darica's eyes focused on some distant image. "Sometimes He dispenses justice through earthly hands, but He always sees that justice is done."

As Jordyn, Siara, and Jayme exchanged puzzled looks, the phone rang.

Jordyn glanced at her watch. "That will be Aunt Bonnie," she said, reaching for the phone.

* * *

Not a tear in the whole damn congregation, Jordyn thought, casting furtive glances at the mourners assembled at the cemetery. *Not even Aunt Bonnie. We're here because we are expected to be. Because social propriety demands it. Especially since Blair was considered a prominent citizen because of his position at the bank. Too bad he wasn't a prominent human being. And now he's a private joke shared by the people of Applewood who know the details of how he supposedly died. Sorry 'bout that, Blair ol' boy.*

Jordyn reached for her sister's hand. She wasn't quite sure how this death was affecting Siara, who had remained unusually quiet since Aunt Bonnie's phone call three nights before. Common sense told Jordyn that Siara was not grieving; twinstinct told her that Siara was struggling to maintain the proper funereal demeanor when, in fact, she felt like…celebrating. That was it…Siara felt like celebrating their uncle's death.

Where their parents' deaths had been an end, Blair's death was a beginning. The time in between had been their emotional purgatory. Dues had been paid. Souls cleansed. Guilts laid to rest.

Now they were free.

"Are you all right, Jordyn?" Luke asked anxiously.

He had come for Jordyn rather than for Blair, and stood inconspicuously among the black-garbed curiosity seekers and social adherents while Bonnie Eldred and the twins, Connor Sanderson, Darica, Jayme, and a stray cousin or two occupied the places of honor afforded the chief mourners.

After the ceremony the crowd scattered as quickly and chaotically as fallen leaves awhirl in an autumn gust. Eventually, when Connor escorted Bonnie and Siara back to the limousine, only Jordyn remained alone at the gravesite. To Luke she was a forlorn figure there by the gaping hole now being filled by the workmen. Though she had seldom spoken of her uncle to Luke, he knew they must be close because they had spent so much time together.

"I'm glad he's dead," she said so matter-of-factly that he wasn't sure he had understood her properly. "It pleases me greatly to see the fucker covered up by dirt. He was so full of shit he'll make dandy fertilizer. Maybe we should have planted him in your cornfield."

"Let me take you home. You've been under a lot of strain these past few days."

"Strain, hell. I've been having a great time. I hated the son of a bitch."

"You don't mean that. You seemed so close."

"The only time Blair and I were close was when I had to fuck him."

"When you had to WHAT?"

"You heard me…fuck…F-U-C-K. Oh, grow up and don't look so damned surprised, Farm Boy. How do you think I managed to finance the studio? I didn't fuck him because I enjoyed it. Guess that makes me an authentic whore, huh? Farm boys shouldn't mess with whores, so go home and play with your plow. I'm going home for a private celebration with my sister. From the looks of it, Aunt Bonnie will probably join us."

She turned and marched toward the limousine, leaving Luke stunned and motionless with disbelief.

CHAPTER TWENTY-FOUR

Sitting at her father's desk, Siara rummaged through the drawers for her stationery. Since none of the roommates had much occasion for casual correspondence, the stationery always seemed to become buried beneath Jayme's notes and stat sheets, Jordyn's ledgers and schedules, Darica's church bulletins, and Siara's own research for the book she and Connor were writing on Sara Teasdale.

The desk had become a centralized filing dump for the roommates, who gravitated toward the coziness of the kitchen to do their actual work, leaving Devon Nealy's study an unused, but revered monument to the man who had worked there and to the woman who had fashioned the room especially for him. The study was in real use only when Connor Sanderson was there to collaborate on the book. The sight of Connor sitting at her father's desk was always comforting to Siara. At thirty-seven he was acquiring the dignifying thick, gray hair and preoccupied manner of a devoted scholar. When his glasses slid to the tip of his nose, he was usually too engrossed in his work even to notice this minor inconvenience. With his head tilted back slightly to enable him to read through the lenses, or his brown eyes peering at her intently over the frames, he reminded Siara more than ever of her father. Of course, she rarely shared this observation with him anymore. He was always so strangely impatient with her when she did.

After finally locating her stationery, Siara began to hum to herself as she picked up the pen and began to write. Sandie would probably be surprised to get the letter. Their correspondence had tailed off considerably since both of them became so involved with their own scholarly pursuits.

"I have truly found my peace with Uncle Blair just as I said I would," Siara wrote to Sandie. "His influence over me ended when the last clod of dirt was thrown over him a year ago. Goodness, has it been a whole year now? I have to say without any remorse that his death was my rebirth, and the weight that was burdening my soul and conscience lies moldering in his grave with him.

"But even in death he somehow continues to plague Jordyn. She and Luke have not seen each other since the funeral, and I have to think that somehow, some way Blair is responsible. Luke always asks about Jordyn whenever he sees Dari, Jae, or me, but he will not call her. Nor will she call him although my twinstinct tells me that she thinks about him often. Mutual obstinacy continues whatever stalemate exists between them.

"Aunt Bonnie, however, must have had a rebirth similar to my own. She is surely enjoying her widowhood with a newly slim figure and a generous bank account, the result of insurance, trusts, and investments made by her dearly departed. At this moment, Aunt Bonnie is 'visiting' (Jyn calls it 'shacking up with') a young Greek vineyard owner she met at some fancy party in Palm Springs.

"These updates are not my reasons for writing, however. I wanted to tell you that you were wonderfully right when you said that some day I would open my eyes to discover men—well, A MAN actually—whose interest in me was obvious even to me. As promised, I intend to do something about it. We have a date, a REAL DATE, tomorrow evening.

"Although he is several years older than I, he is quite handsome and very distinguished. Sometimes when he looks at me, my heart beats so fast I feel flushed and warm all over. After all these years, I think I have finally experienced desire and may even be falling into love!

"I know I could have related this information to you more quickly by phone, but the simple fact is that I wanted an excuse to write his name:

"Dr. Prescott D. Chadburn."

* * *

Sitting cross-legged on the floor of her office, Jordyn sorted through a pile of bills. The mundane tasks of writing checks and reading and answering correspondence were maddeningly tedious, and only her carefully cultivated self-discipline prevented her becoming swamped in overdue paperwork.

As it was, the bills were paid just barely on time, never late, or early. When her schedule became too hectic with classes, meets, and recitals, her roommates volunteered to help. Jordyn might have hired someone to assume responsibility for these necessary annoyances if the studio were turning just a little more profit. However, such a luxurious addition to her overhead would have to wait for a while. She had spent so much already on the additions and renovations. Whatever was left of her share of the insurance and settlement money was now tied up in time certificates and annuities, her own insurance against any future dependence on any man.

At the moment what she needed most were teachers. Her class rolls had increased while the availability of quality teachers had not. Jordyn herself had taken on as much of the overload as she could, and she had pressed a few of her older, more promising students into service as mentors. Until all the work on the studio was complete, only careful scheduling kept the place from becoming a mob scene.

Jordyn was usually at the studio from ten in the morning until after nine at night, six days a week. Nanette, who was physically incapable of handling such long hours, had hired an assistant. Their grind would ease somewhat next week when schools reopened after summer vacation, but then Jordyn would be faced the dilemma of packing all school-age children into the after-school hours.

Her days would then be filled with newly organized adult aerobics classes and students sent to her from the university.

Even Mr. Grayson from the high school had called about her teaching special units of gymnastics, aerobics, and dance to the physical education classes.

Let's face it, Nealy, she thought as she lay back on the floor. *You're overextended and can't take much more.*

She raised her legs into the air and massaged her thighs. Though firm and strong, her legs were tired from the strain of her extended class load. That morning, when she pulled a thigh muscle, she taped her leg and continued dancing.

What I need is a good fuck to loosen me up.

As quickly as she thought of Luke, she forced him out of her mind. The big chicken didn't even pick Lissa up after practice anymore. He sent his mommy.

Well, there are other fucks in the sea, Mr. Farm Boy Johnson. Though it's been so long since I went fishing for one, my bait may be rusty.

"Miss Nealy?"

Jordyn sat up quickly, scattering bills around her on the floor.

"Yes, Beth…what is it?"

"One of the gymnastics kids fell on the bars," the student mentor told her. "She hurt her back. Mrs. Bigelow called an ambulance, but she wants you out there right now."

"Oh, God…" Jordyn jumped up immediately and rushed toward the door.

"Which student?" she called back over her shoulder.

Beth raced to keep up with Jordyn. "One of the intermediate kids…Malissa Johnson."

"Are you sure you won't come with me?" Siara asked as she climbed out of Jayme's Datsun Z. "I won't be in the post office very long, but you know how I like to browse in the bookstore, and I would like to stop by the Chic Shoppe to look for a new dress for tomorrow night."

"Take your time. I have to listen to today's Cubs-Phillies game before I make any profound observations on the Pennant race, and I can do that here just as easily as at home. My car radio will probably pick up the game better, in fact…"

"You are trying very hard to make me feel better about troubling you for a ride."

"It's no trouble at all. I'll just open up the sunroof and pretend I'm soaking up the rays at Wrigley."

"Still, I do appreciate this, Jae. My car has already been in the shop two days longer than the mechanic said it would be. If I had Jyn's courage, I would call and yell at him. But since I have no courage…and since I can't handle your stick shift…I'll just be a bother to my friends."

"You're no bother, Sari. Now scoot. And when you're in the Chic Shoppe, try to find something in blue. You and Jyn are knockouts in blue. Dr. Chadburn will be knocked right out of his socks when he sees you."

"Do you truly think so?"

"Yes, I truly think so," Jayme said, adding to herself, *just as I truly think Connor is the one you should be going out with.*

"Maybe you should come with me to help me pick something out."

"I'm a sports writer, not a fashion editor." Jayme frowned and bit her lip. "Not that fashion editors are that useful."

"Especially the one married to Harlan Oakes?"

"I have a game to listen to. Don't you have some shopping to do?"

"I'm on my way. I'll try not to be too long."

"Take your time. The game is just starting."

Jayme opened her sunroof, switched on the radio, and settled in her seat with her notebook.

Almost September, she thought, *and men are scrambling to capture a Pennant while children are starving in Africa and people are blown to bits in Lebanon. I hope to God you're not one of the casualties, Najib! The trouble with the world is that priorities have gotten screwed up along the way. And my priorities are in no better shape as long as Harlan Oakes is my primary concern.*

"Who's winning?"

Startled, Jayme jerked her head up. Luke Johnson leaned casually against her car and grinned down at her through the sunroof.

"Actually I don't know," she told him. "I wasn't paying much attention. Shouldn't you be home playing farmer on a day like this?"

"Had some banking to take care of. Been looking at a new truck. Do I need to ask who it was you were thinking about?"

"That obvious, huh? Strange, isn't it, how we often fall for those who aren't really worth the effort of caring?"

"So how is Jordyn these days?"

"I was not talking about Jordyn, and she is very busy these days."

"I won't ask what she's busy with."

"It's not what you think. She's usually at the studio until late into the evening, Monday through Saturday. On Sundays she collapses. That doesn't leave much time for socializing."

"If I know Jordyn, she has men shipped in…home delivery smorgasbord."

"Watch it, fella. That's one of my three best friends you're talking about."

"Do you want me to apologize?"

"No. I want you to stop with the snide little digs at Jyn. You're not fooling anyone. Siara, Darica, and I compare notes. We know you're still crazy about her. Love doesn't stop just because we want it to."

"I'll get over it."

"It's been a year, and you don't look over it yet. Why don't you call her?"

"Why should I?"

"Because you want to. Isn't that reason enough?"

"I put up with her rubbing my nose in her numerous affairs, but she finally told me one more that I could handle."

"Her uncle, you mean?"

"You knew about her uncle?"

"Of course I knew. I told you she's one of my best friends."

"And you didn't try to stop her?"

"No one stops Jordyn from doing anything she has her mind set on. You should know that. Just as you should know she would never put herself in a servile situation if she didn't have a damn good reason for it."

"To support her grand lifestyle?"

"To get by, you idiot. Blair was pulling the financial strings for a while, and he was none too honest about how much the twins really had. That's how Darica and I originally came to live with them. They rented out the spare rooms so that they wouldn't have to rely on Blair so much. If it had been just Jordyn, she would have told him to go to hell. But there was Siara, and Sari had plans for grad school...and then the studio was available..."

"You're wasting your time if you're telling me all this thinking I'll change my mind about her being a...a..."

"Is *whore* the word you're groping for?"

"You make it sound sleazier than I actually intended it to be."

"You know how Jyn is. Sex to her is only a physical experience totally separate from emotion...and love. In her mind she was merely trading one favor for another to keep her and Siara going. Like you mow my lawn, and I'll iron your shirts. It's not something I myself would do, but I surely don't condemn her for doing what she felt was necessary in that situation. In fact, I admire her gutziness. Not many women her age would willingly shoulder so much responsibility."

"Too much gutziness can ruin a good woman."

"If you're looking for a doormat, try the housewares section at Wal-Mart."

"I guess I deserved that."

"Yes, you did."

"Is today a day off for you?"

"Yes, it is."

"Would you want to have dinner with me tonight?"

"With what purpose in mind?"

"What purpose does a guy usually have when he asks a girl out?"

"In this case, I can think of two. One, you want to pump me for more information about the girl you'd rather be with...Jordyn. Or two, you want to make Jyn jealous by taking out one of her roommates. Tacky, Luke. Very tacky."

"Or three, maybe I like you and think you're cute."

"If that were the real reason, I'd be immensely flattered and maybe even a little tempted, but the answer would still be no. There's a certain code of ethics that governs roommates, one commandment being 'Thou shalt not date thy roomie's boyfriend.'"

"Jordyn and I don't even date anymore."

"You would be if you weren't so narrow-minded and pig-headed."

"You have such a diplomatic way of phrasing things."

"When all is said and done, you can't deny your true feelings for her. And though she won't admit it, even to us, she feels the same about you. If you don't believe me, believe Siara's twinstinct. It's infallible."

"You're still not going out with me, are you?"

"Dammit, Luke! Haven't you been listening to me?"

"I've been listening," he said, scanning the summer sky, deeply blue…like Jordyn's eyes. "But I sure have been trying hard not to…"

"Jordyn? Where is she? How is she? What happened?"

Jenifer Johnson swept into the hospital like a rampaging comet with her husband drawn along in her jet stream. That this poised and strikingly attractive woman could be in such frenzy surprised Jordyn since Lissa and Luke's mother was usually the very incarnation of composure. In fact, Jordyn had always marveled that a woman of such obvious suavity and sophistication was content with being the wife of a farmer.

Because Mrs. Johnson was always one of the first to volunteer to help with Jordyn's meets and recitals, Jordyn was certain that the lady was eager for any excuse to escape the tiresome confinement of country life. Apparently she wasn't smart enough to avoid getting trapped in the first place although Jordyn could tell that Luther Johnson would have been a temptation to any girl thirty years ago. Luke had come by his height, broad shoulders, and amber eyes naturally.

"The ER doctor is with her now," Jordyn said. "He said for us to wait here until he's finished. The EMTs don't think it's serious because she could move her legs and all, but they immobilized her before bringing her in just to be sure."

"What happened to my daughter?" Luther Johnson demanded, his eyes snapping the same amber fire Jordyn has seen so often in Luke's eyes.

"She was trying a new routine on the uneven bars and fell," Jordyn told him.

"Without proper supervision?"

"Mrs. Bigelow was there, sir, and a student mentor. There was no time for me to ask for details, but I trust Beth and Mrs. Bigelow completely."

"Too much if you ask me."

"She didn't ask you, Luther, so hush." Mrs. Johnson took a deep breath, whether from relief at the information from the EMTs or to bring herself further under control Jordyn wasn't sure. "Jordyn is always very careful about having spotters there for the girls."

Luther hushed, but grudgingly, as he directed a steady, accusatory glare in Jordyn's direction. Jordyn felt uncharacteristically ill at ease with his hostile scrutiny.

Great, she thought, *first he thinks I ruined his son's life, and now he's sure I'm trying to kill his daughter.*

"I'll check with the ER nurse to see how much longer they will be," Jordyn said to the more sympathetic Mrs. Johnson.

Jordyn was thankful for an excuse to escape the immediate vicinity of Luther Johnson's glare. She tapped gently on the ER door until the nurse opened it.

"I know I shouldn't be interrupting, Earla," Jordyn said, "but the girl's folks are here, and it would help a lot if you have some good news for us."

Though Earla Foster was predisposed to abruptness with anyone intruding into her emergency room, her face softened when she saw Jordyn, whose childhood mentor had been Earla's daughter, the always rebellious and rather infamous Mia.

"Looking good, Jyn," Earla said. "We're waiting for x-ray verification, but it looks like just a bit of bruising."

Earla peered down the corridor at the unfriendly amber eyes focused on Jordyn. "Are they hassling you about what happened, child?" she asked.

"Not really. They're just…concerned. She is being more understanding than he is though."

"I could tell. If it helps any, the little girl…what's her name?…Malissa? She says she fell because she was showing off. She had the wind knocked out of her is all, and then she was too embarrassed to get up, especially when someone rushed to call an ambulance."

"Thanks. I owe you another one."

"I'm the one who owes you, child. You check in on me a lot more than my own daughter does."

"I'm closer to home than Mia is."

"Alex Bell invented phones so children can call their mothers. Christmas…Mothers Day…sometimes my birthday…that's all I get."

"Well…you know how Mia is."

"Yeah, I'm afraid I do. Now get along with you and let me get back to work. Good luck with Mt. Crushmore there."

"Thanks, Earla. I'll need it."

Jordyn squared her shoulders and strode confidently back to the Johnsons.

"They're waiting for x-rays, but the doctor is sure there's nothing serious. The nurse said you can see Lissa in a few minutes."

Mrs. Johnson closed her eyes. "Thank goodness!"

Mr. Johnson's hostility did not diminish with the news. "I hope you have good insurance, young lady."

"Luther!" Mrs. Johnson said, embarrassed by her husband.

"I have already instructed admissions to send the bills to me," Jordyn said evenly.

"That's not necessary." Mrs. Johnson leaned forward to pat Jordyn's hand. "We can handle our daughter's bills. Luther always forgets his manners when he's upset."

Mr. Johnson uttered an expletive to corroborate this last remark. A stern look from his wife quieted the angry muttering, but Jordyn understood a few of his words, spoken, no doubt, just distinctly enough for her to hear them, but not loudly enough to infuriate his wife any further. "Bitch thinks she's too good for a farmer."

Mrs. Johnson's face reddened, but Jordyn acted as though she had heard nothing. While this gracious gesture relieved Mrs. Johnson's mortification, Jordyn had another reason for feigning ignorance: she did not want to give Luther Johnson the satisfaction of knowing that his verbal shot had hit its mark.

"I've taken care of everything already," Jordyn said, deliberately maintaining steady eye contact with both parents. "So let's just leave things as they are, okay?"

Mrs. Johnson's protest was interrupted when her son exploded into the emergency room.

"Mom...Dad..." Luke's deep voice reverberated in the corridor. "Where's Lissa? What happened?"

Jordyn's heartbeat quickened as she leaned against the wall to steady herself. A summer in the sun had streaked his hair with gold, and his massive shoulders filled his tee shirt so completely that every muscle was clearly outlined against the black fabric. Slim hips...powerful thighs straining against the faded denim of his jeans...

Suddenly feeling weak, Jordyn pressed her palms flat against the wall for support.

Jenifer Johnson grasped the hands of her visibly alarmed son. "Calm down, Luke..."

"Calm down! You leave a note saying to meet you in the ER 'cause Lissa's been hurt, and you want me to calm down!"

As Mrs. Johnson forced her son into one of the chairs, Jordyn was edging away along the wall toward the emergency room door.

"It's not as serious as we feared," Mrs. Johnson explained. "She had a little accident at the studio..."

Jordyn tapped on the ER door.

"I've got to get out of here," she whispered to Earla. "I'm going back to the studio. Will you call me the very second you know for sure about Lissa?"

"Sure, Jordyn..."

Though puzzled, Earla asked no questions as Jordyn nodded her thanks and walked quickly to the exit doors.

Luke saw her retreat.

Little bitch, he thought, *doesn't even care enough to stay until we're sure Lissa's okay. And here I was thinking that maybe Jae was right. I should've known different…*

CHAPTER TWENTY-FIVE

"Are you sure I look all right?" Siara asked, staring uncertainly down at her new dress.

"You're beautiful, baby. Absolutely gorgeous." Jordyn adjusted the collar on her sister's dress.

Although Jordyn herself would never wear such a lacy, frilly concoction, she thought her twin was quite enchanting in it. Blue was definitely a good color for them, and with Siara's blond hair curled, swept back, and held with a blue ribbon, she was truly beautiful.

For a twelve-year old anyway, Jordyn thought although she would never tell Siara that.

Does Dr. Prescott D. Chadburn like children "in that way"? Just what Sari needs right now…another perv…

"Where is this dude taking you anyway?" Jordyn asked.

"I don't know too much about the place. He said dinner, and since he is a doctor, I'm guessing that the restaurant is probably rather elegant."

Darica entered the room then with her camera. "Are you ready to pose for me, Sari? I promised to take a picture for Jae since she's working tonight."

"Everyone is turning this event into something rather spectacular," Siara said, pressing her palms against her flushed cheeks. "It's just a dinner date."

"Obviously it means more to you than that." Jordyn rearranged a tendril of Siara's hair. "I don't leave the studio early for 'just a date.' Now stand over there and let Dari take your picture."

"You be in it with me."

"No way, Baby. Tonight's your night, and my cut-offs will hardly go well with that dress. You'll have to pose alone on this one. Look sexy."

"How do I do that?"

"Drape yourself on the bureau there, and give us a touch of a pout. Not quite so much lower lip there…there you go…that's it. Shoot, Dari."

Darica snapped the picture. "Should I take another one?"

"Maybe one for Connor," Siara said, fidgeting with a button on her sleeve. "He's working at the library tonight to verify some information we uncovered on Sara T and Vachel Lindsay. I tried to persuade him to wait until tomorrow when I can help, but he was rather abrupt with me. He has become quite grumpy lately."

Jordyn and Darica exchanged knowing glances.

"Maybe he's working too hard," Jordyn suggested casually.

"He does tend to forget that he's getting older."

"You make him sound like he's ready for a nursing home. He isn't that old."

"I know, but I always think of him as being from Daddy's generation…perhaps because Connor has been so much like a father to us since…since the fire."

"I'm sure Connor's delighted that you think of him that way." Jordyn folded her arms and leaned against the wall. "So when is your doctor gonna make his appearance?"

"He isn't coming here." Siara smoothed on more lip-gloss. "I'm supposed to meet him. That's why I was so worried about my car. Thank you for talking to that stubborn mechanic for me, Jyn."

"Back up, Baby. You mean Dr. Date isn't picking you up here?"

"He has a patient in the hospital in Mt. Posey. For the sake of convenience, I'm meeting him in a restaurant there so that he won't have to drive all the way back here to take me back there. Understand?"

"Perfectly." Jordyn's eyes narrowed. "So what's wrong with the restaurants in Applewood?"

"The place we're going to is very special to him…and very exclusive. It is tucked away in the countryside somewhere…like a quaint English inn…I think. I have the directions in my handbag."

"I don't like you being on any strange country road after dark in a car that's ready to call it quits."

"My car is working fine now, I have precise directions to where I am going, and I will keep my doors locked at all times. Please don't worry. I have to go now. Will you girls wait up for me? Jae, too?"

"Only if you promise to be home before dawn."

"Really, Jordyn. This is not that kind of date. Prescott is a gentleman. Well…I'm going now…"

After pausing a moment, Siara hugged both Jordyn and Darica tightly before running out of the bedroom and down the stairs.

Sitting on the edge of Siara's bed, Jordyn rubbed her eyes. "He's married, Dari. Otherwise he would have picked her up here and taken her somewhere more…more public."

"Why didn't you stop her?"

"You saw how excited she was. How could I ruin that for her on only a strong suspicion? Besides, I could be wrong. I haven't exactly been the expert on men lately. Why couldn't the little twit have fallen for Connor instead?"

"What can we do?"

"We can hope that Dr. Prescott D. Chadburn is such a creep, Sari will never want to see him again."

Outside, a hot pink neon sign flashed "Fat's Red Dog Rendezvoo" against naked, gray, and splintered wood. Inside, the candle within the blaringly red, plastic-netted globe splattered crimson spots across their faces.

Siara, however, was burbling with starry-eyed exhilaration.

Prescott had planned his strategy wisely. In Siara he recognized a rare combination of beauty, legality, and innocence. Here was a bud just ready to bloom, and his experienced hand would pluck its fresh loveliness.

However, there was still something of the frightened fawn about this young lady, and he had to proceed carefully or risk scaring her away. Instead of baubles, jewelry, candy, and flowers, he could ply this miss with gallantry, gentleness, and romance.

Lying at the core of his game plan was his loophole, the escape hatch that he could use if this misty-eyed maiden started to cling and pose a problem: he could claim that he had a wife: a shrewish and unsympathetic wife. The irony of the stratagem amused him, and the result of it would keep him out of trouble with the good widow Reba Bingham, who pleased Prescott greatly with her bank account, but not with much else. Though Prescott had recently instigated a financial coup that would supplement his doctor's income quite agreeably, he still did not want to surrender the widow's wealth.

Fortunately lonely widows were usually so grateful for the companionship of a man of Prescott's caliber that they demanded little of the relationship. Nevertheless, even Mrs. Reba Bingham would not tolerate Prescott's little diversion with other ladies. He had had a difficult enough time trying to explain why he needed such an inept, though young and curvaceous receptionist.

He decided to throw Siara a complimentary crumb now. They had been sitting in silence for a few moments, and she was beginning to fidget.

"You are especially lovely tonight, Siara," he said. "I could spend hours gazing at you without saying a single word, and still I would have a wonderful time."

Color tinged her cheeks as Siara lowered her eyes to stare at her hands, clasped tightly together in her lap. "Are you sure I'm not over-dressed, Prescott? I didn't know quite what to expect."

"You are definitely several cuts above the crowd that frequents this place, but don't worry about that. The locals need to look at a real lady now and then. I know this isn't the most elegant spot in the world, but it has one definite advantage. Because the people here don't know me, I am not constantly bothered for free medical advice, charitable contributions, and social invitations. The life of a doctor is not always his own, so I was fortunate to find this place. It has become my haven, and I wanted to bring you here so that I would not have to share you with anyone else. You understand, don't you?"

Siara ventured a shy look into his eyes and then quickly resumed her scrutiny of her hands. "I understand. Actually, I am rather relieved about the…the remoteness. I am uncomfortable in crowds."

He beamed his approval. "Splendid! I am so lucky to have found you, Siara. Most women need to be seen publicly in boisterous and crowded hellholes where any sort of companionable intimacy is impossible. A man feels that they are more interested in being seen by their friends than in being with him."

"I have hardly dated at all. I...I was always too bashful."

"You didn't seem bashful that day in the park when we met. I thought we had a delightful conversation."

"About *Anna Karenina*. I couldn't have talked sensibly about anything else at the time."

"I must admit to a little deception. I jogged by you twice without your noticing. When I was finally desperate enough to stop and rest right there on the bench with you, I saw what you were reading and realized a way to begin a conversation with the most beautiful woman I've seen in all my life. I was interested in you, not Anna."

His declaration emboldened her. "I felt as though Sir Lancelot had swept out of the pages of legend to sit beside me that day."

"Sir Lancelot?" he said, amused. "You flatter me. Wouldn't my age make me more comparable to King Arthur, or even Merlin?"

"You can't judge people in terms of their ages any more than you can on their hair color," she proclaimed firmly to dispel any qualms he might have about her being so much younger.

"You are a rare woman." He raised his beer mug in tribute. "Mature and understanding beyond your years. Though it was your beauty that first attracted me, your intelligence and sensitivity kept me returning to the library for books I never had time to read."

Siara lowered her eyes again. "I must confess I began to watch for you each day."

"Do you know what a soul mate is, Siara?"

"I've heard of the expression, but I've never considered a definition for it."

"A soul mate is one with whom you are totally compatible...spiritually, emotionally, psychologically, intellectually...physically. It's been said that each person on this earth has a perfect soul mate somewhere. The trick, of course, is finding her...or him. Unfortunately most people never do find their soul mates. I was one of the lucky ones who did...last month in a park across from Scheffers."

"That's how I feel, too, Prescott," she whispered, trembling with emotion.

"I dared to pray that you did, my precious Siara...which makes my next revelation even more difficult for me..."

"What is it, Prescott?" she urged softly when he hesitated.

"Siara..." The pain etched on his face wrenched her heart. "Sometimes a man despairs of ever finding his soul mate, and after years of fruitless searching, he's so lonely, he settles for less and ultimately pays an exorbitant price in suffering for his mistake."

"I don't understand what you mean..."

"We must go where we can be alone before I bare my soul to my soul mate. If you reject me, I want no witnesses to the destruction of my heart. But if, as I pray is the case, you understand and forgive me, I want our joy shared only by the two of us."

"Of course, Prescott…"

Though she was still bewildered, her eyes shone rapturously as he pressed her hand against his lips.

Jordyn lay on her bed, swinging her legs in the air and thinking. Thinking of Siara. Of Connor. Of the studio. Of Jae and Dari. Of Fred Astaire, Fred Flintstone, the Smurfs, and Smucker's orange marmalade. Anything else but an amber-eyed giant.

Groaning, she rolled over and buried her face in a pillow. Had a whole year really passed since she last saw him?

She had tried very hard NOT to see him. When his battered Bronco was parked on one side of the street, she walked on the other. When he was in the audience at recitals and meets, she became ultra-focused on the students' activities. When, on rare occasions these days, he came to the studio to pick up Lissa, Jordyn remained closeted in her office with a pile of paperwork while he just as deliberately read a newspaper as he waited in his truck.

Well, it was his loss. Isn't that what girlfriends told each other in situations like this one? He had walked away from her, hadn't he? Jordyn couldn't remember anymore.

Nor was remembering important. She didn't have time for him or any other man right now. Hell, she didn't even time to feel horny.

However, seeing him yesterday has stirred her hormones all over again.

To prove to herself that her need was for any man rather than for him, she called a few of her old boyfriends after Siara left.

Bill, Chris, and Tony weren't home. Bryce had just had oral surgery. Jervis had a new wife.

She could find appropriate entertainment at Burkey's. However, she was too tired to change her clothes for something merely adequate. In spite of his prudery, Luke Johnson was considerably beyond merely adequate.

For that matter, Jordyn had more fun with Luke when they didn't go to motels than she did with all the other guys she spent whole nights in bed with.

She beat her fist against the red satin comforter. A year of rigid self-control had been wiped out with one look into those amber eyes.

"Damn you, Farm Boy!"

She muffled an angry scream with a pillow.

"This is my other place of refuge," Prescott said as he turned off the car. "I rent most of the surrounding land to a local farmer, but I save this little area for me…and now for you."

"Somehow I have the impression that you need refuge from more than just the demands of a doctor's life," she said.

He reached across the seat for her hands and pulled her closer to him.

"Siara, dearest, this isn't going to be easy for me, and I want you to reserve your judgment…and any decisions you might make…until I am finished. Above all, remember how I feel about you…how we feel about each other. These feelings must be our source of strength no matter what happens."

"You are frightening me with all these ominous implications."

"I don't want to frighten you, my dearest, but I do want you to prepare for the tragic flaw in your Sir Lancelot. Siara, may I kiss you?"

"Now?"

"I'm so afraid you won't let me later. If my fear is realized, this kiss will be a memory I will cherish throughout the rest of my miserable life."

"Now I am really frightened, Prescott."

Gently tilting her face up, he lowered his mouth onto hers. Siara kept her eyes tightly closed. The memory of the fiasco she had made out of Stanley Klosterman's kiss was still fresh. The touch of Prescott's skillful lips on hers, however, melted her apprehensions, and instinctively she slid her arms around him.

"You have just given me a memory that is certain to warm my heart even on the coldest nights," he whispered. *Pretty warm elsewhere, too…*

"You sound so certain about there being no memories for us after tonight."

"I am honestly evaluating my own wretched perfidy. I am not worthy of your…dare I say *love?*" *I'll have to dare stopping by Darla's on my way home tonight so that she can finish what this bookish babe has begun…*

"You may say *love*, Prescott, because I feel it, too. So, please, entrust me now with your dark secret, and we'll do whatever needs to be done…together."

"Siara, dearest, you are the treasure of my life."

He paused to take a deep breath. *God, this melodramatic dialogue is making me nauseous, but it seems to appeal to the girl. Capture her mind, and can her goodies be far behind?*

"Please, Prescott, don't prolong my suspense."

"Have you read *Jane Eyre*, my dearest?"

"Of course, though several years ago…in the fifth or sixth grade I think."

"Do you remember the plight that so agonized Rochester when he realized he was in love with Jane?"

"He wanted desperately to marry her, but…but…" Siara sucked her breath in sharply. "But he already had a w-wife. Oh, Prescott, no! Tell me I have misconstrued your allusion."

"I wish I could." He turned away from her and pressed his forehead against the window glass. "So now you see how file, contemptible, and despicable I truly am."

Siara twisted her hands together in her lap and then interlocked her fingers tightly as she considered this disturbing complication in what she had deemed her idyll. If she was not destined to be a romantic heroine, perhaps she was fated to be a tragic one.

"In *Jane Eyre* there were extenuating circumstances," she said finally.

"I claim no such excuses. My wife...Reba...is neither mad nor infirm." He paused before adding softly, "In a physical or mental sense anyway."

"What do you mean?"

"I've said enough already." He straightened in the seat and stared out into the night. "Whatever blame there is should fall squarely on my shoulders. I accept full responsibility for the sorry state of our marriage, though God knows Reba would try the patience of a saint."

"Do you...l-love her?"

"Love? It would be as easy to love a chunk of stone...and easier on my nerves I'll warrant."

"Yet you married her."

"Yes, I married her, and therein lies the mistake I shall pay for, for the rest of my life. If only I had foreseen your presence in my future, I would gladly have waited. But men...especially professional men...reach an age where they feel a connubial liaison is necessary to the furtherance of their careers and lifestyles. There is seldom love, always convenience, and I was willing to make that trade-off at the time."

"Therefore, you see, I've no one to blame for my current agony but myself...though in all honesty, Reba has not been the most warm and sympathetic of partners. Don't get me wrong...I'm not trying to excuse myself. Reba has been an efficient doctor's wife, but a man needs more than efficiency from his life mate. Efficiency he can get from a...from a secretary or receptionist."

"Prescott, perhaps I have no right to ask this..."

He turned to her quickly and cupped her face within his hands. "You have every right to ask me any question you want to ask, my darling, for in spite of the legal bond I'm burdened with, you are the possessor of my heart and soul."

"Then I've got to ask why you don't relieve yourself of this burden you find so irksome."

"I had no reason to before, my darling."

"And now?"

"And now, though you've given me ample reason, I'm afraid that...that I can't, no matter how much I long to do so. For all her faults, she is my legal wife, and her years of efficient service cannot be cast aside for my selfish reasons."

Siara swallowed back a sudden rush of tears. "Then there is no choice for us but one, however painful it might be."

He grasped her hands firmly. "Must tonight be an end when I had so hoped for a beginning?"

"There's no other way. We can't continue like this. It wouldn't be right."

"There is another way…if you can be patient…if you can trust me."

Siara looked at him hopefully. "I do trust you."

"Then bear with me for a while, my dearest. Rather than overwhelm Reba all at once with the trauma of separation, I can accustom her to it gradually. That would be the kinder way, and I'm sure she'll eventually see the wisdom of divorce. I will, of course, see to it that she is well provided for afterward. We…you and I…might have to sacrifice a few luxuries, but at least we'd have each other."

"And in the meantime?"

"The most honorable thing would be for us to refrain from all contact until my matrimonial condition is resolved."

"Yes, that would be the most honorable thing for us to do."

"The problem is that I don't have enough will power to do the most honorable thing."

"There's no alternative…"

"Yes, there is, Siara. Perhaps less honorable, but we're already sacrificing our immediate desires to spare Reba any emotional trauma. We're entitled to some meager happiness…if we do nothing indiscreet until I feel Reba is ready to handle the shock with a minimum of hysterics and ill will."

"Are you saying we should continue to see each other even though you'd still be married?"

"As iniquitous as it sounds, yes, that's what I'm saying."

"My conscience rebels at being the other woman."

"But you aren't the other woman, dearest Siara. For me you are the only woman. Isn't that enough to soothe your troubled conscience?"

"That means a great deal to me, Prescott, but—"

"Before you reject my alternative completely, consider all the unhappy people in the world who are lonely because of circumstances beyond their control. Our circumstances are well within our control, my dearest. It's almost a sacrilege to throw away our potential for immediate happiness together."

"Will it be very long before your wife agrees to…to let you go?"

"A moment is an eternity without you, my beloved. And I'm afraid Reba is very unpredictable in terms of disposition. We could be talking weeks…or months. The ordeal before us will be a hellish trial of patience, darling, and it will be a lot easier to bear if we can do it together."

"But, Prescott…"

"Don't you understand, Siara? A month or two is nothing to a girl your age, but to me it's a major portion of the remainder of my lifetime. I've been without you too long already. If you can't put your own happiness above honor, can you put my happiness above it? We don't have that many years left as it is."

"Please don't talk like that. I can't bear to think about losing someone else I love."

"It's a reality of a May-December relationship that must be faced, darling. Do you really want to further decrease the number of days left for us to share?"

Siara brushed away a tear that had sneaked from her eye. "No, Prescott. I want us to be together always and forever."

"Then you won't banish me from your life?"

"I want you in my life...no matter what we have to contend with."

"Siara...my precious Siara..." He gathered her into his arms and held her against him so that she could not see the triumphant gleam in his eyes.

CHAPTER TWENTY-SIX

Jordyn forced herself to concentrate on the columns of figures in the ledger. Bookkeeping was so damn boring. And too easy to keep her mind off a pair of amber eyes and powerful arms that had held her last night in a dream.

Just held her.

Awakening, Jordyn had remained snugly enfolded within a soporific cocoon until she shook the drowsiness from her head. The transition was like moving from a warm electric blanket to a cold toilet seat.

She had made the transition many times in the month since seeing Luke at the hospital. While Siara became more radiant as her ill-advised romance blossomed, Jordyn became more irritable…too little sleep and too many intrusions into her dreams by those amber eyes.

"Jyn?" Malissa Johnson peeked around the door into Jordyn's office. "Can I wait in here for my mom? Everyone else has gone home, and it's lonely out there."

"Come on in, Liss." Relieved by the diversion, Jordyn quickly closed the ledger. "How are you feeling?"

"Oh, I'm fine. I was never really hurt, y'know." Lissa set her gym tote down by Jordyn's desk. "Except for my pride anyway."

"Did you learn anything from your experience?"

"Not to act like a dweeb, and when Mrs. Bigelow says to wait for a spotter, I should wait for a spotter." Lissa rolled a piece of wood from one hand back into the other. "I'm sorry you got stuck with my hospital bills. It was my fault for showing off."

"Don't worry about it. I have insurance. What's that in your hands?"

"Oh…this? It's the wedge for holding the gym door open during practice. I forgot to leave it by the door when I helped Mrs. B close up. Remind me to put it back, or she'll go nuts trying to find it."

Lissa wandered around the office, peering at Jordyn's awards and trophies on shelves that Connor had recently installed.

"My dad wanted to yank me out of here," she told Jordyn, "but Mom wouldn't let him. She likes you a lot. She says you're very talented and could be a professional dancer if you wanted to be. She used to be one."

Jordyn's eyebrows rose in surprise. "I didn't know that."

"That's how she met Pops. She was dancing in a show where Pops was stationed, and they fell in love. It's kinda strange to think about Pops being romantic. He gets all red whenever Mom kisses him in front of Luke and me. Is Luke like that?"

Jordyn opened the ledger and studied the numbers there. "How would I know that?"

"You two used to be in love. I wish you still were. Luke's been a real grumpy-bear since you broke up, especially this month."

"We were never in love. We just...dated."

"Luke wouldn't be this grumpy if you weren't in love. He's been seeing another girl sometimes, but I don't think he likes her that much. Mom and I don't. She's a real nerdette."

As Jordyn copied numbers into the ledger, she tried to ignore the painful constriction in her chest. "Maybe you can learn to like her. She just might be your sister-in-law someday."

"I don't think so. Luke never smiles when he talks to her on the phone. He always smiled a lot when he talked to you...though sometimes you made him pretty mad, too."

Jordyn pressed the pencil against the ledger so hard the lead broke.

Lissa kept talking. "That day they kept me in the hospital for observation...you came by to see me after visiting hours so that you wouldn't run into Luke, didn't you?"

Jordyn grabbed up another pencil. "I'm always busy here during regular visiting hours."

"You always called me at home when Luke was in the fields."

"So?"

"He and Mom got into a fight about it. He said you were a real...a real bee-itch for not checking on me, but Mom straightened him out. She told him to stop inventing reasons not to like you when it's obvious to everyone else that he still loves you. Then he told her to mind her own darn business...only he didn't say *darn*. You can probably guess what he said instead."

"How much longer until your mother gets here?"

"Am I getting on your nerves?"

"Your topic of conversation is."

"Oh well...I thought I'd give it a shot. I sure like you a whole lot better than the nerdette."

"Thank you. That's a real ego booster."

"Mom might be a little late. She's got PTA tonight. I could call Luke to come get me."

"Don't bother him. If your mom isn't here by the time I finish my posting, I'll take you home."

"Will you park a mile from my house and make me walk so you won't have to look at Luke?"

"Two miles is more like it, sweetie." The clack of the studio's front door was loud in the quiet building. "But it sounds like your mother is here to save you from a long walk."

Smiling, Lissa hid her hands behind her and went to stand by the door. Jordyn stiffened as she recognized the heavy tread in the hallway.

"Dammit, Lissa!" the familiar voice boomed. "How long am I going to have to wait for you?"

"But, Luke…I thought I was supposed to wait in Jyn's office for Mom," Malissa said sweetly as the office door was jerked open and her brother's massive form filled the entryway.

"Mom has a meeting tonight, and you damn well know it!" he bellowed, centering his eyes on his sister. "I've been waiting over thirty minutes."

"Gee, Luke, I'm really sorry," Lissa murmured humbly. "I'll get my stuff, and then we can leave."

"I'll wait in the truck."

"No! You wait here. I've got…a bunch…a bunch of encyclopedias I need you to carry. They're awful heavy…"

"Where are they? I'll get them."

"No! Not yet. I have to…to pee first. Okay? I'll be just a minute. Will you get my duffel for me…over there on the floor? I'll be right back."

Without looking at Jordyn, Luke moved toward the desk to retrieve the bag. Lissa quickly left the office, slamming the door behind her. Scowling, Luke strode to the entryway and pushed against the door, which budged only slightly even after several of his attempts to force it open.

"We've been set up," Jordyn told him quietly as she remembered the wood wedge. "Lissa planned for this to happen."

Luke finally turned to face her. His expression was not amiable. "She's only a little girl. Maybe she had a little help."

"What are you implying, Farm Boy?"

"Not a damn thing. I'm saying straight out it's pretty cheap to use my sister to help you trap a man."

Jordyn propelled herself out of her chair. "You think I arranged this? You egotistical son of a bitch…"

Malissa's voice called out to them from the other side of the door. "For crying out loud, will you two grow up? Jyn didn't have anything to do with this, Luke. Mom and I thought it up so you'd have to talk to each other. So quit shouting and start talking 'cause I'm not letting you out until you kiss and make up."

Luke beat his fists against the door. "Open this door now, Malissa Johnson, or so help me—"

"You can't do anything to me, Luke Johnson," Malissa shouted back. "Mom won't let you. I'm going to the gym now, and when I come back, you guys better be all made up."

"It's not going to work, Liss." Jordyn's voice lacked any trace of anger, a fact that rather surprised Luke. Instead, Jordyn sounded…tired. "Let your brother out. Your devious little plan is very impressive, but it's not going to work like you want it to no matter how long you leave us in here. Liss, are you listening to me? Lissa?"

No response.

Shrugging, Jordyn dropped into her chair. "I guess she really did go to the gym. If you'll forgive my lack of hospitality, I have work to finish. You can amuse yourself in whatever way you want until Liss returns. Then maybe you can talk some sense into her."

"I could kick the door down…unless you're emotionally attached to it in some way…which you must be. You spend enough time here."

"Since when does my schedule concern you? And don't you dare destroy any part of my studio or I swear I'll feed you your balls for breakfast."

He folded his arms and leaned against the door. "You haven't lost any of your charm I see."

"What do you know about charm, Farm Boy?"

"I sure didn't learn anything about it in the time I wasted on you."

"I don't recall any complaints from you."

"Then you weren't paying attention. Maybe you're confusing me with one of your thousands of other bedmates."

"Thousands? Gee, I should get each fuck documented and submit the total to Guinness. Too bad Uncle Blair isn't around to share in the notoriety. You and he rang up the lights on my scoreboard more often than most."

"Damn you, Jordyn."

"Ah, the melody lingers on." With forced casualness, Jordyn sorted through some papers on her desk. "If you'll excuse me, I have work to do. If you're in as big a hurry to be rid of me as I am to be rid of you, you might unscrew the hinges or something. Connor left his toolbox over there beneath the shelves. But I'll have to ask you to replace the door when you've made your escape."

Surprised when he did not respond with some derogatory remark, she turned in her chair. His face was contorted with rage as he advanced toward her. She was not frightened so much as amazed that his anger had transcended a mere vocal attack. Still, as he reached her chair, she instinctively threw up an arm to defend herself. He grabbed her wrist and jerked her into his arms. Though she pummeled his chest with her fists, he crushed her against him as his mouth crashed down onto hers. The kiss was a savage release of a year's suppressed longing, and when Luke finally let her go, she fell back against the desk, exhausted and trembling.

"Satisfied now?" she snapped, trying to regain some semblance of composure.

"No…and neither are you."

"You seem pretty damn sure of yourself, Farm Boy."

"What time tomorrow can I pick you up?"

Jordyn's lips tightened into a thin line. "Eight," she said finally.

* * *

Through the open sunroof, Siara stared up at the moon, a lonely orbed floe adrift in a midnight blue sea. Prescott lay atop her…sleeping, dozing, resting…she wasn't sure which. In books she had read recently to prepare herself for this inevitable night, the lovers usually slept afterward…or smoked cigarettes.

However, neither she nor Prescott smoked.

Prescott's weight against her was making breathing difficult. Somehow this afterglow…was that the proper term?…wasn't very glowing for her. Where was all the body-consuming ecstasy she thought she would feel? Where was Vladimir Horowitz? She had always imagined that she would hear Vladimir Horowitz's *Moonlight Sonata* the first time she made love.

Instead she was stiff and sore…and wondering why Jordyn enjoyed this particular activity so much. Surely Luke…or whoever…couldn't be better at it than Prescott. Prescott was a doctor.

Whatever was wrong had to be her fault.

Prescott had assured her that the next time would be easier for her. She was comforted by the mere implication that she would have a second chance.

Maybe she was frigid.

Maybe she hadn't buried Uncle Blair as deeply as she thought she did.

With the drapes closed and the room dark, Jordyn's hearing was sharper than usual as sounds drifted in to her in the night.

Voices from the motel room adjacent to theirs…cars passing on the highway…the whine of semi tires…a car door slamming…the ice machine humming outside the door…even leaves scraping against the sidewalk as the autumn wind ushered them along.

And beside her Luke's even breathing.

She moved closer to him.

"Are you awake, Farm Boy?" she whispered when his arm tightened around her.

"Mmm…"

"Is that a yes or a no?"

"That depends on what you want to do next." His voice was husky with sleep as his lips brushed against her forehead.

Jordyn's fingers wandered through the mass of hair on his chest and down across his muscled stomach. "Surely you can guess."

"I won't have any strength left for my chores in the morning."

"You need a day off anyway."

"The same might be said for you. That studio's going to kill you if you don't ease up."

"I feel quite lively at the moment," she said, caressing him gently.

He moaned softly and rolled over, pinning her beneath him. "In all this time and with all that's happened, my feelings for you haven't changed."

"Don't spoil tonight with talk like that."

"I want you to know it, Jordyn."

"I want you to know I can't be tying myself down right now. If you want something serious, you're better off with the nerdette. Oh God! Sorry…that slipped."

She could feel his grin against her neck.

"Liss has been bending your ear," he said. "But we'll play it your way… while my patience holds out. The way I see it, my chief competition is your studio, and I can handle that better than your usual mob of men."

"I reserve the right to see other men…if I want to," she said, more from habit than from inclination.

Luke noticed the absence of the usual defiance in her voice.

"And I reserve the right to see other women…if I want to," he told her quietly. "But I won't stop telling you that I love you…or reminding you that I'd marry you next week if only you'd agree."

"So long as we both understand the ground rules."

"I'd appreciate a few concessions from you along the way."

"Like what?" she asked suspiciously.

"Like I don't want to hear about any other men you might want to see. I'm sure I'll find out about them one way or another, but don't rub my nose in it."

"That's reasonable enough."

"And I'd like for you to accept a few of Mom's dinner invitations. You know her well enough by now to realize you won't be breaking bread with Ma and Pa Kettle."

"Your dad and I won't make real friendly dinner companions."

"He'll bull up for a while, but he'll come around. Mom can handle him. So what do you say? Dinner at my house Sunday?"

Sighing, Jordyn buried her face against his chest so that her assent was muffled. "Okay, Luke…"

"Great! Now one more thing…"

Jordyn pushed him away from her. "Don't get carried away, Farm Boy."

"I'm just going to ask if your boss will give you a weekend off sometime."

"Boss? I'm my boss."

"So will you give yourself a weekend off soon?"

"For what?"

"For an uninterrupted weekend away somewhere with a farm boy. We have a lot of catching up to do."

He lowered his lips onto hers and trailed his tongue along her throat and over her breast, where he took her rigid nipple into his mouth. Groaning and wriggling with need, Jordyn immersed her fingers in his hair and wrapped her legs around him.

"You've got a date, Farm Boy," she whispered as he entered her.

Jordyn skimmed her finger across his shoulder. "Luke?"

"Hmm?"

"I want you to know something."

He nuzzled her neck sleepily. "What?"

"I want you to know that if I were the marrying type...which I'm not...but if I were, you'd be the one I'd marry."

His mouth found hers. *That's quite a confession coming from her*, he thought with a smile. *Maybe someday she'll admit that she loves me.*

CHAPTER TWENTY-SEVEN

Prescott put his hands on Siara's shoulders and shook her gently.

"You have to understand that our situation is not...well...normal," he told her, keeping his voice low so that no one else in the Red Dog could possibly overhear. "Do not...I repeat...do NOT come by the office during business hours. Darla...the receptionist...is...the daughter of a family friend. Word could get back to Reba too easily."

Imagine the nightmare, he thought, *if both Siara and the widow show up while Darla is working. I'm having enough trouble keeping my stories and my women straight.*

Siara's lip trembled from his scolding. "How else can I see you when I need you or want to talk to you in person?"

"You'll have to wait for me to call you."

"But that's often not when I most need you!"

"What can possibly be so urgent that it can't wait a while?"

"I would have told you this afternoon, but you threw me out."

"I did not throw you out. I merely told you I was too busy to talk."

"It was your lunch break. Your waiting room was empty."

"I had someone on the table." *Like Darla.* "And then I was going to get some paperwork done so that I could be with you this evening. You really are being childishly petulant, Siara. I expect more maturity from you. I can get these kinds of hassles from Reba."

Biting her lip, Siara lowered her eyes. "I'm sorry. I just feel so isolated from you sometimes."

"It has to be this way."

"It's been nearly four months. We haven't even made love in a bed. The back seat of a car is neither comfortable nor dignified even if it is a Lincoln."

"I'm just as eager as you are, my darling, but it would be inhuman of me to precipitate a separation right now, a week before Christmas. Please be patient."

"I'm trying. It isn't easy."

"Maybe sometime when I can send Darla home early, I'll call you to come by the office then...before I make my hospital rounds. Would you like that?"

"Oh yes, Prescott!"

"My examination tables should be less confining than my back seat, and the stirrups present us with lovely possibilities."

"Do you mean that we could make love in your office?"

"People in our situation must be grateful for whatever opportunities come their way. Now tell me this news of yours that was so important."

Siara's eyes brightened with his interest in her announcement. "Connor and I received a favorable response from a publisher about our Teasdale project. As soon as the book is finished, we'll have a buyer for it. This isn't Connor's first published work, but it's mine, so I wanted to share the news with you."

Prescott peeked at his watch. "That's wonderful. Why don't we go to our little haven in the country to celebrate?"

"Couldn't we go to a motel for a change?"

He pulled at his tie. "I didn't come financially prepared for a situation like that, and I can't use my credit card with my name so prominently featured."

"I'll pay."

"That's highly unacceptable to any respectable gentleman."

"You're being old-fashioned. Please, Prescott…"

"If it means so much to you. But we'll have to take your car. I certainly couldn't explain why my car was parked outside some second-rate motel room…"

* * *

Prescott D. Chadburn spent Christmas Eve with his receptionist in her apartment. Darla gave him a Christmas card containing a Polaroid of herself naked, and a memorable evening in bed. Prescott gave her a crystal jewelry box with a hundred dollar bill inside.

He spent Christmas Day with the good widow, Reba Bingham, and an assortment of her society friends. Later Mrs. Bingham gave him a Rolex; a diamond-studded keychain from which dangled the keys to her house, her BMW, and her cabin retreat in the Ozarks; and a forgettable night in bed. Prescott gave her a crystal jewelry box and the promise of a trip to Paris in the spring.

The day after Christmas was Siara's.

Deeming herself lucky to get even this moment of his time during such a busy social season, Siara smiled with steadfast understanding and gave him a gold watch, inscribed with "Our love is timeless—Siara," and a few hours in a sagging motel bed. Prescott gave her a crystal jewelry box. Inside he placed a poem he told her he wrote especially for her. Actually he had copied it from the Christmas card he received from Reba.

He had one more crystal jewelry box to deliver. This one, however, would not be received so favorably by the woman who wanted to forget her relationship with him. Prescott, on the other hand, delighted in reminding her of it.

* * *

Jordyn lay awake long after Luke had fallen asleep.

To celebrate New Year's weekend, they had returned to the same St. Louis hotel that had been the scene of the monthly weekend vacations that Luke planned to get Jordyn away from the studio for a while.

Beyond insisting to pay the hotel bill every other month, she never protested his initiative because she enjoyed being with him and benefited from the break in her routine.

This new complacency caused her some concern, however. Being with Luke had become too comfortable. She looked forward to being with him too much. Placing that high a priority on any man would be detrimental to her freedom, her future, and possibly her emotions.

In the three months since she and Luke had resumed their relationship, Jordyn occasionally accepted invitations from other men as her personal declaration of independence. Though a couple of these dates ended in bed, Jordyn was horrified to realize that sex with anyone but Luke had become perfunctory and unsatisfying. Young men who were well acquainted with her were astonished when she asked to be taken home early because of a headache or fatigue.

Eventually she stopped accepting invitations from all men but Luke. She told herself that this was a logical, efficient decision. After all, she had only so much time she could fritter away on a man. Shouldn't he be the one who provided the most quality for her time investment?

During the exchange of Christmas presents the week before, however, she had glimpsed within herself the frightening result of her decision.

One of the gifts he gave her was contained within a small jeweler's box. Though Jordyn narrowed her blue eyes in suspicion, her heart thudded wildly as she opened the box. Inside was a pair of diamond studs. Her theatrical training helped her summon an expression of relieved surprise when, in fact, she was disappointed that she had not received an engagement ring.

Later she rationalized that she had merely wanted an excuse to refuse another of his marriage proposals. But lying beside him now with his strong arms around her and his breath a gentle whisper against her cheek, she knew the real reason why she had been disappointed. And she was afraid.

"Farm Boy?" she said, urgently seeking to obliterate these strange and unwelcome sensations with something she was more accustomed to. "Wake up. I want to fuck."

"For crying out loud, Jordyn," he mumbled, rubbing his hand over his eyes. "I've asked you not to say that word."

"And I told you I refuse to euphemize in the totally sappy way you want me to."

When she felt his body tense, she closed her eyes and waited for the beginning of the fight. It was time they had a good fight. Things between them had been peaceable too long.

Instead of the heat of his wrath, however, she felt the warmth of his lips pressed against the hollow of her throat.

"Then I guess we'll have to think of a compromise," he murmured into her ear.

"Damn you, Luke," she said, but her voice was soft as her mouth yielded to his kiss.

* * *

Siara jerked away from Prescott when he reached to unbutton her blouse.

"I know you hate emotional scenes, Prescott," she said, "but we're going to have one unless you force an immediate resolution to our situation. We've been together almost a year now, and there's no discernible change in your marital condition. My conscience and patience are wearing thin."

Prescott drummed his fingers against his steering wheel and resisted the urge to rub his erection. Reba had recently delivered an ultimatum, too, and even Darla was getting possessive. Things were getting too complicated. He had to simplify his romantic life.

Reba was the keeper. A woman with her social position and money was difficult to replace. Of course, he would have to find ways to placate the widow other than by marrying her. Oh, he COULD marry her. Who was to say he couldn't, except one...and she would be delighted to keep her silly mouth shut for once. He would have to weigh one situation against the other to see which would be the most advantageous for Prescott D. Chadburn.

In the meantime, he had to jettison two complications: Darla and Siara.

Darla was easy enough. He could fire her or threaten to fire her if she didn't lighten up. To her he had made no promises that she could throw back in his face, and if she threatened to carry tales to Reba, he would tell the widow that Darla was merely a disgruntled employee trying to cause him trouble.

Siara was the bigger problem. He would miss her beauty and blind adoration; but, in truth, he was growing tired of her constant chatter about their getting married and bored with her limited sexual talents. However, he would have to dump her so that he wasn't around when she realized it. He didn't want to deal with the inevitable scene.

"Very well, dearest Siara," he said, sliding across the seat to take her into his arms. "I will tell Reba tonight. Then you and I must leave to avoid any repercussions that may arise."

"What kind of repercussions?"

"Reba will not go down without a fight, and you know how I loathe situations like that. It will be best for all concerned if you and I absent ourselves from the unpleasantness. We'll go to Reno. Divorces are easier to obtain in Reno."

Siara could scarcely believe that her dreams would be so easily realized. "But can you get away so soon?"

"I'm long overdue for a vacation. I'll arrange for someone to cover for me while we're away."

"I'll have to arrange for time off from the library, and I must tell Connor, too. I've been typing the final draft of our book, and now there will be a delay. He'll be disappointed with me."

"You spend a lot of time these days worrying about Connor. Maybe you should go to Reno with him."

"I worry about Connor like I worry about Jyn, Jae, and Dari. We've been close friends a long time."

"Don't tell him or anybody else where you're going or with whom or why. I don't want your name sullied by scandal. Just tell him you're taking a vacation."

After a moment's thoughtful silence, Siara pressed her face against his chest. He felt her tears soaking through his shirt.

"What's wrong now?" he asked impatiently. "I thought this was what you wanted."

"It is...it is...I'm not really sure why I'm crying."

"Maybe this will make you smile again," he said, guiding her hand into his pants.

When he had undressed them both and was settling himself between her legs, she asked, "Will I get an engagement ring, Prescott?"

He pushed himself into her. "Haven't I always given you everything you wanted?"

Tears sprang to her eyes again as he thrust himself into her.

Siara pressed her hand against her stomach. Sometimes she felt quivery when she talked to Connor. Nerves probably. Her situation with Prescott had caused her many a sleepless night, and Connor himself had been none too affable in the past few months. As one of the few who knew about her and Prescott, Connor had not approved of the relationship although he steadfastly refused to say anything to Siara about it.

Siara thought a romance of his own might bring back the tender smiles she missed so much. For a time he dated a lady professor in the English department, but the smiles did not return.

Siara didn't like the lady professor anyway.

And now she didn't like telling Connor what she had to tell him. Where an hour ago she had been so certain she was doing the right thing, now, as Connor's phone rang, she didn't feel so sure.

"Connor? It's Siara. Did I wake you up?"

"No, Siara, you didn't. I'm giving our final chapters one more look before I turn them over to you for typing."

He never calls me Stacks anymore, she thought. *I wish he'd call me Stacks.*

"About the typing, Connor...we don't have an official deadline, do we?"

"I'd like to have the manuscript in the mail by the end of June. Is there a problem?"

"I...I have to go away for a while..."

"Is something wrong?"

"No. At least I don't think so."

"Does this have anything to do with that lothario you've been seeing?"

"He's not a lothario."

"That's it, isn't it? You're going away with your degenerate boyfriend and leaving Sara T and me hanging."

Siara knew she should be angry with him, but as the volume of his voice increased, her lip began to tremble.

"I'm s-sorry. Really I am. It wasn't my intention to cause you a problem," she said.

"Siara, stop and think about what this man is doing to you…what he has been doing to you…"

"You're not going to talk me out of anything, so don't try." *Why do I suddenly wish he would try to talk me out of it?* "I'm sorry I've disappointed you. I'll try to make it up to you when we…when I return."

The anger in his voice was replaced by weary resignation. "Just be careful, and call me when you return. Don't worry about the manuscript. I'll hire a student to finish the typing."

"Don't do that!" Tears blinded her, and again she couldn't explain them. This was supposed to be a happy time. "I want to do the typing myself. Please…wait until I return. Can a…a week or two make that much difference?"

"Very well. I'll wait. It's our project…yours and mine…and it's special to me for that reason alone. An intrusion of a third party would be like a violation of some kind I guess."

"Thank you."

"I know you have packing to do…"

"I suppose I do…"

"Watch out for yourself," he whispered. "Good-bye…Stacks…"

Siara quickly replaced the receiver and ran up the stairs to her bedroom, where she buried her face in a pillow and sobbed until she was exhausted enough to fall asleep.

"Sari's home early tonight," Jordyn said as Luke turned off the Bronco. "That old bastard of hers must have got what he wanted early."

Luke dropped his arm around her shoulders and nuzzled her ear. "Aren't you being a little harsh on both of them?"

"My sister deserves better, and he deserves worse. I've never met the guy, but I hate him. I wish Connor had a little caveman in him…just enough for him to drag Siara away from that son of a bitch and show her what real love of a real man can do for her."

"Maybe I should try that with you."

"I could've used a little caveman from you tonight. By now I should know that when you say dinner and a movie, you mean dinner and a movie."

"Does every date have to end in bed?"

"Mine do. Ask around."

Luke remained silent though Jordyn could feel the anger building in him. Her life was safer if he thought there were still other men in her life.

"So," she said to soothe his ruffled feelings, "do I get a good-night kiss?"

"Will I have to stand in line?"

"Not tonight."

"How about tomorrow night?"

"What do you mean by that?"

"I have got a dentist appointment late tomorrow afternoon. Maybe we can have dinner afterward?"

"Will we see another movie afterward?"

"If you want to."

"I don't. What I want to do is f—"

Luke quickly placed his hand over her mouth. "We have an agreement about that word, Jordyn."

"It's stupid to be so squeamish about a word so basic to my well-being."

"Do we have a date or not?"

"That depends one whether we get to...to fuse after dinner." She smiled up at him. "You really owe me after shutting me down tonight."

Grinning and shaking his head, he cupped her face within his hands and kissed her soundly. "Okay, Jordyn...tomorrow night will be dinner and a motel."

She returned his kiss. "Do I get a preview of the coming attraction?"

He opened his door and jumped out. "Not tonight," he said, helping her out of the truck. "If I don't get out of here now, you'll get...fused in the truck, and you know how picky I am about the seats."

CHAPTER TWENTY-EIGHT

S iara's hand encircled the doorknob, but she couldn't talk herself into opening the door to Prescott's office. A week before she had been grief-stricken by his deceit. Now she was enraged…as much as she could be anyway.

His failure to meet her for their trip to Reno had hurt, but she solaced herself by supposing that he had ultimately been too honorable to break his marriage vows. She was sure this belief would be bolstered when he refused Jordyn's invitation.

But Jayme discovered that he lied about a wife, so he had to have lied about other things, too. He deserved whatever Jordyn had planned for him that night. Siara was certain now that he would have accepted her sister's offer after all.

Some fragment of vindictiveness guided her to his office after she left Jayme at the drugstore. The satisfaction to be gained by telling him to his face that he was a degenerate lothario would obliterate the disturbing image she had of his laughing at her naiveté.

Such bravado was not an inherent part of her personality, however, and she feared she would make a bigger fool of herself than he had already made of her. She would exit with dignity now and take great pleasure in witnessing what Jordyn had planned for him later.

Siara's hand fell away from the doorknob, and she turned her back on the office of Dr. Prescott D. Chadburn. She had told Jayme that she would walk to the college and call a taxi to take her home.

But there was someone she needed to talk to first.

He was working in the yard behind the house he rented from Dr. Cuthbertson's widow. Siara approached him hesitantly. They had spoken only briefly in the last week, barely long enough for Siara to tell him that she had decided not to go away after all. The manuscript was boxed and ready for the mail now. Frequently plagued by sleeplessness, she had typed all night to tire herself enough that she could sleep.

Connor's strong and confident handwriting had been a source of comfort to her. His astute observations and clever phrasing had brought smiles of appreciation to her lips. Even throughout the parts she herself had written, he had added personal marginal notes to express his opinions of her commentaries and his delight with her interpretations.

Though they had exchanged few words during these past few days, Connor had been, however unwittingly, her mainstay.

He had been her mainstay for a long, long time.

Standing behind him, Siara watched him work. During these few weeks between terms at the college, he was clearing away an accumulation of brush and debris in the tiny grove of trees that separated his house from Mrs. Cuthbertson's larger one. He was burning the litter in a huge barrel, and when the smoke from the fire billowed toward Siara, she was encapsulated within an acrid fog that stung her eyes and choked her into a fit of coughing.

Startled, Connor spun around. "Siara! I didn't know you were here. You should stand upwind, Stacks. It's rather breezy for burning today, but I wanted to get it finished while I have the time."

Taking her hand, he pulled her gently out of the path of the smoke. When he did not release her hand, Siara did not protest.

"I finished typing the manuscript this morning," she told him, her eyes downcast. "I thought perhaps you and I should mail it together."

"I agree." When she continued to avoid his eyes, he squeezed her hand. "Are you all right, Siara?"

"I will be. There's a little poison in my system I need to purge. Prescott and I aren't seeing each other anymore."

"I know."

She glanced up quickly, then away. "Jyn…you've been talking to Jyn…"

"No, I haven't been talking to Jordyn. I'm not so senseless…especially in matters that concern you…that I couldn't deduce what happened."

"I've been such a twiddling fool. That's hurting me more than finding out about Prescott. I guess that means I didn't love him as much as I thought I did."

"Infatuation can be an intense emotion. You had to experience its fugacity before you could realize the depth of true love."

For the first time, her eyes locked on his. "May I tell you something personal?"

"You know you can tell me anything."

"Walking over here, I thought seriously about what qualities I most admire in people. Prescott…as he really is…doesn't possess a single one of the qualities I listed. Then suddenly I realized there is a man who does truly embody all the qualities and values that are so important to me…and he's someone I cherish and enjoy spending time with. If I was a fool to canonize Prescott, I was a complete ninny for not recognizing earlier that you…you are an exceedingly special person to me."

He smiled faintly. "I know…like your father."

"Yes, like my father. But you're not my father. It took me a while to appreciate the difference and perceive the subsequent possibilities."

Connor laid a hand against her cheek. "I've been waiting a long time for that very revelation to come to you."

She covered his hand with hers. "What do we do about it?"

He drew Siara closer to him. "We get a bucket of water to douse this fire, and then you and I shall go inside for a talk that is long overdue…"

"It looks as though your roommates have all beat you home," Connor said as he parked his car behind the four cars already in the driveway…close enough to the road to be hidden by a cluster of trees.

Siara smiled sheepishly. "We have a big evening planned…though it seems so silly now."

Grinning, Connor skimmed his fingertip across her lips. "I'm sure Jordyn is looking forward to it. As a man I should try to dissuade you girls from your plans for the doctor, but I must admit that I appreciate the poetic justice of your scheme. The part of it I don't like is having to give you up for a while…until our lunch date tomorrow anyway."

"It seems strange, our having a real date. WONDERFULLY strange…like when you kissed me earlier."

"Is that a hint for me to kiss you again?"

When Siara smiled and nodded, Connor touched his lips to hers. As the intensity of their newly confessed emotions overwhelmed them, his kiss deepened and probed, and Siara yielded willingly to his exploration.

A dizzying wave of excitement coursed through her. Kissing had never been like this before. This was the kissing that dreams were made of…

"I love you, Stacks," Connor whispered into her hair.

Siara buried her face against his neck. "Connor, I—"

He touched a finger to her lips. "Don't say it until you're sure you feel it, sweetheart. Your emotions have been thoroughly disrupted during the past few days. For now it's enough for me to hope that you and I will really have a future together…as something more than mentor and protégé."

Siara stroked the tender flesh beneath his eyes. "You forgot your glasses. I thought you had to wear them all the time."

Connor grinned. "I was fitted for contact lenses two days ago."

"Contact lenses? Why? You've always maintained that contacts are for people with more vanity than good sense."

"I was becoming desperate. You always equated how I looked in my glasses with your memory of your father, so I decided to rid myself of the cursed things to see if I could attract your attention. Shall I go back to the glasses?"

"Either way you want. It will make no difference in how I feel about you now that I have regained my senses. You do have pretty eyes though."

"Pretty? Egad, I was striving for macho."

Siara brushed her finger over his lashes. "Pretty eyelashes, too. Like Bambi's. You have Bambi lashes, Connor."

Groaning, Connor immersed his face in the silkiness of her hair. "Now I'll have to wear sunglasses…the darker, the better."

Siara sighed happily as Connor's embrace tightened.

"I should be getting inside," she said finally, her voice tinged with regret. "Dari's cooking us a special dinner, and Jyn doesn't like to be kept waiting, especially when she has some kind of mischief planned. Why don't you stay, Connor? If not for the mischief, at least for dinner…"

"Tonight is strictly girls' night, my love. Any man intruding into Jordyn's plan right now could be risking death…or worse. But I will ask you to call me when your adventure is over."

"Are you wanting a thorough report on the evening's events?"

"No. I want to say good night to my lady."

He lifted her hand to his lips and kissed the back of it, then the palm. Then he held her away from him.

"Go inside now, Stacks," he said, his voice husky, "or I'll be taking you back home with me right now, and your roomies will be angry with both of us."

He kissed her lightly and climbed quickly out of the car. Siara took the hand he offered and slid out behind him.

"Call me," he said, squeezing her hand.

"I will."

"I love you."

Smiling, Siara squeezed his hand in response. She watched as he got into his car and backed out of the driveway. Slowly, thoughtfully, she turned and walked toward the house.

"Sari! Baby!"

Siara jerked her head up as Jordyn raced out of the house toward her.

"Where have you been, Baby?"

"Just walking for a while. Just walking…and talking…and getting my heart back on track…"

"Did you walk all the way from town?"

"No. Connor brought me home."

"You smell like smoke." Grabbing Siara's shoulders, Jordyn shook her gently. "Tell me why you smell like smoke."

"What's wrong with you, Jordyn?" Siara's twinstinct flashed an urgent message. "Something bad has happened."

Wrapping a protective arm around her sister, Jordyn led Siara toward the house where Jayme and Darica waited at the back door.

"It's Prescott," Jordyn told her quietly. "He's dead. Somebody…killed him."

Part III: Jayme McCray/1954-1984

CHAPTER ONE

Jim McCray set his daughter on the kitchen counter and handed her a plastic cup filled with raisins.

"Mommy isn't feeling good today, love," he told the child, who was already stuffing raisins into her mouth. "You must play quietly so that you won't wake Mommy up."

Jayme nodded her understanding. Though today was only her third birthday, she had played quietly so many times she knew no other way to play.

Rubbing a hand over his balding head, Jim closed his eyes and swallowed back a sudden lump of emotion that threatened to push the tears right out of his eyes. Some birthday his little girl was having. No party. No games. No balloons. No friends. Just a subdued gathering of grandparents, an uncle, two aunts…and a store-bought cake with a clown on it. A lopsided clown since Jim had hit that pothole on the way from the bakery.

"You're a good little girl, Jae," he said, picking her up and clutching her against him. "Some day Daddy will make it up to you, but for now you and your old man are going to have to work together to make things as easy for Mommy as we can."

Jayme dropped her empty plastic cup onto the floor. Its clattering across the linoleum sounded like machine gun fire in the quiet house.

"Sssshhhh…" Jayme pressed a finger against her lips and shook her head solemnly.

Hugging Jayme even more tightly, Jim fumbled his way into the cookie jar on top of the refrigerator.

"Here, love," he said, shoving a cookie into Jayme's hand and carrying her into the living room. "Gnaw on this while you look at your picture books. I'll be back to read you a story after I check in on Mommy. Daddy came home early today so he could spend some time with his birthday girl before everyone else showed up for supper."

Jayme smiled up at him and wrinkled her tiny nose as Jim set her on the floor amid her books. She stuck as much of the cookie as she could into her mouth and held it there as pushed aside several books in search of her favorite, *Snow White and the Seven Dwarfs*. As she turned the pages, her velvet brown eyes were huge and luminous with fascination even though she was looking at Dopey and Snow White upside down. Jim felt emotion tugging at his composure again. He pressed a kiss against her soft auburn curls and turned away quickly.

What awaited him at the end of the hallway would offer him no comfort.

He softened his footfalls automatically as he neared the door to the bedroom he had shared with his wife for the past six years.

Six years in this house together.

Five in the apartment above her uncle's ice cream parlor while they saved for the house.

A year's engagement until he was sure his job at the newspaper was permanent.

Three years as college sweethearts.

Fifteen years together.

And more often than not these days, she couldn't even remember his name.

Or her daughter's.

Or even that she had a daughter.

After all those barren years, the news of her pregnancy had come to them on the same day as the other news: Rosalie McCray had cancer.

If she had received the recommended radiation treatments in time, she might have escaped this long and agonizing journey into death. But the treatments had to be delayed until after the baby was born, of course. The only other alternative was unthinkable…though Jim would have forsaken his moral qualms had Rosalie elected to follow the doctor's advice to terminate the pregnancy.

"Terminate the pregnancy to save the mother's life," the doctor said to extenuate the unacceptability of abortion.

Rosalie responded to his hushed suggestion with no hesitation.

"Forget it, Doc," she said, squeezing Jim's hand so tightly that his wedding band cut into his finger. "Jim and I have been practicing for a long time. Now that we've finally perfected our technique, we want our reward."

Jayme Rose McCray was born seven months later, on a Saturday.

Rosalie began radiation treatments the following Monday. She received the treatments periodically over the next three years. Her life was not prolonged, but her dying was.

Jim opened the bedroom door and stepped quietly inside. His wife had become so emaciated that her frail form was barely discernible beneath the covers.

"She's had her bath," Rosalie's sister Ronna whispered to him. "I told her she could come to the party if she took a nap first. She thinks it's one of those frat parties from your college days though."

Jim grimaced and nodded. "Retreating to a less painful time. Her reliving the past eases her suffering more than the drugs."

"What can ease your suffering, Jim? Your whole life is spent working or taking care of Rosie. The only time you get out is to take her for her treatments. And poor little Jae must think the world ends at her backyard fence."

"What else can I do?" The anguish in his voice matched the helplessness in his eyes.

"You take that baby and get out now and then. Mother and I can sit with Rosie."

"I should be home with her. There's not that much time for us...for us to be together."

"She's happier in her memories. Maybe you would be, too. And think about that baby. She needs something normal in her life now, and where else is she going to get it if not from her daddy?"

"I know you're right, but I keep thinking that Jae and I will have years where Rosie and I may have no more than weeks or months."

"Jayme Rose is my sister's final gift to you. You are not abandoning Rosie by spending time with your daughter away from here. If Rosie had control of her mind, she'd tell you the same thing."

"Yes," he murmured. "Yes, she would."

He was overcome by an urge to lie on the bed beside his wife, to gather her into his arms and stroke away her misery and reassure her about his love her for. But, of course, that was impossible. Rosalie was much too frail, much too weak. And if she was in one of her foggy states where she did not recognize him, the perception of being handled by a strange man would traumatize her.

"Maybe Jae and I will drive over into St. Louis Saturday," Jim said finally. "Snow White is showing somewhere. Jae would like to see it I think. And she's never seen the Mississippi River...or a riverboat. If you can stay with Rosie on Saturday..."

"You bet I will," Ronna smiled.

* * *

Though doctors were surprised that her wasted body continued to function, Rosalie McCray hovered at the edge of death for another year. The radiation treatments were abandoned in favor of increasing doses of morphine when doctors finally acknowledged that they could not save her life. After consulting with Rosalie's parents and her sister, Jim did not press for continuation of treatment. His wife's illness had progressed past a point where hope was possible. The best he could do for her now was to let her go as peacefully and painlessly as possible.

Those last few days were not painless, however. Rosalie's body had become immune to the numbing effects of even mega doses of morphine, and the pain continued to claw and gnaw away within her. Soon the house was filled with her shrieks of torment. Relief came to her...and to those who could hear her...only when her agony caused her to lose consciousness. A sudden "for sale" sign in the yard of the McCrays' closest neighbors caused Jim no small amount of guilt although Mr. and Mrs. Yeager assured him that they were looking for a smaller place now that their last child was on his own. Their protests and assurances were too profuse to convince Jim, however.

Still, he rejected all suggestions to pack Rosalie off to a hospital. There was nothing to be gained by such a move. His wife should die in her own home, surrounded by those who loved her. A steady procession of relatives and nurses provided by the Cancer Society watched over the dying woman, who sometimes had to be strapped down as her mindless fits of pain caused her to plunge off the bed or to rip out handfuls of her hair.

A huge pair of velvet brown eyes watched the commotion. Though Jayme did not understand what was going on behind Mommy's closed door, she understood the rules. She must play quietly. She must not bother anyone who was busy with Mommy. And she must never go into Mommy's room unless Daddy took her.

Daddy never took her into Mommy's room anymore, though sometimes Jayme stood outside with her ear pressed against the door in hopes Mommy would call for her to come in. Sometimes the most awful sounds came from behind the door. Jayme was sure a monster was in there doing terrible things to Mommy. At night Jayme buried her head beneath pillows to make the sounds go away. During the day, Jim often found his daughter hiding in her closet when he came home from work.

"The monster was hurting Mommy again," she told him as he tried to calm her fears.

Jim had been using words to explain complicated events to the general public for almost fifteen years, but he couldn't explain this tragedy to his own daughter now.

"Don't worry about it, love," he finally told her. "It's not a monster. Mommy's sick and Mommy's hurting, and sometimes she has to…to cry out like that."

"Can't the doctor make her better, Daddy?"

"Not this time, love. Not this time."

He carried her into the kitchen and reached for the cookie jar. Though Jayme didn't really want a cookie, she took one anyway. Grown-ups were always giving her cookies.

"You're such a good little girl for us," Gran McCray would say, passing a cookie to Jayme.

"Such chubby little cheeks!" Grammy Gerber cried as she handed a cookie to Jayme. "We must make sure my Rosie's little girl stays strong and healthy."

"Here, kid. Eat these and stay out of my hair." Nurse Claudene would toss a handful of cookies toward Jayme, then ignore her for the rest of the shift.

Nurse Earla was nicer. "Let's take a cookie break while your mommy's sleeping, honey. You're such a precious little girl. Your mommy is very proud of you for being so quiet when she needs to rest."

Aunt Ronna would set the whole cookie jar on the floor by Jayme. "Poor child. Nothing but a bunch of grown-ups to keep you company, and we're not much fun, are we? Soon you'll be starting school, Jae, and things will be different."

School? Jayme chewed on her cookie thoughtfully. Maybe at school she could learn how to keep that monster away from Mommy.

* * *

Jayme pressed her ear against Mommy's bedroom door.

Nurse Claudene was drinking coffee in the kitchen while Jayme's mother slept. Jayme was glad the monster was leaving Mommy alone today.

"Jayme?"

Jayme's eyes widened. The monster was calling her name.

"Jayme…my baby…"

No, not the monster. Jayme's mommy. Mommy was calling for her.

Jayme reached up for the doorknob. But Daddy didn't want her going into Mommy's room without him.

"Jayme…Jayme Rose…"

But if Mommy was calling for her, Daddy wouldn't be mad, would he?

Jayme peered down the hallway and then cautiously opened the door.

"Mommy?" she whispered.

"Jayme…my baby Jae…"

Jayme tiptoed across the room to the bed. The face that turned toward her stunned her into immobility. Was this Mommy or the monster?

"Mommy?" Jayme gulped and backed away from the bed. "Is that you, Mommy?"

"My baby…"

The monster had swallowed Mommy. Mommy's voice was coming from the monster's mouth.

"Jayme Rose…"

When a bony arm snaked out from beneath the covers, Jayme pressed herself against the wall.

"Jayme…my baby…Jayme Rose…"

Jayme blinked in surprise. There was a tear in the monster's eye. The monster was crying.

"My baby Jae…"

Those weren't monster eyes. Those were Mommy eyes.

Jayme edged toward the bed. "Don't cry, Mommy. I won't let the monster hurt you anymore."

She climbed onto the bed beside her mother. Jim found them there together an hour later.

Jayme was asleep, her head pillowed on her mother's chest.

Rosalie was dead.

On her face was something Jim had thought he would never see again: his Rosie's smile.

CHAPTER TWO

Sitting quietly at the kitchen table, Jayme listened to her daddy and Aunt Ronna talk in the living room. Aunt Ronna had taken her shopping that day…for school clothes…and Daddy was pretending to be interested in all the dresses, slips, and socks. Grinning, Jayme hid her face behind her cookie so that Daddy wouldn't see her grin. His feelings would be hurt if he saw her grinning at him. She knew he'd rather be watching the baseball game than looking at a bunch of dresses, but she felt good knowing that he was pretending to be interested.

"We could have a problem," Aunt Ronna was saying. "I didn't really notice it until today when we were trying to fit her, but Jae is quite the little butterball."

"That's a problem? After all that we've gone through, you're going to worry about a little baby fat?"

"Today's baby fat is tomorrow's blubber."

"Oh, for Pete's sake…she'll outgrow it when she starts school and has more to do than look at her books and watch TV all the time. She hasn't had many chances to run and play and yell her head off like most kids, you know."

"Just the same, maybe we shouldn't be giving her so many cookies. She's got a cookie in her mouth every minute of the day."

Jayme laid down her cookie and folded her hands in her lap.

"And whose fault is that?" Jim asked. "She can't reach the top of the refrigerator."

"I know, I know. I'm as much to blame as anyone else, trying to offer her comfort in a cookie."

"You're making a mountain out of a molehill. She'll slim down when she gets busy with school and starts getting some height on her."

Jayme picked up her cookie and stuffed it into her mouth.

"I hope you're right," Aunt Ronna said. "Children can be so cruel about their…heavyset classmates. Jae doesn't need more heartache in her life."

* * *

"You're fat!"

Jayme frowned and glared at the little boy staring back at her through the fence.

"Am not!" she retorted. "Aunt Ronna says I'm heavyset. That's different."

"Do you play football?" the boy asked hopefully.

"Course not. Girls don't play football."

"You should. You'd be a good linebacker. I play peewee football. Baseball, too. I'm very good."

Jayme was unimpressed. "Why are you standing in Mrs. Yeager's tulip bed? She won't like that."

"This ain't no bed, stupid girl."

"Mrs. Yeager plants her tulips there." Jayme dug in her pocket for some raisins. Aunt Ronna gave her raisins now instead of cookies.

"There ain't no tulips here now," the boy sniffed, "and there ain't no Mrs. Yeager. We live here now, so this here tulip place belongs to me, and I can stand in it if I wanna."

Jayme tilted her head sideways and studied the boy carefully. He was very nice to look at, but...

"You talk funny," she decided finally.

"Ain't nothin' wrong with the way I talk, stupid girl."

"I'm not a stupid girl..." Jayme threw a handful of raisins through the fence into his face.

He countered by hurling two handfuls of dirt at her. Soon the air was filled with the dust of a dirt war. Jayme had never had so much fun, nor had she laughed and giggled and shouted so much. When she finally went into the house, her face was glowing with excitement even through a layer of perspiration-streaked grime.

"What in the world have you been doing, Jayme Rose?" Jim asked, kneeling for a better look at this curiosity beaming up at him.

"I have a new friend, Daddy," Jayme told him breathlessly. "He lives next door now...and you know what, Daddy? We'll be in kindygarden together...and you know what else, Daddy? His name is Harlan Oakes."

* * *

From the pitching mound, Jayme studied an imaginary catcher behind the plate where Harlan awaited her next pitch. They came to the Little League park almost every afternoon during the summer so that Jayme could pitch batting practice to Harlan. After their bucketful of baseballs was empty, Harlan rested in the shade of the dugout while Jayme scampered around the outfield gathering the balls he had hit. Because he was usually ready to resume his practice by the time Jayme finished, she herself received no break. By the end of the afternoon, her clothing was soaked with perspiration and her face was darkly flushed with exertion. Harlan was scornful whenever she suggested that she needed a break, too.

"You need to exercise to melt some of that fat off you," he would tell her as he stepped up to the plate. "Now throw me somethin' low and inside. I been havin' troubles there."

Jayme pretended that she was Sandy Koufax. No...Koufax was a southpaw. She'd have to be Bob Gibson. Bob Gibson would pitch to Harlan Oakes. Harlan Oakes, who already had fans of Applewood talking about their local boy making the Majors some day. And Harlan was only ten years old.

Jayme was certain Harlan would make the Majors. After following him around for five years, she had absorbed his passions for football and baseball. Actually she had become more knowledgeable than he simply because she was smarter than he. Harlan relied on animal instinct and physical ability. He let his coaches do his thinking for him. His coaches and Jayme, who was becoming an adequate neighborhood center and an above-average sandlot catcher. She had power at the plate, too.

"'Cause you got so much weight behind your swing," Harlan told her once as he slapped her on the back so hard she tumbled off the dugout bench. Harlan and the other boys laughed when she fell, especially when Harlan said she looked like a baby elephant wallowing in the dirt.

Jayme didn't tell them how much her finger hurt after she fell on her hand. Later, however, when she returned home, her father rushed her to the hospital emergency room. The finger was broken so badly that most of her hand was put into a cast.

"Good thing it ain't your pitchin' hand," Harlan said when he saw her. "You can still pitch battin' practice."

Jayme pitched for him the very next afternoon. She did everything he asked her to because she wanted to be with Harlan more than she wanted to be with anyone else, except her father. Young ladies in 1961 could not participate in the boys' athletic leagues, but Jayme was always available to help with practices, fill water bottles, or keep stat books…anything that enabled her to be close to Harlan.

"Keep your mind on what you're doin'!" he yelled at her now. "You almost hit me in the kneecaps!"

"You said low and inside."

"Not that much inside, stupid girl," he muttered, pounding the plate with his bat.

Jayme smiled. She didn't mind so much when he called her a stupid girl. That was about the only time he recognized that she wasn't just another one of the guys.

* * *

"You'll come to the game to root for me, won't you, Jayme?"

In her daydreams, Harlan always called her "Jayme." Though she was okay with "Jae," Harlan barked it with the same brusque arrogance he displayed on the fields of battle where he paraded his athletic prowess to an adoring public.

"Jayme" was softer…more pleasant…more romantic…

"Would you go to the dance with me after the game, Jayme?

"You're prettier than other girls in eighth grade, Jayme…even Trina Galena."

"Would you wear my football pendant, Jayme? That means we're goin' steady, y'know.

"Hey, Jae! Coach says he wants to go over Tuesday's stats with you before you set out towels and water bottles. Did you mess up the numbers or somethin'?"

Jayme directed what she hoped was a scathing look at him. "I do not mess up stats, Harlan."

"Geez, Jae, you don't need to bite my friggin' head off. You on the rag or somethin'?"

"Must you be so crass?"

"Aw, Jae…lighten up. If you was a real girl, I'd think you was gonna be a bitch when you grow up. Here…maybe this will make you be nicer to me." He whacked her over the head with a Hershey bar. "Ma packed me an extra one for lunch, and I never ate it."

Jayme accepted the candy gratefully, not because she wanted it, but because Harlan gave it to her.

"Thanks," she said as he jogged off for practice. "I'll treasure it always."

I really and truly will, she thought as she slipped the candy bar carefully into her jacket pocket. *When I get home, I'll put it in the freezer and keep it forever and ever…*

* * *

"If you're not going to dance with me," Jayme asked, "why did you ask me to come to the dance with you?"

The euphoria that had begun that afternoon when Harlan made the dream-come-true suggestion had quickly dissipated when they arrived at the junior high gymnasium.

"Pop said to ax if you needed a ride. He didn't say I had to dance with you, too."

"Did you ever think that dancing with me might be fun?"

"My arms ain't long 'nough to go 'round you, Jae. And you can't dance fast. All that fat jigglin' would cause an earthquake."

He chortled at his own humor and left Jayme sitting alone in the row of chairs that lined the wall. A few minutes later, Jayme saw him dancing with Mary Kay Fahrnhorst, one of the girls from Trina Galena's select group of aspiring debutantes.

Jayme was embarrassed to be sitting alone while everyone else was either dancing or socializing. Those girls who had no dance partners gossiped about those who did…or about Jayme, who was acutely aware of both the smirks and the sympathetic smiles directed her way. If getting up to leave wouldn't have made her plight more conspicuous, she would have eased her bulk out of this nightmare. Instead, she sat with her hands clasped tightly in her lap as she prayed for a merciful miracle that would make her invisible.

"Would you like to dance, Jayme?"

Startled, Jayme snapped her head up. The boy standing in front of her was Oliver Denton, another eighth grade victim of unkind jokes and behind-the-hand snickers because of his size. Where Jayme was tagged with phrases like "Tubs" and "Triple Belly," Ollie was honored with "Runt" and "Pint." In actuality, Ollie was a brilliant student. Though his classmates mocked him, they frequently consulted with him about their homework. He fulfilled their requests with the same stoicism with which he accepted their teasing. Even though Jayme admired his indifference to social acceptance, she quickly realized that the sight of her and Ollie dancing together would cause an orgy of laughter.

"You don't want to dance with me, Ollie," she told him finally. "I'm not exactly light on my feet."

"So? I don't dance well either."

"Then why bother to ask? Did I look that pitiful sitting here alone?"

"I enjoy talking to you. You're the only girl in our class who can carry on an intelligent conversation."

"Oh…well…thank you." Jayme studied the rafters of the gymnasium. "Do we talk enough for you to think that way?"

"You and I are the only ones who will talk in civics when Mrs. McAllister asks her opinion questions. That's like having conversations. You don't want to dance with me, do you?"

"It's not that I don't want to dance with you, Ollie. The thing is I don't dance well. In fact, I've never danced at all. I don't even watch *American Bandstand.* And you have to admit that we'd make a pretty funny-looking couple."

"Then may I sit here with you for a while? We can talk."

"Are you feeling sorry for me?"

He sat down in the chair next to Jayme and folded his arms across his chest. "The only time I feel sorry for you is when you get cow-eyed over Harlan. That's the only time I question your intelligence."

"Cow-eyed!" Jayme squeaked. "I do not get cow-eyed over Harlan. He's immature, egotistical, rude, thoughtless, ill-mannered, and stupid."

"You keep looking around the gym to see who he's with."

"I take a sisterly interest in him. After all, we've been neighbors a long time."

Ollie shook his head. "You might be fooling yourself, but you're not fooling me…or anyone else for that matter…except Harlan."

"Why are we even talking about this? I thought you wanted intelligent conversation."

"I was hoping we could continue that little debate on Vietnam we started up in civics."

"Are you serious?"

"Why are you so surprised?"

"We're at a DANCE."

"I hate dances. Mother makes me come so that I'll learn to function properly in society. Mostly I sit in a corner somewhere and think about how silly most of my classmates are. Except you. This is the first time you've ever come to one of these things, isn't it? I would've noticed if you'd been here before."

"An elephant isn't easy to overlook."

"I don't think thoughts like that about you, and you shouldn't either."

"I've heard all the it's-what's-inside pep talks from my dad. The boys still go for the empty-headed gigglers, no matter what anyone says."

"I'm here with you now because you're interesting to talk to, but if it helps any, you do have pretty eyes…when you're not mooning over Harlan."

At the mention of Harlan's name, Jayme scanned the dance floor for some sign of his muscular, curly-headed form. Maybe he would be jealous if he saw her talking to another boy.

Harlan? Jealous of Ollie Denton? Jayme smiled at the folly of such speculation.

"You have a pretty smile, too," Ollie told her.

Groaning, Jayme slid down in her seat. *Right words, wrong mouth…*

However, she and Ollie continued their debate on Vietnam, and Jayme didn't feel as if she were on public display for the rest of the evening. Still, when Ollie asked her to the dance for next Friday, she declined, saying she and her father had dinner plans with her Aunt Ronna then.

She lied.

Because she had overheard Trina Galena and Mary Kay Fahrnhorst in the washroom…just as they intended.

"Can you even imagine them doing IT?" Trina asked. "Poor Runt would be squished into a pancake if he was on bottom."

Mary Kay giggled. "His thing would be too little to get to her through all the fat anyway. Trina, can you keep a secret?"

"May the Beatles break up if I don't."

"Harlan let me touch his thing."

"Are you serious? When? Where?"

"Tonight…up on the stage behind the curtains."

"What was it like?"

"Big and hard…and kinda scary, but I acted like I really liked it. And you know something else…Harlan says he's already done IT several times…with a high school girl."

"Do you think he's lying?"

"He's too dumb to lie," Mary Kay said. "And he wants to do IT with me."

"Did you say yes?"

"Of course! I'll be the first girl in the eighth grade to do IT…and you can be the second, Trina. You can do IT with Harlan, too. Won't everyone be soooo jealous?"

Mary Kay Fahrnhorst was wearing Harlan's football pendant the very next day.

Two weeks later, the much-traveled necklace was hung around the slender neck of Trina Galena.

CHAPTER THREE

With swaggering impertinence, winter trespassed into spring. As the icy wind penetrated through Jayme's heavy coat, she shivered and tried to close her collar more securely around her neck. Her ears were numb, and her nose dripped in protest to the prolonged exposure. Sniffing rhythmically, Jayme tried to blow some warmth into her fingers. She couldn't write neatly with her gloves on, and she prided herself on a neat and accurate stat book for the Applewood Community High School Wildcats. Her immediate access to the players and their stats, as well as her inherited talent for journalism had earned her the position of sports editor on the school newspaper though she was only a junior. Usually only seniors could be editors.

Harlan, of course, was not impressed with her accomplishments though he always lobbied her for publicity. He needed all the clippings he could get since he had a legitimate shot at the Major Leagues. Jayme was showing no real partiality by writing about him so much for both the school paper and her father's *Sentinel*. Harlan WAS the greatest athlete to pass through Applewood's athletic department.

*Though Harlan was scouted in both football and baseball, he decided that baseball was his easiest tic*ket to fame and fortune. A blind, club-footed orangutan could field his position better, but managers overlooked a lot of transgressions if a player could ring up thirty or more round-trippers a year.

He'll make it, Jayme thought as Harlan stepped up to the plate, *and he'll think back to the old days when I was the only fan sitting here on splinters and freezing to death just to watch him play. Then he'll realize I am his only true love...*

Yeah, he'll do that the same day I squeeze my blubber into a bikini and walk around the city pool.

Jayme would stand a better chance of getting him to ask her to the junior-senior prom.

Hmmm...the prom.

Though Harlan was the escort for the junior attendant, he was actually between girlfriends. Most of his old stand-bys were dating college men now, and the girls who were developing brains had lost interest in him. Except for Jayme, who was thinking that with a little cunning and mental manipulation, she could convince Harlan to take the Girl Next Door to prom.

Yeah...sure...Harlan doesn't have a mental to manipulate.

"Hey, Jae! Coach says to wrap this blanket around yourself. You're turning blue, and that's not one of our school colors."

Jayme smiled her thanks at the player who scaled the bleachers and draped the blanket around her. If only Harlan had been the one to bring it to her. But he would never demean himself that way. He was the star. She was his lackey…flunky…servant…slave. Where most of the other boys had matured enough to appreciate her knowledge and devotion, Harlan remained Harlan.

If I had a brain in my head, I'd accept Ollie's invitation, she thought, hugging the blanket around her. *At least he's taller than I am now.*

But hope continued to spring eternal.

Someday Harlan would come to his senses. Someday. And Jayme must be ready for him when he did.

"Do you need a ride home, Harlan?" Jayme asked as she walked into the school with the team.

"Yeah, I need a ride," he said as he began to undress even before he reached the locker room. "Even if it's in a VW."

"Someday I'll have a Camaro," she said, averting her eyes as he peeled off his undershirt. "But until then, there's nothing wrong with my Bug."

"It ain't the car for you, Jae. It must fit you like a tight girdle."

Jayme clutched her notebooks against her chest and said nothing.

"Aw, you ain't gonna rag up on me, are you, Jae? I was only teasin'."

"Sometimes you hurt with your teasing."

"I don't mean to."

He was unbuckling his belt and unzipping his pants just as he and Jae reached the door.

Jayme poked her finger into his stomach. "You shouldn't be taking your clothes off in a public gym in front of a lady."

"I don't, Jae. Not never. I swear!"

She clenched her teeth. "One of these days, Harlan—"

He was impervious to her irritation. "Don't forget to say in the paper that I got five ribbies today. And that homer I hit…it must've went four hundred feet."

"Two-fifty tops."

"Can't you say four hundred anyway?"

"Even Hank Aaron and Willie Stargell rarely hit 'em that far. If I start exaggerating so blatantly, my credibility with the reading public will deteriorate…a reading public which includes scouts you want to impress."

"Huh?"

"If I pump your stats up in my stories, the big boys will be suspicious and never believe anything else I write about you."

"I wish you'd talk normal so's I can understand things."

"I am talking normal. You're the one who thinks English is a foreign language." Tipping her head sideways, Jayme studied him for a few moments before she added, "Let's see whether you can understand this. I want you to take me to prom."

"Huh?"

"I want you to take me to prom. You don't have a date. I don't have a date. We should go together."

"Do they have a tux big enough to fit you?" he asked doubtfully.

"You'll wear the tux, Sport. I'll wear a formal."

"A formal? You mean like a girl?"

"I am a girl, Harlan."

He scratched his head. "Sometimes I forget. You're just like a regular fella. Now don't go raggin' up. I meant that nice. Me and you's been buddies for a long time, and by now you're just about my best buddy."

Jayme's heart swelled with emotion at this unexpected confession. "Then...then you'll take me to prom? You in the tux, me in the formal?"

"Can we take your car? Pop makes me mow the grass or clean out the garage if I want to borrow his."

"We can take my Bug."

Harlan considered his options. Going with Jae would be as good as going stag. He could spread himself around a lot of girls instead of being stuck with only one.

"It's a deal," he said finally, extending his hand to her.

Laughing, Jayme shook his hand.

She was going to prom with Harlan Oakes.

With three weeks until prom, Jayme was filled with conflicting emotions. Though she lacked any close girlfriends in whom she could confide, she ached to tell someone at school of her forthcoming date with Harlan. However, her common sense maintained her silence. Harlan was keeping quiet about their date, and she must do the same. If anyone were to tease him about being stuck with Jayme McCray, he would change his mind about taking her.

Keeping her mouth shut wasn't easy. Girls like Trina and Mary Kay liked to smile wickedly and ask Jayme who was taking her to prom. This year Jayme smiled just as wickedly and replied, "You'll just have to wait to see."

She would save her triumph for the night she walked into the decorated gym with her arm linked intimately with the arm of Harlan Oakes. What a sight they would make! Harlan supremely handsome in his black tie and tux; she, in her sage green formal with delicate touches of mauve.

The trouble was that finding such a dress in Jayme's size was impossible. The dresses that fit her were in styles that were too mature for a high school prom...unless she were one of the chaperones.

"I'd have just as much luck raiding the closets in an old folks' home!" she wailed to her Aunt Ronna at the end of a long, unsuccessful shopping trip.

"Calm down, dear. We'll find something suitable."

"I want a dress that's more than 'something suitable.' This is PROM, and I'm going with HARLAN."

Jim cleared his throat as he greeted his daughter and sister-in-law at the kitchen door. "Are men allowed into this conversation? I seem to detect a problem brewing here."

"You told me I could have any dress I want, Daddy, but I can't find it!" Jayme's eyes were shadowed with all the anguish that accompanies any major tragedy.

"Maybe you haven't looked in enough stores?"

"We've looked at hundreds of lovely dresses in dozens of shops," Ronna told him, " but we're faced with a slight problem…"

"Oh?" Jim looked expectantly at Ronna and Jayme as he reached for the cookie jar on top of the refrigerator. "Didn't I give you enough money?"

"You gave us plenty of money." Ronna shifted uncomfortably. "The problem is that Jae…Jae is…Jae needs to…"

Jayme shook her head when her father offered her a cookie. "What Aunt Ronna is too polite to say in front of me is that I am too fat to fit any dresses I like. I'm a size nine psyche in a size eighteen body."

"You're not fat, Jayme Rose. Women should have some meat on their bones."

"Let's face it, Daddy. I have enough meat to stock twenty freezers."

"Nonsense. You're a beautiful girl, and Harlan is damn lucky you accepted his invitation."

"It was more like he agreed to my suggestion."

"Which is the smartest thing that boy has ever done. I swear someone dropped him on his head during his formative years. I wish you had accepted Oliver's invitation, Jae. There's the kind of boy a father wants his daughter to go out with."

"The problem is my dress, not my date, Daddy."

"That, love, is YOUR opinion," he said, kissing the top of her head. "Do you know what kind of dress you want?"

"I have a perfect idea. That's why I'm so frustrated about not finding it."

"Then we'll have someone make the dress for you." Jim smiled at his sister-in-law, who was instantly horrified.

"I don't even own a sewing machine, Jim!"

"Don't panic, Ronna. I wasn't thinking of you. But what about that friend of yours, that widow you're always trying to fix me up with. Doesn't she sew things for other people?"

"She's swamped with prom orders already."

"Won't she fit Jae's dress in if you ask her as a favor?"

"Probably. Of course, you could ask her yourself over dinner."

"Can't I pay her extra for her trouble instead?"

"She's none too cheap as it is."

"I'll pay what I have to pay to get Jae the dress she wants…"

Jayme clutched her father's hand. "No, Daddy. You just bought me the Bug for my birthday."

"Hush, love," he said, touching a finger to her nose. "If ever a daughter deserved to be spoiled, it's you…"

* * *

"Do you mind if I sit here?"

Jayme jerked her head up in surprise. No one ever came to talk to her during games. Not that everyone was so considerate about her need to concentrate. None of the girls who attended the baseball games cared to chat with her, and the boys…with whom she could communicate…were busy playing. Except Ollie. But Ollie had an aversion to sports.

However, the new girl in school must be a fan.

"No, I don't mind," Jayme said finally, "but I'm not very good company during a game. I keep the book."

"So that's why you're sitting all the way up here." The girl's voice was tinged with magnolia blossoms.

"I get a better look at the game from the top." Jayme managed a brief smile. "And the bleachers aren't so splintered up here."

Giggling, the girl seated herself beside Jayme. "Do those prissy-missies down there know that?"

"Prissy-missies?" Jayme stared at the girls flocked on the lower bleachers. "You mean Trina and her pack?"

"Oh, I'm sorry." The girl covered her face with her hands. "They're your friends, of course."

"A few a dim maybe," Jayme admitted. "Most are just classmates."

"I'd rather be your friend than just your classmate, Jayme."

"How do you know my name?" Jayme asked, surveying the girl's long blond hair and slender figure doubtfully.

"I heard Mr. Rocosi call you that in history today. I'm in your class."

"I remember seeing you, but I don't remember your name."

"Hanni…Hanni Beaufort. My daddy was just transferred here from Biloxi."

"Well…welcome to Applewood…Hanni." Jayme hurried to record a rally she had fallen behind on…a rally begun by Harlan's double. Jayme drew little stars by his name to remind herself to use him as the lead in her story…like she needed a reminder.

Hanni peered over her shoulder. "You like that boy, don't you?"

Jayme's face flamed with embarrassment. "We're just neighbors."

"I saw you helping him with his math over lunch period."

"I help any of the boys if they need it. Coach will bench them if they aren't passing all their classes. Even Harlan. And keeping Harlan even at a D level is a challenge."

"You're a good friend, Jayme. I hope you will be mine, too. I feel so lonely without a friend to tell my secrets to."

"I feel like that sometimes, too," Jayme admitted, surprised that she had something in common with a girl like Hanni.

"Then we'll be each others' best friends, and I'll feel better about leaving all my friends back in Biloxi. Maybe I can stay at your house tonight so that we can get to know each other better? I'd ask you to stay with me, but our house is still a mess from moving."

"I'll have to check with Daddy, but I'm sure he'll say okay since it's not a school night." Jayme blinked her eyes, totally bewildered by her sudden rush of good fortune. A date with Harlan, a dream dress for prom, and now a best girlfriend, too.

"Great! Maybe we can go to a movie...or cruise around town? You do have a car, don't you? What does everyone do on Friday nights here? That cute boy just hit a ball into the parking lot. Shouldn't you be writing that down?"

Jayme quickly learned that being Hanni Beaufort's best friend involved a lot of listening. The new girl chattered incessantly from the moment she first entered the McCray household. Bashful on this occasion of having a girlfriend to talk to, Jayme was content to listen...and listen...and listen...at least until she was sure what being a best girlfriend was all about.

She felt overly awkward and bulky sitting beside the diminutive Southern belle though Hanni appeared refreshingly oblivious to Jayme's amplitude. Eventually Jayme relaxed enough to venture some of her own personal history and observations. When Hanni, surprisingly, listened just as enthusiastically as she had been talking, Jayme wondered whether she at last had someone her own age in whom she could confide. Hanni seemed receptive to shared confidences.

"I'm going to tell you one of my deepest, darkest secrets," she said in a hushed voice, "one hardly anyone else knows..."

"What is it?" Jayme breathed, thrilled to be so trusted.

Hanni paused for dramatic effect. "My real name isn't Hanni," she whispered finally. "It's Hannabelle Mayline, and everyone in Biloxi calls me Hanna Maye. I absolutely hate it, but now that I'm a Yankee, I want to be just plain Hanni. Now it's your turn to tell me a secret."

"I don't have any secrets, Hanni."

Hanni pointed to Jayme's bulletin board, where Jayme had stapled photographs and newspaper pictures of Harlan. "You don't?"

Color rushed to Jayme's face. "That's no secret," she admitted finally. "EVERYONE knows how I feel about Harlan, except Harlan. He's dumber than dirt about a lot of things...most things...EVERYthing actually."

"You seem close to all the ball players. Do you go out with many of them?"

Jayme laughed. "I'm not exactly the type to inspire their interest in that way, Hanni...though I'm flattered that you asked."

"But you've been places with Harlan, haven't you? He's the best looking boy on the team."

"He and his dad go with Daddy and me to a lot of ball games in St. Louis…"

"I mean a date, silly."

"Not exactly…but…but…Hanni, I DO have a secret I can tell you, but you have to swear not to tell anyone."

Hanni jumped onto the bed and bounced with curiosity. "I swear, I swear, I SWEAR! Tell me, tell me, TELL ME!

"Harlan's taking me to prom." Jayme's lip trembled from the thrill of revealing such exquisite news.

"Prom?" Hanni squealed. "Wow! But why are you keeping it secret? If I was going with the best-looking boy in school, I'd be telling EVERYBODY, especially the prissy-missies."

"Harlan didn't exactly ask me. I knew he didn't have a date yet, so I kinda talked him into taking me. The thing is, with Harlan nothing's a sure thing, and I'm afraid to say anything to anyone. Just one person teasing him even a little bit could make him change his mind. He tends to be pretty fickle."

Hanni was dumfounded. "And you want to go to prom with someone like that?"

"I'd go anywhere, anytime, and for any reason to be with Harlan," Jayme said earnestly.

Hanni nodded knowingly. "You're in love, my new friend. So why aren't you with him tonight?"

"Be serious, Hanni. Look at me. Do I look like someone Harlan Oakes would want to spend his prime dating time with? I'm lucky I'm getting prom night."

Hanni draped an arm around Jayme's shoulders. "Lucky for you I got here when I did. Let Miss Hanni fix things for you. Does Harlan have a date tonight?"

"No. He said he was going to pick up something on the cruising route. Crude, but that's Harlan."

"Call him and ask him to go cruising with us tonight."

"I can't do that! It's so…so obvious."

"To a dummy like Harlan? Use me as your excuse. Tell him I want to see what action this town has, and you don't know exactly what to show me. He'll believe that."

"But he might get the wrong idea about you. He'll think you're a…a prissy-missy."

"I'll take my chances if it will help you. And maybe you can help me back?"

"If I can…"

"I'm the new girl in town, and prom's only two weeks away. I want to go so bad, but all the boys must be taken by now. Since you know so many of them, maybe you can see if one is available to take me?"

"Sure! I'll ask around this weekend. If worse comes to worst, maybe Ollie can take you. He's not the best looking boy in school, but he's the smartest and most polite."

Hanni flopped back on the bed. "I'm so relieved. I was afraid I'd be a wallflower on prom night."

"You could never be a wallflower, Hanni. You're too pretty."

Nodding her agreement, Hanni sat up and passed the phone to Jayme. "Call Harlan now," she ordered. "Let's get this show on the road…"

The quivering anticipation that had settled in Jayme when Harlan agreed to ride around town with them was soon diluted by a vague uneasiness. Hanni had cleverly manipulated the seating arrangement so that Harlan was sitting in front with Jayme. "A big, strong man like you would be cramped in this itty-bitty back seat," Hanni had told him. However, Jayme knew that much of Harlan's interest remained in the back seat anyway.

Hanni, of course, dominated the conversation, prattling in a soft Southern drawl that enthralled Harlan. Jayme could think of nothing to contribute that was not in some way related to sports, and tonight she wanted to be more to Harlan than a buddy with whom he could talk baseball. Any profundities she did render were totally beyond his understanding.

Poor Harlan, she thought with no real sympathy. *It's difficult for him to carry on a conversation when his tongue is dragging the floor.*

Hanni seemed unaware of Harlan's salacious adoration.

However, before the evening was over, she had edged across the back seat so that she was sitting directly behind Harlan. Then she was leaning forward to rest her pretty chin on the back of Harlan's seat.

Jayme was neither so blind nor so busy driving that she failed to notice that her passengers were holding hands, on the side away from her, between the passenger seat and the door.

Later Hanni will give me a good explanation for what's going on, Jayme reasoned.

Nevertheless, later, as the girls lay side by side in Jayme's large canopy bed, Jayme could think of no way to broach the questions that festered in her mind. When Hanni continued to bubble with questions and comments, none of which concerned Harlan in any way, Jayme's apprehensions ebbed. Perhaps the cozy camaraderie between Harlan and Hanni had been the result of her insecurity-fueled imagination?

I'm a real idiot, Jayme finally decided. *Whatever Hanni was doing, she was doing to help me.*

Like a music box winding down, Hanni's chatter dwindled to a few drowsy words. And then to silence.

A smile danced on Jayme's face as she drifted to sleep with thoughts of Harlan that were becoming dreams of Harlan. She barely noticed that Hanni was climbing carefully out of bed.

"Where are you going?" Jayme murmured, refusing to completely leave the sleepy world where Harlan held her in his arms.

"Bathroom," Hanni whispered. "Go back to sleep."

Back to sleep. Back to Harlan. Back to where Jayme could not see her new best friend leave the house to meet the boy next door.

* * *

Over the next few days, Hanni barely mentioned Harlan's name, and Jayme was afraid to. Still, the three of them...Jayme, Harlan, and Hanni...became an inseparable trio. They went to school together. They ate together. They cruised together. They studied together. And Hanni sat with Jayme while Harlan played ball.

The prissy-missies were perplexed. Those girls whom Jayme counted as her friends looked at her with renewed sympathy.

"Miss Southern Fried is using you, Jae," Steffie, one of the friendly girls, tried to tell her.

"Hanni's helping me be with Harlan," Jayme replied evenly.

Steffie shook her head, patted Jayme on the shoulder, and walked away without saying another word.

Since Hanni was being so helpful, Jayme felt guilty about delivering some disappointing news to her new friend: all of the boys she talked to already had prom dates. Hanni, however, did not seem overly distraught about the news.

"My daddy says these things have a way of working themselves out," Hanni said wisely, picking at the splinters in the bleachers. "And I always believe what my daddy tells me."

"What about Ollie? He hasn't asked anyone yet."

"He can go with us, I guess. Oh my...look at the time. I promised Mama I'd be home early to go shopping. You and Harlan have a good time without me tonight, y'hear?"

Jayme immediately forgot about the "with us" part of Hanni's declaration.

"What do you mean? Harlan? Without you?" Jayme asked.

"I can't very well go with you tonight if I have to be with my mama, can I?"

"You mean that Harlan and I will be alone...together?"

"You've been alone with him before. What's the big deal?"

"But alone...together...on a Friday night? Just like real people?"

"Isn't that what you've been wanting?"

"Well...yes..."

"Then go have yourself a good time. You can't use training wheels forever."

"Training wheels?" Jayme asked.

"I've been your training wheels all week, but tonight you're on your own. Go for it!"

"Does Harlan know that you won't be with us tonight?"

Hanni picked at the bleachers more persistently. "He knows."

"And he still wants to go?"

"He does."

"Have you been planning this…to do this for me…all week?"

"Well now, what do you think? But I've got to tell you, Jae, if you blow your chance tonight, there's not much else I can do."

"Thank you, Hanni. Thank you times one million. This could be the most important night of my life…"

Jayme clenched her teeth to stop herself from blurting out some meaningless bit of baseball trivia that could cut into the silence. What in the world did Harlan talk about with other girls? Surely he didn't talk sports with them, and he wasn't smart enough to discuss anything else of any real importance. The answer was, of course, that Harlan didn't go out with girls to TALK to them. Was he planning something other than conversation for Jayme?

The car lurched as Jayme's foot slid off the clutch too quickly. When her hands started to sweat, she wiped them as inconspicuously as possible on her skirt. She had even worn make-up for this momentous night, and now she had to worry that her nervousness would cause her face to perspire, too. Runny make-up and sweaty palms. So romantic.

"Let's drive out to the Bottoms, Jae," Harlan said finally, "so's we can talk."

Jayme jabbed at the brake without clutching, and her car stalled with a violent jerk. Harlan directed his "stupid-girl" look her way.

"Don't you know how to drive this thing yet?"

"I'm working on it," she said more sharply than she intended as she restarted the car.

The Bottoms! Oh God! That means he does want more than conversation. Oh Lord! I don't know how to kiss. I don't know how to be kissed.

Her frenzy of apprehension was washed away by a sudden realization:

Everyone will see us there. Everyone will know that Harlan and I were at the Bottoms together. Thank you times a million, Hanni…

Belix Bottoms. And a line of cars already parked along the road as couples settled in for the next few hours. Down on the bridge, a group of kids sat on the railings, sharing their beer and wine and bragging about prior drunken binges.

Jayme drove slowly along the line of cars and over the bridge. Though she hoped that everyone was getting a good look at her and Harlan, she was equally afraid that they were seen…and laughed about…

Several hundred feet beyond the car parked at the head of the line, Jayme finally parked her VW. It was one thing to be seen with Harlan Oakes at Belix Bottoms. It was quite another to have dozens of witnesses to her first awkward attempts at romance.

"You can save a lotta gas if you turn your car off while we're sittin' here."

"Oh…yes…of course…" Jayme turned off her car and gripped the steering wheel. Normally she would have flung a sarcastic remark back at him in retaliation for his patronizing arrogance, but tonight she meekly accepted his smug air of male supremacy. For once Harlan knew more about something than she did.

Harlan studied the interior of the VW doubtfully. "You sure ain't got much room in this thing, do you?"

Alarmed by what she inferred from his remark, Jayme turned to him quickly. "How much room do you need, for Pete's sake?"

He scratched his armpit. "I s'pose we should get this over with so's I can get to bed early. I got a game tomorrow."

"I know." Jayme's heartbeat quickened until she could feel it throbbing rhythmically within her head. She would have preferred a little more preliminary romance than "I s'pose we should get this over with," but with Harlan she couldn't expect love poems.

Figuring she was smart enough to improvise once he got started, she closed her eyes and waited for him to make the next move.

"I wanna take Hanni to prom," he said.

The throbbing in her head intensified…painfully. "You brought me to the Bottoms to tell me that?" She squeezed the gearshift and imagined that it was Harlan's throat.

"You're the one drivin'."

"You're the one to recommend the Bottoms."

"Everyone's too busy here to bug us here, and I wanna talk to you serious. I wanna take Hanni to prom."

"You're taking me to prom."

"It ain't like we was goin' as dates. Only Hanni's got it in her head we was dates, and she won't go with me unless you tell her yourself it's okay."

"You're taking me to prom."

"You can tag along with us if you wanna. What do you say, Jae? Will you talk to Hanni?"

"Harlan?"

"Yeah?"

"Get out of my car. Get out of my car now."

"How'm I s'pose to get home?"

"Use your…manhood for a pogo stick and hop home."

"Aw, Jae…don't talk to me like that."

"Out, Harlan."

He opened the door. "Are you gonna talk to Hanni for me?"

"Out, Harlan!"

"Okay, okay. I don't know what you're so bent out of shape about." He struggled his way out of the small car, then peered back in at Jayme. "I'll talk to you tomorrow when you ain't such a rag."

"Close the door, Harlan."

He closed the door and walked slowly toward the bridge. As Jayme watched him in her rearview mirror, he stopped and stared back at her.

Good, she thought. *He's having an attack of conscience.*

After a moment of consideration, Harlan strode back to the VW and tapped on her window.

"What now?" she asked impatiently, turning on her car as she rolled the window down.

When Harlan poked his head and shoulders in through the open window, Jayme drew back suspiciously.

"Are you mad 'cause you feel bad taggin' along with Hanni and me?" he asked. "I'll talk Ollie into taggin' along, too, so's it looks like you have a date."

"You're slug slime, Harlan."

"Aw, Jae, I don't like it when you're mad at me, 'specially when I ain't done nothin' I can think of for you to be mad at me."

"Since when did you start worrying about my feelings?"

"I always worry when you're mad at me. You know how I am."

Jayme's face softened. "Yes, I know how you are."

"Then you ain't still mad?"

"I'm still mad, but I suspect I'll get over it."

"I sure hope so, Jae, 'cause I wanna borrow your car to take Hanni to prom."

With a shriek that rivaled the town's tornado siren, Jayme rolled up the window so fast that Harlan's head and shoulders were trapped inside the car. Ignoring his pleas and protests, Jayme edged her car forward. Harlan's frantic dance as he tried to keep pace delighted her.

"This ain't funny, Jae! This ain't funny! Stop the car! I got a game in the mornin'. You're going to make me pull a muscle or somethin'."

When she realized that she could really injure him with her small act of revenge, she stopped the car and released him from the window.

"Get into the car, Harlan," she said in a tired voice. "I'll take you home."

Harlan raced to get into the car before she changed her mind.

Jayme wanted to sneak unobserved into her bedroom, but her father saw her.

"You're home earlier than I expected," he called from the living room. "Did you have a good time?"

Jayme pressed her forehead against the doorjamb. "As good a time as I ever have with Harlan."

"Another bummer, huh? Do you have a headache, love?"

"A little one in my head…a big one next door."

"Maybe things will work out better for you next week when Harlan sees you in your new dress. Ronna brought it by while you were out. It's hanging in your room."

Jayme's face crumbled. "Oh, Daddy…"

She ran across the room and threw herself into her father's arms. Though the force of her hurled weight knocked the wind out of him, he pried the details from her as he tried to soothe away her heartache. Only Jayme's importunities kept him from an angry confrontation with Harlan. At Jayme's insistence, Jim also swallowed the unkind words he had for "that little Southern jezebel."

Jayme herself called Hanni later that night.

"You can go to the prom with Harlan alone…just like you want," she said. "I'll be unable to accompany you because my father is taking me to a fancy night club in St. Louis that night. You know…formal attire and cloth napkins…"

"Jayme, are you sure? I know how you feel about Harlan."

"I know how you feel about Harlan, too. You got what you wanted. You don't need me anymore, and I don't need you as a friend…"

Aware of what probably had happened, many of Jayme's classmates rallied to her support, and Jayme discovered that she didn't really miss Hanni's company at all. Still, when Harlan asked to borrow her VW on prom night, she gave him the keys with a lecture about what would happen to him if he and Hanni slimed up the inside of her car.

Some day, Jayme reasoned, *he'll remember everything I've done for him, and he'll realize why I've done it…and my patience will be rewarded…*

CHAPTER FOUR

Steffie banged her lunch tray down on the table and dropped into the chair next to Jayme.

"Rough morning?" Jayme asked.

"That Harlan. Is he really so dumb, or is he just so cocky he thinks everyone else is dumber than he is?"

"Both." Jayme shrugged and tried to appear indifferent. "What did he do this time?"

"He asked me to prom…like he really thought I'd accept."

"If you want to go with him, go with my blessing."

"Didn't you learn anything last year with Miss Southern Fried? A real friend wouldn't do something like that to you."

"Hanni was sneaky about it. That's what made me mad."

"We suffered no great loss when that bitch went back to Biloxi…though the boys were in mourning for a while. Most of them enjoyed dipping into her magnolia blossoms."

"And Harlan is the biggest dip. I wonder why a fairly intelligent girl like me keeps believing he's worth having."

"We all have big dreams about the way we think things should be. I was like that about Kyle Springer once. Only when I finally got him, I found out what a jerk he is."

"The difference is I know Harlan's a jerk before I have a chance at him."

"He's not going to change, Jae. In fact, he'll probably get worse unless he has a religious experience or something."

"The thing about Harlan is he's so innocent about his jerkiness. Somehow I find that rather endearing."

"You need professional help."

"No time for professional help." Jayme brushed her fingers through her auburn curls. "I have two term papers to research for."

"Two? Oh, Jae, you can't mean that you're writing his term paper…"

"That's the only way he'll pass English, and he has to have the credit to graduate."

"I was teasing before, but I'm serious now. You need professional help…industrial strength professional health…"

* * *

The challenge to Jayme as a writer was to find a subject that Harlan could be interested in and then to write about it in a style simple enough to avoid arousing Mr. Davisson's suspicions about the real author. Nevertheless, Jayme knew that she must sprinkle a few impressive words and phrases throughout the report since Harlan needed at least a C on the paper. The topic she chose for Harlan, "The History of Baseball," was actually too broad for this assignment, but

Harlan was incapable of handling anything more specialized. And Jayme couldn't make him look too good.

However, even Jayme's carefully restrained work was beyond Harlan's aptitude. Still, the discrepancy might not have been so obvious had Mr. Davisson not required his seniors to read their papers aloud in class.

Harlan had never been a good reader, and as he stumbled through his term paper, Jayme knew that even a pea-brain would realize that he had not written it. Nor was he helping his own cause or hers by pausing periodically in his laborious journey through baseball history to glare at her for making his life so difficult.

Mr. Davisson squinted over his glasses at them both just as the final bell rang.

"Miss McCray, Mr. Oakes, remain after class, please!"

Slumping in her seat, Jayme thought, *He knows!* And nothing short of a public execution would appease a man like Mr. Davisson, who refused even to use his students' first names in class.

"Your paper was excellent, Miss McCray," Mr. Davisson began as he stood like a judgmental Zeus before his two students. "Your subject was interesting, your research commendable, and your composition flawless. However, I expect no less from you. You have inherited your father's talent."

"Thank you, sir."

"A writer develops a distinctive style, Miss McCray, as unique as a fingerprint in many cases. Any attempts to disguise that style are usually unsuccessful because there is always some identifying characteristic that will survive all efforts to obliterate it. Do you know why I am telling you all this, Jayme?"

"Yes, sir." Her mouth was dry, and when he condescended to the gentle gesture of using her first name, her throat constricted painfully.

"Such disreputable behavior is not an intrinsic part of your personality, Jayme…which brings us to you, Mr. Oakes."

Mr. Davisson's shaggy eyebrows merged above his nose as his forehead wrinkled with irritation.

"You, sir," he thundered at Harlan, "did not write the paper to which you audaciously signed your name, did you?"

"Huh?"

Jayme rubbed a hand over her face and slumped further in her seat.

"Let me see whether I can make this simple for you, Mr. Oakes. See paper." Mr. Davisson grabbed Harlan's term paper. "Harlan did not write paper. Harlan let Jayme write paper for him. Mr. Davisson knows Jayme wrote paper. Mr. Davisson rips paper into tiny pieces." Jayme covered her face with her hands as Mr. Davisson shredded the paper. "Harlan gets a zero on his term paper. Jayme gets one week of after-school detention, a penalty that will disqualify her from any final exam exemptions. Do you understand now, Mr. Oakes?"

"Yeah, I flunk English."

"Yes. You flunk English. Are you not the least bit concerned that your devious and egocentric manipulation has gotten Jayme into trouble?"

"Please don't blame Harlan, Mr. Davisson," Jayme said, summoning her courage. "I volunteered to help him."

"And a little detention ain't gonna kill her," Harlan said.

"Mr. Oakes, you behavior is unchivalrous and borders on contemptible."

"I ain't sure what that means, Mr. D, but it don't matter 'cause I've signed with the Pirates, and they don't mind if I don't pass English."

Jayme's hands dropped limply into her lap. The Pittsburgh Pirates! Harlan hadn't said a word to her about signing…though he had been cockier than usual after the try-out camps held in area high schools over the last month. Pittsburgh! It was so far away. All their farm clubs were so far away…

"You're dismissed, Mr. Oakes," Mr. Davisson was saying.

Harlan said nothing more to Jayme or the English teacher as he left the room.

"Jayme?"

"Yes, sir?"

"You know it pains me to have to give you this detention, but I have no other choice. I cannot permit attempted deception to go unpunished."

"I know, Mr. Davisson." She avoided his eyes. Harlan's surprise announcement had shaken her composure. Any more unexpected compassion from Mr. Davisson would open the floodgates of her emotions.

"You'll be in college soon, and Harlan will be off God-knows-where doing God-knows-what. I know the separation will be painful for you, but believe me when I say you will benefit from it."

"Yes, sir." Eyes downcast, she hugged her books against her. "May I go now?"

"You may go."

"Thank you, Mr. Davisson."

Jayme stumbled out of the classroom. For the first time in almost four years of high school, she skipped baseball practice. She knew she couldn't watch Harlan without crying.

Blubber blubbering, she thought.

Harlan Oakes left to join the Pirates' farm club at Macon, Georgia, two weeks later.

CHAPTER FIVE

The warm late-September breeze brushed across Jayme's face as she wandered around the campus of Scheffers University. Because she lived at home, she rarely had an opportunity to enjoy the full beauty of the campus. Most of her time was spent in the academic buildings or in the library, and after her classes were over, she worked for her father in the *Sentinel* offices.

Today, however, her political science professor, Dr. Hebris, was absent, and Jayme had an unexpected two-hour break before her News Writing 101 class. In this time she would allow herself to think about Harlan.

She had intentionally overloaded her school and work schedule so that she wouldn't have time to think about him. The ruse worked for the most part though in unguarded moments the pain and loneliness still gnawed at her heart. She wrote him countless letters, but he never responded to any of them. Though Jayme expected no written reply, she hoped for a phone call or two...even though that was all Harlan's own parents had received in the four months he had been gone.

Now that the minor league season was over, she hoped that Harlan would be returning home for the winter. However, Harlan decided to stay in Macon.

Jayme tried very hard to convince herself that he wanted to pick up some experience in winter league ball, but she knew differently...from society news in the Macon newspaper she subscribed to when Harlan left for Georgia.

Harlan Oakes was dating the daughter of Harry Greco, owner of the Macon Pirates. Cydney. Her name was Cydney. Of course. Never a Gertrude or a Thelma or an Ethel. Or a Jayme.

At the library entrance, she stopped to sit on the low brick wall bordering the walkway. From there she could look out over the expanse of the campus lawn that the horticultural students kept so colorfully and creatively landscaped.

Christmas...Harlan will certainly be home for Christmas...maybe Thanksgiving, too.

Did he miss her? Did he even think about her now and then? They had grown up together, for Pete's sake...

Wrinkling her nose, Jayme fanned the air in front of her face as the suffocative smoke from a cigarette drifted her way. Irritated by the intrusion, she whirled around to confront the offender.

The pile of books beside him indicated that he was a student though the creases in his face suggested that he was older than Jayme. His black, shuttered eyes smoldered with unconcealed interest as he stared back at her through haze emitted by a cigarette he pinched between his thumb and forefinger. He was a compact, thickly muscled man with olive-brown skin that was accustomed to the sun. Jayme recognized him as one of the foreign students in her political science class, but she could not remember his name or his country.

"In the sunshine," he said in careful English, "your hair is like burnished copper. My eyes are pleased."

Blinking in confusion, Jayme looked around her to see if he was talking to someone else.

"You were talking to me?" she asked, the offensive cigarette forgotten.

"Perhaps I am too forward." As he drew again on the cigarette, the rising smoke caused him to squint, and tiny wrinkles at the corners of his eyes deepened. "But we are classmates I think. You are in the political science class of Dr. Hebris, are you not?"

"Yes, I am, but I'm afraid I don't know you…I mean I know you're in my class…but I don't know you…" *For Pete's sake, he's going to think I'm a blathering idiot. But why should I be worried what he thinks?*

"You think I am…how to say it?…a wolf, and you are worried for your virtue," he suggested.

"Worried for my virtue? Wait a minute here, fella…"

"Then you are not worried for your virtue. I am in disappointment. I grow weary of girls wanting to…how to say it?…jump Najib's bones."

"Jump your bones!" Jayme squeaked before she realized that he was smiling at her, not maliciously, but with friendly amusement. Jayme returned his smile. "You are…how to say it?…teasing the innocent maiden?"

"And now you tease Najib in return. That is good. My eyes are pleased also by your smile."

Blushing, Jayme stared out over the campus.

"I am Najib Bustani," he continued, "and from Dr. Hebris I know that you are Miss McCray."

"Jayme…I'm Jayme…or Jae…if you like…"

"Jae, I would be so honored if you accept me to buy you coffee."

"You want to buy me coffee?"

"I would not ask if I did not so want."

"But you don't even know me."

"I would like to know the girl with sunset in her hair. The color is that of the sun as it sinks into the sea in my homeland, and the loneliness in my heart is soothed by the memory."

Loneliness. Jayme could understand loneliness.

"I have class in just over an hour," she said, checking her watch.

"The student union is close by. There will be time. And maybe for Najib and Jayme, there will be more time later…"

"Though my family may be considered as wealthy," Najib told her later as he walked her to class, "life is not so easy in Lebanon. These are troubled times within my country. My father sends me here for broader enlightenment he says, though we have excellent universities in Lebanon. I have already three years at the American University there, but I think he wants me removed from the problems for a while. I will do his wishes, and then I will return to Lebanon. All that I learn here I will give to my country."

"I've read a little about what's going on over there," Jayme told him, "but most of our foreign affairs interest in this country is focused on Vietnam right now."

Najib nodded his understanding. "You have men whose blood in spilled upon the Indochina soil, so it is right that you are concerned for them. Someday, though, I fear the eyes of the world will be drawn to Lebanon, for commando forces within our borders will make their voices heard. I soothe my troubled conscience by saying that I will be more prepared to serve my people because of my time here."

"You feel guilty for being here?"

"In the way of one who has deserted his army at the first sound of gunfire."

"What could you be doing back in Lebanon that would make the situation any better?"

"Nothing as a single link that lies unconnected to the chain, but with the other men of my conviction, our chain would be strong. Perhaps my father fears the youthful fire of revolution burns within my veins, and he wishes me time to cool my fervor. His business interests are vast, and such political fever within his eldest son is not so welcome."

"Are you Muslim?"

"No. I am Christian, and with unfortune an adversary to my Lebanese countrymen who are Muslims. I wish it were not so, but it is. Our differences provide the fuel for civil war I fear, but the spark that will ignite it will come from outside our borders."

"Syria?"

He nodded. "And the Palestinians they are in disagreement with. You have read about my country. It is good that you will be a newspaper reporter."

Jayme looked away from him, blushing with embarrassment that she could find no real reason for. "Actually I plan to be a sports reporter."

"A sports reporter?" he echoed, astonished. "Your way will be wasted, Jayme with the sunset hair."

"I have...personal reasons for it."

"Then I shall not criticize though I must lament. We must do what our hearts demand. Perhaps your heart will change. You are young...eighteen perhaps?"

"That's right."

"I am twenty-one. Ah, you look surprised, for my face has the look of an older man of this country. The Lebanese sun is brutal, and I have grown wise and old with much experience in my twenty-one years. I try to tell my father I am too old to be a schoolboy, but he was quite insistent. I do not wish to cause him fatal distress, for his heart is a problem."

"Are you a senior here?"

"Here I am what you call a second-term sophomore, for not all my Lebanese classes count for American credit. That is why I am in a freshman political science course. That is why I can meet the girl with the sunset in her hair. I have not many friends so far. I meet many people…many girls…but I do not wish them as friends."

"Why not?"

"Ways are different here, and I prefer the way of Lebanon in many things. Women I meet here are intrigued by me because I am different, and they are offended if I do not take them to bed within first hour I know them. I do not like that."

"I don't like that either, but the role of women here is very different from that in your country. We don't hide behind veils. Nor must we suffer the indignity of being part of a harem…"

Najib surprised her with his explosion of laughter. "You know the news of my country, my new friend, but there are yet many things which you do not know. In time I will have pleasure to enlighten you."

"I would like that very much," she said earnestly. They were at the door of her classroom now, and she was disappointed that their conversation must end.

"This evening I would be so honored if you accept me to buy you dinner."

When Jayme hesitated, he was quick to reassure her. "Just to talk and to be friends. Najib will not jump your bones. I will bring my roommate to protect you. He is unique, and you will like him. Perhaps you know him at this time. He is a journalism major, too. His name is Rick Girard."

Jayme rolled the name around in her memory. "No, I don't think so. But I haven't really paid that much attention to people in my classes, to tell you the truth…except the ones I already know from high school."

Jayme bit her lip. Though she would like to spend more time with Najib, the thought of eating in front of two strange men unsettled her. Putting food into her mouth with an audience would only emphasize that she had been putting too much food into her mouth all her life.

"I appreciate your invitation," she added finally, "but I work in my dad's office till seven on Thursdays. He usually sends out for dinner for us."

"We can save dinner for another time then, and you can perhaps meet us at Burkey's later for beer and conversation? Conversation with you pleases me, and beer pleases Rick."

Jayme tried not to look too relieved. "That will be great. Only I haven't had too much experience with places like Burkey's."

"That is of no surprise to me. You are nervous about such a place?"

"Frankly yes."

"We will meet you in front at seven-thirty. Your new friends will take care of you. It is not to worry…"

Awakened from a deep sleep by the jangling of the phone, Jim fumbled for the receiver.

"'Lo," he mumbled, laying the phone on the pillow close to his ear.

"Daddy, it's Jae."

Because Jim knew his daughter so well, he could detect apprehension and embarrassment in her voice even though he was not fully awake. He gripped the receiver more firmly as he tried to shake grogginess from his head.

"What's wrong? Where are you? What the heck time is it anyway??"

"A little after midnight, Daddy. We've run into a little misunderstanding here..."

"We? We who?"

"Najib, Rick, and I."

"Who are Najib and Rick?"

"I told you about Najib this afternoon, but you were deep into a story and may not have been listening will all cylinders. And Rick is Najib's roommate."

"What little misunderstanding did you encounter that's important enough to wake up your old man on a work night?

"You aren't making this any easier, Daddy."

"Neither are you, love. So what is the problem?"

"We kinda need for you to pick us up. We're kinda in jail, you see, and my Bug is still at Burkey's, and Daddy, you'll kinda need to bring some bail money, too..."

CHAPTER SIX

Jayme sat on the couch between Rick and Najib as her father paced before them. Every time Jim began to say something, he bit off his words and paced a few moments more. Jayme was concerned not so much about the possibility of an angry lecture as she was about having disappointed her father with her apparent irresponsibility. Having to bail his daughter out of jail had been a colossal embarrassment to the well-respected editor of the local paper. He deserved to rant and rave all he wanted before Jayme explained.

She had cautioned Rick and Najib to remain silent until her father had his say. Equally sheepish about the escapade, both men remained quiet as Jim paced, Najib with his eyes downcast in shame, Rick with his eyes directed at Jim with a curious blend of defiance and respect.

Eventually stopping right in front of Jayme, Jim rubbed his hand over his bald head.

"I seem to be at a loss for words right now, Jayme Rose," he said. "Suppose you give me the details, and maybe somewhere along the way I'll become inspired."

Jayme winced. When he used her full name, he was usually less than pleased with her, and he couldn't be thinking anything too charitable about Najib and Rick either.

"Don't be mad at Rick and Najib, Daddy. What happened was my fault."

"That is not true, Jae..." Najib broke in. Rick had begun to utter a similar protest, though spoken not so gently. Realizing Rick's propensity for profanity, Najib cut him off with a stern glance.

"You gentlemen will have your chance to tell me your versions of tonight's events. Right now I want to hear from my daughter."

Jayme clasped her hands together tightly. Though Jim had spoken with no malice in his voice, his eyes were not congenial as he stared first at Najib and then at Rick. On Rick his eyes rested somewhat longer, and Jayme could imagine what thoughts were forming in her father's mind. Where Najib was well groomed and neatly dressed even after the evening's altercation, Rick was the stereotypical college hippie with shoulder-length hair, bedraggled brown beard, headband, and ragged clothing. Jayme herself had been disconcerted when she first met Najib's roommate, but an evening of conversation had eased her misgivings considerably.

Jim's gaze drifted to his daughter. "I'm waiting, Jayme Rose."

Jayme cleared her throat. "Well...Daddy...here's the thing. We met at Burkey's...for refreshments...and we were sitting in this booth talking..."

"What kind of refreshments are we talking about?"

"B-Beer, Daddy."

"I've had beer in this house all your life, and never once did you express an interest in it. In fact, you declared that the smell of it gagged you. What made you change your mind?"

Jayme cleared her throat again. "I was...well...just being sociable, Daddy. Only it did gag me, and when I said maybe I should try wine instead, Najib and Rick wouldn't let me because they were afraid I'd get sick. So I switched to good ol' 7Up...PLAIN 7Up."

She glanced at her father to see whether he was at all impressed by the boys' concern for her well-being.

He wasn't. "And did your friends switch to good ol' plain 7Up?"

"Well...no...but they're used to beer...not that they're drunks or anything...and we weren't drinking much of anything because we were talking..."

"I see. Go on."

"Well...by midnight the place was getting kinda...lively. Unlike Najib, Rick, and me, some people were there with the serious intention of getting drunk...and most of them succeeded. One of the drunks staggered by our booth, and when he tripped and fell onto our table, he sent our glasses crashing everywhere. Rick and Najib helped this gentleman to his feet while I tried to clean up some of the mess, and then the gentleman made a rude remark about me...something in reference to my similarity to a sow...and Rick told him to shut his face. Then the gentleman made a rude suggestion about what two boars could do with one sow, and Rick tried to shove him on his drunken way. Then the gentleman shoved back, hard enough to knock Rick down. Then Rick got up and knocked the gentleman down. Then someone came out of nowhere to jump on Rick, so Najib jumped in to help, and before we knew what happened, everyone in the place was either fighting or getting knocked down trying to stop the fighting. That's when the cops came and hauled us in. They said we were being public nuisances and being disorderly in our conduct, but that's not the way it was, Daddy. Rick and Najib were defending my honor, so if you have to beat on someone, beat on me. It's my fault."

"I have NEVER beat on you, Jayme Rose!"

"You've never been this mad at me either."

"Do you know the name of the...the gentleman who started this whole disaster?"

"No, sir. But the police kept him in jail. Of course, he was drunk and we weren't. And his father wasn't as wonderful as mine about bailing him out."

When Jayme saw the corners of her father's mouth twitch, she closed her eyes in relief. He realized now that he had no serious reason to be angry, but he still wasn't happy.

"Did you tell all this to the police?" he asked.

"Yes, sir. But they were not very sympathetic."

"Obviously. I just had to fork over three hundred dollars because of their lack of sympathy."

Najib leaned forward. "Rick and I will return money you paid for us as soon as banks become open in the morning. We are indeed grateful for your help."

Jim waved him back. "Let's see what tomorrow brings. I intend to get my money back when I talk to the chief. As my daughter told me when she called, this was a misunderstanding, and I strongly suspect any charges against you will be dropped when the facts are sorted out."

Jayme felt Rick and Najib relax beside her.

"But," Jim continued more sharply, "that does not mean I'm going to aggressively champion your cause down at the station. Nor does that mean I'm pleased or amused about my daughter being in the big middle of a barroom brawl."

"Burkey's isn't usually like that...sir." Rick's protest was tempered by the respectful form of address only after looks of warning from Jayme and Najib.

"Most places like Burkey's don't get really rowdy until around closing time when most people with good sense have gone on to more civilized pursuits," Jim said. "Jayme Rose, you are eighteen...old enough and sensible enough to make your own decisions, but I am requesting that any future visits to Burkey's end well before the bewitching hour."

"Yes, Daddy."

"I'm not overly thrilled with the idea of your drinking...beyond the simple fact that you were doing so illegally. In a college town, no one seems to be overly zealous about carding, so I won't forbid it. A beer here and there, some wine with dinner...okay. But to drink for fun or to pass the time...not okay. That's the kind of drinking that leads to trouble...as you realize now."

"Don't worry, Daddy. Beer really does make me gag."

Jim directed his next words to Najib and Rick. "I don't normally lecture Jae in front of her friends, but you're both intelligent enough to realize why I am now."

Rick nodded sullenly and folded his arms, but Najib leaned forward again, eager to make peace with the father of the girl with the sunset hair.

"We are not wanting to make your daughter into a drunken woman, Mr. McCray. We intend only conversation, for she is pleasant to talk to and has many interesting things to say."

"There are many places other than Burkey's."

"I have to make disagreement, sir. Most restaurants close too early for long conversations such as we enjoy, and we can have no girls in our dorm after ten o'clock on nights before classes."

"Jae's friends are always welcome in this house."

"You are so kind..."

"Kindness has nothing to do with it. I know my daughter well, and I trust her judgment and her honesty. She usually shows good sense in selecting her friends...with one exception anyway..."

When Rick stiffened in response to Jim's remark, Jayme quickly whispered to him, "He doesn't mean you. He means the boy next door."

Harlan.

Jayme twisted a bit of wayward hair around her finger. She hadn't even thought about Harlan the entire evening...

Jim peeked into Jayme's bedroom when he returned from driving Rick and Najib back to their dorm.

"You'll not be cutting your eight o'clock, Jayme Rose, even if you'll be getting only a few hours of sleep now."

"I know, Daddy. I'm finishing my homework right now." Pushing away from her desk, she went to her father and wrapped her arms around him. "Thanks for being so understanding."

"You've been a good girl all your life. I can't see you going bad now. However, your friends may not be thinking I'm so understanding, and that's fine with me. Establishing a few rules of conduct now can prevent problems later, especially where young men are involved."

"Najib and Rick don't count as young men in the way you mean to count them as young men...where I'm concerned anyway."

"Nonsense. Brains of men their age operate on pure hormones. I know. I was that age once myself. I can't see that Rick and Najib are any different."

"They might not be different, but I am. I'm hardly the type to heat up a man's hormones."

"That's more nonsense. You're a beautiful girl with a wonderful personality, wit, intelligence, talent, and—"

"A body to rival Moby Dick."

"You're more huggable than most of those beanpoles around the campus these days, that's all. I'm sure Najib and Rick are aware of it, too. A lot of men prefer voluptuous women."

"Now YOU'RE talking nonsense, but thanks anyway. Now that I have a police record, I need all the ego boosting I can get."

"You don't have a police record. I'll get everything straight with the chief tomorrow."

"You were very sweet to bail out Najib and Rick, too."

"You didn't leave me much choice when you refused to leave the...um...slammer without them."

"It wouldn't have been fair for me to leave without them."

"Najib seems like a fine young man, but I'm reserving judgment on that other fella."

"You have to look past the hair and the beard, Daddy. Rick's a gentle, caring, and intelligent person, but he's going through an anti-establishment phase right now. He thinks he has to be like he is to balance out his father, who is very right-wing establishment I gather. Maybe you know Rick's dad? He owns a paper in Chicago."

"Rick is THAT Girard?"

"No, his dad is THAT Girard. Rick is Richard Joseph Girard III, which is impressive enough to me, but he gets awfully defensive when anyone connects him with THAT Girard. Something about corporate cloning…"

"Knowing the reputation of Joe Girard, I'd have to say he's glad his son is dissociating himself from the dynasty."

"You make Rick sound like total vermin meat, and he isn't. There is an emotional power struggle going on between the two of them, but I truly believe that Rick is a closet conservative dressed in radical rhetoric. I don't even think things are as bad at home as he wants everyone to believe. He is a sophomore journalism major, so he's hardly denying his heritage. All the time he was spouting off about his dad, Najib was grinning and winking at me, so I took most of what Rick said as pure baloney sauce…the kind of stuff a guy would say if he's wanting to look like a rebellious son.

"And he was so genuinely angry when that guy said nasty things about me. I've never had anyone rush to defend me so heroically…except you, of course. Rick…and Najib, too…were…are…so…so…"

Jim raised an eyebrow. "So different from Harlan?"

"A million kinds of different. They make me feel like more than an afterthought."

"Sounds to me like I should get to know these young men better. We can invite them for pizza…and beer tomorrow evening if you like."

"Really and truly?"

"We could have that cardboard-crust delivery stuff…unless, of course, you'd consider making one of those superbly delicious pizzas from Ronna's recipe."

"Is this just a sneaky way to get homemade pizza?"

"Yes, that…and to make sure your gentlemen friends keep their hands off my little girl."

"That's the last thing you have to worry about, Daddykins."

"That boy Rick…he does BATHE, doesn't he?"

"Najib insists on it," Jayme said, laughing as she kissed her father's cheek.

CHAPTER SEVEN

Pushing aside the tangle of sheets, Rick rolled out of bed.

"Back in a minute," he said, reaching the door to the dorm room in only three strides.

Jayme propped herself up on her elbow. "Where are you going?" she asked, reluctant to be left alone in such a strange situation.

"To the john. If you want to go with me, it's okay, but you'll have to make yourself useful."

"No," she said quickly, cursing herself for blushing. "I...I'll wait here for you."

He banged out a heavy-metal-rock rhythm on the door. "Relax, will you? It's okay for you to be here. There's twenty-four-hour open house on weekends. You can stay here all night if you want to."

"I've never been in a men's dorm room before...like this..."

"Why should a dorm bother you after you spent all that time in the men's locker room in high school?"

"I was never in the locker room when the guys were in there. Coach wouldn't allow it."

"Then you never saw a naked man before?"

"No."

"Do you want to now?"

"No!"

"Well, no one's gonna rape you or flash you or anything you here, so relax, will you?" He leaned over and patted her cheek. "If you're gonna be too uptight, I'll stay here and piss out the window."

Jayme's blush deepened. "No. Go...just go."

Grinning, he twirled the ends of his mustache. "And the quivering maiden will eagerly await my return?"

Jayme hurled a pillow at him, but it struck the door he closed quickly behind him. She could hear him chuckling as he walked down the hallway.

This was their first time alone together in the month they had known each other. She couldn't understand why she felt so awkward with him when she felt so comfortable with Najib. Najib was like her fuzzy flannel nightgown where Rick was more like...well, sleeping nude.

Jayme smoothed the wrinkles she had caused by lying on Najib's carefully made bed to watch television with Rick, who had settled into his own burrow of bedclothes. Tonight Najib was out with one of those girls who had expressed interest in jumping his bones.

"Even Najib has primal urges that demand female attention," Rick had explained, "and you've been declared off limits by both of us. There'd be too many problems with roomies going after the same girl, and you wouldn't respect us in the morning anyway...though I'm willing to chance it if you promise not to tell Naj."

Mentally she blessed him for implying that she was worthy of such consideration, but openly she laughed off the suggestion as being ridiculously impossible.

He was gentleman enough to look disappointed. "Your dad would castrate me anyway, and there would go my free meals on Fridays."

The Friday night dinners were becoming a pleasant routine. Jim enjoyed prodding and prying into the minds of his daughter's friends, and frequently their discussions remained animated past midnight. Jayme was an active participant in the conversations that covered a diversity of controversies although much of the talk centered on Vietnam and Najib's homeland.

But never sports.

Never baseball, football, or Harlan.

Jayme was surprised that she didn't mind the omission. What disturbed her, however, was her fascination with Rick Girard. Because this attraction made her feel disloyal to Harlan, she rationalized that it resulted from Rick's being so different from men she was used to.

He was not a clean-cut American athlete though his tall, muscular physique indicated some kind of athletic training. His legs in particular were massive and powerful...the result of pushing his Harley Davidson around, he told Jayme...although later he admitted to wrestling and playing football in high school.

In truth, Rick worked at promoting an unfavorable image. He was an exceptionally intelligent man who maintained a grade point average just high enough to keep him from being kicked off campus and into the war. A war, he said, that was stupid and that was making the United States look stupid. He would split to Canada before THEY would send him off to die. This wasn't HIS war. The war belonged to the pencil-pushing idiots in Washington...let THEM do the fighting, and the poor fools already in 'Nam could come home. Yet Jayme noticed that he swallowed back emotion whenever the National Anthem was played at Scheffers football games.

The paradoxes in him intrigued her.

Though he was just as fastidious about his personal cleanliness as Najib, his hair and beard remained untrimmed and his clothes faded and torn. His side of the dorm room rivaled post-war Germany, yet the Harley in the parking lot was waxed and polished weekly. And every Sunday afternoon he called his father. The conversations didn't last long, and Rick frequently raised his voice in anger, but he always called. Jayme noticed, too, that Joe Girard, a busy newspaperman, was always home to receive the calls.

There was something else even more disturbing to her: she hadn't cared even a little bit that Najib was off having his primal urges taken care of tonight. In fact, she was amused...and pleased to have something to tease him about. Rick's primal urges were more insistent, however, and in his absences Jayme felt…well…as if she'd like to be absent with him. No one else but Harlan had ever had such an effect on her, and the sensation was disquieting.

The door flew open, and Rick hurled himself onto Najib's bed beside Jayme.

"So what do we watch next, sugarplum?" he asked, laughing when Jayme jumped up to close the door.

"Your manners for starters."

Uncertain of whether to rejoin him on Najib's bed or to brave the unknown by sitting on Rick's, she remained standing in the doorway.

"Okay, okay," he said, leaping from Najib's bed to his own. "I'll be a good boy, but you can't blame a man for trying."

She curled up on Najib's bed and tucked the pillows protectively around her.

Am I shutting him out or myself in, she wondered.

* * *

One chilly November day just before Thanksgiving break, Jayme finally got a letter from Harlan. Though there was no return address on the smudged envelope, she recognized the wayward scrawl and the misspellings:

Jay Mukray, 3132 Wimporwil Dr, Apelwould, ILL.

So typically Harlan. And each misspelled word was as dear to her as all the gold at the end of every rainbow.

In the seclusion of her room, she propped the envelope against his framed picture on her desk. This moment must be savored to the fullest. Letters from Harlan were as infrequent and spectacular as the appearance of Halley's Comet, and she could not tear frantically into the envelope and thus bring to an abrupt end the expectancy that had surged through her as soon as she recognized the handwriting.

Did he miss her? And in his missing her, was he realizing that Jayme meant more to him than anything else…even baseball…even Cydney Greco?

Picking up the envelope, she turned it over in her hands a few times before she carefully slit the top edge with her letter opener. Her silver letter opener, a decorative-more-than-useful graduation gift from her Uncle Lester in Virginia. Jayme had never bothered with a letter opener before, but Harlan's letter should definitely be opened with a silver letter opener.

Carefully she pulled the letter out. A roster sheet. He had used the back of an old roster sheet for his stationery. Just what she would expect from Harlan. Adorable, dumb Harlan who had probably spent hours laboring over this simple letter to her.

Dere Jay;

Jayme smiled. He had called her "dear"…uh…"dere." What did it matter if he wasn't an academic whirlwind? She was smart enough for both of them.

Me & Sids coming home for Xmas only Ma'll freek if Sid sleaps in my rume with me. Can she stay with u? We're getin marryd in Feb, so u don't need to freek neether. How come nobody ain't to home when I tryd to call u...

Jayme let the note flutter to the floor.

He's dumped on me again, she thought with no real surprise.

Married. He was getting married. How could he keep a wife when he couldn't even keep a girlfriend longer than a few weeks?

The answer was simple: Harlan might be getting married, but he wouldn't stay married long.

And when Mrs. Cydney Greco Oakes grew tired of Harlan, Jayme would be there to comfort him.

CHAPTER EIGHT

Cydney Greco was a bimbo.

Another diminutive blonde with a diminutive brain. The world was filled with smart blondes, but Harlan could find only the dumb ones. By comparison, "Cyd" made Harlan look like a Rhodes Scholar.

Jayme relieved her frustrations by beating the batter for the pumpkin bread her father liked.

Why are men so dumb about the women they want? she wondered. Even Rick and Najib tended to aim their primal urges at witless wonder-dolls. The bubbleheads were easier to bed on short notice, Rick had recently explained to her. Even though free love was in vogue, intelligent women took longer, so a guy had to be looking for a serious relationship before he'd spend the necessary time with one.

Bubblehead. Cydney Greco was definitely a bubblehead. As far as Jayme could see, Cyd's only talent was whining and complaining about every little thing. The bathroom designated for her use was too small. The soap was too harsh. The towels were too rough. Her bed was too hard, and the sheets chafed her delicate skin.

For all her brainlessness, she was not without a certain amount of manipulative deceit. She became more fragile and more delicate when men were present, and Harlan especially seemed inclined to cater to her every outrageous whim.

If Cydney had shown even the slightest hint of real affection for Harlan, Jayme's attitude might have softened. However, Cyd was preoccupied with only Cyd...though she did smile lovingly enough when Jayme shot pictures of her and her fiancé for the feature story Harlan wanted in the *Sentinel.*

Then there were those occasions when Harlan and Cyd closeted themselves within the privacy of the guest room.

He can't slime up his own sheets, Jayme thought furiously, *so he has to slime up ours.*

But she said nothing as she jerked the bedclothes off Cyd's bed each morning and stuffed the wad into the washing machine. Her only defiance was neglecting to add fabric softener that would make the sheets more tolerable to Cyd's fair skin.

On this particular day, Jayme suffered Cyd's grumping alone, for Jim and Harlan's parents were at work, and Harlan and his agent were meeting with a lawyer about something that did not interest Cyd, who wandered around the McCray household now sighing like a forsaken waif.

Still involved with her Christmas baking, Jayme ignored her guest's apparent distress. Past conversations had been awkward and ultimately futile because Cyd had no knowledge of sports or current affairs, and Jayme had no interest in Cyd.

In a conscience-driven attempt to make Harlan happy by keeping his woman entertained, Jayme offered to teach the future bride how to bake the Nutty Chip Chewies Harlan especially liked.

Cyd, however, was appalled by the idea.

"We have Cook to do things like that," she said. "What if I broke a fingernail or something?"

"We all have our crosses too bear," Jayme said sweetly. "Does the salary of a minor leaguer allow for a cook?"

Cyd shrugged, unconcerned. "Daddy will take care of our necessities until Harlan can."

Harlan will never make enough money to take care of your necessities, girlie, Jayme thought, pummeling her cookie dough as Cyd drooped around the house.

Rick and Najib trooped into the kitchen then. Without knocking. They never knocked anymore, but neither Jim nor Jayme minded the oversight.

An early start on Christmas cheer at Burkey's had livened the young men's spirits, and both were effusively affectionate as they popped hunks of cookie dough into their mouths and dragged Jayme over to the mistletoe they had hung in the doorway on their way in.

After the ego crushing she always suffered when Harlan was around, Jayme was thrilled with the attention and willingly surrendered to the good-natured kisses.

Rick kissed her longer than Najib did. Or was it that she kissed Rick longer than she kissed Najib?

"Why don't you go to Chicago with us, Jae?" Rick sneaked some cookie dough by standing behind her and sliding his arms around her. "My old man won't mind. In fact, he'd probably turn cartwheels 'cause you'd be there to keep us in line when we hit the streets at night."

Jayme smacked Rick's hand though she rather liked his arms around her. "I can't leave Dad here alone on Christmas."

"Bring him also." Najib hiked himself onto the counter. "The hospitality of Mr. and Mrs. Girard extends far. I so discovered when I shared with Rick's generous family the festivities of giving thanks. And there is much excitement in Chicago at night. I joined with Rick and his friend of many years in much amusement. We will be so honored if you share amusements with us."

"Daddy would kill us all if he had to bail us out of jail again." She used the excuse of pouring water into the coffee maker to break Rick's hold on her. "Besides, I have a house guest."

"We have already sacrificed you to her for three days, and we grow lonely for the sunshine of your company." Opening the cabinet doors beside him, Najib passed the coffee mugs over to Jayme. "Of truth, she is not your guest but the guest of one who earns his living playing a game. We do not think you are much enchanted with this visit anyway."

"Still, I promised Harlan."

Rick opened the refrigerator door in search of beer. "Why are you being so damn helpful anyway? What's that guy done for you lately?"

"I was overcome by the spirit of Christmas." Jayme pushed him away from the refrigerator. "No more beer. You guys have a long drive ahead of you. Sit down at the table, and I'll fix you something to eat."

"You're worse than my mom," Rick grumbled, but he sat.

Najib needed no further urging either. "I am so hungry I could eat a house. Rick allowed no time for food this morning. Beer and peanuts is not so good a breakfast."

"Oh, quit griping, Rooms." Rick beat his hands against the table in the familiar rock-'n'-roll rhythm. "I let you talk me into renting a car for the trip to Chicago, didn't I?"

"It is too cold for a motorcycle. I am not accustomed to the weather of Illinois."

"Wait until our first blizzard. The Harley's loads of fun in the snow."

Najib appealed to Jayme. "Rick has a very nice car in Chicago, but he will not drive it, for it was a gift from his father. Instead, he prefers this old motorcycle he bought with money he earned by building highways in the summer."

"It's not an old motorcycle. It's a Harley Davidson classic. Besides, my sisters need the car to get to school."

"Your sisters are not of an age even for their licenses of driving."

"When they are, they will have a car to use. Why wait until the last minute?"

"Enough bickering," Jayme said, hoisting a huge hamper onto the table. "Stuff your mouths full of these sandwiches I have made for you already. I'll make more to replace them."

"That is a basket full of sandwiches for us?" Najib's dark eyes shined with hope.

Rick pulled the hamper closer to him and rummaged around inside it. "Wow, Naj! There's sandwiches, cookies, candy...cinnamon rolls...homemade bread...jelly...honey butter...cupcakes...there's enough in here to feed us for a year."

"It's a Christmas present from Dad and me," Jayme said, passing sandwiches and chips to them. "And Aunt Ronna. I couldn't have finished all the baking and cooking without her. Oh...and out in the garage there's a cooler with some imported beer Dad got for you...only you're not to be drinking it while you're on the road."

"We are very much grateful for the trouble you have gone to in our behalf," Najib said, smiling hugely as he unwrapped a sandwich.

Rick caressed her chin with his fingertip. "That goes for me, too," he said, the softness of his voice causing Jayme to tremble.

"It is strange," Najib said around the sandwich in his mouth, "for we have imported beer in the car for Jim."

"And something for you in the garage," Rick added in that dizzyingly silky voice. "We had to keep it safe and warm."

Jayme covered her tremor of emotion with flippancy. "You got me a Porsche?"

"Even better than a Porsche," Najib told her.

"But if you want one," Rick said, "you can have the one my daddy gave me." He motioned to Jayme to sit down. "Close your eyes like a good girl, and we'll get your present."

Obediently closing her eyes, Jayme listened as her friends banged the door connecting the kitchen to the garage. A few moments later, the door slammed again, and something warm and squirmy was placed in her arms.

She opened her eyes.

A sleepy, rust-colored Persian kitten was regarding her curiously as Rick and Najib babbled their explanations simultaneously.

"Our eyes were drawn to this little one, for he has the color of the Lebanese sunset, as you do…"

"You'll need something warm and furry to keep you company until I get back…"

"We thought perhaps a baby dog…a puppy…but Jim said he prefers a cat inside his house with you and him gone so much each day…"

"You're like a kitten yourself, y'know…cute and cuddly though you can bare your claws when you need to…"

"We have named this little one already. If you do not so like, you may change it, and our feelings with not be hurt…"

"Burkey…his name is Burkey…"

"For that was the scene of our first adventure together…"

Even flippancy could not disguise the tears that sprang to Jayme's eyes as she reached to hug both friends.

"Thank you both so much," she whispered, unable to muster any other words.

Pleased with her response, both Najib and Rick sat down to their sandwiches, Rick pausing long enough to stroke an escaped tear off her cheek.

"We don't often make you speechless, Kitten," he said with a grin.

Jayme cuddled her Christmas present against her cheek. "Kitten? Which one of us are you talking to?"

Cydney Greco made her grand entrance then. By now, Jayme was acquainted enough with her guest's habits to know that Cyd had been listening to them for some time. She had to be sure that Najib and Rick were worthy of her acquaintanceship. And she certainly couldn't enter a room where the attention of the people in it was so focused on something else that they might not even notice her.

"Why, Jae," she said, heavy on the Georgia accent, "I didn't know we had guests. Why didn't you call me?"

Jayme shrugged. "I didn't know you were interested in meeting my friends."

Cyd's quick scrutiny of Rick brought a scornful pucker to her lips, but her eyes lit with interest as her inspection shifted to Najib.

"You are just as wrong as you can be, Jae honey. Hello, there," she said to Najib. "Since I have not been properly introduced, allow me to introduce myself. I am Miss Cydney Lou Greco of the Macon, Georgia, Grecos."

Najib jumped to his feet and bowed to her. "I am pleased to know your acquaintance, Miss Cydney Lou Greco. I am Najib Younis Bustani of the Beirut, Lebanon, Bustanis, and he is my roommate of college, Richard Joseph Girard III of Chicago, Illinois."

Rick did not stand to pay her homage, and she offered him only a glance.

"Don't look now," Rick whispered into Jayme's ear, "but Najib's primal urges are surging. They don't have women like that back in Lebanon."

Grabbing the collar of his shirt, Jayme pulled Rick closer. "Do something," she whispered urgently. "She's a bimbo...an ENGAGED bimbo."

"And spoil the lad's fun? I have to live with him, you know."

Irritated, Jayme pushed Rick away from her none too gently. Najib was just assisting the delicate Miss Greco onto a chair placed close beside him.

"Remember I told you about Cyd earlier, Najib?" Jayme said, trying to remain casual. "She's the one ENGAGED to MARRY the neighbor boy."

Najib did not hear her. Miss Greco had placed her hand over his while murmuring some banality that was holding him spellbound. Soon she was complaining that the kitchen chairs were too hard for her. Wouldn't the sofa in the living room be more comfortable?

Najib followed Cyd into the living room, with only a feeble smile of apology directed at the two friends he left at the table.

When Jayme got up to follow, Rick firmly guided her back to her chair.

"Give it up, Kitten," he said. "When a man's hormones get excited over a bimbo, his brain stops working. That's the difference between lust and love."

"You seem awfully knowledgeable about it."

"Years of experience," he said, "with lust anyway. I'm not ready for the other...yet...unless you want to change my mind."

When Jayme's only response was a distinct tightening of her lips, Rick patted her cheek.

"Lighten up, sugarplum," he said. "He's only flirting. I'll have him out of here and on his way to Chicago in an hour. What's the big deal? You don't usually get this upset when he's...romancing another girl."

"If she'll flirt with Najib, she'll do Lord-knows-what with other guys who don't have to leave for Chicago."

"So? Don't you think the guy's she's engaged to does the same thing?"

Jayme couldn't disagree. "But they're not supposed to," she said lamely. "They're engaged. They're supposed to be in love."

"Love doesn't even make the top ten list of why most people get married these days."

"Harlan deserves better."

"Why are you so damned protective of this guy?"

"Because…because…" Jayme hugged Burkey closer. "Because we're old friends, that's why."

Rick leaned back in his chair. "I'm beginning to understand."

"You don't understand a blessed thing, Rick Girard."

After gently laying Burkey on a chair, Jayme stomped to the sink and banged around some pans she had left soaking there. Rick followed her. Reaching into the soapy water, he grabbed her hands and pulled her over beneath the mistletoe. Jayme was too puzzled to protest.

"He doesn't deserve better," Rick told her, "but you do."

An instant later he crushed her against him, pressing his mouth firmly over hers. The kisses they had exchanged earlier had been nothing like this, and Jayme attempted feebly to push him away. His lips, hard and searching against hers, were making her weak and confused.

The kitchen door opened then.

Harlan flinched from the strange sight before him. A hippie was kissing Jae…like the hippie was a real man and Jae a real girl…

Though Jayme backed away from Rick, her eyes never left his face as she said to Harlan in a breathless whisper, "Your fiancée's in the living room, Harlan."

Scratching his head, Harlan went to join his loving bride-to-be.

Jayme stood in the driveway and waved until Rick and Najib rounded the curve at the end of Whippoorwill Drive. Shivering in the cold, she turned to close the heavy garage door, but she changed her mind when she remembered that she would need to go to the store for food and other essentials for Burkey.

As she hurried into the house, she gingerly touched her lips, which were still bruised and tingling from Rick's kiss. Whenever she dreamed about kisses from Harlan, she imagined that they would electrify her just as Rick's had. If a kiss from Rick could feel so good, a kiss from Harlan must be truly earth-shaking.

Pondering the reason for Rick's sudden display of passion, she decided that the sentimentality of the season and the befuddling influence of beer were responsible. After all, Rick's good-bye kiss had been as chaste and brotherly as Najib's…though Rick's deep brown eyes smoldered with memory as he studied her face before getting into the car…

The kitten was sleeping soundly as Jayme reached into the hall closet for her coat. When she kneeled to rub the tiny triangle beneath his chin, Burkey stretched and licked Jayme's finger a few times before curling back into a purring ball.

"What a wondrous little thing you are," she murmured.

Even more wondrous was Rick's and Najib's caring for her enough to give her such a special gift.

From the living room, however, the words for the cat were not so loving as Cyd's super-sonic whine penetrated Jayme's preoccupation with Burkey.

"I cannot sleep in the same house with that horrible animal, Harlan!"

"Now, hon, that little thing ain't gonna hurt you. Just keep your door shut."

"What about now? Fur balls are floating around everywhere, and my eyes will get red and puffy, and my mascara will run."

"It ain't that bad, Cyd."

"You're so mean to me, Harlan. You don't even care about my health or my safety. That monster could pounce on me at any second and rip my ankle to shreds."

"Aw, Cyd, it's just a little kitty..."

Jayme cupped Burkey's face in her hand. Monster? Pounce? Rip her ankle to shreds? Harlan was right for once. Burkey was just a tiny kitten, not a mountain lion, for Pete's sake.

Well, let Harlan talk some sense into his Georgia peach. Jayme had some shopping to do.

When Jayme returned from the store...her arms laden with cat food, cat bowls, a litter box and litter, and every cat toy Hartz Mountain made...Harlan and Cydney were nowhere in sight. A glance at the closed door of the guest room told Jayme where the couple probably was...and what the couple was probably doing.

Humming loudly to signal to them that they were no longer alone...and to drown out any noises they might be making...Jayme ripped into the package containing a catnip-stuffed mouse and went to look for Burkey.

The kitten was not easy to find, but Jayme knew that cats were naturally curious creatures that liked to sniff around and poke into every nook and cranny of their new territory. Burkey could be just about anywhere.

And Jayme looked everywhere for him...everywhere except the guest room.

Had poor Burkey been sniffing around in there when Harlan and his bimbo went in to slime up the sheets? Poor little kitty, trapped in there, an unwilling witness to all that delirium. Maybe after the little monster pounced on Cyd's ankle and ripped it to shreds, he jumped into Harlan's lap and...

In wicked delight, Jayme hammered on the guest room door with her fist.

"Gee, guys, I hate to disturb you," she said, "but I can't find my kitty. Is he in there ripping you to shreds?"

Jayme stifled a giggle as she heard a muttered expletive from Harlan and a whining plea from Cyd to "Make her leave us alone, Harlan."

A few seconds later, Harlan yanked the door open and stood before Jayme totally naked and exposed...

Jayme quickly averted her eyes.

"Your cat ain't here, Jae." In spite of his irritation, he sounded almost apologetic. "It was botherin' Cyd, so I put it in the garage."

"You what?" There was barely enough breath left in her to articulate the words.

Harlan shifted from one foot to the other. "Cyd gets 'lergic sometimes, so I put it in the garage."

"I just came from the garage, Harlan. Burkey was NOT in the garage, Harlan!" The longer she spoke, the louder her voice became. Harlan stepped back from her. "And the garage door was open, you dimwit! Are you really so stupid you didn't see it, or were you so eager to slobber all over your bimbo fiancée that you didn't see that the garage door was open?"

She meant to slap him, but because he hand was fisted, the blow she delivered to his jaw knocked him down. The effect calmed her enough that she could speak more rationally though the iciness in her voice was more ominous than her shouting.

"I am going out to look for my kitten, Harlan, and when I return, I want you and your dumb slut girlfriend out of my house. Do you hear me, Harlan? Out! Forever!"

Turning abruptly, she slammed out of the house, leaving Harlan to stare after her as he rubbed his jaw.

Chapter Nine

Lying on her bed with her pillow over her head, Jayme felt like a pig wallowing in the mud of misery. Though she had looked around the neighborhood for over two hours, she had been unable to find Burkey. The small victory awaiting her at home, when she discovered that Harlan had taken her seriously enough to move Cyd out of the McCray house, did nothing to alleviate her anguish. She had lost her kitten and banished her heart's desire from her life so resolutely that Harlan would never speak to her again.

Eating a Tupperware canister full of Christmas cookies had not eased her distress one bit.

A soft tapping on her door intruded into her despondency.

"Jae, love…it's Dad. May I come in?"

After leaning over quickly to roll the cookie canister under her bed, Jayme sat up and grabbed a book off her nightstand.

"Come on in, Daddy."

Jim crossed the room and sat beside his daughter. "I managed to get an ad in the lost and found even though it was past deadline. I called up to typesetting right after you called me."

"Thanks, Daddy."

"I see our guest has gone."

Jayme turned over a page in her book. "Guest? Oh, you mean Cyd. Harlan thought it would be a good idea for her to stay at his house after all. If he sleeps on the couch, his mom can't be too upset about Cyd sleeping in his room."

"Would this sudden change in plans have anything to do with the bruise on Harlan's jaw?"

Jayme raised the book to hide her face. "You saw Harlan?"

"He was waiting outside for me when I got home."

"What did he tell you?"

Jim pulled the book away from Jayme's face. "He's really sorry about the cat."

"One dumb animal feeling sorry for another? Only Burkey is by far the smarter of the two."

"Now, Jae…he feels bad about it. He also feels bad because you were so angry."

"I bet."

"Harlan is usually an insensitive cretin, and sarcasm and subtle insults are usually beyond his comprehension…but he can be very sensitive to blatant hostility…especially when it…uh…hits him right in the face."

"I've made progress. I wonder if Cyd can get him to salivate on cue."

"You have every right to be upset, but if I didn't know about Harlan's past transgressions, I might feel obligated to give you a lesson on over-reacting."

"Are you going to make me apologize?"

"Decisions like that should come from your heart, not mine."

"Do I have to tell Harlan he can kennel his fiancée here if he wants to?"

"Save your colorful verbs for the paper, love. I don't like Miss Greco any more than you do, but you did tell Harlan she could stay here…and it's only for a few days."

"Two weeks, Dad. They want to stay until after New Year."

"And she's welcome to stay here…if she wants to. I'll leave a set of keys with Harry and Mamie. You and I, however, will be leaving the day after Christmas. We have an invitation to spend the New Year's holiday with friends."

"We do? Who? Where?"

"Yes…the Girards…Chicago…"

Jayme's book fell to the floor. "Daddy…you didn't call up there!"

"I didn't need to. Joe Girard himself called me with the invitation just as I was leaving work."

"But why? He doesn't know us."

"I'm sure Rick put him up to it." As Jim reached to retrieve Jayme's book, he studied his daughter's face. "The boy didn't waste much time about it either. He'd barely had enough time to reach Chicago when I got the call. Is something going on here that I should know about?"

Jayme grabbed the book from him. "Don't be silly. Najib and Rick want a sober chauffeur for New Year's Eve, that's all. Are you sure you want to take time off work for that?"

"The vacation will do us both good. We've been keeping our noses to the ol' grindstone pretty relentlessly over the past few years. Besides, I'm curious to see Joe Girard's little operation."

"LITTLE operation? *The Chicagoland Ledger* has a daily circulation of nearly half a million."

"Oh, really?"

"You know it, too. Don't pretend you don't."

"Shall I pretend I don't see the cookie canister under your bed?"

Jayme covered her face with the book again. "Please don't tell Aunt Ronna. I promised her that I'd try to cut back on my cookie consumption."

"Your Aunt Ronna can be a bully sometimes. By the way, I listed her number with ours in the ad in case anyone calls about your cat while we're gone. And the Oakeses are offering a reward."

"Do you think Burkey is safe somewhere, Daddy? He's so little, and it's so cold outside."

"He'll turn up somewhere. How far can a kitten go? Now get yourself out of bed and put on your cheerful face. I'll run next door and talk to Harry and Mamie about watching the house, and Harlan's waiting in the living room to talk to you."

"Why does Harlan want to talk to me?"

"I told you he feels bad about the cat. He's the one putting up the reward money...though I think that idea originated in a parental brain."

"Maybe you should chaperon. He might want to rough me up for knocking him down."

"Harlan's not one to bear a grudge, love...he can't hold a thought that long..."

Uncertain of Harlan's true intentions, Jayme entered the living room cautiously. He was sprawled on the couch, watching a Roadrunner cartoon on television and eating Nutty Chip Chewies from a plate balanced on his stomach. The discoloration along his jaw line was distinctive and conspicuous.

"No need for such formality," Jayme said, sitting in a chair across the room from him. "Just make yourself at home."

Harlan's eyes never left the television screen as he scratched at his crotch before picking up another cookie. "Ssshh! That ol' coyote's just 'bout got that damn bird, and I don't wanna miss it."

Oh, for Pete's sake, Harlan...the Roadrunner always gets away. It's an integral part of the whole cartoon motif."

"Aw, Jae..." Harlan's face sagged with disappointment. "Why'd you have to go spoil the end for me?"

He rolled off the couch and ambled over to shut off the television. The plate of cookies that fell to the floor remained on the floor as he resumed his position on the couch.

"So why aren't you with Princess Cyd?" Jayme asked, shaking her head as he picked cookies off the carpet and dropped them wholly into his mouth.

"Whoof?" He sputtered cookie crumbs all over the front of his sweatshirt. "You mean Cyd's a princess. She ain't never said nothin' 'bout it."

"Never mind, Harlan. I'm just surprised that you aren't spending every waking moment with your fiancée."

"This ain't no wakin' moment. She's takin' a nap and don't want me botherin' her. You gave her a headache."

"Gee. I'm real sorry about that."

"Will you tell her that when she wakes up? She's thinkin' you don't like her."

"I don't," Jayme said, knowing that a more subtle reply would be wasted on him.

Harlan's brow creased from the unfamiliar effort of thinking. "You don't? Why you don't?"

"She's a dumb, self-centered, whiny slut...just like I said before. I thought you were paying attention."

"Aw, Jae...you shouldn't talk like that 'bout her. I'm gonna marry her."

"Just WHY are you marrying her anyway?"

"Well…" He scratched his crotch again. "She wanted to. She's nice lookin', and she's got big tits. She fucks real good. And her dad's got a whole lot of money."

Rick was right, Jayme thought. *Love doesn't even make the list.*

"For the sake of good manners," Jayme told him, "I do apologize for going back on my word. I said she could stay here, and if you still want her to, move the slut back in. I guess I can get along with her for a few days…until Dad and I leave for Chicago."

"Why you goin' to Chicago? Bears playin'?"

"Rick's dad invited us up for New Year."

"Rick? You mean that hippie that was kissin' on you?"

When Harlan's lip curled into something approaching a sneer, Jayme hoped that Harlan was…maybe…a little jealous. She chose words she was sure he could understand.

"Did it make you mad to see another man kissing me?"

"Mad? Hell no! Me and Cyd thought it was funny when I told her. Cyd said the hippie was kissing the hippo." Harlan yukked again.

"So, how's your jaw?" she asked, resisting the urge to symmetrize his face by bruising the other side of it.

"You do pack a punch," he said, working is mouth to assure himself that everything was functioning properly.

"Do you realize that in all the years we've known each other, you've never once given me a Christmas present or a birthday gift?"

"Never knew you wanted one…"

"I've known Rick and Najib only three months. They gave me a Christmas present…a WONDERFUL Christmas present…which you lost…"

"I looked and looked for that kitty, Jae. I didn't mean for it to get outside. You should have closed the garage door after you."

Jayme's lips tightened. "And you shouldn't have put him out of the house in the first place. Burkey had more right to be in here than that…that bimbo slut fiancée of yours."

"But Cyd gets 'lergic."

"When it suits her purposes."

"Huh?"

"Never mind, Harlan. You and I function on two different planes of understanding."

"Huh?"

"We think different kinds of thoughts."

"Well…yeah…but I ain't holdin' it against you 'cause you can't help it, and you do the best you can."

Jayme stifled a squeal of frustration.

"If it makes you feel better," he added, "I don't think the kitty's roadkill now or nothin'. Cyd says those fluffy kitties cost big bucks, and someone pro'bly picked it up to keep it."

"You're making me feel tons better..."

"Well...yeah...that's why I came here. I don't like it when you're mad at me."

"Why? You don't need my stories to promote your baseball career anymore."

"I just feel funny when you're mad at me...kinda like I got my shorts on backwards or my jock's twisted..."

Jayme stooped to pick up the cookies still on the floor.

"Someday," she said, tossing Nutty Chip Chewies onto the plate, "you'll realize why you get so disoriented when I'm angry with you."

He popped one of the cookies into his mouth. "Huf?"

"Never mind, Harlan..."

CHAPTER TEN

"We'll be back soon to give you the grand tour of the Palace of Plutocracy," Rick said, setting down Jayme's suitcase.

"It is a much lovely house." Najib carried Jim's bag into the sitting room adjacent to the bedroom where Jayme would be sleeping. "Rick tries hard to pretend he does not like this home of his family, but he cannot fool his roommate of college."

"Naj is easily impressed is all," Rick said. "It's because he lived in a tent somewhere in a Lebanese sand dune."

"My parents will be pleased to learn Americans think so grandly of our homeland." Najib pushed Rick toward the door. "Come. Let us give our good friend time to rest and freshen herself from her journey."

"I was going to help her unpack."

"You will come with me, Romeo." Shoving Rick firmly out the door, Najib directed at Jayme a backward look filled with questions and speculations.

When her friends were gone, Jayme wandered around the rooms she would be sharing with her father, who had left with Joe Girard for a tour of the *Ledger* plant and offices. The guest bedrooms, connected by a sitting room, were located in the "Sleeping Wing," Rick had told her, the twinkle in his eyes belying the tour-guide sophistication in his voice. The richness of the rooms surprised her even though she knew that Rick's family was wealthy. To her a guest room was merely the spare bedroom furnished with secondhand furniture and used by visiting relatives and bimbo slut fiancées of dimwitted baseball players. It was the room where Jim had slept when his wife was so ill, where Aunt Ronna slept those times when Jayme had been sick with scarlet fever, mumps, measles, and chicken pox…a serviceable room, but not a magnificent one.

These guest rooms, however, were magnificent. All ivory, rose, and gold…plush, lush, and luxuriant. She was sure there were fancy designer names attached to everything, but none of them would mean anything to her.

She opened her suitcase on the thick carpeting rather than risk defiling the exquisite lace coverlet on her lace-canopied bed.

And this is Rick's HOME, she had to remind herself. *Hippie Rick with his Harley and anti-establishment rhetoric. Poor guy. He's embarrassed about having so much and embarrassed about liking it.*

The bathroom was bigger than her bedroom at home. More ivory, rose, and gold. And a HUGE bathtub that made her feel not quite so fat, maybe even petite as she later settled in it amid scented bubbles.

Cyd would love this, she thought, trying to raise her leg into the air with the same slow grace displayed by television's bubble-bath girls. Unable to raise her leg high enough, she shrugged and sank lower into the bubbles, grinning with wicked delight because she was here and Cyd wasn't.

Jayme had exaggerated just a wee bit about the extravagance of the Girard mansion and the importance of the Girard name in Chicago. However, now that she had seen everything in person, she realized that she might have been guilty of understatement. In any event, Cyd had ached to share in this little trip. She had pouted and moped around the house for three days in an attempt to persuade Harlan to spend New Year in Chicago.

But there was nothing Harlan could do, for he and Cyd had not been invited. Nor would Jayme intercede in their behalf. Of course, Harlan wasn't the one to ask her. Since Burkey had never been found, he was afraid to ask Jayme for anything until he as sure she was over being mad at him.

Besides, Harlan wanted to spend New Year's Eve sliming up Jayme's sheets with Cyd. Jayme didn't even mind anymore.

Well, not too much.

Smiling, she pulled some fresh clothes out of her suitcase. And her make-up, which she was wearing more often these days. She had brought the best of her wardrobe, too...though her best would never qualify her for *Vogue*. In fact, most of her clothing had stretched out of shape.

What does it matter anyway? Rick doesn't pay attention to my packaging...he pays attention to ME...

"What did you do with Najib?" Jayme asked suspiciously when she opened the door to find only Rick standing there.

"My sisters are teaching him how to play Monopoly."

"Your idea or theirs?"

"Do I detect a little mistrust here, Kitten?"

Jayme stood aside to let him enter. "Why do you call me that?"

"Everyone calls you Jae...even that idiot athlete friend of yours. I want to call you something that's special just between you and me. Besides, like I told you, you remind me of a kitten, so draw in your claws and give me some cuddling..."

She evaded his arms. "I thought I was off limits to you and Najib."

"Najib's interest in you has become brotherly. Mine hasn't. There's no competition anymore, so you're fair game now."

"Oh, goody. I love being prey in your lustful hunt for willing flesh."

"It's not that way at all, not with you."

"Save your smooth talk for the girls who will accommodate you. I won't."

"You certainly are sleazing up my honorable intentions here. I'm not trying to talk you into bed."

"Then what are you trying to talk me into?"

"Well…being my girl."

"Why?"

"Because I like you, dummy…a lot…more than I've ever liked any other girl if you want to know the whole truth. I want to hold you and kiss you without hiding behind a sprig of mistletoe…and you feel the same things for me."

Jayme whirled away from him. "Don't be ridiculous."

"You've got it in your head that you're going to be faithful to that ball player no matter what he does or how you feel about someone else. Does a man who turns kittens out into the cold deserve that kind of single-minded sacrifice?"

"Well…no…but…" Jayme jumped as Rick placed his hands on her shoulders.

"He's getting married, Kit. You're a free woman."

"You don't really want me. I'm not exactly the willowy maiden that stars in men's fantasies."

"Don't stereotype me. You know me better than that. Look me straight in the eyes and tell me you don't feel the attraction between us."

As Rick trailed his fingers up her arm, Jayme fought conflicting urges. The proper thing was to push his hand away, but she had a strange desire to melt into his embrace. Wasn't that what a heroine did in the embrace of her hero? She melted.

Rick slid his arms around her, and Jayme melted.

"Not bad, huh?" he whispered into her hair.

"Okay, so there's an attraction," she admitted finally. "But that doesn't mean that I'm going to surrender EVERYTHING to it…to you…"

"I'm not out to conquer you, Kit. I'll admit I want to sleep with you, but I'm not going to club you over the head and drag you into the bushes. Just give me a fair chance…you can decide how far we go with it…"

His saying he wanted to sleep with her flustered her. She couldn't trust her voice in this moment, so she said nothing. Nor did she protest when he tipped her face up and covered her mouth with his.

This kiss was a gentle question rather than the bold statement he had made beneath the mistletoe a week before. As his soft breath fanned her face and sent a warming tremor through her body, Jayme pressed against him, compelled by a need that was both alien and urgent. When she ventured a look up at him, his eyes told her that he meant to kiss her again and that his next kiss would demand more from her. In that moment, Jayme would have given him anything he wanted.

She was spared this ultimate submission, however, when her father opened the door from the sitting room between his bedroom and Jayme's. Embarrassed by his seeing her in such an intimate clinch, she stepped quickly away, but Rick refused to surrender her hand.

"I was just about to give Jae a guided tour of the old homestead," Rick said easily. "Would you like to join us?"

"Not if your guided tours start off this way," Jim said. "Joe's tour wore me out, and I can't handle the kind of excitement you're generating here."

"Daddy!" Mortified, Jayme jerked her hand away from Rick.

But he recaptured it immediately. "Then we'll be on our way."

"Looks to me like you're on your way already," Jim grinned.

"Daddy!" Jayme squeaked again. "You really didn't see what you think you saw. Let me explain."

Jim rubbed his chin. "Okay. Explain."

"I...we...Rick..." She sighed in defeat. "Never mind. Just never mind."

"Your daughter has a fine way of explaining herself," Rick said somberly.

"It's all those journalistic genes she has," Jim replied, just as seriously. "And you're to stay out of them, understand?"

"Her jeans you mean..."

"Exactly."

"I don't believe this," Jayme muttered as she pushed Rick toward the door. "Come on, Rick. Let's GO."

"I won't keep her out late," Rick called back to Jim.

"Damn right you won't, boy. Dinner's in an hour, and you both better be there...on time."

Grinning, Rick pulled the door closed behind them, but Jayme could hear her father chuckling on the other side.

"I have never been so embarrassed in my whole life," Jayme whispered.

"Next time I'll make sure we're not interrupted."

"What makes you so sure there will be a next time?"

"Your eyes tell me everything I need to know," he said softly.

Jayme was still having some trouble reconciling herself to the fact that Rick had grown up in this mansion he was showing her now. For one thing, any house with enough bedrooms to constitute a "Sleeping Wing" was beyond the comprehension of a mere mortal like her. In the downstairs portion of the wing were the master bedroom suite, and bedrooms belonging to Rick's sisters, Shari and Heather. Upstairs were three bedrooms and the guest suite where Jayme and her father were. Najib occupied one of the upstairs bedrooms...and Rick another.

Though Jayme had been concerned that Rick would use the proximity of his room and the guest suite as an excuse to cut the tour short in pursuit of other diversions, he merely waved toward his door and led Jayme down an elegant spiral staircase. Because his parents were in their rooms dressing for dinner, he didn't show her the master suite either, but he did allow her to peek into his sisters' rooms.

The tasteful richness in each was camouflaged in part by the trappings of teenage girls. Heather's delicately patterned peach-hued wallpaper was covered by a collection of Peter Max posters, and the satin moiré bedspread was hidden beneath an assortment of album covers that spilled onto a path of covers that led to an impressive stereo system pulled from its storage area behind satin-lined cabinet doors.

Shari, at twelve, was three years younger than her sister, and her room symbolized her transition from little girl to teenager. Here posters of Charlie Brown and Snoopy, Betsey Clark urchins, the Beatles and Monkees, and Newman and Redford as Butch Cassidy and the Sundance Kid concealed the pink-flowered wallpaper. A white, hand-stenciled sleigh bed was stacked high with stuffed animals and dolls, one of which was a hippie doll with long, brown-yarn hair and beard and a tie-dyed tee shirt with a peace sign on the front.

When Rick noticed the direction of Jayme's scrutiny, he shrugged and smiled sheepishly.

"Shari cried when I left for school, so I had that doll made to watch over her when I'm away," he said, guiding Jayme toward the corridor before she could ask any questions.

In the sunken dining room, the table was already set with fine china and silver. Overhead a massive crystal chandelier splashed diamonds of light around the spacious room. Since the kitchen was off limits at this busy hour of dinner preparations, Rick led Jayme through double doors to the gathering room, where the Girards held their parties and dances. Opposite the entrance hall where glass doors opened onto a flower court and fountain, there was a grand piano, ivory with gold accents to coordinate with the ivory and gold Italian marble floor. A mirrored bar and wine racks were discreetly concealed in the corner by gold velvet curtains like those drawn across the flower court doors when the Girards were not entertaining. Hanging from the center of the high, domed ceiling was a chandelier identical to the one in the dining room, only larger, and there was a partially enclosed, gold-draped balcony along one wall where, Rick told her, his parents and their guests could enjoy private showings of some currently popular movie.

Jayme's lips parted in awe. She had not yet seen this entryway, for Rick and Najib had met her and her father in the driveway and ushered them up to their rooms through a back entrance by the garage.

"You came in through the 'private entrance,'" Rick explained as he opened another door. "That's Mom's fancy name for the back door."

The two rooms he showed her now were sharp contrasts to the grandeur on the other side of the door. Here there was a cozy atmosphere, created mostly by warm wood paneling and autumn colors. It was one long room actually, separated into two by a through fireplace to create a living room on one side and a family room on the other. Sliding glass doors by the living room opened onto the living terrace, beyond which lay the pool and tennis court

Najib looked up from the Monopoly game as Rick and Jayme came around the fireplace into the family room.

"Just passing through," Rick said quickly.

When Najib raised a dark eyebrow, Jayme blushed furiously and then tried to divert attention by pointing to a cigarette burning in an ashtray at Najib's elbow.

"You promised to give up those nasty things," she said sternly.

"And so I do when I am in the pleasure of your company," he replied without smiling. "But that pleasure is not of mine at this time."

When Heather called his attention back to the game then, Jayme was spared from making any excuses or explanations. However, she couldn't help feeling uncomfortable as Rick motioned her up an oaken stairway.

"Heather has a huge crush on Najib, you know," Rick was whispering from behind her.

Jayme didn't quite trust him there so close and kept a wary eye directed over her shoulder as they climbed the stairs together.

He noticed her caution. "For Chrissake, Kit. I'm not trying to look up your dress."

Jayme stumbled on the top step. She would have fallen if he hadn't slipped his arms around her to aid her balance.

"Ease up, will you?" he said softly. "I don't like it that you're suddenly so uptight with me."

Jayme turned to face him. "I'm trying hard not to be. It's just that everything seems so different now."

"You're not different, and I'm not different. The only thing different is that we're finally admitting that we...appeal to each other."

Her confession was barely audible. "But it's scary. I've never felt this way before."

"Not even for that jock?" he asked gently.

Her brown eyes filled with confusion. "Not even for him."

"Didn't you ever...weren't you ever...intimate with him?"

"Don't be absurd. Who would want to be intimate with me?"

"I would."

She flinched from him. "I...we...can't."

"Don't you ever fantasize about it?"

"No."

"About it with your jock then?"

"Certainly not."

"Why not?"

"That's none of your business."

"You're probably right, but satisfy curiosity anyway."

"Because...I...I don't know enough about it to fill in the details, if you must know, Mr. Snoopy-Nose."

"I see," he grinned. "What DO virgins fantasize about then?"

"Certainly not about the orgiastic free love that turns you and your hippie buddies on!" She stalked away, down the hallway, and then stopped when she realized she didn't know where she was going.

"Those doors next to you lead to my dad's study." Rick stroked his beard as he strolled along the hallway to where she stood.

He opened heavy doors to an exquisitely masculine room that smelled faintly of tobacco…the unburned kind that could radiate a pleasant aroma. All the furniture was heavy, manly, and mostly oak and leather. Bookshelves filled with collectors' editions lined three of four walls. On the fourth wall was an array of plaques, awards, and expensively framed photographs and news stories…all proudly centered by a mounted marlin.

"That's Marvin," Rick told her, pointing to the fish. "I was a freshman in high school when we caught him. That fishing trip was the last time my dad and I spent time together without getting on each other's nerves. Maybe we should go back to the Keys sometime."

The wistfulness in his voice was obvious, and Jayme slipped her hand into his.

"You spend too much time trying to be different from your father and not enough just being you," she said softly.

"For a virgin, you're mighty profound," he said, kissing her hand. "C'mon. We have one more stop."

"Where?"

"My room."

Jayme jerked her hand away. "You just don't listen, do you?"

He wrapped his arm around her shoulders and held her fast. "I might accuse you of the same thing. Nevertheless, all I'm intending is to put on a jacket and tie to keep peace in the family. I promise no attempts at free loving, and I will comport myself in a gentlemanly manner befitting the son of Joe Girard."

"Are you sure you're not adopted?"

Rick laughed. "Do you really think that King Joe would ever willingly adopt someone like me?"

Rick's room surprised Jayme: unlike his half of the dorm room he shared with Najib, this room was scrupulously neat. His bed was made, and all the drawers and doors were closed. No clothes accumulated in tiny piles or over lampshades and chair backs. Mirrors and windows sparkled; the stereo system and television built into the wall gleamed; the paneling and warm wood furniture glistened.

A maid, Jayme finally decided. A maid must clean his room every day. Rick would never waste his time cleaning anything that didn't have a Harley Davidson emblem attached to it.

Another surprise was that the paneled walls were unencumbered by acid rock and anti-war posters. Jayme had expected a spray-painted peace sign or slogan…maybe an old mattress thrown into the corner…empty beer bottles…underground newspapers…

She giggled at the ridiculousness of such counter-culture features in such a cultured house.

"Not quite what you expected, is it?" Rick asked, pushing a button that slid back a section of panel to reveal a mirrored bar. "Would you like a drink before dinner? Or maybe some mood music?" He pushed another button and the stereo clicked into motion, filling the room with the Beatles' "Golden Slumbers"…light fare for acid Rick.

"Sgt. Pepper? Are you sure this is your room?" Jayme asked, frowning when he turned a knob that dimmed the overhead light and lamps on either side of his bed.

"The edict from the king says that while I'm under his roof, I live in a civilized manner. The trade-off is he tries to ignore my hair and beard." He peeled off his tee shirt and disappeared into a huge closet that had been concealed by sliding panels.

When he emerged with a shirt, jacket, and tie in hand, Jayme tried not to stare at his furred and muscled chest. She had never seen him without a shirt before, and she wished now that she had the guts to appreciate his physique more openly. He was built better than Harlan…

Rick intended to wear his jeans with the jacket and tie, so Jayme would be spared any further unveiling. *A rather disappointing turn of events,* she admitted to herself with surprise.

"Would you be offended if I tell you that you're a big phony?" she asked to divert her own interest. "In spite of what you say, you like all this."

"You're right. I am a phony, and I do like all this, but let's keep it our little secret, okay?" He stood before the full-length mirror on his bathroom door and adjusted his tie. "You can take it one step further and say that I make a lousy hippie, too."

"Then why try to be?"

"It's good camouflage. Richard J. Girard III can fade into the crowd and become a real person instead of prince and heir of a newspaper kingdom. I couldn't find a pauper to trade places with."

"Being the heir to a newspaper kingdom shouldn't be such a hardship to a journalism major."

"If the whole scene began and ended with the newspaper business, you'd be right. It's the other bullshit I hate."

"Like what?"

"Like the queen mothers in this city always expecting me to be an escort for some empty-headed debutante at their boring bullshit parties…or sizing me up as husband material for their rich-bitch daughters. And as soon as I was accepted at Scheffers, I got all kinds of invitations from the fancy frat men. None of them knew ME, of course. They wanted Joe Girard's son to pledge their fucking fraternities."

He sat on the bed and motioned for Jayme to sit beside him.

She ignored the gesture. "Promoting this image makes you immune to all that?"

"Do I look like someone Mrs. Titless-Snobworth would invite to her gala occasions? The king's not happy with me 'cause he's into the social scene himself."

He grabbed her hand and jerked her onto the bed.

"I promise not to rape you," he said, "if you play true confessions with me."

"I have nothing to truly confess." With all the dignity she could muster, she sat on the edge of the bed onto which she had been unceremoniously yanked. She was careful to place herself several feet away from Rick as she folded her hands in her lap.

"Bullshit. I'm intrigued by this virginity of yours."

"My virginity is of no concern of yours."

"I disagree. C'mon, Kit. I just unloaded my psychological ego on you. Share your id with me. You can honestly tell me that you've never fantasized about sex...even with that Harwood guy?"

"I told you I didn't...and his name is Harlan."

"What have you imagined yourself doing with him?"

"Hugging and kissing...but that's as far as it went. There...are you happy now?"

"You're ready to sacrifice your whole life for this guy, yet you've never thought about having sex with him?"

"There are kinds of love existing on more noble planes than sliming up bed sheets."

Laughing, Rick fell back on the bed. "You can't believe that this Harwood guy prefers your noble plane to sliming bed sheets."

"His name is Harlan, and he doesn't now...but someday he might."

"Does the phrase 'a cold day in Hell' suggest anything to you?"

"So? Even if he doesn't—"

"You'll make the ultimate sacrifice and slime bed sheets with him...whether you feel the urge or not."

"If the occasion calls for it, even a virgin can summon forth an urge or two," Jayme said.

"You shouldn't need to summon anything forth," Rick told her. "If the right chemistry is there, it blazes naturally...like between you and me."

Jayme leaped up from the bed. "They're probably waiting for us in the dining room."

Rick pulled her back down, closer to him this time. "They're gathering around the bar first, if I know the king. We still have fifteen minutes. You know what I think is bugging you about all this? You're confused because you do have these urges for me, and you don't for Harwood."

She twirled a lock of her hair around her finger. He had cut through the fog to show her what had been nagging her conscience, but still...

"Even if you're right...and I'm not saying you are...I won't...be intimate with you no matter what my urges are."

"I'm simply telling you how I feel, and I want you to do the same."

"I did already."

"Do you ever think about hugging and kissing with me?"

"Yes...I have..."

"Hugging and kissing are good...for now. But you can't expect me to pledge fidelity while you continue to moon around over Harwood. I'm a healthy, red-blooded American male. I have to satisfy my primal urges somewhere, and I refuse to do it to myself. You'll have to be satisfied with knowing that you're the only girl I've ever met who's worth all this trouble just to get hugs and kisses."

"I never once asked you for pledged fidelity," she said, trying not to think about him with other girls. "And I pity the girls who are no more than relief to your primal urges."

He shrugged. "Believe it or not, I'm no more than a free meal and movie to them. It's a fair exchange. Are you going to turn me over so easily to other females?"

"I never said it was easy. It has to be this way, that's all."

"So we've reached an understanding?"

"I'm not real sure what it is though."

"We're kinda going together I guess. You're my best girl, but it's one of those open relationships that's all the rage..."

"That sounds fair...under the circumstances..." *Why is being fair so painful?*

"You're in the driver's seat, Kit. I'm ready to make this a closed relationship any time you change your mind."

"And if I don't change my mind? You can REALLY be happy with things this way?"

"Half a loaf is better than none, as the saying goes. So, do we seal this less-than-perfect understanding with a handshake or a kiss?"

"Handshakes before dinner..."

"So long as you promise me something sweet for dessert..."

CHAPTER ELEVEN

Although Jayme had partly feared, partly hoped that Rick would try to tempt her into more than kisses and hugs, he was excruciatingly restrained. However, he made no secret of the change in their relationship. Over the next few days, he was openly affectionate with her. Not embarrassingly so, but just enough to let everyone know that he had staked a claim on Jayme's heart.

While Joe Girard seemed pleased that his son had settled interest on such an intelligent, stable, newspaper-oriented young lady, Barbara Girard lamented along with Chicago's other "queen mothers" the possible loss of the prince's attendance on society princesses. She was never rude or cruel to Jayme, but neither was she overly friendly, though her daughters were quite amiable. Heather's congeniality sprouted from sheer relief because Jayme posed no romantic threat to the younger girl's impossible pursuit of Najib, who had spoken so freely and so fairly of the girl from Southern Illinois.

And Rick's younger sister worshipped him so devotedly that anything he did was fine with her.

Najib and Jim observed this budding romance carefully. Najib's hooded eyes, so accustomed to veiling secrets that were epidemic in his country, revealed no opinion, and he said nothing that would indicate whether he approved. By way of his parental rank, Jim was more openly watchful. Jayme could do a lot worse than Rick Girard…Harlan, for instance…but Jim was all too aware of inherent tendencies in young men to break the hearts and honor of young ladies. While Jim was relieved that Rick could possibly steer Jayme's heart away from Harlan, he was equally worried that the hippie would misuse his daughter in some foul, traumatic way.

This kind of attention was unfamiliar to Jayme. The only boy who had ever treated her like a real girl was Ollie, but she had never experienced for him the feelings she was having for Rick.

Then there was the unique sensation of being worthy of a man's public attention. Rick actually reached for her hand and held it when people were watching, as if he didn't care it was attached to a lard-filled blimp. When everyone gathered in the viewing balcony to watch *Anne of the Thousand Days* or in the family room for games or television, he wrapped his arm around her shoulders as if it was the natural thing to do. And when the press of people overwhelmed them, he excused himself and Jayme from the gathering and led her from the room, his obvious intention some time alone with her.

Other Girards paid little attention to this subtle exit. Obviously something was going on here, or Rick would not have been so insistent about inviting the McCrays up for New Year's week.

But the eyes of Najib and Jim followed the couple unrelentingly, and Jayme always blushed under their scrutiny. Oddly enough, her blushing eased her father's concerns. He would have been more worried if she hadn't blushed.

Rick and Jayme spent most of their alone time in Rick's room…watching television or listening to his stereo…holding hands…hugging…kissing…

Sometimes his kisses were slow and thoughtful, sometimes urgent and exploratory. On those occasions when his lips were more persuasive, Jayme was amazed that she responded so eagerly. Amazed and alarmed when she herself wanted more from him than these tantalizing kisses provided. When, eventually, his hand strayed to her breasts, she did not deny him. She pushed him away with whispered and regretful protests only when his fingers played along the hem of her dress onto her thigh.

He never argued with her or tried to persuade her to change her mind. But sometimes he went to the bar for the ice bucket and locked himself in the bathroom for a while.

Jayme never knew why. Until she asked him. And he told her.

* * *

"You and I have never been apart on New Year's Eve," Jayme said as she fussed with her father's tie. "I'm not sure I like it that way."

"My tie?"

"No, silly…being away from you tonight."

"Then clarify your pronouns with distinct antecedents, love." He grasped her hands and held them against his chest. "You're a young woman now, Jayme. It's natural for you to venture from the nest. Besides, you have your date for tonight, and I have mine."

Jayme's eyebrows shot up. "YOU have a date?"

"You needn't sound so surprised. It's not the first time in my life I've had one."

"It's the first time in MY life." Stepping away from her father, Jayme folded her arms and studied him.

When she continued to stare at him in silence, Jim asked uneasily, "Has this news upset you, love? Maybe I should have given you some warning, but you've been so busy with Rick. Joe and Barbara set this blind date up for me, but I can cancel if—"

Smiling, Jayme hugged her father tightly. "I'm happy to pieces that you have a date. Sometimes daughters forget that their daddies are men, too, and I had to stand back and look at you through different eyes for a minute. You're a very handsome man, and it's a wonder I haven't had a thousand women clamoring to be my stepmom before now."

"Hold on there, girl. No one's talking step-ANYTHING. This is just a New Year's Eve date. I haven't even met the woman yet."

Curiosity shined in Jayme's warm brown eyes. "Who is she, Dad?"

Jim turned to the mirror for one final inspection. "All I know is that her name is Gwyndolena Ridgeway. Her husband died a year ago, and since then she's been keeping busy with charity work and writing society pieces for the *Ledger.*"

"Are you nervous?"

Sighing, he turned back around to her. "I'm scared to death. Does it show?"

"Not a bit." She hugged him again for reassurance. "If you're lucky, she may not hear your knees knocking together."

He grinned and reached to rumple her hair. Then, remembering how long she had taken to arrange her stubborn auburn curls for the evening, he patted her cheek instead.

"Where will you young people be celebrating this evening?"

"Some night spot called JT's. It's supposed to be a happening place for college kids."

"Tell me I won't be bailing my daughter and her friends out of a Chicago jail."

"Not to worry, Daddykins. Even Rick is acting civilized these days."

"I've noticed. Is there anything special you want to tell me?"

"Not to tell you exactly," Jayme said, her face serious, "but I want to ask you something."

"Just be gentle with your old man."

"Well…" Jayme twisted a curl with her finger. "You loved Mom an awful lot, didn't you, Daddy?"

"I did and I do. My love for her did not die with her."

"In all the time since she died…have you ever been…attracted to another woman?"

"Oh, I suppose I've seen a few I'd describe as attractive."

"That's not exactly what I meant. I meant have you ever in that time…wanted the…uh…companionship of another woman?"

Though Jim blushed deeply, he met her eyes evenly. "I'm human, Jayme. Of course there have been times when I've been…lonely…for a woman."

"But you never did anything about it. You never dated anyone…until tonight. Was it because you loved Mom so much?"

"For a few years, maybe that was part of it. Mostly, though, my priorities didn't allow for it. First you, then my job…there wasn't any time or energy left over for romance."

Jayme's lip trembled. "I never wanted you to be lonely because of me, Daddy. I wouldn't have minded your dating."

"Now, love, don't do that." He wrapped his arms around her and stroked her carefully coiffed curls. "You kept me from being too lonely. I've spent my time on what is most important to me, and I have absolutely no regrets about it. You've filled my life with more joy than most men can ever hope to have."

He stepped away from her and took her hands into his. "Now tell me why the questions, love. Are you afraid I've stopped loving your mother because I'm going out with someone else tonight?"

"No…never that." Jayme avoided his eyes, but only briefly. "I was wondering if it's…well…natural to love someone with all your heart and still be attracted to someone else."

"Ah, I see now. Your 'someone' is Harlan and 'someone else' Rick?"

"It's silly considering that Harlan is engaged to that Georgia bimbo and I'm barely more than fungal growth to him, but I do feel guilty for liking Rick so much."

"Considering that Harlan's brain is filled with fungal growths, perhaps you stand a better chance than you think."

"Daddy, please. I'm serious."

"I know, and I've had many a worry about just how serious you are about Harlan. I don't need to enumerate the reasons why to you, do I?"

"I've enumerated them to myself a million times, but my heart never seems to notice."

"You don't have to forsake old dreams while opening your heart to new ones. Life and love are often trial and error processes. If you and Rick are attracted to each other, then let yourself experience and enjoy all the relationship can give you. Maybe you'll discover that Rick is the man for you after all. Maybe you'll find that Harlan's the only man who can make you happy. Maybe you'll decide that neither one of them is what you really want. I don't know, and neither will you if you close your heart to every boy who isn't Harlan."

"It's okay for me to LIKE being with Rick?"

"Jayme Rose, Harlan is engaged to be married, and though no one in his right mind…which excludes Harlan…expects this marriage to last very long, the fact remains that he is unavailable to you in the way you want him. You owe him nothing…neither love nor loyalty beyond that which you'd give any childhood friend."

"But what if…when…he is available to me?"

"Jayme love, has Harlan ever been available to you?"

Eyes lowered, Jayme shook her head.

Jim tipped her face up. "Don't throw away the happiness Rick is offering you now for the dubious kind of happiness you only wish Harlan will provide. Some things are not meant to be, and those that are will happen in their own time no matter what you do. Rick does make you happy, doesn't he?"

"Yes…yes, he does."

"The continue to let him make you happy and feel no guilt for it. If anyone in this world deserves happiness, it's my little girl…" A knock on the door interrupted him. Jim pushed her gently on her way. "There's your date, picking you up at your door like a proper gentleman."

"I'll think of you at midnight, Daddy," Jayme said, kissing her father's cheek.

"I'm sure Rick will be aiming your thoughts in other directions…"

Fortunately, Rick had the foresight to call ahead for a reservation. JT's bulged with New Year's Eve revelers, most of them college students home for the holidays. Even the dance floor was so jammed that dancing was virtually impossible. Instead the horde jerked en masse as the music from the rock band struggled for recognition above the crowd clamor.

Six of them were squeezed into a semi-circular booth that afforded them some degree of privacy. Jayme was comfortably flanked on one side by Najib and on the other by Rick, who placed his arm possessively around her shoulders as soon as they were seated. She was, however, self-conscious about his attentions in the presence of his other three friends, unknown to her an hour before.

Jayme had heard Rick talk about Leonard Cassidy many times, but the young man who sat at the end of the booth bore little resemblance to what she expected. In appearance, he mirrored Najib's grooming preferences more than Rick's: short, neatly combed hair and a clean-shaven face. He certainly looked more at ease in his three-piece suit than did Rick, who had been tugging at the knot of his tie all evening.

In spite of these differences, however, the two were obviously close and genuinely happy to be sharing the evening's celebration. Leonard's date, a petite brunette named Dorinda, seemed miffed that she was not receiving proper adulation from her companion and sat silent and sullen while the conversation flowed around her. Other than the barest minimum required for politeness, Jayme made no friendly overtures to Dorinda, who plainly thought Rick was out of his mind for bringing someone so plebian and so fat to JT's.

Even Najib's date ignored Dorinda. And Najib's date was Leonard's sister, Lora Donna. (Oh, the scene when Heather learned of Najib's New Year's Eve plans!)

Because no one had been paying much attention to Dorinda, everyone was surprised when she did barge into the conversation…with nothing remotely relevant. The rest of them had been discussing the pessimism of Kurt Vonnegut, Jr.

"I was sure you'd have Tawney with you tonight," she said to Rick. "SHE was expecting to be here with you, too, just like last year."

Rick blinked away a moment's disorientation with the sudden change in conversational direction.

"Tawney? Here?"

"Well, not now, stupid. You never called her. Shame on you, Rick Girard. She's probably home right now, crying her eyes out because you didn't call."

"If I know Tawney, she has a dozen guys lined up to welcome in the new year," Rick said.

Dorinda ignored Leonard's warning scowl. "Is that any way to talk about the girl who intends to marry you some day?"

"Her intentions are not my intentions, so shut your goddamn mouth and quit trying to cause trouble."

"Cause trouble?" Dorinda's eyes widened at the offense. "Me? Why, Rick, I was just concerned for my very close friend Tawney. And for Jayme, too. If she had known about Tawney, she wouldn't have wasted her holiday by following you home."

Rick's arm tightened around Jayme, who stared at her hands, clasped in her lap. Scratching his beard, Rick flashed Leonard a look of sympathy. "What did you do, Len? Wait until the last minute to get a date for tonight?"

Leonard's smile was apologetic. "Looks like I should've waited a while longer."

"Hey..." Dorinda said indignantly. "What do you mean by that remark, Leonard?"

"I mean, darling Dorinda," Leonard's narrowed eyes bore into hers, "shut your goddamn mouth and quit trying to cause trouble."

As Dorinda huffed and angrily folded her arms, Najib patted Jayme's clenched hands and leaned over to Lora Donna. "Perhaps this is a good time for us to dance...if we can find enough space to move."

Nodding eagerly, Lora Donna smiled at Jayme and frowned at Dorinda. Leonard stood up and pulled Dorinda out of the booth so that his sister and Najib could leave.

"We'll dance, too, while we're up," he said to his date as he shouldered their way into the crowd. "And when we return, we'll remember that tonight we're here to have a good time...unless, of course, I accidentally lose you on the dance floor."

"Wanna dance?" Rick asked Jayme when they were alone in the booth.

She shook her head and stared out into the crowd.

He turned her face to his. "I'm sorry for that bit of bullshit, Kitten."

"Why should you be sorry?" She smiled to ease the concern clouding his eyes. "For once someone else was being ill-mannered."

Grinning, he touched his forehead to hers. "Do you want to know about Tawney?"

"You don't need to explain anything. As per our understanding, I know and accept that you have other girls."

"I don't HAVE other girls. I merely reserved my right to SEE other girls from time to time, and I told you why. You're the only one who matters to me."

"Does that make me queen of your harem?"

"You're being a smart-ass now. I knew you were upset."

"I'm not upset."

"You always talk like a smart-ass to hide your hurt, and there's no reason for you to be upset now. Tawney and I saw a lot of each other once, but that was over a long time ago."

"I'm not upset. I have no right to be upset."

"Dammit, Kit, would you stop with the goddamn magnanimity? Can't you just once be jealous enough to demand fidelity from me?"

"Under the circumstances, I've no right to do that either. You made that clear yourself."

"You're supposed to disagree with me."

"Why?"

Exasperated, he banged out a rock rhythm on the table so loudly that the glasses rattled.

"So that I can demand fidelity from you, dammit," he growled, slapping his hands on the table and leaving them there.

"The degree of my infidelity is not so threatening as yours."

"You said 'threatening,' so you must feel threatened," he grinned triumphantly.

"I was merely establishing a point of comparison."

"Why don't we cut through the bullshit and say it like it is?"

"You go first."

"I want to sleep with you tonight. There, I can't be any blunter than that."

"Forget it. And I can't be any blunter than that."

"But, Kit…"

"We have an understanding, remember?"

"Fuck the understanding. I didn't know how hard it would be when I agreed to stop at hugging and kissing." When he saw the corners of Jayme's mouth quiver, he grinned, "And no pun intended, but it is appropriate."

Jayme tugged gently on his beard. "Rick…I like you an awful, awful lot…"

"I like you an awful, awful lot, too, Kit. That's why I want you so damn much. And you want me, too."

"I can't deny that," she said softly, "but I'm just not ready for such a big step in my life."

"It's Harwood again, isn't it?"

"No," she replied, surprised that she could truthfully say it. "What you're suggesting is, to me at least, more than just relieving primal urges. Lately I've been pretty confused about a lot of things I used to be so sure of. I can't be rushed until I get some things straight in my head…and in my heart, too, I guess. I'm sorry this isn't the way you want it to be, but that's the best I can offer you right now. If you want to call Tawney, I'll understand."

Sighing, he pressed his lips against the top of her head. "No Tawneys. I don't like waiting in line. But I gotta tell you, Kit, you're making me crazy."

Jayme's brown eyes sparkled as she met his tender gaze. "You were crazy when I found you."

"Would you mind if a crazy man kissed you here in such a public place?"

"Will Dorinda be upset about Prince Rick kissing one of the peasants?"

"Fuck Dorinda. Which is probably what Len intends to do later. I can think of no other reason why he'd want to take her out on New Year's Eve."

"Are all men sex maniacs?"

"I'm trying to reform. So do I get my kiss?"

When Jayme nodded, his mouth descended onto hers. It was not a kiss intended for a public place, but Jayme didn't care. Who would be paying attention to them anyway?

Dorinda. She and Leonard returned to the booth then, and Dorinda leaned across the table to knock Rick's beer into his lap.

"So sorry, Rick," she purred as Leonard shoved her into the booth. "I was reaching for a napkin to blot my lipstick."

Rick grabbed a handful of napkins for himself. "Dorinda, you're a liar as well as a bitch."

Dorinda smiled sweetly, first at Leonard, then at Rick. "I was doing you a favor, Rick. You looked like you were overheating and needed cooling off."

"Yeah, you did me a favor," Rick said, stuffing napkins into Jayme's hand, "but not in the way you intended. Jae, my love, if you'll help me by blotting the beer out of my lap, I can go back to being overheated."

The flush already on Jayme's face deepened, though she smiled faintly as she wadded the napkins back into Rick's hand. "Maybe later, my stallion."

"Do you really mean it?" Rick whispered into her ear.

Laughing, Jayme pushed him gently away. "You don't let up, do you?"

"Not where a pretty girl is concerned," Leonard said, nudging Dorinda even closer to Jayme to make room for Najib and Lora Donna, who were returning to the booth. Dorinda stopped short of touching Jayme, of course. Peasantry might be contagious.

"There is no room for dancing," Najib said. "Except for...how to say it...chin to chin. Of fortune, I do not mind standing so close to Lora Donna, the lovely one."

Lora Donna melted under his smoldering observation while Dorinda sniffed at such foolishness.

Draining his beer mug, Leonard indicated to their waitress that the drinks should be replenished. "You'll notice," he said, "that Dorinda and I weren't out there long."

Dorinda was quick to catch his implication. "If you're going to insult me all evening, you can take me home now."

"Sorry. You'll have to sit here and be insulted 'cause I'm not going anywhere. I'm here to share this evening with my sister, my oldest and best buddy, and my two new friends, and you don't seem inclined to be agreeable to any of us."

"Well, I never!"

"Yes, you have, Dorinda...many, many times...which is why I let you con me into bringing you tonight. I waited too long to get a congenial date...just like Rick said...and since I couldn't get good company, I went for an adequate lay."

"Adequate!" she squealed, all his other remarks forgotten. "How dare you say I'm only adequate!"

"Truth hurts, doesn't it?" Rick said behind half-lowered eyelids and a faintly complacent smile. When Jayme pinched his thigh, he grimaced and smiled even more.

"Take me home now, Leonard!" Dorinda yelled, propelling herself up so violently she knocked over the glasses clustered in front of her.

"If you want to leave, leave," Leonard told her easily. "I'm staying here with my friends."

Dorinda glared at everyone else in the booth in hopes of coercing some sympathy. However, Jayme was sopping up the beer and ginger ale that Dorinda had spilled, and Lora Donna and Najib were busy studying ceiling fans. Only Rick and Leonard met her glower evenly...no commiseration there. There was an awkward pause while Dorinda struggled to find a face-saving way to leave.

When Jayme opened her mouth, intending to say something in the neighborhood of "Let's all be friends," Rick pinched her thigh, beneath the skirt of her dress. Twice Jayme had to slap his hand before he moved it.

Leonard ended the silence by asking Lora Donna and Najib to stand out of the booth so that he could follow, leaving a clear path of retreat for Dorinda.

"Here's cab fare," Leonard said, slapping some bills into her hand as she passed him.

"You're just about the lowest, meanest, weasel-faced bastard on earth to be treating me like this," she hissed.

"Your estimation of me means very little. I should have come stag tonight. Desperation and tequila made me lose my head for a while."

"Small loss," Dorinda snapped. "And there are scads of guys who did come stag tonight. One of them will be happy to escort me home."

"Did she say 'scads' or 'scabs'?" Leonard asked Rick.

"I thought it was 'crabs,'" Rick said.

Jayme wasn't completely sure what the two friends were meaning with their word play, but it was enough to make Dorinda squeal one more time before she turned her back on them and lost herself in the heaving crowd.

"She didn't even give back the cab fare," Rick said, stroking his beard.

Leonard shrugged. "Still cheaper than keeping her around the rest of the night...in a lot of ways."

The waitress brought the next round of drinks then, and he waited until she was finished tidying the table and serving the fresh drinks before he spoke again.

"While we're on unpleasant subjects, I may as well unload my big news on you, buddy. I've been holding back on it 'cause I know you're gonna shit a brick when you hear...excuse my language, ladies."

Rick's hand searched beneath the table for Jayme's, but his voice was without emotion as he said, "Only two things would work like that on me, Len, and both of them mean you need your head examined. It can't be that you're getting married 'cause you brought Dorinda here tonight, so that must mean…"

"I've enlisted, Rick."

The hand around Jayme's tightened painfully as all eyes focused on Rick. Lora Donna, who had shared this secret with her brother, sneaked an encouraging glance his way, but Leonard was not aware of it. All week he had worried about the best way to break the news to his friend. Leonard feared that Rick would consider enlistment a betrayal of a boyhood friendship where they had shared everything. Leonard had not discussed this major decision with him beforehand though Rick sensed it coming when Leonard did not return to college in the fall. Their brief communications during that time and over Thanksgiving break had carefully avoided any lengthy mention of Vietnam, the draft, and enlistments although Leonard's conscience was in high gear by then. Still, any dissenting word from Rick might have changed his mind, so close was their friendship.

However, their friendship was also close enough that Rick would not intrude into this intensely personal decision even though it ran counter to his own feelings.

"You know I think you're a damn fool," Rick said finally. "And you're likely to become a dead damn fool in a war that's not even ours."

"It's a risk I have to take. Right or wrong, we're in the big middle of it, and as long as we are, it's our war. My political conscience finally overcame my social conscience."

"I'm not going to debate you on it. You know how I feel, and I know how you feel. There's too much apple pie in your blood for you to think different, so nothing short of a complete transfusion will change anything. All I have to say is watch your ass and make damn sure you bring it home intact. So when do you leave?"

"Monday morning."

"Damn. That doesn't give us much time for hell raising…"

Everyone else in JT's was beginning the ten-second countdown to 1970 then. At midnight Rick kissed Jayme, Najib kissed Lora Donna, and Leonard kissed both girls.

When Rick reached across the table to clasp Leonard's hand, Jayme shivered as an uneasy premonition slithered coldly along her spine.

"I was proud of you tonight," Jayme said later as she lay beside Rick on his bed. He had been reluctant to part company with her when they returned home, and Jayme, understanding his need to talk, had not balked at being in his room at three in the morning.

"Proud?" he asked absently, touching a kiss to her forehead just as absently. "Of what?"

"Of you…of the way you handled Leonard's news. I know you were bursting at the seams with protests and dissuasions, but you held it all back."

"What good would preaching have done? He's already enlisted. I can't fault a guy for doing what he feels he has to do, especially when the guy is my best friend. But still…"

"But still?" Jayme prompted as his voice trailed away.

"I'm scared shitless about him going to 'Nam, and we all know that's where he'll end up."

Jayme could muster no words of reassurance, for the memory of the foreboding chill she had experienced at JT's was still fresh. Instead, to comfort him, she pressed his hand against her chest and laid her head on his shoulder.

"Don't do that if you don't intend to see it through, Kitten."

"Hmm?" she murmured, puzzled.

He bounced his fist on the bed in a steady rhythm. "Kit…" he began before increasing the force of his fist pounding. "Damn…I can't handle this. Not tonight."

Quickly he rolled over, pinning Jayme beneath him and taking her mouth with masterful intensity. With one hand against the bottom of her spine, he pressed her more tightly against him. With his other hand, he fumbled at the neckline of her dress, seeking possession of the softness of her breasts.

Startled, Jayme pushed at him weakly. "Rick…don't…please…"

His voice was hoarse. "For once can't you give in to it?"

"Not like this, and not now," she said firmly. "You're half drunk, and Dad's just down the hall."

"We can go somewhere else…"

"No, Rick. You know how I feel."

"You're making me crazy, Jayme. YOU put my hand on YOUR breast, and then you act like I'm out of line for getting ideas."

"I never meant for you to get THAT idea. I was trying to comfort you."

"COMFORT me?" He rolled off the bed and laughed until tears trickled over his cheeks and into his beard. "I'll have to sleep with the whole damn ice bucket on my balls because of your comforting. Go on to your room now. I can't stand any more of your comforting."

Both worried and offended by his banishment of her, Jayme sat up, her lower lip trembling as she turned from him to slide off the bed. He let her get to the door before he stopped her.

"Good night, Kitten," he called softly as he stretched out on the bed and laid a forearm over his eyes. "Happy New Year…"

CHAPTER TWELVE

Suddenly Jim McCray began making trips to Champaign, Illinois, almost every Saturday afternoon. At first, these repeated absences were no source of any great curiosity for Jayme because her father had made many business trips in the past, especially since she had become old enough to fend for herself. Jayme herself was so busy these days that she was barely aware that Jim did not return home until dawn some Sunday mornings.

What she did notice was that he was taking greater care with his appearance, even to the point of asking her to go clothes shopping with him one weekend. And they spent a lot of time choosing men's cologne.

"You're still seeing that Gwyndolena lady, aren't you?" Jayme asked with sudden insight when they stopped for lunch.

"Well..." Jim's bald pate reddened under her scrutiny. "We...uh..."

Jayme's eyes twinkled. "Why, James Lee McCray, you've been meeting your lady in Champaign all this time, haven't you?"

"Well...we...uh..." Jim pulled at the collar of his shirt.

"You said that already, Dad." Jayme laughed and clapped her hands together, delighted by her father's discomposure. "Why the need for all the secrecy?"

He grinned sheepishly. "No need. I just didn't know how to tell you. You've been so wrapped up in other things, I didn't think you'd notice until I figured out a way to tell you."

Frowning, Jayme reached for his hand. "I have been neglecting you, haven't I?"

"Gracious no. All fathers should have a daughter as loving and attentive as mine. But you have your interests to pursue, and I have mine. There's nothing wrong with that. In fact, that's the way it should be in the natural scheme of things."

Jayme patted his hand. "Then tell me about this new interest you're pursuing. Are you in love?"

Jim paid his daughter the respect of considering her question carefully. "Having been as deeply in love with your mother as a man can be, I'd have to say no, I'm not in love with Gwynnie at this point in our relationship, but I could be some day. She's a fine woman, and we get along splendidly. And she...and she...well...never mind with that..."

"She turns you on, huh, Dad?" Jayme laughed when her father blushed again. "So why aren't you on your way to meet her? You're usually on the road by now."

"Even with meeting halfway between here and Chicago as we do, it's still quite a drive, and Gwynnie is...well...what Gwynnie's doing this weekend is packing."

"You're taking a trip together?"

"I'm not going anywhere, except to help her move into her new home. I'm hoping that you, Rick, and Najib will help us at that time."

"Sure, we'll help," Jayme said instantly, sipping her tea. "Where's she moving to?"

"She's moving to Applewood."

Jayme set her glass down so hard that tea splashed over the top. "She's moving in with us?"

"Not in with us. Just to Applewood. She's renting a house from an old college friend of hers…in Lost Hollow."

"Lost Hollow? That's a pretty classy neighborhood."

"Gwynnie's a pretty classy lady, and she can afford to live anywhere she wants to."

"She obviously wants to live close to you," Jayme grinned. "It must be serious for her to move all the way to Applewood."

"There's the potential for something serious, but that's not the entire reason for the move. Chicago's still a little painful for her since her husband died, no matter how busy she keeps herself, and she wasn't blessed with a child as I've been. So she's looking for a change of scenery, and then she had a job offer here…something to keep her busy when she's settled."

"And this new job is…?"

"You know she did some society pieces for the *Ledger.* I told you that. Remember?"

"I remember. The night before I found all that lipstick and make-up on your best dress shirt."

Jim cleared his throat. "Don't be impertinent, Jayme Rose."

"Sorry, Daddy." She made no attempt to hide her grin.

"Anyway," her father continued, rubbing a hand over his head, "I talked things over with Gerald…"

"And the owner of your paper just happens to be a friend of the Girards…or Gwynnie?"

"Actually Gerald knew Gwynnie's husband, but you get the picture. Gwynnie has a few social ties in this area…both she and her husband attended Scheffers…so we hired her to do a weekly society column for us. If our small-town audience responds favorably, we'll try a whole women's news page."

"And if the column bombs?"

Jim studied his daughter's face. "By then Gwynnie should have enough going on with her other pursuits that she can be both busy and contented in Applewood. Does this news about her relocating here upset you?"

"Of course not. I'm glad she will be here so that you won't have to drive all the way to Champaign every weekend. You haven't been worrying about me all this time, have you? I told how I felt the first night you went out with this lady."

"One date might be easier for you to accept than a relationship."

"For Pete's sake, Dad. Anything that makes you happy is acceptable to me. I trust you not to do anything embarrassing to either of us. You're not a slimy old lech or anything."

Chuckling, Jim squeezed Jayme's hand. "That wasn't exactly my main concern. Sometimes children feel...well...like they're being cast aside or abandoned when a single parent begins to date someone regularly. It's important to me that you realize that you are the single, most important part of my life, no matter who comes along or what else happens."

"Don't you think I know that already?"

"You seemed a little unsettled when you thought that Gwynnie might be moving in with us."

"I was surprised, that's all. You'd just told me you weren't quite in love with her yet, and then I thought you were saying that she was moving in. The two ideas seemed incongruous, especially for you."

"If ever you do have a problem with ANYTHING, I want you to come to me with it right away. I don't want any worries or uncertainties collecting in your head. Understand?"

"Understand."

"So you and the boys can drive up to Chicago with me next Friday after your last classes? Gwynnie's renting a U-Haul truck to bring down everything she's going to need before the professional movers take over. We can load up Saturday morning and be back in Applewood by evening so that you kids can do whatever it is you do on Saturday nights."

"We're yours for as long as you need us. We never do anything screamingly exciting on Saturdays anyway."

"Are you sure you're speaking for Rick and Najib?"

"I can convince them if they need convincing. And Rick can see his family to make up for not going home over spring break."

"Does Najib have a...a friend he can take along? We'll have three vehicles to drive back...my car, Gwynnie's, and the truck. Najib shouldn't have to make the trip alone."

"What makes you think Najib would be the one driving alone?"

Jim slowly pushed the food around on his plate. "Is there some problem between you and Rick?"

"I don't know," Jayme said softly, eyes lowered.

"Do you want to talk about it, love?"

"I don't know what to talk about. There's nothing I can put the ol' finger on...just that everything's been a little different since New Year's Eve. We had a little...misunderstanding then, but nothing that should have lasted this long."

"Has he tried anything...ungentlemanly?"

"Quite the contrary."

"You sound a little disappointed, Jayme Rose."

Color rushed to Jayme's face. "Sometimes I am."

"I see. Your feminine ego has been stepped on a little. Is that the reason for this…this…" Jim waved his hands toward Jayme. "This new you?"

"New me?" Jayme asked, bewildered as she looked down at herself.

"You've lost a lot of weight in the last few months."

"I have?" Jayme inspected herself again. Her jeans and skirts had been awfully loose lately. She thought the fabrics were becoming old and stretchy.

"Enough that Ronna and I think you need some new clothes so that you won't look like an orphaned waif," he told her with a smile. "That's another reason for today's shopping trip. Haven't you been dieting intentionally…for Rick?"

"No, honestly I haven't."

Twirling a curl around her finger, Jayme considered the reasons for this physical miracle. The busy schedule she inflicted upon herself had become her natural routine. Drudgery worked better than cookies when she didn't want to think about Harlan…and, later, Harlan's wedding. The wedding she had been "too busy" to attend. And all her unbusy time was spent with Rick and Najib. Sometimes when she collapsed into bed at night, she remembered that she hadn't had time for dinner. And lately she always overslept…never enough time for breakfast.

She felt her father's eyes on her and knew he was waiting for some response.

"I've been too busy to eat I guess," she told him simply. Why bother him with details when he was on the brink of being in love?

"I can't say this news pleases me, Jae. You're not getting the nutrients you need, and—"

Jayme interrupted him. "How much do you think I've lost, Daddy?"

"It's hard to say. Women are better judges of things like that. Your Aunt Ronna mentioned maybe forty, forty-five pounds."

"Forty-five pounds!" A sudden light radiated from her face. "Forty-five whole pounds, and I wasn't even trying!"

"Now look here, Jayme Rose. Don't be getting any foolish notions. I'll not be letting you ruin your health."

"How do I look? Tell me honestly how I look."

"You've always been beautiful…"

"You're talking like a father. Tell me how I look to real people. Do I LOOK skinnier?"

"Yes, you do…though I must admit I didn't much notice it until Ronna said something to me…I guess because I see you everyday where Ronna sees you less frequently."

"Do you realize that I've lost maybe forty-five pounds in the last few months without trying? If I could lose another forty-five pounds in the next three or four months WITH trying, I'd weigh about what all those charts say a five-seven girl my age should weigh."

"Don't get carried away. I'm concerned about your health."

"I'll take vitamins."

"Vitamins are poor substitutes for natural nutrition."

"For Pete's sake, Dad. I've been a blubber-ball all my life. How healthy is that?"

"You have never been a blubber-ball, Jayme Rose, but if you must continue with this weight loss thing, I insist that you check in regularly with Dr. Dennis."

"It's a waste of time and money, but if it will make you happy, okay."

"It will make me happy. So will buying my little girl some clothes that will fit her properly. I don't want you looking like an urchin when you meet Gwynnie. She'll think I'm a poor father."

"No one could ever think that about you, especially not a woman hot for your bod."

"Jayme Rose!"

Laughing, Jayme pushed away her plate. "Let's buy only a few things this afternoon, Dad. I'll need a whole new wardrobe in forty-five more pounds. And then..." The corners of her mouth turned up in pleasant speculation.

"And then what?" her father prompted.

"And then we'll see if Harlan Oakes will notice the girl next door."

Jim rubbed a hand over his head. "Jayme love, Harlan is a married man now, and from all his parents' reports, he and his bride are getting along fine."

"Of course they are. Harlan's gone most of the time during baseball season. But when the season is over and Cyd has him underfoot all the time, we'll see how long the honeymoon lasts."

"You're thinking thoughts that can only bring you heartache."

"He wouldn't be Harlan if he didn't break my heart a dozen times a day."

"I'm beginning to recognize the source of any problems you and Rick might be having."

"Don't be silly. Rick and I have an understanding."

"Maybe Rick doesn't understand as much as you think he does," Jim said casually as he reached for the check.

* * *

The difference in Rick that Jayme had spoken of to her father was perceptible only to her, for Rick was as openly attentive to her in public as he was before. Sometimes they double-dated with Najib if he was inclined to find a date. More frequently the three of them pursued their studies and diversions without intrusion of a fourth party, excepting Jim, who still anchored their Friday night dinner dialogues. At these times, Rick claimed the privilege of sitting closest to Jayme, draping his arm around her, holding her hand, or touching an occasional kiss to her forehead or cheek.

When Jayme and Rick were alone, however, a discernible wariness permeated all his affectionate gestures. Always tender, but never ardent, he made no further attempts at intimacy with her, neither through verbal persuasion nor physical encouragement. If they lay or sat by each other on his bed or hers, he held her hand while carefully maintaining a noticeable space between their bodies.

Some evenings, Jayme and Najib were left alone together. While delighted to have Jayme to himself for a while, Najib was equally ill at ease because he knew why they were alone for the evening. On these occasions, he persevered with steady prattle so that there would be no conversational gaps for Jayme to ask any questions.

Finally Jayme told him, "I know he's out tending to his primal urges, so stop your blathering. Rick and I have no binding commitments between us. It's okay for him to be out with other girls."

Heaving a huge sigh of relief, Najib went about the enjoyable task of bringing smiles to the face of the girl with the sunset hair. The girl whom he had found first, but on whom Rick seemed to have a stronger claim.

The girl who fought against the pain of knowing that Rick was in bed with another girl.

* * *

Jayme did not wear any of her new clothes until the trip to Chicago the following Friday. When Rick and Najib met her in the lobby of their dorm, she had the satisfaction of seeing them both do double takes when they first saw her. She was dressed casually, in jeans and a black knit pullover, but the clothes fit her well and flattered the curves emerging from her bulk.

Rick said nothing, however, as he quickly kissed her lips and stood away from her. Najib salvaged this important debut for her by walking around her for an unhurried inspection.

"We did not know you were attempting such a thing as this," he said, "and your former clothes hid from us what you were doing. My eyes have always been pleased when they behold you, but now they are pleased in twice amounts. You are like the butterfly that has shrugged away its tycoon."

Jayme was so grateful that she did not correct his English. "Thank you, Najib. I wasn't aware of it myself for a while. I usually avoid mirrors…but now that I am aware of it, I intend to continue in earnest."

Najib nodded. "My heart is pleased as well, for it sees that your eyes are now pleased with yourself. It is time that you see that beauty which many have already seen."

Jayme ventured a glance at Rick.

"We shouldn't keep Jim waiting," was all he said as he turned toward the doors to the parking lot.

They arrived in Chicago late, after ten o'clock, and Rick used that as an excuse for not, as he said, "busting in" on his family. Though both Jayme and Rick were puzzled by his decision, they didn't try to change his mind, opting instead to persuade him at least to call his parents before leaving for Applewood the next morning.

Gwendolena Ridgeway's house was as opulent and almost as large as the Girard home, but because of its stripped and packed-up appearance, it seemed cavernous and spooky.

However, Gwynnie herself was like a captured sunbeam flitting around within the gloom. *A visible Tinkerbell,* Jayme thought, stifling a giggle that might offend either her father or his lady. In truth, Jayme liked Gwynnie from the first moment Jim introduced them.

The widow was a comfortable woman, at ease with herself and with those around her. Though Jayme had anticipated a woman of the same stately, statuesque bearing as Barbara Girard, Gwynnie's figure had assumed soft, matronly proportions that emanated a cozy, serene aura.

She and Jayme shared something else that endeared each to the other for a lifetime: they both loved Jim McCray.

Since their arrival, Jayme noticed that her father was continually rubbing his hand over his head, tugging at his collar, and clearing his throat. The reason for his discomfiture eluded her for the moment, for she and Gwynnie had taken to each other so quickly and so easily that he had no cause for concern. At midnight, however, when Gwynnie suggested that everyone turn in so that they could get an early start the next morning, Jayme realized what was on her father's mind.

Why, the old dear, she thought, biting back a grin. *He wants to sleep with Gwynnie, and he's worried about what I'll think.*

"I suppose we'll be doubling up tonight since most of the linens are packed away?" Jayme asked, her eyes sparkling.

Color tinged Gwynnie's cheeks as she looked from Jayme to Jim, back to Jayme. "If everyone doesn't mind? I thought that you and Felicia could sleep in the guest suite. There's a king bed in there, so you won't be crowded. The bedroom at the end of the hall has twin beds for Rick and Najib. And Jim…"

Jayme interrupted her by stretching, yawning loudly, and declaring that her fatigue was life threatening.

"We'll go right to bed is what we'll do," she said, pushing Rick and Najib toward the stairs.

Both Rick and Najib cast strange glances her way, but they preceded her up the stairs without question while Najib's friend, Felicia, followed the group, mildly disappointed that the boys and the girls would be separated for the night.

"Jayme Rose!"

Jayme leaned over the balustrade bordering the second-floor hallway. "Yes, Dad?"

"You're not fooling anyone, love," he called up to her, smiling.

Jayme returned his smile and blew him a kiss. "Neither are you, Daddykins."

Silently fuming at how difficult Rick had become lately, Jayme stared out the window of the rented truck as it lumbered along the interstate. Though the day was fairly cool for early May, Rick had left his window down, and the circulating air chilled Jayme even as it fanned her anger. Her jacket was in her father's Oldsmobile, somewhere ahead of them on the interstate as Najib and Felicia headed back for Applewood at a speedier pace than the truck could manage. Sometime between last night and this morning, Najib had decided that he didn't much care for Felicia's company, and he was eager to take the girl home before meeting Rick and Jayme at Gwynnie's new house.

Jayme's curiosity was piqued, for she had been awake when Felicia sneaked out of the guest suite during the night. Experienced now in the wily ways of girls like Felicia, Jayme guessed that Najib and his traveling partner had planned a rendezvous in one of the vacant rooms. *Men and their primal urges,* she had thought with no sympathy or understanding.

Although she expected Najib to be all smiles and contentment in the morning, he was withdrawn and uneasy. And he carefully avoided all eye contact with Jayme, who didn't have much time for wondering why since Rick chose to start his day by being perverse.

When Jayme reminded him to call his parents, he told her…sharply…to mind her own damn business. He never called his parents, and he barely talked to Jayme, though he tried continually to start a conversation with Najib. However, Najib wasn't talking much to Rick.

The tension was exacerbated when Rick adamantly refused to drive either Gwynnie's Mercedes or Jim's Delta 88, labeling the former as a "plutocratic piss pot" and the latter as a "bourgeois facsimile of a plutocratic piss pot." Neither his language nor his attitude was much appreciated, but Jim did not belabor the point and merely reminded Rick to watch his mouth while ladies were present.

The actual assignment of vehicles warranted no further debate. Jim had chosen the truck for himself only as a courtesy because it was so much more difficult to drive, and now he gladly turned the truck keys over to Rick, pleased that the younger man would do penance for his foul mood by fighting with a stubborn gearshift.

So Jayme and Rick climbed into the truck together to lead Najib through Chicago to the interstate, from where Najib could proceed to Applewood unguided at his own pace. Jim and Gwynnie would follow later in the Mercedes.

"She wants a few minutes to say good-bye to the house," Jim explained softly. "She made a lot of memories here in the twenty years she was married."

Jayme nodded, a knot swelling in her throat. As Jim stepped away from the truck, she instinctively reached for the comfort of Rick's hand.

But he jerked away from her.

"Do you have to be hanging on me every minute?" he growled, struggling to find first gear. "I can't even shift this damn thing 'cause you're in the way."

Crushed by his rebuke, Jayme scooted immediately to the far side of the seat and pressed herself against the door. When they were finally on the interstate, her hurt gave way to anger when she asked him to roll up his window.

"If you weren't running around half naked," he snapped, "you wouldn't be cold now."

He left the window down though his own arms were goose fleshed.

Half naked? Jayme's lips tightened as she continued to glare out the window. Half naked in jeans and a Scheffers tee shirt? Her new Scheffers tee shirt. A medium. A SLIGHTLY snug medium, but she was so thrilled to fit into it, she didn't care. What was wrong with Rick that he accused her of being half naked?

Let him sulk, she finally decided. *In his current mood, he's not worth talking to.*

Her resolve lasted only until Champaign, however.

"I can't take this anymore," she said as she combed her fingers through her hair. "We have to talk about whatever it is that's bugging you so much."

"What makes you so damn sure something's bugging me?" He did not look her way, but Jayme saw his hands tighten on the steering wheel.

"You're acting like a real butt-hole, Richard."

"According to you and my roommate, that's my normal, everyday personality."

"Lately you've been worse than usual. Especially today. And I want to know why."

Because he was silent so long, she thought he wasn't going to respond at all. When he did speak, his voice was hoarse from repressed emotion.

"You're really something, you know. You bring all this on yourself, and then you stand back and pull the innocent routine. I bought your little act at first, but I'm not falling for it anymore."

Jayme stared at him in surprise. "I don't have the slightest idea of what you are talking about."

"Then let me be more direct. You're a prick tease, Jayme. Even worse than that, you're a prick tease who's using me for practice, and I'm damn sure sick of it."

Although Jayme wasn't exactly sure what she was being accused of, she wasn't about to voice her ignorance.

"How dare you say such a thing?" she demanded indignantly, hoping to provoke him into an explanation. He gave her more than a simple explanation.

"I dare because it's true," he said, pausing to gather breath before unleashing his verbal barrage. "You'd get me all worked up, just enough to make me think you might finally give in, and then you'd stop me cold like I had no business even thinking about what I was thinking about.

"So then I got smart enough to realize you weren't going to give in, and I decided, okay, I'll be a perfect little gentleman for my perfect little virgin, and when she sees I'm serious about her, maybe she'll loosen up with me a little.

"But that wasn't good enough for you, was it? You didn't like it unless I was suffering a little, did you? So then you turn up looking like THAT...like you did last night and like you do today...swinging your hips and bouncing your tits at me, and you wonder why I'm being an asshole?

"It's self-preservation 'cause I know it's all show and no go with you, especially now that you're realizing how fine you can look. There's only one guy you figure to be good enough to give the green light to. Is that why you're dropping the pounds, 'cause you realize that's the only way you'd stand an even chance with a brainless fuckwad like Harwood?

"Well, you won't be practicing your womanly tricks on me to use on him later. You're damn lucky I didn't drag you off somewhere and rape you last night. You had it coming. Lucky for me Felicia was very accommodating about double plays."

The denials and protests that had formed on Jayme's lips as Rick vented his frustrations so vehemently were instantly forgotten after this last revelation.

"What kind of double play are we talking about?" When he did not answer, she stretched across the seat and yanked his beard hard enough to make him wince. "Tell me or so help me I'll yank out every whisker you have."

"Is that your kick...you're a glutton for details? Okay, I'll tell you. Felicia serviced Najib and then she took care of me. How many more details do you want?"

"You're despicable!"

"Oh, come off it. You're the one who insisted on that goddamn understanding between us. It leaves a lot of loopholes in a relationship. Felicia's not the only one I've laid since New Year's Eve. You can't pretend you didn't know."

"But under the same roof with me practically in the next room?"

"You might as well have been on Mars for all the good you would have done me."

"You're beyond despicable! And Najib, too, for letting himself be part of your...your ORGY!"

"Don't be so hard on the guy. He was asleep when Felicia came in and started working him over, and by the time he was fully awake, he was too far gone to stop her. He was a lot more squeamish about watching her with me than I was about watching her with him. I think he even left the room for a while."

"I hate you, Richard Girard!" She clenched her teeth to stop their chattering...and closed her eyes to stop the tears.

"A typical female response. You're learning the game well, my dear."

Because they were cruising along a busy interstate at sixty miles per hour, Jayme resisted the urge to slap him.

Instead she told him hoarsely, "When we get to Applewood, you can let yourself out at your dorm. I'm sure you'd rather be sliming around with Felicia than helping Gwynnie move in."

"Fine with me," he said easily. "I didn't volunteer for the job, you know. But how do you intend to get the truck from the dorm to Gwyn's?"

"I'll drive it myself."

"You? That should provide the world with a laugh or two."

"I can drive a clutch, smart-butt. My Bug's a clutch."

"You can fit a hundred Bugs into this truck."

"And you can fit a hundred trucks into your big mouth, you son of a bitch, so shut the fuck up. After today I don't want to see your goddamn slimy face ever again. Understand?"

Her language astonished him, but all he said was, "Fine with me," as he turned his full attention to the road in front of him.

Najib was waiting for her when she lurched to a stop in Gwynnie's hydrangea bush.

"Why are you driving this vehicle?" he asked, jumping onto the running board. "Where is Rick? Has a thing happened?"

"I'm in no mood to discuss Mr. Richard Girard with anyone," she said, opening the door and knocking him off the running board. "Especially with you. I just picked off a stop sign at the end of the street and scared the puddin' out of an old lady by jumping the curb and nearly running her down. My arm's been jerked out of its socket by shifting this damn thing, and now I've squashed Gwynnie's hydrangeas. So leave me alone while I go somewhere to scream my head off. I don't want Dad to see me like this."

Najib grabbed her arm as she walked away from him. "Rick told you of the events of last night, has he not?"

Jayme pulled away from him. "Rick has told me."

"I am most ashamed, Jayme. I must explain."

"I don't want to talk to you now, Najib, but I'll get over being angry with you a whole lot sooner than I'll get over being angry with Rick. You and I will talk then if you still think it's necessary."

"I will so think, if you please."

"Let's start unloading the truck, and maybe I can work my angries out without screaming. I don't want Gwynnie's new neighbors to think the neighborhood is being overrun by banshees."

"Banshees? Who are these banshees?"

"I'll explain it to you later…when I'm talking to you again."

Jim could tell by the look in his daughter's eyes that he should forgo any inquiries about Rick's absence. Restricting himself to conversational trivialities, he helped Najib finish unloading the truck while Jayme and Gwynnie unpacked inside. They all worked steadily until dusk, when Gwynnie declared that enough order had been established within the house that they could take a long dinner break.

While Gwynnie called in a carryout order, Jim flashed inquisitive looks alternately between Jayme and Najib. That his daughter and her friend exchanged few, if any words throughout the afternoon and early evening had not escaped his notice. Common sense told him that their silence was in some way connected to the reason for Rick's absence, but still he ventured no questions beyond who would go for the food.

Najib quickly volunteered.

"I would be so honored to go," he said, accepting Jim's car keys, but waving away the money Jim tried to give him. "Please, no. I would be so honored also if you allow me to pay for our dinner this night. If Jae will permit me her company, my honor will be complete."

Both men turned to Jayme for her reply, and thus cornered by their stares, she shrugged, grabbed up her jacket, and headed for the door with Najib following closely behind her. Her acquiescence, though reluctant, gave him reason to hope that his sentence of silence would soon be commuted.

However, Jayme said nothing to him on the short drive to the restaurant, and she remained in the car when he went inside to pick up the order. When she said nothing on the return trip either, Najib was certain he was forever doomed to her displeasure.

His shoulders sagged as he opened the car door, and Jayme chewed on her lip, suddenly regretful for making Najib bear the brunt of the anger she felt for Rick.

"Wait, Najib…"

His head jerked around toward her, and in the glow of the yard lamp, his dark eyes glistened hopefully.

"You are speaking once again to me?" he asked, pulling the car door closed behind him as he slid across the seat to take her hand.

"I am speaking once again to you." She pulled her hand away from his grasp. "But I'm still not pleased by your part in the orgy last night."

"What I have done I cannot undo, my cherished friend, though my shame today has no boundaries."

Sighing, Jayme shook her head and brushed her fingers through her curls. "It's Rick who should be ashamed. Felicia was your date. If you and she wanted to…uh…be friendly, I have no right to criticize though I am surprised that you were able to function with an audience."

"I cannot explain to a lady of your innocence the hungers of a man, but at times they consume his reason and nobility like the very worst of Hell's fire."

"You don't need to explain your actions to me," she said softly, "but I wish you would explain Rick's. I don't understand why he did what he did."

"Nor do I, though I am trying, and perhaps I see a glimmer of what is troubling him inside."

"He said last night was my fault."

"How could this be true?"

"He accused me of being a...a prick tease."

"Is this accusation a true one?"

"Of course not!" Jayme closed her eyes. "If I was doing that to him, I swear I didn't realize it. The very idea of a bucket of lard like me being able to do the things he accused me of is absurd."

"You underestimate yourself, my dear friend. You're a beautiful woman in every way that is possible."

"Thank you, Najib. You are very sweet to say so, but you and my dad are the only two men who think that way."

"Again you underestimate. Rick is of agreement, and there are more whom you do not see, for always your eyes are focused on that one who plays a game for his money and thinks of women as only dolls with no feelings."

"I can't help how I feel. Lord knows I've tried to reason myself out of it. But I was always honest with Rick. He had his primal-urges girls, and I had Harlan...or my dreams about having Harlan."

"Rick does not want many girls. He wants only the one that fills his heart."

"Not anymore," Jayme said, choking back a sudden sob. "I can't easily forget what he did to me last night. Whatever I was doing either consciously or unconsciously was not enough for him to do what he did."

"You do not see in his heart at this time little things grow and fester and cause him pain he will never admit he feels. He is a much troubled man who is full of fear for Leonard."

"I understand that, but it's no reason for his being such a colossal, all-around jerk...not only to me. He treats his family like puppy poo."

"He writes to Shari, and she to him. She will call him when their parents are not home, and he will glow at the sound of her voice. It is his father who has much upset him into this exile of his own making. Did you know that Mr. Girard called his only son a coward for not following in the way of Leonard?"

"No, I didn't know. Rick never said anything."

"He hides his heart well. But I heard their argument at the time of this new year, for their discussion was very loud and angry. You and Jim were in your rooms packing at this time."

"I can sympathize will all these things that are bothering him. I really can. But lots of people have problems without acting like slug slime to the people who care most for them."

"This is Rick's way...and the way of many men both in my country and in yours. It is better to be obnoxious and strong than sensitive and weak. Such men are uncertain of their manhood."

"Rick? Uncertain of his manhood? You're joking, of course."

"I am most serious. He does not know who is this Rick Girard that hides within his body. He does not want his father's image to be his own even where they are alike, for to be so diminishes Rick to a copy in his own eyes. So he chooses a path that is not always agreeable to him just to be different. He is so stubborn in this one thing I sometimes want to knock on his head."

"He's alienating people…losing friends…"

"This is true. But friends who are deep should see this wall he builds around himself and climb over it."

"Are you saying I should forgive and forget what he did last night?"

"Would you not forgive your athlete friend if he had been the one to do what Rick did?"

"I'm ashamed to say I probably would…but Harlan and I have never been romantically involved. Even with the open relationship that Rick and I had, what he did last night was unforgivable. I was just a few feet away from your orgy, for Pete's sake. He showed ZERO respect for me. I should forgive THAT?"

"Forgiveness is a decision to be found within your own heart. I only want you to try to understand our friend as I have tried. My road is easier to travel because I live with him and see his many moods when he does not think I see. I can tell you that walking with his fear for Leonard is his fear that his father is right."

"About what?"

"Rick wonders if he is a coward. He has said in recent weeks that most conscientious objectors and anti-war demonstrators are cowards hiding behind glorious pacifistic slogans. He has never talked this way before…and he talks this way only to me. To everyone else his…how to say it…mask is still in place."

Jayme was silent as she considered all that Najib had told her.

"If I ask you something, will you tell me the truth?" she said finally.

"I may not wish to reply, but I will never lie to you."

"Whose idea was it…Rick's or Felicia's…for them to…to be together after you and she were done?"

"Felicia has been without innocence for many years. What she suggested to him, he did not refuse."

"I see."

"I do not try to convince you that he did nothing shameful, for we all know this is not true. Rick knows this, too, and hides his disgrace behind his disagreeableness."

"I will not go rushing back into his arms proclaiming my forgiveness. He would only rebuff the gesture anyway."

"I do not ask you to do so. Only, please, do not hate him."

"I don't hate him. I just don't want to see his fuzzy face for a while."

"His heart will be heavy with regret and sadness."

"He can easily find someone else to lighten the load."

"The one he wants is the girl with the sunset hair."

"The girl with the sunset hair has had her fill of Rick Girard. I'll tell you this though: he's very lucky to have a friend like you."

"Perhaps not." Najib slid back across the seat and opened his door.

"Why do you say that?"

"I speak words I know I should say for you to hear," he said without looking at her, "but a selfish part of me would be pleased if you and Rick were forever apart."

"I still don't understand what you mean."

"I have not always liked sharing you with my friend," he said, reaching for the sacks of Chinese food, "and many times I have wished to be the one to bring the starlight to your eyes."

Astonished, Jayme stared at him as he muttered something about the food being cold now as he walked away toward the house.

Chapter Thirteen

N ajib stopped suddenly as he rounded the corner of the library building and
saw Jayme sitting vividly beautiful in the sunlight that glistened within her
hair like gold dust engraining a brilliant sunset. She had lost even more weight,
and her soft and simple dress billowed slightly in the midsummer breeze so that
Najib was blessed with a full glimpse of her shapely legs.

She was oblivious to his scrutiny. She was so lost in her own thoughts that
she was oblivious to everything and everyone within the normal sphere of her
notice.

Najib wished that her thoughts could be so fully focused on him, but he
knew such longings were futile. Since that May evening two months before when
he had so carelessly given her a peek into his heart, both of them had carefully
avoided any mention of what he had revealed to her. Their continuing friendship
depended on this mutual disregard of his lapse.

Najib had not tried to force his way with her even though she and Rick had
neither seen nor spoken with each other since that day. With the three of them
enrolled in summer school and Rick and Jayme sharing the same major, Najib
knew that his friends had to work stubbornly at avoiding each other, and he was
both saddened by their loss and gladdened by his own gain, for now Jayme spent
all her free time…what there was of it…with only her Lebanese friend.

However, on this summer day, Jayme's thoughts were far away from
Scheffers or Najib or Rick. In truth, she seldom allowed herself to think about
Rick anymore unless Najib accidentally mentioned his name. Her self-inflicted
schedule was again her salvation. The intense strength of will she had discovered
within herself and the determination that had kept her on an eight-hundred-
calorie daily diet had also kept Rick Girard out of mind, if not out of memory.

Now that her weight-loss goal was within thirteen pounds of realization, she
was channeling her energies toward another goal: Harlan Oakes.

The more she thought about Harlan, the less she wanted to think about Rick.

A strong mind could convince itself of about anything.

Of course, she didn't tell her father or Najib about the content of these
thoughts. Najib would have his feelings hurt, and her father would be appalled
that she was thinking such serious thoughts about a married man.

A TEMPORARILY married man.

Jayme was counting on his temporary matrimonial state. When the inevitable
happened, she would be ready for him. REALLY ready.

Some days she didn't even eat her full eight hundred calories. And one of the
assistant baseball coaches at Scheffers had given her an exercise program that
she followed religiously, even on those days when she was drop-dead tired. A
flabby body would be as repulsive to Harlan as a fat one.

To keep her father happy, she checked in with Dr. Dennis each month and
faithfully took the vitamins and supplements he prescribed for her. And

Gwynnie, who was delighted to be consulted, provided all kinds of useful assistance, from teaching Jayme how to use a curling brush to tame her wayward curls to instructing the young woman in the most flattering make-up applications. Gifted with impeccable taste in clothing, Gwynnie was also invaluable as Jayme began to build her new wardrobe, funded by her proud father, who excused his indulgence by saying that Jayme needed all her savings for school. Jayme wasn't fooled by his rationalization. Because she had a scholarship and lived at home, her actual school expenses were relatively minor.

Jayme was careful to seek the advice of her aunt, too, for Ronna had been somewhat miffed at Gwynnie's arrival in Applewood. That her sister's place in Jim's heart was being usurped was almost forgivable, for men, by nature, were inclined to fickleness, and Rosie had been gone for many years. However, Ronna fretted openly that the widow was also worming her way into Jayme's affections. Though sometimes Jayme became impatient with her aunt's insecurities, still she hastened to reassure the woman who had guided her with such motherly devotion for so many years. Jayme very much wanted her Aunt Ronna and Gwynnie to be friends, especially since her father and Gwynnie were so obviously in love.

In love...

Jayme raised her face to the sunshine. *Someday,* she vowed, *Harlan Oakes will be in love with me. He has to be. He just has to be.*

Absently she wrinkled her nose and fanned the air in front of her. Cigarette smoke. Najib's cigarette smoke.

She faced him apologetically because she didn't know how long he had been sitting beside her on the low brick retaining wall.

"You shouldn't be smoking those nasty things," she reminded him softly.

"When I see you, I forget many things but your beauty," he said, crushing the offensive cigarette on the sidewalk. "Are you ready for lunch?"

"Just tea for me today," she told him, grasping the hand he held out to her. "I'm too close to give in to a few hunger pangs now."

"I do so hope you will find your destination worthy of this arduous road you now travel, my dear friend."

The brown eyes that met his were determined.

But the longer his dark eyes bore into hers, the more uncertain she became.

* * *

"Hello, Kit."

The voice she had banished so diligently from her mind now caused her hand to tremble even as she tightened her grip on the telephone receiver.

Why was he calling her now after over two months of silence? SOMETHING was going on. Najib had been acting strangely these past few days, even for Najib.

Shock and concern forced her into civility.

"Hello, Rick."

"How've you been doing?"

"Fine, thank you. And you?"

There was silence on the other end. Then she heard his muttered expletive.

"Fuck this idle chitchat," he said. "I'm calling because I need to see you, as soon as you can make it."

Her heart flopped over, and her knuckles whitened as her grip on the telephone tightened even more.

"Why?" she asked.

"Let's call it unfinished business."

Her eyes narrowed suspiciously. "Sorry. I'm busy."

More silence. Then, "Please, Kit. I'm asking you…please…"

The urgency in his voice alarmed her.

"Okay," she said finally. "I'm on my way to meet with Dr. Nealy right now, but I can meet you afterward."

"That's good. Thank you. Call upstairs when you get here, and I'll come down to get you."

"You want me to meet you in your dorm?"

"If you don't mind…"

"I do mind, unless Najib is there."

"He's in classes for the next three hours."

"Then we…we should meet somewhere else."

"Kit…look…I can't go into details right now, but it's a lot more convenient if you meet me here. We can leave the door open if you're afraid of me."

There was no mockery in his voice. She wasn't afraid of him, but of his sudden inexplicable seriousness.

"Okay," she told him, her whole body trembling now. "It'll be a good hour before I can get there though. Dr. Nealy wants to talk to me about one of my papers."

"So long as you're coming. That's all that matters."

He hung up without saying good-bye.

Rick didn't wait for the elevator when Jayme called to tell him she was waiting in the lobby. Instead he took the stairs, two or three at a time, slowing only when he reached the stairwell door. Cautiously he peeked through the small window there. Her back was to him as she faced the elevators, expecting his appearance there. If not for her hair, he would not have recognized her this way.

"You're letting your hair grow," he said softly behind her as he gently touched an auburn curl.

She whirled around. "Rick! You startled me. I was watching the elevator for you."

His heart contracted painfully. Najib had been right, of course. She was a bona fide knockout.

He watched her velvet eyes as she stared at him, her lovely lips parted from the shock of what she saw. He had changed, too. Perhaps more drastically than she. His beard and mustache were gone, as well as the long hair. Except for the torn tee shirt and faded denims, he could easily have been mistaken for one of the Ivy Leaguers he usually scorned.

His eyes were the same though. Darkly brown. Penetrating. Yet softening now as his gaze lingered on her.

"Y-You...y-you..." She found her mouth suddenly too dry to speak.

Gently he cupped her elbow with his hand and guided her toward the elevator. "We'll talk upstairs."

She did not protest when he slid his arm around her waist in the elevator, for she was too unsure of her fragile composure. He felt her uncertainty and resorted to harmless small talk to ease her tension.

"So how did your meeting with Dr. Nealy go?" he asked casually, pressing the button for his floor.

"Oh...f-fine. He's a big help with my writing st-style. That's why I keep signing up f-for his classes I guess."

For Pete's sake, Jayme Rose, she chided herself. *Must you stutter so?*

But Rick didn't seem to realize that she was stuttering. *Or he's too much of a gentleman to mention it. Rick? A gentleman?*

"Your writing style is already earning you a lot of respect in the department," he said, "so Dr. Nealy must be doing something right."

She swallowed back the dryness that had spread to her throat. *A compliment? From Rick Girard?* "Thanks."

"I've been reading the stuff you've been writing for your dad and for the campus paper. You're wasting yourself in sports."

Jayme bristled. "It's what I choose to do."

"Then do it. I was only expressing a regret, not a criticism. You probably thought the same thing along the way or you wouldn't be so defensive about it."

"I am not defensive!"

When she stiffened in mounting anger, Rick pulled her against him and tipped her face up to his. "Retract your claws, Kitten. I didn't ask you here so that we could fight."

"Then why did you ask me here?" she whispered, her irritation evaporating as soon as she looked into his eyes.

"I want to say good-bye."

The elevator doors opened, and he stepped out, leaving her immobilized by his announcement.

"I'll explain when we get to the room," he told her, reaching back for her hand.

She followed him dumbly, filled with sudden and unexpected sadness. The intensity of her reaction surprised her. They had not spoken to each other for over two months, for Pete's sake. Why should she care that he was going away?

In his room she automatically sat on his bed and he beside her. The bed was stripped, and boxes and luggage were packed and stacked neatly in front of his closet. The wall on his side of the room, once covered with rock and anti-war posters, glared nakedly at her now.

It was true. He was going to say good-bye.

A lump formed in her throat, and tears rushed to her eyes, defying all her intentions to remain cool and calm. Somewhat in a panic, she looked at him.

He had been watching her all along.

Now, as he moved his mouth over hers, she did not pull away as she knew she should if she wanted to regain control. He kissed her tenderly though she knew the passion was there for the asking. Tracing his jaw line with her fingertips, she marveled at its smoothness. His face, fully exposed now, was remarkably handsome, even more than she had imagined. He looked like his father. Was that another reason why he grew the beard?

"It's been a while," she said to fill the awkward moment that followed a kiss between those still uncertain of each other.

"Not so long. I've kissed you dozens of times every night in my dreams."

His affectivity unsettled her. But when she looked at him for further explanation, he stood up and strode to the window. Leaning on the sill, he watched the clouds drift lazily in the summer blue sky.

"I've enlisted, Kit," he said finally, without turning to face her, "and I plan to volunteer for 'Nam."

He might as well have hit her in the stomach with a baseball bat.

"B-But...b-but..." She ran her tongue over her lips to dispel the dryness that had plagued her since he met her in the lobby.

He turned to her slowly. "Shari called. Lenny was killed there. The poor fucker was barely off the plane when he was hit."

She remembered then the shiver of premonition that had so disturbed her on New Year's Eve. "I'm so sorry, Rick..."

Closing his eyes, he nodded and turned back to the window. "Yeah, so am I."

She gave him enough time to rein his emotions before going to him.

"When do you leave?" she asked softly, wrapping her arms around him from behind and laying her cheek against his back.

"Not for a couple of weeks yet," he said as he placed his hand over hers. "But Dad's coming for me tomorrow. Lenny...what's left of him...will be buried Friday, and then I figure I owe my folks some at-home time before I leave."

"Are you sure this is what you want to do? You were so against Len's going."

"I was against it because we were sticking our noses into something that was none of our business, but it became MY business when the gooks killed Lenny."

"I can understand what you must be feeling, but you can't take on the entire Viet Cong army yourself."

No, I can't," he agreed, "but I can sure as hell take out a few of the bastards. Unless, of course, Rick the Cowardly Hippie runs chicken once he gets there."

"You're not a coward."

"That, my dear, remains to be seen," he said, facing her and gathering her hands into his. "I was certainly no hero about dealing with my feelings for you, and I want you to know before I leave that I deeply regret it. I was falling in love with you, and I didn't know how to handle it."

Dryness returned to her throat. "In l-love? With ME?"

"I knew you weren't feeling the same thing for me, at least not in equal quantities. That's why I was so damn frustrated about it, especially since I believed that you could feel the same for me if you'd only give it a fair chance. If you want to know the truth of the matter, I still believe it could happen for us, but now's not the time for experimenting I guess. Still and all, it would mean a lot to me if you'd write to me now and then."

"Of course I will. Send me your address when you...when you..." Her eyes held on his until she felt the tears gathering. Quickly she pressed her face against his shoulder.

Feeling the tears soaking his shirt, he stroked her hair and tipped her face so that he had easy access to her lips. Now his kisses were more demanding, and she yielded to him completely, even when he picked her up and laid her carefully on his bed. Covering her body with his, he smothered her face with kisses as he cupped her breasts with his hands. When she didn't push him away, he teased and massaged until he felt the hardened peaks of her nipples through the thin fabric of her summer dress. Still she yielded to him, moaning softly as he kissed her deeply, hungrily, delirious with the hope that at last she would be his, completely and totally his.

Only when he had pushed her skirt up and settled himself between her legs as he fumbled with his belt buckle did the realization of what was about to happen register with her. In that same moment, Harlan's dimpled, smiling face loomed in her mind, and she knew she would have to refuse Rick this final time.

Her tears flowed freely as she pushed him off her and jumped to her feet.

"I can't, Rick," she said, her eyes pleading with him to understand. "I just can't..."

"Kit, PLEASE..."

Sobbing, she shook her head and ran out of the room. Out of the dorm. Out of his life.

She didn't write to him because he sent no letter to her. He did write to Najib, however. Often while he was in boot camp, less frequently after he was shipped to Vietnam. Eventually not at all.

Then one crisp March afternoon, Najib brought news he had received from Rick's family: Rick was MIA.

Missing in Action.

CHAPTER FOURTEEN

Najib moved into the McCrays' spare bedroom in spring of '71, at Jayme's request and with Jim's full blessing. Although Najib had voiced no actual complaints, Jayme knew that he was not overly fond of his current roommate.

Jayme also wanted Najib close by so that they could worry together about Rick.

In her more merciless moments, Jayme wondered if Rick were really an AWOL in MIA clothing. She could picture him hiding out in a hut somewhere, guzzling beer and relieving his primal urges with an accommodating mama-san who could also keep him supplied with the marijuana he'd acquired a taste for in 'Nam.

Jayme read his letters to Najib. Eventually. After she heard that he was missing. She had refused to read them before although Najib offered each to her as it arrived. However, Najib saved them all, perhaps anticipating that one day she would want to read them…she would NEED to read them.

She took the letters to bed with her one night, the same night Najib moved in, for she wanted to hear the reassuring noises of his arranging his belongings in the guest room while she read.

Her dad was at Gwynnie's. He was there a lot these days. Jayme knew they were well beyond the handholding stage, and she was happy simply because her father was. Still, she had trouble imagining either Jim or Gwynnie in the throes of passion. As she and Rick had been. For a crazy moment before she came to her senses and remembered that she loved Harlan.

Harlan, who had not come home for the Christmas holidays or at any other time since, forcing Jayme into prolonged and agonized patience.

She willed her mind back to Rick's letters. She had already read his boot camp letters, the ones full of expletives directed at some "son of a bitch Pollack" sergeant named Lowicki and praise for a "righteous bro" named Bongart. The "Army bullshit" annoyed him, but he had taken instruction quietly and kept his opinions to himself, using Najib and Bongart as safety valves for his irritation.

"Someday," he wrote, "this fucking bullshit may save my ass. At least, that's what Sarge Son-of-a-Bitch keeps yelling at us."

Rick had gone directly from boot camp into the war, ironically just after President Nixon announced that forty thousand American troops would be withdrawn from South Vietnam by the end of 1970. While anti-war demonstrations were breaking out on college campuses all across the United States, Rick was an insistent volunteer for combat, and Bongart was going with him before all the heavy ground troop action was curtailed by Congressional intervention.

Rick's 'Nam letters were alarmingly graphic. Though aggressions had supposedly diminished, he wrote of getting off the plane in Bien Hoa in the wilting heat and immediately hearing the gunshots and mortar rounds from the jungle. As the odor of gunpowder stung his nose, he became acquainted with the taste of fear, slimy and metallic, and always there.

Always there, as he dodged bullets and suffered the indignities of scorpions and leeches, mud and red dust, powdered eggs…

Always there, as he ventured forth on the body counts, putting buddies and parts of buddies into body bags. The intense heat disintegrated corpses that fell apart in his hands, and he realized with sickening clarity why there had been so little of Lenny to ship home.

Why couldn't people learn to make peace, he wondered, with the same enthusiasm as they learned to make war?

Peace-loving hippie Rick was learning all the war tricks. Learning to kill before being killed. Learning to pump bullets into dead bodies to guard against gook booby traps. Learning to jump at shadows and sleep in foxholes filled with water.

Learning that he could soak his fear and grief in Carling's beer or 45 whiskey. Or marijuana. An unbelievable bargain at twenty dollars for two huge bags.

Another bargain, two-buck whores. Vietnamese women who followed the grunts and willingly provided services in the bushes or any other convenient place. At first, he resisted the temptation, but after a while he was too horny to care.

The coherency of his letters gradually declined, in direct proportion to his increasing dependency on the booze and pot.

His last letter, however, was keenly and concisely explicit. Befitting a journalism major. Befitting the son of Richard Joseph Girard, Jr.:

"…We left the relative safety of our base at Lai Khe for God-only-knew-what. Though the CO hadn't told us where we were going, we all noticed the choppers heading north into Tay Ninh province where there was heavy NVA activity.

"Our job was to carve a fire base out of the jungle, and we stripped the area till it lay there like a naked red whore waiting to be fucked by the VC. When our bunkers were dug and sandbagged, we waited, and waited some more until the distant drone of approaching planes and choppers became a deafening cacophony directly overhead.

"What followed was a nightmare of military chaos. Luckily my capacity to feel much of anything was shut down for the duration of this fiasco, but my other senses shifted into overdrive.

"The noise was the worst. Grenades, mortars, M-16s, planes, helicopter gunships—but even worse were the human sounds: men calling, crying, screaming, dying…

"I say the noise was the worst because I could close my eyes to the guts and gore that splashed red against the red dust, and after a while I got used to the smells of gunpowder, blood, and death. When something—or someone—blew up right in my face, I tasted war, too.

"By then everyone had forgotten all the military bullshit that was supposed to save our asses. Men were firing blindly, both at their attackers and at each other. We were more worried about survival than destruction.

"Finally a few of us were able to get a good look through the smoke and the dust at our attackers. I supposed at some future time I'll get a hellacious laugh out of this fuck-up. You see, Naj, the B-52s and Cobra attack choppers were from the good ol' USA. Our CO had led us into an ambush by our own troops.

"Bongart was right there with me, and he had a few choice words to say on the matter. They were his last words. Suddenly beside me there was a big flash that splattered blood and flesh into my face, and there was Bongart with a sucking hole in his chest and bloody foam around his mouth.

"He was dying, and he knew it. And he didn't go easy. All I could do for the poor fucker was prop him up so that he wouldn't choke on his own blood. I tried a few token lies about how he was going to be okay as soon as the medic could get to him, but we both knew it was bullshit.

"Eventually someone somewhere realized we were killing our own, and the fighting stopped. By then Bongart was dead. He was on his way home in a body bag while I was on my way back to Lai Khe.

"This is pretty horrific shit to unload on you, Rooms, but I gotta unload on someone, and Bongart's not here anymore. I sure can't be writing the folks back home about it, and I figure you're used to this kind of shit considering where you're from.

"Would you do something for me? Tell Jayme that I—oh, hell, never mind. She wouldn't be interested in anything I have to say. But I'll tell you that I think of her a lot more than's good for me, and if I go out like Bongart, my last thoughts will be of her..."

Jayme let the letter drift to the floor. Burying her face in her pillow, she allowed her tears to flow unchecked. She had been so unfair to him. Unfair for thinking he was AWOL instead of MIA. Unfair for not letting him make love to her. Unfair for not loving him as much as he needed to be loved.

"I might have loved you like you wanted," she whispered to him, beating a fist against a pillow. "Only there's Harlan. Please understand...there's Harlan..."

To punish herself, she imagined where he might be. The worst was dead, but the Girards would have received that kind of news by now. Maybe wounded and lost in the jungle? Wounded and DEAD in the jungle, hidden from the body counters by all the foliage. *No! He's alive. I know it. I feel it...*

The only other answer was that he was a prisoner of the Viet Cong.

This new possibility frightened her more than anything else in her life, for she had read countless stories about the Viet Cong treatment of POWs.

Quickly she climbed out of bed and padded down the hall to Najib's room. In her haste, she neglected to put on her robe, and her slender legs were fully exposed beneath the over-large tee shirt she liked to sleep in. Najib gasped when he opened his door and saw her standing there as she was. Then he realized that she had been crying.

"The letters, you have read them?" he asked.

Nodding, Jayme settled within the shelter of his arms. Najib pushed the door closed and led her to his bed.

Jayme was relieved when her father slept too late to see that she had spent the entire night in bed with Najib. She awakened just as dawn peeked through the windows. Carefully disengaging herself from Najib's embrace, she tried unsuccessfully to edge out of bed without awakening him.

"Where do you go so early?" he murmured, reaching for her.

"Back to my own room," she whispered, "before Dad wakes up and checks in on his little girl. He'd scalp us both if he found me here like this."

"We have done nothing to cause him anger." Najib's voice was softly regretful.

"I know, but it still looks bad. Not too many men would...well, comfort a girl throughout the night without...well...you know."

"My restraint was nothing so gallant. I would have been making love to you, but you would have been making love to Rick..."

He rolled over and returned to sleep while Jayme tiptoed to her own room.

* * *

Whenever Jayme left her thoughts unguarded, she worried about Rick. Mostly, however, she tried to keep her mind so filled with work and school that she could not dwell on anything painful. When she felt herself on the verge of worry about him, she consciously diverted her thoughts to something else that demanded her undivided attention. She was an expert on drudgery, for there was always something NOT to think about.

Then one day toward the end of March, a year after Rick's disappearance, two news items provided the ultimate distraction:

The wire service reported that Harlan Oakes of the Pittsburgh Pirates' AA farm club in Nashua, New Hampshire, had just been traded to the St. Louis Cardinals, who immediately assigned him to their AAA team in Louisville, Kentucky, only 250 miles away from Applewood.

The news from Mamie and Harry Oakes was even better. Because of a brief hiatus between spring training and the start of the minor league season, Harlan would have a couple of days off before he had to report to his new club.

He was coming home. Alone.

Cydney Greco Oakes had filed for divorce.

CHAPTER FIFTEEN

Lifting the corner of the kitchen curtain, Jayme peeked across to the Oakeses' home. Harlan had said he would stop by some time this evening to see her. She had called him that afternoon to insure that he would indeed SEE her before he left to meet his new team in Louisville. Without a reminder, Harlan could quite possibly forget even that Jayme lived next door, and he wouldn't think of coming over on his own unless he wanted something.

Everything was ready for him. She had baked him Nutty Chip Chewies and encouraged her father to spend the evening at Gwynnie's. With Najib at the library until its closing to work on a research paper, she and Harlan would be quite alone.

She left her bedroom door open so that music from her stereo could be heard throughout the house. Soft, romantic music from a record borrowed from Aunt Ronna. Though Jayme had never heard of Glenn Miller, she could easily imagine herself swaying in Harlan's arms to the mellow melodies.

Drifting into her bedroom to turn the record over for the fifth time, she inspected her appearance for the tenth time. Never before had she taken such great pains with how she looked. *Not even for Rick,* she thought with a major twinge of guilt. *And he wanted me even when I looked my worst.*

She brushed Rick from her mind as easily as she brushed her bangs into place, for she had practiced and practiced this art of refusing to think disturbing thoughts. However, thoughts of Rick were the most difficult to dispel.

So now she concentrated on her appearance. At first she had planned to greet Harlan in form-fitting designer jeans, but such attire was too reminiscent of the old days when she was one-of-the-guys to him. A pants suit wasn't feminine enough, nor did it show off enough of her new shape. Although a dress seemed pretentious, it was the only solution. She could always say that she hadn't had time to change after school and work. Harlan was too blockheaded to detect any subterfuge. Heck, he was too blockheaded even to need an excuse.

The dress she had chosen was a gauzy summer print, full-skirted and cinched at the waist by a wide belt that emphasized her slenderness. In spite of pursuing a writing career in sports, Jayme preferred the softly feminine look to the feminist uniform adopted by most young ladies striving for a career in journalism. In this time of bra burnings, Jayme opted for the traditional, gentle styles that proclaimed her femininity. She wanted no one, especially Harlan, to confuse her with one-of-the-boys Jayme from her high school days.

After setting her stereo so that it would replay without her constant attention, she arranged herself carefully on the living room sofa, draping her full skirt high enough to give Harlan a good look at her legs. She wouldn't have to get up to let him in because he never knocked. He would barge right in and find her on the sofa in all her slender and feminine loveliness. Then he would realize that he had been in love with her all his life, and they would live happily ever after.

Like Prince Charming and Sleeping Beauty. Like Prince Charming and Snow White. Was Prince Charming a bigamist or a philanderer? Harlan is no Prince Charming. He's more like Dopey. Would his kiss even awaken me?

When she felt a gentle pressure against her cheek, she smiled and reached for her prince. Still lost in the fog of her dream, she could not see her prince clearly, but she was certain that he was there and murmured for him to kiss her. He obliged, and she wrapped her arms around his neck and let him kiss her over and over again.

The fog parted then, and Jayme saw Rick standing there, so clearly that she was suffused with the joyous relief of knowing that he was all right. But the relief drained from her quickly when she recognized the sadness on his face and the pain in his eyes as he turned from her and disappeared into the fog.

Though she tried to call to him, something smothered her mouth, preventing her from stopping his retreat. Of course…her prince was kissing her. Jayme tried to push him away so that she could go after Rick, but her prince would not budge. Jayme pushed harder, and when the prince still didn't move, she grabbed his ears…his Dopey ears…and wrestled him to the ground. His cry of pain was matched by her cry of anguish when she saw that Rick was nowhere to be found.

"Jesus Christ, lady…what are you tryin' to do? You axed me to kiss you. And my name ain't Rick."

Jayme sat up on the sofa and shook the grogginess from her head. As Harlan sat up on the floor, she realized what had happened.

So much for first impressions, she thought, kneeling beside Harlan.

"Are you okay, Harlan?" she asked softly, laying her hand on his arm.

"You nearly yanked my ears off, lady. Why'd you go and do that for? You axed me to kiss you. Where's Jae?"

Why, he doesn't even recognize me, she thought. *Would he have kissed me if he had known?*

"Do you always kiss women you don't know just because they ask you to?" she asked, helping him up.

"Sure. Ladies is always wantin' me…wantin' me…" Harlan's eyes bulged. "Jae? Is that you inside that lady?"

Laughing, Jayme pirouetted before him. "It's me all right. So what do you think?"

Harlan walked around her twice before responding. "What did you do with all that fat you had? You must be wearin' a super girdle."

"I lost nearly ninety-six pounds, Dopey. I'm not wearing a girdle."

"You ain't?"

"I ai…I'm not. Do you want to feel for yourself?"

"You want me to feel you?"

Jayme stepped toward him. "Now that you mention it, yes, I do."

Harlan cautiously touched a finger to her hip.

"Is that the best you can do?" she teased, stepping closer to him.

When she moved close enough to him that her breasts pressed against his chest, he jumped back and tumbled onto the sofa.

"Jesus Christ, Jae! What's wrong with you?"

Jayme crossed her arms and tapped her foot impatiently. "What's wrong with ME? You're the one who's acting like a twit. You weren't this shy when you thought I was a stranger sleeping on the sofa."

"You axed me to kiss you."

"What would you do if I asked you to kiss me now that I'm fully awake and can enjoy it?"

"Why would you ax me that?"

"Because I want you to kiss me," she said, sitting beside him. "Now."

"Aw, Jae…"

"NOW, Harlan."

"Aw, Jae…" He kissed her quickly on the cheek. "Do you have anything to eat?"

Jayme fluffed her hair. "Do you like the way I look now, Harlan?"

"You look okay…like a real girl…"

"Then kiss me like you would kiss a real girl."

"You ain't no real girl," he said simply. "You're Jae. Guys don't go kissin' on girls that's been like fellas with them. I ain't no queer. Did you make me some of them chewy things?"

"In the cookie jar."

Jayme fell back on the sofa and covered her face while Harlan rummaged in the kitchen for something to eat.

Squinting into the sunshine, Jayme fungoed a baseball to Harlan, who bobbled an easy catch. The outfield of Scheffers baseball field was sprinkled with baseballs he had misplayed, baseballs that Jayme would be expected to gather when the balls in the bucket beside her were gone. The only difference between practicing with Harlan now and practicing with Harlan before his pro contact was that Jayme was doing the hitting. No one doubted that Harlan Oakes could muscle a ball out of any stadium in the country, but his fielding was such a liability that his advance to the Majors was delayed.

He had matured enough to realize that he needed extra glove work. In fact, he had matured enough to WORRY about his need for extra glove work, even to the point of telling Jayme about it the night before. She had been the one to suggest this practice session before he left for Louisville. Cutting a day of classes seemed a small sacrifice to make to spend some time alone with Harlan. Somewhere along the way, maybe he would begin to realize that she was a girl.

"Ready for a break?" she called to him when he had muffed the last ball from the bucket. "I packed a picnic lunch for us."

Harlan slammed his glove down on the ground and waved away the dust that billowed around him.

"Yeah, let's eat. I sure ain't doin' no good here."

Because he looked so dejected, Jayme's heart swelled with tenderness. Life in the pros was tougher and more competitive than this small-town hero had anticipated, and his wife had deserted him when he needed her most.

Jayme squeezed his hand and led him into the shade of the dugout.

"Don't worry about it," she said, setting him on the bench and wrapping her arm around his shoulders. When he didn't shrug her off, she dared to hug him. "You need to practice is all."

"We been practicin' all morning."

"You have to practice every day, and practice hard."

"I can hit real good, Jae. Why ain't that enough for them anymore?"

"You're getting paid for playing now, and you're not much of an investment if you're losing more games with your glove than you're winning with your bat."

She wished immediately that she hadn't said anything, for his scowl withered her romantic hopes. However, his glower was caused not by anger, but by an arduous and unusual attempt at deductive thought.

"Maybe I should use a bigger glove," he said finally.

Jayme considered his suggestion carefully. "Maybe not...at least not if you're being groomed for first base. Have you ever worked with a SMALLER glove?"

"Smaller? Aw, Jae, ain't I missin' enough balls already with a regular glove? I won't even get leather on them fuckers with a smaller glove."

"Think about this now, Harlan. Would you walk better in oversize clown shoes or in shoes that fit you properly?"

"Well, in shoes that fit. Do you think I'm an idiot?"

Jayme suppressed a grin. "It's the same deal with a glove, Harlan. A smaller glove will be easier for you to handle, and you'll be quicker with it so that you'll actually catch more balls in the long run. Your hand-eye coordination will have less interference."

"You really think so?"

Jayme shrugged. "It's worth a try, isn't it? After lunch, you can practice with my glove. It's smaller than yours, and you'll be able to see whether you can work better with it."

"You want me to use a GIRL'S glove?"

"Just a smaller glove, Harlan...mine...and I'm like one of the guys, remember? It's not like it's pink with daisies on it."

"Well...okay..." Harlan's eyes trailed along her body as he suddenly became very conscious of her arm around him. "It ain't so easy to think of you as one of the fellas no more, not with you lookin' like you look now."

Jayme's heartbeat quickened dramatically. "That's the nicest thing you ever said to me, Harlan."

"Yeah...well...don't go getting' sloppy about it." Suddenly uneasy about her closeness, he slid off the dugout bench onto the concrete floor by the picnic hamper. "So what did you bring to eat? Got any of them chewy things?"

Because he was tired when they finished practicing after lunch, Jayme suggested that he rest in the shade of the dugout while she gathered all the baseballs she had hit his way. There had been no magical transformation in his fielding, but there had been enough improvement that Harlan saw the wisdom of Jayme's advice. His depression had quickly evaporated with his increased, though still meager success, and now as he lay down on the bench and munched serenely on the last of the Nutty Chip Chewies, Jayme marveled that such childlike simplicity could exude from a man like Harlan.

His attention span was as limited as his capacity for worry. No one looking at him now would guess that he was in the midst of a divorce and that he was in grave danger of stagnating in the minors if he couldn't improve his fielding. Yet he possessed a distinct animal magnetism that belied his childlike demeanor, and women were hopelessly drawn to him.

He was both a baby to be protected and cuddled, and a brawny hunk to be craved.

He was dozing by the time she finished. Asleep he looked even more vulnerable to her, and in a sudden rush of bravado, she sat beside him, lifting him enough to cradle his head on her lap. When he did not stir, she became bolder, even venturing to comb her fingers through his wavy hair, still damp with perspiration and curling around his face.

His eyes flew open then, and he stared up at her, momentarily bewildered by the lovely face above him. When he lifted a hand to touch her cheek, Jayme's heart thundered. In the next moment, however, he remembered who she was...only Jae...and let his hand fall as he quickly sat up.

"You ready to go?" he asked, shifting his weight to stand up.

Her voice was quiet as she laid a restraining hand on his arm. "Let's sit here a while."

"What for?"

"To talk."

"What for?"

"Just to talk. Is that asking too much?" Her disappointment had given way to exasperation, and the impatience crept into her voice. "You're leaving tomorrow morning, you know, and I won't get to see you until October."

"Okay. What do you wanna talk about?"

"Why don't we begin with your favorite topic of conversation?"

Warily, he tilted away from her. "You mean fuckin'?"

Jayme rubbed a hand over her face. "No, Harlan. I mean you."

"Me? You writin' another story on me?"

"Can't I show some interest in what's going on in your life without your thinking I want a story?"

"Well, you're a reporter."

"I'm also your oldest, dearest, and most devoted friend, and I want to know what's going on in your head."

"Ain't nothin' much goin' on in there."

Jayme bit her lip to keep from grinning. "I want to know how you feel about things…like were you happy about being traded?"

"Sure. The Cards was always my favorite team. You know that."

"Even so," she said slowly, selecting simple words, "I thought maybe you were sad because the Pirates didn't want to keep you."

"It was Cyd what didn't want to keep me."

Though Jayme searched his face for traces of regret or sorrow, she found none. "What happened with you and Cyd?"

"She thought I should go somewheres else since her and me was splittin', so her dad axed me where I wanted to go. I told him St. Lou, and he fixed for me to go there."

Jayme tilted her head in quiet speculation, surprised that anyone related to Cyd would be so considerate. Papa Greco could have packed Harlan off anywhere. Instead, he sent Harlan home…close enough to count as home in baseball terms anyway.

But Harlan's professional upheaval wasn't what Jayme was most curious about.

"What happened with you and Cyd to cause a divorce?" she asked gently.

Harlan shrugged. "She said she wanted one, so I gave her one is all."

"You didn't ask her WHY she wanted one?"

"Yeah, but I didn't understand it. Somethin' about our ears bein' different."

"Your ears being different?" Jayme shifted her brain into low gear for a moment so that she could think like Harlan. "Do you mean irreconcilable differences?"

"Yeah, that's what she said, but if you ax me, she was wantin' someone fancier than me…y'know, someone who wears a suit all the time. Her and Fenton sure got engaged awful fast if you ax me."

"Fenton?"

"Some guy that works for Cyd's dad. He was always hangin' around Cyd, and she was hangin' around him back. I figured somethin' was goin' on 'cause Cyd didn't wanna sex me up anymore."

Jayme inched closer to Harlan. "Do you think that Cyd and Fenton were…were…"

"Fuckin'? Pro'bly."

"Were you upset about it?"

"I was pissed a little. Cyd and me was married. She was supposed to sex me up whenever I wanted it. I thought that was part of the deal. It's bad enough huntin' for tail on the road without havin' to at home, too."

"Hunting for…for…you mean you were cheating on Cyd while she was cheating on you?"

"I ain't cheated on no one. I was just f—"

"Never mind, Harlan," Jayme interrupted quickly, tugging on her ear. "Why in the world did you and Cyd bother to get married if neither of you was going to honor your vows?"

"Vows? You mean them words we said at the weddin'?"

"Yes, Harlan. I mean those words you said at the wedding."

"Aw, Jae, them words don't mean nothin'. I didn't say them right anyway."

Am I surprised? Jayme thought, scooting close enough to Harlan that she could grasp his hand. When he did not pull away from her, she said, "Let's talk about future things now. Do you think you'll like being single again?"

Harlan shrugged. "Won't be no different to me."

"Do you miss Cyd?"

"Naw. It's kinda nice not havin' to listen to her bitchin' all the time. 'Course, she could sex me up pretty good. I miss that. But lots of girls can fuck good."

"There's more to a relationship with a woman than what takes place in bed."

"Y'mean fuckin' in kinky places like bathtubs and ironing boards?"

Ironing boards? "No, Harlan. I mean there are things other than sex."

"What else is a woman good for…except havin' babies…and that comes from fuckin'?"

Jayme's eyes narrowed. "What about your mom? What about me? Aren't we good for something more than sex and breeding?"

"Well…yeah…but you and Mom don't really count for women."

Jayme grabbed a handful of his shirt and pulled him toward her.

"Harlan…" she began, before realizing that a debate with him would be futile. He was a man of actions, not words. She must let her actions argue for her.

Locking her fingers behind his neck, she pressed her lips against his. The first kiss with him…when she was awake anyway…was not what she dreamed it would be, for she was struggling to quell his struggling as she clamped her mouth tightly over his. Eventually his resistance ebbed, and the kiss became gentle. It still wasn't the sensual delight she had anticipated, however. In fact, her lower lip throbbed from being pinched between her teeth and Harlan's. But progress had been made. Harlan was kissing her back.

When she loosened her grip on his neck, he fell back, panting and staring at her, astonished.

"Wow, Jae…where'd you learn to do that?"

"Did you like it?" she asked casually in spite of her galloping heart.

"Yeah," he said, shocked that this could be true.

Jayme smiled. "Take a good look at me, Harlan. I turned into a woman while you were away. Now it's up to you to do something about it."

"I…I ain't sure what you mean."

She skimmed her fingertip across his lips. "I mean, my dear Harlan, that's I'll be here for you when you return home this fall. If you're a really good boy, I may warm up your winter for you."

Harlan gulped. "Are you really Jae?"

"I'm really Jae, but a new Jae. Not your old sports buddy Jae. I'm all woman now, and it's time you realized it."

His response was to kiss her. Though this time Jayme gloried in the knowledge that he initiated the gesture, she wanted to maintain control. Just as children needed adult guidance, Harlan needed her to be more than a bimbo beneath the bed sheets.

So she allowed him only brief access to her lips before pushing him gently away.

"Let's save everything for this fall," she said. "It will be difficult enough to be away from you over the summer."

Harlan merely nodded, open-mouthed and still dumfounded by this strange twist of events.

Jayme was further encouraged when Harlan stopped in to say good-bye the next morning before his father drove him to the airport. He even kissed her before he left. Nothing that would set off any Richter Scales, but enough to raise Jayme's hopes.

Her hope lasted most of the summer, right up until the August evening when her father broke to her the news relayed to him by Mamie Oakes:

Harlan had married Valma Bergeron, a secretary in the front office of the Louisville Cardinals.

CHAPTER SIXTEEN

Another Christmas, another Mrs. Harlan Oakes.

Jayme slammed her fists into the bread dough and resisted an impulse to stuff a handful of it into her mouth. Since August she had been increasingly beset with urges to cram her mouth full of anything edible. The only deterrent to this gluttony was her hope that her instincts would prove correct again and that this second Mrs. Harlan Oakes would last no longer than the first one.

The trick for Jayme was to catch him between wives. Obviously whatever progress she had made with him in the spring had been severely negated when Ms. Valma Bergeron sank her talons into his crotch. Smiling wickedly, Jayme pummeled the bread dough and conjured an image of Harlan's new bride. Another blonde, no doubt. A dumb, whiny, selfish blond bitch that Jayme would hate on sight.

Jayme was so sure of her prognosis about Valma Oakes that the statuesque brunette beauty Harlan brought into the kitchen later made no immediate impact. Harlan immediately went to the cookie jar and stuffed his mouth with freshly baked Nutty Chip Chewies, so his guest had to cover his breach of etiquette and introduce herself as Harlan's wife.

Harlan had not married a bimbo this time. Valma Bergeron Oakes was a beautiful, intelligent, and gracious lady. Though Jayme tried to muster some animosity toward her, she could summon none. As Jayme's spirits plummeted, she reached automatically for a cookie, which, a moment later, she passed half-eaten over to Harlan. The thing tasted like Play-Doh. Why did Harlan like them so much?

Then she noticed that the sack of sugar bought especially for Harlan's cookies remained unopened on the counter. She had been concentrating so completely on Harlan's new bride, she had forgotten to add sugar to the dough.

Harlan hadn't even noticed.

* * *

Najib returned to Lebanon in January, in spite of his father's importunities that he continue in graduate school. Though Jayme was inclined to reinforce Amin Bustani's pleas, she knew that a sense of duty throbbed strongly within Najib. Jayme had long since given up trying to understand the intricacies of MidEast politics. All she needed to know was that Najib was increasingly troubled by the news of his homeland, enough that he overloaded his class schedules to obtain his undergraduate degree a term earlier than his father planned.

Both Jayme and Najib cried, unashamed, as they said their final good-byes at the airport. She was losing her closest, dearest friend...a surrogate big brother...and he was losing the girl with the sunset hair, a woman who had touched his heart more than she would ever know.

Even though in the following months they frequently exchanged letters, loneliness pressed close around Jayme. Sometimes she sought the familiar comfort of the cookie jar, only to become doubly disconsolate because of her weakness. Where work had been her chief source of solace in those past times when she had needed comfort, she couldn't find enough work now to fill her days as completely as she wanted them filled. The college wouldn't let her carry more than twenty hours a term, and her father refused to give her much overtime because of her extended class load. With Rick and Najib gone, she had no close friends with whom to spend her evenings, and she would not intrude on her father's time with Gwynnie although both Jim and his lady badgered her with repeated invitations.

Then, of course, there was the knowledge that Valma and Harlan were blissfully happy together. Jayme knew because Valma called or wrote regularly. For some reason, Valma liked Jayme and was making every effort to build a friendship with Harlan's boyhood chum. In turn, Jayme liked Valma enough to return the letters and phone calls.

Of course, being able to check up on Harlan was an added incentive.

Still, Jayme was more miserable than she could ever remember being at any other time in her life. Many nights her pillow was damp with tears when sleep finally, mercifully overcame her.

In her more introspective moments, she realized that she still cared deeply for Rick, and with that caring went the guilt of knowing that she had failed him when he most needed her, not only before he left for Vietnam, but afterward when she had wadded her concern for him into a tiny ball to make more room in her heart for Harlan.

By way of Najib and then Gwynnie, Jayme knew that Rick was wounded, but alive in a POW camp near Hanoi. Joe Girard had been lucky to find out even that much about his son, for information about POWs trickled out of North Vietnam, its meager flow dictated by political expediency rather than humanitarianism. Jayme could well imagine the frustration of this journalistic potentate who was accustomed to using his influence to overcome all barriers to information. Any attempt to get even a letter through to Rick proved as futile as Joe Girard's constant pressure on both the Pentagon and State Department, as he begged, threatened, and bargained for further word of his son. All this maneuvering would have amused Rick, for his father had finally realized the limits of his power, and the result was humbling and demoralizing.

Nevertheless, there was enough generic information on the plight of POWs that the Girards, Jayme, and the rest of the nation were concerned. Fresh in their memories was the image of Commander Jeremiah Denton, blinking his eyes to spell out "torture" in Morse Code as the North Vietnamese taped his interview for television. The release of a select few POWs to American anti-war groups in 1968 and 1969 had furnished even more fuel for fear as the repatriated prisoners provided information on their treatment in the camps. Although North Vietnam had acceded to the Geneva Convention, which prescribed the minimum humane standards for treatment of prisoners of war, the captors circumvented this agreement by proclaiming that Americans were actually criminals since no actual state of war had been declared. Confessions were extracted by torture…simple, but excruciating methods of torture. Though trained to follow a code of conduct that required them to resist, to attempt to escape, and to make no statement beyond name, rank, and serial numbers, prisoners soon realized how completely helpless they were in such uncivilized hands. Beyond the mental anguish of captivity, there was also the physical torment of being held under such harsh and primitive conditions.

Now these circumstances had become personal for Jayme and, therefore, more horrific. The prisoner was no longer a faceless, nameless man whose situation caused Jayme such distress simply because he was a fellow American and human being. The prisoner was Rick, and thoughts of his suffering tormented her.

At least there was an upsurge of public sentiment for the prisoners now where before they had been overlooked or forgotten by all but their family and friends. Even though the Hanoi regime had been forced to improve its treatment of Americans because of this widespread support, no one was naïve enough to believe that the changes were immediate and radical.

On the crest of this massive campaign to rally world support for POWs and MIAs, the United States tried to rescue men being held at Son Tay, a camp some distance from Hanoi, only to discover that the Americans were no longer there. They had been moved to compounds in or around Hanoi, but there was little change in the way they were treated.

Back in the States, the National League of Families of American Prisoners and Missing in Southeast Asia continued their support efforts. Thousands of Americans were wearing special bracelets, each one bearing the name of a POW or MIA, each one to be worn until the captives regained their freedom.

Jayme wore one of the bracelets. Not with Rick's name, though she had requested it. Her bracelet bore the name of USAF Captain Charles Stratton, missing as of January 3, 1971, in Laos.

She had sent off her request that spring after seeing a bracelet on the wrist of another journalism student who provided her with information on how to get one. At last, here was something she could do, for she stopped short of joining college anti-war demonstrations that were, to her, hypocritical by reason of their radical, even violent protests vociferated by students who had either bought or cheated their way around the draft and now needed rationalization for their actions.

Rick had not agreed with the war, but in the end, he had gone to it.

Jayme preferred to work within the system to proclaim her increasingly pacifistic beliefs. Knowing that the one real contribution she could offer was her experience as a writer, she began locally with opinion pieces and editorials for the campus paper and for her father. To larger papers in St. Louis and Chicago, she sent letters to the editors, advocating either a swift end to a costly and senseless war or more stringent actions in behalf of the POWs and MIAs. Her pieces attracted some attention, both favorable and otherwise. She knew she had touched some consciences when letters to the editors were written in response to her letters.

When local representatives of the League of Families enlisted her assistance with their literature, she eagerly agreed to help, pounding away at her typewriter sometimes so far into the night that she had time for only a couple of hours of sleep before her first class.

Though Jim joked about how much paper they were going through, he realized the reasons behind Jayme's all-consuming labors and remained silent when he might otherwise have lectured her on not taking proper care of herself. In truth, all this work produced the desired effects: she didn't think so much about Harlan, she felt like she was doing something for Rick, and she didn't miss Najib quite so much.

For Jim there was an unexpected bonus: the attraction of sports writing paled as Jayme became more involved with these events of world importance, and he resurrected his dream that his little girl would succeed him as editor of the Applewood *Sentinel.*

Jayme was so engrossed in these new pursuits that Christmas of her senior year sneaked up on her. Though Harlan and Valma would be coming home, Jayme had not baked a single cookie. Nor did she plan to. Gwynnie and Aunt Ronna assumed full responsibility for this year's festivities, and Jayme was relieved to pass the rolling pin along. Her relentless schedule was beginning to affect her physically, and she was drained emotionally. For the first time in a long time, she could think of things personal to her alone without total desolation of her spirit because exhaustion had blunted her pain.

Her heart was healing, and her obsessive need for work was diminishing proportionally. Though President Nixon had ordered resumption of bombing north of the Twentieth Parallel after a two-month pause and the Paris peace talks had been suspended until January, everyone had reason to believe that peace was imminent. *Let this be a Christmas of hope and rest,* Jayme thought as she unplugged her typewriter and vowed not to touch the thing until after Christmas break. Until then, she intended to vegetate in peace.

With Jim and Gwynnie away caroling with the church choir, Jayme was alone. Leaving only the Christmas tree lights blinking in the dark house, she stretched out on the carpet in front of the tree and laid her head down on folded arms.

Peace and quiet, she mused, *do not come cheaply for anyone...*

Like an Indian with an ear pressed to the ground to detect the approach of buffalo or cavalry, she felt his footfalls before she actually heard him. She breathed deeply to control the thudding of her heart. Harlan was home, and he was coming to her, unrequested. More the dumb buffalo than the gallant cavalry. Nevertheless, she held her breath in anticipation as he approached.

"Hey, Jae!" came the buffalo bellow from the kitchen. "Where are you? I know you're here 'cause I seen your car."

Jayme rolled into a sitting position.

"Living room, Harlan. In front of the tree."

A sudden blast of light throbbed into her eyes as Harlan flipped on the overhead lamp.

So much for atmosphere, she thought. Harlan had disappeared into the kitchen again, and Jayme could hear him clattering through the cookie jar and cabinets. She felt instantly guilty.

"Hey, Jae...who ate all my chewy things?"

Wincing, she jumped up and ran to join him in the kitchen.

"I planned to make you some tomorrow," she began, blushing at the lie. "I wasn't sure when you'd be home...and I...I want them to be fresh."

"But I'm hungry now."

"I'll make you a sandwich. And there are chips in the cabinet."

"Okay," he grumbled, opening cabinet doors until he found the chips. He was stuffing them into his mouth even as he dropped into a chair at the kitchen table. "But I really want them chewy things."

"Tomorrow, Harlan. I'll get up early and make you some before your cartoons come on." Frowning as she opened the refrigerator door, Jayme wondered what happened to her resolve not to bake him any cookies. The answer was simple, of course. One look at those dimples...those blue eyes...those muscles...and her determination turned into pudding.

She was so focused on preparing his sandwich that at first she didn't notice how fixedly he was watching her. When she did become aware of his scrutiny, she was addled enough to spread mustard on her hand.

"For Pete's sake, Harlan," she snapped, grabbing a paper towel. "Why are you staring at me?"

"'Cause you're pretty and I like lookin' at you," he said simply. "Does Jim got any beer?"

"In the fridge...where it always is..." Grasping the sink for support, she reminded herself that was married. "So where's Valma? Why didn't she come over with you?"

Harlan spritzed open the beer can, guzzled half the contents, belched, and wiped his mouth with his sleeve. "She'll be here. She wanted to slop on some new face goop afore she seen you."

"She doesn't need to bother with make-up just for me."

"She feels better if she's gooped up, and she gets goopier as she gets—" His words were garbled by the sandwich he stuffed almost wholly into his mouth.

"Doesn't Mamie feed you?" Jayme asked, sitting with him at the table.

He just grinned and kept eating.

Propping her chin in the palm of her hand, Jayme studied this hunk of uncouth duncery that caused her heart to gallop so. They had absolutely nothing in common but baseball and a shared childhood, and even these meager connections provided little fodder for conversation.

I have absolutely nothing to say to this man, she thought, *yet I want to devote my whole life to him? Love isn't merely blind…it's brain-dead…*

"I hear there's a good chance you'll make the parent club next season," she said, relying on the old conversational standby.

He stared at her oddly. "I ain't joinin' no parent club. Val ain't knocked up…"

I asked for that. She leaned back in her chair and hooked her arms over its back. "I mean that the talk around baseball is that you're ready for the Show next year."

"Yeah, I s'pose."

"You 's'pose'? It's a fair indication the Cardinals are counting on you since they traded their back-up first baseman for relief pitching."

"Yeah, I s'pose."

Suddenly she realized he was responding more absently than usual…even for him…and then she noticed the direction of his stare. Right at her chest, thrust forward now, however innocently, by her current posture. Her shirt was even gaping a bit.

Let him gawk, she decided.

Getting a prolonged shot at her womanly attributes would do him some good. He was a slow learner, but finally he was discovering that Jayme Rose McCray was a woman.

A timid knock on the door brought an end to the lesson.

"Yoo-hoo! Anyone home?"

Valma Oakes peeked around the door and grinned hugely at Harlan and Jayme.

Hugely.

Jayme stifled a gasp of surprise as Valma stepped into the kitchen. Harlan's wife…a former third runner-up for Miss Oregon…had gained a few pounds since Jayme last saw her. Quite a few pounds. So many, in fact, that she was heavier than Jayme had ever been.

Unexpectedly, Harlan and Valma stayed in Applewood until he had to report to St. Petersburg for spring training. Because Harlan had grown fond of the nightlife in sports cities, only the allure of a woman could persuade him to tolerate the inactivity in his hometown in the deader-than-usual months of January and February.

The woman in this particular case was Jayme. However, she found no joy in all the attention she was suddenly receiving from the great love of her heart, for always the wife of the great love of her heart hovered within her conscience.

Harlan, of course, found nothing amiss in the situation, and Jayme knew that he was probably an unfaithful husband, especially now that Valma had ballooned so unbecomingly. Still, Jayme had no desire to be The Other Woman. She wanted to be The Only Woman.

Further complicating the dilemma for Jayme were her feelings for Valma. Jayme LIKED the lady. Liked her, sympathized with her, and understood her torments and uncertainties. Because Harlan was so nearsighted in his relationships with women, their inner beauty meant little to him if the packaging was unpleasant to him.

Throughout the years, Jayme had come to terms with this quirk of his. Valma, however, was naïve enough to believe that since Harlan had married her, he must love her enough that her extra padding would make no difference in his feelings for her. She thought there had to be some other reason for his increasing remoteness. He rarely kissed her anymore, and he never initiated their lovemaking. Though she knew that Harlan had a roving eye, for the first time in their marriage, she feared that some other part of him might be roving, too.

She dumped her fears right into Jayme's lap, but voicing the truth to Valma required more diplomacy that Jayme could muster.

Perhaps down deep in the dark part of her soul, Jayme was thrilled that roles were reversed this time.

Thrilled and ashamed that she could be so shallow and vindictive about someone as kind and gracious as Valma.

So Jayme assured her that Harlan was merely preoccupied with his prospects for the coming season, and when, in late February, Harlan and his wife left for Florida, Jayme tucked a copy of her personal diet plan into Valma's suitcase.

Thus vindicated, Jayme had the further satisfaction of knowing that she had resisted Harlan's advances, but she was equally hopeful that some day she wouldn't have to.

CHAPTER SEVENTEEN

In late January 1973, following the formal signing of the cease-fire agreement between the United States and North Vietnam, the final U.S. withdrawals began, and American and South Vietnamese prisoners were freed. At the time of these peace accords, the United States Department of Defense listed 591 POWs in Southeast Asia, 1380 MIAs, and 1929 servicemen unaccounted for. In "Operation Homecoming," the Communists released only 512 people previously classified as MIAs, and one serviceman who had been listed as unaccounted for. These discrepancies did not go unnoticed though they were overshadowed by joyous reunions taking place across the country as repatriated service men and women were reunited with their loved ones.

One such reunion took place in Chicago when Joe and Barbara Girard brought their son home to stay.

After receiving this news from Gwynnie, Jayme offered a silent prayer of thanks, but she did not dwell on possibilities that might be available to her in Chicago. The path to her future was less clouded now, and it led to St. Louis.

As expected, Harlan remained with the St. Louis Cardinals at the end of spring training. After gently informing her father of her career plans, Jayme sent her resume to all St. Louis city and county papers that covered the Cardinals in depth. Only one was willing to take on a female sports reporter, no matter what credentials she could present…and only after a persuasive phone call from Jim, who was appeased by the knowledge that this particular job was close enough to Applewood that Jayme could live at home. Having already disappointed her father by declining a fulltime position with the *Sentinel*, Jayme did not balk at remaining at home and commuting to work each day.

She would need a new car for the commute because her beloved Bug was gasping through its final miles. With the VW as trade-in and graduation money from Jim, Gwynnie, and Aunt Ronna, Jayme and her father shopped first for her dream car, a Camaro. Initial test drives were surprisingly disappointing, however, and ultimately she fell in love with a metallic blue Datsun 240Z.

On June 4, 1973, Jayme McCray began writing general sports news for the *St. Louis County Crier*. She would get no byline until she proved her worth.

A week after beginning her new job, she received from Gwynnie further word from Chicago.

Richard J. Girard III and Tawney Elizabeth Westbrook were engaged to be married in the fall.

* * *

By October, both Jayme and Harlan had made professional progress. Following a mid-season injury to the Cardinals' regular first baseman, Harlan was thrust into the starting line-up sooner than anticipated. His bat kept him in the line-up though, at times, his defensive play was so horrendous that his teammates called him "Fingers," "E3," and "Holey Oakes." Nevertheless, his offensive stats for the season impressed enough people that he was runner-up in the National League Rookie of the Year balloting.

Harlan's break was also Jayme's. Her childhood association with this new "home-grown" Cardinal made her a logical choice for the feature story about him. Jayme received her first *County Crier* byline, albeit an abbreviated one, for the sports editor was not, as yet, dechauvinized enough to permit a woman's name atop a professional baseball story. Therefore, the byline read "J.R. McCray," and as such it appeared with increasing frequency as Jayme established her capability. She was not above manipulating Harlan so that she had exclusive access to club gossip that further enhanced her position on the *County Crier* sports staff.

Harlan was easy enough to manipulate. Although he would never admit it, he liked having Jayme's familiar, friendly face close by during this difficult first year when he worried constantly that his defense would get him shipped back to the minors. When he was away on road trips, he called Jayme more than he called his wife…whom he called not at all…for Jayme's reassurances meant more to him than Valma's. Jayme knew baseball, and if she told him he was playing well enough to stay in the Show, he did not need to worry.

Also true was the fact that Jae was sure pleasant to look at these days, and Harlan scratched his head many times over the strange sensations she could make him feel. Not that it did him much good to figure that out now. Jayme wouldn't have anything to do with him That Way, but he surely liked being around her…and looking at her.

If only he wasn't married. But he lacked the initiative…and the grounds…to do anything about it.

However, Valma was magnanimous enough to help him out by dying from a brain aneurysm…in late November…when Jayme was in Nebraska covering a Missouri football game, her first road assignment of any consequence.

Valma was buried in Depoe Bay, Oregon, her hometown. Jayme could not get away from the paper long enough to attend the funeral, a circumstance for which she was thankful. Attending the funeral of a woman whose husband she had lusted after for years seemed rather rude.

A few of Harlan's baseball buddies attended the funeral, however. Then they decided to cheer their pal up with a few days in Las Vegas.

When Harlan came home for Christmas, he was not alone. With him was his new bride. She claimed that her maiden name really was Cookie Wacker, and before becoming the third Mrs. Harlan Oakes, she had been a Vegas showgirl.

* * *

"Don't touch me. Don't come near me. Don't even talk to me."

Jayme jerked the paper from her printer so violently that a jagged fragment remained trapped in the machine.

Harlan followed her to the file cabinets anyway. "Aw, Jae, don't be like this with me."

Blindly, she stuffed the paper into a file folder and whirled around to face him. The frustrated rage in her eyes repelled him.

"Why are you even here, Harlan? What do you want from me? A wedding present? Forget it. Two's my limit. What about a congratulatory celebration? I can manage that. Here…" Grabbing a piece of typing paper, she ripped it into pieces and sprinkled them over his head. "Confetti. Congratulations to you. Even better, how about a wedding shower? How rude of me not to give you one. So here's your shower, Harlan…"

She emptied her half-filled mug over his head. He wiped the lukewarm coffee off his face with the sleeve of his jacket.

"You're pissed, ain't you, Jae?"

Dropping into her chair, she stared at him for one incredulous moment before erupting with laughter that squeezed tears out of her eyes. *Thank goodness everyone else in the office has left for the day already,* she thought. *They'd be calling for men in white coats to come and take me away…*

"C'mon, Jae. This ain't funny. I ain't even sure how it happened."

That sobered her. "How can you get married and not be sure how it happened? That's a little extreme even for you. By now you should have the ceremony memorized."

"I don't remember the ceremony, Jae. I don't remember nothin' after the bar."

"What bar?"

"One of them fancy bars in Vegas. Cookie hit on me, and when it looked like I was gonna get lucky, Bailey and Dexter went in the casino to leave us alone. Then Cookie and me had a few drinks, and the next thing I know, I'm wakin' up with her next to me and a goddamn official marriage license starin' at me on the table."

"Are you telling me that this bimbo got you drunk and took advantage of you?"

"That's right. And I think the bitch put somethin' in my drinks, too, 'cause I can hold my booze better than that."

"Did you confront her with this speculation?"

"Huh?"

"If she tricked you or drugged you, you can get the marriage annulled…that's like canceling it."

"I know what annulled means, Jae. I ain't no idiot. I talked to my lawyer, and he explained it all to me."

"I'm surprised you thought of talking to your lawyer."

"I didn't. Bailey told me to get my ass on the phone to my lawyer fast."

Jayme's eyes brightened with hope. "So is your lawyer going to get you out of this marriage?"

"He's still checkin', but he says I'm pro'bly stuck. He offered her money, and she said no way. And she says if I try to dump her, she's gonna sue my ass for a britches contract…"

"Breach of contract, Harlan. 'Gad, she's really got you between a rock and a hard place."

"She's got me by the fuckin' balls, and I don't like it."

"Can't your lawyer get some proof that you were bamboozled into this and get you off?"

"She'd fight me in court, and I'll look like a fuckin' fool. My agent says I'm better off married to her till she does somethin' I can divorce her on. The front office ain't gonna like any bad publicity, and I could lose endorsements, too. It already looks bad enough me marryin' a showgirl a week after Val was buried."

"I've got to tell you, Harlan, if this were anyone else but you, I'd be applauding the poetic justice of this situation."

"Ain't no poems and ain't no justice of no kind."

"But what a story it will make."

Harlan blanched. "You ain't gonna put this in your paper, are you? I wasn't talkin' to you for the paper."

Jayme let him squirm for a moment before answering, "We're a respected NEWSpaper here, not a scandal sheet. Your private exploits aren't newsworthy unless they affect your baseball. However, my silence won't come cheap."

"Name your price. I'll even give you my paychecks."

"Oh, for Pete's sake, Harlan, I don't want your money. I want your help."

"YOU want MY help?"

"Boggles the mind, doesn't it, Sport? The thing is, Bob…the guy who handles the bulk of the Cardinal coverage here…is talking about retirement in the near future, and I want his job."

"How can I help with that?"

"My stiffest competition will come from a geek named Robby Odettes. He's got the inside track because he's been here a year longer than I have and he's a man. So between now and the time Bob retires, I have to prove to my editor that I'll be the better person for the job, and to do that, I have to secure my sources and my access to information even more than Robby can."

"I always tell you everything I know, and I tell the guys you'll do them right in your stories."

"I know that, and I appreciate it…but I still need more inside access…like the locker room."

"Are you nuts? Women ain't allowed in there."

"It's time to open the doors to us, Harlan, and you're going to help me."

"I can't, Jae. The guys'll razz me from here to Tuesday."

"My editor will never consider me seriously if I don't have as much locker room access as Robby, and I HAVE to get the Cardinals beat. Someday you'll understand why it's so important to me. If Robby gets it, I'll never get a chance because he's young and will hang on to it forever."

"But, Jae—"

"Of course, I can always impress my boss with an exclusive on the newest Mrs. Harlan Oakes. I'm sure SHE will be happy to help me score some points with Ernie."

"Okay, okay, I'll get you in."

"And you'll never, ever tell Robby any of the juicy stuff before you tell me?"

"I don't talk to him now when he comes sneakin' around. I think he's a fag."

"Have you mentioned that opinion to your buddies?"

"Naw, but I will if you want me to."

"Probably you shouldn't. That's way too sneaky…and mean…and unfair…"

"If he's a fag and you're a woman, that'd even up things in the locker room. Wouldn't it be fair then?"

Jayme considered this rare bit of insight from Harlan. "Maybe you're right. Lots of sports use handicaps to keep the game evenly competitive, so why not sports writing, too?"

"Huh?"

"Never mind, Harlan. Just drop a word here and there in my behalf, okay? And if you should happen to mention why you don't like talking to Robby…well, you had that opinion long before we had this conversation, right?"

"Right."

She patted his cheek. "Good boy. I know you'll come through for me."

"I wish someone'd come through for me."

"Cheer up, Sport. How long can it last? She'll get tired of you eventually, or she'll slip up enough that you can divorce her without a huge amount of damaging publicity. In the meantime, be a good sport about it. She can't be that bad. You brought her home for Christmas."

"Well…she ain't ugly…and she's got big tits…and she likes fuckin'…"

"There, you see…your favorite trifecta. Already you and she have something in common. Hang loose for a while. Your marriages never seem to last too long."

"This one's lasted too long already."

As Jayme merely shrugged and smiled faintly in response, he was again overcome by the strangeness of what a beautiful woman his buddy Jae had become. His jeans became uncomfortably tight.

"Jae…" He reached to touch an auburn curl. "Since this here marriage don't really count, maybe you and me could be together on the side?"

Regretfully Jayme pushed his hand away. "Forget it, Harlan. If Mrs. Cookie Wacker Oakes decides to divorce you, I don't want my name bandied around in court as the reason why."

"This is really a crock of shit I'm in, ain't it?"

"Couldn't happen to a more deserving guy…"

CHAPTER EIGHTEEN

Cookie and Harlan must have reached an agreement of some kind because they settled into married life with a minimum of commotion once Harlan resigned himself to his situation. Equally resigned, Jayme shrugged off her disappointment and plunged back into her work. Drudgery always helped her keep her mind off thoughts that made her heart hurt.

She was rather surprised that one of those painful thoughts was about Rick being married to Tawney by now. With all her heart, Jayme wanted him to be happy. It was grossly unfair of her to want him to be happy with her in some way. Several times she considered calling him to congratulate him on his marriage, but talking to him now would only make those painful thoughts hurt even more. He probably wouldn't care to hear from her anyway.

And there was Harlan. If she waited long enough, Harlan would be a free man again some day, but catching him in that moment would evidently require both split-second timing and her constant proximity

Because landing the baseball assignment was necessary to insure that constant proximity, she labored indefatigably to elevate her value to the paper. Harlan kept his word about getting her into the locker room. She was greeted not with open arms, but with open towels as the men tried to shock her right back out.

However, she had prepared herself for their resistance. A candid conversation with her father had delineated her options of response. If she stormed the locker room defiantly, shielded behind feminist rhetoric, she would only further alienate those who were so diametrically opposed to her presence. Nor could she adopt the tough-broad persona by matching each athlete obscenity for obscenity, spit for spit, and vulgarity for vulgarity. Her nature countermanded such a guise. Equally ill advised were scathing remarks to deflate cocky egos.

The thing to do, Jim advised, was to be herself: professionally cool with a touch of good humor. Where one afraid of public speaking is urged to picture the audience in their underwear, Jayme was counseled to imagine the locker room crowd fully clothed.

Having never seen a man undressed before, excepting that one glimpse of Harlan, Jayme knew the first revelation might shatter whatever poise she had managed to establish. Therefore, she primed herself for the inevitable shock by studying beefcake magazines that were becoming popular among the liberated female population.

Her strategy worked well enough. When the first towel dropped, she inspected that player's exposed manhood briefly, but unwaveringly, and then proceeded with her questions as if she interviewed naked men every day of her life. She gently, but firmly rejected all propositions and date requests, and she responded with no more than an amused smile when someone tried to embarrass her with a risqué anecdote or joke, many of which she didn't understand anyway.

In time, all attempts to fluster her were forsaken as the team members grudgingly accepted her. Eventually she was a welcomed guest, a little sister they could tease or confide in with the security of knowing that anything said "off the record" would not find its way into print. Because of her byline, J.R. McCray, "the boys" even gave her a nickname: they called her "Junior." All her experience being "one of the guys" was finally reaping benefits.

There were, of course, setbacks and obstacles as she dealt with those intense competitors. And there was one unfortunate scene with Robby Odettes, who accused her of sleeping with the team in general and with Harlan in particular to give her an advantage in what had become a fierce fight for Bob's job.

"Are you jealous of my sources or of their preferring me over you as a sleeping partner?" she said, hating herself for being such a bitch, hating Robby for being such a vindictive liar, and hating Harlan for making her resort to such extremes to insure herself a place with the team.

She tried to soothe her conscience by reminding herself that the boys didn't like Robby anyway. Nevertheless, her conscience continued to trouble her, and when Bob was a month away from retirement and their boss, Ernie Dowell, called both Jayme and Robby into his office, she was relieved by his Solomonesque decision:

Jayme could cover the home games, and Robby would travel with the team to report on road contests.

If Jayme had been a man, the beat would have been hers exclusively, for Robby lacked her flair with words and her affinity with the team.

Ernie, however, could not acclimate himself to sending a woman on regular road trips with a bunch of horny athletes.

He would have felt like a pimp.

* * *

"It's been a while since we've heard from Najib, hasn't it?" Jim asked casually during one of those rare evenings when he and Jayme were home together.

After two and a half years with the *County Crier*, Jayme had taken her first vacation. Robby was packing to leave for his first spring training with the Cardinals, and she gnashed her teeth at the thought of his triumphant reports coming up from Florida. When Ernie suggested that she take some vacation time, she agreed immediately.

Her initial feeling of good sportsmanship over sharing the baseball beat had quickly dissipated as Robby gloated constantly about his upcoming assignment in St. Pete. Moreover, Jayme knew that Harlan and Cookie's fights had become more volatile lately, though Cookie had been the aggressor, even at times pounding on Harlan so strenuously that he appeared in Jayme's cubicle with bruises and cuts. If Cookie was hoping to provoke him into retaliatory fits of violence, she was sorely disappointed, for Harlan was as docile as he was dumb.

In any event, the marriage was rapidly deteriorating, and Jayme had to be near Harlan at the time of its demise, a situation that mandated her attendance on road trips, too.

By now she knew Ernie well enough to realize why he had given Robby the road assignments, so in the future, she must work on Ernie, too, and pray that Cookie didn't die like poor Valma. A divorce would give Jayme more time for maneuvering.

However, her single-minded pursuit of Harlan had relegated many other matters to positions of subordinate priority, and her father's query about Najib now crystallized this sad fact in her conscience.

In this case, she felt the guilt of allowing her friendship with Najib to lapse. They hadn't heard from him since the letter he had written three months before, telling them of his plans to marry a Lebanese girl. Though Jayme had immediately sent a congratulatory card, she had neglected to answer the letter.

In truth, the span of time between letters both ways had gradually lengthened since those first few months of Najib's return to his homeland. While Jayme realized that time and distance apart often doomed pledges of eternal communication made by college friends, she also knew that she could have been a more devoted correspondent. Over the last few months, she had even stopped reading the newspapers as thoroughly as she once had. She had become a headline scanner, reserving the bulk of her reading time for sports papers and magazines that would expand her sports knowledge.

What she knew from the headlines was that Lebanon was a country in turmoil in spite of its efforts to remain neutral in the Arab-Israeli conflicts infecting the MidEast. What she knew from Najib's letters was that he was, so far, safe on the battleground of Beirut.

He did not dwell on politics, for he knew how confusing the situation was to people like Jayme who were not involved in it on a daily, personal basis. Instead, he focused on his own anguish over the self-destruction of his country. He had seen women and children trembling inside their homes, knowing that behind barricades outside, gunmen were crouched with machine guns, grenade launchers, and rifles aimed at random targets. Countrymen had been jerked from their cars in the middle of the day and shot if their Lebanese identity cards listed rival faiths. Much later their bodies would be found rotting in the sunshine, their genitals horribly mutilated and hands roped behind their backs. Truces were basted together; today's ally could be tomorrow's assassin.

In spite of all this news, Jayme was not so worried for Najib as she had been for Rick. In Vietnam, Rick had been totally alone, bereft of both his family and the shelter of their wealth, and, therefore, more vulnerable. Even though Najib was surrounded by bloodshed, his rich and powerful family insulated him. He was where he wanted to be.

Whatever the degree of his safety, he was the closest friend she had ever had, and she owed him a letter. She went immediately to her room and filled ten pages with news about herself, Jim, Gwynnie, and Applewood. She posted the letter early the next morning.

By mid-summer she still had not received a reply. Although she worried about the reasons why, she had a lot on her mind to divert her attention. She was focusing all her energies on getting Ernie to assign only her to the baseball beat.

* * *

The painter left shaking his head.

"Don't look like no sports writer's office to me," he grumbled, mortified that he had been forced to associate himself with such blight upon the masculine world.

Jayme merely grinned as she settled back in her burgundy upholstered chair and propped her feet up on the large desk, painted cream to match the mauve, cream, and burgundy she had chosen for her new office. Actually, her office was little more than her old cubicle with permanent walls and refurbished furniture, the result of a building renovation project by the *County Crier* and Jayme's new position as the one and only Cardinal reporter. Ernie had told her she could decorate however she wanted, within budget.

Robby had left amicably, even cheerfully because a sudden and miraculous offer from the St. Louis *Globe-Democrat* lured him away. He wouldn't have the Cardinals, but the prestige of working under legendary sports editor Bob Burnes appealed to him more.

To move Robby along, Jayme had to turn down the same offer made to her first, then have dinner with an aging personnel officer whose lascivious intentions she deflected by saying that her herpes was active. Ultimately her goal had been realized with no one harmed or inconvenienced, except maybe the *Globe-Democrat* sports staff that was stuck with Robby.

Now her major coup was on the brink of actualization: Harlan would be by to take her on a real, honest-to-goodness dinner date. No "Let's send out for pizza, Jae." No "Let's grab a dog at the park, Jae." No "What do you got in the fridge, Jae?" And best of all, no "You pay, Jae…I ain't got no money on me."

"Maybe you and me can check out that new eatin' place on the Landing tomorrow night," he had said to her suddenly last night after the game. "We ain't got no game then."

Jayme was momentarily stunned by the invitation. No matter how much she had dreamed of it, she never expected it even now that he and Cookie were legally separated and in the middle of a very public divorce after two years of very public marital warfare.

Was he seriously asking her on a DATE?

"You don't have any money, right?" she asked. "You need someone to pick up the tab."

"Naw, I still got some of the 'lowance Raymond gave me for this week, and he gave me one of them credit cards to use so long's I don't get carried away with it."

"I'm glad you have Raymond to handle your money. I hope he's as honest as he is smart."

"If I ain't had Raymond, Cookie'd done spunt all my money."

Spunt? Jayme bit the inside of her cheek to halt the giggle that threatened to bubble forth. *Oh, Harlan, Harlan, Harlan…*

"She was always bitchin' 'cause Raymond handled the money," Harlan continued, "and now she's really pissed 'cause Raymond's got things fixed so's she ain't gonna get as much as she thought in the divorce. He's been plannin' this since the ol' cunt tricked me into marryin' her."

Jayme stared at the ceiling as she twisted a curl around her finger. Though by now she was accustomed to the language of the locker room, sometimes Harlan's choice of words bothered her in the way of a woman who wants to be treated more respectfully by the man she loves.

As always, Jayme's silence made Harlan uneasy. "You ain't mad at me 'cause of Raymond, are you? You're the one which told me a long time ago I should see to it my money's handled right so's I got somethin' when I can't play ball no more."

Her eyes skimmed his lean, tanned form. Whenever he listened to her advice, she was mildly surprised…though, in fact, he did listen to her more often than not, a fact that reinforced what she had known all along: Harlan was excessively manipulable, and she could manipulate him better than most. Better than even Raymond, who was motivated by fifteen percent of Harlan's impressive salary. Now that the path to Harlan's hormones was less cluttered than usual, Jayme would manipulate him, too; but her only incentive was love.

So, of course, she accepted his dinner invitation.

The feeling of being on the brink of a major change in her life was deliciously strong. Still, she couldn't keep another thought of Rick out of her mind. *This must be the way it's meant to be, Rick. You with Tawney, me with Harlan. I hope you're happy now. Please be happy…*

Please think of me now and then while you're being happy?

Why were the tears gathering in her eyes now? This should be one of the happiest moments of her life.

And Harlan was late for it.

But she expected him to be late. Chronic tardiness was as inherent to his nature as his witlessness.

What she didn't expect was his entering her office with a redhead hooked onto his arm.

"Hi, Jae!" he called, beaming his dimples right into the redhead's green eyes. "I just met someone new workin' on this here paper. Her name's Wallis Robins, and I told her you and me'd show her around town tonight."

CHAPTER NINETEEN

Changes, changes, changes, Jayme thought as she tossed an almost-empty mustard jar into the trash before packing the rest of the refrigerator contents into a cardboard box. She had spent the morning moving her things into her new home on Meadow Lane with her new roommates, Jordyn and Siara Nealy. Now she was helping her father pack the last of his belongings. Next week a new family would be living in this house, her home for every moment of her life, and her father would be living in Lost Hollow with his new bride.

After nine years of dating, Gwynnie had finally convinced Jim that he would not be considered a gigolo for marrying a woman with more money than he had. Though the newlyweds expected Jayme to move in with them, she gently declined. They then offered her the deed to her childhood home, but this, too, she refused.

Living there alone amid memories of her first kiss from Rick and a childhood shared with Harlan would be detrimental to her mental health.

There would be too much time for brooding about Harlan and HIS new roommate, the green-eyed she-dragon who had moved in with him barely two months after their chance meeting in the newspaper lobby.

Harlan was manipulable all right, but never by Jayme at the right time.

However, Wallis Robins had her professionally painted talons finely tuned to push every button with perfect efficiency. She bullied him. She teased him. She mothered him. She coddled him. She sexed him up. She catered to his every whim and decreed that he must cater to hers. She manipulated and molded him into a blindly devoted, tail-wagging, jump-through-the-hoop-on-cue puppy.

Jayme slammed the refrigerator door. Moving in with the Nealy twins was the right decision. She really liked them, and they seemed to like her well enough in return.

Here was a new experience: her having close female friends. Jayme traveled so much in a masculine world that there had been few opportunities for any abiding friendships with other girls. There was a whole new perspective to be gained on the mystery of romantic relationships, especially from Jordyn, who was OVERLY candid about her experiences.

Girl talk had a way of alleviating the pain…as long as Harlan was a noodle-headed lump of hormones…which would be forever.

Beneath the pork steaks at the very back of the freezer lay something long forgotten and disguised by a thin coating of frost: the candy bar Harlan had given her so many years ago, the one she had vowed to keep forever.

Reverently she turned the bar over in her hand, this bar of chocolate that was pure gold to her soul, for it was a gift from her true love.

She knew the perfect place for this treasure…this piece of her heart…this fragment of memory…and she dropped it there now, into the trash right next to the almost-empty mustard jar.

* * *

Jordyn's right. I am nuts. I may be even more terminally stupid than Harlan.

Glaring at her image in the mirror, Jayme tugged at the bodice of her dress and muttered as many profanities as she could remember. The dress just had to be pink. PASTEL pink. She looked like a colorless lump of oatmeal in pastels. And the cut of the damn thing befitted some bustless high-school girl, not a fully developed, pushing-twenty-nine woman. In fact, to accommodate her fuller bosom, Jayme had to order a size larger than she usually wore and then have the waist taken in.

Wallis Robins would have realized all that when she selected the dress for her bridesmaid. The fourth future wife of Harlan Oakes had worked on the *County Crier* staff as a fashion reporter for over a year before convincing Harlan that she could handle his money better than Raymond. Being Harlan's live-in lover hadn't hurt her chances...though, to her credit, in the year since her career transition, she had proved to be better than Raymond as Harlan's business manager.

Now his money would be her money, too.

The animosity between Jayme and Wallis thrived as surely as Harlan's bank account. Neither woman troubled herself with any pretense of friendship. Wallis even traveled with Harlan during the season so that Jayme would have very little time alone with him. The zinger had been Harlan's asking Jayme to be Wallis's bridesmaid.

Jim and Gwynnie were surprisingly relieved when Jayme accepted this dubious honor because to them it meant Jayme would finally accept that she had no romantic future with Harlan. Of course, they were so enraptured with life since their own simple chapel wedding that they could be optimistic about World War III.

Jayme's roommates were more realistic, for they had been privy to Jayme's daily heartaches. Where Siara and Darica, her newest roommate, fussed over her emotional stamina, Jordyn was more direct.

"You're friggin' nuts, Jae!" Jordyn had said on more than one occasion. "You know that spiteful bitch is behind it, and you're helping her twist the knife in your own back."

The one minuscule bit of justice that Jayme could find in this particular situation was that Wallis Robins was, in fact, URSULA Wallis Robins. As bridesmaid, Jayme saw the marriage license. Ursula...the she-bear.

In another hour that she-bear would be Mrs. Harlan Oakes, and Jayme...the oatmeal lump in pastel pink...would be immortalized in the group wedding photograph right next to her.

* * *

Chewing thoughtfully on the end of her pen, Jayme studied her notes for a feature story she was writing for the Sunday edition. Even though today was one of her rare and blessed days off, she knew she should be working in her office. There were too many distractions here at home, like Jordyn's clumsy attempts to get dinner started. How could anyone so naturally graceful be so clumsy in the kitchen?

For all the distractions, however, Jayme had to be here today. Deliciously redemptive mischief was afoot, and as an active participant, she was obligated to stick around until its culmination. This whole week had been permeated with the proverbial all-for-one-and-one-for-all spirit as the roommates rallied to avenge Siara's heartache, caused by that armpit of the medical world: Dr. Prescott D. Chadburn.

Though Jayme had often thought about things she would like to do to those who caused her grief, namely Wallis and Harlan, only the emotional injury to someone she loved and Jordyn's contagious, outrageous bravado could provoke her into action. In truth, Jayme's guise as Doris Hudson that afternoon now seemed rather silly, almost embarrassing. However, the results made the ridiculous deception worthwhile: Jayme had a prescription for those magic pills that would enable her to out-sneak Wallis.

Grinning wickedly, Jayme doodled Harlan's name in her steno book.

Let's see how well the she-bear is handling things months from now when I'm still sleeping with her husband...

Jordyn broke into Jayme's hopeful speculations. "Would you believe I'm nervous?"

"Nervous? You? About what?"

"Tonight's extravaganza with the doc. This kind of stuff may work for Doris Day, but I'm not so sure about it working for me."

"I can't believe that you're nervous about something that's so simple compared to stuff that you...and we have done and gotten away with in the past. Remember Hudson Turner? And your nasty uncle?"

"I have a spooky feeling this time though."

"Stage fright, that's all. We're rounding third and heading for home. What could possibly go wrong now?"

A car skidded into the driveway then.

"It's Darica," Jordyn said. "She looks excited about something."

Darica was shouting as she raced into the kitchen. "Jyn! Sari! Jae! You won't believe it! He died and the office burned! God's judgment! It's God's judgment!"

Jordyn grabbed Darica's arm to keep her from destroying the kitchen in a blind stampede. "Calm down, Dari. Who's dead? What office? You smell like smoke. What happened?"

"The doctor was dead," Darica gasped. "Dr. Chadburn was dead. And then the office...on fire...it burned so fast. I was going to talk to him...to appeal to his Christian decency...for Sari...only...only...and the firemen are there now...and the POLICE. He was murdered. I KNOW he was murdered...I need to wash my hands...I MUST wash my hands..."

Jayme's eyes held on Jordyn's. Siara wasn't home yet, and she'd been detached...aloof...even strange since she learned of the doctor's perfidy. For the first time ever, Jayme saw panic flash in Jordyn's eyes.

There was nothing to do now but wait. To ease the strain on Jordyn's nerves, Jayme led a still-babbling Darica to a chair by the kitchen table.

"Sit here, Dari Mouse," she said. "Take a few deeps breaths and calm yourself. Everything will be all right. We all have each other to rely on when the wickets get sticky. Here...drink some of my Diet Rite...there's a good girl..."

"Siara's home!" Jordyn called finally, dashing out to meet her sister.

Jayme and Darica watched from the screen door.

"Poor Sari," Darica murmured. "I hope she feels better now that justice has been done."

Jayme looked sharply at Darica as Jordyn led her sister into the house. The smell of smoke on Siara's clothing did not alleviate Jayme's growing apprehensions.

Part IV: Darica Cervantes/1959-1984

CHAPTER ONE

Armando Cervantes paced the waiting room where, ironically, he had paced only two years before as he awaited news of the birth of his son, Alvito. However, this time his wife was home with that son while Armando's sweet Mariana struggled to bring into the world a baby that...through no fault of its own...would suffer the stigma of illegitimacy.

Dropping wearily onto the black vinyl couch in the sterile white and black room, Armando smothered his face with large, calloused hands. If there was blame to be allotted, it must rest solely on him, for Mariana was guilty of nothing but loving and trusting him too much. She was little more than a child herself...barely eighteen years old...not even half of Armando's years.

He had known her for three years, since she first began working in the corner bakery where he usually drank his morning coffee. From the beginning her infatuation for him had shined in her large, dark eyes...so brilliantly that when Bella Cervantes threw him out of their bedroom after Alvito's birth, Armando was unconcerned.

His and Bella's marriage had been little more than a convenience anyway. She had told him she was pregnant and forecasted all kinds of grievous punishments upon his body and soul if he did not marry her.

So her married her, not so much because of her threats as because he couldn't think of enough good reasons not to marry her.

Only weeks later did he realize that he had been tricked. Signs of a baby never materialized, and neither, of course, did a baby. However, he did not confront her with the obvious complaint. Their first few months together had been amiable enough because she wasn't too sure that Armando wouldn't throw her out when her deception became obvious.

Besides, he knew that she had been more or less forced into trapping a husband. Spinsterhood in their traditionalist Catholic neighborhood in Chicago's Southside was unacceptable, unless the lady in question had joined the sisterhood of the church. At thirty, Bella must have felt the first twinges of desperation, for she was certainly no beauty, and her personality was as pallid as he face.

Her blood, however, was suffused with pure venom.

When Bella eventually became pregnant for real, her vituperative nature revealed itself as certainly and as obviously as her physical circumstance. At first Armando accepted her hostility as a natural consequence of her pregnancy. Once Alvito was born, however, her frequent tirades about the sorry condition of her life with Armando intensified. She continued to keep his house and cook his meals only because he provided their income from his taxidermy business.

As for the intimate part of their marriage, she announced that he was on his own and moved his personal belongings into his shop behind the house.

Nor could Armando find any domestic comfort in his son, who…thanks to Bella's pampering…showed definite signs of becoming a brat.

That Armando finally succumbed to the invitation in Mariana's eyes seemed inevitable. Of course, he never intended that their affair would become as intense as it did, and he certainly never intended for the child to become pregnant.

The child.

Men had been vilified, even arrested for what he had done. No matter how willing Mariana had been to please him, she was legally underage when first he took her.

Her youthful condition was easy enough for him to ignore at the time. The body she gave to him so eagerly was in no way childlike though she came to him untouched by any other man. His passions were so potent that he finally suppressed all previous misgivings.

There were no parents, older relatives, or guardians around to remind him of his illicit lechery, for she had been orphaned as an infant and taken in by an elderly maiden cousin, who died shortly before Mariana's fifteenth birthday. Mariana went to work at the bakery then, living in a one-room apartment upstairs and eventually quitting school so that she could more easily earn money for her survival.

Through it all, no complaints formed on her sweet lips, which always curved in a gentle smile when Armando entered the bakery for his morning coffee and cinnamon roll. She graciously accepted her life as it was and made no demands from it, just as she made no demands from Armando. In truth, she considered herself the most fortunate girl in God's universe when he finally began to pay her the kind of attention she had dreamed of since their first meeting.

Initially, Armando intended no emotional involvement with the girl, but soon his heart was softly captured. Mariana deified him, and he basked in her adulation. Her selfless love nurtured his soul. When she told him she was pregnant, he would have left Bella, but Mariana would not let him desert his family, though it was a family in name only.

Loving him and being loved by him…and now bearing his child…filled her life beyond her expectations. Her only concession to his entreaties was to accept…finally…his financial assistance, for there were doctor bills now, and more rent for a larger apartment for her and the baby.

After chronic morning sickness forced her to miss work with increasing frequency during the early stages of the pregnancy, she had to quit altogether in her sixth month or risk losing the baby that depleted her strength and weakened her health as it grew within her.

Gravely concerned, Armando spent more and more of his evenings with Mariana. His absences were little noticed by his wife, who rarely saw him or cared to see him after supper. However, the sudden decrease in their checking account inspired her to a confrontation. She did not mind Armando's having a mistress…so long as he was discreet…but she sure as hell wouldn't stand for his spending THEIR money on the little tramp…

Armando had never struck a woman before, nor did he now. But the urge flared within his eyes so hotly that Bella was frightened into silence as he reminded her who earned THEIR money.

Sometime in the twenty-one hours of Mariana's painful labor, Armando made his final decisions. Even if Bella refused him a divorce, he would leave her to live with Mariana as either lover or husband. Either way was preferable to the way he was living now, to the way Bella would make him live in the future if he stayed with her. He would give Bella custody of Alvito, of course. Though Armando had tried to develop some strong affection for the boy, Alvito had a real knack for irritating his father so much that Armando avoided him.

Of course, Armando would fulfill his paternal duties to his son, but his heart would be in the home he would make with Mariana…and the baby.

"Mr. Cervantes?"

Armando jerked to attention. Having been through the waiting room experience once already, he could tell from the nurse's face that something wasn't right this time.

"The baby?" he whispered. "Is our baby all right?"

"Your daughter is fine, sir." The nurse avoided his eyes. "Your…daughter's mother…hemorrhaged during the delivery. She has lost a lot of blood. We've called for a priest at her request."

"Take me to Mariana," he ordered hoarsely.

Any hope he talked himself into dissipated as soon as he saw Mariana, lying frail and pallid in the dimly lit ward. When she sensed his presence, the familiar gentle smile quivered about her lips, but she lacked the strength to sustain it. Nor could she fully bestow on him the warm beauty of her large, dark eyes, veiled now by lids too heavy for her to control.

"We have a daughter now, Mando," she murmured.

"Hush, *querida*." He stroked damp curls away from her face. "You should rest, not talk."

"I shall rest enough later. Now we must speak about Darica."

"Darica?"

Her smile flickered, then faded. "Our daughter. I shared the name with you once, but you were more interested in names for a son. Are you very disappointed that we have a daughter instead, Mando?"

"Any child I make with you is a blessing from God."

"I thought there would be more time for us, but God has not approved of what we've done." Her voice was surprisingly stronger, and she managed to open her eyes to stare at him sadly. "Though we have loved, we have sinned, and Darica must not suffer for it. I know what it is to grow up without a mother and a father, and I do not want Darica to feel that kind of heartache. You must promise me that you will keep her with you and love her in double portions to make up for my absence."

"We shall both love her, *querida*...together. I am leaving Bella..."

"No!" Her meager store of energy spent, she closed her eyes again, her voice dwindling once more to a whisper. "You must not leave. Darica will need a mother. Perhaps your wife can learn to love our daughter, but I want Darica to know that I loved her, too. Promise me, Mando. Promise me that it will be as I say..."

As her words became increasingly agitated and garbled, Armando touched a kiss to her forehead.

"It will be as you wish, *querida*," he said softly. "Rest now and do not worry."

Eventually she lay quiet, with her fingers entwined in his. Though he tried to force some of his vitality into her failing body, he felt the life drain out of her.

"The priest is here," the nurse said just as he was wondering whether he should tell someone that Mariana was gone.

He merely nodded and left the priest alone with the Catholic rituals of death. Mariana would not need the help into Heaven, but she would be pleased to get it.

"I wish to see our daughter," he told the nurse, who led him at once to the nursery.

He immediately knew which baby was Darica, for his daughter regarded him now with her mother's bright eyes.

* * *

Though Darica had fallen asleep an hour before, Armando continued to snuggle her awkwardly against him as he swayed slowly in the old wood rocker Mariana had been so proud of. For the past week he had stayed here in Mariana's apartment, returning home only once for clothing. He knew he could not remain here forever...Mariana had been correct in saying that Darica would need a mother...but he was comforted by being here. And he dreaded the battles he knew awaited him when he took Darica home.

Although he was not a rich man, his business was stable enough that had no trouble in borrowing the money to bury Mariana properly. She rested now beneath a weeping willow tree in a small, but pleasantly maintained cemetery. Armando had ordered dozens of her favorite multi-colored daisies for her funeral. Later there would be a headstone...and more daisies...

Originally he had thought, with some regret, that there would be no one but him, Darica, and perhaps the bakery owner at Mariana's funeral. Her shyness had prevented her making friends easily, and she left no living relatives except her daughter. When a respectable number of mourners arrived for the short graveside service, however, he was thankful and relieved...until he realized that curiosity, not respect was the reason for their attendance.

He had not been so discreet after all.

Why were the two people involved in the affair always the last to know how much everyone else knew all along? Still, he did not care that these people knew he had been an unfaithful husband with a girl over half his age. Nor did he mind their knowing the details of Darica's parentage. But he did not want them to label Mariana with any of the stereotypical slurs reserved for "the other woman."

With all the pertinent information permeating the neighborhood like toxic gas, Bella would be in neither a forgiving nor a receptive mood when he returned home with his daughter.

Shifting the baby's weight in his arms, Armando considered his options.

He could not go home at all. If Bella granted him a divorce, he would suffer financially because his wife would wring from him every cent she could. The prospect was not so tolerable without Mariana there to ease the sting of straitened circumstances, and there was still the necessity of a mother for Darica.

The only choice for him was to make whatever peace he could with his wife. The emotional negotiating would be far from pleasant, and he knew he would ultimately lose more than he gained. His sacrifices, however, would be meager payment for the debt he owed Mariana. And Darica.

One child had already suffered for his deeds. Darica would not.

Perhaps his wife would, in time, love his daughter. For all Bella's faults, she was a good mother to Alvito. Maybe too doting and lenient, but those qualities were the natural inclinations of a mother. What woman could deny love to a baby?

Especially one as beautiful as his precious Darica Mariana.

* * *

"I will not have the spawn of your adulterous lust living in my own house!"

Armando reined his temper. Venting anger would only fuel Bella's wrath...and awaken Darica, who lay sleeping in a basket in a corner of the living room. Still, certain indisputable facts needed to be re-established.

Though his voice was whispery soft, the threat in it was obvious enough that Bella flinched when he spoke.

"This house is mine, woman, and the money that keeps it running, puts food in your mouth and clothing on your back comes from the labor of my hands. If you choose to make a point about community property, you'll have to haul me into divorce court to do it."

When he saw panic flicker in her eyes, he was emboldened. Divorce was an abomination to this Catholic-bred woman, something he should have realized when he was weighing his options. However, his intention was not to defeat her, but to gain her cooperation.

"I'm not asking for forgiveness, Bella," he continued more kindly. "The only regrets I have are that Mariana is dead and that you have been embarrassed."

"Embarrassed!" she spat. "How like you to think that your fling caused me only embarrassment. You humiliated me, Armando, and demeaned our sacred marriage vows."

His dark eyes narrowed menacingly. "I willingly accept your damnations for my infidelity, but don't you dare wave your pious righteousness in my face. How sacred could our vows be when you lied and tricked me to the altar? How devout were you when you allowed me into your spinster's bed in the first place? Can you deny that you were planning all along to entrap me with a pregnancy, whether real or fabricated?"

"Of course I can deny it! You...you seduced me. I came to you with my maidenhead intact."

"No other man could withstand the venom from your viper's tongue long enough to assault your maidenhead, and you compound your waspishness with lies. Will you swear with your hand upon your Bible that you did not intentionally deceive me?"

"You're being ridiculous."

"Just as I thought. You can make no denials without lies." He turned his back to her now. "If we were keeping score in this marital war, I'd have to say we're even now."

"What are you saying?"

"I'm saying that you tricked me into marrying you, and I was unfaithful. We're even now."

Grabbing his arm, she whirled him around. "Is that why you humiliated me...to even the score?"

Carefully he pried her fingernails from the flesh of his forearm. "No, my dear. Initially I was lonely for a woman, plain and simple. But Mariana enfolded my heart within her devotion, something I had never experienced a single day of my marriage."

His head recoiled from the force of her slap. "Don't lay blame for your unbridled lusts at my feet! Do you have any idea of how I've suffered? Are you even aware of the snickers, whispers, and stares I've had to endure? I'm branded by mocking eyes every time I enter the church, and now you expect me to be a mother to this...this bastard of yours!"

Grasping the bodice of her housedress, he yanked her toward him. Though his teeth were clenched, he enunciated each word carefully and distinctly. "Don't you ever call that child a bastard again. Understand?"

She nodded meekly. He had raised his voice to her before, but never his hand. When he released her and gently straightened her collar, she shrank back in fright.

"Good God, Bella. Anyone would think I beat you on a daily basis. Maybe if I had, things would be different now."

He dropped onto the sofa and buried his face in his hands. She stood rooted, wanting to leave, but fearing his reaction if she did.

"If you handle this right," he said finally, "all those people who have been whispering about us will nominate you for sainthood."

"What are you talking about?"

"Think about it, Bella. You not only forgive your husband and take him back, you also accept his daughter by a woman he wasn't married to. Two feathers in your cap, Bella. Two jewels for your crown. The whole parish will applaud your compassion and Christian decency."

Bella was duly thoughtful. "Yes...yes, they would, wouldn't they?"

"I promise you no further embarrassments, no more infidelities. You, Alvito, Darica, and I will, for all intents and purposes, become the ideal family. I've never had any complaints with your devotion as a mother."

"You cannot expect me to love the girl as I love Alvito!"

"Not immediately. But you can still be her mother, can't you? She will need a mother."

"You ask too much..." The protest was feeble. Armando knew that he had won her over by projecting a saintly image for her within the parish.

"I'll do my part as husband and father if you'll do yours as wife and mother. You have my word. I will ask for nothing more from you."

Bella did not answer immediately. Instead she paced around the living room until she reached the basket where Darica lay, now awake but quiet. The baby's dark eyes regarded the woman solemnly, seemingly filled with too much knowledge of the events surrounding her.

"When you say I'm to do my part as WIFE and mother," she said finally, "what, exactly, are you expecting?"

"I'll move back into the house...back into our bedroom, too. In time I'll probably claim my marital rights again, when we are used to each other again..."

He expected an argument, but he was surprised.

"Very well, Armando," she agreed quietly a few heartbeats later.

She dreaded the necessity of intimacy with him, and she felt no maternal tugs as she stared down at Darica. What decided the matter for her was the realization that she could cause Armando more misery with the bastard there.

CHAPTER TWO

Darica studied her half-brother with eyes that would have caused a more sensitive youth to squirm with shame. However, Alvito was, as usual, impervious to any attacks of conscience. Even though Darica was old enough now to string words together into meaningful phrases, he knew that HIS mother would never believe any accusations leveled at him by *Bastarda*.

Bastarda was what he and HIS mother called Darica when nobody else was around. It was their secret name for the baby that did not belong in their house. Alvito belonged here, but not *Bastarda*. Bella had coached her son well.

Well enough that he knew he should never let his father hear the secret name...or see any of the secret tricks he played on *Bastarda*.

Like breaking arms and legs off her dolls. Or twisting the head off her stuffed rabbit.

Or pinching her until blue marks dotted her skin. Alvito wanted to make her cry, but *Bastarda* never shed a tear, and for some reason Alvito was infuriated by the failure.

Today he had been close to making her cry. His friend, Enrique, older and therefore worldlier, had just learned the useful art of fashioning a hangman's noose out of clothesline. Intrigued by the mechanics of the device, Alvito searched for a worthy neck to test the noose. *Bastarda* was his first choice, but even his mother might disapprove of hanging the girl, and his father the taxidermist would tan his hide in every sense of the word.

Instead Alvito settled for the stray mutt that *Bastarda* had befriended several weeks before.

When Darica awakened from her nap, her Poppet was a pathetic droop of fur swaying from a tree branch outside her window. Watching carefully for her reaction, Alvito sat cross-legged on the floor by her bed as he calmly plunged his hand into a jar of peanut butter and licked the paste off his fingers.

The faint trembling of her bottom lip rewarded his hour-long wait, but just as quickly her face stilled to that stony mask that so irritated him. Only her eyes revealed the emotions quaking within her, but Alvito received no satisfaction. In truth, if he held her stare too long, he became decidedly uneasy. No rage boiled within the girl's eyes. Darica had learned the rules of their household game early. Tears and tantrums gained her nothing but stinging slaps from Mother Bella's frayed leather belt...or, if Darica was lucky, banishment to her room until her father came in from his workshop and rescued her.

Anger was a luxury forbidden to Darica in this house. Although she was only three years old, she had already resigned herself to her fate. Still, Alvito could sense a stealthy danger in her eyes. Flickering in those dark pools was the prescience...or the hope...that some day wrongs would be righted and that tormenters would be punished.

This was her early gleaning of her Catholic instruction as Armando endeavored to raise her the way his beloved Mariana would have raised her. Unfortunately, he delegated the responsibility for Darica's physical well being to Bella, refusing to believe that any woman could ill treat a child, especially one as lovely as his daughter.

If Darica had complained about her situation in any way, he might have changed his mind, but Darica's way was quiet acceptance lest her tears elicit from her father the same anger she provoked in Mother Bella. Darica needed his love and kindness in this house.

For now, however, Darica must tend to Poppet. Perhaps Papa would stuff him so that she could keep the puppy forever.

Casting one final dark look in Alvito's direction, she went in search of her father while her brother sulked over her lack of cooperation in his quest to make her cry. However, he brightened considerably with the dawning of another terrific idea for another terrific secret trick. After squishing his fingers through the peanut butter, he smeared the goo on the quilt covering Darica's bed. Then he went to tell HIS mother about the mess *Bastarda* had made.

* * *

"I cannot stuff every pet of yours when it dies, *querida*. We have had this conversation before." Armando chuckled as he continued fleshing a deerskin. "Most girls your age mean something different when they ask for stuffed animals."

"Raquel was such a beautiful cat, Papa. I hate to cover her with a bunch of ugly dirt." Darica's sigh of disappointment was well exaggerated for his benefit.

He paused from his work to study his daughter. Now eight, she looked more like her mother each year. Darica had also inherited Mariana's gentleness and piety. There was, however, an indefinable strangeness about the girl that disturbed him.

"It seems to me, Darica, that you go through many pets," he said, returning to his labors.

"Perhaps our neighborhood is not a healthy place for pets," she suggested. *Perhaps Alvito puts rat poison in their food or finds some other way to hurt them so that he can blame his evil deeds on other children in our rough neighborhood.*

If only she could turn away the stray cats and dogs that were drawn to her doorstep. Each time she fed and nursed a new animal back to health, she told herself that Alvito had surely grown tired of his cruel games. Or maybe she could place the animal in a new home before Alvito struck.

Sometimes she was successful. Father Montez and the sisters at St. Anthony had been recipients of many cats to keep the mice away. However, Darica had few other friends upon whom to bestow the gift of a pet. More often than not, she would find her current animal guest dead or maimed in such a way that her father had to put the pitiful thing out of its misery.

When the animal died unmarked, though violently sick, Darica could understand her father's failure to suspect foul play. Strays, he told her, were often unhealthy.

However, many times the animals were obviously tortured. Darica shuddered as she recalled the puppy nailed to a tree…the kitten trapped inside a stew pot with exploding firecrackers…the dog impaled through its neck by the teeth of a garden rake…and Poppet, her first pet, strangled with a clothesline.

In the case of Poppet, Darica almost made her father believe that Alvito was responsible. When she ventured hesitantly in her toddler's talk that "Bito did it," Armando angrily confronted his son, who cunningly shifted the blame to Enrique. Armando might call Enrique's grandmother with an irate complaint, but the old lady who was raising the wayward boy would do nothing simply because she was afraid of Enrique.

Alvito was clever at shifting blame, a talent he seldom needed with his mother, for in Bella's eyes Alvito was nearly perfect.

And Armando's way of coping with the boy was to let Bella take care of everything.

Alvito naturally preferred his mother's coddling to Armando's gruffness anyway. Armando felt no particular remorse for the preference, accepting as only fair that Bella should have Alvito to herself since Darica was her papa's little girl. In truth, Armando and Alvito had little in common, and any attempts at father-son bonding were awkward and unsatisfying for both. In the one part of his life that Armando wished to establish some rapport…his taxidermy business…Alvito showed neither interest nor aptitude. In fact, the boy seemed downright repulsed by the whole idea despite his blood lust for living animals.

Darica was the one to spend more and more of her time in the workshop with her father. Never intrusive, she was content to watch him working or to read or draw animal pictures that decorated all available wall space in the workshop. Armando enjoyed her company and, as she grew older, their conversations, but he had never considered her as a possible protégée.

"Teach me how to do it, Papa," she said now.

"Teach you what, *querida?*"

"How to stuff and mount. You are too busy to do all my pets I wish to keep forever, so teach me so that I can do them myself."

Armando stared at his daughter in stunned disbelief. "This is no work for a little girl. It is messy, and working with animal carcasses is not pleasant."

"I won't mind since when I am finished, the poor dead animals will be beautiful forever."

"Skinning an animal often requires a man's strength."

"I will do only small animals, Papa, until I get bigger. Then I can help you with the deer, elk, and wolves. If I need a man's strength, you will help me, won't you?"

"That's not the point…"

"Then what is the point, Papa?"

"Little girls should know about playing with dolls and jump ropes, not stuffing or tanning animal skins."

"I already know some things from watching you."

"Tell me these things you know."

"You are upset with Mr. Briscoe because he did not have proper field care for this skin, and you are worried about grease burn. Sometimes the skins come to you dry and hard, but then you do not worry because you can make them relax in one of your solutions."

"Is that all you know?"

"Oh no, Papa. Ask me some questions, but remember I am only a little girl."

Armando indicated the tool in his hand. "What is this I'm using now?"

"That is a fleshing knife, and you must hold it just so or you will cut into the skin."

"And this thing here?" he asked, tapping the structure on which the skin rested.

"That is your large fleshing beam that you use for large skins. You use your small one when you are working with small animals or when you're working around the faces of all the animals."

"What size eye would I need for a deer head?"

"I think in the twenties. You used eights on my cats, and my dogs had different sizes up to sixteen for Duke."

A smile flirted around Armando's lips. "What kinds of skins make the best rawhide?"

"You like deer, elk, coyote, and sometimes woodchuck, Papa."

"Well…" Armando laid down his fleshing knife and motioned Darica closer to him. "You've impressed me, *querida*. Have you picked all this up just by watching me?"

"And listening, Papa. You talk to yourself while you work."

"You really want to learn your papa's business?"

"Yes, Papa. I'll even learn to do fishes and snakes though I don't like them so well."

"It's messy work…"

"May I have a work coat like yours…only smaller, of course?"

"I'll have to get you one if you'll be working with me."

"Then…I may help you, Papa?" Darica's bright eyes glistened with joy.

"You can help me with this skin," he said, picking up a knife and guiding Darica's hands in its use. "You have to angle it just right…"

"I know that already, Papa…"

* * *

On her tenth birthday, when Armando took his daughter to a "grown-up" restaurant for dinner, Darica knew that some momentous occasion was at hand. Having been attuned for several years to the abnormal atmosphere in their household, she knew that tonight's revelation must surely pertain to their family situation.

She wondered, briefly, whether her father had decided to ship Mother Bella and Alvito elsewhere. However, she quickly dismissed this idea as both contrary to her father's nature and unforgivably unchristian. A more reasonable speculation was that her father and she would be the ones to move away, a move Darica would shed no tears for. How perfect life would be without the torment of Mother Bella and Alvito! How happy their family would be if there were only she and her father!

"I have been thinking about this moment for many years, *querida*," Armando was saying to her now. "I did not wish to wait too long to answer the questions that have been in your heart, yet I wanted you to be old enough to understand."

"To understand what, Papa?" Darica asked the question merely as a polite cue for her father. For many, many years she had been old enough to understand why her papa would want to leave Mother Bella.

"Even now I'm not so certain that this is the proper time, and I fear you will think many bad thoughts about your papa."

"Never, Papa! I love you more than anything else in this world."

Her vehemence reassured him. Touching his hand to her cheek, he continued.

"I have a story to tell you, *querida*. It is the story of your papa and your real mama…"

Darica listened raptly. The news was both less and more than she had anticipated. Though she was disappointed that she and her father would not be leaving, she was jubilant with the news that a gentler soul than Bella had given birth to her. And how sadly beautiful was this love story of her father and her REAL mother…her mama…the sweet and lovely Mariana.

"Then you do not condemn me for my adultery?" Armando asked, relieved that she had accepted the news so well.

"Only God can condemn anyone, and in this I pray He will be forgiving since you and Mama were so much in love."

She made the entire mess seem so simple. *And perhaps it was*, he thought, *though at the time I was overwhelmed by the confusion of circumstances.*

"Papa," Darica asked him now, "must I still call Mother Bella 'Mother'?"

"What do you wish to call her instead?" Armando immediately thought of several of his own names for the woman.

"She has not been to me as mothers of other girls are to them. I thought she did not like me, and I was sad because all mothers should love their children. Now I understand."

"Has she mistreated you…harmed you…hurt you in any way?"

He looked so thunderously angry at the mere thought that Darica quickly reassured him.

"Don't scowl so, Papa. She has never been nice to me, but she hasn't been so very cruel either. She hasn't acted as my mother would. That's all. And now I wish to call her only 'Bella,' if you don't mind."

"Whatever you are comfortable with, *querida*."

"Will she object?"

"In truth, Darica, she will be relieved. She had a difficult time adjusting to your calling her 'mother' from the beginning. The compromise between us was that you would call her 'Mother Bella' instead."

"I'm sorry that I have been a source of trouble for you, Papa."

"You have been no trouble, *querida*. You have been the light in my dark life."

Shyly pleased, Darica lowered her dark eyes. "I will light a candle for Mama at mass now."

"She deserves to be remembered in the church in such a way."

"Will you take me to visit her? We can take her flowers…"

"Daisies… we'll take multi-colored daisies," Armando said, memory alive in his eyes. "We'll go tomorrow. I regret that my own visits have become less frequent over the last few years."

"This has been a very special birthday."

"God has blessed me with a very special daughter."

When he raised his goblet of wine in tribute to her, Darica touched it with her glass of milk and felt very grown-up.

Tonight was perfect…

If only they didn't have to go home to Bella and Alvito.

* * *

That Armando and Bella would eventually clash over Darica and Alvito seemed inevitable.

Armando felt compelled to intervene in Bella's previously exclusive parental jurisdiction when Alvito got into more and more trouble both at school and with the law. There were actually more altercations with the law, for…as Armando soon discovered…his son spent very little time at school anymore. When Armando confronted Bella about her son's rampant waywardness, she responded at first defensively and then belligerently.

"Vito has explained things to me," she said tightly, "and I am content with his explanations."

"Perhaps you will share these explanations with me so that I, too, may be content."

"You have been content to ignore your son in favor of a bastard daughter. Why should you be discontent now that he has had a few...misunderstandings with the authorities?"

Armando's fists clenched at the condemnation of his daughter rather than of himself, but he checked his temper to focus on the matter at hand.

"Truancy, gang fighting, and robbery are not misunderstandings, Bella."

"He is guilty of nothing but the truancy, and I have spoken with him about that."

"I'm sure you took a firm stand."

Bella's eyes narrowed. "It's not Vito's fault that we live in such a poor neighborhood that the school is inadequate for his needs. They have taught him all they have to teach. A bright boy like Vito is wasting his time there."

"I have yet to see his genius reflected in his report cards."

"You seldom see his report cards! What do you know of your son, Armando? You are strangers living in the same house. Whose fault is that? Not Vito's. I have done the best I can with him alone. You have no right to criticize him or me."

Armando started to point out that he had that he had done a better job alone with Darica than Bella had done with Alvito, but a twinge of guilt intervened. Bella was right in some respects. If he had taken greater interest in the boy, perhaps Alvito would not be in trouble now.

"I am not criticizing, Bella," he said with forced gentleness, "but you must see that we have a problem with Vito, and we must do something now or the problem will become more serious."

If he had hoped to placate her with a conciliatory gesture, he failed.

"How like you to think there is a problem with Vito! There is no problem but that he's too naïve in choosing his friends. I have often warned him that he's asking for trouble by spending so much time with Enrique, but Vito will not listen, and he suffers the blame for what Enrique does."

"Can you really believe that Vito is so blameless? Are you so blind?"

"Blind?" she spat. "You are the one who is blind! Blind to your son's virtues and to your daughter's faults."

Armando's conciliatory mood vanished. "Darica is an angel by anyone's standards, and compared to Vito, she is a saint."

"A saint? Are saints so lazy that they cannot help with housework? Are saints so dishonest that they lie and falsely accuse others for the vile things they themselves have done? Are saints so wanton that they try to seduce their own brothers?"

"Seduce…Darica? Woman, you are out of your mind! The girl is barely fourteen, and I hardly think the nuns are teaching her such things at school."

"Vito has told me that many times she has looked at him in suggestive ways. Perhaps the skill is an instinct that she inherited from her mother."

Bella knew by the fury in his eyes that she had crossed the boundary of his restraint, and she placed distance and a heavy chair between herself and her husband.

"She never lifts a finger to help me with housework," Bella added, trying to sidetrack his anger with a lesser charge.

"Darica assists me in the shop when her homework is finished and her room is clean. I expect no more from her. Nor should you. God knows you expect much less from your son."

"Vito is working…"

"At what? Robbing poor old men?"

"Vito did not do it. No charges were filed."

"Only because Mr. Santiago is afraid that Enrique and his gang…which includes Vito…will do much worse than rob him next time."

"If he is so afraid of Vito, why did he hire him to stock his shelves?" Bella asked, pleased by the amazement registering on Armando's face.

"Santiago hired Vito?"

"Vito is quite excited to be making his own money so that he doesn't have to rely on his father's charity anymore."

"Charity! I have never denied him anything he needed…"

"Except, perhaps, a father." She smiled when she saw him flinch. "You should know I have given him permission to leave school when he has his sixteenth birthday next week. He feels he can learn more toward building his future from working for Mr. Santiago than he can in school. I agree with him. You have forfeited your right to make decisions for my son."

"He is my son, too, and my work pays the bills around here."

"And I still permit your bastard daughter to live here as if she belongs. I don't think either you or she wants me interfering with her any more than Vito and I want you interfering with us. Do you understand what I am telling you, Armando?"

"Yes. Clearly." The urge to strangle the smirk off her face was frighteningly strong. Armando slammed out of the house to save both her and himself from the impulse.

CHAPTER THREE

Darica's concern for her father's health had evolved into a nagging worry over the past few weeks. Though he usually sustained a robust appetite, even for Bella's cooking, lately he ate sparingly. He tired easily, but refused to rest, plodding along instead at a reduced pace that generated half the work in twice the time. However, because of Darica's skilled assistance, the business suffered no lapse of productivity. She matched her father's late hours, gently disregarding his gruff, though half-hearted commands that she go to bed at a decent hour on school nights.

In truth, demands of both shop and school were wearing on Darica, but one look at her father's sagging shoulders and gray face renewed her fortitude. When she begged him on more than one occasion to consult a doctor, he quickly and firmly denied what seemed so painfully obvious to Darica.

"I'm not sick, *querida*. There are many things that burden my heart at this moment. That's all…"

That's all…

Darica pursed her lips to stifle the observations that would only aggravate him further. She was already helping him in the best way possible by working beside him…often in place of him.

Alvito was the source of her father's despair. Darica had tried earlier to warn him about Alvito's perverseness, but Armando had chosen not to listen, for whatever reasons. Now Alvito's unruliness was beyond parental restraint.

Her brother…her HALF-brother and his friends, who boasted the name "Renegados," were terrorizing the neighborhood, and everyone was too afraid of the threatened consequences to call the police. Poor Mr. Santiago was barely earning enough to live on, for Alvito's idea of stocking shelves…on those rare occasions when he showed up for work…was to commandeer candy, soda, and cigarettes for the Renegados. Every week the old man gave Alvito a regular paycheck, yet Alvito stole cash from the register whenever Renegado funds were too low for their wine and beer.

The volume of losses might have eventually convinced the grocer to call the police if Alvito had not had another source of "insurance": Mr. Santiago's granddaughter, Teresa, a gently raised twelve-year-old. Alvito admired the girl's dark-eyed beauty and blossoming figure, and he made sure that Mr. Santiago knew of his admiration.

What Mr. Santiago did not know was that both Alvito and Enrique had already persuaded Teresa to satisfy their admiration. If she did not cooperate, they told her, her grandfather would have a painful accident.

Darica knew the details of Alvito's activities because he bragged to her. He bragged because he knew that she was sickened by what she heard and because he knew that Darica, like so many others, would not turn him in. Not because she was afraid of him, but because she was afraid for her father.

"Go on to bed, Papa," she said now. "I will clean up here."

"It is so late, *querida.* You need your sleep more than I."

"Tomorrow is Saturday. I won't need to get up so early."

"You have early mass."

"Father Montez will forgive me if I'm late. Now go, please, or I shall worry all night and not sleep at all."

Smiling weakly, he did as she requested with no further resistance.

I hope it is just worry for Vito that burdens him so much, Darica thought as she watched his drooping form cross the lawn in the moonlight.

Eventually Vito and his friends would go too far...try too much...somewhere... and be arrested and locked up for a while.

Or maybe the Renegados' skirmishes with their rivals, the Scorpions, would intensify to the point that blood would flow...Vito's blood...

Darica crossed herself and begged God's forgiveness for her unchristian thoughts as she later climbed the stairs to her room.

Even if Papa would rest more easily, I must not think these thoughts...

Opening the door to her room, she gasped and froze as she saw Alvito spotlighted by the reading lamp attached to her headboard. He had been watching for the lights to go out in the shop. He had been ready for her all evening...

Now, as she watched, horrified, he quickened his strokes, pumping his erect penis until the hot, milky fluid streamed onto her pristine white sheets.

"Like what you see, Sis?" he mumbled, grinning at her, his eyes half closed. "Next time I can go off inside your pure little body instead of on your pure little bed."

"Get out, Vito," she whispered, trembling. "Get out, or I'll call Papa."

"The old man doesn't scare me..."

Nevertheless, he rolled off her bed, sweeping his jeans off the floor in one elaborate motion. He merely draped them over his arm, however, as he strolled past Darica, who pressed herself against the door as he started by her.

"You know, Sis," he said, knowing how much she hated being reminded of their relationship, "Enrique told me you was turning into a fine-looking chick, and damned if he wasn't right. Too bad I didn't notice sooner. You could have saved me the trouble of jackin' off..."

Darica slapped him, aggression that surprised them both.

"Get out," she repeated, though her quivering voice only made him bolder.

"Sure, Sis." He squeezed her breast. "But I'll be back. You can dream about me and what you saw tonight until then..."

She slammed the door behind him. Because there was no lock, she braced a chair against the door. Quaking with fear and disgust, she collapsed onto her bed, too late to remember that Alvito had soiled the sheets.

* * *

"Papa, I've made a decision about my future, and I wish to discuss it with you please."

Hands clasped before her, Darica stood beside the fleshing beam as her father worked on a deerskin. Normally at ease with him, she was rather apprehensive now about telling him her plans. He was expecting her to take over his shop when he retired. However, Darica had known for some time that her calling was in another direction. Taxidermy was, at first, merely an excuse to please and be near her father. Now it was something she did for him since he was no longer able to handle the demands of the shop alone.

Although he was speaking of early retirement with increasing frequency, Darica knew he was still at least five years away from anything official. She could give him two and a half more years of assistance before graduating from high school, leaving him more or less stranded for another two and a half years. Acutely aware of the difficulty he might have affording an assistant, Darica had spoken to the sisters at St. Anthony about possible alternatives to her career planning. As expected, the nuns had been understanding and encouraging; and now, as Darica faced her father, she was well supplied with possibilities that would accommodate everyone.

Armando paused in his work and wiped his hands on the towel hanging from his work-coat pocket.

"So, *querida*, you are barely a sophomore, and already you want to plan for your future? I am pleased with your foresight, but fear perhaps this decision you have made is not the one for which I had hoped."

Can he read me so very well? Darica wondered, avoiding his steady gaze.

"I love you so very much, Papa," she said at last, "but for a long time I have felt that my future is not here in this shop, but with the sisters at St. Anthony…"

"What is it you're telling me, *querida?*"

Darica took a deep breath. "I wish to become a nun."

Armando was silent for too long a moment. "Your mother would have been pleased," he said finally.

"And you, Papa? Are you pleased?"

"I have never been a devout man. I raised you in the church because your mother would have wished it."

"And so I have displeased you?" Darica chewed on her lip so that he could not see it tremble.

"You could never displease me," he said softly, holding his arms out to her. "Your decision is not so surprising to me though I did have some hopes that you would take over for me here."

Gratefully Darica snuggled against him. Though theirs was a close and loving relationship, Armando was not the kind of father to be overly demonstrative with his affection.

"I'll still be here to help you until I am through high school, Papa, and then I won't be far away. If you have trouble finding an assistant, Sister Sherwood says I may begin my schooling, but delay my postulancy until you find someone or until you retire."

"I don't need an assistant. I have become lazy since I have had you to rely on, that's all. Don't worry about the shop. Both it and I will be fine. Now tell me, just what exactly lies ahead for you? I am ignorant in these matters."

"The sisters will send me to college…which is a great honor, for many orders cannot afford to send their members to school."

"Then I am doubly proud of you. What will you study?"

"Zoology. I already have some experience in that field thanks to you. By the time I earn my degree, Sister Zabinski will be retiring, and St. Anthony High School will need another science teacher."

"What of your training to become a nun?"

"I can begin when I enter college. Before my postulancy, I will have at least one year as an affiliate of St. Anthony and meet with a sister who is my spiritual adviser. Sister Sherwood is working with me now so that I may begin my postulancy right after high school."

"The sisters are very cooperative."

"Besides you, they have been my only family for many years."

Armando realized the truth of her observation just as he recognized the spiritual glow in Darica's eyes as she spoke of her plans. Certainly no animal carcass would produce such radiance in his daughter.

"Tell me more of your plans," he said, more at ease with her decision. "I don't even know what this postulancy you speak of means."

"For two years I will study with the church as an applicant for admission to the order. I will be a postulant then. For the next two years, I will be a novice, something like a probationary nun, while I study theology, rules, and history of the order itself."

"All this while you have your college studies, too?"

"Yes, Papa."

"Won't it be too much for you?"

"Many sisters have followed the same path with no problem. I can, too. Hard work does not intimidate me, and I don't plan to spend too many evenings at wild college parties."

Armando's laugh was rusty from neglect. Nevertheless, its sound was pleasing to Darica.

"And then you will be a nun?" he asked, still chuckling at the thought of Darica at a wild college party.

"Then I will make my first promises, and I will be considered a sister though I will not take my final vows until three to nine years later."

"I didn't realize that so much time is involved."

"The long wait is necessary. A sister should not take her final vows until she is absolutely certain that is the life she wants. Like marriage…"

"Like marriage SHOULD be," he corrected her with a sad smile. "I don't have to ask if this is what you truly want, for the answer shines in your face already."

"It is what I want, Papa, more than anything else. But I will worry about you."

"St. Anthony is within walking distance…"

"That's not what I mean. I was talking about leaving you alone to work the shop."

"I told you not to worry."

"In this one case, I will not do what you tell me."

"I will look for some part-time help when the time comes. Will you feel better then?"

"Yes, Papa."

"Good. We have settled many things today. Now it's time to get to work."

"May I ask one more favor from you, Papa?"

"Of course."

"Hug me again."

"It is a favor you do me by asking, *querida*," he whispered, wrapping his arms around her again.

Pausing to snoop beside the shop window as he cut across the yard, Alvito saw the embrace between father and daughter.

Why, that old pervert, he thought. *He's porkin' his own daughter. In this one way, at least, I will be following in the old fart's footsteps…*

* * *

Darica dutifully lit a candle for her mother, a tribute that became part of her morning mass ritual when she learned the truth of her parentage. Today she had dawdled over her prayers because both her father and Bella were gone for the day, one of the rare times that they had done anything together. The funeral of a distant cousin was the reason for this marital miracle. Armando went to pay his final respects to a relative; Bella went to protect her interests and Alvito's should Armando, by chance, be the sole surviving heir to a grand fortune.

Their absence meant that Darica would be alone in the house with Alvito for most of this Saturday.

Though Alvito had never done more than threaten her, usually when…by his plan…Darica stumbled onto him when he was in the midst of self-gratification, she was increasingly uneasy in his presence. Of course, he would never try anything while their father was within range of her screams, and she had a measure of safety even while Bella was around.

Today, however, Alvito and Darica would be there alone, and she stalled as long as she could. There was much work to do in the shop.

Stepping outside the church was like stepping away from Heaven. Inside, surrounded by the majesty of God, she was at peace. Beneath the familiar loving eyes of the statue of the Holy Mother, she experienced a sense of belonging that eluded her everywhere else, even in the shop with her father.

Lately she often stared for hours at the eyes of St. Mary. Sometimes the eyes of her own mother, Mariana, communicated with her through the Virgin, and Darica knew that her mother fully approved of the pure and pious life she had chosen.

The walk between St. Anthony and the Cervantes home was much too short, Darica decided, squaring her shoulders as she entered the house. She would change into her work clothes quickly and seek refuge in the shop. If she were lucky, Alvito would sleep until noon today, as he often did. Once she was in the shop, she would not worry so much about him. He stayed out of the shop for the most part because the messiness of the work made him too queasy to maintain his manly and boastful demeanor.

Darica tiptoed past his room so that she would not disturb him if he were awake.

As soon as she opened her bedroom door, she knew how pointless the effort had been, for Alvito was waiting for her on her bed. At least he was fully clothed.

"We've been watching for you." His grin was sickeningly lopsided as he stood up.

Even before the "we" registered in her mind, she was grabbed from behind. Enrique gripped her painfully as Alvito pawed over her.

"Like that, Sis?" Alvito murmured, his eyes closed as he rocked his hips against her. "We'll call this part of the foreplay…"

Darica spat into his face. Fury blazed in his eyes as he slapped her. Only Enrique's grip kept her from falling.

Though she kicked and struggled to get away, they overpowered her, pinning her to the bed and ripping away enough of her clothing to expose her to them. Alvito was the first to force himself into her. Biting back her rage, humiliation, and pain, Darica retreated into Bible verses until, at last, they were finished with her.

"It won't do you no good to squeal to anyone about this," Alvito told her as he calmly tucked his tee shirt into his jeans. "Our dear papa's the only one to give a fuck about you, and if he tries anything with me and Enrique, you'll be an orphan...an orphan bastard slut..."

Enrique followed him into the hallway. "You told me your old man was fuckin' her," Enrique whispered. "She was bleeding plenty when you was done with her."

"I'm three times the size of my old man. She's not used to man-size meat, that's all."

But Alvito knew that *Bastarda* had been a virgin after all, a condition that made the morning's events even more satisfying for him.

Still, she had shed no tears, no matter how violently he had slammed himself into her.

Goddamn her anyway...

God, damn them. God, damn them to Hell. God, damn them...

From Darica the thought was a plea, not an oath.

Automatically she went about the painful business of cleaning herself and the room of any traces of her violation. Only once did she falter...when, as she washed blood off her body, she was struck by a realization more agonizing to her than her physical injuries:

I will never be able to cleanse myself of this sin...I am impure...I am unworthy...oh, God, why have you damned me, too?

In desperation, she dressed hastily and fled to the shop, where she worked steadily into the evening, ignoring the pain in her body, trying to ignore the pain in her soul.

Armando checked in on her when he arrived home after dark.

"It's late, *querida*. Perhaps you should stop for the night. We will finish the museum's woodchuck tomorrow."

"I'll be in shortly, Papa. Go on to bed..."

Darica did not look up from her work, but Armando saw the bruise on her cheek.

"What happened to your face, Darica?" he asked.

"I tripped and fell against the fleshing beam," she said, still avoiding his eyes.

Her clothing hid other bruises and injuries. If Armando had been able to look into her eyes, he would have seen that the divine light there had also been extinguished.

CHAPTER FOUR

"I've changed my mind, that's all, Papa. Is that not considered a prerogative of a woman?"

"But you were so sure you wanted a life in the church, *querida*."

"And now I'm sure I don't."

Armando had noticed a change in his daughter as she spent less time at church and more with him in the shop over the last few weeks. He had even called Sister Sherwood to consult with her about this baffling situation, but the sister was as bewildered as he. All that she could tell him was that Darica was regretful, but adamant about this change in her future plans.

"Is it your concern for me that has altered your intentions?" he asked yet again.

"I have told you many times that you are not the reason. Now, please, we have many things to do."

"Relieve your old man's heart, and give me a REASON why you have changed your mind, a GOOD reason."

The tempo of Darica's work increased as she loaded fresh sawdust into the drumming machine.

"I have searched my soul," she said finally, "and I decided that I lack the devoutness of spirit necessary to become a sister."

"You are the most devout young woman in the church. Even Sister Sherwood—"

"Papa," she interrupted in exasperation, "you asked me for a reason, and I have given you one. Please be satisfied with it because I shall say no more of the matter. I am content with my decision to continue in the shop after graduation...unless you do not want me here?"

"I am delighted with the thought of keeping you here with me, *querida*...so long as you are happy."

"I am happy."

"Is this happiness why you've filled the drumming machine so full of sawdust, there's no room for the skins?"

"You distracted me with your silly questions."

Although Darica's petulancy was softened by her smile, Armando was stunned that his sweet-tempered daughter was capable of such a reaction at all. He asked no more questions of her, but he did not stop worrying.

He was so absorbed in these new concerns that he paid little attention to the work before him. His sudden oath alerted Darica that something was wrong. Running to his side, she saw that he had sliced deeply into his hand with a scalpel.

She grabbed a clean towel to wrap around his hand.

"We must get you to the emergency room, Papa."

"Nonsense. This is nothing."

"Your nothing has already soaked the towel with blood."

"We have too much to do to waste time with it. The bleeding will stop soon. I will be fine."

As she wrapped a second towel around his hand, Darica insisted that he go to the emergency room. However, he was equally obstinate about not going.

"At least lie down for a while, Papa…with your hand elevated on some pillows until the bleeding stops. And then I will bandage your hand."

"I have a load to take to the landfill."

"I can do that."

"It's a nasty, slimy job."

"I've been up to my elbows in animal slime for years."

"The distance is so far. You've never driven the truck when you're alone."

"I can manage. I am f-fully a woman now and must learn to do these things myself if I am to take over the shop when you retire."

Disregarding his further protests, she tenderly bullied him into the house and up to his room. She waved off Bella's indifferent offer of assistance and tended to her father herself.

"Don't worry about anything," she told him when he was settled. "I'll take care of everything."

"Thank you, *querida*. You take good care of your papa." He closed his eyes, and then remembered, "You will need also to pick up Vito at work on your way back in."

"V-Vito?"

"Pick him up at the store. I told Bella I would do it."

"The store is not so far."

"I know, but his mother is concerned that he is too tired when he gets off work. Though I know he is tired from things other than working, I agreed to do as she asked to avoid another argument. Is this a problem for you?"

"No, Papa. N-No problem…"

Darica left quickly, before her father could detect that there WAS a problem. After loading the back of the pickup with bags filled with refuse of their trade, Darica's smock was filthy with grime and blood. In truth, she had been intentionally careless as she worked in hopes Alvito would be as repulsed by her now as he always was by the shop. She would wear her smock to the animal waste landfill and then to the store to pick him up. As an added precaution, she slipped a razor-sharp scalpel into her smock pocket.

She had waited this last month for God to exact His retribution on Alvito and Enrique, but nothing had happened to either of them. During the night, as she lay awake and fearful, even with her heavy bureau dragged into place before her door, she wondered if she were the guilty one. After all, she had embraced the romantic story of her father and mother, with little thought of the adultery they had committed. Was she, like Antigone, caught up in a cycle of tragedy that had its seeds in her father's sin?

However, in her more reasonable moments, she knew that Alvito and Enrique should have to pay for what they had done to her. When God proved less than expeditious in His punishment of them, she considered helping Him out a little. There were many useful chemicals in the shop. She could poison them as they had poisoned her cats and dogs over the years.

Yet even as she rationalized this possibility with the Biblical logic of an "Eye for eye...wound for wound," tattered remnants of her spirituality reminded her that the Lord claimed vengeance as His own dominion.

If only He were quicker about it. Darica was running out of excuses and strategies to avoid any solitary contact with Alvito.

When she returned from the landfill, she sat in the truck outside the store and waited for several minutes, all the while hoping that Alvito would see her and come out on his own. She finally realized that he would delight in making her wait, just as he would relish her having to go inside to ask for him. Only the thought of work piled up at the shop persuaded her to leave the truck.

Mr. Santiago's sad, drooping eyes reproached her. Did he know of her impurity? Had Alvito bragged to him about why she was now unworthy to take vows at St. Anthony?

No.

Her smock drew his eyes. He was smiling at her kindly now as he spoke.

"You are a good girl to help your father so much, Darica. Too bad his son is not so industrious."

"I've come for, Vito, sir. Will you call him, please?"

"Call him? My voice is not loud enough, child. He is not here."

"Papa thought he worked today."

"Even when he is here, he does not work. You may tell your papa that."

"Yes, sir." Relief washed through her. If Alvito was not here, she would not have to give him a ride home.

"You might check the warehouse."

"Warehouse?" The relief left her instantly. If she knew where he was, she would have to go for him.

"The old Herschberger Warehouse on Gilberti Street. It's boarded up, but they have no respect for private property. Enrique came for him hours ago, and they took off like bats out of...well, they were in a hurry. From what I could tell, the big, bad Renegados were going to have themselves a war council."

Darica's heartbeat quickened. "There's trouble with the Scorpions?"

"Forgive me, child. I forget myself sometimes. I should not be worrying you with talk of gang fighting. Don't worry. All they seem to do in their fights is shove each other, yell, and threaten. Like all bullies, they are afraid of any real challenges. Go on home, child, and don't waste your worry on your brother..."

The warehouse gave no sign that it was occupied, even by trespassers. Darica stayed in the relative security of the truck as she surveyed the grounds. She didn't even know why she was here, putting herself into jeopardy. If Alvito would share her with Enrique, he would also pass her around to all the other Renegados.

But something compelled her to be here...like God's hand directing her to something He wanted her to see so that her faith in His justice would be restored.

A fence in the back encircled what had been a parking area. Darica noticed a hole cut in the fence, and then a door, left open, a few paces beyond. The stillness touched her senses. Her heart thundering, she left the truck and DRIFTED toward the door. DRIFTED, for surely God drew her forward to witness His handiwork. Her faith had never before been so intense, but her fingers enclosed the handle of the scalpel in her pocket anyway.

She crossed the threshold into the warehouse cautiously. When her eyes adjusted to the dimness inside, she saw them. Two of them, lying on the concrete floor. One of the boys wore a faded denim jacket with a black and red scorpion on the back.

And the other boy...

With no real surprise, she recognized the body of Alvito...her half-brother...her violator.

The Scorpion lay in blood that crept in dark fingers on the concrete around him. A gash in his neck was the source of this crimson flood.

There was little blood on Alvito. A knife had found his heart.

An overturned table and smashed crates and bottles told her the story of the fight that must have taken place.

Alvito's haven had been VIOLATED. God was meticulous about details.

Which of them had died first? Surely they had not intended more than their usual shoves and threats, but when boys play war with grown-up weapons, someone will be hurt.

Real soldiers, brave soldiers did not leave their buddies to rot upon the battlefield. Enrique and the others would now be making alibis for themselves and practicing how to look surprised when news of this fight came to them.

With no regard for the mess around her, Darica knelt and prayed, not for the souls of the two dead boys, but to thank God for His retribution. In the midst of her prayers, she felt the scalpel hot in her hand. Hot. Uncomfortably hot.

God was giving her this chance to exact her own retribution.

When she was finished, she stared numbly at the bloody mass in her hand. Had God really meant for her to do THIS? She had to get back to the shop immediately.

But first she would help Alvito into Hell.

Beneath the lop-legged table, she stacked broken crates in semblance of a bonfire. With only a little straining, she was able to flop Alvito's body onto the table. Onto the funeral pyre.

Thank goodness...thank GOD...she had built up her strength over the years by lugging and lifting animal carcasses. This strength had not saved her from violation by two boys bigger than she, but now it would help her with retribution for the violation.

Then she saw a half-full bottle of whiskey on the floor. The Devil's unholy water. She used it to anoint Alvito, to accelerate his way into eternal flames.

Calmly she searched through his pockets for matches. Then she watched as flames gyrated in their Devil's dance beneath him, around him, on him...

Blood soaked her smock from the fleshy trophy in her pocket. She must return to the shop quickly. Hopefully her father would still be nursing his injured hand.

As she guided the truck into busier traffic, she heard the sirens. Alvito would be in Hell before the sirens reached the warehouse.

* * *

The deaths of the boys were attributed, rightfully, to gang fighting, which was also the explanation given for the fire in the warehouse. Some gang ritual had been the reason for the funeral pyre on which one of the bodies had been so badly burned. The body, but not the warehouse. The concrete floor had contained the fire even before police arrived on the scene. They had been alerted by the proverbial "anonymous tip."

There was one annoying detail, however.

Autopsy reports claimed that the penis of the burned body had been surgically removed.

Police were not overly anxious to pursue this lead, figuring the coroner's boys were up to a little creative reporting. How the hell could they tell if a dong was missing on a body that badly burned? Even if, by chance, the report were accurate, police were not inclined to waste their limited man-hours on intensive investigations into gang killings. Those punks protected each other. Even rival gangs allied against the cops, and getting details of the warehouse fight that must have happened had been nearly impossible as the gangs closed ranks. Everyone seemed to have an alibi for the time in question.

Besides, so long as the gangs were killing each other, most police and citizens alike believed the punks were performing a public service.

* * *

Days later, Darica sat serenely in her rocking chair as she read her Bible and fingered the bookmark she had just finished the night before in the shop after he father left her alone with her work.

CHAPTER FIVE

By the time Darica was ready for her graduation from high school, the old calling was whispering to her again. Alvito had been dead nearly two years. During that time, Darica had inflicted upon herself a severe regimen of penance. She was deliberately harsh with herself, for in sidetracking Father Montez's confessional, she feared she might be heaping even more sin onto her overburdened soul. Despite this concern, she never once considered revealing to the priest the details of her horrible experiences with Alvito. Even though Father Montez had a direct line to God himself, he was still a man, and the mere fact of his gender intimidated Darica.

Except for Armando, Darica sought only the gentle company of the sisters, who accepted her as part of their special family though they were bewildered that she no longer wished to be one of them. She helped them with housekeeping and clerical work in the church, school, and abbey as well as maintaining her regular schedule in her father's shop. All of these responsibilities added to her school assignments were a Herculean load, especially for a teenager, but Darica welcomed the exhaustion that was surely cleansing her soul of its impurity.

She was not content to limit herself to this mere physical purgation, however. Her attendance at mass was perfect, not just nearly perfect, and she never forgot to light a candle for Alvito as devotedly as she did for her mother. Even Father Montez was moved to comment on how ardently Darica attended to her prayers and rituals.

However, the severest penance of all was that Darica forced herself to be as loving and dutiful to Bella as she was to her father. No matter that Bella did not welcome this new honor. No matter that Bella was even more embittered because her son had died while *Bastarda* lived. Darica meekly accepted her stepmother's abusive remarks while always herself speaking kindly and respectfully to the woman and doing whatever she could to help Bella around the house.

While Bella never expressed any pleasure or gratitude for this change, she was deterred from her usual complaints simply because Darica gave her nothing to complain about. Eventually Bella gave up on even the *Bastarda* taunts, lapsing into a gloomy silence that was golden to both Darica and Armando.

For two years Darica had adhered faithfully to this regimen. Gradually the old tranquility resettled in her soul, and she wondered whether she had purged herself of her awful sins. Surely two years of strict penance was enough? Wasn't God showing her His forgiveness through Bella's blessed silence…her father's improved health…and the sisters' repeated invitations for her to join their order?

At morning and evening masses for over a week now, Darica had knelt and stared into the eyes of the Holy Mother, seeking some sign, some verification that she was worthy of the church again. There were no miraculous revelations; however, there was a profound peace of soul that was in itself a miracle.

Each night she read her Bible as she sat in the rocker that had been her mother's. Each night there was the bookmark to remind her of her sin. Each night she prayed for God's forgiveness…and for Alvito's. His sin was greater, but she had defiled his body as surely as he had hers.

Then one day Sister Sherwood interrupted Darica's prayers before the statue of St. Mary:

Darica was to meet Bella at the hospital immediately.

Armando had had a stroke.

* * *

Darica's penance had scarcely begun.

She did not begrudge her father the constant care he needed since the stroke, and Bella was helping with him…though only because Darica had to work in the shop to provide income for the family.

Nevertheless, having to watch her once strong and proud father enfeebled to the point that the women must tend to him as one would an infant was too big a burden…too harsh a penance…

Darica was now sure that she had incurred God's most intense wrath. How foolish she had been to hope that a mere two years of atonement would purify her blackened soul. Seeing her father so debilitated was the most ruthless penance of all. God had felled them both for their sins…with one stroke. God was very efficient and meticulous about details.

During those nights when Darica was most exhausted in both body and spirit, the urge to weep overwhelmed her. Yet she resisted the tears, choking them back until they knotted painfully within her. Her father slept near her cot, and she did not wish to awaken him. Nor did she want to anger God further by acknowledging His divine justice so piteously.

So much better for her to accept His judgment graciously. By surrendering the rest of her life to His justice, perhaps her stay in purgatory would be commuted.

Darica clung to this possibility as her only hope for eternal salvation as she spent her days in the shop and her evenings and nights tending to her father. Though Darica attended most Sunday masses, Bella curtailed her trips to church on all other days, refusing to take care of Armando unless Darica was working in the shop.

On Sunday mornings, however, Bella and Darica paid Teresa Santiago to sit with Armando while they went to mass together. No sudden, miraculous bonding between them motivated these trips together. Darica went because this was the only way she could attend mass and light candles for her mother and Alvito. Bella, whose own devoutness had long since dissipated, went to keep a suspicious eye on Darica. Bella was afraid that the girl would be meeting boys and getting herself into trouble if her stepmother did not monitor her activities.

That Darica had neither the time nor the inclination for such pursuits did not occur to her. Bella was too certain that Darica meant to escape their situation somehow and leave her father and poor stepmother with no means of support.

If only Vito were alive, Bella thought, letting her tears flow freely, for the parishioners were kinder to her if she let them see how she was suffering. *If Vito were alive, he and I would escape together. Vito would take care of me, and we'd leave the adulterer and his bastard to fend for themselves.*

Darica shed no tears, but the dullness in her large, dark eyes and the droop of her shoulders earned more sympathetic respect than all Bella's tears and complaints. Many times members of the church stopped by the Cervantes home with covered dishes or baked goods…mostly in the evenings, for everyone knew that Darica worked in the shop all day. Bella, though, failed to see at whom the generosity was aimed and entertained their guests with lamentations of her sorry lot in life while Darica politely excused herself to go upstairs to her father.

For nearly a year there was no change in Armando's condition. He could neither speak nor control his extremities though, with Darica, he could communicate with his eyes. Darica knew how much he was frustrated by the necessity of her feeding him, how ashamed he was that she must change his diapers when he soiled himself. Darica tried to ease his embarrassment…and her own…by tending to his needs without once commenting on the task at hand. Instead, she spoke to him softly about the shop or the visitors downstairs suffering Bella's monologues.

Armando closed his eyes in sympathy for the guests. Bella was neither as attentive to nor discreet about his daily needs as Darica, but most surely she would be establishing her qualifications for sainthood at that very moment. Darica smiled at this private joke she shared with her father. He seemed pleased when she smiled.

In the twelfth month after his stroke, however, Armando's eyes emptied gradually of their expression, and Darica knew he was failing. When she decreased her time in the shop to spend more time with him, Bella lashed out at her for her irresponsibility. SOMEONE in the household needed to bring in some money to pay bills.

Darica listened to her stepmother's tirades by day and to her father's uneven, labored breathing by night. The painful knot inside her seemed to swell and grow till she felt ready to explode…like a boil that needed lancing to release all the impurities…to relieve her soul of all its impurities…

She had long since dragged her rocking chair to her father's bedside, for its gentle rhythm soothed her. Lately she slept there instead of on the narrow cot placed in his room for her to use when Bella moved into Alvito's old room.

Darica also retrieved her Bible from her room, after carefully concealing the telltale bookmark in a shoebox on the top shelf of her closet. Each night by dim lamplight, she silently read the Scriptures for the solace they provided, though she was always vigilant for any loopholes that might mitigate her current status in the eyes of God.

As her father drifted farther and farther from her, she began to read aloud to him. Although he had little use for religion, she did not want him entering purgatory unprepared. So she read to him of God's anger, of punishment and retribution…and her own soul was weighted by the words.

He died peacefully one January night. Darica did not know of his passing until morning, for she had been deep within the torments of a recurring nightmare through which God was showing her the agonies of Hell's eternal flames.

Though she tried, with the last vestiges of her self-control, to have her father buried beside her mother, she failed. Bella took charge of the funeral, the insurance, the house…everything but the shop, where she bullied Darica into staying both day and night. If Bella had not needed the money from the shop, she would have thrown Darica out completely. But there was very little insurance money, and many medical and funeral bills.

Darica did not mind the banishment, and she saw no reason not to give Bella most of the shop's profit. She went about her work automatically, and when she grew tired, she rocked in her rocking chair and read her Bible, all the while stroking the bookmark she felt safe using in the shop that Bella avoided as diligently as Alvito had.

Alvito. Vito…Vito…Vito…forgive me. Forgive me, Heavenly Father, for I have sinned.

She rocked throughout each night.

"Wilt Thou be angry forever?…Wilt Thou draw out Thine anger to all generations?"

She rocked instead of sleeping…instead of dreaming dreams that only tormented her and scared her awake again.

"Great is the wrath of the Lord that is kindled against us, because our fathers have not hearkened unto the words of this book."

She rocked until Scriptures whirled in her head like a tornado determined to suck her soul right into Hell.

"The whirlwind of the Lord goeth forth with fury, a continuing whirlwind: it shall fall with pain upon the head of the wicked."

"Thus saith the Lord God; Behold, I, even I, am against thee…"

Darica closed her eyes and rocked. In her memory the eyes of the statue of the Virgin shone on her kindly…mercifully…beacons of love in the black abyss…

"Mother," she whispered. "Holy Mother..."

The Holy Mother was more understanding. Even fathers were men. How sadly shocked she had been to see her father equipped as all men were. Men hurt...even fathers...even the Blessed Father...

Mother...Holy Mother...have mercy on my soul...

As she rocked, serenity settled around her...a cloak of peace...in darkness...rocking...

Mother...Holy Mother...I am safe in your womb...and now I can be reborn to eternal joy...

The cemetery groundskeeper found Darica lying on her mother's grave. She was without a coat in the bitter winter wind, and for a frightful moment he thought she had died of exposure. But then he heard her murmurs...bits of Bible verses...

Bundling her within his own coat, he carried her to his truck. She roused enough from her mutterings to struggle against this stranger...this strange MAN...but the groundskeeper was much stronger than she. Finally she quieted enough that he was able to set her in the truck and drive her to the emergency room.

She had no identification on her. Nor did she seem to remember her name.

Her only responses were whispered Bible verses and the words "Holy Mother."

CHAPTER SIX

Andria Bradford flipped through the copious notes Dr. Garza had given her. She knew this case was being dumped on her not because she was the newest psychologist in the clinic, but because she was a woman. Though in this year of 1978 the majority of the country was accepting the edicts of women's rights, Cliffside Lodge was regrettably antiquated in its executive staff. She had been hired as the stereotypical token female, a girl fresh out of college and with no experience, presumably too green to exert her own personality in spite of her illustrious mother with the influential contacts that had "persuaded" the Cliffside administrator to hire her.

Although compunctious about this maneuvering in her behalf, Andria did not oppose it because Cliffside Lodge was a prestigious clinic catering to a distinguished and affluent clientele despite its old-fashioned attitude toward women.

It had the added advantage of being over eight hundred miles from her mother. Though their relationship was congenial, Andria wanted to establish her own name in her own profession before returning home.

For now, she had to apply herself to her job, even though this first assignment was not the stuff that made reputations.

Darica Cervantes had neither the money nor the position of all the other patients at Cliffside. She, too, was here because of some maneuvering in her behalf. The priest in her parish had prevailed on Dr. Garza, a friend since grade school, to take the girl in as a personal favor. The unspoken compromise was that Darica would be isolated and forbidden to mingle with the rest of the patients…"guests" actually, for Cliffside Lodge epitomized discretion in the wealthy world. Even the name was designed to suggest a resort rather than a mental institution.

Andria admitted to herself that this assignment was ironically appropriate: the token female counseling the token charity case.

I must get this chip off my shoulder, Andria thought sternly, *or I won't do the girl or myself any good. I can't expect to start with the juiciest cases.*

She coaxed a smile to her face as she entered the tiny room, no more than a converted storeroom, but the girl was lucky to have even that in this clinic. At least the walls had been freshly painted a soothing blue, and there was a window, barred, but curtained. Although the furnishings were sparse, they were sturdy and functional.

A wave of sympathy for the girl washed through Andria. Darica was lying fetal position, Bible clamped against her, on the narrow iron-frame bed.

After the caretaker found her in the cemetery, Darica remained a "Jane Doe" at the hospital until Dr. Garza's priest friend and his nuns became worried enough to phone area hospitals and police precincts. The girl's stepmother was singularly unconcerned about Darica's condition, viewing it as only an excuse to avoid work. Therefore, Father Montez and the St. Anthony nuns assumed responsibility for obtaining the help Darica needed.

In a fit of self-righteous anger, Mrs. Cervantes cursed them all and threw Darica's clothing and belongings into two cardboard boxes, one of which was now stored in a corner of the girl's room because the small bureau there barely accommodated her meager wardrobe.

Andria noted that the only animation shown by Darica in the last week was as she pawed like a crazed animal through the boxes until she found her Bible. She had darted from the room, down the hall to the bathroom designated for her use, where she locked herself in. Just as orderlies were preparing to remove the door hinges, she emerged, once more sheltered within her private world of Bible verses. Only when someone tried to take the Bible from her did she again show any emotion, from whimpering to shrieks of anguish.

Surely a symbolic reaction, Andria thought. *Leave it to the Catholics to drive their people crazy with their inflexibility about sin.*

"Darica?" Andria approached the bed cautiously so that her patient would not be alarmed. "My name is Andria, and I am here to help you…"

There was no response. Only the vacant stare of the eyes that could be so beautiful under different circumstances…and the barely perceptible movement of the lips murmuring fragments of Bible verses.

"Darica, I know that you can hear me…"

Andria closed the distance between them and laid a gentle hand on Darica's head.

"I will not hurt you, Darica," she said when the girl flinched. "I want to help you."

Andria repeated these assurances patiently, soothingly, until she felt…through intuition only…that Darica was more at ease with her.

"I am here to help you, Darica, but you must help me help you."

Andria continued to talk to her in hopes of striking some hidden cord of response…as one talks to coma victims…but Darica showed no signs of reply. Eyeing the Bible that Darica gripped so relentlessly, Andria considered reaching her through the Holy Writ, but an attempt to pry the Bible from the girl's fingers would prove destructive rather than constructive, considering Darica's prior reactions.

Andria knew her idea was reasonable, however. All psychologists look for keys to unlock the mysteries of the mind, and for Darica the Bible was the key.

Smiling, Andria pulled a metal stool close to Darica's bed and prepared to take notes. Andria wasn't a Bible scholar, but surely the phrases repeated by the girl were significant. A little homework would give Andria a clue about what was going on inside Darica's head.

To understand the murmuring, Andria had to place her ear so close to Darica's lips that she could feel the girl's breath. Still, she was able to fill a page with notes over the next half hour.

"I'll be back to see you tomorrow, Darica," she said then, touching the patient's face, determined to create a bond, however slight. "I have a room here at the clinic, and I'll be staying here for a while until you improve. If you need me, I'll be right down the hall."

No response.

Andria did not expect one.

But she was a long way from being discouraged.

That evening Andria sat down with a borrowed Bible, determined to identify the passages containing the mumbled phrases. However, being unfamiliar with the specific content of the Good Book, she was unable to locate anything, and her initial zeal over her potentially brilliant idea faded. Nevertheless, the idea itself was sound. The obstacle was her insufficient knowledge of the Bible. A glance at her watch verified that the mall would be closed before she could get to the bookstore to purchase a book of Bible quotations, but she was too impatient to wait until morning.

With only a minor twinge of guilt, she placed a call to the priest of St. Anthony, Father Furtado Montez. After all, he was responsible for Darica's admission to Cliffside. What could she be interrupting anyway? Even though tonight was Friday, he couldn't have a date...

He was participating in a friendly Scrabble tournament with the sisters, but, of course, he wanted to help Darica however he could. Andria read to him the snatches of Bible verses written on her pad. Father Montez knew his business well, and soon a pattern emerged, a pattern she had anticipated.

"Darica is carrying around a heavy burden of guilt for some reason," Andria told him. "You must have heard her confessions. As one professional to another, has she revealed anything to you that would trigger such severe response?"

"Darica was the most seriously devoted young woman in my church, but truthfully I haven't seen her in confession for several years. She spent all her time here praying or helping the sisters."

"Has she ever expressed any remorse for her...her family situation being what it was?"

"You mean because she was Armando's illegitimate child?"

"Yes, that's what I mean." She was relieved that she would not have to euphemize so delicately around the priest.

"Not a trace at any time. In fact, when Armando told her the truth of her birth, she was greatly pleased. If you had met the stepmother, you would understand why Darica was delighted to discover that they were not related by blood."

"Dr. Garza's preliminary said nothing about animosity between Darica and her stepmother, though I could tell that Mrs. Cervantes is rather...vinegary."

"Animosity really isn't the right word for it on Darica's side of the relationship. She accepted the situation rather stoically, in fact. Having never experienced a mother's love, she felt no great loss because of Bella's attitude. And, of course, Darica and her father were totally devoted to each other."

Andria tapped a pencil against her cheek. "The father's death may have been cause enough to trigger her final collapse, but there had to be a pre-existing condition..."

"Isn't that what you're supposed to find out, Miss Bradford?"

Leave it to me to get a smart-ass, chauvinistic priest, Andria thought.

"Yes, sir," she said. "That's what I'm supposed to find out. Did Dr. Garza mention to you that I'm a licensed psychologist?"

"He didn't mention you to me at all. I merely knew of his intentions to assign a staff member to Darica. Why do you ask?"

"I don't want you to worry about the quality of Darica's care."

"I hardly think I need to worry about that at Cliffside."

"Still, perhaps we'd all feel better about my qualifications if you could think of me as DR. Bradford. I am deserving of the title."

"I'm sure you are. I'm very sorry if I offended you."

Because she could not determine whether he was laughing at her or not, she offered no response to his apology.

"One more question before you return to your Scrabble game, sir," she said. "Is it possible that Mr. Cervantes had a sexual relationship with Darica?"

"Certainly not!"

Andria was pleased to hear him sputtering. Perhaps she should have euphemized after all.

* * *

As soon as the mall was open the next morning, Andria purchased three books of Bible quotations and her own Bible. Another idea was forming in her mind though she would not have it functional in time for today's visit with Darica. There would be no miraculous instant cure in this case. Darica's road to recovery would be a painstaking journey. Improvement would be gradual, almost imperceptible, and Andria knew she must guard herself against her own impatience.

For today, she contented herself with sitting beside Darica, talking to her gently, stroking her dark curls soothingly. She continued this routine for nearly a week, until she was sure that Darica was used to having her around. The girl no longer flinched at her touch. In fact, Andria noticed a definite relaxation in Darica's body during the visits.

Here was another interesting pattern that was taking shape. Darica was noticeably more comfortable in the presence of Andria or female nurses. If a male nurse or orderly tried to escort her to the bathroom or brought her meals, she became agitated, almost frantic if the men tried to touch her in any way.

Was the priest wrong about Darica's father?

During this week, Andria also accumulated her own list of Bible quotations to be used in her treatment of Darica. These quotations dealt not with God's anger and retribution, but with His mercy and love.

"Look, Darica," she said, holding her own Bible in front of the girl's vacant eyes. "I brought my Bible so that we can share our favorite Bible verses with each other."

Andria began to read her selections aloud. For several days, there was apparently no change in Darica, but Andria did not alter the calm and patient pattern of her reading. If she was to convince Darica of God's love and mercy, her tone of voice must exemplify those very qualities…even if inside Andria was raging with frustration and doubt.

Then one day, Darica's mumblings grew stronger in rebuttal to verses Andria had been reading to her.

She's arguing with me! Andria thought, relieved and triumphant. *We're dueling with quotations!*

Andria read more insistently now, as she would if emphasizing a point with someone in a normal, rational debate. Though there was no instantaneous outburst from Darica, over the next few weeks her responses became quite audible, quite strong, and often imperious. Theirs was a strange debate to a casual observer, but Andria was certain there was definite progress, however unorthodox the procedure seemed.

Now she focused on eliciting responses on a conscious level, on ridding Darica's eyes of that vacant, disturbing stare.

Her patience was finally rewarded nearly two months later. Their "argument" had been more animated than usual on this day, and midway into what had become a routine exchange for them, Darica suddenly interjected something new:

"He grants ME no mercy. He will not forgive ME."

Pained intelligence flashed through her eyes as she whispered the words, but just as quickly she retreated into her sub-conscious world.

Nevertheless, Andria was elated. The barrier had been broken, and Darica now walked the fine line between reality and withdrawal. Along with the Bible verses now, Darica offered prayers of confession, pleas for forgiveness…

However, she did not address her prayers to God, but to the Holy Mother.

* * *

Andria tapped her pencil against her cheek. "I'm rather ignorant about your Catholic doctrines, Father, so if my questions seem somewhat foolish, please bear with me."

"Of course, Dr. Bradford." Father Montez said. "Anything I can do to help."

"First of all, sir, is praying to Mary part of your standard procedure?"

"I'm not sure what you mean."

"Most Christians pray to the Lord. Do Catholics also pray to the Virgin Mary?"

"That is a common misconception among Protestants. However, we do NOT pray to St. Mary in the sense you mean though she is addressed in certain litanies, like the Rosary. She is our principal saint and as such shares in the holiness of God."

"I was in your church...briefly...last Sunday."

"You are always welcome. Next time please let me know who you are."

"I didn't stay long. I couldn't really understand too much that was going on. You have a highly ritualized religion, sir."

"That goes with the territory, as they say. Each faith has its own rituals and customs."

"I noticed that a statue of Mary was featured almost as prominently as the statue of Jesus. His was rightfully elevated above the tabernacle behind the altar, but hers and Joseph's were close by on His right-hand side, in front of the congregants."

"Beautiful sculptures, aren't they?"

"Yes, sir. But I'm curious about something, and I hope you won't take offense when I say this, but isn't it rather strange to put Mary in such an exalted position when your religion relegates women to second-rate status?"

"Did you call me to debate women's rights?"

"I'm merely trying to get a clear picture of Darica's environment during her formative years."

"Darica was hardly relegated to second-rate status. In fact, she might be construed as one of your 'modern women,' with a promising career in a field that was primarily the realm of men. At least, I know of no other lady taxidermists."

"You said that she could never do anything that was grievously sinful. On what do you base that conclusion?"

"On Darica herself. I watched her grow up. In my entire career, I have never met another woman so totally devoted to the church and its doctrines. At one time, she was even planning to join our St. Anthony order of holy sisters, but then she felt she was needed more in her father's shop."

"Is it possible that even though she was guilty of nothing serious...but was, in fact, the victim of something serious...she became so wrapped up in doctrines that...that, well, even little things assumed grand proportions and she condemned herself to Hell?"

"You're blaming the church for her breakdown?"

"Not actively. But I do believe that her self-esteem was obliterated somewhere along the way. Let's say her stepmother was harassing her at home, though Darica never complained about it. Then at church she's taught that she's sinning for every little thing. She's going to collect a barrelful of guilt until she finally explodes from the pressure."

"Excepting, for the moment, that our doctrines would make her think that she was sinning for 'every little thing,' what you say makes sense. She has always been a serious, sensitive girl."

"I've broken through with her, sir. At least, she's listening when I tell her that God loves her and forgives her for whatever she has done."

"Perhaps if I talked with her and heard her confession…"

"Not at this time. She has shown a definite aversion to the company of men."

"I'm her priest!"

"With all due respect, sir, a man is a man is a man. She's even avoiding, well, let's say 'direct contact' with the Divine Father right now. She says her prayers to the Holy Mother."

"But WHY? That is not the way she was taught."

"As you once said, Father, my job is to find out. Did Darica have one special place in the church where she always said her prayers?"

"She was always in the third pew…on the west side of the church…right in front of…of the statue of St. Mary."

"While all the turmoil was building in her, the Holy Mother was right there for her when she began to feel that God had deserted her."

"As I said, that is not the way she was taught."

"But she WAS taught that a whole lot of normal human behavior is sinful."

Andria grinned when she heard Father Montez begin his sputtering. She interrupted him before he could launch into a lengthy speech of self-defense.

"Was Darica particularly close to any of the nuns?"

Indignation still choked his voice, but he answered evenly enough, "She and Sister Sherwood were close."

"Is Sister Sherwood available for a few sessions? If Darica hears a more qualified female voice talking to her of God's love and mercy, maybe I can keep her in the real world permanently."

"Sister Sherwood is available whenever you need her."

"Excellent. Thank you, sir. I have one final question. Are you absolutely certain about your judgment of Darica's father? Obviously somewhere along the way, a man has terrified…or terrorized her…"

"I am absolutely certain. Though he did not belong to the church, he was always attentive to Darica's school and church activities. As I said, they were devoted to each other. Darica never showed any indication of an unnatural relationship with him."

"Were there uncles…grandfathers…neighbor men close to the family?"

"None to my knowledge. Only her brother…her half-brother, as you know."

"Tell me about him please."

"Darica never expressed any fear of him. She was probably ashamed of him. He terrorized the whole neighborhood and met a violent death indicative of his lifestyle, but in his own home, he wouldn't dare do anything so heinous. His father would have dealt with him harshly had Alvito done anything to Darica."

"Did Darica ever talk about her brother?"

"Seldom, if at all. They weren't close. Alvito was Bella's boy, and Darica was Armando's girl, and that's how the household coexisted peacefully over the years."

"There has to be SOMETHING…"

"Only Darica knows the answers you're seeking, Dr. Bradford."

"And I will find those answers, sir…"

Andria tapped her pencil against her cheek. For a charity case, this one was certainly intriguing.

CHAPTER SEVEN

"Why are you angry with God, Darica?"

Sitting at the most distant corner of her bed, with her back pressed against the iron headboard, Darica curled her legs back, huddling behind the wall they made. If she had not improved in so many other ways, Andria might have been disheartened by this withdrawal. However, Darica was back in the world of conscious intelligence now, and though she might retreat from Andria's sometimes direct questions, she retreated physically rather than mentally. This modified fetal pose was her most repeated signal to Andria that forbidden territory had been breached. Andria ventured into this prohibited realm only a cautious step or two before receding. Because Darica permitted her to trespass a little farther each day, Andria could honestly report progress to Dr. Garza and Father Montez, but the pace was frustratingly slow.

However, Darica must be allowed to set that pace. Any attempt to bully her toward quicker revelations of her anguished soul would fling her right back into catatonia.

The problem was that Dr. Garza was clamoring for Andria to release the patient. Darica had been at Cliffside for eight months, time enough for Dr. Garza to feel that his charitable responsibility had been fulfilled, but not time enough for Darica's total healing. Oh, the girl could probably function well enough in the world outside if she were to lead a completely sheltered life with someone constantly around to watch over her. Whenever Sister Sherwood visited, she told Andria that the sisters were still willing to take Darica into their order and provide her with that very environment. However, Andria knew that even a cloistered life could not guarantee that Darica would not fall prey to the demons within her.

"You can give that girl a few more months now, sir," Andria told Dr. Garza, "or a few years in the future, Father Montez will be calling to ask you to take her in again."

Dr. Garza was sure that Andria's zeal was obscuring her judgment. Nevertheless, he agreed, temporarily. His friend the priest was pressuring him to heed Andria's suggestion, and except for the expense involved, the patient was very little trouble. She kept to the tiny section of the lodge allocated to her and required very little attention anymore. The nurses peeked in on her during their regular rounds, and the orderlies took her meals and clean clothing and bedding and collected her laundry. Other than that, Andria was the only staff member who spent a lot of time with Miss Cervantes, much of it off-duty time when Dr. Garza began to complain.

The administrator had to admit, grudgingly, that Andria's work with the girl was admirable. Otherwise, he would never have allowed himself to be persuaded in favor of the extension.

So he gave Andria four more months…a full year of charity. Even Furtie Montez could expect nothing more. Only PAYING guests were encouraged to stay as long as they needed or wanted to.

Darica Mariana Maria Cervantes was penniless.

After selling the house, the shop, and all furnishings and equipment, Bella Cervantes had left town. Though rumors about her destination ran rampant in the neighborhood, no one actually knew where she was, for she had intentionally left no forwarding address. Her reasons were simple: she wanted no responsibility for Darica foisted on her, and she did not want to share proceeds of the property sales although Armando had listed his daughter as co-recipient of everything he left behind.

With Darica at Cliffside, Bella had had little trouble obtaining power-of-attorney for her stepdaughter, a necessary legal formality that ultimately robbed Darica of any inheritance, however small. When she was well enough to be informed of her stepmother's actions, she accepted the news indifferently. Andria wondered whether the response masked more volatile feelings…though with her father gone, Darica did not care about the house and shop. In fact, if she associated either with some unhappiness in her past, she might indeed be glad about the transactions.

Her only question was about her rocking chair. It had belonged to her real mother, and she expressed noticeable regret over its loss. Andria was pleased by the response, for it showed that Darica was feeling SOMETHING.

Eager to build on this reborn capacity for emotion, Andria and Sister Sherwood appealed to the new owners of the Cervantes house to sell them back Darica's rocking chair. New to the neighborhood and eager to make a good first impression with their new church, the family gave the chair to the women, whose efforts were rewarded by tears of joy in Darica's eyes.

Andria believed that the rocker, as much as anything else, aided in Darica's recovery. The girl looked so serene as she rocked by the window with her Bible on her lap.

But she couldn't spend the rest of her life in a rocking chair. Andria had to prepare her to LIVE, not merely exist outside the walls of Cliffside Lodge.

And there were only four months left.

So today, when Darica hid behind the wall of her drawn-up legs, Andria did not leave her alone. Andria would not badger her; nevertheless, she must be more insistent.

"I've noticed that you pray to the Virgin Mary instead of to the Lord," Andria said casually. "Will you tell me why?"

Darica said nothing for a long, long time. Just as Andria prepared to pursue another method of questioning, Darica whispered, "God doesn't listen to me anymore."

"Isn't He supposed to listen to all who wish to pray to him?"

"Yes. That's why I know I've been evil."

"Perhaps you have misunderstood Him, Darica. No one believes that you are an evil person. Why should God think that you're evil?"

"You don't know everything about me, but God knows, and He thinks I'm evil. He has cast me out as he did Lucifer."

"Can you tell me what God knows about you that I don't?"

When Darica pulled her legs more tightly against her, Andria knew she would get no further answers to this particular line of questions.

"Does the Holy Mother know what God knows, Darica?"

"She knows."

"Does she think you're evil?"

"Yes."

"Still, you pray to her."

"She is merciful and understands that I have suffered enough for the sins of another."

Andria's heartbeat quickened. "Whose sins have you suffered for, Darica?"

Darica pressed her face against her knees. There would be no more revelations today.

* * *

Darica's gaze was fixed on the garden below her window. Though autumn's vivid colors had faded to the brown and gray that presaged winter's onslaught, a few of the lodge's "guests" still ventured into the crisp, fresh air. A solitary man in a wheelchair sat in the garden now, and Darica studied him so intently that she did not hear Andria enter the room.

"What is it that you're watching with so much interest, Darica?" Andria asked, laying a hand on her patient's shoulder.

"Jesus. Jesus is in the garden."

Blinking in confusion and fearing a setback, Andria leaned to look out the window. The man in the wheelchair was longhaired and bearded. And without both his legs. One of Dr. Garza's personal cases.

"That man isn't Jesus, Darica. He's a guest…a patient here…just as you are."

"No, Andria. He's Jesus." No lawyer had ever sounded so sure of his case.

"Did you see that the man has no legs? He lost them in Vietnam. Not too many people think that God…or Jesus…was anywhere near Vietnam."

"Oh." Darica quickly lost interest and resumed rocking in her chair.

Andria knew a good opening when she saw one, however.

"Even though that man isn't Jesus, maybe God intended for you to see him and to think so for a while."

"God is tricking me now?"

"No. He's convincing you."

"Of what?"

"You have told me that you've suffered for the sins of another…"

Darica did not reply, but the quicker rhythm of her rocking showed that she was listening, not retreating.

"Didn't Jesus suffer for sins that He did not commit?" Andria asked.

"Yes."

"But He was not evil."

"No."

"Maybe God intended for you to see the man in the garden to remind you that you are not evil though you have suffered for the sins of another."

Darica stopped rocking and concentrated on this possibility.

"He didn't answer my prayers," she said finally. "He wouldn't forgive me. He wouldn't understand when I tried to tell Him."

"What did you try to tell Him?"

"Papa wouldn't understand when I tried to tell him."

"About what, Darica? Tell me so that I may understand."

Darica's dark eyes focused on Andria. "Maybe you would understand. You're a woman. The Holy Mother understands."

"Will you tell me, too?"

"I...I...can't."

Leaning back in her rocker, Darica closed her eyes. She either fell asleep or feigned sleep. Sighing, Andria left her alone.

* * *

"Are you angry with God because He did not try to understand what happened to you?" Andria asked.

"I cannot be angry with God." Darica folded her hands over her Bible. "One should love and honor Him in every way."

"But you are...a little miffed with Him for not understanding...for letting you suffer when you had tried so hard to be good."

"I deserved to suffer...a little..."

"Because you think you're evil?"

"Because of what I DID."

"What did you do, Darica?"

"I..." She did not finish her statement. Instead she replied by pulling her legs back, building her wall with them.

Andria, however, brought a new antagonist into their conversation.

"If you won't tell me what you did, Darica, will you tell me what Alvito did to you?"

Gasping, Darica buried her face against her knees.

"No...no...no...no...no..."

Her voice faded into silence.

* * *

Grasping Darica's hands, Andria forced her to maintain eye contact.

"I know you don't want to tell me what your brother did to you," Andria said, "but until we have everything out in the open, you're not going to get better. You'll always feel evil though it was Alvito who was evil to you."

"He was my HALF-brother. He was evil."

"Tell me about him, Darica."

"He...He killed my dogs and cats and rabbits...in horrible ways."

"That made YOU feel evil?"

"No."

"But you were mad at him for killing your pets."

"Yes."

"Do you feel evil because you feel this anger?"

"No."

"Did your parents...your father and stepmother...punish him for what he did?"

"No. He lied. They believed him."

"That made you mad, too?"

"Yes."

"How did you show Alvito you were angry?"

"I didn't."

"Why not?"

"He liked to make me mad or sad. I didn't want to make him happy."

"Was killing your pets the worst he ever did to you?"

Darica withdrew her hands from Andria's grasp. "No," she replied with obvious effort as she folded her arms across her chest and began to rock.

"What else did he do?"

"He lied and got me into trouble with Bella many times."

"Is that all?"

"He stole things and beat up on people smaller than he was."

"He beat on you?"

"Not beat on me. But hurt me." Darica turned her head to look out the window.

"How did he hurt you, Darica?"

"He...He...He was with Enrique...his friend Enrique."

"Is Enrique like Alvito?"

"He's not dead."

"I mean in personality, Darica. Were they alike?"

"Yes."

"How did they hurt you?"

The protective leg-wall went up again, and Darica rolled her face back and forth over her knees.

"Answer my question, Darica," Andria said gently, but firmly. "I know remembering hurts sometimes, but we must continue. If I ask you questions that you can answer with yes or no, will you continue? Will you answer?"

Darica kept her face buried, but she nodded her agreement…reluctantly.

"I'm proud of you, Darica. I know you're hurting, and you're brave to continue."

Darica nodded again.

"You told me that Alvito and Enrique hurt you," Andria continued.

"Yes."

"Did they slap or hit you?"

"Yes."

"Did they do more than that?"

"Yes."

"Did they steal from you?"

"No…yes…in a way…"

"Did they rape you, Darica?"

The girl indicated no response either by words or gestures, but she began to tremble, then to shake uncontrollably.

Oh, Lord…oh, Lord…oh, Lord, Andria thought, wrapping her arms around her patient. *It's just what I expected, but it's worse than I expected.*

When Darica quieted, Andria spoke to her softly.

"What they did to you does not make YOU evil, Darica. THEY were evil. You feel dirty and ashamed and defiled because you are moral and decent. What happened to you was not your fault. God is not punishing you. You are punishing yourself."

"B-But…But…I…I…"

"Is there more you need to tell me?"

Darica nodded, her face hidden.

"Did they continue to force themselves on you?"

"No."

"Did they make you pregnant?"

"No!"

"Then what?" Andria forced the frustration out of her voice. Darica would not tell her the story straight out. They had to continue their game of Twenty Questions. But how to ask questions when the questioner had not even a vague notion of what had happened after Darica's ultimate violation? What could be even more traumatizing for the girl than that experience?

Andria quickly reviewed Darica's history.

Oh, Lord!

Alvito had died violently in a vacant warehouse. Surely Darica didn't…she couldn't have…

"Darica…" Andria swallowed back the dryness in her throat. "Did you…did you kill Alvito?"

"No."

Andria exhaled a long, relieved breath. But what else could there be?

"Were you glad that Alvito died?"

"Yes."

"Do you feel guilty because you're happy about his death?"

"No."

Andria sighed loudly enough to make an impression on Darica. "I'm stumped. You must help me if we're going to get anywhere today. Do you trust me not to hurt you, Darica?"

"Yes."

"Then give me something to work with. I need a clue…something…anything you think can tell me more…"

Darica said nothing as she stared bleakly at Andria. Never before had Andria seen such torment on a person's face.

Finally Darica seemed to make her decision.

"The clue is here," she said, handing her Bible to Andria.

Worried that she had caused Darica to regress with today's more aggressive questioning, Andria took the book and flipped through it. When she saw the bookmark, she paused, intrigued by its strangeness, but unable to identify it…at first.

When the realization hit her sharply, she slammed the Bible shut.

Oh, Lord…oh, Lord…oh, Lord…

CHAPTER EIGHT

Although Andria had paced the perimeter of her office countless times, she was no closer to alleviating the confusion weighting her mind than she had been upon leaving Darica's room that afternoon. While she realized that the ultimate breakthrough had occurred with her patient, Darica's "secret" had shaken her badly. She had summoned every ounce of her professional fortitude even to remain in the room following her ghoulish discovery. To leave Darica abruptly, after the girl had shared the most intimate torment of her life, would have been unthinkable in either a friend or a psychologist.

And by now, Andria considered herself both to this troubled young woman.

However, there had been little left for the two to say to each other at that moment. After convincing herself that Alvito had indeed died before Darica saw him, Andria stayed only until the emotional intensity in them both dissipated, until Darica...drained by the afternoon's revelations...fell asleep in the iron-frame bed. Somewhere during that time, Andria knew that she had murmured automatic reassurances to her patient though she couldn't recall exactly what she had said. She remembered only that she had carefully made no promises about what would be done next, no promises that might have to be broken for reasons beyond Andria's control.

I'm letting this situation overwhelm me, she finally decided. *I have to dissect it...work on it part-by-part...bad choice of words there. Oh, Lord. My professors never told me there would be days like THIS.*

Finally she dropped into her chair and grabbed up her pencil.

I must be professional, I must be sympathetic, and I must be successful. Not only for Darica, but also for ME. This is the kind of stuff careers are made of after all. I'll write a case study for the journal...changing the names of those involved, of course. Thank goodness I've been taking so many notes. I'll use Mother's middle name, sort of like a dedication to her. She'll like that. Darica will be "Tanita," and...

Andria thunked her head with her pencil, ashamed of her wayward motivations. Darica was her top priority, and Darica should be her only motivation right now.

So, what to do?

First, she must find out the extent of the illegality of what Darica had done. Less than murder or manslaughter. But how much less? Tampering with evidence? Disturbing a crime scene? Failing to report a crime?

No matter how serious the crime, Andria had no thought of turning Darica into the authorities. Darica had been a very disturbed young woman when she committed the offense, and she had punished herself enough for what had happened. Andria was well justified and LEGAL in this decision because anything Darica told her was privileged communication.

And, Andria finally admitted, that son-of-a-bitch brother of hers had gotten just what he deserved. In truth, it was not unreasonable to believe that thousands of women across the country had similar fantasies about the men who had mistreated or ill-used them.

The moral ramifications were the real issue here. Darica had not only desecrated a human body in a gruesome manner, she had turned part of it into a souvenir. And she was aware of the violation. Otherwise she would not have tortured herself right into a breakdown. In a sense, her own beloved father had betrayed her by not realizing the situation developing in his own home. No wonder she avoided contacts with men. No wonder she appealed to the Holy MOTHER in her prayers.

Andria checked her watch. Plenty of time to sort through a few legal books at the library.

From her window, Darica saw Andria walk through the garden to the parking lot. Was she going for the police? Worse yet, was she going for Father Montez?

No.

Andria had told her everything would be fine. Andria was proud of her for being so brave.

Yet Andria acted strangely when she saw the bookmark.

Darica thought about running away, but she had nowhere to run to. In fact, she didn't even know how to get out of the building. She had always resisted Andria's efforts to take her to the garden. The only times Darica felt the fresh air on her face was when Andria coaxed her onto one of the lodge's balconies.

Andria won't hurt me, Darica finally decided.

She opened her Bible and began to read.

Tonight Darica rather enjoyed the dark as it closed around her. Usually she was a little afraid of the demons it held and would have asked the nurses to leave her light burning at night if she had the nerve to make the request. But tonight the darkness was peaceful, even friendly…like a cozy blanket.

She even felt lighter. Light-hearted. Light-bodied. Light-souled. She had shared her secret, and the pits of Hell had not opened up to swallow her. Andria had told her she would feel better, and she did.

A miracle. It was a miracle.

A shaft of light intruded into the room as the door opened. A touch of the old fears choked a frightened gasp out of her.

"It's only me," Andria said, flipping on the light. "Why are you sitting in the dark?"

"It was…pleasant." Darica blinked away the ache of light-blinded eyes and smiled at Andria. A timid smile. The awkward smile of one who had not smiled in a long, long time.

In fact, Andria had never seen Darica smile.

"How are you feeling tonight, Darica?"

A silly question, considering Darica's smile. But it was their usual conversation starter and would suffice in this awkward moment. Following the soul-deep intensity of their afternoon session, all normal conversation seemed strangely inadequate.

"I feel...good."

"I'm well pleased with our progress today, Darica...though you did give me a bit of a start there."

A shadow crossed Darica's face. "I was afraid."

"Of what?"

"That you might not come back."

"As you can see, I'm here in living color. I never once considered not coming back, but I did need to think about where we go from here."

The color drained from Darica's face. "The police?"

Andria quickly placed a reassuring arm around Darica's shoulders.

"Not to the police or to anyone else. What you tell me is just between you and me. No one else. Not even Dr. Garza, and he's my boss."

Darica's relief was obvious, but concern still wrinkled her brow. "Will you get into trouble for not telling?"

"Between a psychologist and her patient, there is something called privileged communication, which simply means that I can't tell anyone else the secrets you tell me."

"Even if it's very bad?"

"That's right. If it were very bad, I might, under certain circumstances, talk a patient into turning himself in, but ethically I couldn't do it myself."

Apprehension flared in Darica's eyes. "Are you going to talk me into turning myself in?"

"No. I can't see how your spilling your guts to the cops would further justice. I just returned from the library, where I did some checking in a few law books. From what I can determine, what you did to Alvito's body is a misdemeanor."

"The fire. I made the fire. Arson is more than a misdemeanor, isn't it?"

"Arson is a felony. But since the fire was confined to the...uh...funeral pyre...and the warehouse itself wasn't damaged, we won't worry about it. Did you make the fire to cover what you had done to Alvito?"

"No. I ...wanted it to be like Hell for him. It seems crazy now, but at the time it seemed...important."

"You were a very troubled girl then. You had suffered one of the most painful traumas that a woman can suffer. I'm not surprised that you were thinking as you were."

"You're not?"

"Let me tell you something, Darica. There are cases on file of women doing similar things to LIVE men because the men abused them, and there are many abused women out there who have thought about getting even with their abusers in the way that you did.

"Now what you did was wrong, and you've punished yourself for it far beyond what any court would do to you. But your reaction...your desire for revenge...was not so abnormal. I myself have had an urge to crush a man's balls when he's being patronizing and overbearing.

"The thing is you have to be enough in control of yourself that you can prevent your actually doing such things. At the time of...Alvito's demise...it was impossible for you to have that self-control. What we have to do now is work toward giving it to you. We've already made tremendous progress."

"But I'm still confused."

"We've covered a lot of ground today. Let's take a vacation tomorrow."

Disappointment darkened Darica's eyes. "I won't see you?"

"Of course you'll see me. I thought maybe we could get you away from this place for a while."

"But I don't want to leave!"

"Just for a while, Darica. I'm not throwing you out. We can walk around the mall for a while...have lunch...my treat..."

"Thank you very much, but—"

"I won't allow you to refuse. You must begin to reintroduce yourself to the outside world. Goodness knows you've been cooped up here long enough. Give it a try, will you? I'll be right there with you all the time, and I haven't steered you wrong yet, have I?"

"Well...no..."

"Then let's say ten tomorrow morning?"

Though doubtful, Darica nodded agreement.

"Great. Now, there's just one more little thing before I leave..." Andria dragged a stool over by Darica's rocker. "If this will be too painful for you, I'll save it for later. But the more I think about it, the more curious I get..."

"About what?"

Andria whispered her request. "Can you tell me how in the world you made a bookmark out of that thing?"

* * *

Now their conversations were more casual, less intense. A complete portrait of the troubled girl gradually materialized for Andria. The situation with her stepmother and half-brother had been endured with saintly resolve, until Alvito's final abomination. She had found solace in her father's love for both her and her real mother, a woman Darica had idealized over the years to the point that Mariana's identity, in Darica's mind, intermingled transferentially with that of the Holy Mother.

Though Darica had been devoted to her father, she subconsciously felt betrayed by him for not recognizing and stopping Alvito's offenses against her.

Alvito and Armando had been her only real experiences with men, except for Father Montez, who was a distant, nebulous symbol to her though she was a familiar figure around the church. Consequently, she had neither encouraged nor welcomed any attention from her male classmates, who classified her rebuffs as the result of her religious ardor.

Alvito and Enrique extinguished this fervor, and Darica's decline began. Now Andria was responsible for rebuilding Darica's life, for getting her ready for life.

Long conversations. Self-esteem activities. Trips to the zoo, the mall, the movies…the church. Talks with the sisters, then Father Montez. And the final triumph: socializing with a well chosen few of the other Cliffside guests…both male and female.

There was also the borrowed television, Darica's "window to the real world" Andria called it.

However, rather than tuning in the news and popular sitcoms and dramas, Darica developed a passion for reruns of older shows, especially *I Love Lucy* and *Father Knows Best.*

"Lucy and Ethel have so much fun," Darica said to Andria one afternoon.

"Are you envious?"

"A little. Not so much now as I would have been before…before you became my friend."

"Thank you. That's a wonderful compliment. Did you have many friends when you were in school?"

"Not really. Everyone was nice, but I couldn't walk into their houses without knocking and do crazy things with them like Lucy and Ethel."

"Forgive me, but I can't picture you doing crazy things like Lucy and Ethel."

"You're right. I have never had any crazy fun. Nice times, but never crazy fun."

"What kinds of things did you do for 'nice times' when you were younger?"

"I played with my pets…until Vito got to them. Or I hung around Papa's shop or the church."

"No Kick the Can…Hide 'n' Seek…catching fireflies…making clover necklaces…anything like that?"

"No. Not me anyway. Vito…ran wild with the other kids at night, but I wanted to stay away from him…from them, too, I guess."

"Did you like the neighborhood kids?"

"I did not dislike them, but they were…too rough for me. I like gentle things."

"Like skinning and stuffing bobcats?"

Darica smiled shyly. "The skinning and stuffing kept us in a rougher neighborhood. Papa could have afforded something grander I suppose, but not many neighborhoods would have allowed a shop like ours in the backyard. Sometimes I thought Papa stayed there just to irritate Bella."

"You sound like you approved of his irritating her intentionally."

"I guess I do. Is my instinct for revenge so deep?"

"The instinct for revenge is human. You just have to—"

"Control it."

"You have learned well."

"You have taught well."

"Have you ever gone cruisin'?"

"What's that?"

"Driving around aimlessly, honking at strange men when they're cute, listening to the radio. We can even take the top off my car."

"It's freezing outside."

"I have a terrific heater in my car...and we can stop for hot chocolate."

"But that is...crazy!"

"And fun...maybe not quite up to Lucy's crazy fun standards, but you can't start at the top. You with me?"

"Oh, yes!" Darica's smile was her brightest yet.

* * *

"Andria, are there really men like Jim Anderson?"

For the sake of her patient's recovery, Andria bit back a sarcastically negative reply.

"Somewhere," she told Darica instead, "but I haven't stumbled over one yet. Of course, I haven't had a whole lot of time for stumbling."

"My mother would have been like Margaret," Darica said wistfully. "It would have been nice to have a brother like Bud...and sisters..."

"Was your father like Jim?"

"In some ways...to me anyway. But in many ways no. He had much on his conscience."

"By now you know how troublesome that can be," Andria smiled. "Would you like to have a family some day, Darica?"

"I would like to be part of a family...like the Andersons, but I'm afraid that I...that I..."

"Might have trouble in a relationship with a man?"

"Yes."

"It is possible to have a loving, nurturing relationship with a man."

"But could I?"

"Certainly. You are a gentle, caring woman, and with a gentle, caring man, you could have a wonderful relationship."

"With a man like Jim Anderson?"

"Like him, yes. But don't build a fantasy in your mind, or you'll always be disappointed."

"I would like to be a mother like Margaret some day."

"Does that mean you have definitely decided against joining the sisters?"

"I am not worthy."

"Darica! I thought we got that bullshit out of your system."

Darica flinched at the obscenity. "Sisters must be pure."

"Sister Sherwood told you that virginity is not a prerequisite."

"I know. But I no longer have the...desire for that life...not as I did. So much has changed in my mind."

"That is a reason I can accept. You know I'll be releasing you in a few weeks. Shall we start looking for openings in a taxidermy shop?"

"No. I prefer the company of living things these days."

"What will you do then?"

"I can work for the church for a while...filing and typing...cleaning and cooking. The sisters say I may stay with them until I am on my feet." She paused, debating with herself before continuing. "But I am afraid...a little."

"Of being on your own?"

"That makes me nervous, but not afraid."

"Then what frightens you?"

"Enrique has been at the church when Sister Sherwood takes me there for masses."

"Doing what?"

"Working for the church...cleaning...yard work..."

"Has he tried anything with you?"

"No. He has looked at me though, and I was uncomfortable."

"Shall I talk to Father Montez?"

"No! Then we must explain the reasons for my fear, and I am too ashamed. It is enough that Sister Sherwood knows about my impurity."

"Darica..."

"I know I'm not at fault, but still I feel the shame of violation."

"I don't like your having to be around that scum-bag, Darica...especially now."

"Surely he will not try anything at church."

"Are YOU reassuring ME now?"

"I guess I am. I must be very cured."

* * *

Darica hung up the phone. Andria had called every day since Darica's release from Cliffside. Every day for over two weeks. It was nice to have such a friend. It was nice to have a job and to earn money of her own. It wasn't much because the church couldn't afford much, but the sisters were providing her with room and board.

The money was her own, nevertheless, and this weekend SHE would take ANDRIA out for lunch.

However…

Enrique was at the church, too. Every day. A work rehabilitation program. And his stares were becoming increasingly suggestive.

Although Darica tried to ignore him, he went out of his way to run into her at every opportunity. He knew that she was afraid to complain. And he knew why she was afraid.

When she returned from her lunch with the sisters, she saw the note on her desk right away:

"Meet me in the sacristy at midnight or I'll tell Father and the nuns what you did with your brother and me. And what you did to your brother."

There was no signature. A signature was not necessary.

Her hand trembling, she picked up the phone to call Andria. But Andria would storm the church and demand Enrique's dismissal…or arrest. Then Enrique would tell the whole story…to everyone…

Darica counted the money in her handbag. Not much. But it would have to do.

After packing her clothing in the suitcase Andria had loaned her, she walked to the bus station. She had four directions to choose from, and she chose south because the southbound bus left earlier than the others. To Applewood. She did not know the town at all, but that was as far as her money would take her if she wanted a few dollars left over to live on for a few days.

Chapter Nine

With a two-hour layover in Springfield, the trip to Applewood took almost eight hours. While waiting in the Springfield bus station, Darica wrote a note of explanation to Andria, including both an apology for taking the suitcase and the promise of a longer letter when she was settled.

Settled.

Darica considered the word with trepidation as the consequences of her hasty escape descended upon her with full impact. Her total assets were a twenty-dollar bill and some loose change in her handbag. She knew no one in Applewood, and she had no job now. Unless some miracle occurred, she faced an exceedingly serious situation...and Darica was sure that God had no miracles in His pocket for her.

Her own fault, of course, for fleeing from a problem rather than meeting it head on.

Briefly she considered phoning Andria to come for her, but the fact of the matter was that Darica was more inclined to face the unknown in Applewood than the certainty of Enrique's threats.

Still, as Darica stepped off the bus at her final destination, she trembled so uncontrollably that the driver had to assist her. She was reluctant to let him resume his route, for his was the last familiar face around her.

But, of course, he had to go. His bus stopped in Applewood only long enough for unloading and loading.

Applewood didn't even have a full-fledged bus station. Just a small ticket booth inside a corner drugstore and a bench outside beside the bus parking zone.

Though people were still moving around inside the drugstore, the doors were locked for the night, and Darica dropped onto the bench, quaking with confusion. There was no motel in sight, and she had no idea of which way to walk to find one. She wasn't even sure that she had enough money for a motel room.

Darica huddled down within her coat, turning its collar up around her ears. The harsh winter wind seemed suddenly more relentless, her coat less protective.

The streets were nearly empty though the courthouse clock showed only 10:31. Darica watched the traffic lights go through their sequences several times although only two cars crossed the intersection.

Maybe she could sleep on the bench overnight. Weren't small rural communities of Southern Illinois noted for their peaceful environments? Somehow, though, staying on a public bench all night seemed more desperate than she wanted to admit to right now.

The problem was that she had no idea of what else to do. The employees of the drugstore were staring at her strangely as they left for the night, and she was too shy to ask them for help. How long could she sit there on the pretense of waiting for her ride?

Taking a deep breath and squaring her shoulders, she picked up her suitcase and started to walk in the direction she was already facing. Hunger was beginning to gnaw at her stomach, but she didn't see any place open where she could buy something to eat.

The suitcase was becoming unbearably heavy, but Darica trudged on simply because she knew of nothing else to do. Gradually commercial buildings gave way to residential houses, and she realized that she had chosen the wrong direction in which to walk.

However, just as she was considering the advisability of retracing her steps, she saw the small concrete-block building set back away from the street. A twenty-four-hour laundromat. With all the lights shining brightly and cheerfully into the night.

Tears of relief streaked Darica's cheeks as she hurried into the building. Into the warmth. Sagging against a wall, she gratefully surveyed the large room. Under the circumstances, she could hope for nothing more: chairs, tables, a restroom…a well-dented vending machine, so she would have something to eat if she could dig out enough change.

And absolutely no one else in the laundromat to question her being there.

Darica chose a corner for herself well out of sight of the street. After freshening herself in the restroom…the condition of which would have precluded her use of it under normal conditions…she purchased a candy bar from the machine and settled on one of the large tables so that she could stretch her legs out in front of her.

This respite from her dismal situation revived her somewhat, and she began to make plans for the next day. The first thing to do, of course, was to find work. She would just have to apply at every single location in Applewood until someone wanted her.

But what if someone didn't want her? And if someone did want her, what would she live on until her first paycheck? She couldn't stay in this laundromat every night until then.

The enormity of her disaster settled on her again, and Darica bit her lip to halt its trembling. Instinctively she reached into her handbag for her rosary. The beads were always a comfort to her.

Everything will be okay, she told herself. *God does not give us burdens unless He knows we can handle them.*

She had made her peace with Him. Surely He wouldn't let her down now that she had opened her heart to Him again.

Suddenly an idea bloomed for her.

Surely Applewood had a Catholic church. She could seek help there. The church had never failed her. It had always been like a second home to her.

Relieved, she folded her arms and closed her eyes. She could get a few hours of sleep now. Of course, she must awaken early enough to avoid the early-morning laundromat patrons.

When the crunch of gravel beneath car wheels jerked her awake, she bolted off the table in fright just as the spotlight blasted her fully in the face. Terrified, Darica pressed herself against the dryers as a policeman entered the laundromat. One look at Darica's belongings verified to him that she was not there to do her laundry, but he could also tell that she was neither a vagrant nor a vandal, but merely a frightened young woman.

"What's the problem here, miss?" he asked, not unkindly though Darica reacted as if he had screamed obscenities at her. "Maybe you should come with me, miss…"

He stepped toward her, to help her with her suitcase, but Darica fainted, banging her head against the table as she fell.

Darica blinked away the fuzziness in her head. When she remembered what had happened, her eyes filled with alarm. Fully expecting to see iron bars around her, she tried to sit up, but a sudden pain in her head restrained her.

As a cold cloth was laid over her forehead, Darica opened her eyes again. To whiteness. Everything was white. She must be in the hospital. "They" would take her to jail from here.

"May I talk to her now, Earla?" Darica heard a distant voice ask.

A voice right above her replied, "She's still a bit dazed, Father, but you can talk to her."

Father?

Wincing, Darica turned her head.

"I'm Father Jonathan," a man in black told her as he pulled up a stool beside her. "How are you feeling, Darica?"

What miracle was this? "You know my name?"

"Timothy…the young man who brought you here…peeked at your driver's license. A policeman's prerogative, you know."

"Am I…under arrest?" Darica asked weakly.

"Have you done anything wrong, child?"

Darica closed her eyes. *Why does he have to ask me a question like that?*

"I…ran away, Father," she managed to say, hoping the response would suffice.

"We gathered as much."

When he did not ask her to elaborate, Darica opened her eyes again. His eyes were kind, and she was less afraid.

"Are you in any trouble with the law?" he asked gently.

Darica could meet his gaze evenly this time. "No, Father."

He nodded. "Timothy will be relieved to hear that. He didn't act strictly according to procedure in bringing you here and calling for me."

"How…why…?" Darica knew the questions, but she couldn't get them formed properly on her lips.

He seemed to understand though. "You were clutching your rosary in spite of being out cold. Timothy is a member of my parish and guessed that I might be of some help to you."

He placed the beads in her hand and folded her fingers around them.

"I…I do need help, Father."

"Then we will have a long talk in the morning, child. These fine people here want to keep you overnight for observation."

Darica tried to sit up. "But I can't pay—"

"Hush, child. Earla's going to pretend she didn't hear that. We'll work out something. Don't be worrying about it."

"Thank you, Father…"

Darica pressed her rosary against her chest as a tear leaked from her eye. God did have a miracle in His pocket for her after all.

CHAPTER TEN

Upstairs in her new bedroom, in her new home, Darica lay in the darkness, fingering her rosary and counting the blessings that had befallen her over the last week. Surely God himself had guided her to Applewood and to Father Jonathan.

After her release from the hospital, he drove her back to the parish house, a rambling structure next to the church. His living quarters were an apartment over the garage, for a contingent of five sisters from an order in St. Louis occupied the house, though on the day of Darica's first visit, they were busy teaching in the grade school behind the church. However, the priest had arranged for one of the sisters, Sister Elsbeth, to be present during his interview, both for appearance's sake and to put Darica more at ease.

Hesitantly, Darica told them as much as she dared to tell them, saying only that she had fled the improper advances of a man who worked where she did. They knew there was more to the story, but they attributed omissions to Darica's delicate sense of propriety, a rare and admirable quality in a young lady these days.

However, they did want to talk to Andria, for Darica's disclosure about her stay at Cliffside concerned them. Although they did not consider her a closet psychopath, her story was incomplete, and the girl might have special needs that they should know about.

Darica did not object. In fact, she welcomed the opportunity to talk to Andria, who had not yet received Darica's letter.

Darica had left behind quite an uproar with her sudden departure, but all was forgiven when she explained the circumstances. When Andria promised that the authorities or Father Montez would deal with Enrique, Darica asked that nothing be done to him because of her.

"I…I want to stay here in Applewood," she said…with some difficulty, for she would miss Andria. "God guided me here, and I want to stay. He must have plans for me."

"Are you absolutely certain?"

"Absolutely. Father Jonathan will help me find a job and a place to stay, and I will type for their school to repay their generosity."

Andria was still ambivalent about this drastic change, but after eliciting a promise from Darica to return to Chicago if things did not work out, she agreed, even offering to take Darica's rocking chair to Applewood when Darica had a permanent address.

Andria's real motive was to convince herself that Darica would be able to cope in this entirely new world.

The next few days had been busy ones for Darica as she helped the sisters in the school, attended Father Jonathan's masses, and…less confidently…interviewed with potential employers. Her devoutness quickly gained her the respect of the church staff; her knowledge and love of animals earned her a job in Applewood's only pet store.

By the end of the week, she had a new home, too. With three other girls: the twins who owned the house and a girl sports writer.

Because events of the week had taken their toll on Darica by the time she moved in, she was too exhausted to make much of an effort at conversation. Father Jonathan had done most of the talking.

The girls seemed to understand Darica's situation and insisted that she go to bed early, assuring her that they would have a big dinner for her the next evening to celebrate her first day in the pet shop.

They were all so very kind. Especially one of the twins...Siara, was it?...who had helped her unpack.

Maybe they would be like Lucys and Ethels...or Margarets, Kittens, and Princesses...

For the first time in years, Darica felt a tentative tranquility, and she was more certain than ever that God's hand had guided her here. Within this house there was special warmth that had touched her as soon as she entered with Father Jonathan. Perhaps she was so perceptive of the warmth because her heart had been so cold.

Friends.

Maybe she would have FRIENDS now. Not just Andria, though Andria was certainly a wonderful friend to have.

God had forgiven her, sinner that she was. She didn't deserve all these blessings.

If only...

"Alvito, forgive me as I'm trying so hard to forgive you," she whispered. "Father in Heaven, forgive me, for I cannot find it in my heart to forgive Vito though You have forgiven me."

The prayer was a nightly ritual with her. No amount of counseling could completely eradicate the blackness Alvito had colored her soul with. In spite of Andria's subtle and not-so-subtle suggestions, Darica had refused to throw away the bookmark, for it symbolized to her that her greatest humiliation had been avenged.

This appetite for vengeance disconcerted her. Though Andria had told her that it was a common human frailty, Darica felt that she should somehow rise above it, yet she could not.

Controlling it was the trick, Andria had said over and over.

But, Darica reasoned now, if she were truly in control of it, she could make it go away completely. If she could forgive Alvito, she could throw away the bookmark.

And she couldn't. Not yet anyway.

So each night she did the next best thing: she prayed to be forgiven for not being able to forgive.

CHAPTER ELEVEN

Sprawling across Darica's bed, Andria stretched to rid herself of the kinks from her long drive from Chicago.

"Are you happy here, Darica?" she asked.

"I didn't think I could ever be this happy."

Darica rubbed her hand over the arm of her mother's rocker. Now that the chair was here, her feeling of home was complete.

The cozy contentment that shined on her face elated Andria personally and professionally. Seeing joy in the same eyes that had once been so dark and vacant was worth all the professional accolades Andria could ever collect, but she was still gratified to learn that the journal would be soon publishing "Tanita's" case study, a definite psychological success story.

Life was good, and getting better for both of them.

"Tell me everything you should have been writing me about," Andria scolded gently.

"I'm sorry I didn't write you more often. There is just so much to do."

"Things are going well at work?"

"Oh, yes! It is so nice being around LIVE animals all day. Mr. Butler even keeps two cats for pets at the store…Gypsy and Starbuck. They are strays that he found several years ago."

"Just as you used to."

"Only these kitties will be around for a long time. Mr. Butler spoils them terribly."

"I'm sure you help him with that."

"He is such a nice man…so gentle and kind to the animals. He gets so attached to them, he almost hates to sell them sometimes."

"You get along okay with him then?"

"I do. As a matter of fact, he has already given me a raise though I've been there only two months."

"I'm happy to hear that, but I had a little more in mind…like how you're relating to him on a more personal level?"

"Personal level?"

"Are you comfortable around him? Do you have real-life conversations with him?"

"Well, of course we talk. He's my boss, and he's a very nice man."

"How nice are we talking here, Darica?"

"What do you mean?"

"I mean, silly girl, since you and your Mr. Butler seem to be getting along so well, could something big be developing?"

"A promotion?"

"A romance, Darica!"

"Romance? My goodness, Andria, Mr. Butler is over sixty years old."

"Well darn. I was hoping you had met your Jim Anderson."

"I'm not looking for Jim Anderson right now. I'm too busy getting my life together."

"But if you met him, you'd give him a fair chance, wouldn't you?"

"I wouldn't know how to give him a fair chance."

"You can learn."

"Maybe some day. Living with Jordyn will give me a chance for some instructive observation."

"She dates a lot?"

"She could. Boys are always calling for her, but she's been so busy lately with her dance studio, she's turning most of them down. Except for this new boy, Luke. He's a farmer, and he's very nice, though at first I was scared of him because he's so big."

"Two men who aren't priests, and you've called them both nice. I'm encouraged. What about Jordyn's twin? Is she as popular as her sister?"

"She's as beautiful as Jordyn, of course, but she's awfully shy. Sometimes Jordyn and Jayme call us the Mouse Sisters because they say we are so much alike."

"Do you mind being called a Mouse Sister?"

"Oh, no. It makes me feel good to have a nickname...a NICE nickname. They call me Dari sometimes. I like that, too. It makes me feel like...like one of the girls."

"Should I point out that you've always been one of the girls?"

"Not like this. I belong here. For the first time in my life, I feel like I truly belong somewhere. We all watch out for each other and talk about all kinds of things. Sometimes on Fridays, if Jae doesn't have an afternoon game Saturday, we'll order pizza at midnight and stay up until dawn talking and teasing each other. Jyn and Jae are always thinking up fun things for us to do. Sari and I don't get so wild about it, of course, but we get a little wild sometimes."

"How have YOU been even a little wild?"

"Well...we had a picnic in the park last Saturday before Jae left for her game...and we ran all over the playground acting goofy."

"YOU acted goofy?"

"Not intentionally, but when I got stuck in the swing..."

"How do you get stuck in a swing?"

"The baby swing...we were swinging in the baby swings...and I couldn't get out of mine..."

Andria's giggle exploded into laughter. "Darica...Dari...I think your roommates are the best therapy in the world for you."

"They are good friends, even when we're not doing fun things. Sometimes at night I have bad dreams and cry in my sleep, and they don't get mad even if I wake them up. Usually Sari comes in to stay with me until I'm calm again.

Sometimes Jae or Jyn will, too, but they don't understand me as well as Sari does."

"Have you confided your…experiences to her?"

"No, but she understands just the same. I understand things about her, too…like she's not as happy as she deserves to be. She still misses her parents a lot."

"You and she should be good for each other. Did you tell me she's Catholic, too?"

"We go to mass together many times."

"How about Jayme and Jordyn?"

"Jae is Lutheran, and Jyn…well, we'll get her there some day. Usually she throws pillows at us if we try to get out of bed on Sunday mornings."

"I'm concerned about the bad dreams you're having. What kind of bad dreams?"

"Don't be concerned. They're more like flashbacks…about Vito…about things in my head then. I dream like that only when I'm really tired."

"Subconsciously that's when you feel most vulnerable. You've managed to resolve everything in your mind except Alvito."

"I do wish I could be more forgiving."

"Under the circumstances, it's understandable that you aren't. Otherwise I'd have to nominate you for sainthood. But you are improving each and every day. I can see a huge difference in just these two months. Applewood has been good to you."

"God guided me here. I believe that with all my heart."

"How are you getting along with God these days?"

"I've made my peace with Him, and He has blessed me."

"Do you like your new church?"

"Very much. Father Jonathan and the sisters have been so nice to me. Father Montez, Sister Sherwood, and the other sisters at St. Anthony were nice, too, but here it's more like…like family. Maybe that's why they use their first names here. It's more informal. The sisters don't even wear the full-dress habits and wimples here."

"Exactly the kind of church environment you need. All that rigid, ritualistic stuff isn't good for anyone."

"Spoken like a true Protestant." Darica's smile showed that she meant no reprimand.

"Spoken like a psychologist, my dear friend. So tell me, are you going to feed me here tonight, or shall we go out? I'm starving."

"The girls are meeting us at Burkey's tonight for dinner…MY treat. It gets a little rough there later in the evening when the college kids come in for beer, but during the dinner hour, it's very nice."

"'Nice.' There's that word again. I'm going to buy you a thesaurus, Darica. You're going to need some new HAPPY words in your vocabulary."

* * *

Darica closed her Bible but continued to rock, the motion…as always…a balm to her nerves when events of the day were troubling.

Jordyn's eye had been blackened by her date. By a boy named Hudson Turner.

Jordyn…who had dozens of boyfriends.

Jordyn…who had all kinds of experience with men.

Jordyn's roommates were concerned and indignant in degrees according to their proclivities.

Jayme raged hotly. Only Jordyn's insistence that no retaliation be instigated prevented Jayme from forming a posse of the entire Cardinal team and confronting Hudson Turner face-to-face when she drove into St. Louis for the game.

Siara's gentle nature precluded any angry outbursts, but Darica could FEEL how deeply distressed Siara was about her sister. Distressed enough to call their Uncle Blair with a complaint. A nasty man, that uncle. No wonder Siara was so afraid of him. And Jordyn had to cater to his despicable whims.

Darica herself felt so helpless today. There was little she could do but hover at Jordyn's side and make a pest of herself with offers of aspirin, cold cloths, pillows, cookies, milk…

When Jordyn shared with her new roommates the story of her previous encounter with Hudson Turner at the Kappa Chi Nu party, Jayme and Darica were duly impressed. But Darica couldn't help wondering what Andria would have to say about Jordyn's act of revenge. Doing what Jordyn had done must have required all kinds of control, yet her doing it showed NO control? An interesting paradox.

Interesting, too, how there were so many parallels in the roommates' lives.

Siara was afraid of her uncle…Darica could well guess why…and hesitant about dating. Even now she was involved in cathartic dialogues with a psychology student at the local college. Having benefited so much from Andria's help, Darica openly supported Jordyn's and Connor's attempts to persuade Siara into some kind of counseling…even if the counselor was just a psych major.

Now there was a very nice man, Connor Sanderson. Like a beloved older brother to them all. A Jim Anderson type. A very NICE man. Nice…pleasant…sweet-natured…good-humored…thoughtful…

Andria had sent the promised thesaurus with all the HAPPY words highlighted in yellow…

Nevertheless, in spite of the NICE men, there were so many whose sole purpose in life was to cause grief to women.

The roommates talked so often late into the night, sharing SOME secrets…enough that Darica knew she was not the only victim in the household.

Even Jae, who got along so well with all those ball players, was hurt over and over again by that simple-minded Harlan Oakes.

Even Jordyn…beaten and bruised by Hudson Turner.

Even Siara. Poor Sari Mouse, who had given Darica absolutely no details about what Uncle Blair had done to her, but Darica knew. Oh yes, she KNEW.

Darica's hand fumbled inside the Bible until her fingers gripped the bookmark. She squeezed until her knuckles were white from the effort, until her fingernails cut into her palm.

God should really do something about the men who were NOT nice. Yes, He really should.

* * *

I want so much to help, yet there never seems to be anything I can do, Darica thought.

Another roommate in pain, and all Darica could do was hover.

Jayme…poor Jae…being so brave when Darica knew how tormented she was. They had been roommates for over a year now, and Darica knew how much Jayme cared for Harlan Oakes, how profoundly she was hurt by Harlan's constant insensitivity to her feelings.

It wasn't that Harlan wasn't a NICE boy. He was merely STUPID. Even Jayme admitted that he was seriously deficient in mental prowess.

Still, imagine the audacity of his asking Jayme to be a bridesmaid in his wedding! His fiancée had asked just to be mean, and Jayme had refused HER. But Jayme could not refuse Harlan.

Harlan, who was too utterly ignorant to realize how badly Jayme was hurting. If he had even the teeniest bit of sense, he would see that Jayme was prettier…and smarter…and more fun…

"Can I do something to make you feel better, Jae?" Darica asked…again.

"Stop fretting, Dari Mouse." Jayme patted Darica's cheek. "You did a great job taking in the waist on this pastel-putrid dress. Thanks."

"You look beautiful."

"Thanks again. But I know that I look like an oatmeal lump in pastels…which is why the bitch-bride chose this particular color."

"You're more beautiful than the bride can ever be."

"A warthog is more beautiful than the bride can ever be. Unfortunately Harlan seems to prefer warthogs this year."

"It's so UNFAIR!" Darica's lip trembled as tears welled in her eyes.

"Hey…hey…none of that, Dari Mouse. I'm the one who's supposed to be crying."

"Then why aren't you?"

"By now I'm numb to things Harlan does to me. Besides, tears only wash you away. Getting angry instead will give you enough spark to keep you going."

Darica nodded. For all that Alvito had done to her, she had never once shed a tear because of him. Her tears flowed freely for her friends now, however…when they were hurting…when she could do nothing to help them…

Maybe she would be more useful to her friends if she choked back the tears and let the anger knot up inside her again. Maybe then she could help God do things about men who would hurt her friends.

CHAPTER TWELVE

Synchronicity.

Darica's tongue protruded as she concentrated on decorating the twins' birthday cake.

On that and synchronicity.

She had learned about the word just the week before in a magazine article. The theory of synchronicity explained to her how so many similar things could happen to her and to her friends throughout their lives even though they had met each other only three years before when they became roommates.

And now Darica's friend Andria was leaving Chicago to open her own practice "back home" in New York, and Siara's Sandie was also leaving to pursue her career there.

More synchronicity.

Which proved to Darica all the more that she was where she belonged.

Finishing the cake, Darica stepped back to scrutinize her handiwork. Not too bad. She had been somewhat afraid to tackle the job since so many people would see it at the twins' party the next evening. But cooking had become a relaxing hobby for her, and she did want to do something NICE for the twins.

She joined Jayme in the living room then, but Jayme only smiled at her and continued watching television. Because Jayme didn't have many opportunities for watching TV, except for those old, late-late-night movies she was fond if, Darica didn't want to interrupt, so she grabbed up a magazine and settled down to read until Siara finished her shower and came downstairs.

"Shouldn't Jordyn be home by now?" Jayme asked suddenly, during a commercial.

Darica glanced at the clock. "She is later than we expected. Perhaps her uncle if giving her a hard time."

Jayme laughed, though Darica could not understand why.

"My dear Dari Mouse, he's probably giving her a very HARD time...which is why she's late..."

Darica caught onto the pun then and blushed. "Well...no more hard times after tonight. The twins will control their own money. Their uncle is a terrible man to make Jordyn do such terrible things."

"I agree. But the decision was Jyn's. She has a different opinion of...of romance than we do, so we can't hold her decision against her."

"I don't. I hold her decision against HIM."

Frowning, Darica felt the familiar fist of anger clench in her stomach. She knew exactly what Jordyn was doing to please her uncle. Jordyn was a victim, too.

The phone's ringing right next to her startled her, and she fumbled moving the receiver to her ear.

"Is Siara back, Dari?"

"She's in the shower."

"What about Jae? Is she home yet?"

"She got home about an hour ago. Do you want to talk to her?"

"I want to talk to you all. Put Jae on the phone downstairs. Then drag my sister out of the shower and share the upstairs phone with her."

"What's wrong, Jordyn?"

"Don't ask questions now. Just do what I said and hurry!"

Throwing the phone toward Jayme, Darica hurtled up the stairs. Siara was stepping out of the shower as Darica thundered into the bathroom.

"Good grief, Dari…"

Darica quickly tossed a towel around her roommate.

"Quickly. Jordyn is on the phone. Something is wrong. She wants us all to listen."

They ran for the upstairs phone together.

"Jordyn, what is going on?" Siara asked as Darica pried the phone away from Siara's ear, far enough for both of them to hear. "Darica's running around up here like Chicken Little."

"I've killed Blair, Baby."

"What!"

Horrified, Siara and Darica listened as Jordyn told them details of Blair's apparent heart attack. As usual, Jayme and Jordyn did most of the talking…most of the planning…but Siara and Darica gave their whole-hearted support, no matter what.

Darica's knees weakened as she imagined what Jordyn must have endured that evening. Though Jordyn had done nothing wrong, people would surely think otherwise. All because of that awful, awful man. He deserved to die, and Darica thanked God very much for taking care of that detail. However, even in dying, Blair had managed to hurt Jordyn.

Darica gripped Siara's hand for strength. They must all give strength to each other.

Jayme and Jordyn were planning what to do now.

I must listen so that I can help, too. But what can I do? I'm so useless…so helpless…

"Pleasuring himself." Jayme's words caught Darica's attention. How brilliant Jae and Jyn were! Set the scene to look as if Uncle Blair had been doing nasty things to himself. Then he, not Jordyn, would get all the blame. Absolutely brilliant…

If only Darica, too, could do something beyond giving the proverbial moral support…

"But what do I do?" she heard Jordyn wail into the phone then. "I've never seen a man jack off. My proximity makes such a thing unnecessary."

"What's to know?" Jayme was saying. "Wrap his fingers around his whackydoodle, and then vacate the premises."

"If you want it to be convincing, you must do more than that," Darica said quickly, before she lost both the opportunity and her nerve.

Closing her eyes, she recalled scenes of all the times she had seen Alvito's show for her benefit. Here, at last, she had something worthwhile to offer.

She choked out a description of what she had too frequently seen. Siara was staring at her in disbelief, and Jayme was stunned to silence.

"My God, Dari," Jordyn was saying. "How do you know all that?"

"I...I had a b-brother once. Please... none of you ever mention this again. Ever..."

Sagging against Siara then, Darica listened quietly while plans were finalized. They might have to lie, to say that they had been with Jordyn all evening if anyone asked. Fibbing was sinful, but in this case the Lord would forgive them. Wouldn't He?

"All we can do now is wait for Jordyn," Siara said as she hung up the phone.

Darica nodded, but said nothing.

"Do you need to lie down for a while, Dari?"

"I'll be fine. Let's wait for Jordyn downstairs...together, please."

"Of course. Just let me get some clothes on."

As Siara squeezed her roommate's hand then, Darica stared into blue eyes that welled with understanding of what she had endured with her brother.

CHAPTER THIRTEEN

*T*his is too much, Darica thought, rocking and fingering the bookmark.

The ultimate insult. The ultimate frustration.

Jordyn's and Jayme's ordeals had been bad enough, but now Siara was suffering all over again, just when she had pulled her life back together.

Darica had fussed and fretted the entire year of Siara's involvement with that married doctor. But Siara seemed so happy that Darica tried valiantly to ignore the concerns.

Now they had discovered that Dr. Chadburn had been deceiving Siara the entire year with his lies and deceptions.

This is too much when Siara's the one who's hurt, God.

One of the Mouse Sisters was sobbing herself senseless at that very moment. Siara was trying hard to be quiet, but Darica's ears were tuned to Siara's heartache. Jordyn and Siara had their twinstinct, but Darica and Siara shared unspoken conversation, too.

This is too, too much…

Of course, the roommates had rallied around their stricken comrade, and Jae and Jyn had devised another superb retaliatory plan. However, as usual, Darica was a passive participant. There for support purposes only. She lacked the bluster and the bravery to be on the front lines.

Now more than ever, she wanted to be ACTIVELY involved. For her most special friend.

And I will be involved!

Jayme had a three-thirty appointment with Dr. Chadburn the next day. Phase One of their Master Plan. Then Jordyn would instigate Phase Two.

When Jordyn left his office, Darica would have her own little talk with him. If she talked sternly enough and mentioned God, maybe she could touch a cord of decency in him.

If there was no cord of decency to touch…well…

Darica was angry enough now that she couldn't predict what she might do. But God would let her know somehow.

* * *

"Dr. Chadburn?"

The eerie silence of the office bothered her. What if she had waited too long…almost a whole half hour after Jordyn left? What if he was already gone for the day?

However, he would not have left the door unlocked if he were gone.

Taking a deep breath for courage, she opened the door to his inner office.

"Dr. Chadburn?"

Carefully she tiptoed down the hallway, peeking cautiously into each room, giving herself mental pep talks to maintain her resolve.

Approaching the last examination room, she saw his shoes, then his legs…stretched out along the floor.

Darica covered her mouth to stifle her gasp.

He lay on his back, motionless.

"Dr. Chadburn?"

Darica nudged him with her foot. Still no movement. She fumbled for a pulse. None. Dead. Siara's Dr. Chadburn was dead.

Jordyn must have killed him! But how? There were no marks on his body. Unless…

Darica rolled him up far enough to see blood matting his hair. Jordyn would never hit someone from behind. She was much too direct.

Then…who?

Siara? What if Siara had sneaked in and done it. She had been so upset that she might have done it without even realizing what she was doing. Darica better than anyone else knew how possible that scenario was.

Whether Siara had killed him or not, someone might think so and cause her all kinds of trouble.

A sudden thought generated a swelling of gratitude within Darica.

Of course.

Now she knew why God had brought her to Applewood. To help Siara. God was working in His mysterious ways again. God had punished Dr. Chadburn, and now He was giving Darica this unique opportunity to help her fellow Mouse Sister.

She surveyed the examination room. Alcohol. Plenty of alcohol. She soaked the doctor's clothing with it and splashed what was left onto the drapes and into the filled trashcan. This time the fire had to be bigger. Big enough to destroy any evidence of Siara. Big enough to send Dr. Chadburn into Hell with Alvito.

Then she saw the scalpel, gleaming invitingly against the stainless steel counter. How long since she had last held a scalpel?

Testing its weight in her hand, she chewed on her lip as she stared at Dr. Chadburn.

I am in perfect control, and I still want to do it. But what would I do with it? Siara would die of shock if I gave it to her.

And I would have to buy tanning materials. Then I would have to tan it…and everyone would wonder what I was doing. There isn't enough privacy at home. Any suspicion falling on me will only make Siara look guiltier.

I must not…I must not…I must not…

Minutes later she held the bloody tissue in her hand, careful not to drip any blood on her clothing.

Now why did I do that? What do I do with it now? I can't walk out of here with it in my handbag. Leave it here, Dari Mouse. I have made my editorial comment, as Jae would say. What more can I do but light the fire?

As she started to toss the severed member into the trashcan, she was suddenly inspired.

I am beginning to think like Jyn and Jae.

Smiling, she pried the doctor's mouth open and stuffed his manhood into it. Then, after calmly washing her hands and the scalpel, she dabbed the dripping blood off his mouth with the paper towel she had used to dry her hands.

Blood. There's so much blood. Siara would quote Shakespeare right now. "Yet who would have thought the old man to have had so much blood in him...A little water clears us of this deed."

But water will not clear away THIS deed. There is too much blood...too much blood...

A match. I need a match...

There were no matches in the examination room or in the doctor's pocket.

Panic touched her. What if after all this, she couldn't find a match? She searched the other examination rooms and the receptionist's desk. His receptionist must have been an untidy woman, for papers and notes were scattered everywhere. Beneath the papers, though, Darica found a book of matches...from a fancy St. Louis hotel. Receptionists must make very good money.

"Say hello to Vito in Hell, Doctor," she whispered, tossing lit matches onto him and into the trashcan.

The fire spread more quickly than she expected, and the heat drove her into the hallway. Now to get out of there without anyone seeing her.

From the drugstore she heard the fire alarm, and she joined the crowd gathering outside Dr. Chadburn's building. The girls would want details. She would have to tell them something without telling them everything.

This was more serious, more mysterious than Blair Eldred's death. Police would certainly become involved. The less her roommates knew, the safer they would be.

A fit of trembling overcame her then, and she leaned against a tree.

My God, what have I done?

As soon as the police began to disperse the crowd, Darica hurried back to her battered Pinto and drove home as fast as the old car would run.

"Jyn! Sari! Jae!" She called for them while she was still outside, breathless and excited from the ordeal. "You won't believe it! He died and the office burned! God's judgment! It's God's judgment for sure!"

As she slammed into the kitchen, Jordyn grabbed her arm. "Calm down, Dari. Who's dead? What office? You smell like smoke. What happened?"

"The doctor was dead...Dr. Chadburn was dead." Darica struggled for breath. "And then the office...on fire...it burned so fast. I was going to talk to him...to appeal to his Christian decency...for Siara...and the firemen are there now...and the POLICE. He was murdered. I know he was murdered..."

Jayme sat Darica down then, talking to her in a soothing voice until Darica was calm.

Jordyn paced.

Siara was not home yet. All of them were filled with the same apprehension though none gave it voice.

Finally Jordyn called, "Siara's home!" and ran outside to her sister.

"Poor Siara," Darica whispered, staring outside at her most special friend. "I hope she feels better now that justice has been done."

Although Jayme had a question on her lips about Darica's remark, her curiosity was diverted as Jordyn led Siara into the kitchen.

Part V: The Roommates/June-October, 1984

CHAPTER ONE

Locking her fingers behind her head, Jayme stretched and propped her feet on the coffee table.

"Are the Mouse Sisters settled for the night?" she asked as Jordyn came downstairs.

"I think so. Dari's more agitated about this than Sari seems to be. Go figure."

"You know Dari. She tries to mother us all even though she's the baby in our little family. It's her Margaret Anderson complex."

"Margaret Anderson…Doris Day…I'm going to trash every TV in this house."

"Calm down, will you? Here…I made you a Coke-and-whiskey."

Jordyn dropped onto the couch next to Jayme. "Thanks, pal. I need it even if my system's not too used to the hard stuff these days."

"You're probably aware of this already, but I have to say it: this is another fine mess we've gotten ourselves into."

"How bad do you think it is, Jae?"

"That depends. Did you kill him?"

"I would've told you if I did." Jordyn gulped her drink. "You know what I'm afraid of?"

"Siara?"

Jordyn nodded. "And don't tell me it hasn't crossed your mind, too."

"You're right. It has. But is she capable of something that horrendous? She's so gentle-spirited…she balked at even what we had planned for tonight."

"But she was acting so weird when she got home. Maybe she freaked out. The old cliché says it's the quiet types you have to watch out for."

"Wouldn't she have told us? After your adventure with Blair, she has to know we'd take care of her."

"MURDER though? I didn't actually kill Blair. I merely altered the appearance of his natural demise. And if Sari did freak out, maybe she's blocked it out of her mind, and she's in a huge state of denial right now. Maybe she honestly can't remember."

"You're assuming that Sari did it. Is that what your twinstinct is telling you?"

"My twinstinct is fucked up right now. I'm just plain…scared…"

"Let me ask Dad to do some poking around for details. Cops don't always release all the juicy tidbits to the papers, but Dad has some connections that may talk to him off the record."

"Thanks. We may have to do some detecting of our own. Are you up to it?"

"Sure I'm up to it, but I'm leaving for a two-week road trip Sunday evening."

"I'll hold down the fort until you get back. Surely the cops won't have a lead to Siara for a while. Doc Shitburn did us a favor with all his sneaking around with her. Who else is going to know to connect them?"

"Good point. Now I can feel better about having to leave town."

"Are you SURE you're up to this, Jae? We could be in a world of trouble if we're covering for a murderer and someone finds out. It's different for me...I'm her sister."

"And she's the next best thing to a sister for me. All three of you are."

"Thanks." Jayme gulped down the rest of her drink. "I wish the ol' twinstinct was finely tuned tonight. I sure would like to know what's going on inside her head."

Darica climbed out of bed as soon as she heard Jordyn go downstairs. Sleep was impossible in spite of Jordyn's encouragements to rest. Too much had happened. Too many questions needed answers.

Instinctively she stepped toward her rocker, for it was her refuge in trying times. But then she considered that Siara might be lying awake, too, and needing someone to talk to.

"Sari?" she called softly, peeking into Siara's room. "Are you asleep?"

Siara was awake and reading. "Dari! Come in. I couldn't sleep either, but try telling that to Jyn."

"She means well..."

Siara patted the bed for Darica to sit down. "I'm glad you're here. I have some dreadful misgivings rampaging in my mind."

"I thought you might."

"You have the same misgivings?"

"Maybe."

Shyness overcame them both. Without Jayme or Jordyn there to stimulate the conversation, Darica and Siara were hesitant about revealing their opinions for fear of causing offense.

Siara finally took the initiative. "Dari...I am so afraid that...that Jordyn is in some way responsible for what happened to Prescott."

"Jordyn?" Darica closed her eyes to hide her relief. If Siara was worried about Jordyn's involvement, Siara didn't kill Dr. Chadburn after all. Of course, Jordyn would need their help, too, if she had done it, but Jordyn was much stronger than her sister and could cope better. Whichever twin or neither, Darica was satisfied that she had done the right thing with the fire. Maybe not with the scalpel, but with the fire. Finally she had been able to help. God had sent her here for that purpose. To help her friends. To help Him.

Now, however, Siara needed her for something more immediate, for reassurance.

"Jyn would have told us," Darica said finally. "She called us about your uncle."

"But she didn't murder Blair."

"Could Jyn really hurt someone?"

"She's out for the blood of anyone she thinks has hurt the people she loves. Once she almost maimed a boyfriend of mine because she thought he had wronged me. And consider what she did to Hudson Turner when she was still in high school."

"None of that was MURDER. If she had murderous tendencies, your uncle wouldn't have lived to have his heart attack."

"You're right, Dari, and I feel absolutely contemptible for even suspecting anything so hideous about my own sister, but I can't rid my mind of all these troublesome suspicions."

"Does your twinstinct tell you that Jyn killed that awful man?"

"My twinstinct is currently befuddled. This has been a week of confusion and turmoil."

"Oh, I know." Darica squeezed Siara's hand in sympathy.

"We have to remember that IF Jyn did kill Prescott, she did it for me, and I have to protect her no matter what."

"We all will."

"You're so sweet, Dari. But you could get into some serious trouble by becoming involved...if our worst fears are realized."

"I'm willing to face all risks. You, Jyn, and Jae are my family."

"Thank you, Dari. That means so much to us."

Tears glistened on the cheeks of both girls.

"We mustn't tell either Jyn or Jae what we've been discussing," Siara continued. "For one thing, we might be wrong. And if we aren't, Jyn has her reasons for doing what she's doing, and we should wait until she's ready to tell us."

"I agree."

"Jyn and Jae always think they have to protect us because...because we're the Mouse Sisters. And we are more meek and timid than they are. But we must be strong now and watch out for them."

"Them? Do you think Jae helped to kill him?"

"Not actually, but Jyn would trust her with something this audacious. You noticed that Jyn didn't hustle Jae off to bed."

"Jyn thinks she's doing what's best for us."

"Exactly why we have to be so sneaky about doing what's best for her. She likes to think she's omnipotently self-sufficient. That may be why our twinstinct isn't working properly at this time. We can shut each other out when we want to."

"We'll do whatever must be done."

"Thank you, Dari. It's comforting to know that I can count on you, especially in something this serious. I'm glad you came in here tonight."

"I thought you might need me."

"Maybe we're developing mouse-stinct."

Darica smiled, pleased by the implication, but soon awkwardness loomed between them again.

"I…I'll go back to bed now," Darica said finally. "I think I can sleep now."

"Me, too. Thank you again, Dari."

When Siara was alone again, she remembered that in all the confusion, she had neglected to tell her roommates about her and Connor.

Connor.

Smiling, she blocked out the day's unpleasantness with sweet thoughts of him.

Midnight.

Jordyn sat alone in the living room.

Jayme had sacrificed her late-night movies for a little extra sleep, and the Mouse Sisters had been in bed for hours.

However, Jordyn knew that sleep would be a long time coming to her…unless she drank herself into oblivion. And that would be counterproductive right now. She needed to be alert and ready for anything.

For anything.

She listened to the clicks and snaps of the house settling for the night.

At one time, she had thought that losing her parents was the worst thing that could ever happen to her. Now she knew differently. Losing Siara would be the worst.

Jordyn rubbed her stomach. She was feeling queasy again. Too much worry. Too much Coke-and-whiskey drunk too fast.

The phone's ringing scared her, and she yanked the receiver up before anyone was awakened.

Please, God, don't let it be the police.

Luke.

"Don't you have better manners than to be calling at this hour, Farm Boy?" she snapped to cover how frightened she had been.

"Sorry. I thought you might still be up."

"Lucky for you, I am. What do you want?"

"You."

"I'm not in the mood."

"I understand. I heard the news about Siara's doctor friend. How's she taking it?"

"Pretty well, under the circumstances. Of course, she started getting over that sewer-faced son of a bitch a whole week ago. Why are you up so late? I thought you set your clocks on chicken time."

"I've been running a few things through my mind, and I wanted to run them by you before I...chickened out."

"Run fast then. I need some Z's."

"I want you to marry me."

"We've been through this before, and my answer is the same. No."

"I have more to offer this time."

"Like what?"

"My silence."

The queasiness in Jordyn's stomach intensified. "You've always let your actions speak louder than your words, and I haven't complained."

"I'm not getting into a playful exchange of double-entendre with you. The plain fact is that I know now which doctor you saw this afternoon."

Sweat beaded on her forehead. "So? I have nothing to hide."

"And later I saw Siara leaving the doctor's building by the back door."

"You couldn't have!"

"But I did. I took Lissa to Dairy Bar after we left you, and coming back we cut down Belmont Street. That's when I saw Siara."

Jordyn swallowed hard, several times, as the Coke-and-whiskey rose in her throat. The connection. Luke could connect Siara with the doctor...

"Jordyn, are you still there?"

"I...I'm here," she said weakly. "You didn't tell anyone, did you?"

"Not yet. And Lissa was too busy with her magazines to notice."

"Thank you," Jordyn whispered before his words registered with her fully. "What do you mean 'not yet'?"

"As a civic-minded person, I should mention to the police what I saw even though I'm fairly certain Siara couldn't kill anyone."

"Luke, please..." Jordyn fought to regain her composure. "Don't say anything to anyone. Of course Siara didn't do it, but the cops would hassle her anyway."

"I don't know, Jordyn. I like Siara and all, but this is murder and arson we're talking about."

"Please, Luke! I'll do anything!"

"Then you'll marry me."

A statement of fact, not a question.

"That's blackmail, Luke Johnson."

"Obviously that's the only chance I have to make you my wife."

"You fucking son of a bitch! I hate you!"

"And, God help me, I love you...so much I'm stooping to blackmail to get you."

"Never! Siara is guilty of nothing. So take your threats and shove them up your goddamn, fucking, son-of-a-bitch ass."

"Think on it for a while. I've even give you a week to consider, but that's as reasonable as I'm going to be—"

Jordyn slammed down the receiver without answering and ran to the bathroom to surrender to her nausea.

CHAPTER TWO

Normally Darica did not mind being alone in the pet shop after hours, for the animals provided her with plenty of company. Tonight, however, Mr. Butler had taken Gypsy and Starbuck home with him so that Darica could place rat poison in strategic locations in the building. Pampered as they were, the cats were not good mousers, and Darica feared for their health if they were underfoot while she was working with the poison. The rest of the animals were safely in their cages, but they offered her no companionship either. Most were asleep, resting, or indifferent, and Darica felt quite lonely.

Only her scheduled meeting with Father Jonathan here at the shop kept her from leaving for home. She was unable to relax with all the quiet around her. How she missed the birds' normal chirping and squawking and the puppies' and kittens' tumbling all over each other in play. Perhaps the animals sensed her somber mood.

She had spent long hours justifying to herself her actions in Dr. Chadburn's office. Andria had once told her that doing something to an already dead body was not necessarily a serious crime. Of course, arson was felonious, but whatever costs were incurred from the damage to the building were small to her indeed when compared to the safety of her friends. No one besides the doctor had been hurt…that was the important thing. And when a body was dead, whatever else she did to it did not much matter.

Still, there was a touch of guilt nibbling away inside her, and its presence worried her, for she wanted no repeat of the emotional condition that had generated her breakdown. Since the doctor's death, she had been in the confessional twice, but both times she had been unable to voice her most burdensome sins in a way discreet enough to shield the actual deed…and the roommates' involvement.

She and Siara were more certain than ever that Jordyn was involved. They had been watching her carefully. She wasn't sleeping or eating well at all, and the shadows beneath her eyes seemed even darker against her ashen face.

And the phone calls.

Though they rarely called Jayme when she was on road trips, Jordyn had called her three times in the past week…long distance to California…when Jordyn thought Siara and Darica were asleep. They didn't eavesdrop…they were too afraid of getting caught…but they heard enough to know that Jordyn was talking to Jayme.

The surest evidence of all was that she was refusing to see or talk with Luke.

No doubt about it: she was a troubled young lady.

Although Siara and Darica tried their best to be sources of comfort and strength for Jordyn, Jordyn seemed as determined to be a source of comfort and strength for them. They were "nicing" each other to death without saying anything of great importance to each other, even though each was bursting with questions and concerns.

Dr. Chadburn had been autopsied and buried. Siara did not attend the funeral.

None of them WANTED to read the papers. Nevertheless, they forced themselves to scrutinize every published word on the Chadburn murder investigation. So far, the police weren't releasing much information except that they had a few leads.

Leads.

The word scared them all. But all they could do was wait...and worry...

Darica glimpsed the black-garbed figure of Father Jonathan outside the shop then and hurried to let him in.

Good thing I knew he was coming, or he would have scared the bejabbers out of me in my current state of mind.

"The problem is that Mrs. Meadows has been called to Nebraska to care for an ailing brother," he told her when the social amenities had been satisfied. "We need someone to replace her as coordinator of the Fall Festival, and your name was mentioned several times."

"Me? I'm honored, but I have no experience with that kind of thing."

"You're very qualified actually. You've been working in the church long enough to realize its needs, capabilities, and potentials, and you know the people. Your idea of having a petting zoo for the children at the festival impressed a lot of people."

"I want to help in whatever way I can, but this is a rather overwhelming project for me to handle."

"Sister Rosemary and I will assist you, of course...and the committees will do most of the work. Your chief function is to see that all the committees are doing what they're supposed to be doing, when they're supposed to be doing them..."

"I have never been a leader. I'm a better follower."

"Here's an opportunity for you to test your leadership wings with a group of people who already think you're a wonderful young lady."

Blushing with pleasure at the compliment, Darica lowered her eyes. "Thank you, Father."

"May we count on you then?"

"If you will do most of the talking at meetings," Darica said, still not wholly convinced.

Father Jonathan laid his hand against her cheek. "Bless you, child. This will be a good experience for you. Come by the parish house tomorrow, and we'll unload all the paperwork on you..."

When he left, Darica stored the rat poison in the basement and checked the animals one final time before locking up for the night. Smiling with joy, she pressed her fingers against her cheek where Father Jonathan had touched her.

He blessed me. Father Jonathan blessed me. Everything is going to be just fine...

* * *

Jordyn walked through the studio one final time to be sure all her students had left. Jayme would be calling her soon from San Francisco...if Jim had managed to get his hands on any helpful information. Even with the two-hour time difference, it was getting late. The afternoon game had ended almost two hours ago. Jayme should be calling soon.

The phone rang at three different times.

A mother wanting to enroll her daughter in gymnastics.

Then Siara, who was having dinner with Connor again...while Darica was at church meeting with the Fall Festival committees.

Finally Luke. Jordyn hung up on him as soon as she heard his voice.

She paced her office. Surely Jayme would call whether there was information or not. Surely Jayme would call SOON. Jordyn couldn't wait here all night, and she didn't want to take THIS call at home. Siara and Darica had been hovering at her elbow all week.

Finally...blessedly...the phone rang again, and Jayme's voice responded to her greeting.

"Sorry I'm so late. This is a busy time for Dad, and I was put on hold six times while I was talking to him. They have a new owner for the paper, and everything is a mass of confusion there at the moment."

"Everything's a mass of confusion here, too. Did he find out anything?"

"The police are playing this one pretty close to the chest since this is Applewood's first authentic murder. Dad thinks our PD may be in a bit over their heads...which is to our advantage. I gotta tell you...I had to do some quick talking to satisfy his suspicions. First, I asked about the doc's social life, and now I'm asking all these questions about his death."

"What did you tell him?"

"I claimed that a friend of a friend had been interested in meeting the guy...and then my morbid curiosity kicked in when he died."

"He was satisfied with that?"

"Of course not. But he spoils me shamelessly and usually gets me what I ask for. He even managed to get a peek at the police and coroner's reports...with the understanding that nothing is published without authorization."

"Thank God for doting daddies. What was in the reports? Fingerprints or anything that would drag Siara into it?"

"The fire apparently destroyed most of the hard evidence...assuming there was some...in the exam room where the doc was found. There was no mention of useful prints elsewhere, where there was less fire damage. In a doctor's office, there has to be zillions of different prints…even God would need a few days to sort them all out."

"Hopefully there's safety in numbers. With your prints, mine, and Siara's there…well…we'll be up shit creek if anything is traced to our happy home."

"How relieved am I that I used a fake name, address, and phone number in case his appointment book survived the fire? Something that definitely didn't survive was the doc's whackydoodle. It had been whacked off and stuffed into his mouth."

"You're making that up."

"Dad says the police are wondering about some kind of a sex killing…or a ritualistic killing by a 'Nam vet."

"Why a 'Nam vet?"

"Stuffing a man's whackydoodle into his mouth was the fun thing to do among the Viet Cong when they had access to enemy corpses."

"I wish I could have heard Jim explaining all this to you," Jayme couldn't help laughing.

"There was a lot of throat clearing and 'well-you-know-what-I-mean's' from him."

"The sex killing thing…that's definitely more than Siara could ever do, don't you think?"

"If she had a mental lapse or something, who knows?"

"I wanted reassurances."

"Sorry. Are you going to tell Sari and Dari what we know?"

"And scare them to death? Poor Dari would have nightmares for a century."

"How are you holding up?"

"Not great, but adequately."

"Have you talked with Luke?"

"I'm waiting to see if I wake up and discover this is all a bad dream. How are things with Harlan?"

"I made the mistake of telling him that I'd have their baby for HIM. Now, I have to think up excuses for not starting on this particular project for a whole month. I have to take those magic pills that long before I can trust their effectiveness."

"Lucky for you Harlan's so dumb even a bad excuse will do. When are you coming home?"

"Midnight Sunday unless the game runs long for some reason. It always seems to happen on a get-away day. Look…Jyn…I can get a few days off and come home early…as soon as Ernie can fly out a back-up reporter."

"Thanks, but no. I may need you to be here lots more later."

"A serious talk with Siara could clear up a lot of your worries."

"I'm waiting for the proverbial right moment to tell my sweet and gentle sister that I fear she's a psychopathic, body-mutilating sex killer." Jordyn paused thoughtfully. "You never did tell me what actually killed ol' Dr. Cad-burned. Are you holding something back from me?"

"Not intentionally. We were sidetracked. 'Cad-burned.' I like that. You should write heads for the *National Enquirer*."

"Head jobs are only one of my specialties. So what's the poop on the demise of the poop?"

"He was crunched on the back of the head with the legendary heavy, blunt object...probably the metal desk lamp that was discovered behind the exam table. However, according to the coroner, at that point he was still alive. Simply speaking, he was further weakened by loss of blood in his whackydoodle place...and then he was roasted alive."

CHAPTER THREE

Siara's eyes mirrored the candlelight as Connor entwined his fingers with hers. Their carryout dinner from Burkey's lay untouched on Connor's dining room table, for their only hunger was for each other.

However, Connor suffered stoically, for he wasn't arrogant enough to assume that he had captured his true love's heart as completely as she had his. Some remnant of grief must linger within her despite Chadburn's perfidy. She had fancied herself in love with him for many months, and Siara wasn't one to trifle with such a blessed emotion.

In the past two weeks, Connor and Siara had been together every evening, and for him every moment with her was like a taste of Heaven. Still, he detected a touch of worried sadness in her eyes. He didn't pry into her privacy, primarily because he feared that she would confess her abiding love for the doctor.

And she volunteered no confidences.

Although concern for her sister lurked behind every enchanted minute she spent with Connor, Siara hesitated to disclose her worries to him. Over the years, she had burdened him enough with her foolish, imperceptive disregard for his love. For now she and Darica would keep their fears to themselves…while Siara passed each evening falling more in love with Connor.

He told her that he loved her a dozen times a night although he hushed her before she repeated the words to him. His kisses and embraces aroused exquisite longing within her, yet he discouraged consummation of their joy.

His restraint obviously tormented him, but he refused to rush Siara into any commitment. Even though his control was equally frustrating for her, she blessed him for it because it proved to her that his love was deep and true.

As Prescott's never was.

Her eyes clouded with the thought of the doctor. Not from sorrow for him, but with anxiety for Jordyn.

Nevertheless, Connor saw her eyes dim and fought back a surge of jealousy. He should be rejoicing about his future with Siara rather than lamenting her past with another man. A man who was dead now. But a man who continued to intrude into Connor's paradise.

Seeing his mouth tighten, Siara stroked his face until his warm, endearing smile returned. He pressed her palm against his lips and closed his eyes.

"Have I done something to upset you?" she whispered fearfully.

"No, Stacks…never," he said, kissing her hand and caressing her fingers.

"You would tell me if I did? You more than anyone else know that I'm not so receptive to hints and innuendoes, and I never want to muddle our relationship again."

"You're not muddling, my love. I'm just afraid of letting my baser instincts get the upper hand on me."

"Baser instincts? You're the epitome of gentlemanly behavior..." A disappointed sigh escaped her lips and drew his laughter.

"Ah, my precious Stacks...may I hope that my desires are reciprocated?"

Siara forced herself to meet his gaze. "I'm new to this desires business, Connor. All I know is that you make me feel so different from any way I've ever felt before...as if a rosebud has burst into bloom in the deepest part of me."

"But didn't you and he...I'm sorry, Siara. I shouldn't ask such a question. Those baser instincts of mine were taking over again."

Although Siara blushed scarlet, she held his eyes with hers. "Don't apologize. You have a right to know. Yes, Prescott and I did have a physical relationship, but now that I have opened my eyes to the kind of love you give me, I realize that Prescott and I were never intimate in spite of all that physical closeness."

"Yet you still grieve for him..." The words escaped before he could stop them.

"I don't grieve, Connor. I feel sorry for him, and I profoundly regret allowing him to deceive me so easily. But I don't grieve for him."

"Still, sometimes you look so troubled..."

She laid her hand against his cheek. Merely touching him brought her more pleasure than any of her interludes with Prescott.

"I haven't wanted to unload my troubles on you, but perhaps I'm causing you more distress with my silence. I'll admit that Dari and I could benefit from some sage advice."

"I'm no sage, but I'll share with you any wisdom I've managed to accumulate over my many years."

"For the moment, I'll ignore your subtle reminder about the difference in our ages. The plain truth is that we're very much afraid that Jordyn is involved in Prescott's death in some way."

"Twinstinct?"

Siara shook her head. "She's shutting me out, and that worries me all the more."

Uneasiness prickled through Connor. "How involved do you think she is?"

"I think..." Siara took a deep breath. "I think the very worst...that she may have killed him. Not intentionally, of course, but she was furious with him...because of me...and she has a proven track record for vindictiveness. So far as we know, she was the last one in the office with him."

Connor pushed away from the table and paced around the room. "This is all speculation, of course? Has there been anything in the papers to fuel your suspicions?"

"Dari and I have made ourselves read every single word that's been written about Prescott's death, but the reporters don't seem to know any more than we do. What should we do, Connor?"

He returned to his seat and recaptured her hand. "You girls have laid a heavy one on me this time. I've been so engrossed in the miracle of our new relationship that I never once considered any connection between the murder and us. My deepest concern was that you continued to grieve over a lost love."

"And now you know that's not true."

Because she was so breathtakingly beautiful, his restraint melted alarmingly. Tenderly he guided her from her chair onto his lap.

"I think that until we have some definite proof...or until Jordyn confides in us...we should give her the benefit of the doubt," he said, nuzzling her neck. "We owe her that much."

"You're right...of course..." Siara's voice weakened as he continued to brush his lips against her neck. "I have felt exceedingly disloyal because of my suspicions..."

"Let me ponder our problem for a while, my love. Later. Right now something else is occupying all my attention..."

"Is making that damn baby the only thing you think about?" Jayme growled, throwing her clothes into her suitcase.

"But, Jae..." Harlan trailed after her as she stalked around her hotel room. "You said you'd do it. So let's get started. We done wasted two weeks."

"I said I'd do it, and I will. But not NOW. I have too many other things on my mind. You said you wanted a boy. If a woman gets pregnant when she's worried about something, there's a ninety percent chance the baby will be a girl. If we're going to do this thing, we should do it right, don't you think?" *Geez, if he buys that excuse, he's dumber than even I thought.*

"Sorry, Jae. I don't know about women things."

For Pete's sake... "Well...I've been reading a lot on baby making. When the time is right, I'll let you know."

"Will you be getting' over bein' worried soon?"

"Not if you don't stop bugging me." She shot her red pumps across the room, into the suitcase.

"Jim ain't sick, is he?"

"He's fine. He's great. He's ecstatic. The paper is sold, and he's happy with the new owner. And he can finally think about retirement with a clear conscience because the new owner will take over as editor, too. So why are you bothering me with more questions?"

She stuffed more clothes into the suitcase without folding them.

"'Cause you're actin' weird, and you're in such a hurry to get outta here. You ain't even ridin' on the plane home with us guys. How come you ain't?"

"I'm taking an earlier flight. Since when are my worries any of your business?"

"Aw, Jae, don't be such a rag. I worry about you when you're actin' weird."

As always, any expression of concern from him surprised her and dissolved her protective coating.

"I'm sorry I snapped at you, Sport. Don't worry about me. I have a few personal matters to tend to at home, and then I'll be fine."

"Good. I don't want anything screwin' up the kid."

Jayme shrieked and threw a sneaker at him.

He dodged it easily. "Why'd you go do that for?"

"I was aiming for the suitcase."

"The suitcase was behind you."

"No wonder I missed." She dumped the last of the toiletries into the bag and forced it closed. "So, I guess your charming wife is all excited about the baby?"

"I guess so."

"You GUESS so? This whole thing was her idea."

"She's been real busy with some business deal she says is gonna make us real rich. That's why she didn't come on this road trip."

"You're already rich, Harlan." *Richer than a boob and a bitch should be.*

"Wallis says we can't never have too much money 'cause I can't play forever. Say...maybe she bought the *Sentinel*..."

"Don't even suggest such a thing!"

"Applewood is my hometown...and she did like workin' on a paper."

"Since when did you get so analytical?"

"Huh?"

"Never mind, Harlan. Let's go. You'll have to carry my bags for me. Heavy lifting makes women sterile."

"Sure, Jae." He dutifully picked up her suitcases.

Good grief, she thought. *This is going to be fun.*

Good grief again. What if he's right about the paper? Daddy never did tell me the name of the new owner...

"I can give you three different programs on the day of the festival." Jordyn paced the living room and paused periodically to peer outside. "Gymnastics... dance...aerobics. Tell me what you want and when, and I'll have it ready."

Darica quietly continued scribbling her festival notes as Jordyn rambled and paced. With Siara at Connor's for the evening and Jayme on her way home from Houston, Darica felt a keen sense of responsibility for Jordyn tonight.

"Shouldn't Jae be home by now?" Jordyn asked in the midst of her festival brainstorming.

"It's only eight-thirty. She said around midnight."

"It FEELS like midnight. I wonder what Sari and Connor are up to?"

"Should we call them?"

"Good Lord, no. They've been slow enough getting past the goo-goo eyes phase." Jordyn peeked around the drapes again. "I don't want to interrupt if Connor finally worked up the nerve to make his mo—oh, God, no! No!"

Darica set aside her pad and pen. She had never seen Jordyn look so scared. "What's wrong, Jyn?"

"A cop car just pulled into the driveway."

CHAPTER FOUR

From the hall closet, Jordyn grabbed a cardigan, which she yanked on over her tight tee shirt and buttoned all the way up to her neck. Finding a Kleenex in the pocket of the sweater, she used it to wipe off as much make-up and lipstick as she could before the doorbell rang.

"Follow my lead, Dari," she whispered to the white-faced girl, "and be your usual shy and speechless self."

Taking a deep breath for courage and composing her face into the reserved expression of her sister, Jordyn opened the front door to a visibly uneasy policeman: Travers Warren, whom Jordyn had dated when she was in college. Would Siara know him, too? Probably not. Jordyn met him when he broke up a rowdy party she was attending.

"Miss Nealy?" he asked.

"Yes?" *Please, God, don't let him recognize which Miss Nealy I am.*

"SIARA Nealy?"

"Yes." Jordyn stifled a sigh of relief. *If he wants to haul Siara off to jail, he'll get me instead.*

Darica watched the scene silently. *She thinks he's come for her, so she's pretending to be Sari while Sari is safe with Connor.*

"I'm Detective Travers Warren." He peered around her into the house as he flashed his badge. "Is Jordyn home?"

"No, she isn't."

He looked disappointed. "Is she...on a date?"

"As a matter of fact, she is. She didn't make two dates for the same night again, did she?"

"No...I'm here on business...but I hoped that...I mean I thought that...maybe Jordyn would be here. We...dated once."

"She'll be sorry she missed you." *Get on with it, dickhead. Maybe the best defense is a good offense. As I remember, he's not much of a self-starter.* "You said you're here on business. You must be investigating Prescott's death."

He was pitifully relieved that she provided him with such a gracious opening. "I do have some questions I have to ask."

"Of course. Please come in."

Jordyn stood aside to let him enter the house. After introducing him to Darica, she motioned that he should seat himself beside her on the sofa as Darica tried to shrink out of sight in a corner chair while remaining close and attentive enough to help if needed.

"I've been expecting you," Jordyn continued, "but I'm afraid I won't be much help."

"You were...uh...romantically involved with the doctor for a while?" he asked carefully. The twins were well known in Applewood, and this one was the quiet, studious one. The librarian. Obviously no sex killer, and he didn't want to offend her with anything too untactful.

"Yes, we dated for a while." *He* must *know SOMETHING. Steady, Jyn. Remember...you're not supposed to know any details that haven't been in the paper...*

"We traced you...and a few other women, to be frank...through inscribed jewelry and cards we found at the doctor's house."

That fucking watch! "Jewelry? Cards? Women? Oh my..."

"I'm sorry if I have given you unhappy news."

"I knew there were other women, but you make it sound like multitudes."

"That depends on your definition of 'multitudes.' The old guy did get around. May I ask how involved you and he were?"

"Well..." She lowered her eyes in a semblance of shyness. *Don't get efficient on me now, Travers. What was inscribed on that damn watch? Knowing Sari, it was something mushy. How little involvement can I get by with confessing to?* "I was...quite infatuated with him at one time."

"When was the last time you saw him?"

"Hmm, let me think..." *When was the last time they were out in public? Thank God that scumbag seldom took her anywhere but to the bushes...unless I count the Red Dog...and anyone frequenting that place won't be too helpful to the law.* "I guess that would have been two...three months ago for dinner."

"And you saw him no more after that?"

Does he know about later meetings? "Not socially. I ran into him a few times quite by chance. Applewood is such a small town."

"May I ask why you broke off your relationship with him?"

"I discovered that my infatuation wasn't as deep as I thought it was. He had other women, and by then I was becoming involved with someone else myself." *Please, God, don't let him ask me who. Then he'll call on Connor and find Siara there.*

"Dr. Sanderson from the university?"

I'll get you for this, God. "Why, yes. How did you know?"

"I read in the paper that you wrote a book together, and then I saw you with him last week in the grocery store."

"Oh my..." Jordyn lowered her eyes since she couldn't force a blush. "Were we that obvious?"

"Obvious enough," he grinned. "I confess to overhearing your conversation about squeezing melons."

"Oh my!" *Go, Connor, go!* "Please forget you heard it?"

"Only if you'll forget that I heard it."

"You're very kind. Thank you."

"Thank you for being so cooperative. I have only one more question…the ol' where were you on the afternoon of June 14?"

"At the library…and then I met Jordyn and our other roommate, Jayme, in town before coming back here for a special dinner Dari was fixing. Jae isn't home many evenings during the summer, and we like to do something special when she is. Right, Dari?"

Dari swallowed a few times before she had the strength to respond verbally though she was nodding like a bobblehead doll. "Yes. Right."

"Prescott's death was our primary topic of conversation at dinner that night is why I remember it so well. News travels so quickly in this town, especially bad news." Jordyn decided to do some probing of her own then. "We've been very curious about the murder. The papers haven't been very helpful."

"We can't release a lot of the information at this time. I can tell you, though, that I have met many people who didn't like him much."

"Poor Prescott. I feel so incredibly sorry for him even though he was a stereotypical cad."

As she wiped away an invisible tear, Travers seemed surprisingly sympathetic. "I apologize for upsetting you with this grisly business."

"You're just doing your job."

"If it helps any for you to know, he suffered no pain. He was unconscious when…when…well, to spare you indelicate details, I'll simplify the scenario and say that he was unconscious when the fire killed him."

"Fire? Isn't that arson rather than homicide?"

"Not when a death is involved." He debated with himself about how much he could ethically reveal to this young lady whom he wanted to impress simply because she was Jordyn's sister. "We're working on an assumption that the murderer thought he had killed the doctor and then tried to cover everything up with the fire. Is your friend all right?"

Darica was bent forward, with her face buried in her hands.

Poor thing, Jordyn thought. *She's too gentle-natured to be hearing all this.*

Rocking herself in the chair, Darica managed…with great effort…to nod.

"All this gruesomeness is affecting her," Jordyn said. "My parents died in a fire, and I've confided in Dari so often, she really takes things like this to heart."

"I've upset you both now. I really am sorry."

"We understand. It's unpleasant, of course, but we do want you to find the murderer." *Unless it's Siara.*

"I never thought I'd get an opportunity like this in Applewood. I'm not exactly Mike Hammer. To tell you the truth, the only reason I was promoted to detective is that no one else really wanted such a dead-end job. I've mostly continued with patrolman's duties. I'm getting some help from the state boys and DCI, but they're really more interested in Chicago and East St. Louis."

Thank you, God! I owe you! "I'm sure you're doing an outstanding job, but your modesty is refreshingly sweet…Travers."

"Thank you…Siara." Locking his fingers together, he studied the ceiling. "Actually, I do have one more question for you."

Oh, God… "Yes?"

"Is Jordyn still seeing that farmer?"
Jordyn started breathing again. "They have discussed marriage."
"It was bound to happen. Even to Jordyn."

"You never know with Jordyn. Even if she becomes engaged, you might be able to talk her into a good time or two. Call her sometime." *And I can pump you for information.*

"I might do that. Thanks. You'll tell Jordyn I was asking about her?"
"Of course."

Well pleased with the results of her performance, Jordyn escorted him to the door. She stood in the doorway until his car backed out of the driveway.

"We pulled that off rather well, didn't we, Dari?" she said, shrugging out of the cardigan. "Dari? Darica?"

Darica wasn't in the living room anymore.

Poor Dari. She probably collapsed in her room with her Bible as soon as Travers left. Tonight had to be a major drain on her delicate nature.

Her satisfaction with the evening's events faded then as she remembered one other complication that she must deal with immediately.

Travers did not suspect them, and he must be given no other reason to suspect them.

Quickly she punched Luke's number.

Good! I woke him up, she thought when she heard his groggy voice.

"Let's get this over with, Farm Boy," she said. "I'm accepting your proposal, and you're keeping your fucking mouth shut about Siara."

"It's not that simple, sweetheart."

"You haven't spoken to the cops already!"

"No, but I haven't been particularly pleased by your hanging up on me and slamming doors in my face."

"A momentary lapse in etiquette. You've won. You're getting what you want, so be a gracious winner."

"We'll set the date tonight and start making wedding plans tomorrow."

"You sound like you don't trust me."

"I don't."

"I'm hurt."

"Get your calendar out, Jordyn. We're setting the date now."

"If I have to get married, I want a big wedding with Siara, Jae, and Darica as bridesmaids."

"Fine."

"Big weddings take time to plan."

"Pick a date, Jordyn."

"What's today?"

"July 1."

"Oh, too bad. I've always wanted to be a June bride. How about June 30...1985...or later?"

"Nice try, but forget it. We'll get married this year or no deal."

"Okay then...New Year's Eve. We can have one bang-up reception on New Year's Eve."

"That's six months away!"

"It will take that long to plan a big wedding, Luke," she said in her sweetest, most reasonable voice. "Ask your mother. She'll tell you."

"What guarantees do I have that you won't back out if there's a break one way or another in the case?"

"What do you want...a signed contract?"

"That's not such a bad idea."

"Oh, come on..."

"I'll make an appointment with our lawyer this week, and you'll sign a letter of intent."

"He'll think we're crazy."

"He's a local boy, and he knows your reputation. He'll think I'm merely protecting myself from your fickleness."

"You son of a bitch."

"You're going to spoil me with all those sweet endearments."

"My pleasure."

"I'll pick you up for dinner tomorrow night."

"What makes you so goddamn sure I'll have dinner with you?"

"You are now my fiancée, and we have plans to make. So be ready at seven...or else."

"Fuck you, Farm Boy!"

"If you're a real good girl, maybe after dinner," he said, hanging up on her before she could hang up on him.

Upstairs, in her rocking chair, Darica was curled around her Bible.

I killed him...I killed him...I killed him...oh, God, this is a cruel trick you played on me this time...

CHAPTER FIVE

"I don't know what to think, Connor," Siara said, watching him arrange a stack of records on his stereo. "For a bride-to-be, she hasn't been overly enthusiastic about wedding plans. Luke's been asking me to remind her that this or that needs tending to, and then I have to nag or beg her to do it."

Vladimir Horowitz's Beethoven sonatas filled the room as Connor joined Siara on the sofa. When she skimmed her fingertips gently over the skin around his ears and neck, he looked at her, slightly panicked.

His constraint continued to bewilder her. She had done everything she could think of…and almost everything Jordyn could think of… to convince him that she was ready for ultimate intimacy with him. And by now he should know that Prescott was out of her system.

However, Connor persisted with his frustrating self-control for a basic human reason: he was afraid of disappointing Siara. And though he was sure he loved her more than any other man had ever loved any other woman, he didn't have THAT much experience with women in general. What if he disappointed her even more than the doctor did? He could lose her forever. She was so vulnerable at this phase of her life, and if he hurt her in any way, however unintentionally, he would never forgive himself.

He preferred the suffering of restraint to the eternal agony of causing Siara pain.

For her part, Siara was desperate enough to ask Jordyn for seduction tips. Now, as she burrowed into Connor's embrace, she was determined to throw aside her own inhibitions to scale the walls of Connor's self-control.

"Jordyn has always been militantly opposed to marriage," Connor was saying now, his eyes lighting up with surprise as Siara nibbled a trail along his neck. "She is merely compensating for accepting the proposal by acting indifferent to wedding plans."

Siara nuzzled and kissed around the collar of his shirt. "Do you really think that's all it is?"

"Of course." Connor cleared his throat. "You…you're not still…truly worried…that she's a…a murderess…are you?"

She unbuttoned the top three buttons of his shirt. "Since that police detective's visit, nothing catastrophic has happened…even if she did pretend to be me. Actually, Dari's the one who's been acting peculiarly. If she's not working, she's at the church till all hours. We see her less than we do Jae, and when Dari is home, she just stares into space and says nothing unless we ask her something."

"The f-festival is monopolizing her every waking m-moment…" As Siara slipped her hand inside his shirt, he grasped her exploring fingers. "May I ask just what you think you're doing?"

She kissed him sweetly. "I'm seducing you, Connor."

"Siara...Stacks...we can't...we shouldn't..."

Siara's bravado evaporated. "Am I so bad at seduction...or do you just not want me like that?"

"Want you! Given the choice between air to breathe and making love to you, I'd choose you without a moment's hesitation."

"Then why are you stopping me?"

"I love you too much."

"Now I'm REALLY confused."

"I'm not sure even I can explain it." He pressed her hand against his chest. "You're very young, Siara."

"I'll be twenty-seven in a couple of weeks. How old do you want me to be?"

"You're an outstandingly beautiful woman..."

"And you're outstandingly handsome."

"For an old man, you mean."

"Is our age difference a problem for you?"

"Indirectly perhaps." Gently he disentangled her fingers from the hair on his chest. "You could have any man in the world, Stacks...men far richer...far better looking...and built better than I am..."

"Do any of these men love me more than you do?" she asked softly.

"That would be impossible. My love for you is as omnipotent and infinite as all the love beating within the heart of God."

"Then there is no problem here, Connor. I love you in equal measures, and I want you to make love to me now..."

Overcome with emotion, he pressed his face against her softness. "I had such noble intentions," he groaned as he laid her back on the sofa. The swell of her full breasts beneath him unleashed his passions, and she whispered her surrender and her love.

He undressed them both, and the night became their paradise as they explored each other totally, deeply, body within body, soul within soul. She was sweetness in the dark to him, and to her he was a dream bursting into reality.

Never in her life had Siara experienced anything so powerfully exquisite, and she was crying and gasping and whimpering from the sheer joy that Connor was sending throughout her body. She felt as if she was on the brink of something truly wonderful...as though she could jump off the edge of a cliff and fly right into Heaven.

His very soul seemed to be moving deeper and deeper into her, and it was impossible to tell where he ended and she began. From somewhere within her, a seed of ecstasy began to grow, filling her with a joy more intense than anything she had ever imagined was possible. She was intrigued by it...and puzzled...and then the seed burst into full bloom and shook her with waves of the purest pleasure ever experienced by mortal woman.

She cried out Connor's name just as he was calling hers, and they rode the rapturous waves together. They seemed to be melting together. There was nothing else in the world but Connor and Siara and this magical blending of body and soul. She could feel the hot stream of his semen spurting into her for the longest time as her body sucked at his manhood, pulling it deeper and deeper into her. It was like he was pouring all his love, all his soul into her. She wrapped her legs around his, wanting to hold him there forever. Both of them were helplessly exhausted despite the waves of energy rippling through them…fusing them together into one blazing light of infinite love as from his stereo *Moonlight Sonata* serenaded the perfection of their union.

Jayme paid the motel clerk and wrapped her fingers reverently around the key that was handed to her.

The Key. To the motel room she was sharing with Harlan this very night. The Key to their future?

So what if she had to pay for the room herself? The alternative…Harlan's grand idea, of course… was to "get down to it" at his stylishly ostentatious house in Ladue. Wallis's presence in the house mattered little to him.

At least he had taken a shower before leaving the park. Sometimes he didn't if he thought he'd miss the Three Stooges on cable.

However, tonight Jayme had specifically ordered that he take special care of his hygiene while she finished her story on the game. Of course, he failed to place any romantic importance on this particular night, but Jayme planned to change his mind.

Some secret part of her had hoped that he might acknowledge this special evening with flowers, or even a card. However, the best she got was his yawned utterance, "Let's get this over with so's I can get home to bed. I'm tired, and you already made me miss the Stooges."

At least HE had been able to be home between the road trip and tonight's game. That morning, Jayme had gone right from the plane to her office, then to the game.

And now to the motel.

Although her roommates understood, her father had been less than pleased. Of course, she hadn't told him the REAL reason why she was staying over in St. Louis. She simply told him she was too tired to make the long drive home. Still, he had been uncharacteristically perturbed that she wouldn't be in Applewood tonight, however late her arrival would have been.

She tried not to think about displeasing her father for whatever reason she had displeased him. Tonight her lifelong dream would be realized. Tonight would be full of magic, romance, and love.

Sure…Harlan intended to leave for home as soon as his duty was performed. However, Jayme planned to dazzle him with love so brilliant and satisfying that he would forget about returning to his bitch-wife.

For tonight anyway.

Jayme didn't expect a miracle. One night at a time was more realistic.

In preparation for this night, she had bought an ultra-sheer black negligee…to make a memorable first impression.

And then…

Harlan had never been too lonely for female company. Was his personality magically transformed when he was in bed with a woman? Tonight would he whisper gentle, loving compliments and endearments to her to ease her nervousness?

For she was, indeed, exceedingly nervous.

Awkwardly, she had excused herself to change in the bathroom. She took a bath instead of a shower so that she could soak in scented bubble bath. Then, a thorough dusting with scented powder…the too-expensive stuff from Famous Barr…as recommended by Jordyn, the expert counselor in these matters. A carefully light application of make-up…and…

Harlan pounding on the door to tell her to hurry the hell up…he didn't have all night.

Smiling, she fluffed her auburn curls. *But we do have all night, my dimwitted darling,* she thought, shivering with the delicious memory of all the daydreams…all the fantasies she had of Harlan making slow, sweet, body-shaking love to her.

Acquiring enough knowledge on the logistics of lovemaking had taken her a few years of reading and listening to Jordyn's experiences before Jayme knew what to fantasize about. Initially, the face of Rick Girard had a nasty habit of intruding into her finest fantasies…as it still did sometimes in her most unguarded moments.

But now there was only Harlan…

He had left the lights on.

Good. The better to see me with…

But he had also left his clothes on. Mostly. His pants were pushed down around his ankles, and he was already erect.

From anticipation? Not a chance.

From staring at a picture of Wallis in a sheer teddy. He had been stroking himself while staring at it. His wife's suggestion no doubt.

Jayme strangled on a cry of anguish. Somehow she had to salvage this evening, this dream turning into a nightmare.

His eyes raked over her. At least his face showed his approval.

"Lay down," he ordered.

"The bed isn't even turned down."

"So?"

"So don't you think we should turn the bed down. It seems...more polite."

Shrugging, he yanked back the bedspread, blanket, and sheet with one impatient motion.

"Let's do it," he said. Which, Jayme noted, were the exact words he uttered before most ball games.

Trying to arrange herself seductively, she lay down on the bed.

He might as well yell, "Play ball!" Maybe things will improve when we are swept away by towering waves of passion during foreplay.

Another uninvited thought of Rick loomed then as she remembered all the times he had managed to liquefy her vital organs. Since she had not loved Rick as she loved Harlan, surely soon...very soon...Harlan would start doing wonderful things to her eager body.

She realized then that Harlan was shoving her gown up around her hips. Fumbling attempts to undress her? Not a chance. With the speed of a Nolan Ryan fastball, he settled between her legs and propelled himself into her.

Jayme smothered her screams of pain with a pillow as Harlan rammed into her again and again. She tried to push him away, but his thrusts were too strong. Mercifully, he did not take long to finish, and when at last he pulled away from her, she curled into a tight ball and wept as a hot stickiness trickled between her legs.

He belched twice, farted once, and zipped his pants before noticing that she was crying.

"What's the matter with you now?" he asked.

Shaking her head, she sobbed anew and rolled her face into the pillow to hide her humiliation.

"C'mon, Jae. You don't cry if nothin' ain't wrong."

"You...you hurt me..." She shifted so that he could see the bloodstained sheet.

"You mean I'm too big for you to handle?"

"You egotistical jerk! I was a virgin, you idiot, and you ripped me apart!" She rearranged her gown more decorously and turned her back on him.

"Aw, Jae...why didn't you tell me? I would've been more careful."

Though her anger began to fade, she kept her back to him. "Really?"

" 'Course. I ain't no monster."

No, he isn't a monster. He's just a moron. She turned to face him. "It wasn't exactly what I was expecting."

"You should've told me."

"I thought you'd notice on your own."

"I ain't had much 'perience with cherries, not for a long time. I forgot you were too fat to fuck in school. How come you ain't done it since you got skinny?"

The moment of truth. "I was saving myself for you."

"Why would you wanna do that?"

"Because...because..." *Because I love you, you pea-brain. Why can't I say it?* "Because I thought you'd want me to."

"Never thought about it one way or another."

"What do you think about it now that I've told you?"

"I think you should've told me before we fucked. We're buddies. I don't like hurtin' you."

Then why do you do it so often? "That's all you have to say?"

"What else do you want me to say?"

That you love me, you twit! "Is there more to it that this...than what you did to me?"

"To real fuckin', yeah. But we's just makin' a baby. This ain't for fun."

"I see." Jayme picked the gossamer fabric of her gown. "You'd better put a little fun into it, Harlan, or you can forget about the baby-making. It hurts too much this way."

"We can't do that. Wally'll be mad at both of us."

So frigging what? "I'll continue only if you promise to be more gentle. I need some preliminary action."

"Huh?"

"I need more warm-up before the game."

"You mean foolin' around afore the fuckin'?"

"Exactly."

"Wally gets mad if she thinks I'm porkin' anyone but her for fun."

"Those are my terms, Harlan."

"Next time won't hurt you so much."

"The right way or no way, Harlan."

"Okay...okay. Just don't tell Wally. She can make things real bad at home if she's mad at me."

"I have no problem with that. Shall we kiss on it?"

"What for?"

"Never mind, Harlan. Just go."

"Go where?"

"Home. Go home. I want to be alone now."

"You ain't takin' me back to my car?"

"Take a taxi."

"I ain't got no money."

"For a millionaire ball player, you're certainly broke often enough. I should be able to claim you as a dependent on my taxes."

"I don't like axing Wally for extra money. She axs too many questions that make her mad when I answer."

Why don't you admit you married a selfish, greedy, bossy bitch? "Get the cab fare out of my purse. I'm going to soak in a tub of hot water."

"You just took a bath."

"That was before you ripped me apart. I'm rather sore right now."

"Sorry I hurt you, Jae. Really."

Because he did look contrite, Jayme patted his cheek to reassure him.

I carry good sportsmanship to ridiculous degrees, where Harlan is concerned anyway. "Just go, okay? I'll see you tomorrow before the game."

Nodding, he left without another word. A victory of sorts for Jayme, for under normal circumstances, he would have expected her to drive him to his car whether she was hurting or not.

Progress, she wondered, *or grasping at straws?*

She filled the bathtub with hot water and eased herself into the soothing steam.

In the next room, the motel radio blared out the major events of the day on the Top-of-the-Hour Network News. Mondale. Ferraro. Reagan and Bush. The Summer Olympics in Los Angeles. A follow-up on the McDonald's massacre in San Ysidro, California.

A woman from a major political party was running for Vice-President.

Nations were waging athletic wars on Olympic fields.

Children were being gunned down over their Big Macs.

And my top story of the day is a disastrous, disappointing romp with a dimwit. I'm nuts. I am terminally and inexorably nuts.

The radio seemed to agree with this introspective revelation.

The first song after Top-of-the-Hour Network News on this More-Music-Less-Talk station was by Alan Parsons Project: "Old and Wise."

My own personal dirge, she thought, sinking lower into the steam. *I'm nuts. I am terminally and inexorably nuts.*

* * *

Luke parked his truck at the edge of the cornfield. Drumming his fingers on the steering wheel, he waited for Jordyn to say something…ANYTHING. Even her sarcasm or anger was preferable to her silences. Since she had accepted his marriage proposal, she'd had very little to say to him although she denied him neither her company nor her body. After all, appearances had to be maintained.

No one in Applewood must suspect that she was marrying him for any reason other than the usual one. Since she placed no meaningful value on sex, Luke couldn't claim a victory in their physical relationship either.

He knew he was getting just what he deserved. Blackmailing her into marriage was despicable. Using Siara to bait his threat was beyond despicable. When he had first considered the possibility of the arrangement, he rationalized that Jordyn would quickly forgive his treachery, for he intended to show her that being engaged to him wasn't such a bad deal. He had plied her with roses, expensive dinners, theater tickets, and an engagement ring that exceeded his common sense.

Yet the silences continued.

Finally she had agreed to tour his farm, her home after they were married, but she would only "stop by" on her way to the studio this morning. Even though Luke knew she wanted a handy excuse to escape, he hoped that her attitude toward him was softening. However, she had said scarcely a word throughout the entire circuit, and he worried that she would be miserable on the farm and that their marriage was doomed before it even took place.

The alternative was to withdraw his threat. He could never turn Siara in anyway, for he truly liked and respected his future sister-in-law. The idea of her harming anyone was so ludicrous that Luke felt perfectly justified in not informing authorities about what he knew and had seen.

Nevertheless, Luke wanted Jordyn for his wife, and he had long ago wearied of waiting patiently for her to change her mind about marriage.

Now she was understandably outraged, but maybe...eventually...Luke could make her happy enough that she would forgive him.

I'll never forgive him for this. Never.

Jordyn's eyes swept over the neat rows of corn, brilliantly green in the morning sunshine. His spread was grander than she had expected; still, the thought of being imprisoned on a farm galled her. *If he thinks I'm giving up my studio, he's dumber than Harlan Oakes. He's damn lucky I agreed to marry him...*

Jordyn rubbed her hand across her belly. Nausea again.

Now here was this new consideration. Somewhere along the way, she'd gotten careless. Though she had no official verification yet, she knew what the problem was.

And she would rip out her tongue before she told Luke. He would be disgustingly happy to know that his fiancée was pregnant with his child.

"How dutiful of you to fit me into your busy schedule," Jim McCray grinned as Jayme leaned over his desk to kiss his cheek.

"I'm a busy paper person, Daddykins. You of all people should be more understanding."

"I've been wanting to introduce you to the new owner. You'll be surprised...pleasantly I hope. He's joining us for lunch. Will you go tell him we're almost ready to go, love? He's made a temporary office out of the old paste-up room."

"I'm to introduce myself?"

"You're a paper person. You can handle it."

Jayme gingerly walked down the long hallway to the old paste-up room. She was sorer today than she had been the night before.

"Come on in," a voice responded to her knock.

Jayme opened the door. The *Sentinel's* new owner and future editor sat at a scarred wooden desk.

"Hello, Kit..."

Rick Girard.

CHAPTER SIX

Jordyn poured a diet soda into a glass of ice for her sister and then, after a moment's consideration, poured milk for herself.

"How long has it been since we've been home alone like this?" Siara asked, opening a package of Oreos.

"More months than I can remember." Jordyn debated with herself on the advisability of snacking on an apple rather than on cookies, but the Oreos won easily. Milk was hard enough to choke down plain.

"Your...date with that police detective was over in record time."

Jordyn shrugged. "He gave me what I wanted early in the evening. Why waste more time on him?"

"Why waste any time on him? You're engaged."

"Luke's engaged. I'm merely getting married."

Jordyn stared at Siara over the rim of her glass. With Darica still at church and Jayme in St. Louis, now was the perfect time to encourage sisterly confidences, but Jordyn could think of no tactful way to ask, "Did you kill the old fart or not?" Instead she settled for the safer subject of Connor.

"So how long will your honey be out of town?"

"Until the weekend, but it seems like forever." Siara's face clouded. "I know I'm being irrational, but I worry about another fire. First Mama and Daddy...then Prescott. What if there's another fire, and Connor's in it—"

Jordyn interrupted before Siara's fears reached overdrive. "Connor will return to you safe and sound, so don't worry. Even a nuclear conflagration couldn't keep him away from you now. You two should be the ones getting married, not Farm Boy and me."

"Why did you agree to marry Luke if you really don't want to?"

"He made me an offer I couldn't refuse."

"He promised you money? Or real estate?"

"Services rendered. Don't worry about my marital arrangement either, Baby. If I have to be married, I could do a lot worse than my farm boy...and don't you be telling him I said that."

Siara was relieved, not so much because of what Jordyn said, but because of the softening of her voice as she spoke. No twinstinct was necessary to verify Connor's theory: Jordyn was not so opposed to her forthcoming marriage as she wanted everyone, especially Luke, to believe.

"You mentioned Prescott and the fire," Jordyn was saying casually as she stuffed an Oreo wholly into her mouth. Chewing the cookie gave her a few minutes to plan her strategy. "It's common knowledge by now that the fire killed him..."

The panic that flashed in Siara's eyes sent an icicle of fear through Jordyn's heart.

She did it, and now she knows I know, Jordyn thought. *I must let her know I'll protect her and her secret until the day I die...*

She did it, and now she's going to confess to me, Siara was thinking. *I must assure her that I'll protect her and her secret until my dying breath...*

"I understand that the fire destroyed a lot of evidence," Siara said carefully. "The newspaper has reported no progress in the investigation."

"Travers is pretty depressed about the whole thing," Jordyn said around the cookie in her mouth. "He knows he and his colleagues in this town aren't equipped to handle anything beyond traffic violations, wild college parties, and an occasional prowler."

"I once read that if a murder isn't solved in the first couple of weeks, the...the perpetrator is usually never apprehended."

Jordyn nodded. "So says Travers the Dick."

"You went out with him only to question him subtly about...about Prescott's demise, didn't you?"

"If you hadn't been shutting out my twinstinct, you would know that already."

"I was shutting YOU out?" Siara bumped her glass down on the table. "YOU have been shutting ME out. I've been so worried about it that Connor has been urging me for weeks to have a candid conversation with you."

"So why didn't you?"

"Because...because I was afraid of what you might tell me."

"Likewise. So you didn't roast the pig?"

"Of course not."

"Me either." Jordyn rammed her hand into the Oreos bag and withdrew a fistful of cookies. "Down deep I knew you couldn't bump the bastard off, but it's a relief to know for sure."

"Since down deep I thought you could bump the bastard off, you can appreciate how relieved I am. No more secrets?"

"No more secrets."

Siara squeezed her sister's hand. "I'm so glad we had tonight together like this. But since I didn't kill Prescott, and you didn't kill Prescott, who did?"

Jordyn crammed two Oreos into her mouth. "Since we didn't do it, and we can safely rule out Jae and Dari, that leaves only a trillion or so other women and probably a few men who wanted the fucker fried."

Siara stared at the crumbs spewing from her sister's mouth. "Good grief, Jyn! You've eaten enough cookies for two people...and not in a mannerly way, I might add."

"Which brings us to another secret..."

Before she could share this newer suspicion, however, Darica trudged through the kitchen on her way upstairs. Her head drooped sadly as she plodded by the twins without speaking. Only her forlorn nod gave any indication that she was even aware of their presence.

Siara pressed her hands against her cheeks. "This festival is too much for her, Jyn. She's been like a zombie for days."

"She refuses all offers of help, so she must be enjoying it even if it's killing her."

"Like you and your studio?"

"In the early days. I can hire people to do the boring work now, which leaves time for more creative projects...like...well...how do you feel about being an—"

The phone rang then, and Siara leaped up squealing, "Connor! That's Connor!"

"—aunt?" Jordyn finished, but Siara was already bubbling into the living room phone.

Shrugging, Jordyn pounded on the Oreo bag a few times, then dumped cookie crumbs and pieces directly into her mouth.

For all its opulent dimensions aglitter with crystal, silver, and gold, The Chalet exuded a comfortable coziness that settled around the old friends as they sipped after-dinner coffee. Tonight was their first opportunity for an uninterrupted private conversation since Jayme discovered who had bought the *Sentinel*.

Rick Girard had finally succeeded in arranging a date with Jayme...in St. Louis after an afternoon game...when Harlan expected her to spend more time with him in a motel room, breeding...or attempting to breed. She could not dignify their still-painful, still-disappointing interludes as lovemaking.

Although Harlan was more careful about her comfort, nothing he did aroused in her all those divine feelings she had so eagerly anticipated. Lacking experience in these matters, she was unable to isolate the source of the problem though she willingly accepted the failure as hers. To think that Harlan Oakes was a lousy lover was blasphemous.

Nevertheless, Jayme began to seek excuses to avoid his company, and Rick's invitation was a perfect opportunity for a night away from Harlan.

If she were to be completely honest with herself, she would admit that she had not experienced such a totally pleasurable evening since the last cozy evening she spent with Rick.

There had been changes, of course. He had become a practicing member of the very institution he once scorned, a common societal phenomenon among many of the 'Sixties anti-establishment crusaders. He was gentler now, less inclined to sarcasm though he retained his quick wit and ready humor.

When Jayme last saw him in college, he had shaved his beard and cut his hair before leaving for the Army, and he now maintained this neatly groomed appearance. The tattered blue jeans and tee shirts had been replaced by expensive and expertly tailored three-piece suits that he wore with the same casual indifference.

Around his eyes deep lines bespoke the suffering he had endured in Vietnam and since, yet there was no bitterness in his voice as he told Jayme, briefly, of his life since they parted company at Scheffers fourteen years before.

He had been wounded in both legs by enemy fire and then taken prisoner by the Viet Cong. When he offered few other details about his war experiences, Jayme did not pry. These kinds of confidences could not be forced. She had done enough reading to know that Vietnam veterans were particularly reticent about their personal ordeals, and their reception back home had been so inexplicably and unforgivably hostile that few of them were encouraged to break their silences.

"A buddy of mine summed up the situation perfectly when he said that the doves hated us for fighting, and the hawks hated us for losing," Rick told her.

He was more expansive about what had happened to him since Operation Homecoming in January of 1973.

Because the medical care he received in the POW camp had been negligible, he was fortunate even to be alive, for infection was rampant in the lower parts of both his legs when he was released. In fact, both limbs were so irreparably damaged that doctors immediately amputated them just below his knees.

Jayme's eyes widened at this bit of news. Though he walked painstakingly with a cane, she had never once considered that his affliction was so severe.

"They're doing wonderful things with prostheses these days, and the doctors were very lucky to be able to save my knees. Having knee joints makes the fake legs thing a whole lot easier to handle." He steeled himself for the moment when she averted her eyes from his steady stare as so many did to cover their awkwardness.

Instead, she placed her hand over his and met his eyes fully. "I'm sorry. I didn't know. You're managing very well, and I know how hard you must have worked to become so...so adept."

He brushed a stray curl away from her face. "I'm adept at many things. I hope you remember."

This time she did lower her eyes, and he laughed, but not unkindly.

"My sweet Kitten..." He raised her hand to his lips. "I must admit to you, however, that I was not a good patient in the early going. I put Mom and Dad through some real hell for a long time..."

He had been sullen and withdrawn for many weeks after the double amputation, refusing to cooperate with prescribed physical and mental rehabilitation, embarrassing his parents when they attempted to reacquaint him with Chicago society, rebelling again against establishment standards by letting his hair and beard grow and wearing only his oldest, rattiest clothes...

The announced engagement had been the contrivance of Tawney and his parents. Tawney wanted access to the Girard checkbook even if a legless husband was part of the deal. His parents were desperate for ANYTHING that would inspire him to fight against his decline. What better therapy than the comfort and stability of marriage?

When Rick had neither agreed nor disagreed with them, they proceeded with wedding plans. For all their diligence, however, they overlooked one critical detail: Rick's attendance at the ceremony.

He simply disappeared on the eve of his wedding.

Since his return home, he had resumed the marijuana habit acquired in Vietnam, and he paid his supplier a hundred dollars to help him escape.

A week later, Rick's father paid the supplier a thousand dollars to bring Rick home.

Rick was too stoned and drunk even to realize he was home again. Terrified of what their son had become, the Girards admitted him first to a private medical hospital, then to an equally private mental health clinic.

For two more years he fought the doctors, the counselors, his sisters, and his parents at every turn. His progress was negligible, if that. In fact, each rebellious antic jerked him further from recovery.

The breakthrough came when his mother, exhausted from nearly three years of coping with this stranger who was her son, collapsed in tears before him. Not the genteel weeping of society-minded matrons, but the body-racking sobbing of a mother losing her only son. Her unrestrained grief rekindled a spark of humanity in his soul.

That evening he roused enough interest in the outside world to sort through a box of letters, magazines, and newspapers left in his room. His family had kept him supplied with current periodicals although he never read them. And the letters had remained unopened...letters from Najib mostly, though none that were too current. When Rick had not replied, Najib eventually stopped writing.

"It's regrettably too easy to lose touch with people you care about," Rick said, caressing her fingers, "especially when the distance between you is so great."

Jayme blushed, knowing that the distance he spoke of was not necessarily measured by miles or kilometers.

"How is Najib?" she asked to divert his attention from the warmth his touch brought to her body. "I'm ashamed to admit that our correspondence dwindled to nothing, chiefly because of my own neglect."

"Still worried about his country, but hopeful enough to repopulate it. He's been married these past eight years and has two sons and a daughter."

"Then you write to him regularly now?"

"We write, yes, but not so regularly. Mail in and out of Lebanon is chancy, at best."

"I'm glad he's doing well. I'm glad YOU'RE doing well..."

"The thanks go entirely to my family. They never gave up on me. My mental recovery, when I wanted to recover, was more arduous than physical therapy. I had to remain at the clinic for another year full-time, then part-time for retreats for the next two years. That's a lot of wasted years I can never regain and never return to my family. I went to work for Dad, at first to repay some of that major debt, but before I knew it, I was metamorphosing into a clone of my old man...and not unwillingly. For all his pomp and circumstance, he does a lot of good in a lot of places...and he's a damn fine newspaperman."

"Shari and Heather...how are they?"

"Married and both pregnant. Are you going to ask me about the weather in Chicago now?"

"Why would I care about the weather in Chicago?"

"As a diversionary tactic to prevent my confessing to you the real reason why I'm back in Applewood."

Jayme studied the design woven into the tablecloth. "The p-paper isn't the real reason?" *Am I quick with the witty repartee or what?*

"Working for Dad gave me lots of opportunities for discovering what's been going on in your life. I've read nearly every published word you've written. You're a very good sports writer, Kit, but your best work was the writing you did for the POWs and MIAs."

"I'll thank you for the compliment if you promise me this isn't going to develop into a lecture on my choice of genre."

"No lectures...merely an observation. Why didn't you call any of the times you were in Chicago?"

"I thought you were married. Gwynnie never gave me the update that you weren't."

"She probably didn't know. We've already established how old friends can lose touch, and when I plunged out of society, I pretty well dragged my folks with me."

"You're brutally honest with yourself."

"Part of the therapy. And part of the reason why I'm here. Would you have called me if you had known I wasn't married?"

Offense, girl. Offense. "You could have called me."

"I was waiting to see what was happening with you and that ball player. When it looked like ol' Hobart was going to stay married this time...and then the *Sentinel* came up for sale...well...I could wait forever for another set of events so perfectly suited for reintroducing myself into your life. Of course, money was no object. Big bucks can be very useful sometimes, and I now respectfully yield to their influence. So here I am. My question now that I've bared my soul and intentions to you is what are you going to do about it?"

Jayme gulped her coffee, scalding her tongue in the process. "D-Do? Me? I…"

Rick's fingertip traced tiny circles on her wrist. "Once upon a time you and I wasted a whole lot of time playing games with each others' minds and hearts…and bodies, too, for that matter. I don't intend to make the same mistakes again. I'm going to be unfashionably honest with you, and I expect the same from you."

"We never lied to each other…did we?"

"More to ourselves I guess. But we concealed a lot of honest emotion from each other. One thing I learned in therapy is the value of laying everything out in the open. Psychiatrists are very big on naked souls."

"Is it only my soul that you want naked?" *For Pete's sake, what am I saying? I've been around Jordyn too long.*

Rick grinned. "Of course not, but I'm willing to be patient. Therapy also taught me not to expect overnight miracles. All I'm asking now is an honest assessment of where you stand with Hobart and where I might stand with you."

"Harlan's married, VERY married."

"That doesn't answer my question. Do you still have a thing for him, as the saying goes?"

"I'm embarrassed to tell you what that thing is right now."

"We're laying everything out in the open now, remember? Tell me."

"Well…" Jayme studied the napkin in her lap as she told him briefly of the status of her relationship with Harlan.

Rick rubbed a hand over his face. "I really can't say that I'm surprised by this, but you'll understand if I think you're totally brainsick where Hobart is concerned."

"Many people have told me the same thing, and these days I'm agreeing with them."

"A glimmer of hope," he grinned, lifting her hand to his lips again. "I expect the *Sentinel* to turn a respectable profit, but you realize I could make more…and easier money back in Chicago. You're the reason why I'm back in Applewood."

"I don't understand why…though I thank you for the sentiment…"

He signaled to the waiter to bring them more coffee. "I was unfair to you when I accused you of being a prick tease and using me for practice. If I'd been more of a man then, I would have looked around my bruised ego and realized that you weren't experienced enough with men off the baseball field to do all the things I accused you of."

"I wasn't exactly fair to you either, so we're even. Sometimes a person gets so wrapped up in a dream, she can't appreciate reality."

"Instead of driving you away with my jealous anger, I should have moved heaven and earth to prove that very thing to you." He waited until the waiter had served them fresh coffee before he continued. "You were very special to me once, Kit. You still are, and I'm not satisfied to live on the memory of what we had if there's any chance for us to make even better memories with each other in the future."

"Fourteen years is a long time. People change. We're different people, you and I. It's unrealistic to think that we can pick up on a good memory and continue as if those fourteen years never happened."

"Don't you think that I more than most am aware of those fourteen years? It's because we are different people that I'm hoping that a relationship between you and me will work this time. This isn't something I've decided overnight. I've been thinking about it a long time...and, I'll admit through a lot of women."

"I'd rather not hear about your other women, please," Jayme said, surprised by a twinge of jealousy.

He was encouraged by her reaction. "Be fair. I heard you out about Hobart."

"Harlan. His name is Harlan."

"Who cares? The point is that I did listen...and I will listen even if what you tell me rips my heart right out of me."

Jayme folded her arms. "Okay, I'm listening. Tell me about your women."

"Don't be like that. It's not like I was trying to be an Olympic-class stud. Maybe at first I was out to prove something, but after a while I wanted something more meaningful. I never found it, though once or twice I tried to talk myself into believing I had. The bottom line was...and is...I had already found what I wanted...who I wanted...many years ago in you."

"Again, I thank you for the sentiment, but I'm not sure I can handle the responsibility."

"Your only responsibility is to yourself. I'm not asking you to run off to the marriage license window with me tonight. I am asking that you give me...give US...a fair chance."

"And Harlan?"

"I'm painfully realistic about him. As long as you want to continue...seeing him in the way that you are seeing him, I won't say a damn thing to dissuade you. However, I would like a fair and equal share of your time and attention. If, at the end of...let's say a month...no, two months because of your road trips...either of us thinks we're wasting our time together, we'll go our separate ways with no hard feelings and still be friends."

"Are you talking about dating or...something more?"

"I've acquired more patience, but if the mood is right...and to keep things fair and equal...we shouldn't deny ourselves the 'something more' you're thinking of...unless..." He studied her face intently. "Tell me truthfully, Jayme...are you repulsed by the thought of intimacy with a double amputee? It's something I've dealt with before."

She was appalled that he would even think such a thing about her. "For Pete's sake, Rick. That's not even close to what I was thinking."

"Then tell me what you are thinking. Are you plain not interested in starting up with me again?"

"No!" She blushed at the forceful certainty of her reply. "I mean...I mean...oh, I don't know exactly what I mean except that I've enjoyed being with you tonight more than I've enjoyed any other evening since we were together in college...and lately I keep remembering how badly I once wanted a Camaro and how disappointed I was when I finally had a chance to test drive one. I'm not making much sense, am I?"

"Quite the contrary. I understand perfectly, and I'm encouraged beyond my wildest hopes," he whispered, cradling her chin within his hand.

Jayme closed her eyes, amazed that this simple gesture filled her with so much joy when an evening in bed with Harlan left her pitifully empty.

"You're taking an awful chance with me," she said finally. "We were close before, and I could never come through at the moment of truth...no matter how much I wanted to."

"A risk I'm willing to face."

"So what do we do now?" she asked nervously.

"You return to the motel room you've booked for tonight, and I'll return to Applewood. I know you have an early flight, but I hereby claim your first day back as my own. Fair enough?"

Smiling, Jayme nodded.

Rick motioned for the check. "Great. Now I'll escort you to your car and collect a good-night kiss or two..."

Jayme couldn't help shivering from the anticipation of feeling his lips against hers again...and his kisses didn't disappoint her.

After a half dozen of them, he opened her car door for her. "You need to go now, Kitten," he said softly, "or I won't be letting you go at all..."

She nodded, not wanting to let HIM go...and surprised by the feeling.

When she was in her car, he leaned down and kissed her one more time. "I love you," he whispered, "and I haven't stopped loving you in these fourteen years."

Then he quickly closed the door before she could say anything...before she had to say anything.

After she fumbled her key into the ignition, she started her car and reluctantly pulled away from him.

By the open window, Darica swayed in her rocking chair as raindrops spattered off the sill to dampen her nightgown.

Can God's tears extinguish the Hell fires that consume me now? she wondered. *He gave me a second chance, and once again I disappointed Him with my sins. Black night. Blacker soul. What to do? What to do? Oh, dear Lord, what shall I do?*

Her fingers crawled across the fine paper of her Bible and enclosed the old, familiar bookmark.

Alvito. Dr. Chadburn. My soul is tormented while theirs have found peace. If Hell can offer peace...

At least they are at their journeys' ends while I struggle through each day with an anguished heart. A seed of evil was planted within me, and I can do nothing to stop its insidious growth.

What to do? What to do? Oh, dear Lord, what shall I do?

Even Hell's peace must be a respite from Hell on earth.

She eyed the stack of papers on the small table she used as a desk. Earthly responsibilities to dispose of before she could grapple to the death with her soul.

CHAPTER SEVEN

Panting, Jordyn lifted herself off Luke's moist, limp body. She liked the afterwards…the afterglow…when they both were sloppy, sleepy wet from sex.

Industrial strength fucking.

Though Farm Boy held onto that ridiculous misnomer: *lovemaking.*

As if she would degrade herself enough to love any man. Especially one who was blackmailing her into marriage.

Jordyn rolled onto her side, her back to Luke as she hugged the edge of the king-size bed. No cuddling afterward, though she knew that was what he wanted.

Of course, there could be certain advantages to her situation.

Farm Boy was an outstanding bed partner. And he was sparing no reasonable expense or effort toward insuring their future happiness, even to the point of setting up this surprisingly elegant, doublewide mobile home for them on his land until they could build a home of their own.

Then there was the little bun in her oven to consider. A doctor in Willow Grove had verified her suspicions: she was definitely pregnant. She and Luke would have a Valentine's baby.

How hysterically ironic! It'll save me the expense of buying my new hubby a Valentine.

However, she wasn't going to tell him about the baby until her condition was so obvious, even Darica could tell what was happening. The blackmailing bastard deserved no special consideration…

When Luke smoothed his hand over the curve of her shoulder, she started.

"I thought you were asleep," she said, curling away from him."

"I don't get a whole lot of sleep lately."

"Guilty conscience, Farm Boy?"

"What about you? Do you really think Siara is mixed up in the doctor's death?"

"I KNOW she isn't."

"So why haven't you called off our engagement?"

"You could still cause us a shitload of trouble by flapping your jaws to the cops."

She heard him sigh, and then he was silent for so long that she thought he had, indeed, fallen asleep. But he startled her again by speaking slowly, softly, in the way of one reluctant, yet determined to rid his conscience of a burden.

"The only excuse I can offer is that I love you too much and want you too much to worry about ethics and principles. Even if I really thought that Siara was involved, I could never make trouble for her…or for you…and I've hated myself more each day for using you both in such an underhanded way. What I'm trying to say is I'm giving you your freedom. You don't have to marry me, and you don't have to worry about my causing you and your sister any trouble."

He was the one to be startled this time, for he fully expected her to gather her clothes and leave his life forever. Instead, she whirled toward him in a furious blaze.

"Isn't this just like you, you goddamn prick, to give me your pretty little speech now! The whole goddamn town knows about our wedding and the big New Year's Eve reception, and you decide to get magnanimous. Well, I'll be damned if I let you embarrass me like that! We'll get married as planned, and that's the way it's going to be whether you and your fucking conscience like it or not!"

Now she did gather her clothes and stomp away, into the bathroom to dress.

Folding his arms behind his head, Luke stretched out on the bed and smiled as he listened to her bang around.

She wants to marry me, he thought happily, *but she'll cut her throat before she admits it to anyone...especially to me...*

* * *

"Go back to your own room now, Harlan." Jayme pushed him with her feet to get him out of bed.

But Harlan burrowed deeply into the bedclothes. "I'm tired, Jae...and Wally flew back to St. Louis for some business thing. Can't I sleep here tonight?"

"No, you cannot sleep here. I prefer to sleep alone tonight." *I can't believe I'm saying this to him...and meaning it.* She kicked at him again. "Go, Harlan. Now. We've finished our business. I need some rest. My body needs some rest."

"You ain't still hurtin' when we do it, are you?"

Pleased by his concern, she tried to simplify her reply for his benefit. "Not hurting exactly...just uncomfortable..."

"Then you ain't doin' somethin' right. And you should be pregnant by now."

Jayme slammed a pillow against his face. "Get out of my room, Harlan. Now!"

"Okay, okay..."

Muttering to himself, he dragged on his clothes, and then, as he buckled his belt, he tried to make peace with her.

"I know you're doin' the best you can. We'll try again tomorrow."

"Like hell we will."

"Huh?"

"Not tomorrow. I plan to have a headache."

"But we gotta."

"We don't 'gotta.' I need time away from you. I haven't had a good night's sleep this whole road trip, and I need a night alone."

"Why?"

"To think."

"You need a whole night for that?"

"I don't expect you to understand anything about thinking, Harlan. In fact, this time I don't understand so much myself."

"They why do you do it?"

"Never mind, Harlan. Just leave, okay? We'll talk tomorrow."

"About what?"

"About us…you and me."

"What's to talk about?"

"Let me ask you something. If I were to tell you that I stand a snowball's chance in Tijuana of getting pregnant right now, would you still want to be with me like this?"

"If you ain't getting' pregnant?"

"If I'm not getting pregnant and probably won't be getting pregnant."

"Why would we wanna do it if you ain't getting' pregnant?"

"Somehow I thought you'd say something like that. There's the door, Harlan. Use it."

"NOW what have I done?"

"Good-bye, Harlan…" Jayme grabbed up her handbag from the floor and fumbled through it for a business card.

He stood there, staring at her for a moment, rather reproachfully…for Harlan anyway. "We've wasted a lot of fuckin' if you ain't getting' pregnant."

"Out, Harlan!"

He left then, muttering…and she resumed the search through her handbag, at last remembering that she had tucked the card safely into her wallet, behind her MasterCard. Thoughtfully she weighed both cards in her hand, staring at them for guidance. Then she picked up the phone and punched 0.

"Hello…I'm making a credit-card call to Applewood, Illinois…Yes, I have the number here…"

She read from information Rick had written for her on the back of one of his business cards.

"Wake up, sugarplum," she said when Rick answered the phone, "it's me…"

"I was just lying here thinking about you."

"And now I'm lying here thinking about you."

"Not exactly how I wanted to spend time in bed with you, but it will do…for now."

"And for later?"

"You tell me."

"I'll be home in a couple of days. I'll tell you then…in person…"

"And Hobart?"

"I just sent Hobart back to his own room…permanently…"

Chapter Eight

With Siara's head just beneath his, Connor peeked around the doorway into Jordyn's office.

"May we buy you lunch, ma'am?" he asked, rubbing his chin against Siara's silky hair.

Smiling, Jordyn stretched and glanced at the empty cookie bag on her desk. "You bet. I'm starved."

She turned her chair so that she could better see them, cuddling on the threshold. "Something tells me this is a special occasion."

"It is, Jordyn! Oh, it is!" Siara posed in the doorway, her left hand pressed conspicuously against the jamb. "Notice anything?"

Yelping, Jordyn catapulted out of her chair. "You're finally engaged!"

"Yes...finally..." Connor blushed as Jordyn planted a loud, sloppy kiss on his cheek and then one on her sister's. "Not nearly soon enough, yet I fear too soon..."

"You're talking like Shakespeare," Siara said, giving her sister a closer look at the ring.

"You, my love, are a euphoriant that would inspire any bard." He sighed as he watched the girls chatter over the ring. "I only wish that my salary were more conducive to a larger diamond."

"But, Connor...sweetheart!" Siara slid her arms around his neck. "This is absolutely the most beautiful ring in the whole world! Oh...no offense, Jyn."

"None taken, Baby. You do have the most beautiful ring in the world, and I have the gaudiest...which suits us both just fine. Have you set a date yet?"

"Well..." Siara studied her shoe tops. "We...I...had an idea about a date...but if you don't like it, please tell us, and we'll understand."

Jordyn was puzzled by her sister's hesitancy. "I can't see that any date is a problem so long as it's after Fall Festival."

"Even if it's YOUR wedding day?"

"Siara very much wants to have a double wedding with you," Connor explained quietly. "But if you have a problem with it, we shall, of course, understand and make other plans."

"I think it's a wonderful idea!" Jordyn said, wrapping an arm around each of them.

"You do?" Siara whispered with relief.

"I do. It will give Applewood society someone else to stare at and take some of the heat off me."

"Maybe we can even wear identical wedding gowns? Since you haven't looked for one yet, we could still do that...couldn't we...oh no..." Siara noticed the strange look on Jordyn's face and was immediately remorseful. "I'm sorry,

Jyn. Of course we don't have to look alike. My asking you to share your special day with me was forward enough without suggesting matching dresses, too."

Jordyn patted her sister's shoulder. "It's not what you think, Baby. It's just that we can't look exactly alike in December unless you happen to be pregnant now, too."

"Pregnant!" Connor and Siara exclaimed together.

"The baby's due in February, so by the end of December, I'll be a real blimpette."

"That's wonderful news…about the baby I mean," Siara said. "Why didn't you…or our twinstinct…tell me sooner?"

"And why," Connor asked pointedly, "are you and Luke waiting so long to get married?"

Jordyn met Connor's stare evenly. "Luke doesn't know yet, and neither of you is to tell him."

"Why haven't you told him?" Connor asked.

"It slipped my mind?"

"Shouldn't you be telling him soon?" Connor continued.

"I will. I will." Jayme retrieved her handbag from her desk. "So, let's get this celebration underway. Shouldn't we invite Jae and Dari?"

"Jae and her friend Rick will meet us at Burkey's though we haven't yet told them the real reason for this spontaneous get-together," Connor said. "Jae had just returned home from her road trip and was meeting Rick right away…so we invited him, too, rather than postpone our announcement."

"Good," Jordyn said. "It will give us a chance to get to know him better. He must be a major stud if Jayme's kicking Harlan to the curb for him."

"We called Dari at the pet store," Siara added with a worried voice, "but she politely declined. She sounded so tired. I'm more worried than ever, Jyn. She's even quieter than usual, and she's so reclusive. She's locking her bedroom door now."

"She's extremely busy is all," Jordyn said. "Locking her door is Dari Mouse's way of telling us to leave her alone so that she can get her work done. I'm willing to bet my engagement ring that this is the last festival she ever handles. Now…c'mon…let's eat. I'm hungry for two, you know!"

Gypsy and Starbuck rubbed themselves around Darica's ankles, pausing occasionally to stare at her plaintively when she continued to ignore them. Upstairs in the pet shop, the animals were rustling about as they settled for the evening. Mr. Butler had gone home already, leaving the evening feeding and cleaning in his assistant's capable hands.

However, his assistant was struggling to complete her chores. As she sat on the bottom step of the basement stairway, she rested her forehead against a post and closed her eyes. She was exhausted. Exhausted from a busy day in the shop. Exhausted from the relentless demands of organizing the Fall Festival.

Exhausted from dodging worried questions and offers of assistance from her roommates, boss, and church friends.

Exhausted from carrying a soul laden with sin.

Exhausted from a lifetime of struggling against evil tendencies that were so obviously an inherent part of her.

My soul is a sponge, she thought, *absorbing evil until I'm saturated with sin.*

What a hypocrite I am to disguise myself with piety, to fool my friends into thinking I'm good and kind. Even Andria thought I was good and kind. She said I am a blameless victim. Blameless victims don't sin over and over again.

Yet God has used me as an instrument of retribution. Does he intend for me to be an instrument of retribution against myself?

A clattering from a corner of the basement summoned her attention. Tired of being ignored, the cats had been enticed by the challenges of the basement shelves. One of Gypsy's leaps had knocked some cans and boxes to the floor.

"Naughty kitty," Darica said automatically, rising wearily to clean up the mess.

Fortunately there was nothing spilled or broken, and Darica began to rearrange everything on the shelves. When she saw the box of rat poison, she paused and stared, first at the box, then at the ceiling.

God has provided me a sign.

CHAPTER NINE

"Not bad," Jayme said, surveying Rick's apartment. "A little bare yet, but not bad."

Rick motioned her onto the couch. "My parents will bring the rest of my stuff next month when they drive down for the Fall Festival. I was lucky to find something partially furnished on short notice...and with a landlord agreeable to letting me install the grab bars and rails I need. Money does talk."

"Do you use your wheelchair much?" Jayme asked, shivering as Rick dropped onto the couch beside her.

"Just inside the apartment...when I take my legs off." He noticed her shivering. "Are you cold? I can adjust the AC..."

"I...I'm not cold." She leaned toward the coffee table. "Do you mind if I pour us some of this wine I brought to warm you...as an apartment warming present?"

Grinning, Rick ran his finger along the underside of her arm. "Am I making you nervous?"

Jayme jumped, splashing wine onto the table. "Nervous?" she asked, blotting at the wine with a napkin. "Why do you think I'm nervous?"

"Lucky guess. However, I have the perfect ice-breaker, guaranteed to calm your jitters."

Jayme contemplated him skeptically. "What is it?"

Taking the napkin from her hand, he drew her into his arms. Gently, his lips pressed against hers, and then he claimed her mouth more insistently. The smallest peep of surprise issued from her before she surrendered to his kiss...to him...

"That was no ice-breaker," she whispered, stroking his face. "That was an ice-MELTER."

"I enjoyed it myself," he grinned. He settled back on the couch and pulled her close. "Let's snuggle for a while, drink some wine, and drift along on whatever moods move us."

"Are you going to get me drunk and have your way with me?"

"I was hoping to do that without getting you drunk. It's better if we can remember everything in the morning."

"I...we..."

"Wine?"

"Please."

He poured wine for both of them and raised his glass to her. "To us?"

"To us." She touched her glass to his and then gulped at the wine.

"Easy, Kitten..." He took the glass from her as she choked. "Do I make you that nervous?"

"Not you specifically. The situation..."

"I will never force you into anything you don't want."

"I wouldn't be here if I thought you would."

"Then relax. Let's talk about more prosaic things for a while. Like furniture."

"There's not much here to talk about," she said, reaching for her wine again.

"Exactly. And what's here isn't something I want to live with for very long. Maybe on your next day off, you'll go furniture shopping with me?"

"Sure. I like spending other people's money."

"I like the idea of our picking out furniture together."

"You might change your mind the first time we disagree on chintzes."

"So long as we agree on the bed."

Avoiding his eyes, she drained her wine glass, and then refilled it, her hand shaking so much that he had to help her again.

"You...you mentioned prosaic things," she prompted, struggling for control of her melting body.

"Actually this is a good time for me to ask you a few questions about something for the paper."

"That sounds prosaic enough." *At least until I get over this damn trembling virgin sensation. Can virginity grow back?*

"I'd like to make an immediate impact at the *Sentinel*," he was saying, "so I've been doing some investigating of my own on a news item that had stalled considerably though it still has news potential. I've been looking into the Prescott Chadburn murder."

Jayme choked on her wine again.

"I thought you might be a little shocked," he said, rubbing her back gently until she was breathing evenly again. "He dated your roommate?"

"Dated and that's all..."

"I'm sure of that...especially after meeting her today."

"Then why do you need to ask ME questions?"

"You were asking questions yourself once. Why the curiosity?"

"Merely a breakdown in communication. Jyn and I were a little concerned that Sari had stumbled into something. Not SERIOUSLY concerned, but enough to motivate us to ask a few questions."

"Were you satisfied with the information you received?"

"Completely. You don't consider one of us a suspect, do you? Is that why you really asked me here?"

"No and no." He eased her back until his arms encircled her again. "First of all, I was never suspicious of any of you. Except for Harwood, you have good taste in friends."

"His name is Hobart."

He grinned and kissed her lightly. "I stand corrected. Anyway...after I met you friends, any lingering doubts about your rooming with cutthroats were erased. They seem like the kind of roommates I'd chose for you myself...after choosing myself, of course."

"More wine?" she asked, angry with herself for her inability to relax enough to reciprocate his subtle, suggestive teasing.

"No…and no more for you either." He took her glass from her and set it on the coffee table. "I don't want you dulling your senses. You know the real reason why I invited you here tonight, don't you?"

She subdued her nervousness enough to meet his gaze evenly. "It's the same reason why I accepted," she whispered. "But…"

"But?"

"I have to tell you…I'm not very good at…it."

"Did Hobart tell you that?" he asked, anger flashing in his eyes.

"He didn't have to…I could just tell…"

"I'll see what I can do about changing your mind. Can you handle my being a foot and a half shorter in bed?" He tried to keep his voice light as he placed her hand on his knee.

"I'd be lying if I told you I hadn't thought about it," she told him softly, laying her head against his shoulder and entwining her fingers with his. "But all thoughts have been overwhelmingly pleasant…even the one about the tripod."

"The tripod?"

"You'll think I'm terrible."

"I've dealt with every kind of squeamishness possible, Kit. I can deal with tripods."

"No squeamishness, sugarplum. You were the tripod, and I had this delightful image of you…naked…and ready for me…and…well…like a tripod."

"You flatter me, Kitten," he laughed. "I'd fall flat on my face."

"Maybe not. I'll be there to cushion your fall…"

"Are you seducing me?" he asked, wrapping a bit of her hair around his finger.

"You seduced me first."

"I hope you feel adventuresome. It's difficult for me to get proper leverage from some angles without my bars…"

"I…I know only one angle."

"We'll improvise. You'll understand if I don't sweep you up into my arms and carry you to the bedroom."

"So long as you don't expect me to carry you…"

There was no awkwardness between them as they helped each other undress, not even when he took off his prostheses. Jayme was too busy noticing that even now he was more muscular than Harlan…from therapy to maintain his upper body strength and the muscles in his thighs.

As he stretched out beside her, his eyes trailed up and down the length of her body. His dark, warm-brown eyes, when they met hers again, were full of love and wonder…and hunger.

She expected a flurry of passion, but at first his touch was slow and easy as he savored every inch of her.

To the question in her eyes he said, "I have waited a long, long time for this moment, Kitten, and I'm not going to rush through it like some horny school boy getting laid for the first time. I love you, and this moment deserves all the respect and attention I can give it..."

In the dim light of the bedroom, her eyes were darkly brilliant pools of emotion. Touching tender kisses to her eyes...her lips...her neck, he murmured his love for her. Her touch was hesitant, but no less eager, and he helped her by guiding her hand and whispering encouragement, teaching her how to touch him as he learned how to touch her.

His mouth covered hers hungrily now, and she yielded herself to his need. He devoured the softness of her lips...the sweetness of her mouth...as she met his desire with her own. She quivered sweetly beneath his touch, mostly from a passion that equaled his, but he knew a little from apprehension, too. These emotions were powerful and pervasive to them both.

She would not stop him this time...

Jayme entangled her fingers within the mass of damp hair on Rick's chest, opening and closing her hand gently, rhythmically like the ecstatic kneading of a contented kitten.

So THAT'S what all the fuss is about, she thought. *No wonder Jyn is such a sex maniac.*

"You okay?" Rick whispered sleepily.

"Oh my yes..."

"I was a little worried at first. You seemed frightened..."

"I thought it would hurt."

"Hurt?" Rick raised himself onto his elbow. "Did Hobart hurt you? I'll cut the bastard's balls off..."

Jayme touched her fingers to his lips. "No more Hobart," she murmured, snuggling closer to him.

He brushed the hair back from her face. "You've made me a very happy man tonight, Kitten."

"Then I was...okay for you?"

"You were galaxies beyond okay, sweetheart."

"So were you," she said, stroking his face and outlining his lips with her fingertip. "I...I never felt like that before...or DID that thing that happened last..."

"Climaxed you mean?"

"Yes...that..."

"Then I was your first time after all," he grinned, "for that anyway."

"Yes, you were," she said, returning his smile.

"In a way, you were my first time, too...for making love anyway. And imagine my surprise to discover it's a whole lot better than just having sex."

She nodded, understanding him perfectly. Which must mean…

He saw the confusion on her face. "Gives you something to think about, doesn't it, Kit?" he said as he kissed her. "You already know that I'm in love you…and now you're realizing that you're in love me, too."

"But…"

He stroked her hair. "The funny thing about loving a dream is that it goes away when you finally open your eyes to something that's been right there for you all along. Think about that for a while, too, okay?"

"Right now?"

"Did you have something else in mind?" he asked, kissing her neck and massaging her breasts until their tips were hard with desire for him. Her gentle moan of pleasure was all the answer he needed.

He made slow, sweet love to her again…and later, she woke him up for more.

Even without the lovemaking, though, she was content just to be with him, beside him, and in his arms. In the morning, they shared a shower. He had to sit on a shower chair, but they made their adjustments. He was relieved when she showed no signs of revulsion when she saw his stumps so closely in the morning light. However, later, as she knelt to help him with his prostheses, he could tell something was troubling her, and he drew her up, onto the bed beside him.

"What's on your mind, Kitten?" he asked softly.

"I…I can't help thinking part of this is my fault," she told him finally, indicating his legs. "Maybe if we hadn't broken up…and I hadn't been such a—"

"Don't," he said, touching his fingers to her lips. "I had to go to 'Nam and work out issues I had in my thick-skulled head…and you had to work Hobart out of your system. Things happened as they needed to happen for us. We're together now. That's what matters most."

She wanted to tell him that she loved him, but now…so soon after Harlan…she was afraid the words would ring hollow to him. He seemed to understand.

"Your eyes tell me everything I need to know," he whispered, kissing her. "For now…"

He laid her back on the bed and slid his hand inside her robe. "Do you think anyone will notice when we're late for work?"

Drive time to and from St. Louis was always prime thinking time for Jayme.

Maybe too much time for thinking this morning. Throughout most of her magical night with Rick, a subconscious worry had been tugging for attention, and now it crystallized for her in the light of day.

"I'll cut the bastard's balls off," Rick had said of Harlan.

Prescott Chadburn retained his balls, but something darn close to them was gone.

Cut off and stuffed into the doctor's mouth...like those soldiers in Vietnam...

The Vietnam veteran she had just spent the night with was surely eager for information about the doctor's death.

* * *

Jordyn double-checked the costume designs for her students' performances at the Fall Festival. One month to go, and everything was on schedule...so far. The costumes could be easily finished in a month. She had intentionally kept them simple, yet attractive, and as inexpensive as possible. The families of many of her students were stretching their budgets even to send their children to Jordyn.

Glancing at her body...again...she made an impatient face. The slight bulge of her stomach, the increasing fullness of her breasts...obviously she couldn't perform at the festival. She shouldn't even be wearing leotards anymore.

Grimacing, she reached for the chambray work shirt she had taken from Luke's closet. The oversized shirt hid the bulges.

As she ran her hand over her stomach and gazed lovingly at her feet, she smiled wryly. Soon she wouldn't be able to see her feet at all.

"Nothing wrong with a pleasantly plump woman."

Jordyn whirled around to see Luke leaning against the doorjamb.

"Don't you ever knock?" she snapped, buttoning the shirt quickly.

"But your door is always open, sweetcakes," he drawled, kissing her lightly as he slid his hands beneath her shirt.

"Quit that! Someone will see!"

"Since when did you become so proper?" He gently pinched the flesh at her waistline. "If you think you'll discourage my interest in you by getting fat, you're wrong. There will be just that much more to love on."

"More than you think, Farm Boy."

"You aiming for two hundred pounds by our wedding?"

"No, Mr. Smart-Ass," she said, walking away from him. "I'm pregnant."

Casually she opened a file cabinet and pretended to sort through papers there. There was no reaction from him at first, but moments later he tenderly turned her toward him and wrapped his arms around her.

"Jordyn...honey...I don't know what to say. This is too perfect to be true."

She glowered up at him. Why the big oaf had tears in his eyes. That would never do. She didn't want to make him happy, especially that happy.

When he noticed her hostile expression, he stepped away from her, color draining from his face.

"It is my baby, isn't it?" he whispered hoarsely.

Anger and nausea boiled within her. "How the hell should I know? Haven't you heard of community property?"

He slammed his fist into the file cabinet, leaving a conspicuous dent, then turned and stomped out of her office.

As she dropped into her desk chair, Jordyn pretended she was pleased by upsetting him so much.

CHAPTER TEN

Oblivious of the paint she was smearing on her face, Siara rubbed her nose and stepped away from the bedroom wall to inspect the color. With Jordyn moving out to Luke's farm soon, some changes would be taking place:

Connor would be moving in with Siara, into the house on Meadow Lane, and Jayme and Darica would take over the smaller house Connor had been renting from Mrs. Cuthbertson.

Jayme had already surrendered her bedroom to Siara's redecorating, for that room was the largest of the four bedrooms. The revolving living conditions had sent Jayme's belongings into Siara's room and Siara in with Jordyn.

However, plans might have to be altered if Luke and Jordyn didn't make up soon.

Siara wasn't exactly sure what had caused this latest upheaval in the relationship between Luke and her sister. Jordyn had said only that Luke walked out on her when she told him she was pregnant. Twinstinct told Siara there was more to the story than that, and she and her beloved Connor had a plan to get things resolved once and for all. Interfering was a prerogative of a twin sister, especially since Jordyn's stubbornness and fierce independence were traditionally detrimental to her happiness where Luke was concerned.

For a couple that so obviously belonged together, Luke and Jordyn were certainly at odds often enough.

How ironic that I'm the one to find contentment and joy in love, Siara thought dreamily.

When she heard the soft swish of painting behind her, she spun around. Quietly, unnoticed, Darica had entered the room and taken up a paintbrush.

"You shouldn't be doing that, Dari. You have enough to do already."

"I want to help," Darica mumbled. "I want to help YOU."

"That's very sweet, but I'll agree only if you allow me to help you with some of the festival work."

Darica shook her head. "That is my responsibility."

"And this is MY responsibility. I didn't hire it done because I wanted to do it myself for Connor and me."

"I wish to help because I love you."

"I love you, too, but you have more of a burden now than I."

Darica's shoulders sagged. *Does Siara see the sin that fills my soul?*

"I know you have some typing to do," Siara was saying. "I can do that tonight while Connor grades papers."

"I don't deserve your kindness..."

"Nonsense! You can be as obstinate as Jyn sometimes. I'm serious when I say I won't let you paint for me now unless you let me type for you later."

Darica dipped her brush into the paint. "Very well. You may type for me tonight."

"Thank you." Siara smiled and returned to her own painting.

Darica smoothed color onto the wall before her. "Vanilla Cream" over "Baby Bonnet Blue." White over blue. No matter how much white there was, the blue still lurked beneath the pristine surface.

I can't paint my soul with goodness and hope the evil will go away. It will be there always…

But I am the instrument of retribution for my sins. God has sent His sign to me.

* * *

Scanning the hotel room to see if she was overlooking anything, Jayme packed her suitcase, leaving out only what she would need for the night and next day. This had been the final road trip of the season. Tomorrow was the final game. She would not be covering the Play-offs or World Series this year. Ernie claimed those privileges because he had relatives in Baltimore, and the wire services could feed them information on the other games. In Ernie's' absence, Jayme was needed at the editor's desk although she intended to take some time off in October. The season had been a grind, and she wanted more time with Rick.

There had been a final plea from Harlan, who couldn't quite believe that Jayme was putting an end to their project. As usual, there wasn't a single thought in his head for Jayme. He had lamented all "that wasted fuckin'" and the fact that Wallis was "pretty damn ragged about it." Jayme couldn't help a moment of satisfaction over that bit of news.

And Harlan couldn't help being surprised when Jayme told him that she had a boyfriend now, a SERIOUS boyfriend.

"You wanna be with him instead of fuckin' with me?" Harlan said.

"Yes…and no one is more amazed than I am to hear me say that," Jayme told him. "But that's the way it is."

I just hope I'm not trading one heartache in on another, she added to herself.

She had managed to convince herself that she was looking for trouble where there was none when she considered any connection between Rick Girard and Prescott Chadburn. A subtle question to Rick had established that he never met the doctor, so Jayme shut down those flights of fancy that had Dr. Chadburn being the one to amputate Rick's legs and send him into a severe mental decline that culminated in his killing the doctor in retaliation.

I should write fiction with this imagination, Jayme thought, pressing a fist against her forehead.

The fact of the matter was that she should trust Rick until he gave her a reason not to. How many chances had she given Harlan over the years? And

Harlan had managed to disappoint her in some way nearly every day since she first knew him.

Rick was never disappointing. He paid for their dates...he held doors for her and stood when she entered a room even though standing wasn't always that easy for him...he talked intelligently to her and really listened to what she had to say...he sent her flowers when she was on the road and when she returned home from being on the road...

He set off little brush fires in her body whenever he touched her...full-scale atomic blasts when he made love to her.

And he respected her and loved her.

Now that she was peeking around that disappointing dream of Harlan she had held onto so stubbornly all those years, she realized that she loved Rick, too...and probably had loved him all along.

If she had really loved Harlan, things would have fallen into place somehow without her working so hard to make them happen. True love just happened...and then blossomed into something beautiful on its own, even after fourteen years.

But she still had to have a serious face-to-face conversation with her true love when she returned home.

CHAPTER ELEVEN

"I've been set up!" Jordyn glowered at Connor as Siara entered Burkey's with Luke. "You didn't want to consult with me about a wedding present for Sari at all."

"That's not entirely true," Connor said easily, wrapping his fingers around her wrist when she tried to get up to leave. "The best gift any of us can give Stacks is to fix things up between you and Luke. Both of you are too mule-headed to do what needs to be done."

"What makes you so damn sure I want things fixed?"

"Siara's twinstinct is good enough for me. And if you don't behave like a lady over the next few minutes, I'll personally turn you over my knee and wallop the daylights out of you right here." Ignoring her indignant sputtering, he rose to kiss his fiancée. "Hello, my love. I ordered beer for you, Luke. I hope that's acceptable. I'm not so knowledgeable about your preferences as I am Siara's."

Luke bobbed his head in response, then returned Jordyn's glare.

"I'm here only because Siara asked me to be here as a favor to her," he said.

Jordyn snorted contemptuously. "How gallant…especially from a man who used my baby sister's relationship with Dr. Chadburn to blackmail me into marriage."

Siara gasped in surprise as Luke lowered his eyes in shame.

"I apologized for that," he said quietly, relieved by the diversion of the waitress's bringing their drinks. "Besides, I offered you your freedom." His eyes raked over the bulge at her midriff. "Now I know why you didn't accept."

Wringing her hands together, Siara looked to Connor for help. "This isn't going well at all."

Connor laid his hand on hers. "All is not lost, my love. If only for your sake, I'm sure both Jordyn and Luke with make an honest attempt to clear the air between them since we're all here anyway."

"Why the hell should I listen to a goddamn thing that bastard has to say?" Jordyn blazed, until she saw Connor's steady stare. "Sorry for the unladylike language, Connor," she muttered meekly then.

Connor ignored Luke's how-did-you-do-that? expression. "At the risk of sounding like a marriage counselor, both Stacks and I believe there's something between you two worth salvaging. Otherwise, one of you would have broken the engagement over this latest tiff…whatever its cause…instead of continuing the engagement without speaking to each other."

"A mere oversight," Jordyn said, removing her engagement ring.

However, she did not pass it to Luke, and he did not indicate that he wanted it.

"I never made any secret of how I felt for Jordyn." Luke directed his statement to Siara. "That was my fatal mistake. She rips the heart out of men who care for her."

Jordyn straightened angrily in her chair but spoke quite sweetly to Connor. "HE walked out on ME when he found out he'd knocked me up. What a chivalrous show of devotion, huh?"

"And SHE freely admitted that the child in question may or may not be mine," Luke told Siara.

"Jordyn!" her sister admonished. "How could you say such a thing when both you and I know that Luke is the only possible father?"

"What makes YOU so sure, Baby?"

"Because I KNOW."

"So what if he is? He accused me first."

Siara looked to Luke for an explanation.

"What else was I to think?" he asked. "She's flaunted her other men at me all the time we've dated. I told you that."

"And I told you that my sister has a tendency to exaggerate to you," Siara said quietly.

"Siara Dawn Nealy! How can you say such a thing about me?" Jordyn slapped her palms on the table and leaned toward her sister.

"Deny it, Jordyn," Siara challenged.

Jordyn muttered an expletive and folded her arms.

"Obviously," Connor said to Jordyn and Luke, "this whole mess between you is the result of sheer obstinacy and subsequent jumping to conclusions…both of you. If you didn't love each other so much, I'd tell you to forget the whole thing and look in the personals ads for other mates."

"I never said I love him," Jordyn pointed out.

"You agreed to marry him," Siara pointed out.

"He blackmailed me."

"And he rescinded the blackmail. You chose to remain engaged."

"I'm pregnant."

"Even that wouldn't get you to the altar if you didn't want to be there. Admit it, Jyn. You love Luke very much."

"I love lots of people."

"You have a damn fine way of showing it," Luke interposed, still angry.

"I've shown you just fine on numerous occasions, Farm Boy, and you never complained."

"The trouble with that is you were showing lots of other men, too."

"So what if I was? You got your share."

"I refuse to share my fiancée with other men!"

"You haven't shared me with other men for a long time now. If you'd come down off your manure pile, you'd realize it."

"Damnation! You have to be the most exasperating woman it's ever been my displeasure to deal with!" Luke stood up, grabbed Jordyn's hand, and shoved the ring back on her finger. "Let's go."

"Where?"

"Where do you think…Farm Girl?"

Connor and Siara watched them leave.

"Jordyn didn't tell him she loves him," Siara said sadly.

"Don't expect miracles, my love. Besides, I think he knows it now."

* * *

"And so we've invited Dari's friend Andria to fly in for Fall Festival weekend," Jayme told Rick as she wandered around his living room and sipped at a can of Diet Rite. "Dari could use some perking up."

Leaning back, Rick lifted his legs onto his new couch. "Darica looks vaguely familiar to me. I wish I could figure out why."

"You probably crossed paths in Chicago somewhere. I'm surprised you can't remember. You're not one to forget a beautiful face."

"I'm going to forget your beautiful face if you don't get yourself over here real soon. What's bothering you anyway? You've been like a caged coyote all evening…a chatty caged coyote jabbering about everything under the sun but what's bothering you."

"You do talk pretty to me. Careful or I'll become spoiled."

"What can I say? I'm a romantic kind of guy."

Jayme smiled faintly and then studied her soda can.

"Don't make me get up and come after you," he said softly. "Take-offs and landings on these things aren't among my greatest accomplishments."

"I'm sorry. I didn't mean to be…rude." She sat on the coffee table and faced him.

"I had visions of your sitting on the couch with my head nestled in your lap, or I would never have stretched out like this."

"Sorry."

"Would you stop apologizing and tell me what's wrong? Something's been nagging at you since we made love before dinner." Panic washed over his face. "Is it Harlan? Are you telling me you're going back to him?"

"No!" she reassured him quickly. "I realize now that you're the man I'm in love with. Heck, you've even been the man of my dreams all along, but I kept trying to put Harlan's face on it."

Rick propped himself up on his elbows, his face glowing with happiness. "Really?"

"Yes, really," she said, reaching to stroke his cheek. "But I promised myself that I'd get something straight with you…about you…even if I made you angry by asking."

He lay back down. "Fire away. Nothing you could say now would make me angry with you."

Jayme leaned over and took his hand. "Keep that in mind when I ask you why you're so interested in Prescott Chadburn."

"I told you already. I want a spectacular launch of my tenure with the *Sentinel*, and that story has a strong local impact."

"That's all?"

"Of course that's all. What else could there be?"

"You yourself discovered that Jyn and I investigated a little on our own. One of the things we learned that was that the doctor's...manhood had been sliced off and stuffed into his mouth...something that was a common Viet Cong ritual."

"True."

"Well...you were awfully curious about him...and you are a veteran..." Jayme covered her face with her hands, preparing for either his confession or his indignant denials. When she heard him struggling to sit up, she lowered her hands.

"You've been thinking I offed the dude?" he asked, leaning cradle her face within his hands.

"The thought crossed my mind is all. Not that I think you're a cold-blooded killer, but I've read about 'Nam vets freaking out and doing weird things."

"I've already gone through my weird phase."

"Then you didn't..."

"Never even knew he existed until I read in the *Sentinel* about his death."

"Are you angry with me for thinking as I was?"

"Actually I'm very pleased that you love me enough to confront me and get it out of the way. That took a lot of guts and a lot of love, Kit..."

"Oh, I do love you..." she whispered.

He pulled her over to the couch with him, and she snuggled close as he trailed kisses along her neck until his lips found hers. Then he set her away from him and gazed deeply into the velvet pools of her eyes.

"I would like some more brutal honesty from you now," he said. "You're sure Harlan is out of your system?"

"Except for being friends...just friends...nothing more."

"Even if he were suddenly single again?"

"Nothing I could ever have with him could come close to what I have with you. I'd be nuts to change my mind."

"With all due respect, you do have a rather nutty track record where he's concerned."

"I'm all grown up now though it took me thirty-three years to get there. You're the one I want to cross the finish line with. Even without your legs, you're twice the man he is...and I mean that in every good way possible."

"You have just made me the world's happiest man," he said, kissing her deeply. "And now I'm not scared shitless about showing you copies of something I turned over to the Applewood police this afternoon. If you can get my briefcase for me, sweetheart...there under the coffee table..."

She handed him his briefcase, and he handed her a manila envelope from inside it. Inside the envelope were private investigators' reports...and a photocopy of a marriage license.

A 1963 marriage license issued to Prescott Durwood Chadburn and Ursula Wallis Robinson.

"Surely this isn't..." Jayme looked to Rick for verification.

He nodded. "Surely it is. If you read the PI reports, you'll see there is no record of any divorce for them in any of these United States...or Mexico or Puerto Rico.

CHAPTER TWELVE

Rick's plan to initiate his ownership of the *Sentinel* with a blockbuster story was successful beyond even his expectations. Since Harlan Oakes was the hometown golden boy, interest was even more rampant than usual as headlines about Wallis, Harlan, and Prescott D. Chadburn displaced the usual banner topic at this time of year in Applewood: the Fall Festival at the end of the week.

What Rick's private investigators failed to uncover, Wallis eagerly provided. She was desperate to gain any break available, for she confessed only to hitting the doctor with a desk lamp. She declared herself to be totally innocent of setting the fire and rearranging Chadburn's body parts.

As for her attack on the doctor, she claimed self-defense. The good doctor had been a cad inclined to violence from the beginning of their relationship, in 1963 when he was a twenty-two-year-old medical student and she, a sixteen-year-old high-school sophomore who discovered that she was pregnant soon after they began dating. Wallis threatened all kinds of public ruin and damnation if he did not marry her. Since she was underage and he could not afford a scandal, he complied, as did her parents, who wanted her out of their lives.

Soon afterward, during one of their frequent fights, he punched her repeatedly in the abdomen, and she miscarried.

Perhaps that had been his intention all along, for he then packed his belongings and simply disappeared.

After that, Wallis never bothered herself overmuch with the legality of her marital situation, beyond making a few generous people feel sorry enough for her that she was able to get through college with a minimum of financial worries. She chose journalism as a career because she had an aptitude for it and because a press pass could open many doors that would otherwise be closed to her.

When Harlan came along with so much money and so few brains, she grasped the golden opportunity with both hands. Prescott Chadburn was a dim memory, until he suddenly decided to move his practice to Applewood. He had seen Wallis on a talk show devoted on that particular day to baseball wives.

WEALTHY baseball wives.

Opening an office quickly was easier in the small college town of Applewood, which was close enough to St. Louis to give him easy access to Wallis Oakes. And because Applewood was Harlan's hometown, she spent some time there herself.

After re-establishing secret communication with his wife, he threatened to reveal their marriage if she did not provide him with certain financial gifts.

On the day of his death, they had fought…again…violently. Wallis grabbed the desk lamp and smashed him over the head with it. Fearing that she had, indeed, killed him, she fled, living in constant fear of the discovery until she learned that someone else had apparently come along after her and done the actual killing.

The police were not inclined to believe the latter part of her story.

Rick had done them a favor by using his own money and resources to uncover Wallis for them while not mentioning in the paper that he, not they, was responsible for the break in the case. Therefore, the police intended to hold onto Mrs. Harlan Oakes...a.k.a. Wallis Robins...a.k.a. Ursula Wallis Robinson Chadburn.

Wallis was desperate.

When Harlan fully understood that he and she were not legally married, he was in no big hurry to remarry, as Wallis begged him to. His parents and his lawyer advised him to distance himself as much as possible from "that woman." Being the victim of a woman's treachery was one thing. Remarrying that woman while she was held on a murder charge was quite another.

Faced with the possibility of having a court-appointed attorney as her only defense, Wallis appealed to Jayme, who...surprisingly...felt sorry for the jailed woman. How like Harlan to desert someone if the need was not his own.

Jayme pointed out to him that Wallis, by virtue of years of service, deserved some support from him now, even if it was only financial support. As his business manager, she was probably entitled to a legal percentage of his earnings anyway, even if she lost her claim to community property.

"You think I oughta marry her again, Jae?" Harlan asked.

"That's entirely up to you and how you feel about her. One way or another, I'm sure there will be another Mrs. Harlan Oakes around very soon. However, what you should do now is pay for her to retain a decent lawyer. And if you want my further advice, you'll get your own lawyer busy...or hire another agent or business manager...before vultures descend on your bank account."

"Thanks, Jae," he said humbly. "You always come through for me."

"Sure, Sport. Any time."

He shuffled his feet. "Maybe you and me can go to the festival this weekend?"

"I told you I have a boyfriend now, Harlan. I'll be with him this weekend."

"Nights, too?"

"Most definitely nights, too."

"Well, damn. Things sure do change in a hurry, don't they, Jae?"

Jayme laughed. "Sometimes they take fourteen years to change in a hurry."

"Huh?"

"Never mind, Harlan..."

* * *

Mild weather descended on Applewood just in time for Fall Festival weekend. Trees on the church grounds were touched with autumn colors, and bars of sunlight sliced through the leaves, bathing the citizens of Applewood with welcomed warmth.

The doors to the school's auditorium were propped open, and people flowed steadily between activities in the gym and those on the lawn. When the October sun set gloriously beyond the horizon, the peaceful afternoon gave way to more energized anticipation as the festival continued at a quicker pace with even larger crowds.

"Our Father is smiling on our fundraising efforts this year," Father Jonathan said. "We've never had such total-community participation before. You've done an outstanding job, Darica."

"Thank you, Father," Darica murmured, excusing herself to circulate methodically from booth to booth, activity to activity, checking to see that all was well, that everything was running smoothly.

In an ocean of smiles and laughter, no one would miss her somber face.

Jayme and Rick were with their families, enjoying the festival or helping Jayme's Aunt Ronna at the Cancer Society craft booth.

Siara and Connor were working in the Mosby Scheffers' booth, making and selling ice cream and handing out information to potential students.

Jordyn was with Luke and Lissa...or with her students when they were scheduled to perform.

None of them would miss Darica.

Luke's parents were in St. Louis at the airport to pick up Sandie and Andria, who by virtue of their professional association and Illinois ties had become close friends.

Coincidence. Synchronicity. Fate. God's plan. His hand touched them all.

At first, Darica had been rather agitated when her roommates sprang the surprise of Andria on her. But then she recognized the hand of God upon them again.

Of course...

Andria would help everyone understand.

The roommates would be very sad, but Andria could help them understand.

Darica must hurry though. Before Andria arrived in Applewood. Before Andria tried to interfere with God's plan.

No one will miss me if I go now.

She drove home quickly. From the trunk of her car, she took the plastic bag of cookies she had made the day before when she was alone in the house. The bag of cookies and a bottle of grape juice.

Cookies and juice.

Wafers and wine.

Last rites would do her no good.

But maybe the Eucharist...one last time...

For a moment she would be mystically united with Christ. Then Satan could reclaim her soul for eternity.

After leaving a wrapped package in Siara's bedroom, she settled in her rocking chair and read her favorite Bible passages, all the while chewing the cookies and washing them down with grape juice.

I am God's instrument of retribution against all sinners. I am a sinner.

Cookies and juice.

Wafers and wine.

Darica was careful to eat all the cookies. To make sure her plan worked. To make sure she left none for someone else to eat by mistake.

One murder was burden enough on her soul. Two if she counted her own.

She had made the cookies with rat poison from the pet shop basement.

CHAPTER THIRTEEN

"Look at this mess," Rick said, motioning to the boxes stacked around him and Jayme in his apartment. "No wonder Mom and Dad preferred to stay with Jim and Gwynnie."

"You wanted your stuff around you," Jayme told him, sitting on one of the boxes.

"Not exactly like this."

"So we'll unpack a few things tonight and do the rest tomorrow."

Rick kissed the top of her head. "Does that mean you're staying with me tonight?"

"Someone has to help you. Besides, I'd be lonely at home. Jordyn stays at Luke's, and Siara stays with Connor...and Darica's dead asleep with exhaustion I bet. She even left the festival early. Did you notice?"

"I was too busy noticing you."

"Sure you were. I was so fascinating, you left me to run back to the paper."

"Only for a few minutes to tuck things in for the night. And since the U.S. Embassy bombing in Beirut last month, I've been keeping a close eye on the wire." Soberly, he touched his lips to the palm of her hand. "I've been waiting for the right time to tell you this. I guess this is as good a time as any."

"Najib..." Jayme's hand tightly enfolded his as her heart constricted painfully.

"His oldest son was kidnapped and is being held by a terrorist faction for a sizable ransom."

"But Najib has never been a radical political force. He's just a concerned Lebanese citizen. Why are they picking on him?"

"Family money...and the power that by reputation usually goes with it. Some of his countrymen feel that the Bustani family is too closely associated with Western capitalism. Or, considering the turmoil on the streets there every day, R.J. could have been at the wrong place at the wrong time."

"R.J.?"

"The boy...Richard James. Hell, his name could have made him a target, too. It's not real MidEastern, is it?"

"But it's very much Najib." Jayme's eyes misted. "What can we do?"

"All we can do is watch the wire services and try to get a call through...though I do have an idea I've been kicking around for a few days."

"You sure kick around a lot of ideas for a man with no feet. What's this one?"

"It depends on a lot of things, chief among them you. Would you consider a career change now? You've been wasting yourself in sports..."

"And?"

"And I've been thinking about going to Lebanon for a while, as a special correspondent for the *Sentinel* and for my dad. Obviously I'd be somewhat limited physically. I want you to go with me as my co-correspondent."

"To Lebanon? You and me?"

"I do take you to the finest places, don't I? I wouldn't be thinking about it except for Najib, and if things get too dangerous, I'll ship you home."

"Think again, bucko. If we go in together, we come out together."

He rested his head against hers. "Then you'll consider it?"

"Yes…for you and for Najib…and for the fringe benefits I hope you'll provide with the assignment."

He grinned and tipped her face up for a kiss. "I hope Jim doesn't mind postponing his retirement for a few more months. Of course, he'd probably be more inclined to let his little girl go if she were married to the guy she's going with."

Jayme's eyes widened. "What are you saying?"

"I'm asking you to marry me. Gee, I thought you were smarter than that. Maybe I won't take you after all."

"Try to leave without me. I'll chop you off at the knees."

"Someone beat you to it, precious. We'll have to have a quicky wedding and leave within the next month. We won't be here for the twins' wedding."

"Maybe I can get them to videotape the thing for me…or maybe even move up the date so that we can all get married at the same time. We have to find a man for Dari. I can't see her living alone."

"The twins will watch out for her for now," he said, pulling her up. "We'll take over custody when we return home. Kiss me?"

"With all this unpacking to do?"

"We can do it tomorrow."

"No way, sugarplum. We can't even reach the bedroom."

"Considering what I had in mind, that does present a problem. We'll make a path."

Quickly they worked through the boxes between them and the bedroom, all the while touching, joking, reveling in the new intimacy of two people who have pledged their futures to each other.

"The marlin!" Rick exclaimed suddenly. "Dad's letting me have Marvin!"

"Oh, goody…" Jayme noticed then that he was abruptly pensive. "What is it, honey?"

"I remember now," he said, staring at her strangely. "The marlin… Alonzo…no…Armando Cervantes mounted it for us. His little girl…Darica… worked in the shop with him."

"Dari? That explains why she looked familiar to you."

"There's more. I remember now. Dad mentioned it to me because of Marvin… because of Armando Cervantes. His son was killed…supposedly…in a fight by rival street gangs. Someone mutilated his body by cutting off his whanger and setting him on fire..."

"Surely you can't be implying that Dari...of all people..."

"Later she was at Cliffside...the private clinic where I was treated."

"Just to visit Andria. Andria worked there for a while before returning to New York."

"Are you sure?"

"That Andria worked there? Sure. I remember the name because it sounded like something out of a Gothic novel."

"You're being deliberately obtuse, Kit. Are you sure Darica was just visiting?"

"Well...no. Dari has never talked much about her life in Chicago. We always had the impression that she had a lot of bad memories about...about...well, we never pried, and she never offered, and it never mattered...oh, damn...it's just not possible. She couldn't have afforded a place like that anyway."

"There are too many coincidences not to check it out."

"I'm never going to have a moment's peace until YOUR suspicions are laid to rest, am I?"

"Call her."

"It's after midnight. She's probably asleep."

"Call her, Kit. If she did it, she needs some MAJOR professional help as soon as possible."

"Oh, all right...but IF...and that's a HUGE if...if she had anything to do with it, let's remember she needs a hospital, not a jail cell." Jayme jerked up the phone and punched their home number. Though she let the phone ring two dozen times, there was no answer. "That's strange. I'm sure she went home."

"Could she and Andria have gone somewhere?"

"Andria would have gotten in too late. She and Sandie were going directly to the Johnsons' for the night."

"I don't like the feel of this, Kitten."

"Me either. Let's go."

While Rick made the necessary phone calls...to the authorities and to the twins...Jayme gulped back an explosion of grief, stumbled into her room, and collapsed on her bed. A sharp-edged box beneath her dug into her painfully, and she yanked it from under her.

On top was a note written by Darica's hand to Siara:

"Mrs. Oakes did not kill the doctor. I did, though I thought he was already dead and I had to help him into Hell with Alvito. Now I must pay for my own sins. The cycle of sin will end with me. Andria can help you understand. Do not grieve, Sari Mouse, for God has shown me that this is the only way. I love you all, Dari Mouse."

Tears spilling down her cheek, Jayme opened the box. Lying inside in a nest of cotton was Darica's bookmark...the expertly tanned male member...the missing part of her brother's body...

CHAPTER FOURTEEN

A grief-stricken trio in black, the remaining roommates gathered in their living room after Darica's funeral. With them were Connor, Luke, and Rick…their individual sources of strength and reason over the past few days of insanity and heartache. Andria was with them, too, for Darica had promised that Andria could help them understand.

And they very much needed to understand.

"Darica never want you to know that I was her psychologist before I was her friend," Andria explained to them through her own grief. "She had found so much happiness here, she didn't want your opinion of her to be sullied by what she'd gone through in Chicago. I can tell you these things now because her…her last note pretty well waived our patient-psychologist privilege."

"What happened to her would have made no difference to us!" Siara's lips quivered as she buried her face against Connor's shoulder. "We loved her."

"Darica was never secure in her happiness." Andria picked at her gloves, lying in her lap. "I've already told you all that was in her mind when I first treated her. She considered herself a major-league sinner. Through treatment, she was able to realize that she was really a worthy person…though down deep where it counts, she must never have been completely convinced. Discovering that she was directly responsible for a death sent her into a tailspin from which she could not recover."

"I should have noticed that…that she wasn't well," Jayme murmured, covering her face with her hands as Rick protectively hugged her close.

"I'm the one who should have noticed." When a tear escaped from her eye, Jordyn didn't try to conceal it, and Luke touched it tenderly off his face with his fingertip. "I was here every day, Jae. You weren't."

"But we were the Mouse Sisters," Siara sobbed anew. "I should have known…like with twinstinct…"

"Stop it, all of you!" Andria ordered sternly. "The worst and most unnecessary thing you can do is blame yourselves. Darica was trapped in her own private Hell, and she took great pains to conceal it from you. You couldn't have known. In fact, you should be tremendously comforted with knowing that her only years of complete contentment were here with you."

"It's all still so hard to believe." Shuddering, Jayme pressed closer to Rick. "That THING in the box…and Dari…"

Andria herself shivered, amazed that she and Darica had once had such a matter-of-fact discussion about making "that thing in the box."

"In her confused state, she thought she was leaving that package for Siara," Andria explained. "She forgot that you had temporarily moved into Siara's room."

"She wanted me to have THAT?" Siara said, horrified.

"She felt that she shared a special bond with you, so she also wanted to share her deepest secret with her Mouse Sister."

Jordyn leaned to hug her sister. "No offense, Jae, but I'm glad YOU found that thing. You'll recover faster than Sari from that kind of surprise."

Jayme nodded her understanding. "Still and all, I'm not such a tough old broad. I've had nightmares or insomnia every night since." She smiled weakly up at Rick. "Lucky for me I wasn't sleeping alone."

"I recommend to you all that you talk about your feelings candidly with each other and with your fiancés to get you through this period," Andria said. "Counselors, too, if necessary. I plan to have a long chat with Sandie soon. I should have realized that Darica wasn't completely cured and prescribed continuing therapy for her. And I should have maintained closer ties with her after I moved to New York. Above all, I should have insisted that she dispose of that grisly bookmark."

Luke sat on the arm of the sofa, beside Jordyn, who laid her head in his lap now as she spoke, "As you explained to us, Andria, the worst thing you can do is to blame yourself. If we couldn't see her...her decline here, you surely had no way of knowing all the way in New York. We just thought she was overworked and overstressed from the festival."

"I hope Father Jonathan has someone to talk to," Siara murmured. "He was quite unnerved himself."

"We can have a long talk with him when we talk to him about moving up our wedding day and coordinating with Jayme's pastor," Jordyn said. "I have this strange need to spend a little more time at church anyway."

"Dari would be pleased by that miracle," Jayme said softly.

Then they were all silent, each lost in a personal memory of Darica. The ringing of the phone broke the quiet, and at Jayme's nod, Rick reached to answer it. His mouth tensed slightly as he handed the receiver to Jayme.

"Harlan," he said.

Jayme's face expressed her apologies to everyone as she took the phone.

"What is it now, Harlan? This is not a good time to be calling me....So? You hired her a fancy lawyer, didn't you?...What do they have on her now?...No kidding?...Who?" Jayme eyes locked on Jordyn's. "No kidding?...You do what you have to do, Sport. I won't even be around then. I'm getting married in two weeks and then going to Lebanon for an extended honeymoon....No, not Lebanon, Illinois....I have to go now, Harlan. I'll see you at the wedding, and I expect a very expensive wedding gift for Rick and me after all the money I've spent on yours..."

She passed the phone back to Rick and looked around the room, her eyes stopping on Jordyn. "The Applewood PD is still pretty stunned by the recent turn of events in its one and only murder case, but Wallis is out on bail as the D.A. decides exactly what to charge her with beyond aggravated assault. Whatever he decides, she is also in trouble in St. Louis with the S.E.C. for some shady business maneuvers made with the able assistance of a certain bank official who will be indicted tomorrow. Care to guess who that certain bank official is?"

"Hudson Turner!" the twins said together, dissolving into giggles.

Among others in the room, only Connor and Jayme knew enough to catch the joke.

"Now would be a good time for us to open a bottle of that Riunite you girls are so fond of and toast to memories past and future of friends old and new," Connor said, rising and pulling Siara up with him.

"I've always thought there was more to that Hudson Turner story than I was told," Luke said. "Will you let me in on the secret now?"

"You'll never believe it," Connor told him, nodding toward Jordyn.

"If it involves my wife-to-be, I'll believe anything."

They all laughed...nervous, uncertain laughter of people who had endured a tragedy together and were ready to look toward the future again.

The roommates disappeared into the kitchen and emerged with glasses and two bottles of wine. Jordyn had a glass of milk and a box of vanilla wafers.

"Cookies and milk, hon?" Luke asked her.

"Baby on board," she responded with a smile. "Besides, you said you'd believe anything about me, so get real comfortable, Farm Boy honey. Sari, Jae, and I are about to take a trip down Memory Lane in Dari's honor, and you all are invited."

"Something tells me that two bottles of wine won't be enough," Rick said, smiling into Jayme's eyes.

"It never is," Jayme told him, stroking his cheek.

She laid her head against his shoulder and looked at her roommates...and roommates-in-law.

"You once told me that love doesn't make the top ten list of reasons why people get married," she said softly. "Look around this room, and tell me what you think now."

"I changed my mind when you agreed to marry me."

Jayme laughed. "Even Harlan was smart enough to realize that things can change in a hurry."

Rick touched his lips to her forehead, then his glass to hers. "Thanks be to God for that..."

Printed in the United States
40775LVS00005B/28